I0785115

Mary Roberts Rinehart

Mystery Cases of Letitia Carberry, Tish

OK Publishing 2021

Mary Roberts Rinehart

Mystery Cases of Letitia Carberry, Tish

The Adventures & Mystery Cases of Letitia Carberry, Tish: The Chronicle of Her Escapades and Excursions & More Tish

Published by

MUSAICUM

Books

- Advanced Digital Solutions & High-Quality book Formatting -

musaicumbooks@okpublishing.info

2021 OK Publishing

ISBN 978-80-272-7767-4

Contents

The Amazing Adventures of Letitia Carberry

by

Mary Roberts Rinehart

The Amazing Adventures of Letitia Carberry

Chapter I
What Happened to Johnson

Strictly speaking, this is Tish's story, but Tish is unable to write it, being laid up, as you probably know from the newspapers. But we all three felt that a record of the affair ought to be kept while it was fresh in our minds, although goodness knows we're not likely to forget any of it. A good many people wondered, when the story came out, how Tish had come to be mixed up with it at all, but as Tish herself says, it was very simple.

The people at the hospital had become demoralized, and some firm hand had to take hold. Besides, Tish was a member of the Ladies' Committee, and felt responsible.

Tish says the first thing she knew about it was a piercing scream, just outside her room, I This was followed by a number of short, sharp cries, feminine, and steps running past her bedroom door. Now, as Tish also remarks with truth, one hears a variety of strange sounds in a hospital at night, and at first she thought it was the woman across the hall, who had had her appendix removed that afternoon, and who had been very unpleasant as a neighbor all evening. But when the noise kept up, and only died away to be followed by somebody crying hysterically down the hall, Tish was roused. She sat.up in bed and threw her small traveling clock at Miss Lewis.

(Miss Lewis was Tish's nurse, a splendid woman, but a heavy sleeper. She slept on a cot in the room, and until Tish learned that it did not hurt the clock to throw it, she had been obliged to ring for one of the night nurses to come in and waken her. So now she threw the clock.)

Miss Lewis picked the dock from off her chest and sat up, yawning, to look at it.

"Twenty minutes after one. Miss Carberry," she said. "Would you like some buttermilk?"

Now Tish was not really ill. She was taking a rest cure last autumn while her apartment was being painted and papered, and while she recovered from a twisted knee. She'd bought a second-hand automobile some months before, and learned to run it herself, and the knee was the result of her being thrown out over the steering wheel and ten feet beyond the potato wagon she had collided with. Although, as Tish says, it is a strange thing that her knee was twisted, when she brought up standing on her head in three inches of muddy water and a family of tadpoles.

Both Aggie and I went to see her daily, the three of us being old friends, although not related, and she was always glad to see us, although she grew sarcastic when Aggie casually remarked that except for the meeting of the anti-vivisection society, we might also have been flung over the potato wagon. Well —

"Would you like some buttermilk?" asked Miss Lewis again, beginning to draw on her ki-mono. Tish says that provoked her and she reached for the clock again, but of course Miss Lewis had it in her hand.

"No," she snapped. "Go out in the hall and see what has happened."

Miss Lewis yawned again and groped around in the half light for her slippers. It was more than Tish could stand. She hopped out of bed in her bare feet and limped to the door.

The hall was almost dark and across it the woman with the appendix-or without-was groaning. But half way along, where the night nurse has her desk and keeps her papers and where the annunciator for the patients' bell is fastened to the wall, Tish saw a group of five or six nurses, gathered about somebody in a chair. One of them came running past with a glass of something, and the crowd opened to admit the girl and the glass and closed again. Miss Lewis came and looked over Tish's shoulder.

"Gee!" she said, and ran down the hall with her slippers flapping and her braid switching from side to side. Just then the woman across gave another groan, and it being dark and the scream still echoing in her ears, Tish reached inside the door for her cane and hobbled out in her nightgown.

The girl in the chair, she said, was as white as milk, and her lips were blue. She was half-lying, with her head against the back of the chair, and a violent shudder now and then was the only sign of life about her. One of the other nurses was stroking her hands and talking to her in a soothing tone.

"Now listen, Miss Blake," she said. "It couldn't be. We all have these queer feelings here. It's the nervous strain and loss of sleep. I'll never forget the first time I had to do it."

"Nor I," said another girl, "I went with you. Do you remember? It was that dwarf, that died in J. We'd forgotten something, and you had to go and leave me alone."

"Hush!" another nurse broke in, and Miss Blake began to shudder again. "If we had some hot coffee for her-will you drink some coffee if we make it. Miss Blake?"

The girl in the chair shook her head and Miss Lewis dragged one of the nurses from the group and whispered to hen Tish heard part of the answer.

"Went up with Linda Smith and as usual Linda forgot something-she's been overworking; went to raise the window for fresh air-she says she heard a sound, but didn't notice- it-when she turned around" — then more whispering that Tish couldn't catch.

"No!" Miss Lewis said, and looked queer herself. "Then, if it's true, it is still —?"

"Yes."

Miss Blake sat up just then and tried to wipe her blue lips with her handkerchief, but her hands shook so that one of the nurses did it for her. She mopped the girl's pallid forehead, too, and put her arm over her shoulders protectingly.

"You're going off duty, girl," she said. "About all the hard work in the place has been falling to you lately, and if we don't take care we will be minus the class flower."

Tish says the girl tried to smile at that and was very pretty. I can answer for her looks myself, having seen her often enough later. She had soft, wavy, black hair and Irish-blue eyes, and she was rather small. Partly for that and partly because she was so young, we fell into the way of calling her the Little Nurse. But to go back to Tish's story.

"You're sure you didn't doze off?" one of the girls asked, pressing forward. But the Little Nurse shook her head.

"Asleep! There?" she said, in a low voice. "Could you?"

"What enrages me," Miss Lewis burst out, glaring at the group through her glasses, "is ,why Linda Smith left her there alone."

"She forgot something," said Miss Blake.

"She usually forgets something!" Miss Lewis began. "When she dies, Linda'll forget —"

"Hush!" somebody whispered. "Here she is."

Miss Smith came quickly along the hall, her arms full of bundles. She stopped when she saw the group and ran her eye over it.

"Weill" she said, "what is it? Fudge?"

One of the girls detached herself from the group and started for her. Miss Smith was a tall, raw-boned woman, with short, curly hair and a rugged but good-natured face, and Tish says she stood smiling at them.

"I suppose you know," she said. "The spiritualist from K has 'passed over.' Didn't want to go, poor old man. Said he had three wives waiting in the spirit world."

The other girl came up to her then and caught her by the elbow and whispered to her. Tish was standing in the shadow, leaning on her cane, and she didn't know from Adam what was the matter, but she was covered with goose flesh.

"Nonsense!" said Miss Linda Smith suddenly. "She's been dozing."

Miss Blake got up and steadied herself by the back of the chair, looking across at the other woman.

"I'm afraid not, Miss Smith," she said. "You-remember when-when the orderlies carried up poor old-Johnson. They-laid him on the table in the mortuary, didn't they?"

"Yes," said Miss Smith, half smiling. "They usually do. They don't generally throw 'em out the window."

Miss Blake clutched the chair tighter, Tish says, and her lips trembled.

"I want you to come with me and see," she said. "We-covered the body with a sheet, didn't we?"

"Yes," Miss Smith stopped smiling.

"And then you left, and I was alone. I —I tried not to mind. I haven't been here very long. But I was afraid, after a minute or two, that I was-getting faint. I —seemed to fed eyes on me."

Some of the girls nodded as if they understood.

"So I went to the window and threw it up to get air. Then I thought I heard something moving behind me. I —I felt it, like the eyes, rather than heard it. And —I didn't look around at once; I couldn't. It was so far from ' the rest of the house, and —I was alone with it. And when I turned —" She stopped and moistened her lips with her tongue, and her face was ghastly — 'Ht was gone. Miss Smith. Gone!"

Now Tish isn't easy to frighten, but at that moment the appendix woman gave a deep groan and she says her heart jumped once or twice and turned over in her chest. The nurses were all standing huddled together in a little group, and one of them kept looking over her shoulder.

"Gone!" said Miss Smith, and sat down in a chair suddenly, as if her legs had given way. Wha-what have you done?"

Sent for Jacobs, the night watchman," one of the nurses explained. "Doctor Grimm and Doctor Sands are in the operating room — a night case, and the medical internes had a row with Mr. Harrison and left last night. We'll be in nice shape if G ward gets busy."

"What's G ward?" Tish asked, edging over to Miss Lewis.

"G ward," said Miss Lewis coolly, "G ward is where the stork drops that part of the population that has only half the legal number of parents. You'll have to go back to bed, Miss Carberry."

"I'll do nothing of the sort," said Tish, and glared at her.

Tish told us the rest of the story the next morning, sitting propped up in bed with Aggie on one side and me on the other. We'd brought her some creamed sweetbreads, but she was so excited she could not eat The change in her was horrible; she had passed through a crisis, and she showed it.

"You'd better let us take you home, Tish," Aggie pleaded, when Tish had finished. "This is no place for a nervous woman."

Tish took a mouthful of the sweetbread and made a face over it.

"Heavens," she said, "it's easy seen salt's cheap. No, I am not going home. I shall stay to see the end of this if it's the end of me."

"Listen, Tish," Aggie said miserably. "Hasn't my advice always been good? Didn't I beg you on my bended knees not to buy that automobile? Didn't both Lizzie and I protest with tears against the motor boat, and you'll carry that scar till your dying day. And now-now it's spirits, Tish. Don't tell me it wasn't."

"Where's that Lewis woman?" was all Tish would say. "Speaking of spirits reminds me I haven't been rubbed with alcohol yet."

But I'd better tell Tish's story in her own words:

"Once for all, before I begin, Aggie," she ordered-Tish is a masterful woman —"you open the collar of your waist and put a pillow behind you. I'm not going to be broken in on in the middle of this by your fainting away. Faint if you want, but get ready beforehand. Lewis is not usually around when she's wanted."

"I don't want to hear it if it's as bad as that," Aggie protested, opening the neck of her waist. "Lizzie, reach me that pillow."

"I don't know that I want to hear it myself, Tish," I said. "You'd better do as Aggie says and come home. You're a wreck this morning, and I've telephoned for Tommy Andrews."

Tommy is Tish's doctor, the son of her cousin, Eliza Peabody Andrews, a nice enough boy, but frivolous. He is on the visiting staff at the hospital, and makes rounds once a day, I believe, with an attentive interne at his elbow and the prettiest nurse he can find carrying the order book.

Tish set the sweetbread on the bedside table with a bang and looked at me for an instant over her glasses.

"Don't be a fool, Lizzie," she said. "Do you think Tommy Andrews can make me do anything I don't want to? Do you think the entire connection could move me one foot if I didn't want to go?"

"You can't spend another night here," I put in, somewhat feebly.

"Can't I?" she said grimly. "Not only I can, and will, but you and Aggie are going to take turns here with me, night and night about, until this is cleared up. Mark my words, last night was not the end."

She turned over on her side then, and proceeded to have her back rubbed with alcohol. And while Miss Lewis rubbed, she told us the story.

"Miss Lewis wanted me to go back to bed," she said, when she had reached that point, "but I refused to go. (You needn't take the skin off, Miss Lewis.) I stood there in my gown, and I watched them making up their minds to go to the mortuary. That's up a narrow flight of stairs from this end of the hall, not far from this very room. Nobody was anxious to lead off, but Miss Blake seemed determined to go back and prove she hadn't been asleep, and at last they moved off huddled in a group and left me there. (You haven't got a spite against my right shoulder, have you?) Miss Lewis followed them."

"I didn't," said Miss Lewis sourly. Tish turned and looked up at her over her shoulder.

"You looked as if you were going to, and you know it," she asserted. "And don't interrupt me. Miss Lewis followed, and seeing I was felling to be left alone, and feeling somewhat creepy along the back, I followed her."

"Really —!" Miss Lewis began.

"We went up the staircase, and if you and Aggie go out and look, you'll see how it leads. There's a hall up there, with a few private rooms along one side, and a small ward across. The mortuary is up a flight of about eight steps, at the far end.

"The hall was dark, and all the light came from the mortuary. The door was open, and it seemed bright and cheerful enough. I was feeling pretty sure the black-haired girl had dozed and had a dream, when I saw Miss Smith, who was in the lead, stoop and pick something up, and hold it out to the other nurses,

" That's queer!' she said, and her eyes were fairly starting out of her head.

"What is it?" said I, limping forward.

The nurses were staring at the thing she held.

" 'It's impossible?' she muttered, 'but-that's the bandage I tied Johnson's hands together with!' Miss Lewis, will you let Miss Pilkington sniff that alcohol for a moment?"

"Fiddle!" Aggie protested feebly. "I'm not at all upset" Then she put her head back on her pillow and fainted, as Tish had arranged, with decency and order.

Well, to go on, it seemed that Tish began to lose her courage about that time, and when one of the braver nurses came running back, after a hasty look, and said that Miss Blake was right, and there was no body in the mortuary, there was almost a stampede. And then it was, I believe, that heavy steps were heard on the staircase, and it proved to be Jacobs, the night watchman.

Now, Tish was in her nightgown, and I fancy, although she never confessed it, that she fell into some sort of a panic and darted into one of the empty rooms. She herself says Miss Lewis pushed her in, out of sight, and closed the door, but Miss Lewis indignantly denies this.

"I stood inside the door, in the darkness," Tish said. "The night watchman was just outside, and I could hear everything that was said, plainly. He didn't believe the body was gone, and said so. I heard him go toward the mortuary door, and the young women followed him. I could feel a chair just beside me, and my knee was jumping again, so I sat down.

"That was when I saw I'd stepped into an occupied room. There was a man in his night clothes standing not ten feet away, in the middle of the room, and I jumped up in a hurry.

" 'Good heavens!' I said, 'I didn't know there was anybody; here I You'll have to excuse me.' "

Tish is an extraordinary woman. She was apparently quite cool, but I happened to glance at Miss Lewis, and she was pouring a small stream of alcohol into the lap of Aggie's black broadcloth tailor-made. She was a pasty yellow-white.

"The man didn't say anything, although I could see him moving," Tish went on, "I thought he was rude. I got the door open and stepped into the hall, almost into the arms of the Blake girl.

" 'Well, were you right?' I asked her.

"She nodded. 'Absolutely gone, without a trace!' she said with a catch in her voice. 'Maybe he wasn't dead,' I suggested. There's a lot of catalepsy around just now.'

" 'He was dead,' she insisted. 'Quite dead. He's been dying for a week.'

"Well, what with the watchman and lights moving around, I wasn't so nervous as I had been, and I was pretty much interested.

" There's one thing sure, my dear,' I said, 'he won't go far in that state. I'll just hobble down and get my wrapper on and we'll have a search. I stepped into that room in my nightgown and I daresay the man in there nearly died himself-of the shock.'

"The man in Iheref she said. Why, all these rooms are empty, Miss Carberry!"

We stood staring at each other.

" 'There's a man in there,' I repeated. 'He stood up and stared at me when I went in.'

"She got very white, but she walked right over to the door and pushed it open. I saw her throw up her hands, and the next minute she had fallen flat on her face in the doorway, and the night watchman was running toward us with a lighted candle."

Tish leaned over and took a drink of water.

"This bed's full of crumbs. Miss Lewis," she grumbled. "It's queer to me that the only part of this hospital toast that is crisp is the part I get in the bed!"

Tor heaven's sake, Tish," I said impatiently, "I suppose she didn't faint because there were crumbs in your bed!"

"No," Tish said, hitching herself over to the other side of the mattress. "She fainted because the body of the missing spiritualist was hanging by its neck to the chandelier, fastened up with a roller towel."

"Dead?" Aggie asked, opening her eyes for the first time.

"Still dead," Tish replied grimly.

Chapter II
The Little Nurse

Aggie was really frightfully upset. Aggie is rather emotional at any time, and although she herself is a Methodist, her mother's only sister had been a believer in Spiritualism. (They dug her up ten years after she died, to make room for somebody else, and Aggie's mother said her hair had grown to be fully ten feet long, and was curly, whereas in life it had always been straight. We may sneer at Spiritualism all we want, but things like that are hard to account for.)

Well, of course, Aggie declared that no human hand had strung poor old Johnson to the chandelier by a roller towel around his neck, and although Tish ridiculed the idea, she had to admit that the fourth dimension had never been accounted for, and that table levitation was an accepted fact, and even known to the ancient.

We sat there gloomily enough while Miss Lewis fixed Tish's hair and massaged her knee. In the middle of the massage Tommy Andrews came in, whistling.

"Morning, Aunt Tish," he said. "Morning, Miss Aggie, morning. Miss Lizzie. How's the knee? Looks as handsome as ever."

"She's been walking on it," said Miss Lewis sourly, and giving the knee an extra jab.

Tommy gave Tish a ferocious frown over his glasses.

"Humph!" he said. "I told you to keep off it! Miss Lewis, if she is obstreperous again, just tie her down with a half-dozen roller towels."

"Roller towels!" Tish ejaculated. "Why, it was a roller towel that-that —"

"So you said," Aggie said somberly, and we stared at each other, we hardly knew why.

Tish told Tommy the whole story as he strapped her knee with adhesive plaster. He hadn't heard it, and he was as much puzzled as we were. It was Aggie who remarked afterward how his face changed when Tish mentioned Miss Blake.

"Blake!" he said, glancing up quickly, "not the little nurse with the dark hair?"

"Yes," Tish said.

"Damn!" said Tonuny. "To have left her alone, like that!" And to Miss Lewis: "Is she ill to-day?"

"She's in bed, but she's not sleeping," said Miss Lewis, with more feeling than I'd have expected. "I was going to ask you if you would see her. Doctor. Since the shake-up yesterday, we have no medical internes, and the surgical side is full up."

"She-she didn't ask for me!" said Tommy, with his brown eyes kindling. But Miss Lewis shook her head.

"She's hardly spoken at all. She just lies there with her eyes wide open and her face white, watching the door. An hour ago one of the nurses pushed it open quietly, for fear she was asleep. Miss Blake lay and watched it moving, and when Linda-Miss Smith went in, she fainted again."

Tommy took a turn up and down the room. "She's had a profound shock," he said. "I'm not afraid of it, unless —" He stopped at the window and stood looking out.

"Unless what?" said Tish, but he didn't answer. Instead, he stalked over and rang the bell.

"I'll have the hall nurse relieve you. Miss Lewis," he said. "We can't leave my aunt alone, and somebody must see to Miss Blake. There's some natural explanation for what happened last night, and we must find it and tell her."

Aggie began to tell about the aunt with the hair, but before she had even buried her, the door opened and Miss Blake herself came in.

"Did you ring?" she asked. She was dead white, lips and all, with deep circles around her eyes, but her step was brisk and her voice cheerful. As Tish said, if you could only have heard her and not seen her, nobody would have believed what had happened.

Tommy gave her one look, and hauled a chair forward.

"Sit down," he ordered. "You are not fit to be on duty."

"Thank you, but —I am all right again," she said, hesitating.

"Please sit down," said Tommy, with a note in his voice which I never heard him use to Tish. And she took the chair, glancing around at all three of us and then at him.

"Miss Blake," he said, "I have decided to become your medical adviser!"

"Thanks very much!" she said, with the ghost of a smile.

"On one condition," he went off, polishing his glasses very hard with his handkerchief. "Tfou will have to obey orders."

"That's the first lesson in the training school," she assented, the smile deepening. "Always obey the doctor's orders."

"Stuff!" said Tommy sternly. "If I order you to bed this minute, you'll not go! The trouble is. Aunt Tish and Honorary Aunts Lizzie and Aggie," he said, addressing us each in turn, "the trouble is that in a hospital medicine is a drug on the market. It's too accessible. So are doctors. They're always on tap, like city water, plentiful and free and therefore subject, like the said water, to the scorn and contumely of the beneficiaries."

"Indeed, Doctor," Miss Blake began, but he interrupted her.

"Now, Miss Blake," he said, "at your earnest solicitation I am about to undertake your case, and the first condition is —"

"Obedience?" She shot a glance at him from under her long, dark lashes, and Aggie raised her eyebrows across the bed at me.

20

"Exactly," he said. "The three aunts, actual and honorary, are witnesses. You have promised obedience. The first condition is — you are to leave the hospital immediately and go to a place I know just out of town, a nice place, with a dog and kittens-no. Aunt Tish, not a cat and kittens, a —"

But Miss Blake stood up suddenly, she was paler than before.

"Not that," she said almost wildly.

Tommy came over and put his hand on her shoulder. "We can dispose of the animals," he said gently. "Can't you see yourself, little girl, that you are about at the end of your string? Quiet nights, sleep, fresh milk-you won't know yourself in a week."

"I can not go," she said, and stood looking straight ahead with such misery in her face that Aggie's eyes filled up.

"You can take your vacation," Tommy persisted, gently, "I'll take you out myself in my machine."

"I don't want to go. Doctor; I —I can't be spared just now. Don't send me away! Don't!"

She began to cry, wildly, hysterically, with her shoulders quivering and her whole body tense. I was considerably upset, and Tommy looked dumbfounded. After all, it was Miss Lewis who knew what to do. She is a large woman, and she simply took the little nurse into her arms and petted her into quiet. Finally, she coaxed her into the hall, and as the door closed behind them, the four of us sat' silent.

Aggie was sniveling, and wiping her eyes, and Tish turned on her in a rage.

"What in the name of sense are you bleating, about?" she demanded.

"The child's in trouble,"said Aggie. "I —I never could see anybody cry, and you know it, Tish,"

"I know something else, too," said Tish grimly, sliding her feet out of bed carefully; and reaching for her cane. 'That young woman knows more than she's telling. Tommy Andrews.' We're not through with this yet."

Now Tommy will always have his joke with Tish, and they differ on a good many subjects, politics, for one thing, and religion. Tommy not believing very much in a future existence, and maintaining that no medical man ought to-it made them more saving of life in this. But he has a great respect for Tish's opinion.

"You may be right," he said. "There must be some reason —, but whatever it is-it's not to her discredit. I'll swear to that."

"Listen to the boy!" Tish sneered, picking up the traveling clock and putting it back on the bedside table again. "That's what a pretty face will do. Suppose it had been Lewis, who stood there, crying into a starched apron and saying she couldn't leave-don't, don't ask her?"

"Why should she leave when she has you, dear Aunt Letitia?" asked Tommy, and Tish reached for the clock again.

Well, we talked the thing over, but we couldn't come to any conclusion. There didn't seem to be any matter of doubt that Johnson, having died peaceably and in order, had been carried to the mortuary and laid on the table, there to await the final preparations for burial. And the fact was incontestable that shortly after, the said Johnson, as Tommy put it, was hanging by the neck to the chandelier in a room fifty feet away and down eight steps. We all agreed up to that point. As Tommy said, the Question then became simply, did he do it himself or was it done for him?

Aggie was confident that he had done it himself.

"Why not?" she demanded. "Isn't it the constant endeavor of the people who have-passed over, to come back and prove their continued existence on a spirit plane? Shall I ever forget that the third night after Mr. Wiggins died —" Aggie was once engaged to a roofer, who passed over' by falling off a roof —"can I ever forget that a light like a flame of a candle rose in one comer of the bedroom, crossed the ceiling and disappeared in my sewing basket, where I kept Mr. Wiggins' photograph? Why should not Mr. Johnson, before deserting the earth plane for the spirit world, have come back and proved his continued existence? Why?"

Tommy lighted a cigarette and puffed at it. "Well," he said, "I should call it indecent of him if he did, and bad taste, too. Maybe he didn't think much of his body, bat it had lasted pretty well and carried him around a good many years. And to have his spirit cast off its outer garment and hang it to a chandelier — it was heartless! Heartless!"

Chapter III
Another Roller Towel

Now Tish is a peculiar woman. Once she starts a thing, whether it is house-cleaning or learning to roller skate, she keeps right on at it She learned to skate backwards, you may remember, although she nearly died learning, and lay once twenty minutes insensible on the back of her head. And as Tish acknowledged later, she had made up her mind to find out who or what had hung Johnson by the neck to the chandelier.

So after Tommy had gone, she got into her roller chair and asked me to ring for Miss Lewis.

"What time do you go to your lunch?" she' asked her sharply, when she came.

"I don't eat lunch," said Miss Lewis.

"It's making me stout Besides, there's never anything fit to eat."

"Humph!" said Tish, "I guess the meals provided in this training school are above the average. I myself engaged the housekeeper. You'd better have lunch to-day."

"But —"

"At twelve o'clock," said Tish firmly. "Any nurse who takes care of me eats three meals a day."

Miss Lewis stood in the doorway, with her cap over one ear, and stared at Tish, and Tish glared back.

"I prefer not," she said defiantly, giving her apron belt a twitch.

"At twelve o'clock!" Tish repeated, and then Miss Lewis gave it up.

"Very well," she said unpleasantly. "Does 'it make any difference what I eat?"

"None whatever. And now send me the Smith woman," said Tish calmly. "And shut the door. There's a drought."

Miss Lewis slammed out. And whatever reason Tish had for wanting to get rid of her at noon, she deigned no explanation. In ten minutes Miss Smith knocked at the door and came in. She looked tired, but cheerful.

"Do you want me. Miss Carberry?" she asked.

"If you are not busy," said Tish in her pleasantest manner. "Sit down. Miss Smith. Lizzie, Aggie, this is the Miss Smith I told you about. You will pardon the curiosity of ,three old women, won't you. Miss Smith, and answer a question or two about last night?"

"Certainly." She looked surprised, and I fancied amused.

"In the first place," Tish asked, getting a pencil and sheet of letter paper from the table, "has any investigation been begun?"

"I think not," said Miss Smith. "There are always queer goings-on in a hospital, and besides, there has been a stir-up in the management, and things are at sixes and sevens. Two internes left last night, and the superintendent is pretty busy this morning."

"Indeed," said Tish, and wrote something down. "Where is the-er-body now?"

"It went to the anatomical board this morning. He had no relatives and no money. If he isn't claimed in a certain time, he'll be sent to the college dissecting room-"

Aggie shuddered.

"And now, Miss Smith," said Tish, leaning back in her roller chair, "would you mind telling me exactly what happened last night?"

"Not at all!" said Miss Smith, smiling. "We have a rule here that when a patient dies in one of the wards at night, the day nurses for that ward go with the body to the mortuary and prepare it for burial. The night nurse, having charge of several wards, can not easily leave. I am in charge of K ward, and Miss Blake is my assistant."

'She's not in K ward to-day," said Tish.

'No, she is relieving the hall nurse here for her off duty- Miss Blake is not well, and this is lighter."

"One moment," said Tish, "what is the K ward's night nurse's name?"

"Miss Durand."

"What time did Mr. Johnson die?"

"Shortly after midnight. It was marked twelve-ten on the record."

"And you were called at once?" I —think not, Miss Smith said slowly. "It was nearly one o'clock."

"Is that customary?" Tish demanded.

"Not usually," said Miss Smith, "but it is not extraordinary, either the night nurse may have been giving a fever bath, or something else she could not leave."

"You are very indulgent to the curiosity of , three old women," Tish said with her pleasantest smile. "Will you be amiable a little longer, and tell us what happened in the mortuary?"

"Well, really, nothing happened to me. Doctor Grimm had seen Johnson and pronounced him dead; he had been called from the operating room to do it, although Johnson was a medical case. The. night orderlies, Briggs and Marshall, took the body to the mortuary and waited with it until Miss Blake and I arrived."

"Briggs and Marshall," Tish put down.

"The lights were on, and Briggs was smoking. We had a few words over that, because the orderlies are not allowed to smoke on duty, and tobacco makes my head ache."

Tish leaned forward in her chair and looked at Miss Smith.

"Do you often have words with the orderlies, Miss Smith?"

Miss Smith smiled cheerfully.

"Quite often," she said. 'They're such a stupid lot."

"You don't think it possible that these men may have retaliated by playing a practical joke on you?"

Miss Smith considered.

"No," she said, "I don't. When I found the linen closet up there locked and went downstairs for sheets, they were both at work in the wards. Anyhow, they might be willing to play a ghastly trick on me, but I don't think they would try to frighten Miss Blake. She's very well liked."

"And after you went for the sheets?"

That's all I know. Miss Carberry. The rest you heard Miss Blake tell."

"Are you sure," Aggie broke in suddenly, leaning forward, "are you sure, Miss Smith, that he didn't do it himself?"

Miss Smith stared. "Why, he was dead. Miss Pilkington," she said. "He'd been sick for months, and if he was alive as I am this minute, he couldn't hang himself by the neck, the way he was hanging, with nothing to stand on near, or any chair kicked away. The center of the room was clear when we found him, and the nearest thing was the foot of the bed, a good eight feet away."

"He was a —Spiritualist, I think?"

"Yes — yes, indeed," Miss Smith laughed. "It would have made you creepy to hear him, lying there carrying on whole conversations with nobody near, and raps on his bed until the nurses balked at changing the sheets!"

Aggie shivered. "Gracious!" she said, "I hope they don't send him back here for the dissecting room. I shan't be easy until he is safely buried."

"OK, you needn't worry about that," Miss Smith said cheerfully, getting up to go. "We wouldn't be likely to get all of him anyhow."

Well, as Tish said, she hadn't learned much she hadn't known before, except that Johnson had been left in the ward fifty minutes after he died, instead of ten. But although the people in the hospital seemed disposed to let the affair alone after sending the body away, and to get back to its business, which, as Miss Smith said, is full of curious things anyhow, Tish, as I say, having taken hold, was not going to let go.

Promptly at noon by the traveling clock, Miss Lewis having taken herself off, Tish lifted herself out of her wheel chair and reached for her cane.

"You can stay here, Aggie," she said, "and if Lewis comes back, I'm seeing Lizzie to the elevator."

"She won't believe a word of it," Aggie objected.

"Then think up something she will believe. Lizzie is coming with me."

I wasn't surprised when Tish turned to the left, in the corridor, and hobbled to the foot of a flight of stairs. She stopped there and turned.

"We're going up to see that room in daylight, Lizzie," she said, "but I want you to read this first. You're a practical woman, and if any of your family ever grew a head of hair after they died, at least you don't brag about it."

She took a page of the morning paper, folded small, from the sleeve of her dressing-gown, and pointed to a paragraph.

"Amos Johnson, once a well-known local medium, died last night at the Dunkirk hospital, after a long illness. Johnson was sixty-seven years of age, and had lived in retirement and poverty since the murder of his wife some years ago, a crime for which he was tried and exonerated. The woman's body was found in the parlor of the Johnson home, hanging to a chandelier by a roller towel knotted about the neck."

Tish was watching me.

"Well, what do you make of that, Lizzie?" she asked.

"Coincidence," I said, with affected calmness. "Many a man's hung his wife to something when he got tired of her, and when you come to think of it, a roller towel is usually handy."

We didn't look at each other.

Chapter IV
The Footprint on the Wall

Well, Tish and I examined the room, and I must say at first sight it was disappointing. It was an ordinary hospital room, with two windows, and a bureau between them, a washstand, a single brass bed, set high and not made up, the pillows being piled in the center of the mattress and all covered with a sheet, and two chairs, a straight one and a rocker. Except that the heavy chandelier was bent somewhat from the perpendicular, there was no sign of what had happened there.

Tish sat down in the rocker and looked thoughtfully about the room.

"Under ordinary circumstances," she said, "if you hang a broadcloth skirt on a chandelier to brush it, you'll have the whole business and half the ceiling about your head in a minute. And yet, look at that, hardly bent!"

The room had evidently not been disturbed since Johnson had been found there. The straight chair had been drawn beneath the chandelier, and Tish pointed out the scratches made by the feet of whoever had cut down the body. Over the back of the chair still hung the roller towel, twisted into a grisly rope.

Tish picked it up and examined it.

"Pretty extravagant of material, aren't they?" she said. "No Ladies' Aid that I ever saw would put more than two yards of twelve-cent stuff in a roller towel. Look at the weight of that, and the length!"

"There's something on it," I said, and we looked together. What we found were only three letters, stamped in blue ink.

"S. P. T.?" said Tish. "What in creation is S. P. T.?"

She sat down with the towel in her hand, and we puzzled over it together.

"It's the initials of the sewing circle that sent it in," I asserted "That S. stands for Society."

"I've got it," said Tish. "Society for the Prevention of Tetanus."

"That doesn't help much," I said. "We could find out by asking; I daresay the nurses know."

But Tish wouldn't hear of it She said the towel was the only clue we had, and she wasn't going to give it to a hospital full of people who didn't seem to care whether their corpses walked around at night or not

She rolled up the towel under her arm, and in the doorway she turned to take a final survey of the room.

"Well," she said;, "we haven't examined the dust with the microscope, but I think it's been worth while It would be curious, Lizzie, if his murdered wife's initials were S. P, T."

"They couldn't be," I said. "Her last name was Johnson, wasn't it?"

But Tish wasn't looking at me. She was staring intently at the wall over the head of the bed, and I followed her eyes.

The wall was gray, a dull gray below, and a frieze of paler gray above. The dividing line between the two colors was not a picture molding-the room had no pictures-but a narrow iron pipe, perhaps an inch in thickness, and painted the color of the frieze. Why a pipe, I never asked, but I fancy its roundness, its lack of angles and lines, had been thought, like the gray walls, to be restful to the eyes.

Directly over the head of the bed, the pipe-molding was loosened from the wall, as if by a powerful wrench, and sagged at least four inches.

"Look at that!" said Tish, pointing her cane. "Lizzie, I want you to help me up on the bureau."

"I'll do nothing of the sort, Tish," I snapped. "You ought to be ashamed with that leg."

But she had pulled out the lowest drawer and was standing on it by that time, and there wasn't anything for it but to help her up. She caught hold of the pipe-molding between the windows, and jerked at it.

"I thought so," she said. "It doesn't give a hair's breadth! Lizzie, no picture ever pulled that molding down like that."

Well, it was curious, when you think about it. It's easy enough to read Mr, Conan Doyle's stories, knowing that no matter how puzzling the different clues seem to be, Mr. Doyle knows exactly what made them, and at the right time he'll let you into his secret, and you'll wonder why you never thought of the right explanation at the time. But it is different to have to work them out yourself, and to save my life I couldn't see anything to that bended pipe but a bended pipe.

Tish's next move was to crawl upon the, bed, and that time I helped her willingly. She stood for quite a while, gazing at the pipe, with her nostrils twitching, steadying herself with one hand against the wall to put on her glasses with the other.

"Humph!" she said. "I can't quite make it 'out There are prints against the wall just underneath, but it doesn't seem to be a hand."

I got up beside her and we both looked. It was a hand, and it wasn't. It seemed like a long hand with short fingers. Tish leaned down and rubbed her hand on the headboard of the bed, which was dusty, as she expected, and then pressed its imprint against the wall beside the other. They were alike, and they were different, and suddenly it came to me, and it made me dizzy.

'I know what it is now, Tish," I said as calmly as I could. "That's the mark of a foot!"

Tish nodded. She'd seen it almost as soon as I had.

"A foot," she repeated gravely, and we climbed off the bed in a hurry and went out into the hall.

Tish had left her cane in her excitement, and she refused to go back for it alone. I went with her, finally, and we stood at the bottom of the bed and looked at the foot, with its toes pointed up toward the ceiling, and Tish's hand beside it.

"You know, Lizzie," she said, clutching my arm, "if there were a fourth dimension, we could walk up walls easily."

And we went down to her room again.

It was careless of us to forget Tish's handprint on the wall, for when things got worse, and they discovered the two marks, somebody suggested that no two hands make exactly the same print, and they had an expert take an impression of it As Tish said, she expected to be discovered every time she had her pulse counted, and the strain was awful. They might have accused her, you know, of carrying off old Johnson and stringing him up, for they reached a state when they suspected everybody.

Chapter V
When Aggie Screamed

Now Aggie has hay fever, and the slightest excitement, any time in the year, starts her off. So when we heard her sneezing as we went down the stairs, we were not surprised to find Tommy Andrews In front of her with an order book on his knee, and Aggie trying to hold a glass thermometer in her mouth.

'I can't," she was protesting around the thermometer. "Justh try sneething yourself with a—a—choo."

Her teeth came down on it just then with a snap and her face grew agonized.

"There!" she said. "What did I tell you?" And pulled the thermometer out minus an end.

"Where's the rest?" Tommy demanded.

"I—I swallowed it!"

Tommy jumped up. and looked frightened.

"Great heavens, it's glass I" he said. "What in thunder-why, there it is in your lap!"

"I swallowed the inside," Aggie said stiffly. "I should think that's bad enough. It's poison, isn't it?"

Tommy laughed. "It won't hurt you," he said. "It's only quicksilver."

But Aggie was only partly reassured. "I daresay I'll be coated inside like the back of a mirror," she snapped. "Between being frightened to death until I'm in a fever, and then swallowing the contents of a thermometer, and having it expand with the heat of my body, and maybe blow up, I feel as though I'm on the border of the spirit land myself."

In spite of Tommy's reassurances, she refused to be comforted, and sat the rest of the afternoon waiting for something to happen. She ate no luncheon, and she absolutely refused to go home. Aggie is like most soft-mannered people, trying to make her do something she doesn't want is like pounding a pillow. It seems to give way, and the next minute it's back where it was at first, and you can pound till your hands ache. So when she said she was going to stay at the hospital until she felt sure the mercury wasn't going to blow up or poison her, we had to yield.

We got the room next to Tish's and put her to bed, and she lay there alternately sneezing and sleeping the rest of the day. I went out during the afternoon and brought a nightgown for her and one for myself, and the mentholated cotton wool for her nose. The walk did me good, and by the time I got back I was ready to sneer at footprints that go up a wall and Johnson hanging to a chandelier.

As I left the elevator at Tish's door, I met Miss Linda Smith and stopped her. "Is there anything new?" I asked.

"Nothing, except that Miss Blake has been sent back to bed," she said. "She's a nervous little thing anyhow, and she has not been here very long. When she has had almost three years, as I have, she'll learn to let each day take care of itself-not to worry about yesterday or expect anything of to-morrow."

"And how about to-day?" I asked, smiling at the contradiction of her pessimistic speech and her cheerful face.

"And to work like the deuce to-day," she said, and went smiling down the hall.

I had brought in some pink roses, and when I'd put Aggie's nightgown on her and the wool in her nose, I had Miss Lewis take me to Miss Blake's room.

It was close at hand. If you know the Dunkirk Hospital, you know that the nurses' dormitory is directly beside the main building, and connected with it by doors on every floor. One of these doors was at the end of Tish's corridor, and Miss Blake's room was the first on the 'other side.

Miss Lewis knocked and tried the door, but it was bolted.

"Who's there?" asked a startled voice, quite close, as if it's owner had been standing just inside.

"Miss Lewis, dear."

"Just a moment."

She opened the door almost immediately and admitted us. She had on only her night gown and slippers, and her hair was down in a thick braid. I have reached the time of life when I brush most of my hair by holding one end of it in my teeth, so I always notice hair.

"You're up," said Miss Lewis accusingly.

"Only to be sure the door was fastened," she protested, and got into her single bed again obediently.

"Now don't be silly!" Miss Lewis said-"Why should you lock that door in the middle of the afternoon? I thought you were the girl who rescued the kitten from the ridge pole of the roof!"

"That was different," said Miss Blake, and shut her eyes.

"I don't want to disturb you," I said. "Only-my friend and I felt sorry that she caused you such a shock last night. And I want you to have these flowers."

She seemed much pleased and Miss Lewis put them on the table by the bed, beside another bouquet already there, a Huge bunch of violets and lilies of the valley. Violets and lilies of the valley are Tommy's favorite combination!

"Doctor Andrews been here this afternoon?" Miss Lewis asked, looking up from arranging the roses.

"Once-twice," said the little nurse, with heightened color.

"I see," said Miss Lewis. "And the husband of thirty-six telephoning all over the city for him."

"The husband of thirty-six!" I repeated, astounded. They both laughed, and Miss Blake looked for a moment almost gay.

"He is not a Mormon," she said. "It's a case of 'container for the thing contained.' Thirty-six is a room."

I think the laugh did the little nurse good, but when we left, a few minutes later. Miss Lewis halted me a few steps from the door. We heard her cross the room quickly and the bolt of the door slip into place.

"Queer, isn't it?" asked Miss Lewis. And I thought it was.

Tommy Andrews came back late that night to see Aggie, but she had stopped sneezing and dropped into a doze. He beckoned me out into the hall.

"How is she?" he asked. "Having been quick-silvered inside, I daresay she's been reflecting! Never mind. Miss Lizzie —I couldn't help that."

"Tish wants to see you. Tommy," I said. "She-we found something this afternoon and I don't mind saying we are puzzled."

"More mystery?" he asked, raising his eyebrows. "Don't tell me somebody else has shed his fleshy garment and hung it up — "

"Please don't," I said, looking over my shoulder nervously. The hall was almost dark.

"Look here," Tommy suggested in a whisper, "I'll make a bargain with you. I'll go in and listen to Aunt Tish without levity —I give you my word, no frivolity-if you'll come over and play propriety while I see Miss Blake."

Seeing me eye him, he went on guiltily: "She's —sick, you know, and I've been there two or three times to-day already. If it gets out among the nurses — please, dear, good Aunt Lizzie!"

Now, I'm not his aunt. For that matter, I'm a good ten years younger than Tish, but he's a handsome young rascal, and when a woman gets too old to be influenced by good looks, it's because she's gone blind with age, so I agreed on one condition.

"Yes, if you'll see Tish first," I said, and he agreed.

That was how we happened to be in Tish's room when Aggie screamed. Tish had just got to the footprint-on-the-wall part of her story, and even Tommy was looking rather queer, when Aggie sneezed. Then almost immediately she shrieked and the three of us were on our feet and starting for the door before she stopped. As we reached the hall, a nurse was running toward us, and the stillness in Aggie's room was horrible.

It was dark. Which was strange, for Fd left the night light on at Aggie's request. Tommy pushed into the room first.

"Where's the light switch?" he demanded. "Are you there. Miss Aggie?"

There was no answer, but in the darkness every one heard a peculiar rustling sound, such as might be made by rubbing a hand over a piece of stiff silk. It was the nurse who found the switch almost instantly, and I think we expected nothing less than Aggie hanging by her neck to the chandelier. But she was lying quietly in bed, in a dead faint.

When she came to, she muttered something about a dead foot and fainted again. By-eleven o'clock she seemed pretty much herself once more and even smiled sheepishly when Tommy suggested that it had been the fault of the thermometer. She thought herself that she had dreamed it, and Tish and I let her think so. But both of us had seen the same thing.

Just over the head of Aggie's bed the pipe molding was wrenched loose and pulled down out of line!

Chapter VI
Candle and Skylight

Tish sent Miss Lewis in to sit with Aggie, and the three of us, including Tommy, met in Tish's room. She had brought her alcohol tea-kettle with her, and she insisted on making a cup of tea all around before we talked things over.

"Besides," she remarked, measuring out the tea, "it's about a quarter of twelve now, and we may need a little tea-courage by midnight."

"If that's the way you feel," Tommy said, from the bed, holding his empty cup ready for the tea. "I can get something from the medicine cupboard outside that has tea knocked out in the first round."

"Not whiskey. Tommy!" Tish said with the tea pot in the air.

"Certainly not! Spiritus frumenti," Tommy said with dignity, and Tish was reassured. But I knew what he meant, my great uncle having conducted a country pharmacy and done a large business among the farmers in that very remedy.

When we'd had our tea and some salted wafers, Tish drew up a chair and faced Tommy and myself.

"Now," she said, "what did Aggie see?"

"Personally," Tommy remarked, balancing his teaspoon across the bridge of his nose, and holding his head far back to do it, "personally, I'm glad she only saw-or felt —a foot. It proves her really remarkable quality of mind. The ordinary woman, in a stew like that, would have seen an entire corpse, not to mention smelling sulphur." r

Tish took the spoon off his nose and gave him a smart slap on the ear.

"Thomas!" she said, "you will either be serious or go home. Do you remember what we told you about the room upstairs, a foot-mark on the wall not three feet from the ceiling?"

Tommy nodded, with both hands covering his ears.

"Do you realize," Tish went on, "that that room is directly over the one Aggie is occupying?"

"Hadn't thought of it," said Tommy. "Is it?"

"Yes. Tommy Andrews, Aggie may or may not have dreamed of that ice-cold foot, but one thing she did not dream; Lizzie and I both saw it. The pipe molding over Aggie's bed is pulled loose from the wall and bent down."

Tommy stared at us both. Then he whistled.

"No!" he said, and fell into a deep study, with his hands in his heavy thatch of hair. After a minute he got off the bed and sauntered toward the door.

"I'll just wander in and have a look at it," he said, and disappeared.

It was Tish's suggestion that we put the light: out and sit in the dark. Probably Tommy's nearness gave us courage. As Tish said, in five minutes it would be midnight, and almost anything might happen under the circumstances.

"And as honest investigators," she said, "we owe it to the world and to science to put ourselves en rapport. These things never happen in the light."

We could hear Tommy speaking in a low tone to Miss Lewis, but soon that stopped, although he did not come back. Even with the door open, a dimly-outlined rectangle, I wasn't any too comfortable. Tish sat without moving. Once she leaned over and touched my elbow.

"I've got a tingle in both legs to the knee," she whispered. "Do you feel anything?"

"Nothing but the slat across the back of this chair," I replied, and we sat silent again. I must have dozed almost immediately, for when I roused, the traveling clock was striking midnight, and Tish was shaking my arm.

"What's that light?" she quavered.

I looked toward the hall, and sure enough the outline of the door was a pale and quavering yellow.

The door frame is moving!" gasped Tish. "Fiddle!" I snapped, wide awake. "Somebody's out there with a moving light. Where's-Tommy?"

"He hasn't come back. Lizzie, go and look out. I can't find my cane."

"Go yourself!" I said sourly.

Well, we went together, finally, tiptoeing to the door and peering out. The light was gone; only a faint gleam remained, and that came down the staircase to the upper floor.

"Damnation!" said Tommy's voice, just at our elbow. And with that he darted along the hall and up the stairs, after the light.

Now Tish is essentially a woman of action. She's only timid when she can't do anything.'

And now she hobbled across to the foot of the stairs, with me at her heels.

"That was no earthly light, Lizzie!" she said in a subdued tone. "Do you remember what Aggie said, about the light when Mr. Wiggins died?"

I'd been thinking about it myself that very moment.

"I'd feel better with some sort of weapon, Tish," I protested, as we started up, but Tish only looked at me in the darkness and shook her head. I knew perfectly well what she meant: that no earthly weapon would be of any avail. Considering what we thought, I think that we got up the staircase at all is very creditable.

The light was there, coming from one of the empty rooms, and streaming out into the dark hall. There was somebody moving in the room. We heard a window closing, and then the footsteps coming toward the door. The next moment the light itself came into the hall. It was a candle, and Miss Blake was carrying it!

I made out Tommy's figure flattened in a doorway, and then the light disappeared again as Miss Blake went into the next room, the one where Johnson had been found. She was there a long time, and once we heard her exclaim something and the light from the doorway wavered, as if the candle had almost gone out.

She went into each private room, then into the ward, and finally there remained only the mortuary. Tish clutched my arm. Would this bit of a girl, in her long white wrapper, her childish braid, her small bare feet thrust into bedroom slippers, would she dare that grisly place?"

She did not keep us in doubt long. She went directly to the foot of the mortuary steps and stood, her candle held high, looking up. Then she began to mount them, slowly, as if every atom of her will were required to urge her frightened muscles. Tommy stirred uneasily in his doorway.

The large double doors to the mortuary stood partly open. She pushed them back quietly and hesitated, candle still high. Then she went in, and by the paling light we knew she had gone to the far end of the room. Tommy came out from the doorway and tiptoed down the hall. We could see his outline against the gleam.

The stillness was terrible. We could hear her moving around that awful place, could hear, even at that distance, the soft swish of her negligee on the floor. And then, without any warning, she spoke. It was uncanny beyond description, although we heard nothing she said.

"My God!" said Tish, forgetting herself.

There was a sound immediately after. Tish said it was a thud, as if a chair had been upset, but I insisted that it sounded more like a window thrown up with terrific force. The light went out immediately, and we heard footsteps running away from us.

"Tommy!" Tish called. But nobody answered. We were left there alone in the darkness, shivering with fright.

I am very shaky about what happened next. I remember Tish fumbling for her cane, and saying she was going to follow Tommy, and my holding her back and telling her not to be a fool-that the boy was safe enough. And I remember seeing a light behind us and the old night watchman coming up the staircase with his electric flash, and trying to tell him something was wrong in the mortuary.

And then, as my voice gave way, we heard a shout overhead, and immediately the crash of broken glass and a thud into the hall just ahead of us. The watchman pushed us aside and ran.

Tommy was lying unconscious on the floor with the pieces of a broken skylight all around him.

Chapter VII
Insinuations and Recriminations

Miss Lewis had heard the crash and came running, with the hall nurse from the floor below. Tish was sitting on the floor among the pieces of glass, with Tommy's head on her knee, crying over him, when they got there. He opened his eyes just then, and lay staring up at the hole in the skylight above, as if he was puzzled. Then he turned his head and saw who was holding him, and made an effort to sit up.

"You-needn't look so tragic, Aunt Tish," he said. "I'm —I'm all right," and fell back on her lap again.

Miss Lewis got down and began to feel him for broken bones.

"Skull's whole, thank goodness!" she muttered. "Can you move your legs. Doctor?"

Tommy lifted them in turn, making grimaces of pain. Then he lifted his right arm. It fell as if he couldn't support its weight

"I've bruised my shoulder," he said, and lay back with his eyes closed.

"Get his coat off," ordered Miss Lewis, and I knelt to help her. But Tommy resisted.

"I'm all right," he said crossly. "I'll look after it later myself."

"Tommy!" said Tish. "Let them take your coat off."

"I won't have it off," he insisted, and when she persisted he was almost vicious.

Miss Lewis sat back on her heels and shook her head at me.

"He's a little dazed," she said. "How in the world did it happen?"

"I was walking on the roof," said Tommy more agreeably, "and I stepped on the skylight by mistake. It was dark underneath. It was a dam fool thing to do!"

The hall nurse and Miss Lewis exchanged glances, and the hall nurse looked at me and smiled.

"He is still dazed," she said, smiling. "How could he step on the skylight? It has a four-foot fence around it!"

We waited for him to explain further, but he let it go at that, and lay for a little while with his mouth shut hard and a queer thoughtful look on his face. He roused pretty soon, however, and grunted as if his shoulder pained him. Then he made Tish get up, and after a minute or so he sat up himself. He sat there gazing at the skylight, and a few drops of rain came down through the opening. Tish and I shivered. We were only partly dressed.

He saw it and was on his feet at once, pretty much himself.

"Now don't let's have any fuss about this, please," he said, addressing us all. "I forgot the sky-light. That's all. I'm not hurt. Aunt Tish, and you and Miss Lizzie must go to bed this instant."

"What are you going to do?" Tish demanded sharply. "Going up on the roof again?"

"I'll be down pretty soon," he evaded. "Jacobs and I will just straighten this mess a bit."

I caught a look of intelligence between the two of them, and Jacobs spoke up.

"If the doctor'll lend a hand —"

"Tommy," Tish said suddenly, "the shoulder of your coat is soaked with blood!"

Tommy put his hand up and felt it.

"I've got a scratch somewhere up there," he said coolly. "It isn't going to be touched until the two ladies in negligee and curl papers are safe in bed with hot-water bottles at their feet. Miss Lewis, Miss Carberry is using her knee again!"

"I'd use a switch if I had one," said Tish, almost with tears in her eyes. But Tommy has the same will that she has herself, and we were downstairs between blankets, I on the couch in Tish's room and Tish in bed, with our feet against hot-water bottles, and drinking cups of hot milk, almost before we knew it.

But Tommy and the watchman did not clean up the broken glass in the upper hall. Whatever they did, that glass was still there the next morning, and none of us disturbed the general belief that it had been broken by the hail-storm that came just before dawn.

I was so hoarse the next morning that I could hardly speak, and Tish kept me on her couch. Her knee was stiff again, too. Including Aggie, although she had slept through the skylight incident, we were pretty well used up, and Tish would not let us go home. It was just as well. She should hardly have faced the events of the next two days without us.

Aggie had her breakfast in bed, but Tish and I had Briggs, the orderly who carried in our trays, set out a table for us, and were really .very snug. Tish was as cross as two sticks until she'd had her tea, when she grew more companionable.

"I want to ask you something, Lizzie," she said as she poured her second cup. "How, when we saw Tommy go into the mortuary, as plain as day, could he fall down from the roof?"

"Well," I said, buttering my toast, "you know about the what-you-call-'ems in India, They send up a rope into the sky and then a boy up the rope, and after he has disappeared they give the rope a jerk and he falls, apparently from nowhere. It's some sort of optical illusion."

Don't be a fool," Tish observed sharply. I've been thinking it over in bed. There must be a fire-escape there somewhere."

"Oh!" I hadn't thought of a fire escape.

"Now, then," said Tish, "suppose there is a fire-escape, and the Blake girl went up by it to the roof, and Tommy followed her. Which is what happened, Lizzie. I'm nobody's fool; I've got eyes in my head. If that young woman had jumped off the window sill, Tommy Andrews would have jumped too. Now, then, why did the Blake girl go to the roof?"

"Maybe she wanted air," I suggested. Tish waved her napkin at me.

"Air!" she snapped. "When you want air, do you generally climb a fire-escape to a roof, when there's a staircase up to it, and entice young men to fall down through skylights and break their shoulders? Lizzie," —she leaned over —"Lizzie, that young vixen pushed him through that skylight and I can prove it!"

"No!"

"Yes." She got up and, going to the cupboard, lifted down her best hat.

"T-ook here!" she said, and took from its crown a brass candlestick, the base bent almost double.

"I was sitting on that when I held Tommy's head last night. It came down with the skylight," she said. "That's the candlestick the Blake girl was carrying. What do you make of it?"

I was speechless. Tish tinlocked the lower bureau drawer and put the candlestick in it, beside the roller towel marked S. P. T. and something else, which I learned later was the bandage Linda Smith had found in the upper hall, and identified as the one that had tied Johnson's hands.

Now," she said, locking the drawer again, I'm going to have a little chat with Miss Blake. It's my belief that she let old Johnson die from neglect, or gave him poison by mistake. And now he's haunting her-or she's haunting him, which is what it looks like."

But we had no chat with Miss Blake that day. The day nurse, taking her a tray of breakfast, found her delirious in bed, with a raging fever. Miss Lewis went over to see her.

"She's been preparing for this for some time," she said when she came back. "She was queer yesterday-you remember. Miss Lizzie '—and last night she did a funny thing. She got the night nurse to give her a bottle of morphine-enough to kill a horse. And I found' it under her pillow this morning, almost half of it gone!"

"Great heavens!" Tish said. "Why, the girl's a potential murderess!"

Miss Lewis turned, with a pillow in her arms. "Not a bit of it," she said. "There's something queer about this place lately, and I don't care who hears me say it. But folks will have to make insinuations against Ruth Blake over my dead body!"

She glared at Tish, and Tish at her.

"I have reasons to doubt that Miss Blake is all you think her," said Tish stiffly. But Miss Lewis came and stood over her unpleasantly. , "I'm not for making any trouble. Miss Car-| berry," she said, "but this house was calm enough until two days ago, and Ruth Blake has been here six months, and what's more, I notice one thing. The most of the excitement has been around where you are. Maybe you're psychic, as they call it, and don't know it. Maybe it's—something else. But it wasn't Miss Blake who first saw Johnson hanging by his neck, and it wasn't Miss Blake the skylight all but fell on, and it wasn't Miss Blake's nephew that fell through the skylight, and it wasn't in the room of Miss Blake's best friend next door that a death-cold foot —"

But Tish put her fingers in her ears and fled to Aggie.

Nevertheless, Miss Lewis had set me to blinking.

Chapter VIII
Overheard in the Dormitory

Aggie's hay fever was bad that morning, and she stayed in bed. Tish and I went in and sat with her after breakfast, and she was very disagreeable.

"I shall certainly tell Tobby whad I thig of hib," she grumbled. "I told hib I could dot hold that therbobeter. That is what gave be that dreab. If it was a dreab!"

"Certainly it was a dream," said Tish.

"I'b dot so sure!" Aggie retorted.

Well, relieved of the hay fever, Aggie's story was something like this:

She had been asleep, and was dreaming' she had turned into a thermometer herself, and as she> got hotter, having too many blankets on, she said she felt herself expanding until her head touched something that she thought was the head of the bed. But she said in her dream she kept on expanding, and she was just saying to Tommy Andrews, in a fury, that if it grew any hotter she'd burst, when something gave way at the head of the bed with a sort of tearing sound, and she wakened. She said it was a full minute before she was certain she wasn't a thermometer and hadn't expanded right up through the top. Then she reached up to turn over her pillow, and just beside her was a dead foot. She had thought she was still dreaming and had actually caught hold of it. But it disappeared under her fingers, dissolved, as you might say, and there was no body. Aggie was positive about that. It was then she sat up and screamed.

Well, we kept the knowledge of what had happened to Tommy from her, and left her sitting up in bed using a nasal spray. Tish was wonderfully better after breakfast, and we walked up and down the corridor, she without the cane and hardly a limp.

It was Tish who suggested that we go into the nurses' dormitory and ask how Miss Blake was, and after we had located Miss Lewis, gossiping with the day nurse in a corner, we slipped in. Patients are forbidden in the dormitory.

The door to Miss Blake's room was closed, but somebody was inside, talking. Tish and I waited outside, and we could hardly help hearing what was said. It was a woman's voice,, familiar enough, but I couldn't place it.

"You must stay in bed, Ruth," she was pleading. "Oh, my dear, how can I forgive myself!"

'Tret me up!" Ruth Blake's voice, insistent and querulous. "They are hanging him up by the neck —" her voice died away in a groan.

The other woman broke into frightened sobbing, and Tish put her hand on the knob. But I held her back.

"I have killed her!" said the voice. "Always thinking of myself! Ruth! Listen to me!"

"Through the skylight!" babbled Ruth. "I tell you, he is dead!"

"Ruth!" begged the voice, and more sobbing, growing gradually quieter. Then silence, as if the sick girl had dropped asleep.

Tish and I slipped away, and back through the connecting door to our room. Once there, by common mute consent we left the door into the corridor open and took up such positions as enabled us to watch the people who passed along the hall. Ten minutes brought nobody. Then we heard the door open, and brisk steps coming along the hall.

"Well," said Miss Linda Smith, in her cheerful way, "Well, how's the knee this morning. Miss Carberry?"

"Better," Tish replied genially.

"That's fine," said Miss Smith and hurried along, humming a bit of a song. Tish and I looked at each other. In spite of the cheerfulness, of the eyes bathed in cold water and carefully powdered, it was Miss Smith's voice we had heard in the Blake girl's room.

But when we got to talking it over we couldn't see that what we had heard had really any importance. Miss Smith had left the girl alone in the mortuary, and was reproaching herself for having done it. That was all. But as Tish said, what did she mean by saying she was always thinking of herself? It was hardly, as Tish pointed out, an act of supreme selfishness to go down and get an armful of sheets to cover a corpse!

Tommy came in at eleven o'clock, freshly shaved and linened, and apparently as well as ever. He had been over to see Miss Blake first, but found her sleeping, which he considered a good sign. I noticed that he kept his right hand in his pocket, and did not use the arm at all. He said the shoulder was stiff, naturally, and that he must have been sleep-walking himself to get over that fence and through the skylight the way he had.

"Sleep-walking!" said Tish sharply. "Do you think that that girl was sleep-walking?"

"I certainly do," said Tommy.

"Then you are a fool," said Tish. "If she was sleep-walking, so was the burglar who took my disciple spoons last fall. Sleep-walking!"

"I wish you —"

"You're wishing me bad luck if you feel the Way you look!" said Tish shrewdly. "Now, Tommy, I'm going to get to the bottom of all this, and so are you. It will take twice the amount of effort separated as united. Don't try any evasions with me-half a truth is worse than a good lie. Now-out with it. What really happened on the roof last night?'"

"I wish I knew!" said Tommy, and looked at us gravely. "You saw what there was to see up-stairs. I happened to see Miss Blake going up the stairs with the candle, and I noticed something strange in her expression. I followed her and you followed me. She went into each room and then to the mortuary. That's proof, isn't it, that she was sleep-walking? I've worried over it all night, and I'm sure of it. Anyhow, why should she take a candle, when there is electric light everywhere? I tell you, the shock of the night before was on the girl's mind while she slept."

Tish had got out her sheet of letter paper. Well?" she said, putting something down. I saw her go into the mortuary, and I heard her talking; I couldn't make out what she said. Then there was a crash, and I ran. When I got there one of the stained glass windows was wide open, and she was climbing up the fire-escape outside. The candle had gone out. Aunt Tish, that fire-escape up there is the merest skeleton, and it is five high stories from the ground. Awake, she couldn't have done it."

"Humph!" said Tish. "It isn't hard at night, when you can't see how far it is to the ground." Then, seeing that Tommy was looking sulky, she added: "Still, you may be right."

"Up to that point," said Tommy, "I'm perfectly dear. I was out on the escape by the time she got to the roof, and I lost her there. I saw her again, however, when I climbed on the roof, and went toward her. I've heard a lot about the danger of waking sleep-walkers suddenly, and I spoke to her quietly. I said 'Miss Blake.'"

"Yes?"

"Well," he confessed, "that's about all I remember. Or no, it isn't. The girl was asleep, and not responsible. She turned like a flash when I spoke, and cried out, and —I think she threw her brass candlestick at me! Then —I seemed to be falling forward-and when I knew anything again I was in the hall below."

"Having fainted over a four-foot fence!" Tish observed sharply. "Tommy, that won't do."

"I give you my word. Aunt Tish," he said, "I haven't any idea how I got over that fence and through that skylight."

"I have!" Tish said, and put away her note-paper. We both stared at her and Tommy even smiled.

"Exactly," he said. "I've thought of that, but how do you account for the fact that not a patient left his ward or private room last night? That every servant and nurse was in his proper place? Jacobs and I took pains to find that out. And that I've got as pretty a bite in my right shoulder as you would care to see?"

"Bite!" Tish exclaimed, and reached feebly for the note-paper.

"Bite!" I repeated. "Then it must be an animal —!"

"Who knows?" Tommy said quietly. "Jacobs and I got it cauterized. I don't want the internes to get hold of the story-they're apt to talk to the nurses. I hardly know what to do next Since Mr. Harrison had the trouble last night with the two medical men, he is too busy holding down his job to have much time for anything else. If there is to be anything done, I rather think it's up to me" "It's up to us!" said Tish firmly.

Chapter IX
Orderly Briggs and Disorderly Bates

After all, it was my suggestion that we bring in Briggs, the orderly, and ask him about the night Johnson's body was moved. Tish acknowledges this, and if she does not realize how much poor Briggs helped us in unraveling the mystery, I am not one to remind her. But Briggs was on night duty, and went to bed after carrying the breakfast trays on our floor.

Tish, however, having approved of my idea, had appropriated it as her own-which is a way most self-willed people have, and she insisted that Tommy send for him.

He came about twelve o'clock, looking rather surly, and presenting a general appearance of having his coat and trousers on over his night shirt.

"Come in, Briggs," said Tommy, when he knocked. "Sorry to wake you, old man."

"I wasn't sleeping," he replied sourly. "The noise in the place is enough to waken the dead."

"Perhaps," said Tish, "perhaps that's what ailed Johnson!"

Briggs turned quickly and looked at her. He was a tall man, with a heavy black mustache and powerful stooped shoulders. He had one drooping eyelid, that gave him an unpleasant appearance. Whether it was consciousness of this, or shiftiness, which was Tish's theory, he never looked directly at one. As Tish said, his gaze seemed to stop at your collar, but if you averted your eyes you were sure to have the feeling that he'd darted a stealthy glance at you and got away with it before you could catch him.

"No," he said, after a moment, "nothing will waken Johnson but the trumpet on the last day."

"Do you know, Briggs," Tish said coolly, "I have my own little theory about that night? You don't like Miss Smith, and you and Marshall prepared a little surprise for her. Shame on you, Briggs."

He positively looked straight at her. It was so surprising that it presented him in a new light with a sort of aureola of outraged virtue.

"No, mam," he said. "You're right, I don't get along with Miss Smith, but as for playing a trick of that sort —!" He took his handkerchief out and wiped his forehead. "I wouldn't have done it on anybody," he said; "and as for Johnson —" he glanced at Tommy, half ashamed —"I tell you, the things I've seen about that man's bed would make me respect him, dead or living. Raps on the foot-board, and his bedside stand with two legs in the air, beating time like a drum. No, mam, if you think I did that, you think I'm a braver man than I am."

"Humph!" said Tish, and put down "Raps and bedside stand. Johnson."

"Suppose," Tommy suggested, "now that you are here, you tell us exactly what happened the night Johnson died."

"He died at ten minutes after twelve on Tuesday night, sir. I was staying by a delirious patient in the next ward. Doctor. Miss Durand, the night nurse, was busy and asked me to watch him. It wasn't until an hour after he died that I was notified to take Johnson's body to the mortuary. I called Marshall from the floor below, and we took the body up on the elevator. Jacobs runs the elevator after midnight, it being not used except for emergency, night operations, ambulance cases coming in, or a death.

"We put the body on the receiving table, and Marshall uncovered the face. Maybe we were both nervous, having talked many a time during his sickness with the old man, and him saying he'd come back and bring us some sign from the spirit world, after he'd 'passed over.' Anyhow, Marshall uncovered his face and looked at him, and he said, "Johnson, now's your time to make good. Here you are and here we are. Come over with the sign!' "

Briggs looked at Tommy and Tommy nodded.

"Sign," wrote Tish. "Then what happened, Briggs?" Neither of us would have been a bit surprised if he had said the dead man moved a foot, or that unseen hands pulled the pipe-molding loose and bent it down before their very eyes. But Briggs shook his head.

"Nothing-then," he said, "but when I heard about what happened later, I had a talk with Marshall. I don't believe in fooling with things you don't know anything about."

"Briggs," Tommy said suddenly, "you say the body lay in the ward almost an hour before removal. Why was that?"

"Because," Briggs replied significantly, "there was no nurse in that ward when he died, or for nearly an hour after. The ward was in charge of a convalescent typhoid named Bates."

"Why was that?" Tommy demanded. But Briggs only shrugged his shoulders, with his good eye fixed about four inches bdow Tommy's chin.

When he got no answer, "Bring Bates here," Tommy said sharply, and during the interval until the two men appeared he walked somberly up and down, his face thoughtful.

Bates was hardly prepossessing. He shuffled in in a pair of carpet-slippers much too large, a pair of faded trousers, and a garment that was evidently his nightshirt with the tail tucked in. But Bates was shrewd if unshaven, as we found out.

"Bates," said Tommy, "you are a patient in K ward?"

"Yes, sir."

"You helped to look after Johnson, the man who died night before last?"

"Sometimes-when the nurses were busy."

"Have you heard anything about-of what happened after his death?"

Bates smiled.

"There's been a good bit of talk going around, sir," he said. "He'd got the ward worked up some-talking about coming back after he'd chipped in. One of the men claims to have seen him looking in the window near his bed last night, and there's a story about his corpse being found hanging-but that's ridiculous, sir."

"It's true. Bates."

Bates' jaw dropped. "Oh, no, sir. Surely not!" he said, and changed color.

"Now, Bates," Tommy said, "we are men of sense, you and I. We know Johnson didn't do it himself, don't we?"

"Yes, sir." Not as convinced as he might have been.

"Then it was done for him." "Yes, sir."

"Presumably by somebody in this house."

"Yes, sir."

"Bates, was any one missing from your ward during either last night or the night before, that you know of?"

Bates thought "No, sir," he said. "I don't sleep much; that's my trouble, insomnia. I can hear a kitten stir in my ward-not, of course, that we're liable to kittens, sir. Night before last I was up and dressed all night, wandering around, and last night, as you know, I sat up with that railroad case. The boy was out of his head."

"Then, either night, no patient could have stolen out from K ward into the house and been absent for any length of time without your knowing it?"

"It's hardly possible," Bates said. "Mr. Briggs or I would know for sure, sir."

"Do you help in the other wards on the men's floor?"

"Yes, sir."

"Are there any delirious patients?"

"None able to stand or walk about."

"I see," Tommy said thoughtfully, "And now. Bates, is it correct that Miss Durand, the night nurse, left her ward for fifty minutes, knowing that Johnson was dying?"

"Fifty-five minutes, sir." Bates' shrewd eyes said more than his words.

It was, possibly, for night supper?" That's at two o'clock." Bates knew a good bit about the hospital, and enjoyed showing his knowledge.

You have no idea why she left?" No, sir. Miss Smith came to the door, and they went away together. Miss Smith looked upset and nervous, as if she'd been crying-if you'll excuse my saying so, sir."

"Did you notice in which direction they went?"

"They went down-stairs. When they came back Miss Smith was looking more cheerful, and she had a bundle in her hand."

"What sort of a bundle?"

"Darkish. It might have been clothing. Miss Durand was frightened when she found Johnson had died, and she asked me not to say she had been away."

"Thanks, Bates. You'd better go back now," said Tommy, "and Bates, if you hear or see anything that strikes you as curious, let me know, will you?"

Bates promised and flapped out, with Briggs behind him. Tommy called Briggs back. "Briggs," he said, "I have asked the superintendent to let me put on a few guards to-night. This thing has gone beyond a joke. Mr. Harrison will give us the scrubbers, Frank, from the elevator and two assistants from the laundry. The internes have volunteered, also, that makes eleven; with you and myself, thirteen."

"Thirteen!" said Briggs. "Would you mind making it fourteen, Doctor?"

Tommy looked surprised.

"Briggs!" he said. "Surely you —" Then he took a good look at Briggs' pasty face and nodded. "All right," he said. "We can have Hicks from the ambulance. And just a word," he said, as Briggs made for the door. "We are not talking, Briggs. Most of these men are watching for a thief. Do you understand? And I'd be glad to have your help in placing them where they'll do the most good."

Chapter X
An Ape and some Guinea-Pigs

Miss Lewis came in a few minutes after Briggs had gone, and, closing the door behind her, looked at Tommy.

"Miss Blake is conscious," she said. "Temperature only ninety-nine, pulse a hundred and forty."

"Good!" Tommy said heartily. It was evident to us all how relieved he was. "But I don't like the pulse." He was brushing his hair back with Tish's brush. "She's had a terrific shock of some sort."

"Yes, sir," said Miss Lewis, still with her back to the door.

Tommy leaned over and kissed Tish's cheek. He was delighted at the mere prospect of seeing the Little Nurse, and showed it. "Now, try to be good until I come back, both of you," he said. "All right, Miss Lewis, we'll have a look at our patient in the dormitory."

Miss Lewis looked flushed and uncomfortable.

"I'm sorry, Doctor," she said. "Miss-Miss Blake doesn't—she has asked for Doctor Willson instead."

"What!" said Tommy, and turned a dark red.

"She's asked for Doctor Willson," repeated Miss Lewis. "There's no mistake. I've been coaxing her for ten minutes."

"She's still delirious," Tish snapped. "And it is not necessary to coax people to retain my nephew's professional services. Miss Lewis."

"Why, that's all right," Tommy said with affected cheerfulness. "Willson's a fine chap —she couldn't do better."

"Fiddle!" Tish was angry. "Who is Wilson, anyhow?"

"Big fellow, dark eyes-very distinguished looking man," said Tommy humbly. Tommy is handsome, if being straight and slim and young count for anything, but I daresay one could hardly call him distinguished. Tish and I differ about this. "Good gracious. Aunt Tish, the girl ought to have the privilege of selecting her own medical adviser."

"Humph!"

"Suppose you go back to the dormitory. Miss Lewis," Tommy said, "and say to Miss — Miss Blake that she's made a wise choice, and I'll send Willson to her as soon as he comes in. And ask her if she will let me see her for a moment, not professionally."

Miss Lewis looked doubtful, but she went. When she came back, in five minutes, she was evidently irritated, and her cap was more than ever on one ear.

"She's sitting on the side of the bed, half dressed," she grumbled, "and she says she won't see anybody."

"Then she doesn't want-Willson?" asked Tommy, looking relieved.

"No. Says she's all right, and if people don't stop bothering her she is going out somewhere in the country where they have a dog and kittens! That's what she said! Not cat and kittens —"

Sensible girl," said Tommy, happy again. She-hasn't changed her mind about seeing me?"

"No, nor about locking the door. And what's more —" She stopped and glanced at Tommy. "I'd like to speak to you a moment in the hall, Doctor."

"What sort of shilly-shallying is that?" demanded Tish. "Can't you speak to him here?"

"I can not," said Miss Lewis, glaring back at Tish, her thumbs inside her apron belt. "It isn't considered shilly-shallying in this hospital for a nurse to make a report to a doctor, and if you'll read the rules on that door —"

"I'll speak to you in the hall," said Tommy. "Miss Lewis is right. Aunt Tish. If it's in line with what we've been discussing, I'll tell you."

But Tish isn't a woman to take chances. Afterward, she justified her looking through the keyhole on the plea that she was making a scientific theory to fit the case, and if it were not for keyholes many a murderer would have gone unhung to his grave. At the time, however, I was rather horrified.

She had plenty of time to tell me what she saw, as it happened, for Tommy did not come back until late in the afternoon, after the guinea-pig incident.

Tish says that when she'd got them in focus, as you may say. Miss Lewis was pulling something out of her sleeve. It was a knife, Tish says, with a short, thin blade that looked as sharp as a razor.

"One of the knives from the operating-room, Doctor," Miss Lewis said. "I thought I'd better not let the old ladies see it."

I daresay that was when I saw Tish's back stiffen.

"Great Scott!" said Tommy.

"I found it on the floor under her bed," Miss Lewis went on. "She didn't see me pick it up. Tommy was staring at the blade.

"It's been used," he said. "Look at this!"

"Exactly," said Miss Lewis. "It's from the operating room, Doctor, and they don't put away their knives in that condition."

"What do you mean by that?" Tommy demanded sharply. But Miss Lewis only looked at him.

"I don't mean anything against Ruth Blake, if that's what you are indignant about," she said. "But I'm glad I found that knife. There's enough talk. Doctor."

They moved down the hall then, so that was all Tish heard. But she added, "Knife, blood-stained," to her sheet of paper.

Aggie being half drowsy and altogether sulky, we took a little time to go over the notes Tish had made, and they pointed as many different ways as a porcupine-Johnson, with his raps and his talk about coming back, taken from the mortuary and hung by his neck with a roller towel marked S. P. T.; the coincidence of Johnson's wife murdered a few years before and hung up the same way; Miss Blake wandering around at night with a brass candlestick and a blood-stained knife from the operating room, and Tommy Andrews falling or being pushed through a skylight and coming out of the excitement with a bite instead of a fracture! And then there were smaller things, though strange enough-the twisted pipe-molding and the footprints on the wall up-stairs in the room where Johnson's body was found; the loosened molding in Aggie's room and her story about the foot; the fact that Johnson was left to die in the care of a convalescent typhoid and the ward left alone for fifty-five minutes; Linda Smith and her speech to Miss Blake, not to mention the darkish bundle.

It was Tish who advanced the gigantic ape theory. She'd been reading The Murders in the Rue Morgue, and some of the clues seemed to fit, especially Tommy's shoulder. The loosened molding helped out the theory, and as Tish said, also the stringing up of Johnson's body, which, if you left out the supernatural, had apparently been done by something tremendously strong, but without intelligence.

Well, the more we thought of it the more certain we felt. The footprint part of it, too, we considered corroborative evidence, until we got the encyclopedia and learned that the great apes have the equivalent of four hands, and not a foot at all.

But Tish was undaunted. "Mark my words, Lizzie," she said, "they've lost a chimpanzee or a gorilla from the Zoological Garden-not that they'll acknowledge it. You remember when the lion got loose and ate a colored woman out the Ralston road, and how the papers denied everything until they found the beast dead of indigestion in a cellar? But that is what has happened."

Well, I thought it likely enough myself, and Tish called up Charlie Sands, who is on a newspaper and is another of Tish's nephews.

Lizzie and I," said Tish over the 'phone, have reason to believe that there is a great ape —a-p-e —ape! Monkey, monkey-yes. A large monkey loose, and we want you to trace it."

There was a long pause. Tish said afterward that Charlie claimed to have fainted at the other end of the wire, and to have had to be restored with whisky and soda. However, which is more to the point, he promised to find out for us what he could, and Tish hung up the receiver.

"He'll do it, too, Lizzie," she said, "although he spoke to me gently, as if he thought my reason had entirely gone. But, as he said, it won't hurt to scare up the Zoo people anyhow. They're very casual about their animals."

Now, two things were discovered that afternoon, neither of them to be explained by anything we knew. The first one was that Tommy Andrews and Mr. Harrison, the superintendent, making a careful examination of the roof, found a spattering of dried blood leading from the broken skylight to the ridge pole, where it ceased abruptly. The second one was made by Aggie and myself.

About three o'clock that afternoon Aggie got into her clothes and insisted on coming into Tish's room, which was inconvenient, Tish expecting the message from Charlie Sands at any moment. Aggie was nervous, but her head was clearer. She'd been thinking things over, and she knew now that what had happened the night before had been a message from the roofer.

"Then the least said about it the better!" Tish snapped. "If he hasn't any better sense than to materialize his foot, and you a woman of your years and respectability, he'd better go back where he came from."

For heaven's sake, Tish," Aggie pleaded, looking over her shoulder. "He may be listening to us now!"

"I don't care if he is," said Tish recklessly. "If he'd materialize a will, now, leaving you that house in Groveton! But a foot!"

"I'm not so sure it was a foot," Aggie said restlessly. "I've been thinking, Tish-he was a large man, you know. It may have been a hand."

Now at that moment the telephone bell rang, and Tish signaled to me to take Aggie out at once. I got up and took her by the arm.

"I'll walk up and down the corridor with you, Aggie," I said. "You need exercise."

"I don't care to walk," she objected, trying to sit down. "See who is at the telephone, Tish. I expect my laundress is through washing and wants her money."

"I'd like you to see the hospital," I said desperately as the 'phone rang again. "The-the guinea-pigs, Aggie." Miss Lewis had told me about them.

Now, Aggie loves a guinea-pig. It's a queer taste, but she says they neither bark like dogs nor scratch like cats, and they have a nice way of wiggling their noses.

"Guinea-pigs!" she said in an ecstasy. "Where?"

"In the laboratory," said I, and led her out of the room.

She put on all her wraps and Miss Lewis took us to the laboratory, which is a small brick building set off by itself in the hospital yard, with Aggie cooing in anticipation and wanting to send out and buy a cabbage for them. Doctor Grim, who was the surgical interne, met us as we were crossing the yard, and volunteered to let us in.

"You know," he said, feeling in his pocket for the keys, "they're not attractive as some guinea-pigs and rabbits I have known under happier circumstances. They scratch a good bit-some think it's fleas; some say it's germs."

"Germs?" Aggie asked, puzzled.

"Oh, yes," he said, opening the door and leading the way into a narrow hall. "Some of them have been inoculated with several different kinds of germs. That's why we keep this place so well locked up, for fear the germs may escape. You know," —he unlocked the second door and threw it open, "you know, suppose you were walking up the street and met a solid phalanx of say sixteen billion typhoid germs, or measles! It would be horrible, wouldn't it?"

He stepped into the room and looked about him.

"Come in," he said. "It's a little close. We had a tear-up among the resident staff, and nobody has been here to-day. Hello!"

He threw open the shutters, and a broad shaft of gray daylight lighted the room. Aggie gave a cry of dismay. The doors of the small cages around the walls were all open, and in the center, a pathetic heap of little brown-and-white and black-and-white bodies, lay the guinea-pigs.

Doctor Grim picked one up and examined it closely.

"I'm damned!" he said, and put it down. "Throats cut, every one of them! And where are the rabbits?"

Aggie sat down and began to blubber, but Miss Lewis scolded her soundly. "There'll be plenty more where they came from," she said sharply. "What does concern us is-how would anybody or anything get in here with both doors and all the windows locked, and not a chimney."

Aggie wiped her eyes and got up.

"You laughed at me last night, Miss Lewis," she said with dignity, "but I wish to remind you that to the fourth dimension there are no locks, no bars, no doors or walls."

"When they invent that," said Miss Lewis, opening the door to let us out, "they'll have to invent something like these X-ray-proof screens, or a woman won't dare to change her clothes."

"And what's more," said Aggie, turning in the doorway, "the hand that slew those innocent little creatures is the one I touched last night!"

"Hand!" cried Miss Lewis. "It was a foot then."

But Aggie was holding her shoulder over her face and hurrying across the yard. At the far side she threw back a contemptuous sneeze.

Tish's commission to Charlie Sands had an unexpected result. She was almost bursting with it when I got back.

"Listen," she said while Aggie got her spray, "doesn't this bear out what IVe been saying right along? The Zoo people say positively that none of their animals has escaped. But they took such an interest in his inquiry that Charlie grew suspicious and bribed a keeper. He sent this up by messenger from the office:

" 'Dear and revered spinster aunt,' " she read —"the young rascal! 'I couldn't tell you this over the 'phone, for it's our exclusive property, and will be published to-morrow morning, with photographs of the late deceased, etc. Hero, the biggest ape in captivity, pining for his keeper, Wesley Barker, who has been away, committed suicide in his cage last night by hanging himself with a roller towel. He was found dead when the assistant keeper unlocked the cage at six o'clock this morning. Nobody knows how he got the roller towel. Charlie.'

" 'P. S. —I've got the roller towel, a fine long one and marked S. P. T. Do you think the letters stand for Suicidal Purpose Towel?' "

Tish looked at me triumphantly over her reading-glasses.

"You see, Lizzie, what a little logical thinking will do. If it hadn't been for me, you and Aggie would have gone to your graves expecting to be able to come back at any time and hang from chandeliers or do any of the ridiculous buffoonery that seems to be expected of returned spirits. We search for a ghost and we find a gorilla."

She meant ape, of course, but the other was alliterative.

"I'm not quite clear about it yet, Tish," I said, with my head in a whirl. "If his cage was locked, and the keepers say he hadn't been free, and if Miss Blake —"

"If! If r said Tish impatiently. "I haven't had time to figure it all out, of course. But mark my words, Lizzie, the mystery is solved. We shall sleep to-night."

But, as a matter of fact, we never even went to bed.

Chapter XI

If It Had Not Been for Love

It is curious to think that if Tish had been able to finish her story to Tommy Andrews that evening, and to have given him Charlie's letter to read, the thing that occurred that night could scarcely have happened. For with Tommy knowing what he did, he could have put two and two together and have gone about things in a different way. Aggie, of course, is a fatalist, and believes it would have happened anyhow.

In the first place, Tish felt so sure that everything was cleared up that she told Aggie the whole story, ending with the suicide at the Zoo. Aggie sat with her mouth open, and didn't speak except to sneeze until Tish was through. Then she surprised us.

"Maybe you are right, Tish." she said. "I know I hope so. I don't know much about gorillas, but I guess they're mostly hairy, aren't they?"

"Mostly," said Tish grimly. "I haven't heard of any Mexican hairless ones."

"Well, the hand by my bed-you needn't sneer, Tish; you can call it a foot if you prefer foot —"

"Listen to the woman!" cried Tish. "I haven't called it anything."

"The hand-or foot-was not hairy!" said Aggie, and stuck to it. She is that kind. Tish says she has a small mind, but I think there are some large minds that can only hold one idea at a time.

Well, we told the whole thing again to Tommy, who had heard about the guinea-pigs from Doctor Grim, and who listened gravely, and Tish was just getting out Charlie's letter to read to him, when Miss Lewis came in.

"Drat that woman!" Tish muttered. "She's never around when she's wanted, and always butting in when she isn't. Well, what is it?"

"Miss Blake is better,. Doctor," she said. "She is sitting up, dressed, and-she's leaving her door unlocked. That's a good sign."

"Thanks, very much," said Tommy, looking conscious.

"It's supper hour now," remarked Miss Lewis. "If, when I come back, you would care to go over to the dormitory —"

"I suppose she hasn't asked for me?"

"No. But she asked if you were in the house."

"Thanks," said Tommy again. "When you come back, then. Ah-thanks, very much."

Miss Lewis left and Tish spread out Charlie's letter. "Dear and revered spinster aunt," she began. But Tommy was looking at his watch.

"How long does she usually take for supper?" he asked. "Excuse me for interrupting. Aunt Tish."

"About an hour," said Tish grimly. "She says she's been ordered to chew her food thoroughly. 'Dear and revered —' "

"You know," said Tommy, "she may get tired and go to sleep, or something like that."

"Not while she's eating," said Tish.

"I mean Miss Blake. I —I think I'll just run over for a moment now, if you don't mind."

"Not alone!" Tish got up and reached for her cane, but Tommy pushed her back in her chair.

"No, indeed, dear Aunt Tish," he said. "You must not use that knee. Nor Miss Aggie either —"

"Aggie has no intention of using my knee," said Tish crossly. Tommy was sending me messages with his eyes. I'm notoriously weak as to love affairs.

I'll go," I volunteered, obeying Tommy's signals, and go I did, leaving Tish clutching her cane with one hand and the letter with the other! Aggie was, as usual, oblivious and quite calm.

It was my suggestion that I play propriety from just outside the door. Tommy went in, and I heard a rustle from the window, as if she had turned to look at him.

"I —my aunt is just outside," he began, hesitating. I am not his aunt, as I have said.

"Won't you ask her in?" She had a low, sweet voice.

"Certainly, if you wish," he said, and made no move to do it. "You dismissed me to-day," he accused her.

"I didn't need a doctor."

"I need not have come professionally. I am here now only-well, because I couldn't stay away."

She said nothing to that, as far as I could hear.

"I came also," he said, "to ask you not to stay here alone to-night."

What do you mean?" she asked sharply.

"Only that you might do the same thing again to-night —walk in your sleep, you know."

I heard her chair move, as if she had turned abruptly and faced him.

"Why do you say that?" she demanded. "You know I was not asleep last night."

"I assure you —" he began, clearly startled. "I —really thought —"

"Please!" she said, and there was another silence. Then I realized she was crying softly.

"Don't do that!" pleaded Tommy. "Don't!"

"I thought you were killed!" she said, in a smothered tone. "All the rest of the night I sat and wanted to die. I thought I had killed you!"

"Where did you sit?" asked Tommy gently.

"It doesn't matter, does it?"

"Very much-to me."

"I was-here," she said, after a hesitation.

"You were not here," said Tommy. "Between that and morning, I was here four times. Where were you?"

"I was safe," she said. 'Why do you question me so?"

"Because," he said gently, "I was in the laboratory at two o'clock this morning. Jacobs helped me with a —wound on my shoulder. I had looked everywhere for you and failed to find you. I thought I heard somebody moving across the hall, and we made a casual search. We found nothing, nobody. But during the fifteen minutes that that door was unlocked, somebody entered the building, and cut the throats of eleven guinea-pigs, piling them in the center of the room. And-on the floor underneath them I picked up this afternoon a small pink rosette, apparently off the toe of a woman's bedroom slipper."

"Ah!" she said, as if she found it suddenly hard to breathe. And then she burst out unexpectedly. "After all, was it so terrible? They-they were only guinea-pigs!"

"Yes," said Tommy gravely, "they were only guinea-pigs."

He came out the next moment and went back along the hall into the hospital, having quite forgotten me. His chin was sunk on his breast, and he walked heavily. He was as bewildered as I had been. We saw him only once again that evening, and then only for a minute. He was preparing to station his guards through the house, much to Tish's disgust.

"It's idiotic," she confided to Aggie and me that night as Aggie was getting ready for bed. "Isn't the creature dead? Do they expect it to come back from the spirit world and do a materializing seance for them while they wait?"

"That's all very well, Tish," said Aggie, turning on all the lights and getting into bed, "but that hand was not hairy."

"Foot, you mean," said Tish. "If that is a footprint on the wall of that room up-stairs, it was a foot you touched last night."

At nine o'clock that night Tommy had a talk with Miss Durand, the night nurse of K ward. She denied being out of the ward between twelve-ten and one o'clock, and characterized Bates' whole story as a fabrication.

"He's always making trouble. Doctor," she told Tommy. "He brings in tobacco and morphine and sells it to the men, and you take his word against mine!"

And Tommy said that Bates, with Miss Durand's outraged eyes on him, reduced the time of her absence to ten minutes, and might have gone further if Tommy hadn't turned away in disgust.

Chapter XII
The Carbolic Case and a Brown Coat

Tommy was very gloomy that night. He went about placing guards, with his mouth set in a grim line and his eyes hard. A few of the nurses knew what was going on, but with the exception of the three of us, none of the patients had been told.

To Tish's assurance that the trouble was over, that the death of Hero, the ape, meant the end of the disturbance, Tommy turned a tolerant smile and a deaf ear. I would have given a good bit to have had Tish's conviction, but no theory that was based on Hero at the Zoo could possibly involve Miss Blake. And Tommy and I knew that Miss Blake was involved.

I had not told Tish the particulars of Tommy's visit to the girl's room, or about the rosette he had confronted her with. To be candid, Tish was disagreeable about my having gone with Tommy, and only relaxed when, at supper time, a package came from Charlie Sands, and proved to contain the very towel with which the giant ape had been killed,

"Thought you might like it," Charlie wrote. "I snitched it while the keeper's back was turned. Gruesome, but interesting, isn't it? The beast was almost human, and as far as I know this may be the towel with which he performed his final ablutions-or do apes ablute?"

Tish laid it solemnly out on the bed and, going to the dresser drawer, brought out the one that had, as you may say, suspended Johnson. They were absolutely alike, even to the position of the S. P. T. which distinguished them both.

Tommy came into Aggie's room about eleven o'clock and sat, as usual, on the foot of the bed. He had lost his customary air of good-natured raillery, and looked tired.

"I've placed them all," he said. "Counting myself, there are fourteen of us, and I don't think a germ could escape from any of the wards without my knowing it."

"How about the private rooms?" I asked. "There's as apt to be mischief done by pay patients as by charities."

"You're right, there. Well, every corridor is under secret surveillance. The doors into the nurses' dormitory are being watched on every floor, and we have a man on the roof."

"Humph!" said Aggie, from the bed. "You'd do better to have a barrel of holy water. Things that dissolve under your fingers, just as the clock strikes midnight-it was midnight, Tish. The clock in the hall is five minutes fast by my watch."

"Fiddlesticks!" Tish said tartly. "Then the sun's too fast; you'd better have it regulated. No, Tommy, it would have been more to the point if you'd taken all these precautions last night. You are too late."

"I hope so," Tommy observed and got off the bed. "I'll come around now and then and keep you posted." He started toward the door and stopped, looking at me. "You haven't seen-Miss Blake? She has not come from the dormitory?"

"No."

He looked relieved at that and went out, and for an hour we saw nothing of him.

A little before midnight Miss Lewis brought in on a tray three glasses of buttermilk and some crackers.

"I knew none of you were sleeping," she said. "This will do you good. I don't mind saying my nerves are all twittering. This house is enough to set you crazy. If you go around a comer unexpectedly, you come across a figure ducking into a doorway. A nurse from L ward just fell across one of the moppers squatting in a corner by the pantry and threw a bowl of chicken broth at him, thinking it was Johnson himself."

"They might as well calm themselves," Tish observed, sipping her buttermilk. "Nothing will happen."

"Then why don't you take off your clothes and go to bed?" Aggie asked, but Tish scornfully refused to answer.

"I'm not expecting anything myself," observed Miss Lewis, straightening her cap at the mirror. "These things have a way of petering out-and yet, on the other hand, things in a hospital usually go in threes. If we have one burned case, we'll get two more. Shot cases will come in threes every time, and as for suicides! Well, I've seen three carbolic acids every time I've seen one. And that reminds me," she said, turning from the mirror and with a dive thrusting a foot-rest under Tish's leg, "a carbolic case has just piped out in one of the wards. There are things I'd rather do than go up and lay it out."

And at that instant the hall nurse appeared in the doorway and spoke to her.

"Miss Lewis," she said, "you are to go to the mortuary with that case. Miss Grimes is having an attack of hysteria."

Miss Lewis turned and surveyed us through her spectacles. "Can you beat that?" she demanded. "Wouldn't a self-respecting mongrel pup rebel at a life like this?" She jerked her head-and her cap fell over her ear with the facility of long practice. "All right," she said to the nurse, "I'm coming, but —" she turned in the doorway and waved her hand to us. "If I am found strung up with an S. P. T.," she said, "I'll not hang alone, believe me."

An S. P. T.! We all three stared at each other, and Tish tried to call her back. But she had gone. Could it be, we wondered, that Miss Lewis knew the meaning of the three letters? And if she did —

At five minutes of midnight Tommy stopped in to see us.

"Nothing yet," he said. "Heaven knows, I hope there won't be anything at all, but there's an uneasy feeling in the house — I've had to make a few changes. The man on the roof refused to stay."

"Naturally," Tish observed, with the lofty air she'd had all evening. "If the wind blew he would declare he heard groans."

"Exactly what he did say," replied Tommy. "Says he heard groans and felt eyes looking at him. But we had the roof searched, and found nothing. I put Hicks, the ambulance man, there instead. He hasn't any nerves."

"I beg your pardon. Doctor," said the hall nurse, from the doorway. "But-Hicks wants to see you."

"Just for a moment," a voice came from behind the nurse. "I'll go back up there, Doctor, if I've got to kick myself up, but —"

"Well?"

"Doctor, as sure as I'm a living man, something is singing on the roof."

"Singing!" said Tommy.

"Half singing, half chanting. I —I'm going back. Doctor. Nothing ain't ever scared me yet. But-it's singing 'Nearer, my God, to Thee' —not the words. Just the tune."

"Did anybody else hear it?"

"They heard something in the mortuary. They said it didn't sound exactly like singing. But I heard it as plain as I hear you, sir. It — it's horrible."

"Are the nurses still there?"

"No, sir. Miss Lewis was sent to take Miss Grimes' place, but she insisted on having her night supper first. Mr. Briggs is in the mortuary with the-you know, until she comes."

"I'll go up with you to the roof," said Tommy, and went at once.

Aggie had been getting white around the lips during the whole scene, and when Hicks said "Nearer, my God, to Thee," she almost keeled over against her pillows. The moment Tommy had gone, she burst into tears, declaring that something awful was going to happen, that being the tune they had sung at the roofer's funeral.

Tish, however, was stonily calm, although I could see she was shaken. She had got out her Irish lace, and sat making picots as if her life depended on it.

"I don't for the life of me see what you are bleating about," she snapped. "If you argue from hearing that tune that he's coming back to-night, there will be more ghosts walking that this hospital can hold. It's been sung at a good many funerals. And another thing, if he was as good as you think he was, he's sitting around with a harp, learning celestial melodies, not coming back to string up innocent corpses with roller towels, and break skylights. It's only the bad ones that aren't satisfied where they are and come back."

It is hard to say just why that line of reasoning made Aggie dry her tears, but it did, and she sat up and finished her buttermilk. It was when I was reaching her the crackers that I heard a creak, and knew that somebody had stealthily opened the door into the nurses' dormitory. Tish heard it, too, and put down her crocheting.

All our lights were on, while the hall was dark. This time we saw no candlelight, but we each felt who it was. I stepped to the door and looked out.

Miss Blake, fully dressed, was on the narrow staircase to the floor above, and at the top somebody with an electric flash was barring the way.

"Sorry, Miss," said Jacobs, the night watchman. "We have orders not to let anybody pass here to-night."

"But I must!" she pleaded. "I can't endure this suspense another moment, Jacobs! Where is Doctor Andrews?"

"On the roof. Miss Blake."

"Oh, no, not on the roof!" she cried. "Let me pass. I must pass."

"Sorry," he said, not moving. "My orders —"

Suddenly, from somewhere overhead came a woman's scream, a shrill note of horror that left my ears aching, my heart beating madly. It rose and fell and then rose again, and the silence that followed was the silence of paralysis.

Immediately after, there was the sound of scurrying feet. Tish and I never knew afterward how we got up the stairs, or were almost the first on the scene.

The hall was dark, as on the floor below, but from the mortuary a bright light streamed down the short, wide flight of steps that served as its approach.

On one side of the receiving table Tommy was standing. On the other. Miss Lewis stood, as if frozen, with one hand turning down the covering sheet. But the body on the table was not wrapped in a shroud. It was the figure of a tall man fully dressed, and with the head and shoulders tightly wrapped in what looked like a brown coat.

Tish gripped my arm, shaking so she could scarcely speak. "Johnson!" she said. "Oh, my God, Lizzie, it's Johnson!"

But it was not. When they had untied the sleeves, tightly knotted about the neck, Tommy himself gave a cry of horror.

It was Briggs, the orderly, dead about ten minutes, and with his ribs crushed in like a broken barrel.

The "carbolic case" was lying in placid peace under the table, its bandaged hands folded, its jaw relaxed, its half-shut eyes looking calmly up at the horror overhead.

Tish and I put Miss Lewis to bed that night and Tish sat with her until morning. It was dawn whep Tommy came in. They had found nothing-except one curious fact:

The brown coat that had covered poor Briggs' head had belonged to Johnson. The pockets were full of his private papers.

Chapter XIII
Jacobs' Elevator

As I have said. Tommy came in about dawn. Miss Lewis had dropped into an uneasy sleep, and Tish was dozing in the chair beside her, Aggie was stretched out on the couch, with a cubeb cigarette burning in a saucer beside her, and was resurrecting her mother's sister again when he came in. He beckoned me out into the hall after he had told us about the coat.

"Miss Blake is ill again," he said. "The second shock, after the first, you know."

"Not seriously. Tommy?" I asked, putting my hand on his arm.

"I don't know," he said miserably. "People don't go from one fainting attack into another without — I guess you've seen how it is. Miss Lizzie. I — it would kill me if any harm came to her!"

"No harm is coming to her," I reassured him. "If the strain has had this effect on Miss Lewis, who has about the same nervous system as a cow, of course it would go hard with a finely organized girl like Miss Blake. And — don't be foolish, Tommy. No finding of surgical knives in that girl's room, or of rosettes where they don't happen to belong, is going to make her guilty of anything wrong. If she's in trouble, it's not of her own making."

He fairly put his arm around me and hugged me, to the horror of a passing nurse.

"Blessed are the spinsters!" he cried, "for they are the salt of the earth! Do you really think that?"

"I do," I said firmly. "And shame on you, Tommy Andrews, for having thought anything else. I shall stay with her for an hour or two."

"If you will," he said gratefully, and we started toward the dormitory.

On the way over. Tommy told me more clearly what had happened. The body of the "carbolic case" had been taken to the mortuary by Jacobs and Briggs, Marshall, the other night orderly, having refused to go. On the way up, Jacobs, who was running the elevator, complained that it was out of order. It was an old-fashioned lift, moving always very slowly, and built on the familiar cable and wheel principle. Twice during the ascent the cage stopped entirely.

Near the top floor the cage began to vibrate wildly and Briggs had been obliged to steady the wheeled table containing the corpse.

Jacobs, who had told Tommy the story, said that both he and Briggs were alarmed, fearing that one of the cables had broken; while he worked with the lever in the cage, Briggs looked up apprehensively through the metal grill in the center of the cage. The car was still shaking from side to side, and refused to obey the lever. Jacobs turned to Briggs and threw up his hands.

"It's stuck!" he said. "Either it's going to drop, when it gets ready, or —"

He said Briggs wasn't listening, but was standing looking up at the grill with his face blue-white. Jacobs looked up, too, but he was a second too late. He had a sense of something white moving just out of his range of vision, and then the car ceased vibrating.

Briggs was still staring up and the car was moving again as if nothing had happened to it. At the mortuary floor he had touched Briggs on the arm, and he shivered and helped him wheel the table out of the cage. Then Briggs asked him to lower the cage until he could see the top, but there was nothing there. After that they took the body to the mortuary.

"What did Briggs think he saw?" I asked nervously, holding to Tommy's arm. The hall was dark.

"It's rather fantastic," Tommy said, "but — he declared there was a bare foot planted directly on the grill of the cage."

"A foot!" I gasped.

"A foot," said Tommy soberly. "And I'm going to tell you what I wouldn't care to tell Aunt Tish or Miss Aggie, I've been on top of the cage myself, just now, with a candle. There are innumerable footprints in the dust, distinct marks of a naked foot. But it is always the right foot!"

I shivered. "Tommy!" I quavered. "The mark on the wall where Johnson was found was — the print of a naked right foot."

"I know," he replied, and fell to thinking. "Well," he said, after a moment, "I'd better go on. Jacobs moved the cage down, but there was nothing on it, or in the shaft over their heads. It ends just above that floor, and as the doors to the shaft were all locked, if anything had been above the cage, it could hardly have got away. Briggs himself said that he thought it was an optical illusion, and was apparently not nervous when Jacobs went down to get Miss Lewis. He was gone some time, Miss Lewis, as I have said, having insisted on being fortified with food before she went up."

Finally, as we knew, he had got Miss Lewis and they went back to the mortuary. Briggs was sitting there quietly, with his pipe lighted and a newspaper on his knee. But he was neither reading nor smoking and Jacobs said he was staring overhead, with a queer expression on his face, as if he were listening to something.

He started to say something to Jacobs, but Jacobs signaled him to be cautious and pointed to Miss Lewis. Briggs had nodded and resumed his pipe. Everything was quiet and peaceful, Jacobs insisted. Tommy and Hicks had appeared sometime before and had gone up the stairs to the roof. The man who had been sent to guard that corridor, one of the laundry men, was dozing in a chair half way down. Jacobs, not being needed in the mortuary, went down to him and roused him by shaking. He and the laundry man were talking when Miss Lewis came down to the empty ward across from them, and turning on the lights, went in search of something she needed.

Jacobs was positive there had not been a sound from the mortuary, except that a gust of air from its open windows had swept along the hall, and the glass-topped doors slammed shut. There had been no outcry, no struggle. When Miss Lewis went back briskly, and opened the doors, she found Briggs apparently gone, and the sheeted figure on the table as before.

It was only when she turned down the sheet that she discovered the truth-the body of the murdered orderly on the table and the corpse not to be seen. It was then she screamed.

"We have sent for the police," Tommy finished. "We didn't want any publicity, but now it has to come. It's beyond us. The Strange thing is," he said, "at the time it happened, every corridor, every ward, every possible means of access to the mortuary was guarded."

"Yes, and with the one nearest it sound asleep!" I commented scornfully. "And goodness knows how many of the others!"

"Jacobs was in the upper hall," he contended, "and whoever was asleep beforehand, none of them was asleep after Miss Lewis shrieked. Miss Lizzie. There are only two means of access to the mortuary, one is the fire-escape and the other the steps. Jacobs was just beyond the steps all the time, and Hicks and I were on the roof near the fire-escape. Nobody left by those two exits. That's positive."

"There is another door in the mortuary," I said. "What is that?"

"Mortuary linen closet," said Tommy. "Always kept locked, and still locked."

"You haven't examined it?"

"The linen room woman carries the key, and she is away over night."

"Nobody was missing in the house?"

"We made a tally immediately, with the guards all watching every door and window. Two internes and I made the count ourselves, not a soul was missing.'

"He was-strangled?'

"No. That's one of the queerest things about It. He had been squeezed —his chest is caved in, and I think the autopsy will show that a point of one of the ribs entered the heart. Death was almost instantaneous."

"And the brown coat?" I asked. "How did it get there?"

"God knows," said Tommy, and rapped at Miss Blake's door.

Chapter XIV
Bag and Baggage

Tish stared at me the next morning when I told her the story Tommy had told me, and laid the key of the mortuaiy linen closet on her breakfast tray.

"The Blake girl is still out of her head," I finished up, "and I found the key, as I tell you, on her dresser, labeled as you see it. I don't want you to show it to Tommy, Tish."

"Tommy!" said Tish scornfully, and pushed away her breakfast untasted. "I tell you, Lizzie, if I had had charge of things last night, that poor wretch would have carried in this tray this morning, with the tea slopped over everything as usual. Tommy is a nice boy, but he's stupid."

"But I don't understand," said Aggie from the bed. "If you think, Tish Carberry, that finding the key to a linen closet is going to prove anything against that pretty little nurse, I'll tell Tommy about it myself."

"Exactly," said Tish, coldly. "And if you do, I wash my hands of the whole affair. As far as I'm concerned in that case, she can go under suspicion the rest of her life."

"Suspicion of what?" Aggie demanded tartly. "She didn't kill Briggs, I suppose. Even if she could have broken his ribs, as Tish says, and she's a perfectly respectable girl-you can see that in her face-she was right on the stairs here when it happened, wasn't she?"

Tish got up and put the key of the linen closet in the lower bureau drawer.

"Don't be any more of a fool than you can help, Aggie," she said, and shut the drawer. "I don't think Miss Blake killed Briggs, or got up on the wall and made a footprint a foot and a half long near the ceiling, or hung Johnson by the neck to a chandelier. And if my nephew chooses to be so head over ears in love with the young woman that he's no more capable of logical thought than a guinea-pig, I shall look into the thing myself."

"Guinea-pig," said Aggie. "Now then, that's another thing, Tish. The rabbits —"

"Lizzie," Tish said, snubbing her completely. "Will you see if Miss Durand is off duty yet? I want to talk to her. Lewis won't be back from breakfast for an hour. She can't Fletcherize and tell that story at the same time."

The hall nurse promised me to find Miss Durand and send her to Tish's room, and started at once in the search for her. She turned to say, over her shoulder and with bated breath, that detectives were in the building now, that Tommy was with them, and that there was a story that they'd found some curious prints on the wall in the room where Johnson's body had hung.

"A foot, and just beside it a woman's hand," she said. "I hear they are going to take impressions of all the hands in the hospital to-day!"

I carried this to Tish, and she affected indifference. But she was visibly uneasy and at different times I caught her staring fixedly at her palm.

At eight o'clock Miss Durand came in looking tired and white, Tish asked her to sit down and offered her a little port wine, but she refused.

"No, thanks," she said. "I'm off to bed soon, and if I can only sleep —I didn't sleep much yesterday."

"Too noisy, I daresay," said Tish. "Poor Briggs complained of the same thing in this very room yesterday."

"Oh, it wasn't the noise. I —I got to thinking." She tried to smile. "There have been so many strange things happening!"

"I should think so," said Aggie. "That poor Miss Blake! Do you think —"

Tish fixed her with a cold eye, and Aggie's voice trailed off to nothing. She looked frightened.

"Miss Durand," said Tish, suddenly hitching her chair forward, "I should like you to tell me why you left Johnson to die alone end why you absented yourself from your ward for fifty minutes."

Miss Durand turned even paler, and got up. "I didn't understand that you —"

"Sit down," said Tish. "I guess you know I'm chairman of the Ladies' Committee here, and you'd better tell me than tell the police. I don't start with the belief that half the hospital's guilty and the other half accessories to the crime, and that's what the police will do, according to my experience."

You may ask Bates —" she began. So I may," said Tish cheerfully. "And if you are around he'll say you were away a scant ten minutes and if he's alone, he'll swear to an hour or more."

"It was less than an hour, I'd swear to that anywhere," said Miss Durand. "It couldn't have taken so long!"

"What couldn't have taken so long?" Tish demanded.

Miss Durand looked around at the three of us and seemed to be thinking.

"What do you mean by saying I'd better tell you than tell the police?" she asked.

"Just this," Tish said briskly getting out her sheet of note-paper. "I flatter myself I can see as far through a stone wall as most people, especially if there's a crack to look through. I've been looking at this particular stone wall off and on since four o'clock this morning, and-well, I think I begin to see daylight."

"Humph!" said Aggie. "Then the least I can say, Tish —"

"Now, Miss Durand," Tish began, biting a point on her pencil. "We'll get at this systematically. Did Briggs have any enemies in K Ward?"

"He wasn't popular. I guess old Johnson hated him about the most."

"Ah!" said Tish, and put that down. "Did you know Johnson was dying when you left the ward?"

"He'd been dying for twenty-four hours and had been unconscious for six," she defended herself. "Nobody can tell when that sort will make a clean get-away."

"Good gracious!" Aggie ejaculated, and even Tish looked shocked. Miss Durand was clearly not in Miss Blake's class: seen in the morning light, her face looked hard as well as tired.

"I see," said Tish, and put down "clean getaway." "Now, Miss Durand, why had Linda Smith been crying when she came to you at midnight that night?"

"She said she had had some words with the head nurse. She had missed a lecture that evening."

"Why did she miss the lecture?"

"I don't know."

"Don't know or won't tell?" asked Tish, over her note-paper.

"Don't know," snapped Miss Durand, and for all I didn't like her, I thought she was telling the truth.

"Now, Miss Durand," Tish observed, sitting back and fixing her lame leg on its hassock, "I'd be glad to hear why Miss Linda Smith took you away from your wards that night, and where you went."

"She had forgotten to attend to something, and she came back to fix it."

"What?"

Miss Durand stared at Tish and Tish leaned back, with her pencil stuck through the knob of her hair, and stared at Miss Durand. As I have said somewhere else, Tish is a masterful woman, and Miss Durand felt it

"She had forgotten to turn in Johnson's clothes," she said. "That is always done after a death: the clothes are held in the office for the friends to get We went to the basement clothes room."

"But Johnson was not dead!"

'The chances were he' would die that night. The clothes should have been ready in case relatives had wished to remove the body at once."

"The trip to the clothes room would take about ten minutes, I daresay," Tish said dryly. "Why didn't she go alone?"

"I —I hardly know. She was nervous and upset You see, her three years is almost up, and she and the superintendent are on bad terms. She has always said that he would make use of any small mistake she made, to keep her from getting her diploma."

"When would she get it, everything going well?"

"Next week."

"Very good," said Tish, and put something down. "Now then, what happened in the clothes room?"

"I didn't go in."

"Where were you?"

"The morning milk cans were being delivered. I went to the other end of the basement, past the engine room, and got a glass of milk. I was thirsty."

"I see. And that took forty minutes?"

"No," said Miss Durand. "When I got back to the clothes room, I couldn't find Miss Smith. The cellar man, sitting on the stairs, said she had not gone up. I was worried, and we both searched for her. We couldn't find her."

"But you did find her. You went back to K ward together."

"I didn't find her," said Miss Durand. "When I came back to the stairs, she was sitting there, with a bundle in her lap. She was white. The cellar man asked her if she felt sick."

How did she explain her absence?"

She didn't," said Miss Durand with her curious smile. "She's a very queer woman, Miss Smith is,"

"Humph!" Tish said, and put down a line or two. "Well, I reckon the next thing to do is to see Miss Snuth. She looks pleasant enough, btft you can't tell by looking at a toad how far it can hop."

Miss Durand got up and prepared to go. She still wore her curious smile.

"I think it has hopped a good ways, Miss Carberry," she said. "Linda Smith has gone, bag and baggage, nobody knows where!"

Chapter XV
To the Zoo

Aggie being better, and having declared that no power on earth would make her spend another night in the place, we planned to leave about noon that day. But Tish's astonishing conduct drove all idea of going from our minds.

In the first place, Miss Lewis came in from breakfast looking a little bit better, and insisted on giving Tish's knee its massage, as usual. But Tish was sitting poring over the notes she had made, and wouldn't even so much as look up.

"Get away," she snarled, with her pencil in her teeth. "There's nothing wrong with my knee."
Miss Lewis looked at me.

'There was something wrong with it yesterday," she said, with her thumbs tucked inside her belt and her spectacles flashing. "It's got cured pretty quick, I think."

"I don't employ you to think," said Tish, hopping past her and opening the lower bureau drawer.

"You needn't employ me at all."

"That's a fact," Tish said. "It hadn't occurred to me. You go in and take care of Miss Pilkington to-day. Miss Lewis. There's nothing pleases her like being taken care of."

"There's nothing the matter with Miss Pilkington, either," snapped Miss Lewis, but Tish was getting down on her knees by the drawer, groaning as she did it, and she only threw an absent reply over her shoulder. "Oh, well," she said, "you know what I mean. I didn't mean to offend you. You're a good nurse, but I've got something else on hand.! Give Miss Pilkington a bath and put talcum on; she'll take to it like a baby."

Miss Lewis opened her mouth to refuse, thought better of it, and went to Aggie's room. Tish drew a long sigh.

"Thank heaven!" she said. "They'll keep each other busy for the rest of the day."

Which they did. Aggie emerged from her room when Tish and I, breathless and dirty, got back late that morning. She was powdered and manicured, curled and French-puffed, and she knew the history of every private case on the floor; name, age, family scandal and operation. She was primed to talk, but by that time Tish and I had no time to stop. Things were approaching a climax.

Well, Miss Lewis and Aggie off our hands, Tish emptied the lower drawer and spread its contents on the floor in front of her. First of all, she laid out the two roller towels, with the S. P. T. showing. Then followed the brown tweed coot, secured by a dollar to Jacobs, the small surgeon's knife, the dented brass candlestick, the bandage Linda Smith had picked up in the upper hall, the linen room key, and Charlie Sands' letter about Hero at the Zoo. Then with the sheet of note-paper in her hand, she began to play a sort of checkers with the different things. The two S. P. T. towels she put together and using this combination as a king, she proceeded to jump the other articles, one by one, moving them around aimlessly in the intervals and consulting her notes.

At the end of the game, as well as I could make out, the king had it. At least, the two towels seemed to have Charlie Sands' letter checkmated in a comer, and the other articles lay in a humiliated heap on Tish's lap.

"Well," I said, "I see the towels win, although I think you cheated once."

Tish stuffed the notes into the bosom of her dress and tumbled the other things back in the drawer. Then she got up, making horrible faces as she straightened her knee.

"I'm sorry if s raining, Lizzie," she said,

'We'll have to go out."

"Where!" I asked sarcastically. "To the matinée?"

"To the Zoo," she replied, and hauling down her bonnet from the cupboard, stuck it on her head. "Shall we need a taxicab?"

"Probably, if you intend to go out in your nightgown," I said coldly.

But if I expected Tish to be confused, I was disappointed. With her bonnet still on, she put on her shoes and stockings, her black broadcloth skirt, a lamb's wool vest and her long fur coat. It wasn't until she was finished that she remembered her nightgown underneath everything.

"It's a little long, isn't it?" she said, when she'd started for the door, with six inches of white trailing all around her. "Pin it up, Lizzie; that's a good girl."

"I'll do nothing of the sort," I said. "If you want to make a goose of yourself with a knee that you are forbidden to step on, and maybe a taxicab accident with you fixed like that underneath, I'm not going to be a party to it."

"Very well!" said Tish', and getting a pair 'of scissors, she was about to cut off eight inches of her best French gown, when I weakened and got the safety pins. It was plain, Tish was in no mood to stop at trifles. I made her as respectable as possible, at least on the surface, and by that time, seeing she was determined to go, I got ready and went with her.

Now, a patient can't leave a hospital without a card being sent down, signed by the interne and countersigned by the superintendent, and brought back by the elevator boy for the signatures of his family, his friends and the police bureau, or something almost as complicated. But not knowing anything of this, Tish and I went down in the elevator, past the door-man and out the front door, called a taxicab and drove away with perfect ease and calmness.

We went to the Zoo. That is generally known now, although that Tish went in her nightgown is here for the first time set forth. But what we did at the Zoo I do not know exactly. I might as well have been back with Aggie, being bathed and talcumed. Tish let me pay the taxicab, pointed to a chair in the ante-room, and spent twenty minutes in the private office of the superintendent

I was rather bitter about it. In the first place, I don't like Zoos, and in the second place, after I had been there ten minutes, a man in uniform came in and examined all the corners of the room and turned over every chair. When he came to the one I was in, he said, "Excuse me, ma'am, but you haven't noticed a small green snake with red and yellow markings anywhere around here, have you?"

I was frozen in my chair.

"No," I replied as calmly as I possibly could, "Unless I absent-mindedly put him in my hand-bag!"

"Oh, I didn't mean that, lady," he hastened to explain, "I meant-he may be curled on the rungs of your chair."

I got up at that almost instantaneously and he tilted the chair over. "Not here," he said, disappointed. "Little devil, this is the third time this week!"

Is he-is he poisonous?" I asked. Well," he said thoughtfully, "personally, I shouldn't care to sit down on him in the dark."

He went out and dosed the door, and when Tish came back, she declares I was standing in the middle of the room with my skirts held up, and turning slowly around in a circle.

There was a glitter in Tish's eye that I had never seen there before, as we drove back to the hospital. I attempted to explain a little of how I felt at being left in a place like that, where at any moment something might break loose for the third time that week, and why I was turning around, but she told me tartly not to bother her.

We returned to the hospital in silence, and I paid for the taxicab. It was not until we were back in Tish's room, and had put her into her chair and got a hot-water bottle under her knee, which had gone on a strike about that time and refused to bend at all, that I spoke.

"Well?" I asked.

"Well-what?"

"Have they lost anything? Any animals?"

"No," said Tish calmly. "I knew that before I went there. Aggie, what day was it the two medical internes left?"

"This is Friday," I said. "It was Tuesday evening, Tish."

"I thought so," she observed. "Now reach me my notes, Lizzie, and go call Bates."

Chapter XVI
Tommy Tells Why

Bates came unwillingly. His shrewd face was pale and twitching, and he insisted on knowing why he was wanted.

"I can not tell you, because I do not know, Mr. Bates," I said. "Miss Carberry wants to speak to you. That is all."

"I haven't time," he said. "I'm helping out in the wards to-day. One of the day orderlies has to take Mr. Briggs' place to-night, and he has gone to bed to get some sleep."

But I got him to go finally, and we went together along the hall, his carpet-slippers flap-ping loosely as he walked, his shirt open at. the throat and showing his lean brown neck. I thought to myself uneasily that the man looked like, at least, a potential criminal him-self. But just as we reached Tish's door Tommy came out

I sent Bates in, for Tommy had put his hand on my arm,

"What has she been up to?" he asked, as the door closed "She's sitting in there in a kimono, with her foot on a stool, and she's got her bonnet on,"

"We've been out," I said tartly. "Or she's been out. I only went along. We went to the Zoo, Tommy, and she left me to sit on snakes with green and red markings —"

"What!"

"Well, it only happened that L didn't And she's got hold of something: I never saw her in such a state,"

"The Zoo!" cried Tommy and whistled. Then he smiled. "I see," he said; "The Murders in the Rue Morgue, eh? Well, what happened?"

"I haven't any idea. She's got some sort of a scent, and she's got her nose to the ground and running like mad. If she's interfered with to-day, shell bite."

"I see," said Tommy again thoughtfully. "Well, good luck to her."

"How is Miss Blake?"

He lowered his voice. "She's conscious, but don't tell Aunt Tish, please. She wants to ask her some questions, and I don't want her disturbed. She's very weak." He looked down at a little case he had in his hand, and then at me. "I'm going to give her a hypodermic," he said, "and the nurse is doing something else. Would you mind coming over with me?"

Well, of course, I'd wanted to hear what Tish asked Bates, but as I've admitted before, I'm a good bit of a fool where there's a love affair on hand, and I'm fond of Tommy.

"All right," I said, and we went. I thought I heard Tish's voice raised angrily as we left the door, but the next moment there was only the quiet hum of Bates speaking.

The little nurse was lying in bed with her eyes closed. She looked white, but her lips had more color than the day before. She opened her eyes as we came in, and put out her hand to me.

"You're very good," she said, "You see I am better." Tommy beamed.

"And just in time!" said I. "One more fainting fit, and Doctor Tommy Andrews would have been tied up in a strait-jacket."

She colored a little and looked at him.

"I've been telling her," said Tommy, catching my eye, "about Miss Lewis and the mouse last night. A girl with a set of lungs like that is lost in a hospital. She ought to be in a garage blowing up auto tires."

"And-everything was quiet last night?"

"Not a sound-except the aforesaid yell. Never knew the house quieter." He reached over and caught her wrist. "Nerves as tight as a string!" he said. "You're going to have a hypodermic and relax a bit."

"Since you will be my medical adviser —" she said, half shyly, and held out her right arm.

Tommy fixed the hypodermic and came over to the bed. "Ready!" he said, but instead of the right arm, he leaned across and drew up the short white sleeve of the left She made a quick movement, but was too late.

"Good heavens!" Tommy said, and we both stared. The arm was covered with bruises from elbow to shoulder!

Tommy walked back with me to Tish's room, but at first he said nothing, and neither did I. The girl had offered no explanation, and he had asked none. The poor little arm had been too pathetic.

Just before we reached Tish's door, however, he stopped.

"The sheer brutality of it!" he said. "She's only a bit of a girl, and she's been through something horrible. But I'm not going to ask her about it, and I won't have her questioned by anybody else. If I'm satisfied, it's nobody else's affair."

"Listen to the egoist!" said I. "And why is it your affair only."

"Because I'm going to many her, if shell have me," he said hotly. "And after I have her, and can protect her, I'm going to kill whoever put those finger-prints on her arm."

"Finger-prints!" I cried.

"Yes, finger-prints," he said, and opened the door.

Bates had gone, and Aggie and Tish were together. Tish still wore her bonnet, and she had a crimson spot on each cheek.

"Tommy," she said, the moment we entered. "I've sent for the linen woman, and I want you to stay by. As soon as I've seen her, we're going to the Blake girl's room."

"Oh, no; you're not," said Tommy calmly. "You'll go there over my dead body."

"That wouldn't be much of an obstacle!"

"She's very ill. I won't have her disturbed," said Tommy, and set his jaw. They both have the Carberry jaw. Tish made an impatient movement. "Oh, well, 'I can manage without her. Is the top of the elevator flat?' " she added.

"The center is, I believe," Tommy was doubtful. "What on earth —"

"Never mind!" said Tish grandly, and the linen woman knocked.

"Mrs. Jenkins?" asked Tish.

"Yes'm," said Mrs. Jenkins. She was a tall woman, in black, with a white apron and a thimble as badges of office.

"I wanted to ask you for the key to the mortuary linen closet, Mrs. Jenkins," said Tish.

Mrs. Jenkins fidgeted, and glanced at Tommy.

"I'm sorry," she said. "I —haven't got it just now."

"Indeed!" Tish raised her eyebrows.

"Aren't you responsible for that closet? I have a particular reason for asking."

Mrs. Jenkins turned to Tommy. "Since you're here, Doctor Andrews," she said, "I suppose it's all right, but we don't give the keys to any of the closets to patients usually."

"Since you haven't got it, that needn't disturb you," Tish said sharply. "If you wish a reason, however, I'm a member of the Ladies' Committee of this hospital, and as I am undertaking a special inquiry into things that have happened here lately, I want that key."

"Mrs. Jenkins looked dazed. She had never seen a female detective, I daresay, and to see one sitting before her in a kimono over a nightgown, with a black bonnet with jet bugles over one ear, and her foot out on a stool, clearly bewildered her.

"I'm sorry," she said respectfully, when she'd recovered, "but the key that usually hangs in the mortuary is lost, and I gave Miss Linda Smith the other one."

"Hah!" cried Tish, "When?"

"Yesterday, I think. I'm not sure."

'Thank you very much, Mrs. Jenkins. I'll not keep you any longer." And as the linen woman went out, Tish got up and reached for her cane.

"Now then. Tommy," she said, "I'll trouble you to take Lizzie and Aggie somewhere and keep them, so I can think. Take them out and get them some soda water."

"Soda water! Perhaps you would like me to go back to the Zoo," I observed with biting sarcasm. But it was lost on Tish.

"I shouldn't advise it," she said. "It's raining again. Just get out-go anywhere, so you go. And come back in an hour."

"I've half a mind —" Aggie began nastily.

"Why, so you have!" said Tish. "Shut the door behind you." And as Aggie, who was the last, slammed out, we heard Tish opening the lower bureau drawer.

Chapter XVII
On the Roof and Elsewhere

We came back in an hour to find Tish waiting with her bonnet still on, and in a more agreeable frame of mind. She asked Tommy and me to go around the hospital with her, but refused to take Aggie, who retired sulking to her room. Tish rolled up the S. P. T. towels and led the way herself, a strange gleam in her eye. Considering what she had in mind, it was a courageous thing she was doing, but I don't mind admitting now that there were moments that day when I thought she had lost her reason.

She led the way to the mortuary first, with her bundle under her arm, and Tommy and I trailing at her heels, like two bewildered lambs after a wild-eyed sheep. Seen in daylight, there was nothing horrible about the mortuary. There were no bodies there, and the daylight came in in churchly fashion through the two large stained glass windows in the end. Indeed, the room looked like a small chapel, being finished in dark wood, with pale walls, chairs in a row around the edge of the floor, and only the row of tables in the center instead of pews, to spoil its ecclesiastical appearance.

At the far end, to the left, and near the windows, was the door to the linen closet. Tish gave the room only a casual glance, and stalked across to the linen closet She hesitated a moment and grasped her stick closely. Then she inserted the key she had carried up with her, and slowly turned it.

The door flew open immediately and I took a hasty step back. But it had been pushed only by the draft of air from a small window at the side, which was open, and except for piles of neatly folded linen, the closet was empty. Tish looked slightly disappointed, but not discouraged. She went in and stuck her head out through the open window, looking in every direction.

"Exactly," she said and prepared to close and lock the closet again. But she waited to close the small window first, and when she turned. Tommy had stooped over something lying on the floor just inside the door.

"Look!" he said, holding it out on his palm. "Briggs' old pipe, with the stem gone! The one he was smoking when —!"

If he expected Tish to be impressed he was disappointed.

"There's nothing astonishing about that!" she said calmly, and proceeding to climb out one of the stained-glass windows on to the fire-escape —although it was the fifth floor and Tish had always declared she'd rather bum up than put a foot on one of the things-she ran nimbly up and over the cornice to the roof.

It was a very ordinary roof. One part was flat, and evidently used occasionally as a breathing spot. There were benches around and a flower pot or two, and directly in the center was a four-foot iron fence, enclosing a skylight. Two men at work there showed where Tommy had gone through, and when I glanced at him he was staring at it with a rueful smile.

"When you remember," he said, "that I weigh a hundred and seventy pounds, and that I went over that fence head first, it makes you wonder what grudge old Johnson had against me. I was decent enough to him, if Briggs wasn't."

"Do you mean that-that Briggs was cruel to him?" I asked Tommy.

"With a refined form of cruelty, yes. The sort that lets an old man go without sugar in his tea, and won't hear him begging for ice-water."

"Then I'm glad he's dead," I snapped, "and if I'd been Johnson, I'd have —"

Tish had wandered across the roof, and was standing on a part of it about two feet higher, than the rest, looking at a second and smaller skylight.

"What's this. Tommy?" she called.

"Elevator, I think," said Tommy, and we went over. Tish was looking around her with speculative eyes.

"I guess this is about right," she said. "I miss my guess, unless — Tommy, get down with your ear to the roof and see if you hear anything."

"It's dirty," said Tommy.

"I guess you'll wash without spoiling," Tish snapped. "It ain't a Carberry trait to be afraid of dirt. Get down."

Tommy pulled up his trousers legs and got down gingerly, and I followed suit. I daresay we looked queer, both kneeling, and each with an eager ear to the tin. The two men at the other skylight stared at us over the railing nervously.

We didn't hear anything, and Tish looked disappointed. But she didn't stop her half hop, half run, over the roof. At the end of fifteen minutes she was back at the top of the fire-escape, ready to descend. But going down was different from going up, and I guess we were both relieved when Tommy said there was a staircase.

When we got to the bottom, I was clear out of breath, and even Tommy was panting. But Tish hadn't turned a hair. Some sort of inward excitement was stimulating like a fever, and knowing Tish, I felt she would cave in like a pricked balloon when it was over.

The next thing she demanded was to be put on the top of the elevator cage. But Tommy absolutely balked at that and Tish seemed to realize herself that it wouldn't do.

"I'll go for you," Tommy said. "I'm willing to sacrifice myself for you any time. Aunt Tish, but you can see for yourself that a self-respecting woman in her prime can't ride on top of an elevator without causing comment. It isn't being done in our set this winter. Aunt Tish."

Tish gave in, or pretended to, and we went back to her room. Aggie was there, dressed but sulky, and we had tea all around and tried to talk about indifferent things. We told Aggie we had been up to see the mortuary, whereon she insisted on seeing it, too, and Miss Lewis and I took her.

We left Tish still working over her notes, with a cup of tea in one hand, which she was absently stirring with her lead pencil, and went up-stairs. Tommy had gone to see Miss Blake again.

We showed Aggie the mortuary and she got weak in the knees and had to sit a few minutes. It must have been fifteen minutes, therefore, when supporting her between us, we led her down the steps and rang for the elevator. It travels, as I say, very quietly, and when it came into view, all we could do was to stare, our mouths open.

Riding majestically on top of it, one hand in a dignified manner holding to the cable, the other clutching her stick, and with her head thrown back and staring up, was Tish! She went past us without seeing us, and a moment later we heard her say calmly:

"Stop now, Frank. Stop!"

Almost immediately on that she said, "Go down! Go down, I tell you! Go down!"

The cage went down past us, with Tish still holding on, still looking up. But on her face there was the most terrible expression of mingled fright and satisfaction I ever saw.

The next moment there began, from above, a shower of sticks, pieces of plaster, and finally, a small creature that looked like, and proved to be, a dead rabbit Aggie began to scream and to tear at the elevator doors, but luckily they held.

Well, as the newspapers have told, the idiot of an elevator man kept on to the first floor in his excitement, and it's -a great wonder Tish was not brained. But nothing hit her, and! she got to the lower floor in safety. If she had waited until the cage was lowered sufficiently, she would not have been hurt, but just as the top was still four feet from the floor, the rabbit landed, and Tish jumped and broke her arm.

Chapter XVIII
Common Sense

Well, that's all there was to it. As I said at the beginning, this is really Tish's story. She told us the whole thing that night sitting up in bed, with the Chief of Police and the hospital superintendent on one side of the bed, and Miss Lewis and I on the other. Aggie lay on the couch with a cubeb cigarette burning beside her, and stared at Tish with admiration mixed with awe.

"In the first place," said Tish, to the Chief of Police, "here are the two towels that figure in the case. One of them is the one that hung Mr. Johnson's body three nights ago to the chandelier, the other is the one with which the ape, Hero, is supposed to have committed suicide at the Zoo the following night. As you see, the two towels are alike. Do you know what S. P. T. stands for?" she asked.

"I can't say I do," said the Chief of Police, and picked up one of the towels.

"Humph!" said Tish. "Well, it means 'Sick Patient Towel,' and they are used in hospitals for tying up delirious patients. The trouble was, there wasn't a delirious patient in the hospital strong enough to walk, let alone tie up a body to a chandelier.

"But before I learned from Bates what S. P. T. meant, I'd been to the Zoo. That was yesterday morning. Maybe you believe that a lonely monkey will commit suicide; maybe he will, I don't know. But when he hangs himself with a roller towel from the Dunkirk hospital, I want to know how he got that towel."

"Oho!" said the Chief of Police, "so the little rascal got loose, did he?"

"He did not," said Tish tartly. "They said he was lonely for his keeper. Very well, said I, where is his keeper? Where is this man he was so fond of that he couldn't live without him? The answer, gentlemen, was that this keeper was a patient in the Dunkirk hospital, as the result of being crushed almost to death by the beast that was supposed to be pining for him! The keeper's name was Wesley Barker!"

"Barker!" said Tommy. "Why, that was the big Englishman —! Go on. Aunt Tish."

"I came back to the hospital with a strong desire to talk to Wesley Barker, but Wesley Barker was not in the hospital. He had been dismissed three days ago. Bates recalled taking his dismissal card to the elevator man, about seven o'clock Tuesday evening. That put Barker out of the case, apparently, but I sent for Jacobs and asked him how easily a man could get into the building at night. He said it was impossible. The doors are always locked, the basement entrances and fire-escapes lead from the courtyard, and the courtyard is locked and in charge of a gate man. That seemed to cut out Wesley Barker, as I say. If he was out, he could hardly get back without using dynamite.

"I got out my notes again, and went over then I couldn't see how Miss Blake and Miss Linda Smith were mixed up in it. They were the day nurses in K ward. Miss Smith in charge and Miss Blake assisting. I had several notes on them: Tuesday at midnight Miss Smith coaxed the night nurse to go to the basement with her, where the patients' clothes are kept in lockers: she was missing for a time, and when Bates saw her later she carried a 'darkish bundle,' possibly clothing. Why?"

The Chief of Police looked wise; he had a way of wriggling his nose like a rabbit.

"The next morning, Miss Blake being ill, we heard Miss Smith crying in her room and blaming herself for the girl's condition," Tish went on. "Again, why?"

"On Wednesday night Miss Blake, still weak and ill, made a complete search of the third floor. Not another nurse in the house would have gone there, or to the mortuary and later to the roof, as she did. Some strong purpose sent the girl, of course-but what?

"That night, following Miss Blake to the roof, my nephew was thrown through a skylight. Later he confessed to a bite on the shoulder. The same night, apparently in a spirit of wanton mischief, the guinea-pigs in the laboratory were killed and three rabbits were taken away. Miss Blake had been there. My nephew confessed later to finding a rosette from her slipper there. Again-why?"

Tish stopped and looked at the Chief of Police, who sat stroking his chin.

"How would you have gone about the case, Mr. Chief of Police?" Tish demanded.

"Probably much as you did," he said, looking at her with a patronizing smile. "It's a simple matter when we know the answer, to say that two and two make four, but you are giving me the four, and asking me whether you reached that conclusion by adding three and one, or two and two, or four and nothing. Given a certain number of clues, the logical mind often achieves remarkable results, but it is usually the trained mind. That you succeeded so well, my dear lady, I consider remarkable. Remarkable!"

"Given the same clues," Tish persisted, "you'd have reached the same result?"

"Undoubtedly."

"Well," said Tish, mildly. "It's strange that I couldn't There were a few gaps my mind wouldn't jump. And I noticed your men here seemed to feel the same way. It seemed like some distance from a roller towel in the Zoo to Johnson's brown tweed coat."

The Chief of Police looked uneasy.

"By exactly what mental process did you connect the two?" he asked, wriggling his nose.

"I didn't," said Tish cahnly. "While you and your men were measuring finger-prints and reassembling Mr. Johnson from where he'd been scattered to, I did what any person with common sense would have done, I went to Miss Blake and asked her!"

Chapter XIX

Miss Lizzie's narrative stops here. My Aunt Letitia, during her convalescence in the hospital, having been discovered poring over books of aerial navigation, and having written to the Wrights, offering to turn over a second-hand automobile of standard make, a thirty-foot motor launch, and an equity in money, for one of their model biplanes. Miss Lizzie and Miss Aggie hurriedly took her to Mount Clemens for a series of baths.

"I shall take up Miss Lizzie's narrative with the story told to my Aunt Letitia by Miss Blake, now my wife. Miss Blake was young, only nineteen, and had been in the hospital only six months. Miss Smith was the head day nurse in K ward, with Miss Blake as her assistant. Miss Smith had almost completed her three years' course, and was not popular with the officers. She was, however, a good nurse, and unlike Miss Blake, was dependent on her earnings for her support.

"On Tuesday evening, trouble between the two medical internes and the hospital superintendent, Mr. Harrison, reached a climax. The three men had a wordy argument on the staircase near K ward, and Linda Smith (who was not over-scrupulous) had shut herself in a small supply room near to listen. The ward was in charge of Miss Blake, who was serving the patients' suppers from a table in the center of the long room. Behind a screen, in the second bed from the far end of the ward lay Amos Johnson, peacefully dying. Beyond him, in the end bed, lay a delirious patient named Wesley Barker, an Englishman, who had been sent in from the Zoological Garden, badly injured by the great ape, Hero, since dead.

"Barlcer was tied down. Two long towels, one over his arms and one over his legs, were knotted beyond his reach under the edge of the bed. His fractured ribs had healed, but he was still delirious. His delirium in the last day or two had taken on an acuter form, and was mania. Articulate speech had changed to noisy ape-like chatterings. He made strange facial grimaces, and being tied, had more than once tried to bite his nurses.

"Miss Blake filled a feeding cup with broth, and having attended to the other patients, went behind Johnson's screen to feed the maniac in the last bed. To her horror, the bed was empty!

"Nervous, but not excessively alarmed. Miss Blake called Linda Smith, and they searched the ward. Barker had gone, perhaps by creeping behind the heads of the beds to the doorway, and there, watching his chance, escaping to the fire-escape by a hall window near. Although only late September, it was cold, and he wore only the clothing he had worn in bed, a hospital nightshirt.

"Miss Blake wished to raise an immediate alarm, but Linda Smith refused. She was responsible: an investigation would show she had been absent from her ward without reason, and for some time. She was in disfavor already, and she could not risk losing her diploma. She had an invalid sister dependent on her. By threats and tears she made Miss Blake promise to say nothing of Barker's escape and to help her find him.

"It was almost dark by that time, and the girls were in despair. Linda Smith went down the fire-escape to the courtyard, and found the gate man staring through the bars at the river.

"I dropped a rubber sheet out the window," she said, "but I don't see it. What are you looking at?"

"The gate man pointed to the Center Street bridge, which crosses the river near the hospital. There's a woman out there in white,' he said, 'and she looks as if she might be thinking-there, look at that!'

The bridge was practically deserted. She and the gate man saw the figure move back a step or two, run forward and dive over the rail. The gate man unlocked the gate and ran out, but the toll house is at the east end of the bridge, and by the time he had raised the alarm there was nothing to be seen. Linda Smith went back to Miss Blake, and had hysteria in the K ward linen room.

Discovery meant disgrace to her, so she made up her mind not to be discovered. Barker had had no family and no friends. No one had visited him except the assistant keeper, and he had not shown any particular solicitude. Linda Smith thought she saw a way out, and half frightened, half coaxed Miss Blake into helping her. Remember, they both thought Barker was dead, and Linda Smith threatened in case of discovery, to throw herself off the roof. Miss Blake's part, therefore, was the acquiescence of a young and terrified girl, in a situation that would have shaken older and stronger nerves.

The two medical internes left at seven o'clock, as a result of the dispute with the superintendent. At ten minutes past seven, Linda Smith sent down a dismissal card for one Wesley Barker, with the forged signature of one of the departed internes. At twenty minutes past, the yellow ticket came back from the office, the ticket which would permit Wesley Barker to pass the door man and leave the hospital for good. Linda Smith destroyed it.

At seventy-thirty the night nurse. Miss Durand, was told that one of the heaviest burdens had been taken from her, and went to work cheerfully. But at ten o'clock that night Linda Smith, lying awake in bed in her room in the dormitory, saw Wesley Barker climb up the fire-escape outside her window, stopping now and then, monkey fashion, to swing out over the dizzy height by his hands.

The girl was almost frenzied. She got up and dressed and went to the roof. To her horror she found the superintendent, Mr. Harrison, smoking there and she almost fainted when she got back to her room. But the superintendent was not molested. There was no alarm.

At midnight she formed the resolution of getting Barker's clothes from the basement clothes room and putting them on the roof, in the hope that he would put them on and go away. Properly dressed, even if he went back to the Zoo, she could claim that he had been taken away by somebody in a carriage, and might still put through the deception. In any event,-his clothes could not be left there. Their discovery meant her disgrace.

She had forgotten, however, that Barker had been brought in in the ambulance, and had no clothes. Afraid to go to the basement alone, she asked Miss Durand to go to the clothes room with her, giving as an excuse that she had forgotten to send Johnson's clothes to the office, a rule in case of death, and on finding nothing there in Barker's name, she did the only thing she could think of — took Johnson's old brown suit, which, with his worn shoes and not very clean linen, was tied in a bundle with a piece of bandage and marked with the dying spiritualist's name.

Miss Durand had disappeared, carrying the bundle. Miss Smith searched the far comers of the basement, but found nothing. Finally, she and Miss Durand went up-stairs again, to find that Johnson had been dead for some time. Bates, the convalescent, had seen them go and saw them return. He had, however, been detected a day or so before by Miss Durand selling cocaine to a colored man in one of the wards, and later, under Miss Durand's eye, he said she had been absent ten minutes. As a matter of fact, it had been fifty.

Linda Smith went back to her room at once. She knew she and Miss Blake would be called to attend to Johnson in the mortuary, and she waited for the summons. The ghastly trick of hanging the poor old body to the chandelier followed in due course.

Thinking Barker still dead, it had been as great a shock to Ruth Blake as to the others. It was not until the next morning that Linda Smith told her Barker was still alive, and somewhere in the building. There was only one comfort: Linda had put the bundle of clothing on the roof, and it had disappeared.

The other things followed in quick succession. Miss Blake, half frenzied, conceived the idea of putting food heavily doped with morphia, on the roof, along the fire-escape, anywhere that the maniac might find it. She hardly knew what she hoped to do by this: she was in an abnormal frame of mind by this time: ill, sleepless and unable to eat. The food disappeared, but if the morphia had any effect, it was in daylight, when he probably slept, hidden away under the roof or in the linen closet

The following night, she searched the fifth, or mortuary floor, carrying a candle. She had suspected, from the night before, that Barker was hiding in the linen closet, and Linda Smith got the key. The plan had been that Miss Smith should go with her, but she was given a special case that night, and Miss Blake, courageously enough, went alone.

Barker was in the closet, and when she opened the door he seized her arm in a murderous grip that left it blue and swollen. She tried speaking to him, and releasing his hold, he darted out through the closet window and leaped to the fire-escape. Miss Blake pluckily followed him to the roof, but he had disappeared. As Miss Lizzie has told, I followed Miss Blake. Just before I reached her, she cried out and flung her brass candlestick at something behind me. The next instant I was grasped from behind and thrown head first through the skylight.

I did not know I had been bitten in the shoulder. I thought I had been stabbed, until Jacobs and I together cauterized the wound that night in the laboratory. Probably during the time we were there, the door being unlocked. Barker entered and hid in the building. Miss Blake was there at the same time, having watched Jacobs and myself enter, and being fearful of further harm. She did not see anything of Barker, however, and went back to the roof, where she sat huddled until dawn, waiting for Barker to appear again. But he did not come, and at daylight, shaking with cold, she went back to her room. There she had a chill, followed by violent fever and delirium, and there I believe Linda Smith came, bringing a surgical knife stained with blood, that she had found on the roof, and which Miss Lewis subsequently found in Miss Blake's room.

The condition of the two girls by that time was pitiable. Miss Blake, younger and more nervous, had entirely succumbed: Miss Smith, sleepless and unable to eat, was still making a fight to cover the whole thing and to drive Barker away from the building. They could not discover where he hid in the daytime, but at night evidences of his ape-like mischief were everywhere apparent. He swung by his feet from the pipe-molding of the walls, squatted on the foot-board of the bed in private room thirty-six, making hideous grimaces —a story which caused the nurse in charge to mark 'delirious' on the record of a perfectly rational woman-leaped at giddy heights about the fire-escape and the roof, and alarmed Miss Aggie into her story of a ghostly; foot. The man's strength was almost superhuman.

Johnson died on Tuesday night, and it was on Wednesday night that I was thrown through the skylight Toward dawn of Thursday morning. Barker went to the Zoo, distant about a mile from the hospital. By that time he had donned Johnson's trousers, but remained in his bare feet Access to the monkey house proved easy. The assistant keeper, sleeping in a small room just inside the entrance, was not aroused until too late. The key to Hero's cage hung over his bed, it being his habit to go in to see the ape several times during the night. On that night, he opened the cage at one o'clock, and spoke to the ape, who had been sulky all day. He locked the door and went back to bed, hanging the key up again on its nail. It was still there in the morning at six o'clock, but the ape was dead. In spite of his tremendous strength and length of arm, he had been literally crushed to death, and then hung to the top of the cage by a roller towel which did not belong to the Zoo.

The police were put on the case, and had already arrested the assistant keeper, who had been heard to say that either the ape would get him or he would get the ape.

On Wednesday night, Briggs, who had been most unpopular with Barker, met his death in an almost similar manner, his ribs being crushed in. In this case, however. Barker's ingenuity utilized the useless brown coat, the two towels being gone. Previous to that time, he had rocked the elevator in impish mischief, or possibly wrath. It was this incident which caused my Aunt Letitia to suspect a space under the roof at the top of the elevator shaft, as a hiding place.

The result of her courageous investigation is well known: mounted on top of the cage, she was taken to the upper position of the shaft, and there found what she had been looking for, an unboarded spot behind the elevator wheel. She was disappointed, however, in finding the space too dark for inspection, and in hearing or seeing nothing suspicious.

Being a courageous woman and convinced that what she sought was there in the cavelike recess, my Aunt Letitia threw her slipper with all the strength she could summon, and was answered by a growl.

My wife has just read this and confirms most of it. She suggests, however, that I have omitted our theory of how Briggs was murdered without discovery, while Jacobs was in the hall nearby and I myself guarded the only other means of exit, the fire-escape.

Barker probably took refuge in the linen closet, arriving at the mortuary floor ahead of the slow progress of the cage, by scurrying up the cable. He hid in the closet, and by throwing the coat over Briggs and squeezing him in his muscular arms, he prevented any outcry. Immediately after, he locked himself in the closet again, where he smoked Briggs' pipe, perhaps in itself the object of the attack.

On the alarm being raised. Hicks and I came in through the window, and Jacobs through the door. This left the fire-escape and the roof unwatched, and he climbed out the window of the linen closet, swinging himself easily to the fire-escape.

"The rest of the story we know. Barker was found, exhausted and half starving, and was promptly put in a padded cell, where, a week later, he died, probably from an infection, having cut his left foot badly, possibly with the very knife that killed the laboratory guinea-pigs. The injured foot, which he had crudely bandaged, probably explains why only prints of a right foot were discovered. With the removal of suspense Miss Blake recovered, and is now with me, enjoying the lilies and onion fields of Bermuda. My Aunt Letitia is at Mount Clemens, taking a series of baths and —I am informed by Miss Lizzie-carrying on what she believes is a clandestine correspondence with the Wright brothers. Miss Aggie's hay fever left with the first frost. I am sorry to say that Miss Linda Smith has never been heard from."

Three Pirates of Penzance

Chapter I
A Cigarette Case, a Shoe, and a Menu Card

It was three o'clock in the morning when we got back to the lake, and it was twenty minutes before Carpenter heard us and started the ferry across. Tish had lost her glasses in the excitement at the Sherman House, and she did not see that Carpenter had forgotten to put the bar across the end of the boat. Aggie and I screamed, but it was too late: she drove the car down the bank in the moonlight and she did not stop in time. The first we knew we were sitting waist-deep in Lake Penzance, with Tish still holding the steering wheel and the stars making little twinkles in our laps.

As Tish said afterward, it was a fit ending to a sensational night, but, what with the wetting aggravating Aggie's hay fever, and my having bitten through the side of my tongue when the machine struck the bottom of the lake, it more nearly finished us. The engine drowned with a gurgle, and after Carpenter's first yell there wasn't a sound. Then we heard him come to the end of the ferry-boat and look down at us, and the next moment he had dropped the lantern and was doubled up on the dock, laughing like the fool he is.

"Are you both there?" said Tish, without turning her head.

Aggie sneezed, as she always does after a shock, and a wave moved slowly in and raised the water level with my breastbone.

"We are both here," I said, with a bitterness that was natural under the circumstances. "No thanks to you, Tish Carberry. There's no fool like an old fool."

"What do you mean?" Tish demanded fiercely, twisting around in the water with her dust cap over her eye. "Who was it said I ought to buy the dratted thing? Drive it yourself if you think you can do any better."

"Row it," I corrected. "It's finished for good as a touring car, but by putting an awning over it we might make it into a tolerable gasoline launch."

Aggie was crying.

"I told you something would happen," she sniffled. "You'll kill us all yet, Tish Carberry —and me in my foulard silk that spots with a drop of rain!"

But Tish wasn't paying any attention. She picked up the wrench that she had kept by her as a sort of weapon and stood up on the seat Tish is a large woman.

"Abraham Carpenter," she snapped, with as much dignity as she could with her clothes glued to her, "if you do not stop that noise I will brain you."

Carpenter eased down gradually, and, holding his sides, he leaned over the end of the ferry.

"What'll I do, Miss Tish?" he asked, beginning to jerk again, but with an eye on the wrench. "I can go around to the other dock and get a rowboat, but it'll take time."

"Don't bother about the other dock," Tish snapped. "Get that board there on the ferry and put one end of it down to the automobile. Then turn your back."

That's the way we got out. I went up the board first, on my hands and knees, and barring a few splinters I got up very nicely. Aggie came next, and as the board was getting wet she had more trouble. But Tish had the worst, for by that time the board was as slippery as a toboggan; twice she got as far as the middle, only to slide back on her stomach, and the last time she refused to try again. She sat down on one of the seats, with the water up to her waist, and said that she was skinned alive, and that she wished there was a tide to come up and drown her and the miserable machine. We got her up finally by throwing her a rope to put under her arms, and once up she collapsed on the ferry-bench. It was then that Aggie missed the money. Carpenter had slid down the board and was preparing to salvage the cushions when Aggie clutched at her stocking and yelled.

"It's gone!" she screeched, and then she sat plump down on the floor of the ferry-boat and began to cry.

"What's gone?" Tish demanded.

"The money," Aggie said, feeling frantically around the tops of her shoes. "When we went over the edge something broke —I felt it-and the money's gone."

Tish had both her arms in the air and the rope over her shoulder, but she stopped struggling and stared at Aggie.

"Grone!" she said in an awful voice. "Aggie Pilkington, every dollar of that money was graft money. Only the prospect of stuffing it between that red-haired man's teeth has kept me alive through this terrible night. Don't tell me you've lost it."

"We can give him a check," said Aggie ' feebly.

"We can!" Tish snorted, and not another word did she say until Carpenter had taken us across the lake and we stood dripping on the front porch of the cottage, while Aggie got the key from under a flower-pot. Then Tish looked across the moonlit lake to where the cushions of the machine floated in a nest of stars at the end of the ferry-dock.

"We averaged thirty miles an hour coming home,!" she said triumphantly, "and for the first time I feel that I have mastered the machine."

Wet as we were, we remembered to put the lantern in the window as we had promised, and we thought we saw a skiff shoot out in the starlight from the other side of the lake. Tish and I took some hot milk, and Aggie had a raw egg and some more baking soda, and we went to bed. The stars were fading by that time, but after I got into bed I distinctly heard footsteps on the gravel below my window.

"Are you sure you said the first house on the left?" Tish called to me. And then we heard Mr. Ostermaier's voice from the upper window next door, and we knew it was all right. I crawled out and tried to see into the preacher's parlor, but the shade was partly down. I could only make out a sleeve of Mrs. Ostermaier's kimono. I was disappointed after all we had gone through.

She-Mrs. Ostermaier-came over the next morning after breakfast, while Aggie's foulard silk was hanging on the clothes-line. She had been down with the other cottagers, looking across to where the red leather of Tish's machine stuck up above water-level.

"Be careful," Tish said under her breath when she saw her; "she's got something' in her hand!"

"What a terrible accident, and how lucky nobody was hurt!" Mrs. Ostennaier began, holding the thing she was carrying against her skirt and staring from the three of us to Aggie's foulard. "The spots did run, didn't they? I told Mr. Ostennaier they would He thinks you are wonderful women, to go around the country as the three of you do at all hours of the night."

Just then the sunlight caught the thing she held in her hand, and I knew in a moment what it was-it was Mr. Lewis' silver cigarette case Tish saw it too, and ran her needle into her finger.

"We had an exciting night too," Mrs. Ostermaier went on. "Dear me, Miss Carberry, you've jabbed your finger!"

"An exciting night?" I asked, to keep her attention from Aggie Aggie had just seen the cigarette case and she had gone blue around the nose.

"Most exciting. About three o'clock this morning-about the time you three ladies were having such a dreadful experience-still, as couple came to our cottage and wakened Ostermaier. I think they threw gravel through the window. They wanted to be married."

Tish sat up and tried to look scandalized.

"I hope your husband didn't do it," she said. I had to pinch Aggie; she was leaning forward with her eyes bulging.

That put Mrs. Ostermaier on the defensive. "Why not?" she demanded. "They had a license, and they were of age. I believe in encouraging young love; Mr. Ostermaier says it is the most beautiful thing in the world. Cousin Maggie and I were witnesses, and we threw rice after them. It was barley, really, but we didn't discover that until this morning."

Aggie gave a sigh of relief; we had guessed, but it was the first time we had really known.

"I told Mr. Ostermaier that it gave me quite a thrill the way he looked at her as Harold pronounced them man and wife. "All the world loves a lover,' and Cousin Maggie has been reading Ella Wheeler Wilcox diligently all morning.

She turned to go and we breathed easier. Now that we knew they were safely married — Mrs. Ostermaier turned and started back.

"I nearly forgot what brought me," she called. "My Willie found this in the bed of your automobile, Miss Tish." She held out the cigarette case and Tish took it and dropped it into her work-basket.

"It belongs to my nephew, Charlie Sands," she said, looking Mrs. Ostermaier in the eye. Tish has plenty of courage, but I felt calamity coming.

"So I told Mr. Ostermaier," the creature said, with a smile. "But he insists on remarking the coincidence that the initials on the cigarette case are W. L. and that the young man's name on the license was Walter Lewis."

I have always thanked Heaven that at that moment her Willie fell off the dock, and although the child was not drowned, still, as Tish wrote to Maria Lee, her niece, "he had swallowed enough water to wash the initials off the tablets of his mother's memory." And so far as we know, although the papers came out with great headlines about the marriage, and another article about the post-office having been robbed-we had nothing whatever to do with that-and about three men disguised as women making their escape toward Canada in a red automobile and having run over a pig at Dorchester Junction —I told Tish at the time it was a pig, but she insisted it was a cow-although the papers came out with all this, nobody ever suspected the truth except Carpenter. He happened to find a menu from the Sherman House at Noblestown floating in the body of the car, and the good-for-nothing took a trip to the city and traced us.

He did not say anything, but about a week later he came to the cottage and put a package on the table in the kitchen.

"It's been puzzlin' me for four days. Miss Lizzie," he said, fumbling with the string of the bundle. "I sez to Mrs. C, sez I, 'It ain't possible,' I sez. 'She sez she lost her shoe when the automobile went into the water, and she's a truthful woman; and yet, two days after, the chambermaid at the Sherman House finds it high and dry under a bureau, forty miles away. It's spooky,' I sez."

Aggie was pouring hot water into the teapot, and she kept on pouring till it went all over the place.

"Nonsense," said Tish. "That shoe doesn't belong to Miss Lizzie,"

But I looked at Carpenter's face and I knew it was hopeless.

"You've been a good friend to us, Mr. Carpenter," I said "We've always felt we'-ve owed you something. Here's a little present, and thank you for the shoe."

He took the money and we looked each other straight in the eye. Then he grinned.

"For twenty dollars, Miss Lizzie," he said, "I'd be willing to swallow my tongue backward. And the shoe ain't the tongue kind."

Chapter II
A Blue Runabout and a Bad Bridge

Both Aggie and I had objected when Tish talked of buying an automobile. But the more you talk against a thing to Tish the more she wants it. It was just the same the time her niece, Maria Lee, went to Europe for the whole summer and offered Tish her motor-boat. Aggie and I protested, but the boat came, and Tish had a lesson or two and sent to town for a yachting cap. Then, one day when we were making elderberry jelly and ran out of sugar, Tish offered to take me to the mainland in the boat. That was the time, you remember, when the stopping lever got jammed, and Tish and I circled around Lake Penzance for seven hours, with people on different docks trying to lasso us with ropes as we flew past, and Aggie in hysterics on the beach below the cottage.

People of Penzance still speak of that day, for we figured out that we had enough gasoline to run one hundred and sixty miles, and after Peter Miller, at Point Lena, had lassoed us and was dragged for a quarter of a mile before he caught hold of a buoy and could let go of the rope, we got desperate. I was at the wheel and Tish was trying to stop the engine, pouring water over it and attempting to stick an iron rod in the wheels. And just as she succeeded, and the rod shot through the awning on the top of the launch like a sky-rocket, I turned the thing toward shore where it looked fairly flat.

"I'm going to get to land," I said with my teeth clenched. "I don't care if it crawls up and dies in a plowed field; I'm going to get my feet on dry land again."

I had not expected it to stop so suddenly, but it did, and Tish and I and the granulated sugar landed some distance ahead of the boat and well above high-water mark; in fact, Tish broke her collar-bone, and that entire summer, whenever the doctor had to peel off the adhesive plaster, Tish would get ugly and turn on me.

Well, we should have known about the automobile. I had a queer feeling when I started out that morning. Tish had had the car out the day before by herself for the first time — both Aggie and I had had the good judgment to refuse-and she got home safely, although she had a queer-looking mark on her right cheek, and one of the mud-guards didn't look exactly right. She said she had had a lovely ride, and we helped her push the machine into the wash-house, where we had had Carpenter knock out a side, and then she went to bed and had a cup of tea. Aggie heard something moving that night, and she found Tish sitting up on the side of her bed, holding like death to the back of a chair and turning it around like a wheel. Aggie got her back to bed, but Tish only looked up at her and said, "Four chickens!" and went to sleep again.

The next morning her left leg was quite stiff from what she called the clutch, and she sat on the porch peacefully and rocked. But at noon she went to the wash-house, and when she came back she was pale but determined.

"I'm going to take it out," she said solemnly. "If I don't I'll forget everything I've learned. Besides, we've been coming here every summer for ten years, and there are plenty of places we have never seen."

Aggie looked at me, but we knew it would have to come some time, and so we all went in and tied up our heads.

"We needn't go fast," Aggie said when she was putting on her bonnet. "We have all afternoon, and one doesn't really enjoy the scenery unless one goes very slowly."

Tish's face was pallid but resolved.

"It's a great deal easier to go fast than slow," she remarked. "I haven't quite got the hang of going slow. But there's one comfort about going fast: you get around much quicker."

At the foot of the stairs she stopped and called up.

"I'm going to take a tablespoonful of blackberry wine," she said. "I feel chilly in the small of my back."

Aggie and I didn't say anything, but we each took a tablespoonful of blackberry wine also.

Tish had written out a list of things to do to start the car, such as "Turn A," "Push forward B," and so on. And she had pasted bits of paper marked A and B on the levers and plugs. So I read:

"Turn A; push up B; crank, and release C."

It started nicely.

"Just one thing," Tish said over her shoulder as we passed the Ostermaier cottage, and they waved to us from the porch: "Don't scream in my ears; don't lean over and clutch me around the neck; and if we run over anything, try to look as if you didn't know we had."

Luckily she had not noticed my traveling bag. After the affair of the launch I was prepared for anything, and I had packed up three nightgowns, a balsam pillow, a roll of bandage, a bottle of arnica, a cake of soap, my sewing box and a prayer-book. Aggie had some sandwiches; so we felt we were prepared for everything, from sudden death to losing a button.

We got on to the ferry safely enough. Carpenter, who runs the cable drum of the ferry with a gas engine, examined the machine with a great deal of interest on the way over.

"It's a pretty hot day. Miss Tish," he called as we were starting off the boat. "You'll have to watch her; she'll boil."

Tish looked worried, but she said nothing,

"What is there to boil?" Aggie whispered tome.

"The gasoline," I told her; "and if it boils it'll explode, I'm no mechanic, but I know that much."

After a few moments' silence Aggie leaned forward.

"Tish," she said.

"Don't take my mind off this machine!" Tish shouted back. "Isn't that a buggy coming?"

"It's too far off to see. It's either a buggy or a wagon," I said. "Tish, where's the gasoline tank?"

But Tish wasn't listening. "Why doesn't that man turn out? Does he want the whole road?" she snapped. There was a silence while we neared the buggy ahead. Then Tish leaned over and began jerking at levers.

"I can't stop the thing," she gasped, "and there isn't room to pass!"

There wasn't time to pray. I saw Aggie shut her eyes, and the next moment there was a terrific jar. Aggie and I were flung together in a corner of the seat, a man yelled, and the next minute we had leaped out of the ditch again and were going smoothly along the road. I glanced behind. The man had halted his horse and was standing up in the buggy, staring after us.

"I didn't think I could do it," said Tish complacently.

"Only the grace of God took you into that ditch and out again, Tish Carberry," I snapped. "And if you are going to do any more circus performances I want to get out."

She could stop the car well enough when there was no crying need to, and now, to our alarm, she stopped every now and then and got out and held her hand over the front of the machine, like testing the oven for cake. Finally she said:

It's boiling!"

Aggie got ready to jump.

"It'll explode, won't it?" she quavered.

"I don't see why it should explode," Tish replied, wetting her finger to see if it sizzled when she touched it. "But it's hot enough, in all conscience A good rain would cool it."

The sun was blazing down on us, however, and there was no sign of rain. I said I would just as soon be blown up as melted down, and we got in again. The machine would not start. We all took a turn at the handle in front, but it was like winding a clock with a broken spring.

That is where the man and the girl and the little Pomeranian dog enter the story. For they came along in a blue runabout car just as Tish threw her book called Automobile Troubles over the fence and said she was going to walk home. The book said: "Beginners having trouble with their engines should look under the headings Ignition, Carburation, Lubrication, Compression; Circulation and Timing." As Tish remarked, the only one that was understandable was Circulation, and anybody could tell without a book that the car wasn't circulating to any extent.

Just as Tish threw the book away the young man in the blue runabout stopped and got out.

"In trouble?" he asked. "Can I do anything for you?"

"It was boiling," said Tish. "I suppose something has melted inside."

"Oh, I think not." He looked at the car, pushed something, went round and turned the handle-crank, Tish called it, and it's a good name-and the engine started.

"You didn't have your gas on," said the young man. "And don't worry; you're sure to heat up on a day like this, but nothing will melt"

'Or explode?" asked Aggie. 'Or explode."

He looked at the girl and smiled, and when we started off they were still there, watching us. The dog yelped, and the girl smiled and waved her hand. Aggie, who is far-sighted, turned around a second time. "He reminds me of Mr. Wiggins," she said with a sigh, still looking back. Aggie was engaged years ago to a young man in the roofing business, who fell off a roof.

After a minute, "He's kissing her!" she gasped. After that she nearly broke her neck watching them out of sight. Aggie is romantic. I turned around, but I had on my near glasses.

I don't know how we lost the Noblestown Pike. Tish blamed it on having to drive with one eye shut, on account of something getting into the other. Aggie's nose was sunburned and swelling, and I would have given a good bit for something heavy in my lap to anchor me. When I was a girl I rode horseback, and with any kind of a steady horse you can tell when the next jolt is coming; but Tish's machine has a way of coming up and hitting you when you are off guard, so to speak.

To go back, after an hour or so we found we were on the wrong road. It kept growing narrower, and when at last it became only a dusty country lane Tish realized it herself. There was a rickety farmhouse about two hundred feet from the road, with a woman bending over a washtub outside the door. I stood up and made a megaphone of my hands.

"Which way to the Noblestown Pike?" I yelled, while Tish got out and stuck a wet finger on the hood over the engine.

The woman looked up and pointed sullenly in the direction from which we had come. We looked at the road. There wasn't a spot to turn-not another road in sight to back into. It was hotter than ever. The engine hummed like a teakettle on a hot stove, and there were little clouds of blue smoke coming from somewhere or other about it. Aggie said she thought the gasoline tank was on fire.

"If it is you'll soon know it," said Tish grimly. "It's under the seat. I'm going to back up on to this bridge business over the gutter. I think I can make it."

"Do you know how to back up?" I asked; and just at that minute the woman left her tub and started to run down the walk.

Tish backed. With an awful grinding of wheels she got the right lever finally; the machine gave a jerk that would have decapitated a chicken, and we backed slowly on to the timbers that bridged the gutter and made a road toward the house. When it gave the first crack we shouted-Aggie and I. It might not have been too late, but Tish put on the emergency brake by mistake and for a minute we hung on the verge. Then we began to settle. We went down slowly, with Tish above us and rising; and when we stopped, there we were, Aggie and I and the rear of the machine, a good four feet below Tish and the engine, with something grinding like mad and clouds of smoke everywhere.

When we crawled out the woman who owned the bridge was standing on the bank looking down at us, and her face was something awful.

"You'll fix that bridge before you leave!" she said, shutting her mouth hard on the last word.

"You'll fix that automobile before I'm through with you!" said Tish, pointing at the thing, which looked like a horse sitting down in a gutter.

"Oh, rats!" the woman said rudely. "That's four of them things that's gone through that bridge this week, and I'm good and sick of it. Ain't there any other bridges in Chester county?"

"Not like that," retorted Tish, eying the ruins. "You don't call that a bridge, do you?"

"It was," said the woman.

She came forward and a ferocious-looking dog stepped from behind her.

Tish looked at the dog.

"It wasn't much of a bridge," she said, more politely. "If you've got any men on the place I'll give them a dollar apiece to get my machine out of there."

"No men around," said the woman shortly. "Theodore," —to the dog —"don't you go around bitin' until I give you the word. Sit down."

The dog sat down.

"Before you leave," she said to Tish, "you'll mend that bridge or I'll know the reason why. Meantime your automobile is trespassin', and the fine is twenty dollars."

Then she sat down on the bank and began to tickle the dog's ears with a blade of grass.

"Theodore," she said, "if them three old maids think they can bluff us, they don't know us, do they?"

I had stood about as much as I could, so I walked around in front of her and glared at her.

"I wouldn't sit so close to the automobile if I were you," I remarked emphatically. "Something is likely to explode."

"I feel like it," she said. "When I get mad I'm good an' mad. Anyhow, I own this place, and I'll sit where I please. Theodore, let's put the washing-machine on wheels and go round the country bustin' down folks' bridges and playin' hell generally!"

An oath always rouses Tish. She got the engine stopped. Then she came around beside me with her goggles shoved up on her forehead.

"Woman," she said sternly, "how dare you mention the place of punishment so lightly!" Tish had been superintendent of a Sunday-school for thirty years.

The woman stared at her. Then she got up slowly.

"I wasn't alludin' to the next world," she said bitterly. "Ninety-five degrees of heat, seven inches of dust, five miles to a telephone and ten miles to town, with an automobile sittin' down in your front yard-that's all the hell I want"

Then she walked up the path. We stared after her; between her shoulder-blades her blue wrapper was wet through with sweat, and the dog trailed at her heels. Aggie, who is always sentimental, took a step after her.

"I say," she called. "If we come back for you some nice afternoon, will you let us take you for a ride?"

But she got no answer. To our amazement, the woman turned around at the top of the path and put her thumb to her nose!

We did not see her again for some time, but after Tish had climbed in twice and started the engine, to see if the car couldn't climb out — the only result being that it almost turned over —the woman appeared again. She carried a board that looked like a breadboard nailed to a broom-handle, and on it, in fresh ink, as if she had done it with her finger, were the words: Trespassing-fifty dollars."

"You said twenty before," I protested. That was for those little dinky, one-seated affairs," she said, jabbing the broom-handle into the dirt beside the road. "Two seats, forty dollars; two seats and a folded back buggy-top, fifty." She adjusted the sign carefully, looked up and down the road, and then went back to the house.

So we sat down on the bank and Tish explained how she happened to do it. I am a Christian woman, and Aggie is so gentle that she has to scratch twice to light a match, but I must say we were bitter. We told Tish we didn't care how she happened to do it, and that some day she would be punished for a temper that made her throw away books that she would be sure to need some time; and that, anyhow, an unmarried woman of fifty has no business with an automobile.

"It's my belief," Tish retorted, "that she keeps her old bridge for this very purpose. She could make a good living off it, and all the work she'd have to do would be to build it up after every accident."

"Oh, no," Aggie said bitterly. "We are going to repair it, I believe."

The back of my neck began to smart from the sun, and the dust eddied around us. A white hen came down the path, hopped on to the sloping step of the machine, perked its head at us, and then, with a squawk, flew up into Tish's seat behind the wheel. I was thirsty and my neck prickled.

Early in the afternoon we had a difference of opinion about who should walk the five miles to telephone for help, and after that we did not speak to each other. Tish talked to the machine and Aggie to the chicken. Every now and then Tish, after staring at the machine for a while, would get up and pick up the soundest of the bridge timbers, put it under the dropped end of the car and push with all her might.

"Call this a bridge?" —push —"Why, this is nothing" —push —"but a rotten old fence-rail!" —bang! —the timber broke. Tish stood with her back to us and kicked the pieces; then she turned on us. "As far as I'm concerned," she snapped, "the thing can sit there till it takes root. You're very much mistaken if you think I'm going to walk to that telephone, after bringing you out on a pleasure trip."

"Pleasure trip!" Aggie retorted. "I can get more pleasure out of a three-dollar rocking-chair. The next time you ask me to go on a pleasure trip, Tish Carberry, just push me off the porch backward. It's a good bit quicker."

By four o'clock I had a rash out all over my shoulders and chest, and my mouth was so full of dust that my teeth felt gritty. I had not cared particularly about going up to the house, but every few minutes between three and four the woman had come out, pumped some water, making a mighty splash, and gone back into the house again. It was more than human nature could stand. At a quarter after four o'clock I got up from the baked earth, glared at Tish, looked through Aggie, and walked with as much dignity as I could muster up the path to the well. There was a sign hung on it by a string around the nail in the top. It read: "Water, one dollar a tin. For automobiles, five dollars a bucket."

The woman came out and pumped some. The water ran cool and clear into a trough and then spread over the ground in dreadful waste. I could have lapped it up out of the trough; every bit of skin on me and lining membrane in me yelled "Water!" and—I had no money with me! The woman stood and waited, Theodore beside her.

"That's an outrage," I fumed. "How dare you put up such a sign! I—I shall report you!"

"Who to?" she inquired. "I ain't askin' you to drink it, am I? It's my well, ain't it?"

"I'll send the money to you by mail." I had lost all my pride. "I'll come back and pay you."

"Cash in advance," said the creature; and, pumping enough into a tin basin to have cooled me inside and out, she put it down for the dog to drink!

Chapter III
A Difference of Opinion and a Bargain

I have always felt that we did the right thing that night. It was all very well for Charlie Sands, Tish's nephew, when he heard the story, to say: "And they talk about giving women the vote! Why, for sense they would substitute sentiment; they would buy their opinions at the department stores along with their bargains, and a little two-penny love affair could upset the Government!"

Tish was raging.

"It does not matter whether you approve or not, Charlie," she said loftily, "as long as our consciences approve."

"Approve!" He nearly fell back out of his chair. "My dear ladies, you should every one have been jailed! As for conscience, I'd give a thousand dollars to have a conscience that would set the seal of its approval on assault and battery, highway robbery and abduction."

"The end justifies the means," I retorted; "and when did you get a conscience, Charlie Sands?"

"I think I got one Aunt Tish used to have," he said, and I got up and went into the house.

Well, I left the dog drinking, to go back, and at that instant I happened to look at Tish, who was standing on the bank waving her handkerchief at something in the road. I stepped to the comer of the house and saw what it was—creeping along a lane we had not noticed was the blue runabout car. Creeping is the word. It would crawl forward a dozen feet and stop, and it kept on repeating the performance. But what puzzled me was a spot of pink, just in front of the car and moving slowly forward.

At the end of the lane the pink spot hesitated and then turned our way. Once beyond the hedge, it proved to be the girl with her pink motor veil. She was walking with her hands in the pockets of her ulster, and she was limping. About a dozen feet behind her, and stopping every now and then so as not to overtake her, came the runabout. It was very peculiar. The young man had his jaws set tight, and as he was staring at the girl, and as she was staring straight ahead, neither of them saw us on the bank just above their heads.

The girl-she was a very pretty girl, although streaky just then-had a tight grip on the Pomeranian. She had it tucked under her arm and it was wriggling and yelping to be free. Just after the blue machine had turned the comer the little beast got loose, and with a yelp he dashed to the car and into the empty seat.

The girl stopped. So did the car. She faced about and the young man. gazed over her head.

Suddenly the girl looked up and saw us, and with a quick glance she spied the lamps of Tish's machine around a curve. No one would have guessed from the front end of the thing that the rear had died in a gutter.

"Oh!" she said. "Oh, I'm so glad you're here! Are you going back to town?"

"We are not going anywhere," Tish replied shortly, "unless your young man can help us."

"He is not my young man," the girl retorted, with distinctness; "but if there isn't very much the matter I daresay he can do something."

"I am not an automobile expert," he said, "but I probably can help a little, as, for instance, stuffing a puncture with rags until we get back to the city." The girl flushed. It was evidently a personal allusion.

"We haven't any rags," said Aggie, "and it isn't a puncture."

"There are two things we might do," said the young gentleman as he eyed our machine critically. "I might go to the nearest telephone and have help sent out from town, but as it's almost sunset it's pretty late for that; or, with a jack and a little help, we might fix it ourselves."

"A jack!" Tish said with scorn. "What kind of a jack —a bootjack or a jackass? I daresay they have them both at that farmhouse; I know they have one."

"A jack — a, lever," explained the young man, beginning to work at the lock of the toolbox. "Where are you going-to Noblestown?"

"To the lake," I replied. Tish was fumbling for the keys to the machine which she kept in a pocket in her petticoat, "We have a summer cottage there."

"I'll make a bargain with you," he suggested. "The-the-er-young lady refuses to go back in my car. We-the fact is, we have had a small difference of opinion, and-she insists on walking home. If I get your machine in shape, will you take her to the city?"

We would have taken her anywhere short of a planet to get away ourselves, and that was how it began; for the young gentleman took off his coat and fell to work immediately. Once, when he had raised the car on the jack and Tish was holding the ends of the boards that he shoved under, while Aggie and I pushed, something gave way and the whole thing settled back with a jerk. Mr. Lewis — that was his name-lifted the broken fence-rails off Tish and helped her to her feet.

"There's something almost alive about automobiles occasionally," he said. "They are so blamed vicious."

"If it was alive," Tish gasped, hunting for her glasses, "I'd kill it." But it never occurred to her that she was going to drown it that very night!

By seven o'clock we had lifted the thing on five fence-rails and the breadboard sign, and Mr. Lewis announced it was now or never. The girl had not come near us. She had taken off her veil and smoothed up her hair, and was busy with a bit of a silver mirror. She was very pretty.

Mr. Lewis got into the car and put on the power. There was a terrible grinding, but nothing moved. From behind, the three of us shoved, and Aggie said between gasps that if anything gave way her niece was to have her amethyst pin.

"Anne!" cried the young gentleman. But Miss Anne was powdering her nose and we all saw her turn it up.

"Anne!" called the young man who was not her young man, "you'll have to help here."

"Help yourself," said Anne coolly, and, moistening her finger, she proceeded to wipe the powder off her eyebrows.

Mr. Lewis shut off the engine, got out of the car and put on his coat. The girl did not turn her head, but she was watching through the mirror, for as he picked up his cap she rose lazily, put away her toilet things and started in our direction.

"What shall I do?" she asked Tish, ignoring him.

"Push," said Tish sharply — "unless you are too lame."

"My being lame won't matter, unless you wish me to kick the machine out," retorted the girl sweetly; and with that, the power being on, she put her brown arms against the car and her shoulder-muscles leaped up under her thin dress, and before I had planted my feet in the ditch the car rose, clung for a minute to the edge, and was over into the road. The girl said nothing. She looked at her hands, stepped out of the ditch, patronizingly helped Aggie out of it, and swung up the path with her head in the air. When I saw her again she had taken the sign off the pump and thrown it in the grass, and was washing her hands unconcernedly while the woman stood in the door and yapped at her.

If she had a mite of sense she would have gone back to the city in the blue car and let us go home to bed. But when she had come back to the road and the young man suggested it-not to her, of course, but casually to us — she whistled to her dog and started to limp down the road. You can't do anything with It girl in that state of mind, I took her in the tonneau with me, and Aggie, who prefers a love affair to a scandal and always reads the marriage licenses with the obituaries-Aggie went in the blue car to keep Mr. Lewis from being lonely.

Chapter IV
The Appetizers and the Hotel Bureau

We didn't talk very much. Tish was anxious to show she could drive, for all she had sat us down in a ditch, and after she took a wrong turning and stampeded a herd that was being milked in a barnyard, I could not keep my mind off the road. Once I looked at the girl, and there were tears running down her nose and dropping into her lap. I gave her my smelling salts, which I always carry in Tish's machine, and after a while she reached over and slid her hand into mine.

"I shouldn't care if the car went to pieces," she said. "I'd be happier dead."

"If you are always as unpleasant to that young man as you were this evening, I doubt it," I snapped.

"Didn't you ever quarrel with your husband before you were married?" she demanded, looking at me sideways.

"I thank Heaven I never had a husband," I replied, and with that she looked uncomfortable and drew her hand away.

"Is your-friend married?" she inquired. And it took me a moment to realize that she meant Aggie and that the minx was jealous. Aggie is fifty, and so thin that when she wears a tailor-made suit she has to build out with pneumatics. You remember, at the Woman's Suffrage Convention, how Mrs. Bailey pinned a badge to Aggie, and how there was a slow hissing immediately, and Aggie caved in before our very eyes?

Mr. Lewis checked our wild career after a few miles by getting ahead of us, and we got into town about eight. But after we had left the girl at her house-an imposing place, with a man at the door and a limousine at the curb —it was too late to go back home. Aggie and the blue car were waiting down the street, and they piloted us to the hotel.

Now, Tish belongs to the Ladies' Relief Corps of the G. A. R., and when Mr. Lewis said we looked tired and that he was going to order supper for us all, and three Martinis, Tish said it was all right, although she didn't see why we needed guns. It looked like a safe place. But they were not guns-that's part of the story.

While we were washing for supper Aggie told us what the quarrel was about.

"They are-were — engaged," she said, "and the girl's father is Robertson-the boss of the city, Mr. Lewis called him. And Mr. Lewis is the youngest councilman-they call him 'Baby' Lewis, and he hates it-and there's something to be voted for to-morrow; and if Mr. Lewis is for it he is to get the girl."

"And the girl refuses to be sold!" Tish said triumphantly. "Quite right, too. I admire her strength. That's the typical womanly attitude these days-right before anything, honor above all." Tish waved the hairbrush and then she turned on the maid. "Girl," she snapped, "why is this brush chained?"

"The ladies steal them," said the girl. Tish stared at the chain.

"You are so quick, Letitia," Aggie protested. "It was the other way round. The girl was angry because he wouldn't sell his vote, even for her."

Tish sat down in a chair, speechless; but just then Mr. Lewis came to the door and said that supper and the Martinis were ready. The Martinis proved to be something to drink, and after Mr. Lewis had raised his hand and sworn there was no whisky in them we drank them. He said they were appetizers, and the other day Tish said she was going to write to the Sherman House for the recipe before she has the minister to dinner next week.

Never did I eat so delightful a meal. Tish forgot her sprained shoulder and the splinter under her nail, and Aggie talked about the roofer. And the food! I recall distinctly shaking hands with Tish and agreeing to come to the hotel to live, and asking the waiter to find out from the cook how something or other was made. And when Aggie had buried the roofer, and Tish said it was funny, but Mr. Lewis had four brown eyes instead of two, he suggested that we must be tired, and a boy took us to our room. Room, not rooms. We could only get one. The last things I remember are our shaking hands with Mr. Lewis, and that Tish tried to get into the elevator before the door was opened.

About eleven o'clock I heard some one groaning and I sat up in bed. It was Aggie, whom, being the thinnest, we had put on the cot. She said her nose was smarting from the sunburn and she had heartburn something awful. We rang for some baking soda, and she drank some in water and made a plaster for her nose with the rest. After a while she felt better, but we were all wide awake and the heat was terrible. We could look out the window and see there was a breeze, but not a breath came in.

We sent for the bell-boy again, and he said there wasn't another room and nobody he could move around to give us a room on the breezy side of the house.

We took the rules and regulations card off the door and fanned with it, but it did not help much. After half an hour or so Tish got up, pushed the washstand in front of a door that connected with the next room and crawled up on it.

"If I had a chair," she said, measuring the distance with her eye, "I could see if that corner room next door is occupied. I could tell by that boy's face that he was lying."

Aggie was trying to hold down the baking soda, so, although I didn't feel any too well myself, I held the chair and Tish climbed up on it.

"What did I tell you?" she demanded when she got down. "That room's empty, and what's more there's nobody belonging there. There's nothing on the dresser but the towel; and there's a breeze coming in that sends the curtains straight into the room."

The connecting door was locked, and Tish put a bed sheet around her and tried the hall door. That was locked, too. And all the time we were getting hotter and hotter, and by putting our ears to the keyhole we could hear the breeze blowing on the other side. It was too much for Tish.

I'm going over the transom," she announced, after we had tried the dresser key in the door without any effect And go over she did, after putting on her stockings to keep her legs from being scraped.

It was much cooler. We brought in our clothes and Aggie's cot, and spread up the bed in the room we had left. Then we locked the connecting door again, and after Aggie had had some more baking soda, in and out, we went to bed.

Well, as I was saying, I went to sleep. I was awakened by Tish sitting up in bed and clutching me somewhere about the diaphragm., By the light from the hall over the transom I could see Aggie sound asleep, with her mouth opened, and Tish's arm stretched out and pointed at the yellow hotel bureau. I sat straight up and looked. I couldn't see anything, and at first I thought Tish was dreaming. Then I saw it too. The front of that bureau on the left side moved out a good six inches, stayed that way while I could count ten, and then closed up again without a sound.

Tish had put a leg out of bed, but she jerked it in again, and just at that awful moment a clock outside boomed twelve. And then, over in her corner, Aggie began to talk in her sleep.

"Turn around and run over it again," she said, with startling distinctness. "It isn't quite dead."

Tish put her hand up and held her shaking lower jaw.

"I—it's those dr-dratted Martinis," she quavered. "I've-no—d-doubt Mr. Lewis meant well, Lizzie, but I've b-been feeling very strange all evening."

"Your stomach being upset needn't affect my eyes," I retorted in a whisper. "I saw it move."

"Are you sure?" she insisted. "I didn't say anything, Lizzie, but while we were eating supper down-stairs I distinctly saw the piano move out six feet from the wall and go back again."

I didn't say anything to Tish, but the fact was that I distrusted my own vision-not that I had seen anything so ridiculous as pianos walking, but I had had a peculiar feeling in the dining-room that my eyes were looking in different directions, and when I focused them on anything I saw double at once. It had got so bad that when I wanted my fork I had to shut my eyes and feel for it. And so, neither of us being certain the bureau had moved, and nothing more occurring, we lay back again. The next minute Tish clutched me and I looked over. Something had happened to the bureau.

It looked phosphorescent, or as though it was on fire inside. There was a glow all around it. The keyholes stood out like dots of flame, and every crack gleamed. It was the most awful thing I have ever seen.

"Look!" gasped Tish, and, reaching over the side of the bed, she picked up a shoe and flung it with all her might at the thing. The thump was followed by a thud inside the bureau. Aggie stirred.

"The milkman's knocking," she said thickly, and sat up and yawned with her eyes shut. Tish and I leaped out of bed and I turned on the light. That gave us new courage, and the dresser stood there, just like any other dresser, with a towel on its yellow-pine top and fly-specks on the mirror. Tish and I looked at each other and smiled in a sickly way. We felt foolish. But Tish wasn't satisfied. She picked up a hair-brush and banged it on the top.

"Coming, Mr. Gibbs," bawled Aggie, still with her eyes shut, and she began to fumble around on the floor for her slippers.

"Wake her!" Tish commanded. "There's something moving in this thing. Lizzie, give me that pitcher of scalding water."

Of course there wasn't any hot water nearer than the bath-room, which was three turns to the right, one to the left and down a flight of stairs.

And at that minute the bureau spoke.

"Don't, for God's sake, ladies!" it said

Chapter V
The Reporter and the Red-haired Man

I screamed, and, as was perfectly natural, I backed away from the thing. My foot tripped over Tish's water-pitcher, and my sitting down was what wakened Aggie. She says she never will forget how she felt when she saw me prostrate and Tish holding a chair aloft and begging the bureau to come out so she could brain it. Of course she thought Tish had gone crazy, what with the sun and excitement of the day.

"Tish!" she screeched.

"Come out!" said Tish to the bureau. "Make no resistance; we are armed!"

As Aggie says, when she saw the left-hand side of that bureau move slowly forward like a door when Tish spoke to it, she thought she had a touch of sun herself. But when she saw a human figure crawl out of that place on its hands and knees, and opened her mouth to scream, her breath was gone as completely as if she had been hit in the stomach.

The figure got to its feet, and it had neither horns nor tail. It had curly, light-brown hair and blue eyes, and it was purplish red as to face. We stood paralyzed while it stood erect and blinked. Tish lowered her chair slowly and the apparition dropped down on it. It was masculine and shaking. Also young.

"Ladies," it said, "could I —could I thank you for a drink of water? I have been almost stifled."

When the haze cleared away from my eyes I saw that the young man had on a light gray suit, and that in his hand he carried his collar and an electric flashlight. Perspiration was pouring off his face and we could see that he was as scared as we were.

"Give him a drink, Lizzie," Tish said firmly, "and then press that button."

But the young man jumped to his feet at that and looked at us squarely.

"Ladies," he said earnestly, "please do not raise an alarm. I am not a thief. The manager of the hotel put me in that bureau himself."

"The hotel must be crowded," Tish scoffed. "I hope they don't charge you much for it."

From the street below came a sudden confusion of men's voices and the sound of feet on the pavement. The young man threw up his hands.

"Madam," he said to Tish, "you look like a woman of large mind." Tish stopped putting the bedspread around her and stared at him. "By your unfortunate-er-invasion here tonight you are preventing the discovery of a crime against civic morality. The council-manic banquet down-stairs is over; in a few minutes Robertson-well, probably you don't understand, but I represent the Morning Star. The Civic Purity League has learned that in this room, after the banquet, a bribe is going to be offered. That bureau has been ready for a month. Ladies, I implore you, go back to the other room!"

It was too late. At that moment there were voices in the hall and somebody put a key into the lock of the door. There was no time to put the light out. The young man dropped behind the foot of the bed, the door swung open and a red-haired man stepped into the room.

"Suffering cats!" he exclaimed.

"Go out immediately!" I said, pointing to the door. Tish was unwinding herself from the counterpane. She took it off airily and fling it over the foot of the bed, so that it covered the young man. It looked abandoned, but the necessity was terrible. As Tish said afterward, fifty years of respectable living would not have prevented the tongue of scandal licking up such a spicy morsel as that compromising situation.

The red-haired man retreated a step or two, opened the door part way, and went out and looked at the number. Then he came in again.

"Madam-ladies," he said, "this room belongs to me. There must be some mistake."

"I don't believe it belongs to you," Tish snapped. "Why haven't you got some brushes pn the dresser?"

"If you were a gentleman," Aggie wailed from the cot, "you would go out and let us get to sleep. I never put in such a night. First the other room is too hot, and we crawl over the transom to get a cool place, and then —"

"Over the transom," said the red-haired gentleman. "Do you mean to say —" Then he laughed a little and spoke over his shoulder.

"I'm sorry, Lewis," he said, "but my room's taken."

"Kismet," said our Mr. Lewis' voice, but it sounded reckless and strained. "Fate has crooked her finger; I'm going home."

'Don't be an ass," said the red-haired gentleman. "These women in here came over the transom from the next room. It's empty."

"Good gracious!" Aggie gasped. "I left my forms hanging to the gas-jet!"

The red-haired man backed into the hall, but he still held the door.

"I'm going home," said our Mr. Lewis again. "I'm sick of things around here, anyhow. I've got a chance to get an oriange grove cheap in California."

"Fiddlesticks!" retorted the red-haired man, "Why don't you stick by the plum tree here at home?"

On that the door closed, and we could hear them talking guardedly in the hall.

"The wretches!" Tish fumed. "Oh, why haven't women the vote? I tell you" —she fixed Aggie and me with a gesture —"the day of conscience is coming. Women stand for civic purity, for the home, for right against might!"

It was the "right against might" that we repeated to her afterward, when we had stolen-but that is coming soon.

"But he loves the girl," said Aggie, beginning to sniffle. "I—I think as much of ci-civic purity as you do, Tish Carberry, but I th-think he is just p—pig-headed."

"The girl's a fool and so are you," said Tish, beginning to take the counterpane off the reporter. And at that second there was a knock and the red-haired man opened the door again.

"I beg your pardon," he apologized, "but will you give me the key to the other room?"

We did. Aggie unlocked the connecting door and brought back the key to our old room and the things she had left on the gas-jet. In the excitement she threw the key on the dresser and was just about to reach the other articles through the crack in the door when Tish caught her arm.

Chapter VI
A Bribe and a Bride and It's All Over

Now I am not defending what followed. But the Lewis man had been nice to us, and, as Tish said tartly to Charlie Sands, women who had lived in single blessedness as long as we had, learned to think quick and act quicker. As to the law, we sent a check to the farmer whose pig we killed-and with pork at its present price it was ruinous, although we were glad it had not been a cow; and as to using our missionary money to make up for the packet Aggie lost-as we said, we considered that it had been used in missionary work. It was hardest, of course, on the Morning Star reporter. Only a week or so ago we had to go to Noblestown to get a new handle for the meat-chopper. We were in the machine outside the store, and when we saw him it was too late. Tish was wearing his necktie-having gathered it up with her clothes that awful night, and not knowing his name she could not send it back to him-and she clapped her hand over it. But he saw it.

"Good afternoon," he said, grinning.

"What do you mean by addressing us?" Tish demanded, trying to pull the collar of her duster over the tie.

"You don't mean to say you've forgotten me already!" he exclaimed, looking grieved. "Don't you remember-your-our room at the Sherman House?"

"Certainly not," Tish said haughtily.

He pulled out a card and scribbled something on it. "My card," he said. He leaned over from the curb and gave it to Tish.

"Don't bother about the tie," he said. "I never liked it anyhow. But —I lost a scarf pin that night. I—I suppose you don't know anything about it?"

Out of the comer of her eye Tish saw Aggie make a clutch at her neck, and she threw her a warning glance.

"I am afraid you have made a mistake," she said stiffly, and just then the hardware man brought out the handle. Tish was so excited that she started the car without paying for it, and when we looked back he and the reporter were staring after us; and the reporter distinctly said, "Those women will be wealthy some day."

"Why didn't you let me give him his pin?" Aggie demanded when we were safely out of sight. "I —I feel like a thief."

"Fiddle! And confess?" said Tish. "We'll send it to him. I've got his card."

But all he had written on it, after all, was, "A. Dresser. Private Bureau." Charlie Sands has promised to return the pin.

Well, all this time I have left the three of us huddled in our nightgowns on the side of the bed, with sheets draped over us, and the Morning Star gentleman with his ear to the connecting door and taking down every word that was said, in shorthand. Robertson was offering the girl, and enough money for Mr. Lewis to marry on, for his vote on something or other. I reckon the balance between a man's honor and his cupidity hangs pretty even anyhow, and when you throw a girl to one side or the other it swings the scale. The Lewis man was yielding and Tish was breathing hard.

"The hussy!" she muttered.

"Did you notice how pretty her hair was in the sunlight?" whispered Aggie.

Somehow it came over me then how young the girl was, and what kind of moral sense could one expect of a girl with that red-headed scamp for a father?

Strangely enough, the plot was gentle Aggie's. Aggie is like baking powder-she rises when she gets heated up. And she was mad clear through. We had no trouble gathering our clothes in our arms, although I could not find my shoe, which Tish had thrown at the bureau. Then we sat and waited. At the last minute Aggie got a little weak and wanted blackberry wine, but I had nothing in the satchel but arnica.

All we intended to do was to get the yellow notebook-to meet strategy with strategy. The rest, while unexpected, followed naturally. But when I look out the window from my desk and see Aggie's placid face, and Tish's austere Methodist profile, it is difficult to associate them or myself with the three partly dressed creatures who — But to go back.

We had locked the door into the hall and each of us had her clothes. When the two men in the next room went out Mr. Morning Star turned to us with a chuckle.

"Thanks for your forbearance, ladies," he said, "we've got that villain Robertson where he ought to have been a dozen years ago. And as for Lewis —" He shut his notebook with a bang, and there was something in his face besides exultation. "To buy a girl like that I" he said-and I knew. He wanted the girl himself.

Aggie was to ask to see the notebook and then toss it over the transom into the corridor. While the reporter was trying to get out the locked door into the hall we could escape into the adjoining room, lock the connecting door, walk around easily and get the notebook, and then make our escape comfortably.

It would have been all right, but Aggie can not throw. The first attempt failed by seven feet. The young man was so astonished, however, that he stood with his mouth open, and the second trial sent it through.

"What in the name of Heaven did you do that for?" he demanded, thinking Aggie had suddenly gone mad. Then he rushed to the door. It was locked and I had the key! We were all in the next room and a bolted door between us before he realized what had happened.

We had expected, of course, to get the notebook, to dress, and to leave in the machine quietly, but from that time on there was no time to think of the conventions. The young man began to hammer on the door and other doors opened along the hall. Then a bell-boy came up and ran off in a hurry for a key. I saw Tish putting on her ulster over her petticoat, and Aggie and I did the same. The next thing we knew we were down in the empty lobby, and Tish had forgotten the spark plugs!

We got started finally with a steel hairpin , for a plug, and as we moved away I heard the chase coming down the stairs after us. They were howling "Stop thief!" We were hardly well under way when the bell-boy came in sight with the bureau man at his heels and a collection of people in all sorts of costumes following.

Tish says we did forty miles an hour going down the main street. I should have guessed more than that. I had a fearful exaltation: Aggie had advanced her speed limit since morning from four miles an hour to the capacity of the engine, and kept bawling to Tish a phrase she had caught from Charlie Sands.

"Tetter out!" she cried„ over and over. "Letter out!"

We stopped on a quiet side street and listened, but there was no noise of pursuit. Tish got out and stuck her wet finger on the hood, but it wasn't boiling.

"There's nothing coming," she said. "I'm going to stop long enough to put on my stockings.

"I don't see why you couldn't have flung your own shoe, Tish," I snapped. "What use is one shoe? —unless I lose a leg, and that's as like as not before this night's over."

"Do you see where we are?" Aggie asked. "Isn't this where we brought Miss Anne?"

It was, for Anne opened the door just then and peered down at the car.

"Is that you, father?" she called. She came down the steps, and the light from the hall fell full on us. I've must have looked rather strange, with Tish putting on her stocking in the driving seat and the most of our clothing in our laps instead of on us.

"Something has happened!" she said, catching her breath. "Ted!"

"Something has happened," Tish retorted grimly, and held up the notebook. "Here's the Morning Star's shorthand report of the interview in which your Ted sold his honor for a mess of pottage-you being the pottage."

"Oh, no," said Miss Anne, going wobbly. "Oh, he wouldn't —he didn't do such a thing!"

"Upon my soul!" I broke in. "Weren't you fighting him all day to do it?"

"You couldn't understand," she said, looking at me with the eyes of a baby. "I didn't want him to do it; I wanted him to want to do it."

"Well, if that's being in love, thank Heaven for the mind of a spinster," I retorted angrily.

"You've won," Tish said. "You've got him kneeling at your feet, as you wanted. But he went down in the mud to do it. And the only reason the newspapers won't be slinging some of that very mire to-morrow is because three elderly women, who ought to have more sense, have resorted to thievery and lost their reputations and parts of their garments to save him!"

"I hate him," said the young woman, with her chin quivering. "I knew all along I should hate him if he did it. I —I'll never marry him."

And with that she turned and started up the steps. Half way up she turned.

"I'm sorry you went to so much trouble," she said, "I don't think he is worth saving."

Aggie's early experience with the roofer stood her in good stead then. She understood; Tish and I never would have. She got out of the machine and went up into the vestibule, and a minute later, against the hall light, we saw the girl's head on Aggie's shoulder. Then they both came down again with their arms wrapped around each other, and Aggie asked me to move over.

"We're going to Mr. Lewis' apartment," she announced, with a thrill in her voice. She was maudlin with romance. "It will be proper enough, I think, with three chaperons. She wants to see him."

"Not until I put on my other stocking," Tish put in grimly. "And we don't get out of the machine; I've been compromised once tonight."

"They are both young," Aggie rebuked her gently. "I think, having begun this thing, we ought to see it through. We will have to be mothers to her, for she has none."

Well, we passed Mr. Robertson at the comer of the next street, and the girl shrank back and covered her face. And then she directed us, and we overtook the other one as he was going into his doorway. The girl jumped out and ran after him. We distinctly heard him say, "Anne! Darling!" And then, what with anxiety and excitement, Aggie took the worst sneezing spell of the summer, and the rest was lost.

He was terribly ashamed and humiliated, and he said he would take the girl away and be married right off, only he had that wretched package of bribe money that made him think, every time he saw it, how unworthy he was of her! He was going to put it down a sewer drop, but Tish suggested that they be married and go on a honeymoon, and let us return the bribe to Mr. Robertson.

So he gave us the package; and, as you know, Aggie lost it later. Then he asked us if there was a minister in the summer colony at Penzance expect an organ prelude and floral decorations. Get in."

I did not mind their sitting back with me, and his kissing her hand whenever he thought I was not looking. But the thing I objected to was this: I distinctly overheard him say:

"I was desperate to-night, sweetheart; and, oh, my love, you saved me!"

She saved him!

At a crossroads near Penzance, Tish made them get out, and we directed them to a landing where they would find a rowboat. We all kissed the bride; and Mr. Lewis said he had nobody to cheer him on his way, and wouldn't we kiss him, too. So we did, and after they had gone we prepared,for Carpenter's sharp eyes by going into the bushes and putting on the rest of our clothes.

It was the first thing Carpenter said that caused the accident. He brought in the ferryboat and came up the bank to us.

I've been expectin' you," he said, with a grin. "I was thinkin' you might come over by the Carrick Ferry, and the folks there wouldn't know you."

"I guess they'd take my money without i knowing me," Tish said sharply.

"Well," he drawled, with a sharp eye on the three of us, "I didn't want you to have any trouble. We got a telephone message from Noblestown not very long ago to look out for an automobile containing three female desperadoes. The police wants them."

That was when Tish sent the car over the end of the ferry.

Well, as I said early in the narrative, after Tish and Aggie had dried off and gone to bed I stood at my window and tried to see into Ostermaier's parlor, but all I could see was the sleeve of Mrs. Ostermaier's kimono.

As I stood there shivering, the door opened and two shadowy figures came out of the house and crossed the lawn. Just under my window they stopped and the tall shadow held open its arms. The smaller one went into them with a little cry, and they stood there a disgraceful time. Then they lifted their heads and looked lip at our cottage.

"Bless their dear, romantic hearts!" said the girl. I was glad Tish was asleep.

"They should have been pirates!" said the man. "They are true old sports. I suppose they've had their catnip tea by now and are sound asleep. Beloved!" he said, and held out his arms again.

Pirates! I went back to bed in a rage, but I couldn't sleep. Somehow I kept seeing that young idiot holding out his arms, and I felt lonely. Finally I filled the hot-water bottle and put it at my back.

"It's all over, Aggie!" I called-but the only response was a snore that turned into a sneeze.

That Awful Night

Chapter I
The Green Kimono

Nothing would have induced me to tell the scandalous story had it not been for Letitia's green kimono. But when it was found at the Watermelon Camp, two miles from our cottage, hanging to the branch of a tree, instead of the corduroy trousers and blue flannel shirt that one of the campers said he had hung there overnight, it seemed to require explanation. For one of the men at the Watermelon Camp knew the kimono.

He brought it up the next morning, hanging over his arm, and asked Letitia for the trousers and shirt! He said that the young man who owned them had to wear a blanket until we returned them, not having any other clothes in camp. Also, he said there was a particular kind of bass hook in one of the pockets, and if there was any reason why we could not return the trousers, would we be kind enough to send back the hook.

Now Tish is a teacher in the Sunday-School and has been for thirty-five years. But she looked up from the bowl she was wiping-we had made a pretense at breakfast, although nobody could eat-and she lied.

"I don't know what you mean by coming here for your corduroy trousers and flannel shirt," she said, with a three-cornered red spot in each cheek. "As for that kimono, I never saw it before!"

Then she dropped the bowl. She had to pay twenty cents into the cottage exchequer for it afterward, and she explained that she felt the bowl going, and the falsehood slipped out before she knew what she was saying. Anyhow, it did no good, for the young man in knickerbockers and a bathing shirt held up the kimono, grinning and pointing to the laundry tag. It said "Letitia Carberry," as plain as ink could make it.

Aggie weakened at once. It is always Aggie that weakens. She sat down on the porch step and began to cry. She had been crying off and on all morning, having lost her upper teeth when the boat-but that brings me to the boat.

Just as Aggie threw her apron over her face, we saw old Carpenter, the boatman, coming up the path. I caught Tish's arm as she was escaping into the house. "Not a step," I whispered sternly. "If they arrest one of us, they take us all."

"You see, it was like this," the young man was saying, "Carleton, one of our fellows, was out in his motor canoe last night, and it upset. When he came in, he says he hung his trousers and shirt out on a branch to dry. Anyhow, when he got up an hour or so ago, his clothes were gone, and this-er-garment was there instead." He was staring very hard at Tish. "He didn't notice the change, being half asleep, and he got his feet in the sleeves all right, but when it came to drawing it up, he noticed something strange about it"

At the name "Carleton" Aggie threw me an agonized glance from her apron. She would not speak without her teeth, and Tish was stooping over the pieces of the bowl. I am a Christian woman, but seeing Aggie weak-kneed and Tish as shaky as gelatine, I hoped that Carpenter, the boatman, would have apoplexy or fall and break his leg before he reached the porch. I turned on the young man at the foot of the steps.

"If you think," I said indignantly, "that three ladies, past their youth and with affairs of their own to look after, have nothing better to do than to wander around at night stealing clothing that they could not possibly wear, and leaving in exchange articles that they er-cherish, go in and examine the house."

Carpenter had come up and stood respectfully by, listening, and to my horror I saw that he held the other half of Aggie's broken oar.

"He won't go into my room!" Aggie said suddenly, and with amazing clearness, considering her teeth.

"Nonsense," I snapped. "This young man has seen an unmade bed before." But Aggie had gone pale, and suddenly I remembered. The handle of the very oar Carpenter carried was lying on a chair beside her bed. All that terrible night she had held on to it as a weapon.

The young man in the bathing shirt only smiled, however, and shifted Tish's kimono to the other shoulder.

"Certainly, if you say you haven't seen Carleton's clothes," he said easily, "the matter is settled. No doubt the same breeze last night that blew the kimono down to the camp and hung it on the branch of a tree took the trousers to make a sensation on one of the nearby islands. I am sorry Carleton didn't know they were going traveling, he would at least have had them brushed."

While I was glaring at him Carpenter stepped forward and placed the oar blade on the porch. When Aggie saw the name "Witch Hazel" she opened her mouth like a fish, and I daresay if I had not pinched her she would have told the whole miserable story then and there. Not that I am ashamed of it —I am not too old, thank the Lord, to know real love when I see it-but Aggie has no sense of proportion, and in her telling, what was pure romance would have become merely assault and battery, with intent to compound a felony.

"I reckon. Miss Lizzie," Carpenter said, addressing me, "that you and Miss Tish and Miss Aggie didn't take the Witch Hazel out last night and forget to bring her back, did you?"

Aggie shut her mouth and swallowed.

"Certainly," I retorted sarcastically. "We decided to take a midnight row yesterday evening, but the boat leaked. In the middle of the lake it filled and sank under our feet."

Tish gave me an awful look, and snapped:

"I suppose if we'd taken your boat out, we'd have brought it back, not being mermaids."

"That's what I argued down at the camp," he meditated. "I said to them, 'you boys have been up to some devilment or other, and I'll git you yet. It ain't likely that them three old-them three ladies that can't row a stroke or swim a yard would take the Witch Hazel out in the middle of the night in a storm, sink the boat, and swim home four miles in time to put up their crimps and get breakfast.' "

"Thirtainly not," Aggie said with injured dignity, "I can't thwim a thtroke."

Carpenter spat on one of our whitewashed cobblestones. "It's what you might call ree-mark-able," he observed. "Not another soul on the island, and won't be 'til the Methodist camp meeting next week; one of the boys at the Watermelon Camp with a blanket on instead of his pants and a bandage on his head, and the Witch Hazel stole last night by somebody who cut through her painter with a pair of scissors and takes her out with two oars that ain't mates."

The young man with the kimono dropped it carelessly into Aggie's lap and straightened with a glance at her stricken face.

"Scissors!" he repeated. "Oh, come, Abe, you're no detective. How the mischief do you know whether the rope was cut with scissors or chewed off?"

Abe dived into his pocket and brought up two articles on the palm of his hand.

"Scissored off or chewed off," he said triumphantly. "Take your choice."

There, gleaming in the sunlight, were TisKs buttonhole scissors and Aggie's upper teeth!

"Found them in four feet of water at the end of the boat dock," he said, "where I left the Witch Hazel last night. If them teeth ever belonged in a fish, then I'm a dentist."

I remember the next ten minutes through a red haze; I knew in a dim way that Aggie had clutched at her teeth and disappeared; I heard from far off Tish's voice, explaining that Aggie had dropped the scissors in the water the previous afternoon, and had lost her teeth while lying on the dock trying to fish them up —the scissors, of course-with a hairpin on the end of a string. And finally, with the line of the waterfront undulating before my dizzy eyes like a marcel wave-which is a figure of speech and not a pun —I realized that Carpenter and the sleeveless and neckless young man from the camp were retreating down the path, and I knew that the ordeal was over.

I believe I fainted, for when I opened my eyes again Tish was standing in front of me with a cup of tea, and she had been crying.

"You needn't feel so badly about it," I said, when I had taken a sip of the tea. "There are times when to lie is humanity."

"It isn't that," Tish whimpered, breaking down again, "but-but the wretches didn't believe me!"

"No," I echoed sadly, "they didn't believe you."

"I could think of so many better ones now," she wailed.

"Never mind," I said, with a feeble attempt to console her, "they won't jail us for lying, any-how. We are reasonably safe, Tish, unless Mr. Carleton has Aggie arrested for assault and battery."

But he did not. The only court concerned was the marriage license court, from which you will know that this is a love story. Even if it does begin with a mangy dog.

At least Aggie said it was mange; her parrot had the same moth-eaten look before it died. But Tish has always maintained that it was fleas. She says they breed in the grass, and attack dogs in swarms in hot weather.

Chapter II
It was the Dog

The dog was put ashore under our very-noses, by the crew of a passing launch. :We were knitting on our veranda that afternoon, looking across at Sunset Island, which is four miles away. Carpenter was not in sight, and from down the beach came the yells and splashes that told that the college boys at the Watermelon Camp were bathing. We were sitting with our backs to them, when Tish said suddenly :

"There is a launch coming in."

There was, a very fine one, although handsome is as handsome does, as the colored man said about the hippopotamus. For as the launch steamed past, a man in a white uniform threw something with a thud on to the dock. It was a dog. The next moment they headed out into the lake again, paying no attention to Tish, who ran down the path and tried to signal them with the raffia basket she was making.

The dog came up and sniffed at her.

Now we never had any dogs on the island, even in the season. Tish's uncle had been bitten by a dog once, and although he never had hydrophobia, he was always strange afterward. They say that when he coughed it was exactly like a bark, and the very sight of a cat upset him terribly. Also, although the family never said much about this, I have heard that after he died they found quite a collection of bones in his upper washstand drawer. And my grandmother saw him once eating raw meat mixed with onion, between slices of bread! So when we bought the island, and sold parts of it for cottages, we always put in the agreement of sale: "No intoxicants, no phonographs and no dogs."

You may imagine how we felt, therefore, when we saw the dog following Tish up the path, and biting at her heels. (When a dog bites at your heels, and isn't wagging his tail, he is not playing; he is in earnest. It is much like that line in The Virginian —"When you say that, smile!". But this dog did not smile.)

Tish shouted to us, as she came, to run and shut Paulina, her cat, in the spare room, and to give her her catnip ball (the cat, not Tish). And then she came up and dropped on the porch step and covered up her feet, and the creature sat down before her and dared her to move.

That was the most terrible afternoon of my life. He sat there and drooled over the step, and growled now and then, and Tish told about her uncle, and Aggie said she knew a man who had been attacked by a bulldog, and the only way they got him loose was to give him-the dog —a hypodermic of poison and pry him off after he died.

To make matters worse, there did not seem to be a soul on the island. The boys from the camp had disappeared; Carpenter's cabin was closed and locked- At tea time the dog heard Paulina wailing up-stairs and he made a hole in the screen door and went after her. He had chewed almost through the guest room door before Aggie called him off with the chops for supper.

That decided us.

About eight o'clock that evening, while the creature was gnawing at a leg of the dining-room table, we held a whispered conference, and Tish came forward with a plan. It was very daring, and Aggie immediately objected. "It's all very well," she said, "to sit here in a rocking-chair and talk about rowing four miles to Sunset Island, with not one of us knowing anything about a boat, and Lizzie told by that fortune teller last spring that she would die by drowning. Not only that. How are you going to get the dog into the boat?"

Tish leaned forward cautiously. The Dog was still gnawing in the next room.

"Chloroform him!" she whispered. "Wait until he gets sleepy. Then take Lizzie's bath sponge, soak it with your chloroform liniment, Aggie, and when he's stupefied, carry him down and dump him in the boat."

"Why not let Carpenter do it, in the morning?" Aggie objected. She was green with nervousness.

"Carpenter!" Tish snorted. "If he ever sees that flea-bitten creature he will keep him."

(Carpenter, being an original settler, had never subscribed to the liquor, phonograph and dog clause.)

At eleven o'clock the Dog turned over on his side and went to sleep. We were ready. My sponge, saturated with Aggie's liniment and impaled on the end of Tish's umbrella, was held to his nostrils, and we each drew a long breath. But we had counted without Aggie's hay fever. Just as the creature seemed about settled and was growing limp, Aggie began to sneeze, and by the time the paroxysm was over the dog was awake and had eaten part of the sponge. It was a terrible disappointment. As Tish said afterward, we should have anaesthetized Aggie first

However, perhaps it was for the best, after all, for it made him very ill, and when, after Tish had washed the floor, she prodded him with the wooden handle of the mop and he only groaned, he had ceased to be formidable.

"It's now or never," Tish said, with determination, and put on her overshoes. It had been raining, and luckily Aggie put her plaid shawl around her shoulders. What we should have done later without that shawl I shudder to think. Tish put on a knitted cape and I tied a scarf over my head. Then, with the dog-no longer a capital D —wobbling at the end of a clothes-line, we started.

At the last minute Tish had a spell of conscience and hunted up a bottle of cleaning fluid to put in the boat.

"It's mostly gasoline," she said. "If it's mange it won't do any harm, and if it's fleas it will kill them- We can put it on just before we leave him on Sunset Island. You start pouring it at his nose and work along his back. The fleas will drop off his tail. Every creature deserves a chance."

None of us thought of the ether in the stuffy although, as it turned out, it did not hurt the dog. It was never used on the dog.

We got to the dock without incident, Aggie ahead with the dog, and Tish and I feeling for the rope of Carpenter's skiff. Tish had the scissors, in case we couldn't untie it. Just as we found it and stooped, something splashed. Tish straightened and gripped me by the arm.

"Did you throw anything in?" she demanded in an awful tone.

"Stop pinching me, Tish Carberry!" I snapped, "or I will."

There was silence for a minute; then there was a swirling whitish appearance at our very feet, and something dark raised itself up in the water and stood waving its arms. Then it gave a gurgle or two, choked, coughed and finally sneezed. We knew the sneeze; it was Aggie!

It was when she got her breath that she said the incredible thing, the thing she flatly denied afterward, but for which she was obliged to pay five dollars into the fine box.

"That damned dog pulled me in!" she gurgled. "I've thwallowed —" She clapped her hands to her mouth, and we knew at once. Her teeth!

We pulled them both out grimly-Aggie and the dog, and Tish ordered Aggie to the house for dry clothes at once. "And it might be as well, Agatha," she added coldly, "if you would wash your mouth out with soap. You can buy new teeth, but you can not buy another immortal soul."

Agatha sloshed a half-dozen steps up the dock. Then she turned on us both in the darkness.

"If you had thwallowed two gallonth of dirty water, tho that you can feel it thaking in you when you walk, and had lotht your thell back comb and your betht upper teeth, you wouldn't care, Tith Carberry, whether you had an immortal thoul or not."

Then she thtalked-stalked, I mean, up to the house. Tish was furious, but luckily, I have a sense of humor. With Aggie's soul hanging fire, so to speak, I sat down on the dock in the rain and laughed. That was the beginning of my deterioration; from that instant, when I braved rheumatism and Tish's displeasure, to that later moment just at dawn, when we came back to the dock again, draggled, dirty and guilty, I was forty-nine years young, reckless, disdainful of consequences, unmindful of wet feet and the proprieties, forgetful even of law and order. That awful, glorious night, when young Love-but that's the story.

Chapter III
A Wet Young Man

Well, Tish and I got the boat loose, and Tish dropped the scissors into the water. Then when we got in, Tish insisted on rowing with her face to the bow of the boat. She said she couldn't see where she was going if she didn't, which, of course, was true enough. We dragged the dog in by his tail and then sat and waited for Aggie. When she did come she was sulky, and almost the only words she said that entire night were "Kill him!" And that was under stress of great excitement, at three o'clock in the morning.

The night was very black, but a light on the boat-landing at Sunset Island gave us our direction. Tish and I rowed, I behind her, and as she had an unexpected habit of scooping the top off a wave with her oar and throwing it over my face and chest, finally, in desperation I turned my back to her. It was really easier rowing that way, although we did not keep very good time. But, as I explained when Tish objected, it was really safer, for by rowing back to back we could see in both directions at once.

When we were about a mile from shore, Aggie spoke for the first time.

"The boat 'th leaking!" she said.

"Gracious!" I exclaimed, and felt my petticoats. They were sopping.

"Nonsense!" Tish sneered. "It's the water Lizzie's been ladling in with her oars." Then she caught a wave with her oar, and poured it down my back. At that minute the dog moved uneasily in the bottom of the boat and crawled up on the seat in the bow, where he sat and wailed.

We should have gone back. I said so then, but Tish is like all-the Carberrys-immovably obstinate. When I tried to row back to the landing, she was rowing for Sunset Island, and all we did was to make as much splash as a paddle-wheel steamer, and not move an inch in either direction. And just then Tish broke an oar.

"There!" she snapped, turning on me, of course. "Just look what your pig-headed-ness —"

She never finished. She was staring, petrified, at the rim of the boat, which was just visible. There were two white splotches on it that looked like hands. The more I looked, the more I knew they were hands! And then the boat tilted to that side until we all screamed, and a head and shoulders appeared, fell back out of sight, upreared themselves with a mighty heave, and-dropped into the boat.

It was a man —a young man. Even in the darkness he gleamed white from head to foot. We shut our eyes and screamed. When we stopped he had sat down on the dog, discovered him, slid him with a splash into the bottom of the boat and had settled himself comfortably in the bow.

"I'm sorry I frightened you," he was saying, "but —I'd been swimming for a good while, and your boat was an oasis in the dusty desert"

"Get back into the water instantly!" Tish commanded, turning her profile to him. "Have you no shame?'

"Oh, as to that," he said aggrieved, "I —I have something on, you know. Of course, they are wet, and they stick to me, but —"

"Give him thith," Aggie broke in, and unwound herself from her shawl. I passed it to Letitia over my shoulder, and Letitia averted her face and held it out to him.

"Thanks, awfully," he said. "After all that exercise, the night air is cold on a fellow's back."

At that Letitia turned on him in a rage.

"Will you open that shawl out and cover yourself?" she asked furiously. "Cover yourself. Your hack I Look at your legs I"

"As long as you sit quiet and behave yourself, you may stay in the boat," I added with as much composure as I could get over my trembling lips. "Otherwise, I warn you, we have a dog."

At that I think he prodded the dog with his foot, for he set up a nauseated whine-the dog, of course-and the young gentleman laughed.

"Your dog is quite safe, madam," he said. "I wouldn't bite him for anything." Then he leaned forward in the darkness and stared at Tish and myself.

"Upon my soul!" he muttered, and then aloud: "How in the name of all that is nautical did you ladies get as far from shore as this, when you are rowing in different directions?"

Tish refused to answer, and fell to rowing madly with her one oar, so that we turned around and around in a circle. Aggie had not said a word since she gave the young man her shawl. She was sitting in the stem with the jug in her lap and her handkerchief over her mouth.

"This is a wonderful piece of luck," he said finally. "I must have been blown up the lake. I hope I didn't startle you?"

"Not at all," I said, as coolly as I could. At least he didn't have a revolver: there was no place to hide one, or a knife either. "Are you out for a pleasure trip? Or did you have any definite objective point?" This scathingly.

"Just land," he said. "Any old land will do. Near a boat-house, if possible."

"We are going to Thunthet Island," Aggie lisped, encouraged by his good humor.

This seemed to surprise him, but after a minute he threw back his head and laughed: it was almost a chuckle. Certainly, if he was a lunatic, he was a cheerful one.

"To Sunset Island, then!" he exclaimed. "Forward, and God with us!"

The rain was over, and by the starlight we could make out a little more about our intruder. He seemed large and not bad looking, and he had a nice voice. (It was a disappointment, when we finally saw him in the daylight, to find that his hair was red, but it was offset by an attractive smile and exceedingly good teeth. Next to a nice nose, I like a man to have good teeth.) But, of course, some of the greatest rascals have all the physical attributes at the expense of the moral ones. As to his good humor, every one knows that a man can smile and smile and be a villain still. He wanted to take the oars, but an oar is a mighty effective weapon: neither Tish nor I would give ours up. Finally —

"I suppose you haven't any gasoline with you?" he inquired, leaning forward and hugging the shawl under his chin.

"Ther'th a quart bottle of cleaning fluid —" Aggie began, but Tish interrupted her.

"Agatha!" she said.

"I suppose you don't know of a boat-house near where we could steal some, do you?" he reflected.

Tish lifted her oar out of the water and leaned on it. There is no space here to set down what she said, but she did it thoroughly. She told him what she thought of his going around in his present costume; she told him that two of us were Methodist Protestants and one an Episcopalian, and that we would not assist him to steal anybody's gasoline, or his wife or his silver spoons: and she ended up by demanding that he go back where he came from immediately: that we could not compromise ourselves by landing him anywhere in his existing undress—only Tish called it negligee.

He listened meekly.

"If that's the way you feel," he said finally, "of course I'll drop back into the water. Browning's an easy death. But if during your excursion you happen to come across a motorboat containing a girl, I wish you would tell her that I did the best I could."

He stood up and began to take off the shawl. Tish poked at him with her oar.

"Don't be a young idiot," she snapped. "We're not making you walk the plank. What about the young lady?"

"It's rather a story," he said, drawing the shawl around him again and sitting down. "But the idea is this: when a fellow starts to elope with a girl, and then funks it, by getting drowned or running out of gasoline or anything of that sort, and leaves her sitting in a dead motor-boat in the middle of the night, she's —she's apt to be touchy about it."

"Lord have mercy!" said Tish. "You were abducting a young woman!"

"Penitentiary offense," he confirmed coolly.

"When she didn't want to be eloped with!" I added. I confess I had a queer thrill up and down my back.

"Well," he considered, "hardly that. She only thought she didn't. She has been told so many times that she mustn't like me that now she thinks she doesn't. Pure power of suggestion. If she hadn't pitched a can of gasoline overboard in a temper, we'd have been miles away by this time," he finished, with his first suggestion of gloom.

In the darkness I heard Aggie draw a long breath. Aggie is romantic, having been engaged a long time ago to a young man in the roofing business, who fell off a roof.

"How you mutht love her!" she said, and one could imagine her clasping her hands. "And how alarmed the mutht be for you."

"She said she hoped I would drown," he said, more cheerfully, "but that's only girl's talk. When she gets over thinking she doesn't like me, she's going to be crazy about me. When a girl hates a fellow, she's next door to loving him."

" 'Out of the mouths of babes and sucklings,' " Tish snorted with scorn, and just then the dog began to whine again and tried to crawl up into Aggie's lap. The young man in the shawl started to say something about having a minister waiting at Telusah, and stopped suddenly.

"It isn't raining now," he said, "and yet this boat is filling. Does she leak?"

She did, we knew it then. The water that had been sloshing around in the bottom was almost to the top of our overshoes, and an instant later Aggie, with a fine disregard of the proprieties, had her feet up on the thwarts. We are all vague about the next few minutes, but after a great deal of screeching and tip-ping of the boat, our young man, with the shawl belted around him as a petticoat, was in Tish's seat, rowing like mad, and we were all bailing like mad with our rubber shoes.

We headed the boat straight for Sunset Island, which was as near as any place, but in spite of us it kept on getting fuller. And just when Aggie had lifted her jug into her lap to lighten her end of the boat, and the water was well above our shoe tops, and climbing, and Tish was muttering the alphabet under the impression that she was praying, the boat stopped suddenly and the young man said:

"Why don't you women bail? What are you doing? Tickling the ribs of the boat? We'll never get to shore at this rate!"

Aggie began to sniffle, and the man in the shawl stood up and peered over the water.

"Lillian!" he shouted. "Wave the lantern! Coo-ee!"

We all heard it. From far down the lake came a distant "coo-ee" that was not an echo. The shawl man muttered something and lurched where he stood: the boat tipped, of course, and more water came over the edge.

Aggie began fervently, "For what we are about to receive, O Lord, make us duly thankful," when the boat bumped without warning into something.

It was just in time. As I, the last, was hauled into the motor-launch, the Witch Hazel slid greasily under the surface, to rise no more.

(The loss of the Witch Hazel was deplorable, and later on we sent Carpenter, anonymously, money to buy a new boat. He has one, which he calls the Urticaria, but the ghost of the Witch Hazel still walks, a sort of Pond's Extract in his memory.)

Chapter IV
Cleaning Fluid to the Rescue

It was some time before we could realize that eternity had ceased staring us in the face and had taken a back seat, so to speak. The first thing Tish said was that, man or no man, her shoes were going to come off, and while Aggie was wringing alternately her hands and her petticoats, I happened to notice the Shawl Man. He was standing holding his garment around him and staring over the dark water ahead.

"You needn't feel so badly," I said to him. "We're only glad Aggie had the shawl, and now, if you can run the launch, why don't you hunt up your own, with the young lady in it?"

"This is the boat!" he said heavily, and, sitting down, he dropped his chin in his hands.

Well, there was no girl. Dark as it was, we could all see that Tish looked up suspiciously from where she was stuffing her wet shoes with her stockings to keep them in shape.

"I don't see any clothes either," she said tartly. "I suspect your lady friend tied them into a bundle and swam ashore with them in her teeth!"

"I left her there in that chair!" he affirmed. He looked dazed. "She-she didn't want to —to go, you know, and she threw the extra gasoline can overboard. When we stalled there was nothing to do but swim ashore, borrow a skiff, and steal some gasoline from the boat-house on one of the islands. I wasn't going to sit out there in a dead motor-boat and let her people stand on the bank in the morning and pot at me with a target rifle."

"Thirtainly not!" said Aggie, who had shamelessly allied herself with him.

"Not only that," he went on defiantly, "but when a man cares for a girl the way I care for-her, he either carries her off and marries her or he dies trying."

"And quite right, I'm thure." Thus Aggie. She was still clutching her jug; the dog, the first to be saved, had sniffed the cork, got a whiff of the ether, and retired with a moan to the corner.

"If she tried to swim to shore," began the Shawl Man, and groaned But Aggie had not forgotten her lisp in her role of comforter.

"Nonthenth!" she said. "Probably Mithther Carleton came along with hith motor canoe and took her home. He'th alwayth mooning around the lake late at night."

The Shawl Man jumped to his feet and the boat rocked.

"Denby Carleton!" he said. "Hell!"

Then he went to pieces. As Tish wrote to her niece, Martha Ann Lee, afterward, "his composure went to pieces on the rocks of adversity, and sank in a sea of woe." He raged up and down the launch, muttering strange and awful things, and every now and then he stooped over the engine in the middle of the boat and gritted his teeth and turned something. And the engine would draw a quick breath and turn over on its other side and settle down to sleep again. And then, when he finally gave up, he declared he was going to swim after the canoe and kill Carleton for stealing the girl and throwing his clothes overboard.

(Yes, we found a soft hat floating, and the rest were gone.)

He stood up on the front peak of the launch and began to untie the shawl, but Tish pulled him back and told hifti if the girl wanted Mr. Carleton instead of him he was well rid of her. And she asked him his name. This brought him around a little. He said, "Mansfield, Donald Mansfield," and stalked back and sat down in the stern squarely on the dog.

"Keep away from that dog!" Aggie exclaimed. "He hath mange."

"Mange!" said Aggie.

"Upon my word, Aggie Pilkington," Tish sniffed, "if the creature has mange, why on earth are you still hugging that jar of gasoline?"

Then, of course, the Shawl Man, who shall be Mansfield now, gave a whoop and seized the jug.

"Ith cleaning fluid," Aggie protested.

"Thereth ether and alcohol —"

"Never mind what's in it," he said excitedly. "I know this engine. It'll run on the gas out of a bottle of Apollinaris." And while he poured the stuff into the tank he explained his plan. If the engine ran on the mixture, and didn't get something that he called a "bun on," we could get back to Sunset Island, which I gathered belonged to the girl's father, get into somebody's boat-house (preferably the father's) and obtain some gasoline. Also, he would try to find some clothes. It shows how thoroughly demoralized we were that not one of us objected to his stealing anything he needed, and that Tish asked him to bring her a blanket if he happened on one!

The engine would not start at once. And after he had explained that he had only one hand to crank with, having to hold on the shawl with the other, we turned our backs, and almost immediately there was an explosion. The boat jumped out of the water and dropped back with a thud. I could not scream. Then there came a series of reports, and I sat waiting for the floor to separate and drop me into sixty feet of water and mud and crawly things with the family burial lot full, provided my body was ever found, unless they moved Cousin James beside his first wife, where he ought to be anyhow. And then I realized that we were moving.

We did not float. We got to shore by a distinct species of leaps; once or twice I am quite sure we left the surface of the lake. If that stuff had ever been put on the dog, the fleas would have killed themselves jumping. And all the time there was a combination of odors that as Tish said afterward reminded one individually of burnt brandy sauce and an operating room, and collectively of something that has died in the alley. And whenever we stopped Mr. Mansfield would do something that he called "spinner again."

When we got near enough to shore we could see that the big white Lovell house was lighted up, late as it was, and there were people on the boat dock with lanterns. Mr. Mansfield saw it too, and changed the course of the launch, so. we stopped at a smaller landing, half a mile or so down the beach, and tied up there.

"You are perfectly safe here," he said, "and I'll be back in ten minutes. The only way Major Lovell could recognize this boat in the dark would be by the sound of the engine, and if he heard this racket he'll take us for a battle in a moving picture show. Just sit tight and keep warm."

He threw the shawl to us and dived into the darkness. Somebody was shouting at the Lovell dock, but we sat In safe obscurity and listened to the wash of the water against the piles. The absurdity of the situation began to dawn on me, and the sight of Tish and Aggie, luminous in the starlight-it had stopped raining-trying to get into their wet shoes, made me fairly hysterical. To add to it all, the patter of Mr. Mansfield's bare feet on the boards of the dock waked our sleeping dog, and with a series of staccato barks he was at our unlucky young man's heels. He seemed to have a fondness for feet.

"If you could see yourself, Lizzie, I might understand your mirth," Tish said scathingly. "But I fail to see anything funny."

"Then for goodness sake, Tish," I cried, "stop dangling that shoe on your toe and see what is the matter with your figure. It has slipped up under your chin."

"Good heventh!" said Aggie. "They are coming down the beach after uth!"

It was true. The lanterns had left the Lovell dock and were bobbing wildly along the water-front in bur direction, guided by the barking of the dog. Of all the hours of that awful night, that was the most terrible. We sat there shivering and helpless and watched Nemesis chasing and bobbing down on us. About half way to us the first lantern stopped and fired a gun, and back along the beach new lanterns kept adding themselves to the line that stretched out like the tail of a comet.

Tish thought she was very cool, but both Aggie and I distinctly heard her say that the stars had stopped raining. And once she said that she had always been a respected member of the community, and that nobody in his sober senses would believe her if she told the true story. And when the first lantern was so close that we could see a vague outline of the man behind it, desperation gave me a courage that has appalled me since.

I went over to the engine and tried to "spinner."

What is more to the point, I did it. The wheels began to revolve with a sickening speed: the whole frame of the boat jarred and quivered. I sank back on my knees and closed my eyes.

"We're not moving," Tish said with awful calmness.

And at that a white figure hurled itself from . the darkness at the end of the landing and flew down the dock to us. It had a can in one hand and a lantern in the other. It hesitated a second to throw off the rope, which was why we hadn't moved, of course, and, as the engine was going full, he had only time to catch one of the awning supports as it flew past. It went as if it had been shot out of a gun, and when Aggie and Tish and I had assorted ourselves from a heap on the floor, we were well out from shore.

It was lucky that Aggie took one of her awful sneezing spells just then, as she always does when she is excited, for by the time she was breathing easily again the shore was well behind and Mr. Mansfield had put on the shawl again.

Chapter V
The Cave-man and His Woman

It is a little difficult, looking back, to explain our state of mind that night. It was only our second taste of romance-Aggie's roofer being too far back to count. Now, with six months of perspective, I think we were intoxicated with adventure to the point of abandon. For when Mr. Mansfield offered to take us home, before starting on his pursuit of the motor canoe, we refused to go. As Tish said:

"No doubt when you do overtake them, Mr. Mansfield, the young woman will feel the need of some of her own sex, women of-er-maturity and experience, to advise her. I consider it our duty to go."

"Oh, leth go!" said Aggie. "Mr. Carletonth a large man. Do you think you will have to fight him for your lady?" Aggie's tone was cheerfully bloodthirsty, and she clutched the end of the broken oar like a club. Aggie, the apostle of peace!

"Frankly, I should like to see the end of the affair myself," I admitted. "I should like to see the young lady's face when she finds you eloping with three maiden ladies, and —I am curious to know how your cave-man theory works out."

He was working over the engine, and we were headed down the lake. While I was speaking he moved to the other side of the launch, and it tilted villainously. He loomed very large in the darkness, and the strength of his bare arms and heavy chest, his sinewy legs, made him not unlike his prototype.

He did not answer me at once. He had found some cigarettes in the boat, and he lighted one. Only when it was well aglow did he show that he had heard me.

"The original cave man was no fool," he observed, calmly looking ahead. "A man doesn't carry a woman off unless he's crazy about her, in the first place. If he's got sufficient force of character to dare her daddy's stone club — jail, in this case-and enough physical strength to hold her to him with one arm and fight off pursuit and rivals with the other, it-well, it doesn't matter much what the girl thinks of him in the beginning: she'll die for him, in the end."

Aggie positively thrilled in the darkness beside me, and even Tish was silenced by the vision of this masculine point of view. As for me, just at that instant I quite agreed with the young savage I

"Ith-ith the very pretty?" Aggie ventured, after swallowing hard.

"I don't know," he said indifferently, straining his eyes ahead. "Oh — yes, I suppose she is. I never thought about it. I haven't thought of anybody else — anything else, for the week I've known her."

"The week!" we all repeated faintly.

"When her groom lifts her off her horse, I want to kill him. If that ass Carleton gets her to Telusah first and marries her, I'll take her from him. She's my woman."

Tish stood right up in the boat and pointed her finger at him. "You d-don't know what you are talking about," she stuttered. "How —how dare you speak of taking a married woman from her husband!"

"Figs!" he said disrespectfully. "In the first place, if the engine holds out, we'll rim them down at least a mile from Telusah, and in the second place, while I judge you are talking by the book and not by experience — a, few words said over a man and a woman don't make them husband and wife. It gives the woman the man's name, but-the man don't necessarily get the woman. Mine-or nobody's," he added under his breath.

Tish collapsed into her chair. I admit I felt queer all over, and Aggie's heart had fluttered back to the thin young man with the curled-up mustache and a dimple in his chin, who had fallen off a roof.

"Mister Wigginth usthed to talk exactly that way!" she said softly.

That is the way we went down toward Telusah: the prehistoric gentleman in the bow steering and watching the engine, now and then stopping it dead to listen for the throb of the motor canoe ahead. Aggie twitteringly in the past, with her bare feet tucked under her for warmth and the broken oar in her lap; Tish blazing with indignation and excitement, and I saved by my sense of humor from going into violent hysteria and embracing the hot-headed, mad, ridiculous and altogether satisfactory young animal at the wheel. I merely said:

"I wish somebody had wooed me like that thirty years ago. I wouldn't be earning my own living, young man."

"That's what she wants to do-stay single and work for a livelihood," he said with disgust. "I told her it was all fool nonsense; that the place for her kind of woman was in some man's home —"

"Cave," I suggested.

"Bearing his children —"

"Silence!" Tish shouted, and even Aggie was roused out of a dream.

He shut down the engine just then, and we all heard it: a faint throbbing that one felt in the ears, rather than heard. He leaped up on the peak of the boat and stared into the darkness ahead.

"Better than I expected," he said with suppressed excitement "They're not a mile ahead. I wish I had a stick of some sort: I may have to knock that chump on the head."

Luckily he did not see Aggie's oar, and to his everlasting honor be it said, he went dauntlessly into the battle with his bare hands. "And bare arms and legs," Tish ironically suggests that I add.

For battle it was.

We overtook the canoe somewhere about Long Point, and our lantern showed two people, as we expected. It was Mr. Carleton, who evidently hadn't dressed to elope, and who wore the shirt of a bathing suit and a pair of corduroy trousers, and the Girl. She was in a white party frock of some sort She stopped paddling and stared up at us defiantly as we must have loomed black behind our lantern. She was very pretty, and she had two triangular red spots in her cheeks. Our gentleman pulled the shawl around him and stepped on the thwarts, and even at that distance we could see the angry fear in the girl's eyes.

"Lillian," Mr. Mansfield said cheerfully, "I am not going to do that puppy with you the honor of asking you to choose between us. I give you your choice-either get into the launch comfortably, or stay where you are-in which case I shall run you down and pick you out of the water."

"You coward!" said Mr. Carleton from the stem of the canoe. "You can't try your high-handed methods with me. Run us down if you like. It's a penitentiary offense to kidnap a girl and marry her."

"Oh, piffle r said Mr. Mansfield rudely. "I suppose you didn't intend to marry her yourself at Telusah!"

"I intended to return her to her parents in safety, by way of the trolley," retorted Carleton stiffly.

The Mansfield man threw back his head and laughed.

"Did you hear that, Lillian?" he called. "That's love for you! Why, the idiot didn't even intend to marry you! He was going to take you home to your people!" He laughed again in pure delight.

But the girl had plenty of spirit.

"I don't intend to be married at all," she flared at him. "Certainly not to you, Donald Mansfield. Run us down if you like. I would rather die than marry you."

"You hear what she says," said Carleton, from the darkness. "If you are a gentleman you will take your boat and your ruffianly accomplices back to where you came from-or to hell, as far as I'm concerned."

"Ruffian yourself," Tish said furiously, but I pulled her down. There was silence, then —

"Lillian," Mr. Mansfield said very gently, " 'Lady' Carleton is right. If it's as bad as that I'll take you home. I had a sort of fool idea that you would know it was inevitable — that you were my woman. If I've been a bit raw about it, it's because the thing seemed so clear to me. Give me your hand."

"I shall not get into the launch," the girl said haughtily.

"Your hand."

"Confound you, Mansfidd, can't you see she hates you?" This was Carleton, of course.

"The girlth a fool," Aggie muttered angrily, behind me. In the instant that I turned my head, something happened —I don't know just what For the girl was alone in the canoe, we were alone in the launch, and just below me the water was boiling into white spray. Now and then an arm shot into the air, or a leg, and occasionally, not often, both heads were above water at the same time. And it was then that Aggie, the president of the Civic Club and corresponding secretary of the Working Girls' Home, with her draggled skirts pinned up above her bare feet, stood up suddenly and banged Mr. Carleton on the head with what was left of her oar!

But if that was amazing, the most surprising thing followed. The Girl stood up in the canoe and —

Oh, youVe killed him!" she screeched. Oh, Don! Don!" Donald being the Mansfield man!

Then, of course, the canoe turned over, and the rest of what she was saying ended in a gurgle.

Chapter VI
"I Will Go with You"

We got them all into a launch finally, for there was only five feet of water, which explained much that we had not understood about the fight, and they were as disconsolate looking a lot of lovers as I ever wish to see. Mr. Carleton sat in the stem and held his head, which Aggie's oar had almost broken, and the girl dripped and shivered in a comer by herself and stared at the Mansfield man, who was coaxing Tish for one of her petticoats so he could give the girl his shawl.

Aggie was for trying to explain to the girl how we came to be there at all, and without our shoes at that. But it was such a long story, beginning with the dog that had fleas ("mange," says Aggie) and extending through robbery to attempted murder ("I only meant to stun him," says Aggie), that I advised her not to begin it.

The launch would not start after all, and it developed that the propeller shaft was choked with weeds. This meant that the Mansfield man must crawl overboard, get on his back under the launch (which is much more unpleasant, I should think, than getting under an automobile), and clear off the shaft. And while he was holding his breath under the boat, and while Tish had turned her back on everybody and with the aid of the lantern was trying to take a splinter out of the sole of her foot, the Carleton man got up dizzily and went over to the girl.

"Surely, Lillian," he said, steadying himself by the awning frame, "you-you don't intend to let that —"

"Please go away," she said. "I don't want to talk. How funny you look with that bandage around your head." And then, to me (she had accepted the presence of three bare-footed maiden ladies in the launch without comment): "Oh, do you think he might be caught in the weeds and-and drown?"

But he did not drown. He came magnificently over the edge of the boat in a few minutes, with a string of green water-weeds clinging to his head. Aggie, who, as you have seen, is romantic, muttered something about "grape leaves in his hair," which she said afterward was Ibsen, although the only use I have ever known for grape leaves was to wrap pats of butter in, in the country.

He turned the launch around and we started for home. I do not recall that any one spoke on the way back, except Tish, who asked me if I had any castor oil at the house: she wanted it to soften her shoes if they dried stiff. The Girl sat by herself and watched the big fellow in the shawl-toga. And once or twice, when he glanced up and saw her, he smiled over at her, but he did not go near her or speak to her.

It was pale dawn when we stopped at the dock of the Watermelon Camp. We, who had been sodden shadows in the night, were now damp and shivering outlines. Mr. Mansfield, having given the girl the shawl, drew arotmd him still closer the awning curtain with which he had draped himself, and Aggie, still clutching the oar, held up one hand in the gray light to hide the deficiencies of her mouth. No one stirred in the camp.

Mr. Carleton got up stiflly and glanced around at all of us. Then he stalked over to the man at the wheel, who was staring ahead and whistling under his breath.

"Will you give me your word to take her home?" he said.

"Ask her if she wants to go home." He threw this over his shoulder, between whistles, as it were. Then the girl, looking very pretty, but slim and slinky in her wet things, went over to the Mansfield man and put her hand on his shoulder.

"I —I think I will go with you, Don!" she said. And that practically ends the story.

We left Mr. Carleton on the dock, staring after us through the mist, and we all went back to the cottage and put the girl to bed. We gave Mr. Mansfield a pillow by the sitting-room wood fire, and Tish's green kimono to sleep in. And after that we all three took a mustard foot-bath and some camphor sprinkled on sugar and went to bed.

Aggie wakened me at nine o'clock the next morning by hunting in my bureau for her second best teeth, and it was then that we found our lovers had gone. In the girl's room there was a letter of thanks. She said she did not wish to disturb us after that awful night, but that she could not sleep, and that she and Mr. Mansfield were going down to Telusah to be married.

Tish read the letter aloud and stared at us, while Paulina whined for her breakfast.

"Upon my soul," Tish gasped, when she could speak. "Instead of clapping him into jail, she's going to marry him!"

"Do you thuppoth he went to Telutha in that kimono?" Aggie said in a husky whisper. She had taken a terrible cold.

But Mr. Mansfield did not go to Telusah in Tish's kimono.

After all, the beginning of this story is also the end. For now you can understand why Tish dropped the bowl when the young man brought her kimono back from the Watermelon Camp and asked for Mr. Carleton's trousers!

I have told the story in defense of Tish and the rest of us. I wish to brand as false the story told by the man from the hotel who happened to be fishing for muskalunge early that morning. He said, you remember, that he saw. Miss Carberry in her green kimono leave our cottage just after dawn and go stealthily along the beach through the mist to the Watermelon Camp. When she got there, he said, to his horror he saw her strip off the green kimono and hang it to a tree. Just then the mist shut down and he saw nothing more.

In his anxiety for Miss Carberry's sanity he was on the point of landing to investigate, when he hooked the largest 'lunge of the season (registered weight at the hatcheries, thirty-seven pounds four ounces), and when he looked again at the shore all he saw was a red-haired man hurrying along the beach in a pair of corduroy trousers and a bathing-shirt!

Tish closed the incident with one comment.

"Young millionaire!" she snapped when she saw the newspapers. "Young scamp, I say, stealing poor Mr. Carleton's sweetheart and then his trousers. As for my green kimono, after all we did for him, he might at least have had the grace to roll it up and stick it imder a barrel. I shall bum it."

But she did not. Aggie saw it only the other day, put away in a lavender silk sachet, with a bundle of newspaper clippings, a half-eaten bath sponge, and a particular kind of bass hook, which we had found on the sitting-room floor.

THE END

Tish: The Chronicle of Her Escapades and Excursions

by
Mary Roberts Rinehart

Mind Over Motor

How Tish Broke the Law and Some Records

I

So many unkind things have been said of the affair at Morris Valley that I think it best to publish a straightforward account of everything. The ill nature of the cartoon, for instance, which showed Tish in a pair of khaki trousers on her back under a racing-car was quite uncalled for. Tish did not wear the khaki trousers; she merely took them along in case of emergency. Nor was it true that Tish took Aggie along as a mechanician and brutally pushed her off the car because she was not pumping enough oil. The fact was that Aggie sneezed on a curve and fell out of the car, and would no doubt have been killed had she not been thrown into a pile of sand.

It was in early September that Eliza Bailey, my cousin, decided to go to London, ostensibly for a rest, but really to get some cretonne at Liberty's. Eliza wrote me at Lake Penzance asking me to go to Morris Valley and look after Bettina.

I must confess that I was eager to do it. We three were very comfortable at Mat Cottage, "Mat" being the name Charlie Sands, Tish's nephew, had given it, being the initials of "Middle-Aged Trio." Not that I regard the late forties as middle-aged. But Tish, of course, is fifty. Charlie Sands, who is on a newspaper, calls us either the "M.A.T." or the "B.A.'s," for "Beloved Aunts," although Aggie and I are not related to him.

Bettina's mother's note: —

> Not that she will allow you to do it, or because she isn't entirely able to take care of herself; but because the people here are a talky lot. Bettina will probably look after you. She has come from college with a feeling that I am old and decrepit and must be cared for. She maddens me with pillows and cups of tea and woolen shawls. She thinks Morris Valley selfish and idle, and is disappointed in the church, preferring her Presbyterianism pure. She is desirous now of learning how to cook. If you decide to come I'll be grateful if you can keep her out of the kitchen.
>
> Devotedly, ELIZA.
>
> P.S. If you can keep Bettina from getting married while I'm away I'll be very glad. She believes a woman should marry and rear a large family!
>
> E.

We were sitting on the porch of the cottage at Lake Penzance when I received the letter, and I read it aloud. "Humph!" said Tish, putting down the stocking she was knitting and looking over her spectacles at me —"Likes her Presbyterianism pure and believes in a large family! How old is she? Forty?"

"Eighteen or twenty," I replied, looking at the letter. "I'm not anxious to go. She'll probably find me frivolous."

Tish put on her spectacles and took the letter. "I think it's your duty, Lizzie," she said when she'd read it through. "But that young woman needs handling. We'd better all go. We can motor over in half a day."

That was how it happened that Bettina Bailey, sitting on Eliza Bailey's front piazza, decked out in chintz cushions,—the piazza, of course,—saw a dusty machine come up the drive and stop with a flourish at the steps. And from it alight, not one chaperon, but three.

After her first gasp Bettina was game. She was a pretty girl in a white dress and bore no traces in her face of any stern religious proclivities.

"I didn't know—" she said, staring from one to the other of us. "Mother said-that is-won't you go right upstairs and have some tea and lie down?" She had hardly taken her eyes from Tish, who had lifted the engine hood and was poking at the carbureter with a hairpin.

"No, thanks," said Tish briskly. "I'll just go around to the garage and oil up while I'm dirty. I've got a short circuit somewhere. Aggie, you and Lizzie get the trunk off."

Bettina stood by while we unbuckled and lifted down our traveling trunk. She did not speak a word, beyond asking if we wouldn't wait until the gardener came. On Tish's saying she had no time to wait, because she wanted to put kerosene in the cylinders before the engine cooled, Bettina lapsed into silence and stood by watching us.

Bettina took us upstairs. She had put Drummond's "Natural Law in the Spiritual World" on my table and a couch was ready with pillows and a knitted slumber robe. Very gently she helped us out of our veils and dusters and closed the windows for fear of drafts.

"Dear mother is so reckless of drafts," she remarked. "Are you sure you won't have tea?"

"We had some blackberry cordial with us," Aggie said, "and we all had a little on the way. We had to change a tire and it made us thirsty."

"Change a tire!"

Aggie had taken off her bonnet and was pinning on the small lace cap she wears, away from home, to hide where her hair is growing thin. In her cap Aggie is a sweet-faced woman of almost fifty, rather ethereal. She pinned on her cap and pulled her crimps down over her forehead.

"Yes," she observed. "A bridge went down with us and one of the nails spoiled a new tire. I told Miss Carberry the bridge was unsafe, but she thought, by taking it very fast —"

Bettina went over to Aggie and clutched her arm. "Do you mean to say," she quavered, "that you three women went through a bridge —"

"It was a small bridge," I put in, to relieve her mind; "and only a foot or two of water below. If only the man had not been so disagreeable —"

"Oh," she said, relieved, "you had a man with you!"

"We never take a man with us," Aggie said with dignity. "This one was fishing under the bridge and he was most ungentlemanly. Quite refused to help, and tried to get the license number so he could sue us."

"Sue you!"

"He claimed his arm was broken, but I distinctly saw him move it." Aggie, having adjusted her cap, was looking at it in the mirror. "But dear Tish thinks of everything. She had taken off the license plates."

Bettina had gone really pale. She seemed at a loss, and impatient at herself for being so. "You-you won't have tea?" she asked.

"No, thank you."

"Would you-perhaps you would prefer whiskey and soda."

Aggie turned on her a reproachful eye. "My dear girl," she said, "with the exception of a little home-made wine used medicinally we drink nothing. I am the secretary of the Woman's Prohibition Party."

Bettina left us shortly after that to arrange for putting up Letitia and Aggie. She gave them her mother's room, and whatever impulse she may have had to put the Presbyterian Psalter by the bed, she restrained it. By midnight Drummond's "Natural Law" had disappeared from my table and a novel had taken its place. But Bettina had not lost her air of bewilderment.

That first evening was very quiet. A young man in white flannels called, and he and Letitia spent a delightful evening on the porch talking spark-plugs and carbureters. Bettina sat in a corner and looked at the moon. Spoken to, she replied in monosyllables in a carefully sweet tone. The young man's name was Jasper McCutcheon.

It developed that Jasper owned an old racing-car which he kept in the Bailey garage, and he and Tish went out to look it over. They very politely asked us all to go along, but Bettina refusing, Aggie and I sat with her and looked at the moon.

Aggie in her capacity as chaperon, or as one of an association of chaperons, used the opportunity to examine Bettina on the subject of Jasper.

"He seems a nice boy," she remarked. Aggie's idea of a nice boy is one who in summer wears fresh flannels outside, in winter less conspicuously. "Does he live near?"

"Next door," sweetly but coolly.

"He is very good-looking."

"Ears spoil him-too large."

"Does he come around-er-often?"

"Only two or three times a day. On Sunday, of course, we see more of him."

Aggie looked at me in the moonlight. Clearly the young man from the next door needed watching. It was well we had come.

"I suppose you like the same things?" she suggested. "Similar tastes and-er-all that?"

Bettina stretched her arms over her head and yawned.

"Not so you could notice it," she said coolly. "I can't thick of anything we agree on. He is an Episcopalian; I'm a Presbyterian. He approves of suffrage for women; I do not. He is a Republican; I'm a Progressive. He disapproves of large families; I approve of them, if people can afford them."

Aggie sat straight up. "I hope you don't discuss that!" she exclaimed.

Bettina smiled. "How nice to find that you are really just nice elderly ladies after all!" she said. "Of course we discuss it. Is it anything to be ashamed of?"

"When I was a girl," I said tartly, "we married first and discussed those things afterward."

"Of course you did, Aunt Lizzie," she said, smiling alluringly. She was the prettiest girl I think I have ever seen, and that night she was beautiful. "And you raised enormous families who religiously walked to church in their bare feet to save their shoes!"

"I did nothing of the sort," I snapped.

"It seems to me," Aggie put in gently, "that you make very little of love." Aggie was once engaged to be married to a young man named Wiggins, a roofer by trade, who was killed in the act of inspecting a tin gutter, on a rainy day. He slipped and fell over, breaking his neck as a result.

Bettina smiled at Aggie. "Not at all," she said. "The day of blind love is gone, that's all-gone like the day of the chaperon."

Neither of us cared to pursue this, and Tish at that moment appearing with Jasper, Aggie and I made a move toward bed. But Jasper not going, and none of us caring to leave him alone with Bettina, we sat down again.

We sat until one o'clock.

At the end of that time Jasper rose, and saying something about its being almost bedtime strolled off next door. Aggie was sound asleep in her chair and Tish was dozing. As for Bettina, she had said hardly a word after eleven o'clock.

Aggie and Tish, as I have said, were occupying the same room. I went to sleep the moment I got into bed, and must have slept three or four hours when I was awakened by a shot. A moment later a dozen or more shots were fired in rapid succession and I sat bolt upright in bed. Across the street some one was raising a window, and a man called "What's the matter?" twice.

There was no response and no further sound. Shaking in every limb, I found the light switch and looked at the time. It was four o'clock in the morning and quite dark.

Some one was moving in the hall outside and whimpering. I opened the door hurriedly and Aggie half fell into the room.

"Tish is murdered, Lizzie!" she said, and collapsed on the floor in a heap.

"Nonsense!"

"She's not in her room or in the house, and I heard shots!"

Well, Aggie was right. Tish was not in her room. There was a sort of horrible stillness everywhere as we stood there clutching at each other and listening.

"She's heard burglars downstairs and has gone down after them, and this is what has happened! Oh, Tish! brave Tish!" Aggie cried hysterically.

And at that Bettina came in with her hair over her shoulders and asked us if we had heard anything. When we told her about Tish, she insisted on going downstairs, and with Aggie carrying her first-aid box and I carrying the blackberry cordial, we went down.

The lower floor was quiet and empty. The man across the street had put down his window and gone back to bed, and everything was still. Bettina in her dressing-gown went out on the porch and turned on the light. Tish was not there, nor was there a body lying on the lawn.

"It was back of the house by the garage," Bettina said. "If only Jasper —"

And at that moment Jasper came into the circle of light. He had a Norfolk coat on over his pajamas and a pair of slippers, and he was running, calling over his shoulder to some one behind as he ran.

"Watch the drive!" he yelled. "I saw him duck round the corner."

We could hear other footsteps now and somebody panting near us. Aggie was sitting huddled in a porch chair, crying, and Bettina, in the hall, was trying to get down from the wall a Moorish knife that Eliza Bailey had picked up somewhere.

"John!" we heard Jasper calling. "John! Quick! I've got him!"

He was just at the corner of the porch. My heart stopped and then rushed on a thousand a minute. Then: —

"Take your hands off me!" said Tish's voice.

The next moment Tish came majestically into the circle of light and mounted the steps. Jasper, with his mouth open, stood below looking up, and a hired man in what looked like a bed quilt was behind in the shadow.

Tish was completely dressed in her motoring clothes, even to her goggles. She looked neither to the right nor left, but stalked across the porch into the house and up the stairway. None of us moved until we heard the door of her room slam above.

"Poor old dear!" said Bettina. "She's been walking in her sleep!"

"But the shots!" gasped Aggie. "Some one was shooting at her!"

Conscious now of his costume, Jasper had edged close to the veranda and stood in its shadow.

"Walking in her sleep, of course!" he said heartily. "The trip to-day was too much for her. But think of her getting into that burglar-proof garage with her eyes shut-or do sleep-walkers have their eyes shut? —and actually cranking up my racer!"

Aggie looked at me and I looked at Aggie.

"Of course," Jasper went on, "there being no muffler on it, the racket wakened her as well as the neighborhood. And then the way we chased her!"

"Poor old dear!" said Bettina again. "I'm going in to make her some tea."

"I think," said Jasper, "that I need a bit of tea too. If you will put out the porch lights I'll come up and have some."

But Aggie and I said nothing. We knew Tish never walked in her sleep. She had meant to try out Jasper's racing-car at dawn, forgetting that racers have no mufflers, and she had been, as one may say, hoist with her own petard-although I do not know what a petard is and have never been able to find out.

We drank our tea, but Tish refused to have any or to reply to our knocks, preserving a sulky silence. Also she had locked Aggie out and I was compelled to let her sleep in my room.

I was almost asleep when Aggie spoke: —

"Did you think there was anything queer about the way that Jasper boy said good-night to Bettina?" she asked drowsily.

"I didn't hear him say good-night."

"That was it. He didn't. I think" —she yawned —"I think he kissed her."

Tish was down early to breakfast that morning and her manner forbade any mention of the night before. Aggie, however, noticed that she ate her cereal with her left hand and used her right arm only when absolutely necessary. Once before Tish had almost broken an arm cranking a car and had been driven to arnica compresses for a week; but this time we dared not suggest anything.

Shortly after breakfast she came down to the porch where Aggie and I were knitting.

"I've hurt my arm, Lizzie," she said. "I wish you'd come out and crank the car."

"You'd better stay at home with an arm like that," I replied stiffly.

"Very well, I'll crank it myself."

"Where are you going?"

"To the drug store for arnica."

Bettina was not there, so I turned on Tish sharply. "I'll go, of course," I said; "but I'll not go without speaking my mind, Letitia Carberry. By and large, I've stood by you for twenty-five years, and now in the weakness of your age I'm not going to leave you. But I warn you, Tish, if you touch that racing-car again, I'll send for Charlie Sands."

"I haven't any intention of touching it again," said Tish, meekly enough. "But I wish I could buy a second-hand racer cheap."

"What for?" Aggie demanded.

Tish looked at her with scorn. "To hold flowers on the dining-table," she snapped.

It being necessary, of course, to leave a chaperon with Bettina, because of the Jasper person's habit of coming over at any hour of the day, we left Aggie with instructions to watch them both.

Tish and I drove to the drug store together, and from there to a garage for gasoline. I have never learned to say "gas" for gasoline. It seems to me as absurd as if I were to say "but" for butter. Considering that Aggie was quite sulky at being left, it is absurd for her to assume an air of virtue over what followed that day. Aggie was only like a lot of people-good because she was not tempted; for it was at the garage that we met Mr. Ellis.

We had stopped the engine and Tish was quarreling with the man about the price of gasoline when I saw him —a nice-looking young man in a black-and-white checked suit and a Panama hat. He came over and stood looking at Tish's machine.

"Nice lines to that car," he said. "Built for speed, isn't she? What do you get out of her?"

Tish heard him and turned. "Get out of her?" she said. "Bills mostly."

"Well, that's the way with most of them," he remarked, looking steadily at Tish. "A machine's a rich man's toy. The only way to own one is to have it endowed like a university. But I meant speed. What can you make?"

"Never had a chance to find out," Tish said grimly. "Between nervous women in the machine and constables outside I have the twelve-miles-an- hour habit. I'm going to exchange the speedometer for a vacuum bottle."

He smiled. "I don't think you're fair to yourself. Mostly-if you'll forgive me —I can tell a woman's driving as far off as I can see the machine; but you are a very fine driver. The way you brought that car in here impressed me considerably."

"She need not pretend she crawls along the road," I said with some sarcasm. "The bills she complains of are mostly fines for speeding."

"No!" said the young man, delighted. "Good! I'm glad to hear it. So are mine!"

After that we got along famously. He had his car there —a low gray thing that looked like an armored cruiser.

"I'd like you ladies to try her," he said. "She can move, but she is as gentle as a lamb. A lady friend of mine once threaded a needle as an experiment while going sixty-five miles an hour."

"In this car?"

"In this car."

Looking back, I do not recall just how the thing started. I believe Tish expressed a desire to see the car go, and Mr. Ellis said he couldn't let her out on the roads, but that the race-track at the fair-ground was open and if we cared to drive down there in Tish's car he would show us her paces, as he called it.

From that to going to the race-track, and from that to Tish's getting in beside him on the mechanician's seat and going round once or twice, was natural. I refused; I didn't like the look of the thing.

Tish came back with a cinder in her eye and full of enthusiasm. "It was magnificent, Lizzie," she said. "The only word for it is sublime. You see nothing. There is just the rush of the wind and the roar of the engine and a wonderful feeling of flying. Here! See if you can find this cinder."

"Won't you try it, Miss-er-Lizzie?"

"No, thanks," I replied. "I can get all the roar and rush of wind I want in front of an electric fan, and no danger."

He stood by, looking out over the oval track while I took three cinders from Tish's eye.

"Great track!" he said. "It's a horse-track, of course, but it's in bully shape-the county fair is held there and these fellows make a big feature of their horse-races. I came up here to persuade them to hold an automobile meet, but they've got cold feet an the proposition."

"What was the proposition?" asked Tish.

"Well," he said, "it was something like this. I've been turning the trick all over the country and it works like a charm. The town's ahead in money and business, for an automobile race always brings a big crowd; the track owners make the gate money and the racing-cars get the prizes. Everybody's ahead. It's a clean sport too."

"I don't approve of racing for money," Tish said decidedly.

But Mr. Ellis shrugged his shoulders. "It's really hardly racing for money," he explained. "The prizes cover the expenses of the racing-cars, which are heavy naturally. The cars alone cost a young fortune."

"I see," said Tish. "I hadn't thought of it in that light. Well, why didn't Morris Valley jump at the chance?"

He hesitated a moment before he answered. "It was my fault really," he said. "They were willing enough to have the races, but it was a matter of money. I made them a proposition to duplicate whatever prize money they offered, and in return I was to have half the gate receipts and the betting privileges."

Tish quite stiffened. "Clean sport!" she said sarcastically. "With betting privileges!"

"You don't quite understand, dear lady," he explained. "Even in the cleanest sport we cannot prevent a man's having an opinion and backing it with his own money. What I intended to do was to regulate it. Regulate it."

Tish was quite mollified. "Well, of course," she said, "I suppose since it must be, it is better-er,—regulated. But why haven't you succeeded?"

"An unfortunate thing happened just as I had the deal about to close," he replied, and drew a long breath. "The town had raised twenty-five hundred. I was to duplicate the amount. But just at that time a —a young brother of mine in the West got into difficulties, and I —but why go into family matters? It would have been easy enough for me to pay my part of the purse out of my share of the gate money; but the committee demands cash on the table. I haven't got it."

Tish stood up in her car and looked out over the track.

"Twenty-five hundred dollars is a lot of money, young man."

"Not so much when you realize that the gate money will probably amount to twelve thousand."

Tish turned and surveyed the grandstand.

"That thing doesn't seat twelve hundred."

"Two thousand people in the grandstand-that's four thousand dollars. Four thousand standing inside the ropes at a dollar each, four thousand more. And say eight hundred machines parked in the oval there at five dollars a car, four thousand more. That's twelve thousand for the gate money alone. Then there are the concessions to sell peanuts, toy balloons, lemonade and palm-leaf fans, the lunch-stands, merry-go-round and moving-picture permits. It's a bonanza! Fourteen thousand anyhow."

"Half of fourteen thousand is seven," said Tish dreamily. "Seven thousand less twenty-five hundred is thirty-five hundred dollars profit."

"Forty-five hundred, dear lady," corrected Mr. Ellis, watching her. "Forty-five hundred dollars profit to be made in two weeks, and nothing to do to get it but sit still and watch it coming!"

I can read Tish like a book and I saw what was in her mind. "Letitia Carberry!" I said sternly. "You take my warning and keep clear of this foolishness. If money comes as easy as that it ain't honest."

"Why not?" demanded Mr. Ellis. "We give them their money's worth, don't we? They'd pay two dollars for a theater seat without half the thrills-no chances of seeing a car turn turtle or break its steering-knuckle and dash into the side-lines. Two dollars' worth? It's twenty!"

But Tish had had a moment to consider, and the turning-turtle business settled it. She shook her head. "I'm not interested, Mr. Ellis," she said coldly. "I couldn't sleep at night if I thought I'd been the cause of anything turning turtle or dashing into the side-lines."

"Dear lady!" he said, shocked; "I had no idea of asking you to help me out of my difficulties. Anyhow, while matters are at a standstill probably some shrewd money-maker here will come forward before long and make a nice profit on a small investment."

As we drove away from the fair grounds Tish was very silent; but just as we reached the Bailey place, with Bettina and young Jasper McCutcheon batting a ball about on the tennis court, Tish turned to me.

"You needn't look like that, Lizzie," she said. "I'm not even thinking of backing an automobile race-although I don't see why I shouldn't, so far as that goes. But it's curious, isn't it, that I've got twenty-five hundred dollars from Cousin Angeline's estate not even earning four per cent?"

I got out grimly and jerked at my bonnet-strings.

"You put it in a mortgage, Tish," I advised her with severity in every tone. "It may not be so fast as an automobile race or so likely to turn turtle or break its steering-knuckle, but it's safe."

"Huh!" said Tish, reaching for the gear lever. "And about as exciting as a cold pork chop."

"And furthermore," I interjected, "if you go into this thing now that your eyes are open, I'll send for Charlie Sands!"

"You and Charlie Sands," said Tish viciously, jamming at her gears, "ought to go and live in an old ladies' home away from this cruel world."

Aggie was sitting under a sunshade in the broiling sun at the tennis court. She said she had not left Bettina and Jasper for a moment, and that they had evidently quarreled, although she did not know when, having listened to every word they said. For the last half-hour, she said, they had not spoken at all.

"Young people in love are very foolish," she said, rising stiffly. "They should be happy in the present. Who knows what the future may hold?"

I knew she was thinking of Mr. Wiggins and the icy roof, so I patted her shoulder and sent her up to put cold cloths on her head for fear of sunstroke. Then I sat down in the broiling sun and chaperoned Bettina until luncheon.

Jasper took dinner with us that night. He came across the lawn, freshly shaved and in clean white flannels, just as dinner was announced, and said he had seen a chocolate cake cooling on the kitchen porch and that it was a sort of unwritten social law that when the Baileys happened to have a chocolate cake at dinner they had him also.

There seemed to be nothing to object to in this. Evidently he was right, for we found his place laid at the table. The meal was quite cheerful, although Jasper ate the way some people play the piano, by touch, with his eyes on Bettina. And he gave no evidence at dessert of a fondness for chocolate cake sufficient to justify a standing invitation.

After dinner we went out on the veranda, and under cover of showing me a sunset Jasper took me round the corner of the house. Once there, he entirely forgot the sunset.

"Miss Lizzie," he began at once, "what have I done to you to have you treat me like this?"

"I?" I asked, amazed.

"All three of you. Did-did Bettina's mother warn you against me?"

"The girl has to be chaperoned."

"But not jailed, Miss Lizzie, not jailed! Do you know that I haven't had a word with Bettina alone since you came?"

"Why should you want to say anything we cannot hear?"

"Miss Lizzie," he said desperately, "do you want to hear me propose to her? For I've reached the point where if I don't propose to Bettina soon, I'll —I'll propose to somebody. You'd better be warned in time. It might be you or Miss Aggie."

I weakened at that. The Lord never saw fit to send me a man I could care enough about to marry, or one who cared enough about me, but I couldn't look at the boy's face and not be sorry for him.

"What do you want me to do?" I asked.

"Come for a walk with us," he begged. "Then sprain your ankle or get tired, I don't care which. Tell us to go on and come back for you later. Do you see? You can sit down by the road somewhere."

"I won't lie," I said firmly. "If I really get tired I'll say so. If I don't —"

"You will." He was gleeful. "We'll walk until you do! You see it's like this, Miss Lizzie. Bettina was all for me, in spite of our differing on religion and politics and —"

"I know all about your differences," I put in hastily.

"Until a new chap came to town —a fellow named Ellis. Runs a sporty car and has every girl in the town lashed to the mast. He's a novelty and I'm not. So far I have kept him away from Bettina, but at any time they may meet, and it will be one-two-three with me."

I am not defending my conduct; I am only explaining. Eliza Bailey herself would have done what I did under the circumstances. I went for a walk with Bettina and Jasper shortly after my talk with Jasper, leaving Tish with the evening paper and Aggie inhaling a cubeb cigarette, her hay fever having threatened a return. And what is more, I tired within three blocks of the house, where I saw a grassy bank beside the road.

Bettina wished to stay with me, but I said, in obedience to Jasper's eyes, that I liked to sit alone and listen to the crickets, and for them to go on. The last I saw of them Jasper had drawn Bettina's arm through his and was walking beside her with his head bent, talking. I sat for perhaps fifteen minutes and was growing uneasy about dew and my rheumatism when I heard footsteps and, looking up, I saw Aggie coming toward me. She was not surprised to see me and addressed me coldly.

"I thought as much!" she said. "I expected better of you, Lizzie. That boy asked me and I refused. I dare say he asked Tish also. For you, who pride yourself on your strength of mind —"

"I was tired," I said. "I was to sprain my ankle," she observed sarcastically. "I just thought as I was sitting there alone —"

"Where's Tish?"

"A young man named Ellis came and took her out for a ride," said Aggie. "He couldn't take us both, as the car holds only two."

I got up and stared at Aggie in the twilight. "You come straight home with me, Aggie Pilkington," I said sternly.

"But what about Bettina and Jasper?"

"Let 'em alone," I said; "they're safe enough. What we need to keep an eye on is Letitia Carberry and her Cousin Angeline's legacy."

But I was too late. Tish and Mr. Ellis whirled up to the door at half-past eight and Tish did not even notice that Bettina was absent. She took off her veil and said something about Mr. Ellis's having heard a grinding in the differential of her car that afternoon and that he suspected a chip of steel in the gears. They went out together to the garage, leaving Aggie and me staring at each other. Mr. Ellis was carrying a box of tools.

Jasper and Bettina returned shortly after, and even in the dusk I knew things had gone badly for him. He sat on the steps, looking out across the dark lawn, and spoke in monosyllables. Bettina, however, was very gay.

It was evident that Bettina had decided not to take her Presbyterianism into the Episcopal fold. And although I am a Presbyterian myself I felt sorry.

Tish and Mr. Ellis came round to the porch about ten o'clock and he was presented to Bettina. From that moment there was no question in my mind as to how affairs were going, or in Jasper's either. He refused to move and sat doggedly on the steps, but he took little part in the conversation.

Mr. Ellis was a good talker, especially about himself.

"You'll be glad to know," he said to me, "that I've got this race matter fixed up finally. In two weeks from now we'll have a little excitement here."

I looked toward Tish, but she said nothing.

"Excitement is where I live," said Mr. Ellis. "If I don't find any waiting I make it."

"If you are looking for excitement, we'll have to find you some," Jasper said pointedly.

Mr. Ellis only laughed. "Don't put yourself out, dear boy," he said. "I have enough for present necessities. If you think an automobile race is an easy thing to manage, try it. Every man who drives a racing-car has a *coloratura* soprano beaten to death for temperament. Then every racing-car has quirky spells; there's the local committee to propitiate; the track to look after; and if that isn't enough, there's the promotion itself, the advertising. That's my stunt-the advertising."

"It's a wonderful business, isn't it?" asked Bettina. "To take a mile or so of dirt track and turn it into a sort of stage, with drama every minute and sometimes tragedy!"

"Wait a moment," said Mr. Ellis; "I want to put that down. I'll use it somewhere in the advertising." He wrote by the light of a match, while we all sat rather stunned by both his personality and his alertness. "Everything's grist that comes to my mill. I suppose you all remember when I completed the speedway at Indianapolis and had the Governor of Indiana lay a gold brick at the entrance? Great stunt that! But the best part of that story never reached the public."

Bettina was leaning forward, all ears and thrills. "What was that?" she asked.

"I had the gold brick stolen that night-did it myself and carried the brick away in my pocket-only gold-plated, you know. Cost eight or nine dollars, all told, and brought a million dollars in advertising. But the papers were sore about some passes and wouldn't use the story. Too bad we can't use the brick here. Still have it kicking about somewhere."

It was then, I think, that Jasper yawned loudly, apologized, said good-night and lounged away across the lawn. Bettina hardly knew he was going. She was bending forward, her chin in her palms, listening to Mr. Ellis tell about a driver in a motor race breaking his wrist cranking a car, and how he-Ellis-had jumped into the car and driven it to victory. Even Aggie was enthralled. It seemed as if, in the last hour, the great world of stress and keen wits and endeavor and mad speed had sat down on our door-step.

As Tish said when we were going up to bed, why shouldn't Mr. Ellis brag? He had something to brag about.

IV

Although I felt quite sure that Tish had put up the prize money for Mr. Ellis, I could not be certain. And Tish's attitude at that time did not invite inquiry. She took long rides daily with the Ellis man in his gray car, and I have reason to believe that their objective point was always the same-the race-track.

Mr. Ellis was the busiest man in Morris Valley. In the daytime he was superintending putting the track in condition, writing what he called "promotion stuff," securing entries and forming the center of excited groups at the drug store and one or other of the two public garages. In the evenings he was generally to be found at Bettina's feet.

Jasper did not come over any more. He sauntered past, evening after evening, very much white-flanneled and carrying a tennis racket. And once or twice he took out his old racing-car, and later shot by the house with a flutter of veils and a motor coat beside him.

Aggie was exceedingly sorry for him, and even went the length of having the cook bake a chocolate cake and put it on the window sill to cool. It had, however, no perceptible effect, except to draw from Mr. Ellis, who had been round at the garage looking at Jasper's old racer, a remark that he was exceedingly fond of cake, and if he were urged —

That was, I believe, a week before the race. The big city papers had taken it up, according to Mr. Ellis, and entries were pouring in.

"That's the trouble on a small track," he said —"we can't crowd 'em. A dozen cars will be about the limit. Even with using the cattle pens for repair pits we can't look after more than a dozen. Did I tell you Heckert had entered his Bonor?"

"No!" we exclaimed. As far as Aggie and I were concerned, the Bonor might have been a new sort of dog.

"Yes, and Johnson his Sampler. It's going to be some race-eh, what!"

Jasper sauntered over that evening, possibly a late result of the cake, after all. He greeted us affably, as if his defection of the past week had been merely incidental, and sat down on the steps.

"I've been thinking, Ellis," he said, "that I'd like to enter my car."

"What!" said Ellis. "Not that —"

"My racer. I'm not much for speed, but there's a sort of feeling in the town that the locality ought to be represented. As I'm the only owner of a speed car —"

"Speed car!" said Ellis, and chuckled. "My dear boy, we've got Heckert with his ninety-horse-power Bonor!"

"Never heard of him." Jasper lighted a cigarette. "Anyhow, what's that to me? I don't like to race. I've got less speed mania than any owner of a race car you ever met. But the honor of the town seems to demand a sacrifice, and I'm it."

"You can try out for it anyhow," said Ellis. "I don't think you'll make it; but, if you qualify, all right. But don't let any other town people, from a sense of mistaken local pride, enter a street roller or a traction engine."

Jasper colored, but kept his temper.

Aggie, however, spoke up indignantly. "Mr. McCutcheon's car was a very fine racer when it was built."

"*De mortuis nil nisi bonum,*" remarked Mr. Ellis, and getting up said good-night.

Jasper sat on the steps and watched him disappear. Then he turned to Tish.

"Miss Letitia," he said, "do you think you are wise to drive that racer of his the way you have been doing?"

Aggie gave a little gasp and promptly sneezed, as she does when she is excited.

"I?" said Tish.

"You!" he smiled. "Not that I don't admire your courage. I do. But the other day, now, when you lost a tire and went into the ditch —"

"Tish!" from Aggie.

"—you were fortunate. But when a racer turns over the results are not pleasant."

"As a matter of fact," said Tish coldly, "it was a wheat-field, not a ditch."

Jasper got up and threw away his cigarette. "Well, our departing friend is not the only one who can quote Latin," he said. *"Verbum sap.*, Miss Tish. Good-night, everybody. Good-night, Bettina."

Bettina's good-night was very cool. As I went up to bed that night, I thought Jasper's chances poor indeed. As for Tish, I endeavored to speak a few word of remonstrance to her, but she opened her Bible and began to read the lesson for the day and I was obliged to beat a retreat.

It was that night that Aggie and I, having decided the situation was beyond us, wrote a letter to Charlie Sands asking him to come up. Just as I was sealing it Bettina knocked and came in. She closed the door behind her and stood looking at us both.

"Where is Miss Tish?" she asked.

"Reading her Bible," I said tartly. "When Tish is up to some mischief, she generally reads an extra chapter or two as atonement."

"Is she-is she always like this?"

"The trouble is," explained Aggie gently, "Miss Letitia is an enthusiast. Whatever she does, she does with all her heart."

"I feel so responsible," said Bettina. "I try to look after her, but what can I do?"

"There is only one thing to do," I assured her —"let her alone. If she wants to fly, let her fly; if she wants to race, let her race-and trust in Providence."

"I'm afraid Providence has its hands full!" said Bettina, and went to bed.

For the remainder of that week nothing was talked of in Morris Valley but the approaching race. Some of Eliza Bailey's friends gave fancy-work parties for us, which Aggie and I attended. Tish refused, being now openly at the race-track most of the day. Morris Valley was much excited. Should it wear motor clothes, or should it follow the example of the English Derby and the French races and wear its afternoon reception dress with white kid gloves? Or-it being warm-wouldn't lingerie clothes and sunshades be most suitable?

Some of the gossip I retailed to Jasper, oil-streaked and greasy, in the Baileys' garage where he was working over his car.

"Tell 'em to wear mourning," he said pessimistically. "There's always a fatality or two. If there wasn't a fair chance of it nothing would make 'em sit for hours watching dusty streaks going by."

The race was scheduled for Wednesday. On Sunday night the cars began to come in. On Monday Tish took us all, including Bettina, to the track. There were half a dozen tents in the oval, one of them marked with a huge red cross.

"Hospital tent," said Tish calmly. We even, on permission from Mr. Ellis, went round the track. At one spot Tish stopped the car and got out.

"Nail," she said briefly. "It's been a horse-racing track for years, and we've gathered a bushel of horse-shoe nails."

Aggie and I said nothing, but we looked at each other. Tish had said "we." Evidently Cousin Angeline's legacy was not going into a mortgage.

The fair-grounds were almost ready. Peanut and lunch stands had sprung up everywhere. The oval, save by the tents and the repair pits, was marked off into parking-spaces numbered on tall banners. Groups of dirty men in overalls, carrying machine wrenches, small boys with buckets of water, onlookers round the tents and track-rollers made the place look busy and interesting. Some of the excitement, I confess, got into my blood. Tish, on the contrary, was calm and businesslike. We were sorry we had sent for Charlie Sands. She no longer went out in Mr. Ellis's car, and that evening she went back to the kitchen and made a boiled salad dressing.

We were all deceived.

Charlie Sands came the next morning. He was on the veranda reading a paper when we got down to breakfast. Tish's face was a study.

"Who sent for you?" she demanded.

"Sent for me! Why, who would send for me? I'm here to write up the race. I thought, if you haven't been out to the track, we'd go out this morning."

"We've been out," said Tish shortly, and we went in to breakfast. Once or twice during the meal I caught her eye on me and on Aggie and she was short with us both. While she was upstairs I had a word with Charlie Sands.

"Well," he said, "what is it this time? Is she racing?"

"Worse than that," I replied. "I think she's backing the thing!"

"No!"

"With her cousin Angeline's legacy." With that I told him about our meeting Mr. Ellis and the whole story. He listened without a word.

"So that's the situation," I finished. "He has her hypnotized, Charlie. What's more, I shouldn't be surprised to see her enter the race under an assumed name."

Charlie Sands looked at the racing list in the Morris Valley Sun.

"Good cars all of them," he said. "She's not here among the drivers, unless she's —Who are these drivers anyhow? I never heard of any of them."

"It's a small race," I suggested. "I dare say the big men —"

"Perhaps." He put away his paper and got up. "I'll just wander round the town for an hour or two, Aunt Lizzie," he said. "I believe there's a nigger in this woodpile and I'm a right nifty little nigger-chaser."

When he came back about noon, however, he looked puzzled. I drew him aside.

"It seems on the level," he said. "It's so darned open it makes me suspicious. But she's back of it all right. I got her bank on the long-distance 'phone."

We spent that afternoon at the track, with the different cars doing what I think they called "trying out heats." It appeared that a car, to qualify, must do a certain distance in a certain time. It grew monotonous after a while. All but one entry qualified and Jasper just made it. The best showing was made by the Bonor car, according to Charlie Sands.

Jasper came to our machine when it was over, smiling without any particular good cheer.

"I've made it and that's all," he said. "I've got about as much chance as a watermelon at a colored picnic. I'm being slaughtered to make a Roman holiday."

"If you feel that way why do you do it?" demanded Bettina coldly. "If you go in expecting to slaughtered —"

He was leaning on the side of the car and looked up at her with eyes that made my heart ache, they were so wretched.

"What does it matter?" he said. "I'll probably trail in at the last, sound in wind and limb. If I don't, what does it matter?"

He turned and left us at that, and I looked at Bettina. She had her lips shut tight and was blinking hard. I wished that Jasper had looked back.

V

Charlie Sands announced at dinner that he intended to spend the night at the track.

Tish put down her fork and looked at him. "Why?" she demanded.

"I'm going to help the boy next door watch his car," he said calmly. "Nothing against your friend Mr. Ellis, Aunt Tish, but some enemy of true sport might take a notion in the night to slip a dope pill into the mouth of friend Jasper's car and have her go to sleep on the track to-morrow."

We spent a quiet evening. Mr. Ellis was busy, of course, and so was Jasper. The boy came to the house to get Charlie Sands and, I suppose, for a word with Bettina, for when he saw us all on the porch he looked, as you may say, thwarted.

When Charlie Sands had gone up for his pajamas and dressing-gown, Jasper stood looking up at us.

"Oh, Association of Chaperons!" he said, "is it permitted that my lady walk to the gate with me-alone?"

"I am not your lady," flashed Bettina.

"You've nothing to say about that," he said recklessly. "I've selected you; you can't help it. I haven't claimed that you have selected me."

"Anyhow, I don't wish to go to the gate," said Bettina.

He went rather white at that, and Charlie Sands coming down at that moment with a pair of red-and-white pajamas under his arm and a toothbrush sticking out of his breast pocket, romance, as Jasper said later in referring to it, "was buried in Sands."

Jasper went up to Bettina and held out his hand. "You'll wish me luck, won't you?"

"Of course." She took his hand. "But I think you're a bit of a coward, Jasper!"

He eyed her. "Coward!" he said. "I'm the bravest man you know. I'm doing a thing I'm scared to death to do!"

The race was to begin at two o'clock in the afternoon. There were small races to be run first, but the real event was due at three.

From early in the morning a procession of cars from out of town poured in past Eliza Bailey's front porch, and by noon her cretonne cushions were thick with dust. And not only automobiles came, but hay-wagons, side-bar buggies, delivery carts-anything and everything that could transport the crowd.

At noon Mr. Ellis telephoned Tish that the grand-stand was sold out and that almost all the parking-places that had been reserved were taken. Charlie Sands came home to luncheon with a curious smile on his face.

"How are you betting, Aunt Tish?" he asked.

"Betting!"

"Yes. Has Ellis let you in on the betting?"

"I don't know what you are talking about," Tish said sourly. "Mr. Ellis controls the betting so that it may be done in an orderly manner. I am sure I have nothing to do with it."

"I'd like to bet a little, Charlie," Aggie put in with an eye on Tish. "I'd put all I win on the collection plate on Sunday."

"Very well." Charlie Sands took out his notebook. "On what car and how much?"

"Ten dollars on the Fein. It made the best time at the trial heats."

"I wouldn't if I were you," said Charlie Sands. "Suppose we put it on our young friend next door."

Bettina rather sniffed. "On Jasper!" she exclaimed.

"On Jasper," said Charlie Sands gravely.

Tish, who had hardly heard us, looked up from her plate.

"Bettina is betting," she snapped. "Putting it on the collection plate doesn't help any." But with that she caught Charlie Sands' eye and he winked at her. Tish colored. "Gambling is one thing, clean sport is another," she said hotly.

I believe, however, that whatever Charlie Sands may have suspected, he really knew nothing until the race had started. By that time it was too late to prevent it, and the only way he could think of to avoid getting Tish involved in a scandal was to let it go on.

We went to the track in Tish's car and parked in the oval. Not near the grandstand, however. Tish had picked out for herself a curve at one end of the track which Mr. Ellis had said was the worst bit on the course. "He says," said Tish, as we put the top down and got out the vacuum bottle-oh, yes, Mr. Ellis had sent Tish one as a present—"that if there are any smashups they'll occur here."

Aggie is not a bloodthirsty woman ordinarily, but her face quite lit up.

"Not really!" she said.

"They'll probably turn turtle," said Tish. "There is never a race without a fatality or two. No racer can get any life insurance. Mr. Ellis says four men were killed at the last race he promoted."

"Then I think Mr. Ellis is a murderer," Bettina cried. We all looked at her. She was limp and white and was leaning back among the cushions with her eyes shut. "Why didn't you tell Jasper about this curve?" she demanded of Tish.

But at that moment a pistol shot rang out and the races were on.

The Fein won two of the three small races. Jasper was entered only for the big race. In the interval before the race was on, Jasper went round the track slowly, looking for Bettina. When he saw us he waved, but did not stop. He was number thirteen.

I shall not describe the race. After the first round or two, what with dust in my eyes and my neck aching from turning my head so rapidly, I just sat back and let them spin in front of me.

It was after a dozen laps or so, with number thirteen doing as well as any of them, that Tish was arrested.

Charlie Sands came up beside the car with a gentleman named Atkins, who turned out to be a county detective. Charlie Sands was looking stern and severe, but the detective was rather apologetic.

"This is Miss Carberry," said Charlie Sands. "Aunt Tish, this gentleman wishes to speak to you."

"Come around after the race," Tish observed calmly.

"Miss Carberry," said the detective gently, "I believe you are back of this race, aren't you?"

"What if I am?" demanded Tish.

Charlie Sands put a hand on the detective's arm. "It's like this, Aunt Tish," he said; "you are accused of practicing a short-change game, that's all. This race is sewed up. You employ those racing-cars with drivers at an average of fifty dollars a week. They are hardly worth it, Aunt Tish. I could have got you a better string for twenty-five."

Tish opened her mouth and shut it again without speaking.

"You also control the betting privileges. As you own all the racers you have probably known for a couple of weeks who will win the race. Having made the Fein favorite, you can bet on a Brand or a Bonor, or whatever one you chance to like, and win out. Only I take it rather hard of you, Aunt Tish, not to have let the family in. I'm hard up as the dickens."

"Charlie Sands!" said Tish impressively. "If you are joking—"

"Joking! Did you ever know a county detective to arrest a prominent woman at a race-track as a little jest between friends? There's no joke, Aunt Tish. You've financed a phony race. The permit is taken in your name—L.L. Carberry. Whatever car wins, you and Ellis take the prize money, half the gate receipts, and what you have made out of the betting—"

Tish rose in the machine and held out both her hands to Mr. Atkins.

"Officer, perform your duty," she said solemnly. "Ignorance is no defense and I know it. Where are the handcuffs?"

"We'll not bother about them, Miss Carberry", he said. "If you like I'll get into the car and you can tell me all about it while we watch the race. Which car is to win?"

"I may have been a fool, Mr. County Detective," she said coldly; "but I'm not a knave. I have not bet a dollar on the race."

We were very silent for a time. The detective seemed to enjoy the race very much and ate peanuts out of his pocket. He even bought a red-and-black pennant, with "Morris Valley Races" on it, and fastened it to the car. Charlie Sands, however, sat with his arms folded, stiff and severe.

Once Tish bent forward and touched his arm.

"You-you don't think it will get in the papers, do you?" she quavered.

Charlie Sands looked at her with gloom. "I shall have to send it myself, Aunt Tish," he said; "it is my duty to my paper. Even my family pride, hurt to the quick and quivering as it is, must not interfere with my duty."

It was Bettina who suggested a way out-Bettina, who had sat back as pale as Tish and heard that her Mr. Ellis was, as Charlie Sands said later, as crooked as a pretzel.

"But Jasper was not-not subsidized," she said. "If he wins, it's all right, isn't it?"

The county detective turned to her.

"Jasper?" he said.

"A young man who lives here." Bettina colored.

"He is-not to be suspected?"

"Certainly not," said Bettina haughtily; "he is above suspicion. Besides, he-he and Mr. Ellis are not friends."

Well, the county detective was no fool. He saw the situation that minute, and smiled when he offered Bettina a peanut. "Of course," he said cheerfully, "if the race is won by a Morris Valley man, and not by one of the Ellis cars, I don't suppose the district attorney would care to do anything about it. In fact," he said, smiling at Bettina, "I don't know that I'd put it up to the district attorney at all. A warning to Ellis would get him out of the State."

It was just at that moment that car number thirteen, coming round the curve, skidded into the field, threw out both Jasper McCutcheon and his mechanician, and after standing on two wheels for an appreciable moment of time, righted herself, panting, with her nose against a post.

Jasper sat up almost immediately and caught at his shoulder. The mechanician was stunned. He got up, took a step or two and fell down, weak with fright.

I do not recall very distinctly what happened next. We got out of the machine, I remember, and Bettina was cutting off Jasper's sweater with Charlie Sands' penknife, and crying as she did it. And Charlie Sands was trying to prevent Jasper from getting back into his car, while Jasper was protesting that he could win in two or more laps and that he could drive with one hand-he'd only broken his arm.

The crowd had gathered round us, thick. Suddenly they drew back, and in a sort of haze I saw Tish in Jasper's car, with Aggie, as white as death, holding to Tish's sleeve and begging her not to get in. The next moment Tish let in the clutch of the racer and Aggie took a sort of flying leap and landed beside her in the mechanician's seat.

Charlie Sands saw it when I did, but we were both too late. Tish was crossing the ditch into the track again, and the moment she struck level ground she put up the gasoline.

It was just then that Aggie fell out, landing, as I have said before, in a pile of sand. Tish said afterward that she never missed her. She had just discovered that this was not Jasper's old car, which she knew something about, but a new racer with the old hood and seat put on in order to fool Mr. Ellis. She didn't know a thing about it.

Well, you know the rest-how Tish, trying to find how the gears worked, side-swiped the Bonor car and threw it off the field and out of the race; how, with the grandstand going crazy, she skidded off the track into the field, turned completely round twice, and found herself on the track again facing the way she wanted to go; how, at the last lap, she threw a tire and, without cutting down her speed, bumped home the winner, with the end of her tongue nearly bitten off and her spine fairly driven up into her skull.

All this is well known now, as is also the fact that Mr. Ellis disappeared from the judges' stand after a word or two with Mr. Atkins, and was never seen at Morris Valley again.

Tish came out of the race ahead by half the gate money-six thousand dollars-by a thousand dollars from concessions, and a lame back that she kept all winter. Even deducting the twenty-five hundred she had put up, she was forty-five hundred dollars ahead, not counting the prize money. Charlie Sand brought the money from the track that night, after having paid off Mr. Ellis's racing-string and given Mr. Atkins a small present. He took over the prize money to Jasper and came back with it, Jasper maintaining that it belonged to Tish, and that he had only raced for the honor of Morris Valley. For some time the money went begging, but it settled itself naturally enough, Tish giving it to Jasper in the event of-but that came later.

On the following evening-Bettina, in the pursuit of learning to cook, having baked a chocolate cake-we saw Jasper, with his arm in a sling, crossing the side lawn.

Jasper stopped at the foot of the steps. "I see a chocolate cake cooling on the kitchen porch," he said. "Did you order it, Miss Lizzie?"

I shook my head.

"Miss Tish? Miss Aggie?"

"I ordered it," said Bettina defiantly —"or rather I baked it."

"And you did that, knowing what it entailed? He was coming up the steps slowly and with care.

"What does it entail?" demanded Bettina.

"Me."

"Oh, that!" said Bettina. "I knew that."

Jasper threw his head back and laughed. Then: —

"Will the Associated Chaperons," he said, "turn their backs?"

"Not at all," I began stiffly. "If I —"

"She baked it herself!" said Jasper exultantly. "One-two. When I say three I shall kiss Bettina."

And I have every reason to believe he carried out his threat.

Eliza Bailey forwarded me this letter from London where Bettina had sent it to her: —

> *Dearest Mother*: I hope you are coming home soon. I really think you should. Aunt Lizzie is here and she brought two friends, and, mother, I feel so responsible for them! Aunt Lizzie is sane enough, if somewhat cranky; but Miss Tish is almost more than I can manage —I never know what she is going to do next-and I am worn out with chaperoning her. And Miss Aggie, although she is very sweet, is always smoking cubeb cigarettes for hay fever, and it looks terrible! The neighbors do not know they are cubeb, and, anyhow, that's a habit, mother. And yesterday Miss Tish was arrested, and ran a motor race and won it, and to-day she is knitting a stocking and reciting the Twenty-third Psalm. Please, mother, I think you should come home.
>
> Lovingly, BETTINA.
>
> P.S. I think I shall marry Jasper after all. He says he likes the Presbyterian service.

I looked up from reading Eliza's letter. Tish was knitting quietly and planning to give the money back to the town in the shape of a library, and Aggie was holding a cubeb cigarette to her nose. Down on the tennis court Jasper and Bettina were idly batting a ball round.

"I'm glad the Ellis man did not get her," said Aggie. And then, after a sneeze, "How Jasper reminds me of Mr. Wiggins."

The library did not get the money after all. Tish sent it, as a wedding present, to Bettina.

Like a Wolf on the Fold

I

Aggie has always been in the habit of observing the anniversary of Mr. Wiggins's death. Aggie has the anniversary habit, anyhow, and her life is a succession: of small feast-days, on which she wears mental crape or wedding garments-depending on the occasion. Tish and I always remember these occasions appropriately, sending flowers on the anniversaries of the passing away of Aggie's parents; grandparents; a niece who died in birth; her cousin, Sarah Webb, who married a missionary and was swallowed whole by a large snake, —except her shoes, which the reptile refused and of which Aggie possesses the right, given her by the stricken husband; and, of course, Mr. Wiggins.

For Mr. Wiggins Tish and I generally send the same things each year-Tish a wreath of autumn foliage and I a sheaf of wheat tied with a lavender ribbon. The program seldom varies. We drive to the cemetery in the afternoon and Aggie places the sheaf and the wreath on Mr. Wiggins's last resting-place, after first removing the lavender ribbon, of which she makes cap bows through the year and an occasional pin-cushion or fancy-work bag; then home to chicken and waffles, which had been Mr. Wiggins's favorite meal. In the evening Charlie Sands generally comes in and we play a rubber or two of bridge.

On the thirtieth anniversary of Mr. Wiggins's falling off a roof and breaking his neck, Tish was late in arriving, and I found Aggie sitting alone, dressed in black, with a tissue-paper bundle in her lap. I put my sheaf on the table and untied my bonnet-strings.

"Where's Tish?" I asked.

"Not here yet."

Something in Aggie's tone made me look at her. She was eyeing the bundle in her lap.

"I got a paler shade of ribbon this time," I said, seeing she made no comment on the sheaf. "It's a better color for me if you're going to make my Christmas present out of it this year again. Where's Tish's wreath?"

"Here." Aggie pointed dispiritedly to the bundle in her lap and went on rocking.

"That! That's no wreath."

In reply Aggie lifted the tissue paper and shook out, with hands that trembled with indignation, a lace-and-linen centerpiece. She held it up before me and we eyed each other over it. Both of us understood.

"Tish is changed, Lizzie," Aggie said hollowly. "Ask her for bread these days and she gives you a Cluny-lace fandangle. On mother's anniversary she sent me a set of doilies; and when Charlie Sands was in the hospital with appendicitis she took him a pair of pillow shams. It's that Syrian!"

Both of us knew. We had seen Tish's apartment change from a sedate and spinsterly retreat to a riot of lace covers on the mantel, on the backs of chairs, on the stands, on the pillows-everywhere. We had watched her Marseilles bedspreads give way to hem-stitched covers, with bolsters to match. We had seen Tish go through a cold winter clad in a succession of sleazy silk kimonos instead of her flannel dressing-gown; terrible kimonos-green and yellow and red and pink, that looked like fruit salads and were just as heating.

"It's that dratted Syrian!" cried Aggie-and at that Tish came in. She stood inside the door and eyed us.

"What about him?" she demanded. "If I choose to take a poor starving Christian youth and assist him by buying from him what I need-what I need! —that's my affair, isn't it? Tufik was starving and I took him in."

"He took you in, all right!" Aggie sniffed. "A great, mustached, dirty, palavering foreigner, who's probably got a harem at home and no respect for women!"

Tish glanced at my sheaf and at the centerpiece. She was dressed as she always dressed on Mr. Wiggins's day-in black; but she had a new lace collar with a jabot, and we knew where she had got it. She saw our eyes on it and she had the grace to flush.

"Once for all," she snapped, "I intend to look after this unfortunate Syrian! If my friends object, I shall be deeply sorry; but, so far as I care, they may object until they are purple in the face and their tongues hang out. I've been sending my money to foreign missions long enough; I'm doing my missionary work at home now."

"He'll marry you!" This from Aggie.

Tish ignored her. "His father is an honored citizen of Beirut, of the nobility. The family is impoverished, being Christian, and grossly imposed on by the Turks. Tufik speaks French and English as well as Mohammedan. They offered him a high government position if he would desert the Christian faith; but he refused firmly. He came to this country for religious freedom; at any moment they may come after him and take him back."

A glint of hope came to me. I made a mental note to write to the mayor, or whatever they call him over there, and tell him where he could locate his wandering boy.

"He loves the God of America," said Tish.

"Money!" Aggie jeered.

"And he is so pathetic, so grateful! I told Hannah at noon to-day—that's what delayed me-to give him his lunch. He was starving; I thought we'd never fill him. And when it was over, he stooped in the sweetest way, while she was gathering up the empty dishes, and kissed her hand. It was touching!"

"Very!" I said dryly. "What did Hannah do?"

"She's a fool! She broke a cup on his head."

Mr. Wiggins's anniversary was not a success. Part of this was due to Tish, who talked of Tufik steadily-of his youth; of the wonderful bargains she secured from him; of his belief that this was the land of opportunity-Aggie sniffed; of his familiarity with the Bible and Biblical places; of the search the Turks were making for him. The atmosphere was not cleared by Aggie's taking the Cluny-lace centerpiece to the cemetery and placing it, with my sheaf, on Mr. Wiggins's grave.

As we got into Tish's machine to go back, Aggie was undeniably peevish. She caught cold, too, and was sneezing-as she always does when she is irritated or excited.

"Where to?" asked Tish from the driving-seat, looking straight ahead and pulling on her gloves. From where we sat we could still see the dot of white on the grass that was the centerpiece.

"Back to the house," Aggie snapped, "to have some chicken and waffles and Tufik for dinner!"

Tish drove home in cold silence. As well as we could tell from her back, she was not so much indignant as she was determined. Thus we do not believe that she willfully drove over every rut and thank-you-ma'am on the road, scattering us generously over the tonneau, and finally, when Aggie, who was the lighter, was tossed against the top and sprained her neck, eliciting a protest from us. She replied in an abstracted tone, which showed where her mind was.

"It would be rougher on a camel," she said absently. "Tufik was telling me the other day —"

Aggie had got her head straight by that time and was holding it with both hands to avoid jarring. She looked goaded and desperate; and, as she said afterward, the thing slipped out before she knew she was more than thinking it.

"Oh, damn Tufik!" she said.

Fortunately at that moment we blew out a tire and apparently Tish did not hear her. While I was jacking up the car and Tish was getting the key of the toolbox out of her stocking, Aggie sat sullenly in her place and watched us.

"I suppose," she gibed, "a camel never blows out a tire!"

"It might," Tish said grimly, "if it heard an oath from the lips of a middle-aged Sunday-school teacher!"

We ate Mr. Wiggins's anniversary dinner without any great hilarity. Aggie's neck was very stiff and she had turned in the collar of her dress and wrapped flannels wrung out of lamp oil round it. When she wished to address either Tish or myself she held her head rigid and turned her whole body in her chair; and when she felt a sneeze coming on she clutched wildly at her head with both hands as if she expected it to fly off.

Tufik was not mentioned, though twice Tish got as far as Tu — and then thought better of it; but her mind was on him and we knew it. She worked the conversation round to Bible history and triumphantly demanded whether we knew that Sodom and Gomorrah are towns to-day, and that a street-car line is contemplated to them from some place or other-it developed later that she meant Tyre and Sidon. Once she suggested that Aggie's sideboard needed new linens, but after a look at Aggie's rigid head she let it go at that.

No one was sorry when, with dinner almost over, and Aggie lifting her ice-cream spoon straight up in front of her and opening her mouth with a sort of lockjaw movement, the bell rang. We thought it was Charlie Sands. It was not. Aggie faced the doorway and I saw her eyes widen. Tish and I turned.

A boy stood in the doorway —a shrinking, timid, brown-eyed young Oriental, very dark of skin, very white of teeth, very black of hair —a slim youth of eighteen, possibly twenty, in a shabby blue suit, broken shoes, and a celluloid collar. Twisting between nervous brown fingers, not as clean as they might have been, was a tissue-paper package.

"My friends!" he said, and smiled.

Tish is an extraordinary woman. She did not say a word. She sat still and let the smile get in its work. Its first effect was on Aggie's neck, which she forgot. Tufik's timid eyes rested for a moment on Tish and brightened. Then like a benediction they turned to mine, and came to a stop on Aggie. He took a step farther into the room.

"My friend's friend are my friend," he said. "America is my friend-this so great God's country!"

Aggie put down her ice-cream spoon and closed her mouth, which had been open.

"Come in, Tufik," said Tish; "and I am sure Miss Pilkington would like you to sit down."

Tufik still stood with his eyes fixed on Aggie, twisting his package.

"My friend has said," he observed-he was quite calm and divinely trustful —"My friend has said that this is for Miss Pilk a sad day. My friend is my mother; I have but her and God. Unless-but perhaps I have two new friend also-no?"

"Of course we are your friends," said Aggie, feeling for the table-bell with her foot. "We are-aren't we, Lizzie?"

Tufik turned and looked at me wistfully. It came over me then what an awful thing it must be to be so far from home and knowing nobody, and having to wear trousers and celluloid collars instead of robes and turbans, and eat potatoes and fried things instead of olives and figs and dates, and to be in danger of being taken back and made into a Mohammedan and having to keep a harem.

"Certainly," I assented. "If you are good we will be your friends."

He flashed a boyish smile at me.

"I am good," he said calmly —"as the angels I am good. I have here a letter from a priest. I give it to you. Read!"

He got a very dirty envelope from his pocket and brought it round the table to me. "See!" he said. "The priest says: 'Of all my children Tufik lies next my heart.'"

He held the letter out to me; but it looked as if it had been copied from an Egyptian monument and was about as legible as an outbreak of measles.

"This," he said gently, pointing, "is the priest's blessing. I carry it ever. It brings me friends." He put the paper away and drew a long breath; then surveyed us all with shining eyes. "It has brought me you."

We were rather overwhelmed. Aggie's maid having responded to the bell, Aggie ordered ice cream for Tufik and a chair drawn to the table; but the chair Tufik refused with a little, smiling bow.

"It is not right that I sit," he said. "I stand in the presence of my three mothers. But first —I forget-my gift! For the sadness, Miss Pilk!"

He held out the tissue-paper package and Aggie opened it. Tufik's gift proved to be a small linen doily, with a Cluny-lace border!

We were gone from that moment —I know it now, looking back. Gone! We were lost the moment Tufik stood in the doorway, smiling and bowing. Tish saw us going; and with the calmness of the lost sat there nibbling cake and watching us through her spectacles-and raised not a hand.

Aggie looked at the doily and Tufik looked at her.

"That's —that's really very nice of you," said Aggie. "I thank you."

Tufik came over and stood beside her.

"I give with my heart," he said shyly. "I have had nobody-in all so large this country-nobody! And now —I have you!" Aggie saw-but too late. He bent over and touched his lips to her hands. "The Bible says: 'To him that overcometh I will give the morning star!' I have overcometh-ah, so much! —the sea; the cold, wet England; the Ellis Island; the hunger; the aching of one who has no love, no money! And now —I have the morning star!"

He looked at us all three at once-Charlie Sands said this was impossible, until he met Tufik. Aggie was fairly palpitant and Tish was smug, positively smug. As for me, I roused with a start to find myself sugaring my ice cream.

Charlie Sands was delayed that night. He came in about nine o'clock and found Tufik telling us about his home and his people and the shepherds on the hills about Damascus and the olive trees in sunlight. We half-expected Tufik to adopt Charlie Sands as a father; but he contented himself with a low Oriental salute, and shortly after he bowed himself away.

Charlie Sands stood looking after him and smiling to himself. "Pretty smooth boy, that!" he said.

"Smooth nothing!" Tish snapped, getting the bridge score. "He's a sad-hearted and lonely boy; and we are going to do the kindest thing-we are going to help him to help himself."

"Oh, he'll help himself all right!" observed Charlie Sands. "But, since his people are Christians, I wish you'd tell me how he knows so much about the inside of a harem!"

Seeing that comment annoyed us, he ceased, and we fell to our bridge game; but more than once his eye fell on Aggie's doily, and he muttered something about the Assyrian coming down like a wolf on the fold.

II

The problem of Tufik's future was a pressing one. Tish called a meeting of the three of us next morning, and we met at her house. We found her reading about Syria in the encyclopædia, while spread round her on chairs and tables were numbers of silk kimonos, rolls of crocheted lace, shirt-waist patterns, and embroidered linens.

Hannah let us in. She looked surly and had a bandage round her head, a sure sign of trouble-Hannah always referring a pain in her temper to her ear or her head or her teeth. She clutched my arm in the hall and held me back.

"I'm going to poison him!" she said. "Miss Lizzie, that little snake goes or I go!"

"I'm ashamed of you, Hannah!" I replied sternly. "If out of the breadth of her charity Miss Tish wishes to assist a fellow man —"

Hannah reeled back and freed my arm.

"My God!" she whispered. "You too!"

I am very fond of Hannah, who has lived with Tish for many years; but I had small patience with her that morning.

"I cannot see how it concerns you, anyhow, Hannah," I observed severely.

Hannah put her apron to her eyes and sniffled into it.

"Oh, you can't, can't you!" she wailed. "Don't I give him half his meals, with him soft-soapin' Miss Tish till she can't see for suds? Ain't I fallin' over him mornin', noon, and night, and the postman telling all over the block he's my steady company-that snip that's not eighteen yet? And don't I do the washin'? And will you look round the place and count the things I've got to do up every week? And don't he talk to me in that lingo of his, so I don't know whether he's askin' for a cup of coffee or insultin' me?"

I patted Hannah on the arm. After all, none of the exaltation of a good deed upheld Hannah as it sustained us.

"We are going to help him help himself, Hannah," I said kindly. "He hasn't found himself. Be gentle with him. Remember he comes from the land of the Bible."

"Humph!" said Hannah, who reads the newspapers. "So does the plague!"

The problem we had set ourselves we worked out that morning. As Tish said, the boy ought to have light work, for the Syrians are not a laboring people.

"Their occupation is-er-mainly pastoral," she said, with the authority of the encyclopædia. "Grazing their herds and gathering figs and olives. If we knew some one who needed a shepherd —"

Aggie opposed the shepherd idea, however. As she said, and with reason, the climate is too rigorous. "It's all well enough in Syria," she said, "where they have no cold weather; but he'd take his death of pneumonia here."

We put the shepherd idea reluctantly aside. My own notion of finding a camel for him to look after was negatived by Tish at once, and properly enough I realized.

"The only camels are in circuses," she said, "and our duty to the boy is moral as well as physical. Circuses are dens of immorality. Of course the Syrians are merchants, and we might get him work in a store. But then again-what chance has he of rising? Once a clerk, always a clerk." She looked round at the chairs and tables, littered with the contents of Tufik's pasteboard suitcase, which lay empty at her feet. "And there is nothing to canvassing from door to door. Look at these exquisite things! —and he cannot sell them. Nobody buys. He says he never gets inside a house door. If you had seen his face when I bought a kimono from him!"

At eleven o'clock, having found nothing in the "Help Wanted" column to fit Tufik's case, Tish called up Charlie Sands and offered Tufik as a reporter, provided he was given no nightwork. But Charlie Sands said it was impossible-that the editors and owners of the paper were always putting on their sons and relatives, and that when there was a vacancy the big advertisers got it. Tish insisted-she suggested that Tufik could run an Arabian column, like the German one, and bring in a lot of new subscribers. But Charlie Sands stood firm.

At noon Tufik came. We heard a skirmish at the door and Hannah talking between her teeth.

"She's out," she said.

"Well, I think she is not out," in Tufik's soft tones.

"You'll not get in."

"Ah, but my toes are in. See, my foot wishes to enter!" Then something soft, coaxing, infinitely wistful, in Arabian followed by a slap. The next moment Hannah, in tears, rushed back to the kitchen. There was no sound from the hallway. No smiling Tufik presented himself in the doorway.

Tish rose in the majesty of wrath. "I could strangle that woman!" she said, and we followed her into the hall.

Tufik was standing inside the door with his arms folded, staring ahead. He took no notice of us.

"Tufik!" Aggie cried, running to him. "Did she-did she dare-Tish, look at his cheek!"

"She is a bad woman!" Tufik said somberly. "I make my little prayer to see Miss Tish, my mother, and she —I kill her!"

We had a hard time apologizing to him for Hanna. Tish got a basin of cold water so he might bathe his face; and Aggie brought a tablespoonful of blackberry cordial, which is soothing. When the poor boy was calmer we met in Tish's bedroom and Tish was quite firm on one point-Hannah must leave!

Now, this I must say in my own defense —I was sorry for Tufik; and it is quite true I bought him a suit and winter flannels and a pair of yellow shoes-he asked for yellow. He said he was homesick for a bit of sunshine, and our so somber garb made him heart-sad. But I would never have dismissed a cook like Hannah for him.

"I shall have to let her go," Tish said. "He is Oriental and passionate. He has said he will kill her-and he'll do it. They hold life very lightly."

"Humph!" I said. "Very well, Tish, that holding life lightly isn't a Christian trait. It's Mohammedan-every Mohammedan wants to die and go to his heaven, which is a sort of sublimated harem. The boy's probably a Christian by training, but he's a Mohammedan by blood."

Aggie thought my remark immoral and said so. And just then Hannah solved her own problem by stalking into the room with her things on and a suitcase in her hand.

"I'm leaving, Miss Tish!" she said with her eye-rims red. "God knows I never expected to be put out of this place by a dirty dago! You'll find your woolen stockings on the stretchers, and you've got an appointment with the dentist tomorrow morning at ten. And when that little blackguard has sucked you dry, and you want him killed to get rid of him, you'll find me at my sister's."

She picked up her suitcase and Tish flung open the door. "You're a hard-hearted woman, Hannah Mackintyre!" Tish snapped. "Your sister can't keep you. You'll have to work."

Hannah turned in the doorway and sneered at the three of us.

"Oh, no!" she said. "I'm going to hunt up three soft-headed old maids and learn to kiss their hands and tell 'em I have nobody but them and God!"

She slammed out at that, leaving us in a state of natural irritation. But our rage soon faded. Tufik was not in the parlor; and Tish, tiptoeing back, reported that he was in the kitchen and was mixing up something in a bowl.

"He's a dear boy!" she said. "He feels responsible for Hannah's leaving and he's getting luncheon! Hannah is a wicked and uncharitable woman!"

> "Man's inhumanity to man,
> Makes countless thousands mourn!"

quoted Aggie softly. From the kitchen came the rhythmic beating of a wooden spoon against the side of a bowl; a melancholy chant-quite archaic, as Tish said-kept time with the spoon, and later a smell of baking flour and the clatter of dishes told us that our meal was progressing.

"'The Syrians,'" read Tish out of her book, "'are a peaceful and pastoral people. They have not changed materially in nineteen centuries, and the traveler in their country finds still the life of Biblical times.' Something's burning!"

Shortly after, Tufik, beaming with happiness and Hannah clearly forgotten, summoned us to the dining-room. Tufik was not a cook. We realized that at once. He had made coffee in the Oriental way-strong enough to float an egg, very sweet and full of grounds; and after a bite of the cakes he had made, Tish remembered the dentist the next day and refused solid food on account of a bad tooth. The cakes were made of lard and flour, without any baking-powder or flavoring, and the tops were sprinkled thick with granulated sugar. Little circles of grease melted out of them on to the plate, and Tufik, wide-eyed with triumph, sweetly wistful over Tish's tooth, humble and joyous in one minute, stood by the cake plate and fed them to us!

I caught Aggie's agonized eye, but there was nothing else to do. Were we not his friends? And had he not made this delicacy for us? On her third cake, however, Aggie luckily turned blue round the mouth and had to go and lie down. This broke up the meal and probably saved my life, though my stomach has never been the same since. Tish says the cakes are probably all right in the Orient, where it is hot and the grease does not get a chance to solidify. She thinks that Tufik is probably a good cook in his own country. But Aggie says that a good many things in the Bible that she never understood are made plain to her if that is what they ate in Biblical times-some of the things they saw in visions, and all that. She dropped asleep on Tish's lounge and distinctly saw Tufik murdering Hannah by forcing one of his cakes down her throat.

The next month was one of real effort. We had planned to go to Panama, and had our passage engaged; but when we broke the news to Tufik he turned quite pale.

"You go-away?" he said wistfully.

"Only for a month," Tish hastened to apologize. "You see, we-we are all very tired, and the Panama Canal —"

"Canal? I know not a canal."

"It is for ships —"

"You go there in a ship?"

"Yes. A canal is a —"

"You go far-in a ship-and I —I stay here?"

"Only for a month," Aggie broke in. "We will leave you enough money to live on; and perhaps when we come back you will have found something to do —"

"For a month," he said brokenly. "I have no friends, no Miss Tish, no Miss Liz, no Miss Pilk. I die!"

He got up and walked to the window. It was Aggie who realized the awful truth. The poor lonely boy was weeping-and Charlie Sands may say what he likes! He was really crying-when he turned, there were large tears on his cheeks. What made it worse was that he was trying to smile.

"I wish you much happiness on the canal," he said. "I am wicked; but my sad heart-it ache that my friends leave me. I am sad! If only my seester —"

That was the first we had known of Tufik's sister, back in Beirut, wearing a veil over her face and making lace for the bazaars. We were to know more.

Well, between getting ready to go to Panama and trying to find something Tufik could do, we were very busy for the next month. Tufik grew reconciled to our going, but he was never cheerful about it; and finding that it pained him we never spoke about it in his presence.

He was with us a great deal. In the morning he would go to Tish, who would give him a list of her friends to see. Then Tish would telephone and make appointments for him, and he would start off hopefully, with his pasteboard suitcase. But he never sold anything-except a shirt-waist pattern to Mrs. Ostermaier, the minister's wife. We took day about giving him his carfare, but this was pauperizing and we knew it. Besides, he was very sensitive and insisted on putting down everything we gave him in a book, to be repaid later when he had made a success.

The allowance idea was mine and it worked well. We figured that, allowing for his washing, — which was not much, as he seemed to prefer the celluloid collar, —he could live in a sort of way on nine dollars a week. We subscribed equally to this; and to save his pride we mailed it to him weekly by check.

His failure to sell his things hurt him to the soul. More than once we caught tears in his eyes. And he was not well-he could not walk any distance at all and he coughed. At last Tish got Charlie Sands to take him to a lung specialist, a stupid person, who said it was a cigarette cough. This was absurd, as Tufik did not smoke.

At last the time came for the Panama trip. Tish called me up the day she packed and asked me to come over.

"I can't. I'm busy, Tish," I said.

She was quite disagreeable. "This is your burden as well as mine," she snapped. "Come over and talk to that wretched boy while I pack my trunk. He stands and watches everything I put in, and I haven't been able to pack a lot of things I need."

I went over that afternoon and found Tufik huddled on the top step of the stairs outside Tish's apartment, with his head in his hands.

"She has put me out!" he said, looking up at me with tragic eyes. "My mother has put me out! She does not love Tufik! No one loves Tufik! I am no good. I am a dirty dago!"

I was really shocked. I rang the bell and Tish let me in. She had had no maid since Hannah's departure and was taking her meals out. She saw Tufik and stiffened.

"I thought I sent you away!" she said, glaring at him.

He looked at her pitifully.

"Where must I—go?" he asked, and coughed.

Tish sighed and flung the door wide open. "Bring him in," she said with resignation, "but for Heaven's sake lock him in a closet until I get my underwear packed. And if he weeps-slap him."

The poor boy was very repentant, and seeing that his cough worried us he fought it back bravely. I mixed the white of an egg with lemon juice and sugar, and gave it to him. He was pathetically grateful and kissed my hand. At five o'clock we sent him away firmly, having given him thirty-six dollars. He presented each of us with a roll of crocheted lace to take with us and turned in the doorway to wave a wistful final good-bye.

We met at Tish's that night so that we might all go together to the train. Charlie Sands had agreed to see us off and to keep an eye on Tufik during our absence. Aggie was in a palpitating travel ecstasy, clutching a patent seasick remedy and a map of the Canal Zone; Tish was seeing that the janitor shut off the gas and water in the apartment; and Charlie Sands was jumping on top of a steamer trunk to close it. The taxicab was at the door and we had just time to make the night train. The steamer sailed early the next morning.

"All ready!" cried Charlie Sands, getting the lid down finally. "All off for the Big Ditch!"

We all heard a noise in the hall—a sort of scuffling, with an occasional groan. Tish rushed over and threw open the door. On the top step, huddled and shivering, with streams of water running off his hair down over his celluloid collar, pouring out of his sleeves and cascading down the stairs from his trousers legs, was Tufik. The policeman on the beat was prodding at him with his foot, trying to make him get up. When he saw us the officer touched his hat.

"Evening, Miss Tish," he said, grinning. "This here boy of yours has been committing suicide. Just fished him out of the lake in the park!"

"Get up!" snapped Charlie Sands. "You infernal young idiot! Get up and stop sniveling!"

He stooped and took the poor boy by the collar. His brutality roused us all out of our stupor. Tish and I rushed forward and commanded him to stand back; and Aggie, with more presence of mind than we had given her credit for, brought a glass containing a tablespoonful of blackberry cordial into which she had poured ten drops of seasickness remedy. Tufik was white and groaning, but he revived enough to sit up and stare at us with his sad brown eyes.

"I wish to die!" he said brokenly. "Why you do not let me die? My friends go on the canal! I am alone! My heart is empty!"

Tish wished to roll him on a barrel, but we had no barrel; so, with Charlie Sands standing by with his watch in his hand, refusing to assist and making unkind remarks, we got him to Tish's room and laid out on her mackintosh on the bed. He did not want to live. We could hardly force him to drink the hot coffee Tish made for him. He kept muttering things about his loneliness and being only a dirty dago; and then he turned bitter and said hard things about this great America, where he could find no work and must be a burden on his three mothers, and could not bring his dear sister to be company for him. Aggie quite broke down and had to lie down on the sofa in the parlor and have a cracker and a cup of tea.

When Tish and I had succeeded in making Tufik promise to live, and had given him one of his own silk kimonos to put on until his clothing could be dried-Charlie Sands having disagreeably refused to lend his overcoat-and when we had given the officer five dollars not to arrest the boy for attempting suicide, we met in the parlor to talk things over.

Charlie Sands was sitting by the lamp in his overcoat. He had put our railway and steamer tickets on the table, and was holding his cigarette so that Aggie could inhale the fumes, she having hay fever and her cubebs being on their way to Panama.

"I suppose you know," he said nastily, "that your train has gone and that you cannot get the boat tomorrow?"

Tish was in an exalted mood-and she took off her things and flung them on a chair.

"What is Panama," she demanded, "to saving a life? Charlie, we must plan something for this boy. If you will take off your overcoat —"

"And see you put it on that little parasite? Not if I melt! Do you know how deep the lake is? Three feet!"

"One can drown in three feet of water," said Aggie sadly, "if one is very tired of life. People drown themselves in bathtubs."

Tish's furious retort to this was lost, Tufik choosing that moment to appear in the doorway. He wore a purple-and-gold kimono that had given Tish bronchitis early in the winter, and he had twisted a bath towel round the waist. He looked very young, very sad, very Oriental. He ignored Charlie Sands, but made at once for Tish and dropped on one knee beside her.

"Miss Tish!" he begged. "Forgive, Miss Tish! Tufik is wicked. He has the bad heart. He has spoil the going on the canal. No?"

"Get up!" said Tish. "Don't be a silly child. Go and take your shoes out of the oven. We are not going to Panama. When you are better, I am going to give you a good scolding."

Charlie Sands put the cigarette on a book under Aggie's nose and stood up.

"I guess I'll go," he said. "My nerves are not what they used to be and my disposition feels the change."

Tufik had risen and the two looked at each other. I could not quite make out Tufik's expression; had I not known his gentleness I would have thought his expression a mixture of triumph and disdain.

" 'The Assyrian came down like a wolf on the fold, and his cohorts were gleaming in purple and gold!' " said Charlie Sands, and went out, slamming the door.

III

The next day was rainy and cold. Aggie sneezed all day and Tish had neuralgia. Being unable to go out for anything to eat and the exaltation of the night before having passed, she was in a bad humor. When I got there she was sitting in her room holding a hot-water bottle to her face, and staring bitterly at the plate containing a piece of burned toast and Tufik's specialty —a Syrian cake crusted with sugar.

"I wish he had drowned!" she said. "My stomach's gone, Lizzie! I ate one of those cakes for breakfast. You've got to eat this one."

"I'll do nothing of the sort! This is your doing, Tish Carberry. If it hadn't been for you and your habit of picking up stray cats and dogs and Orientals and imposing them on your friends we'd be on the ocean to-day, on our way to a decent climate. The next time your duty to your brother man overwhelms you, you'd better lock yourself in your room and throw the key out the window."

Tish was not listening, however. Her eye and her mind both were on the cake.

"If you would eat it and then take some essence of pepsin —" she hazarded. But I looked her full it the eye and she had the grace to color. "He loves to make them," she said —"he positively beamed when he brought it. He has another kind he is making now-of pounded beans, or something like that. Listen!" I listened.

From back in the kitchen came a sound of hammering and Tufik's voice lifted in a low, plaintive chant. "He says that song is about the valleys of Lebanon," said Tish miserably. "Lizzie, if you'll eat half of it, I'll eat the rest."

My answer was to pick up the plate and carry it into the bathroom. Heroic measures were necessary: Tish was not her resolute self; and, indeed, through all the episode of Tufik, and the shocking denouement that followed, Tish was a spineless individual who swayed to and fro with every breeze.

She divined my purpose and followed me to the bathroom door.

"Leave some crumbs on the plate!" she whispered. "It will look more natural. Get rid of the toast too."

I turned and faced her, the empty plate in my hands.

"Tish," I said sternly, "this is hypocrisy, which is just next door to lying. It's the first step downward. I have a feeling that this boy is demoralizing us! We shall have to get rid of him."

"As for instance?" she sarcastically asked.

"Send him back home," I said with firmness. "He doesn't belong here; he isn't accustomed to anything faster than a camel. He doesn't know how to work-none of them do. He comes from a country where they can eat food like this because digestion is one of their occupations."

I was right and Tish knew it. Even Tufik was satisfied when we put it up to him. He spread his hands in his Oriental way and shrugged his shoulders.

"If my mothers think best," he said softly. "In my own land Tufik is known —I sell in the bazaar the so fine lace my sister make. I drink wine, not water. My stomach —I cannot eat in this America. But —I have no money."

"We will furnish the money," Tish said gently. "But you must promise one thing, Tufik. You must not become a Mohammedan."

"Before that I die!" he said proudly.

"And-there is something else, Tufik, —something rather personal. But I want you to promise. You are only a boy; but when you are a man —" Tish stopped and looked to me for help.

"Miss Tish means this," I put in, "you are to have only one wife, Tufik. We are not sending you back to start a harem. We-we disapprove strongly of-er-anything like that."

"Tufik takes but one wife," he said. "Our people-we have but one wife. My first child-it is called Tish; my next, Lizzie; and my next, Aggie Pilk. All for my so kind friends. And one I call Charlie Sands; and one shall be Hannah. So that Tufik never forget America."

Aggie was rather put out when we told her what we had done; but after eating one of the cakes made of pounded beans and sugar, under Tufik's triumphant eyes, she admitted that it was probably for the best. That evening, while Tufik took his shrunken and wrinkled clothing to be pressed by a little tailor in the neighborhood who did Tish's repairing, the three of us went back to the kitchen and tried to put it in order. It was frightful-flour and burned grease over everything, every pan dirty, dishes all over the place and a half-burned cigarette in the sugar bin. But-it touched us all deeply-he had found an old photograph of the three of us and had made a sort of shrine of the clock-shelf —the picture in front of the clock and in front of the picture a bunch of red geraniums.

While we were looking at the picture and Aggie was at the sink putting water in the glass that held the geraniums, Tufik having forgotten to do so, Tish's neighbor from the apartment below, an elderly bachelor, came up the service staircase and knocked at the door. Tish opened it.

"Humph!" said the gentleman from below. "Gone is he?"

"Is who gone?"

"Your thieving Syrian, madam!"

Tish stiffened.

"Perhaps," she said, "if you will explain —"

"Perhaps," snarled the visitor, "you will explain what you have done with my geraniums! Why don't you raise your own flowers?"

Tish was quite stunned and so was I. After all, it was Aggie who came to the rescue. She slammed the lid on to the teakettle and set it on the stove with a bang.

"If you mean," she said indignantly, "that you think we have any geraniums of yours —"

"Think! Didn't my cook see your thieving servant steal 'em off the box on the fire-escape?"

"Then, perhaps," Aggie suggested, "you will look through the apartment and see if they are here. You will please look everywhere!"

Tish and I gasped. It was not until the visitor had made the rounds of the apartment, and had taken an apologetic departure, that Tish and I understood. The teakettle was boiling and from its spout coming a spicy and familiar odor. Aggie took it off the stove and removed the lid. The geraniums, boiled to a pulp, were inside.

"Back to Syria that boy goes!" said Tish, viewing the floral remains. "He did it out of love and we must not chide him. But we have our own immortal souls to think of."

The next morning two things happened. We gave Tufik one hundred and twenty dollars to buy a ticket back to Syria and to keep him in funds on the way. And Tish got a note from Hannah: —

Dear Miss Tish: I here you still have the dago-or, as my sister's husband says, he still has you. I am redy to live up to my bargen if you are.

HANNAH.

P.S. I have lerned a new salud-very rich, but delissious.

H.

In spite of herself, Tish looked haunted. It was the salad, no doubt. She said nothing, but she looked round the untidy rooms, where everything that would hold it had a linen cover with a Cluny-lace edge-all of them soiled and wrinkled. She watched Tufik, chanting about the plains of Lebanon and shoving the carpet-sweeper with a bang against her best furniture; and, with Hannah's salad in mind, she sniffed a warning odor from the kitchen that told of more Syrian experiments with her digestion. Tish surrendered: that morning she wrote to Hannah that Tufik was going back to Syria, and to come and bring the salad recipe with her.

That was, I think, on a Monday. Tufik's steamer sailed on Thursday. On Tuesday Aggie and I went shopping; and in a spirit of repentance-for we felt we were not solving Tufik's question but getting rid of him-we bought him a complete new outfit. He almost disgraced us by kissing our hands in the store, and while we were buying him some ties he disappeared-to come back later with the rims of his eyes red from weeping. His gentle soul was touched with gratitude. Aggie had to tell him firmly that if he kissed any more hands he would get his ears boxed.

The clerks in the store were all interested, and two or three cash-boys followed us round and stood, open-mouthed, staring at us. Neither Aggie nor I knew anything about masculine attire, and Tufik's idea was a suit, with nothing underneath, a shirt-front and collar of celluloid, and a green necktie already tied and hooking on to his collar-button. He was dazed when we bought him a steamer trunk and a rug, and disappeared again, returning in a few moments with a small paper bag full of gumdrops. We were quite touched.

That, as I say, was on Tuesday. Tufik had been sleeping in Tish's guest-room since his desperate attempt at suicide, and we sent his things to Tish's apartment. That evening Tufik asked permission to spend the night with a friend in the restaurant business —a Damascan. Tish let him go against my advice.

"He'll eat a lot of that Syrian food," I objected, "and get sick and miss his boat, and we'll have the whole thing over again!"

But Tish was adamant. "It's his last night," she said, "and he has promised not to smoke any cigarettes and I've given him two pepsin tablets. This is the land of the free, Lizzie."

We were to meet Tufik at the station next morning and we arranged a lunch for him to eat on the train, Aggie bringing fried chicken and I sandwiches and cake. Tish's domestic arrangements being upset, she supplied fruit, figs and dates mostly, to make him think of home.

The train left early, and none of us felt very cheerful at having to be about. Aggie sat in the station and sneezed; Tish had a pain above her eye and sat by a heater. We had the luncheon in a large shoebox, wrapped in oiled paper to keep it moist.

He never appeared! The train was called, filled up, and left. People took to staring at us as we sat there. Aggie sneezed and Tish held her eye. And no Tufik! In a sort of helpless, breakfastless rage we called a taxicab and went to Tish's. No one said much. We were all thinking.

We were hungry; so we spread out the shoebox lunch on one of the Cluny-lace covers and ate it, mostly in silence. The steamer trunk and the rug had gone. We let them go. They might go to Jerusalem, as far as we were concerned! After we had eaten,—about eleven o'clock, I think,—Tish got up and surveyed the apartment. Then, with a savage gleam in her eye, she whisked off all the fancy linens, the Cluny laces, the hemstitched bedspreads, and piled them in a heap on the floor. Aggie and I watched her in silence. She said nothing, but kicked the whole lot into the bottom of a cupboard. When she had slammed the door, she turned and faced us grimly.

"That roll of fiddle-de-dees has cost me about five hundred dollars," she said. "It's been worth it if it teaches me that I'm an old fool and that you are two others! If that boy shows his face here again, I'll hand him over to the police."

However, as it happened, she did nothing of the sort. At four o'clock that afternoon there was a timid ring at the doorbell and I answered it. Outside was Tufik, forlorn and drooping, and held up by main force by a tall, dark-skinned man with a heavy mustache.

"I bring your boy!" said the mustached person, smiling. "He has great trouble-sorrow; he faint with grief."

I took a good look at Tufik then. He was pale and shaky, and his new suit looked as if he had slept in it. His collar was bent and wilted, and the green necktie had been taken off and exchanged for a ragged black one.

"Miss Liz!" he said huskily. "I die; the heart is gone! My parent —"

He broke down again; and leaning against the door jamb he buried his face in a handkerchief that I could not believe was one of the lot we had bought only yesterday. I hardly knew what to do. Tish had said she was through with the boy. I decided to close them out in the hallway until we had held a council; but Tufik's foot was on the sill, and the more I asked him to move it, the harder he wept.

The mustached person said it was quite true. Tufik's father had died of the plague; the letter had come early that morning. Beirut was full of the plague. He waved the letter at me; but I ordered him to burn it immediately-on account of germs. I brought him a shovel to burn it on; and when that was over Tufik had worked out his own salvation. He was at the door of Tish's room, pouring out to Aggie and Tish his grief, and offering the black necktie as proof.

We were just where we had started, but minus one hundred and twenty dollars; for, the black-mustached gentleman having gone after trying to sell Tish another silk kimono, I demanded Tufik's ticket-to be redeemed-and was met with two empty hands, outstretched.

"Oh, my friends,—my Miss Tish, my Miss Liz, my Miss Ag,—what must I say? I have not the ticket! I have been wikkid-but for my sister-only for my sister! She must not die-she so young, so little girl!"

"Tufik," said Tish sternly, "I want you to tell us everything this minute, and get it over."

"She ees so little!" he said wistfully. "And the body of my parent-could I let it lie and rot in the so hot sun? Ah, no; Miss Tish, Miss Liz, Miss Ag,—not so. To-day I take back my ticket, get the money, and send it to my sister. She will bury my parent, and then-she comes to this so great America, the land of my good friends!"

There was a moment's silence. Then Aggie sneezed!

IV

I shall pass over the next month, with its unpleasantnesses; over Charlie Sands's coming one evening with a black tie and, on the strength of having killed a dog with his machine, asking for money to bury it, and bring another one from Syria! I shall not more than mention Hannah, who kept Tish physically comfortable and well fed and mentally wretched, having a teakettle of boiling water always ready if Tufik came to the apartment; I shall say nothing of our success in getting him employment in the foreign department of a bank, and his ending up by washing its windows; or of the position Tish got him as elevator boy in her hospital, where he jammed the car in some way and held up four surgeons and three nurses and a patient on his way to the operating-room —until the patient changed his mind and refused to be operated on.

Aggie had a brilliant idea about the census-that he could make the census reports in the Syrian district. To this end she worked for some time, coaching Tufik for the examination, only to have him fail-fail absolutely and without hope. He was staying in the Syrian quarter at that time, on account of Hannah; and he brought us various tempting offers now and then —a fruit stand that could be bought for a hundred dollars; a restaurant for fifty; a tailor's shop for twenty-five. But, as he knew nothing of fruits or restaurants or tailoring, we refused to invest. Tish said that we had been a good while getting to it, but that we were being businesslike at last. We gave the boy nine dollars a week and not a penny more; and we refused to buy any more of his silly linens and crocheted laces. We were quite firm with him.

And now I come to the arriving of Tufik's little sister-not that she was really little. But that comes later.

Tufik had decided at last on what he would be in our so great America. Once or twice, when he was tired or discouraged, Tish had taken him out in her machine, and he had been thrilled-really thrilled. He did not seem able to learn how to crank it-Tish's car is hard to crank-but he learned how to light the lamps and to spot a policeman two blocks away. Several times, when we were going into the country, Tish took him because it gave her a sense of security to have a man along.

Having come from a country where the general travel is by camel, however, he had not the first idea of machinery. He thought Tish made the engine go by pressing on the clutch with her foot, like a sewing machine, and he regarded her strength with awe. And once, when we were filling a tire from an air bottle and the tube burst and struck him, he declared there was a demon in the air bottle and said a prayer in the middle of the road. About that time Tish learned of a school for chauffeurs, and the three of us decided to divide the expense and send him.

"In three months," Tish explained, "we can get him a state license and he can drive a taxicab. It will suit him, because he can sit to do it."

So Tufik went to an automobile school and stood by while some one drew pictures of parts of the engine on a blackboard, and took home lists of words that he translated into Arabic at the library, and learned everything but why and how the engine of an automobile goes. He still thought-at the end of two months-that the driver did it with his foot! But we were ignorant of all that. He would drop round in the evenings, when Hannah was out or in bed, and tell us what "magneto" was in Arabic, and how he would soon be able to care for Tish's car and would not take a cent for it, doing it at night when the taxicab was resting.

At the end of six weeks we bought him a chauffeur's outfit. The next day the sister arrived and Tufik brought her to Aggie's, where we were waiting. We had not told Hannah about the sister; she would not have understood.

Charlie Sands telephoned while we were waiting and asked if he might come over and help receive the girl. We were to greet her and welcome her to America; then she was to go to the home of the Syrian with the large mustache. Charlie Sands came in and shook hands all round, surveying each of us carefully.

"Strange!" he muttered. "Curious is no name for it! What do we know of the vagaries of the human mind? Three minds and one obsession!" he said with the utmost gentleness. "Three maiden ladies who have lived impeccable lives for far be it from me to say how many years; and now-this! Oh, Aunt Tish! Dear Aunt Tish!"

He got out his handkerchief and wiped his eyes. Tish was speechless with rage, but I rose to our defense.

"We don't want to do it and you know it!" I said tartly. "But when the Lord sends want and suffering to one's very door —"

"Want, with large brown eyes and a gentle voice!" he retorted. "My dear ladies, it's your money; and I dare say it costs you less than bridge at five cents a point, or the Gay White Way. But, for Heaven's sake, my respected but foolish virgins, why not an American that wants a real job? Why let a sticky Oriental pull your legs —"

"Charlie Sands!" cried Tish, rising in her wrath. "I will not endure such vulgarity. And when Tufik takes you out in a taxicab —"

"God forbid!" said Charlie Sands, and sat down to wait for Tufik's sister.

She did not look like Tufik and she was tired and dirty from the journey; but she had big brown eyes and masses of dark hair and she spoke not a single word of English. Tufik's joy was boundless; his soft eyes were snapping with excitement; and Aggie, who is sentimental, was obliged to go out and swallow half a glass of water without breathing to keep from crying. Charlie Sands said nothing, but sat back in a corner and watched us all; and once he took out his notebook and made a memorandum of something. He showed it to us later.

Tufik's sister was the calmest of us all, I believe. She sat on a stiff chair near the door and turned her brown eyes from one to the other. Tish said that proper clothing would make her beautiful; and Aggie, disappearing for a few minutes, came back with her last summer's foulard and a jet bonnet. When the poor thing understood they were for her, she looked almost frightened, the thing being unexpected; and Tufik, in a paroxysm of delight, kissed all our hands and the girl on each cheek.

Tish says our vulgar lip-osculation is unknown in the Orient and that they rub noses by way of greeting. I think, however, that she is mistaken in this and that the Australians are the nose-rubbers. I recall a returned missionary's telling this, but I cannot remember just where he had been stationed.

Things were very quiet for a couple of weeks. Tufik came round only once-to tell us that, having to pay car fare to get to the automobile school, his nine dollars were not enough. We added a dollar a week under protest; and Tish suggested with some asperity that as he was only busy four hours a day he might find some light employment for the balance of the day. He spread out his hands and drew up his shoulders.

"My friends are angry," he said sadly. "It is not enough that I study? I must also work? Ver' well, I labor. I sell the newspaper. But, to buy newspapers, one must have money —a dollar; two dollars. Ver' leetle; only —I have it not."

We gave him another dollar and he went out smiling and hopeful. It seemed that at last we had solved his problem. Tish recalled one of her Sunday-school scholars who sold papers and saved enough to buy a second-hand automobile and rear a family. But our fond hopes were dashed to the ground when, the next morning, Hannah, opening the door at Tish's to bring in the milk bottles, found a huge stack of the night-before's newspapers and a note on top addressed to Tish, which said:-

> *Deer Mother Tish*: You see now that I am no good. I wish to die! I hav one
> papier sold, and newsboys kell me on sight. I hav but you and God-and God
> has forget!

TUFIK.

We were discouraged and so, clearly, was Tufik. For ten days we did not hear from him, except that a flirty little Syrian boy called for the ten dollars on Saturday and brought a pair of Tufik's shoes for us to have resoled. But one day Tish telephoned in some excitement and said that Tufik was there and wanted us to go to a wedding.

"His little sister's wedding!" she explained. "The dear child is all excited. He says it has been going on for two days and this is the day of the ceremony."

Aggie was spending the afternoon with me, and spoke up hastily.

"Ask her if I have time to go home and put on my broadcloth," she said. "I'm not fixed for a wedding."

Tish said there was no time. She would come round with the machine and we were to be ready in fifteen minutes. Aggie hesitated on account of intending to wash her hair that night and so not having put up her crimps; but she finally agreed to go and Tish came for us. Tufik was in the machine. He looked very tidy and wore the shoes we had had repaired, a pink carnation in his buttonhole, and an air of suppressed excitement.

"At last," he said joyously while Tish cranked the car —"at last my friends see my three mothers! They think Tufik only talks-now they see! And the priest will bless my mothers on this so happy day."

Tish having crawled panting from her exertion into the driver's seat and taken the wheel, in sheer excess of boyish excitement he leaned over and kissed the hand nearest him.

The janitor's small boy was on the curb watching, and at that he set up a yell of joy. We left him calling awful things after us and Tish's face was a study; but soon the care of the machine made her forget everything else.

The Syrian quarter was not impressive. It was on a hillside above the Russian Jewish colony, and consisted of a network of cobble-paved alleys, indescribably dirty and incredibly steep. In one or two of these alleys Tish was obliged to turn the car and go up backward, her machine climbing much better on the reverse gear. Crowds of children followed us; dogs got under the wheels and apparently died, judging by the yelps-only to follow us with undiminished energy after they had picked themselves up. We fought and won a battle with a barrel of ashes and came out victorious but dusty; and at last, as Tufik made a lordly gesture, we stopped at an angle of forty-five degrees and Tufik bowed us out of the car. He stood by visibly glowing with happiness, while Tish got a cobblestone and placed it under a wheel, and Aggie and I took in our surroundings.

We were in an alley ten feet wide and paved indiscriminately with stones and tin cans, babies and broken bottles. Before us was a two-story brick house with broken windows and a high, railed wooden stoop, minus two steps. Under the stoop was a door leading into a cellar, and from this cellar was coming a curious stamping noise and a sound as of an animal in its death throes.

Aggie caught my arm. "What's that?" she quavered.

I had no time to reply. Tufik had thrown open the door and stood aside to let us pass.

"They dance," he said gravely. "There is always much dancing before a wedding. The music one hears is of Damascus and he who dances now is a sheik among his people."

Reassured as to the sounds, we stepped down into the basement. That was at four o'clock in the afternoon.

I have never been fairly clear as to what followed and Aggie's memory is a complete blank. I remember a long, boarded-in and floored cellar, smelling very damp and lighted by flaring gas jets. The center was empty save for a swarthy gentleman in a fez and his shirt-sleeves, wearing a pair of green suspenders and dancing alone —a curious stamping dance that kept time to a drum. I remember the musicians too-three of them in a corner: one playing on a sort of pipes-of-Pan affair of reeds, one on a long-necked instrument that looked like a guitar with zither ambitions, and a drummer who chanted with his eyes shut and kept time to his chants by beating on a sheepskin tied over the mouth of a brass bowl. Round three sides of the room were long, oil cloth-covered tables; and in preparation for the ceremony a little Syrian girl was sweeping up peanut shells, ashes, and beer bottles, with absolute disregard of the guests.

All round the wall, behind rows of beer bottles, dishes of bananas, and plates of raw liver, were men, —soft-eyed Syrians with white teeth gleaming and black hair plastered close and celluloid collars, —gentle-voiced, urbane-mannered Orientals, who came up gravely one by one and shook hands with us; who pressed on us beer and peanuts and raw liver.

Aggie, speaking between sneezes and over the chanting and the drum, bent toward me. "It's a breath of the Orient!" she said ecstatically. "Oh, Lizzie, do you think I could buy that drum for my tabouret?"

"Orient!" observed Tish, coughing. "I'm going out and take the switch-key out of that car. And I wish I'd brought Charlie Sands!"

It was in vain we reminded her that the Syrians are a pastoral people and that they come from the land of the Bible. She looked round her grimly.

"They look like a lot of bandits to me," she sniffed. "And there's always a murder at a wedding of this sort. There isn't a woman here but ourselves!"

She was exceedingly disagreeable and Aggie and I began to get uncomfortable. But when Tufik brought us little thimble-sized glasses filled with a milky stuff and assured us that the women had only gone to prepare the bride, we felt reassured. He said that etiquette demanded that we drink the milky white stuff.

Tish was inclined to demur. "Has it any alcohol in it?" she demanded. Tufik did not understand, but he said it was harmless and given to all the Syrian babies; and while we were still undecided Aggie sniffed it.

"It smells like paregoric, Tish," she said. "I'm sure it's harmless."

We took it then. It tasted sweet and rather spicy, and Aggie said it stopped her sneezing at once. It was very mild and pleasant, and rather medicinal in its flavor. We each had two little glasses-and Tish said she would not bother about the switch-key. The car was insured against theft.

A little later Aggie said she used to do a little jig step when she was a girl, and if they would play slower she would like to see if she had forgotten it. Tish did not hear this-she was talking to Tufik, and a moment later she got up and went out.

Aggie had decided to ask the musicians to play a little slower and I had my hands full with her; so it was with horror that, shortly after, I heard the whirring of the engine and through the cellar window caught a glimpse of Tish's machine starting off up the hill. I rose excitedly, but Tufik was before me, smiling and bowing.

"Miss Tish has gone for the bride," he said softly. "The taxicab hav' not come. Soon the priest arrive, and so great shame-the bride is not here! Miss Tish is my mother, my heart's delight!"

When Aggie realized that Tish had gone, she was rather upset-she depends a great deal on Tish-and she took another of the little glasses of milky stuff to revive her.

I was a little bit nervous with Tish gone and the sun setting and another tub of beer bottles brought in-though the people were orderly enough and Tufik stood near. But Aggie began to feel very strange, and declared that the man with the sheepskin drum was winking at her and that her head was twitching round on her shoulders. And when a dozen or so young Syrians formed a circle, their hands on each other's shoulders, and sang a melancholy chant, stamping to beat time, she wept with sheer sentiment.

"Ha! Hoo! Ta, Ta, Ta!" they chanted in unison; and Tufik bent over us, his soft eyes beaming.

"They are shepherds and the sons of shepherds from Palestine," he whispered. "That is the shepherd's call to his sheep. In my country many are shepherds. Perhaps some day you go with me back to my country, and we hear the shepherd call his sheep —'Ha! Hoo! Ta, Ta, Ta!' —and we hear the sleepy sheep reply: 'Maaaa!'"

"It is too beautiful!" murmured Aggie. "It is the Holy Land all over again! And we should never have known this but for you, Tufik!"

Just then some one near the door clapped his hands and all the noise ceased. Those who were standing sat down. The little girl with the broom swept the accumulations of the room under a chair and put the broom in a corner. The music became loud and stirring.

Aggie swayed toward me. "I'm sick, Lizzie!" she gasped. "That paregoric stuff has poisoned me. Air!"

I took one arm and Tufik the other, and we got her out and seated on one of the wooden steps. She was a blue-green color and the whites of her eyes were yellow. But I had little time for Aggie. Tufik caught my hand and pointed.

Tish's machine was coming down the alley. Beside her sat Tufik's sister, sobbing at the top of her voice and wearing Aggie's foulard, a pair of cotton gloves, and a lace curtain over her head. Behind in the tonneau were her maid of honor, a young Syrian woman with a baby in her arms and four other black-eyed children about her. But that was not all. In front of the machine, marching slowly and with dignity, were three bearded gentlemen, two in coats and one in a striped vest, blowing on curious double flutes and making a shrill wailing noise. And all round were crowds of women and children, carrying tin pans and paper bags full of parched peas, which they were flinging with all their might.

I caught Tish's eye as the procession stopped, and she looked subdued-almost stunned. The pipers still piped. But the bride refused to move. Instead, her wails rose higher; and Aggie, who had paid no attention so far, but was sitting back with her eyes shut, looked up.

"Lizzhie," she said thickly, "Tish looks about the way I feel." And with that she fell to laughing awful laughter that mingled with the bride's cries and the wail of the pipes.

The bride, after a struggle, was taken by force from the machine and placed on a chair against the wall. Her veil was torn and her wreath crooked, and she observed a sulky silence. To our amazement, Tufik was still smiling, urbane and cheerful.

"It is the custom of my country, my mothers," he said. "The bride leave with tears the home of her good parents or of her friends; and she speak no word-only weep-until she is marriaged. Ah-the priest!"

The rest of the story is short and somewhat blurred. Tish having broken her glasses, Aggie being, as one may say, *hors de combat,* and I having developed a frightful headache in the dust and bad air, the real meaning of what was occurring did not penetrate to any of us. The priest officiated from a table in the center of the room, on which he placed two candles, an Arabic Bible, and a sacred picture, all of which he took out of a brown valise. He himself wore a long black robe and a beard, and looked, as Tish observed, for all the world as if he had stepped from an Egyptian painting. Before him stood Tufik's sister, the maid of honor with her baby, the black-mustached friend who had brought Tufik to us after his tragic attempt at suicide, and Tufik himself.

Everybody held lighted candles, and the heat was frightful. The music ceased, there was much exhorting in Arabic, much reading from the book, many soft replies indiscriminately from the four principals-and then suddenly Tish turned and gripped my arm.

"Lizzie," she said hoarsely, "that little thief and liar has done us again! That isn't his sister at all. He's marrying her-for us to keep!"

Luckily Aggie grew faint again at that moment, and we led her out into the open air. Behind us the ceremony seemed to be over; the drum was beating, the pipes screaming, the lute thrumming.

Tish let in the clutch with a vicious jerk, and the whir of the engine drowned out the beating of the drum and the clapping of the hands. Twilight hid the tin cans and ash-barrels, and the dogs slept on the cool pavements. In the doorways soft-eyed Syrian women rocked their babies to drowsy chants. The air revived Aggie. She leaned forward and touched Tish on the shoulder.

"After all," she said softly, "if he loves her very much, and there was no other way-Do you remember that night she arrived-how he looked at her?"

"Yes," Tish snapped. "And I remember the way he looked at us every time he wanted money. We've been a lot of sheep and we've been sheared good and proper! But we needn't bleat with joy about it!"

As we drew up at my door, Tish pulled out her watch.

"It's seven o'clock," she said brusquely. "I am going to New York on the nine-forty train and I shall take the first steamer outward bound—I need a rest! I'll go anywhere but to the Holy Land!"

We went to Panama.

Two months afterward, in the dusk of a late spring evening, Charlie Sands met us at the station and took us to Tish's in a taxicab. We were homesick, tired, and dirty; and Aggie, who had been frightfully seasick, was clamoring for tea.

As the taxicab drew up at the curb, Tish clutched my arm and Aggie uttered a muffled cry and promptly sneezed. Seated on the doorstep, celluloid collar shining, the brown pasteboard suitcase at his feet, was Tufik. He sat calmly smoking a cigarette, his eyes upturned in placid and Oriental contemplation of the heavens.

"Drive on!" said Tish desperately. "If he sees us we are lost!"

"Drive where?" demanded Charlie.

Tufik's gaze had dropped gradually-another moment and his brown eyes would rest on us. But just then a diversion occurred. A window overhead opened with a slam and a stream of hot water descended. It had been carefully aimed-as if with long practice. Tufik was apparently not surprised. He side-stepped it with a boredom as of many repetitions, and, picking up his suitcase, stood at a safe distance looking up. First, in his gentle voice he addressed the window in Arabic; then from a safer distance in English.

"You ugly old she-wolf!" he said softly. "When my three old women come back I eat you, skin and bones,—and they shall say nothing! They love me-Tufik! I am their child. Aye! And my child-which comes-will be their grandchild!"

He kissed his fingers to the upper window which closed with a slam. Tufik stooped, picked up his suitcase, and saw the taxi for the first time. Even in the twilight we saw his face change, his brown eyes brighten, his teeth show in his boyish smile. The taxicab driver had stalled his engine and was cranking it.

"Sh!" I said desperately, and we all cowered back into the shadows.

Tufik approached, uncertainty changing to certainty. The engine was started now. Oh, for a second of time! He was at the window now, peering into the darkness.

"Miss Tish!" he said breathlessly. No one answered. We hardly breathed. And then suddenly Aggie sneezed! "Miss Pilk!" he shouted in delight. "My mothers! My so dear friends—"

The machine jerked, started, moved slowly off. He ran beside it, a hand on the door. Tish bent forward to speak, but Charlie Sands put his hand over her mouth.

And so we left him, standing in the street undecided, staring after us wistfully, uncertainly-the suitcase, full of Cluny-lace centerpieces, crocheted lace, silk kimonos, and embroidered bedspreads, in his hand.

That night we hid in a hotel and the next day we started for Europe. We heard nothing from Tufik; but on the anniversary of Mr. Wiggins's death, while we were in Berlin, Aggie received a small package forwarded from home. It was a small lace doily, and pinned to it was a card. It read:—

For the sadness, Miss Pilk!

TUFIK.

Aggie cried over it.

The Simple Lifers

I

I suppose there is something in all of us that harks back to the soil. When you come to think of it, what are picnics but outcroppings of instinct? No one really enjoys them or expects to enjoy them, but with the first warm days some prehistoric instinct takes us out into the woods, to fry potatoes over a strangling wood fire and spend the next week getting grass stains out of our clothes. It must be instinct; every atom of intelligence warns us to stay at home near the refrigerator.

Tish is really a child of instinct. She is intelligent enough, but in a contest between instinct and brains, she always follows her instinct. Aggie under the same circumstances follows her heart. As for me, I generally follow Tish and Aggie, and they've led me into some curious places.

This is really a sort of apology, because, whereas usually Tish leads off and we follow her, in the adventure of the Simple Life we were all equally guilty. Tish made the suggestion, but we needed no urging. As you know, this summer two years ago was a fairly good one, as summers go, —plenty of fair weather, only two or three really hot spells, and not a great deal of rain. Charlie Sands, Tish's nephew, went over to England in June to report the visit of the French President to London for his newspaper, and Tish's automobile had been sent to the factory to be gone over. She had been teaching Aggie to drive it, and owing to Aggie's thinking she had her foot on the brake when it was really on the gas, they had leaped a four-foot ditch and gone down into a deep ravine, from which both Tish and Aggie had had to be pulled up with ropes.

Well, with no machine and Charlie Sands away, we hardly knew how to plan the summer. Tish thought at first she would stay at home and learn to ride. She thought her liver needed stirring up. She used to ride, she said, and it was like sitting in a rocking-chair, only perhaps more so. Aggie and I went out to her first lesson; but when I found she had bought a divided skirt and was going to try a man's saddle, I could not restrain my indignation.

"I'm going, Tish," I said firmly, when she had come out of the dressing-room and I realized the situation. "I shan't attempt to restrain you, but I shall not remain to witness your shame."

Tish eyed me coldly. "When you wish to lecture me," she snapped, "about revealing to the public that I have two legs, if I do wear a skirt, don't stand in a sunny doorway in that linen dress of yours. I am going to ride; every woman should ride. It's good for the liver."

I think she rather wavered when they brought the horse, which looked larger than usual and had a Roman nose. The instructor handed Tish four lines and she grabbed them nervously in a bunch.

"Just a moment!" said the instructor, and slipped a line between each two of her fingers.

Tish looked rather startled. "When I used to ride —" she began with dignity.

But the instructor only smiled. "These two are for the curb," he said —"if he bolts or anything like that, you know. Whoa, Viper! Still, old man!"

"Viper!" Tish repeated, clutching at the lines. "Is-is he-er-nasty?"

"Not a bit of it," said the instructor, while he prepared to hoist her up. "He's as gentle as a woman to the people he likes. His only fault is that he's apt to take a little nip out of the stablemen now and then. He's very fond of ladies."

"Humph!" said Tish. "He's looking at me rather strangely, don't you think? Has he been fed lately?"

"Perhaps he sees that divided skirt," I suggested.

Tish gave me one look and got on the horse. They walked round the ring at first and Tish seemed to like it. Then a stableman put a nickel into a player-piano and that seemed to be a signal for the thing to trot. Tish said afterward that she never hit the horse's back twice in the same place. Once, she says, she came down on his neck, and several times she was back somewhere about his tail. Every time she landed, wherever it might be, he gave a heave and sent her up again. She tried to say "Whoa," but it came out in pieces, so to speak, and the creature seemed to be encouraged by it and took to going faster. By that time, she said, she wasn't coming down at all, but was in the air all the time, with the horse coming up at the rate of fifty revolutions a second. She had presence of mind enough to keep her mouth shut so she wouldn't bite her tongue off.

After four times round the music stopped and the horse did also. They were just in front of us, and Tish looked rather dazed.

"You did splendidly!" said Aggie. "Honestly, Tish, I was frightened at first, but you and that dear horse seemed one piece. Didn't they, Lizzie?"

Tish straightened out the fingers of her left hand with her right and extricated the lines. Then she turned her head slowly from right to left to see if she could.

"Help me down, somebody," she said in a thin voice, "and call an osteopath. There is something wrong with my spine!"

She was in bed three days, having massage and a vibrator and being rubbed with chloroform liniment. At the end of that time she offered me her divided skirt, but I refused.

"Riding would be good for your liver, Lizzie," she said, sitting up in bed with pillows all about her.

"I don't intend to detach it to do it good," I retorted. "What your liver and mine and most of the other livers need these days isn't to be sent out in a divided skirt and beaten to a jelly: they need rest-less food and simpler food. If instead of taking your liver on a horse you'd put it in a tent and feed it nuts and berries, you wouldn't be the color you are to-day, Tish Carberry."

That really started the whole thing, although at the time Tish said nothing. She has a way of getting an idea and letting it simmer on the back of her brain, as you may say, when nobody knows it's been cooking at all, and then suddenly bringing it out cooked and seasoned and ready to serve.

On the day Tish sat up for the first time, Aggie and I went over to see her. Hannah, the maid, had got her out of bed to a window, and Tish was sitting there with books all about her. It is in times of enforced physical idleness that most of Tish's ideas come to her, and Aggie had reminded me of that fact on the way over.

"You remember, Lizzie," she said, "how last winter when she was getting over the grippe she took up that correspondence-school course in swimming. She's reading, watch her books. It'll probably be suffrage or airships."

Tish always believes anything she reads. She had been quite sure she could swim after six correspondence lessons. She had all the movements exactly, and had worried her trained nurse almost into hysteria for a week by turning on her face in bed every now and then and trying the overhand stroke. She got very expert, and had decided she'd swim regularly, and even had Charlie Sands show her the Australian crawl business so she could go over some time and swim the Channel. It was a matter of breathing and of changing positions, she said, and was up to intelligence rather than muscle.

Then when she was quite strong, she had gone to the natatorium. Aggie and I went along, not that we were any good in emergency, but because Tish had convinced us there would be no emergency. And Tish went in at the deep end of the pool, head first, according to diagram, and *did not come up.*

Well, there seemed to be nothing threatening in what Tish was reading this time. She had ordered some books for Maria Lee's children and was looking them over before she sent them. The "Young Woods-man" was one and "Camper Craft" was another. How I shudder when I recall those names!

Aggie had baked an angel cake and I had brought over a jar of cookies. But Tish only thanked us and asked Hannah to take them out. Even then we were not suspicious. Tish sat back among her pillows and said very little. The conversation was something like this: —

Aggie: Well, you're up again: I hope to goodness it will be a lesson to you. If you don't mind, I'd like Hannah to cut that cake. It fell in the middle.

Tish: Do you know that the Indians never sweetened their food and that they developed absolutely perfect teeth?

Aggie: Well, they never had any automobiles either, but they didn't develop wings.

Lizzie: Don't you want that window closed? I'm in a draft.

Tish: Air in motion never gave any one a cold. We do not catch cold; we catch heat. It's ridiculous the way we shut ourselves up in houses and expect to remain well.

Aggie: Well, I'b catchig sobethig.

Lizzie (*changing the subject*): Would you like me to help you dress? It might rest your back to have your corset on.

Tish (*firmly*): I shall never wear a corset again.

Aggie (*sneezing*): Why? Didn't the Iddiads wear theb?

Tish is very sensitive to lack of sympathy and she shut up like a clam. She was coldly polite to us for the remainder of our visit, but she did not again refer to the Indians, which in itself was suspicious.

Fortunately for us, or unfortunately, Tish's new scheme was one she could not very well carry out alone. I believe she tried to induce Hannah to go with her, and only when Hannah failed her did she turn to us. Hannah was frightened and came to warn us.

I remember the occasion very well. It was Mr. Wiggins's birthday anniversary, and we usually dine at Aggie's and have a cake with thirty candles on it. Tish was not yet able to be about, so Aggie and I ate together. She always likes to sit until the last candle is burned out, which is rather dispiriting and always leaves me low in my mind.

Just as it flickered and went out, Hannah came in.

"Miss Tish sent over Mr. Charlie's letter from London," said Hannah, and put it in front of Aggie. Then she sat down on a chair and commenced to cry.

"Why, Hannah!" said Aggie. "What in the world has happened?"

"She's off again!" sniveled Hannah; "and she's worse this time than she's ever been. No sugar, no tea, only nuts and fruit, and her windows open all night, with the curtains getting black. I wisht I had Mr. Charlie by the neck."

I suppose it came over both of us at the same time-the "Young Woodsman," and the "Camper Craft," and no stays, and all that. I reached for Charlie Sands's letter, which was always sent to Tish and meant for all of us. He wrote: —

Dear Three of a Kind: Well, the French President has came and went, and London has taken down all the brilliant flags which greeted him, such tactful bits as bore Cressy and Agincourt, and the pretty little smallpox and "plague here" banners, and has gone back to such innocent diversions as baiting cabinet ministers, blowing up public buildings, or going out into the woods seeking the Simple Life.

The Simple Lifers travel in bands-and little else. They go barefooted, barearmed, bareheaded and barenecked. They wear one garment, I believe, let their hair hang and their beards grow, eat only what Nature provides, such as nuts and fruits, sleep under the stars, and drink from Nature's pools. Rather bully, isn't it? They're a handsome lot generally, brown as nuts. And I saw a girl yesterday-well, if you do not hear from me for a time it will be because I have discarded the pockets in which I carry my fountain pen and my stamps and am wandering barefoot through the Elysian fields.

Yours for the Simple Life,

CHARLIE SANDS.

As I finished reading the letter aloud, I looked at Aggie in dismay. "That settles it," I said hopelessly. "She had some such idea before, and now this young idiot —" I stopped and stared across the table at Aggie. She was sitting rapt, her eyes fixed on the smouldering wicks of Mr. Wiggins's candles.
"Barefoot through the Elysian fields!" she said.

II

I am not trying to defend myself. I never had the enthusiasm of the other two, but I rather liked the idea. And I did restrain them. It was my suggestion, for instance, that we wear sandals without stockings, instead of going in our bare feet, which was a good thing, for the first day out Aggie stepped into a hornet's nest. And I made out the lists.

The idea, of course, is not how much one can carry, but how little. The "Young Woodsman" told exactly how to manage in the woods if one were lost there and had nothing in the world but a bootlace and a wire hairpin.

With the hairpin one could easily make a fair fish-hook—and with a bootlace or a good hemp cord one could make a rabbit snare.

"So you see," Tish explained, "there's fish and meat with no trouble at all. And there will be berries and nuts. That's a diet for a king."

I was making a list of the necessaries at the time and under bootlaces and hairpins I put down "spade."

"What in Heaven's name is the spade for?" Tish demanded.

"You've got to dig bait, haven't you?"

Tish eyed me with disgust.

"Grasshoppers!" she said tersely.

There was really nothing Tish was not prepared for. I should never have thought of grasshoppers.

"The idea is simply this," observed Tish: "We have surrounded ourselves with a thousand and one things we do not need and would be better without-houses, foolish clothing, electric light, idiotic servants-Hannah, get away from that door! —rich foods, furniture and crowds of people. We've developed and cared for our bodies instead of our souls. What we want is to get out into the woods and think; to forget those pampered bodies of ours and to let our souls grow and assert themselves."

We decided finally to take a blanket apiece, rolled on our shoulders, and Tish and I each took a strong knife. Aggie, instead of the knife, took a pair of scissors. We took a small bottle of blackberry cordial for emergencies, a cake of soap, a salt-cellar for seasoning the fish and rabbits, two towels, a package of court-plaster, Aggie's hay-fever remedy, a bottle of oil of pennyroyal to use against mosquitoes, and a large piece of canvas, light but strong, cut like the diagram.

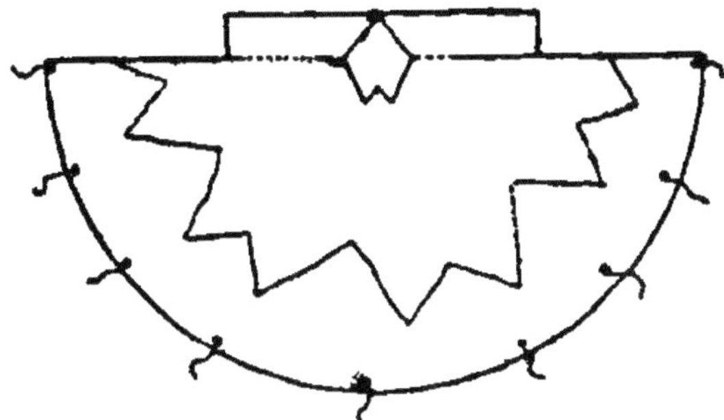

Tish said it was the regulation Indian tepee, and that a squaw could set one up in an hour and have dinner cooked inside it in thirty minutes after. She said she guessed we could do it if an Indian squaw could, and that after we'd cut the poles once, we could carry them with us if we wished to move. She said the tent ought to be ornamented, but she had had no time, and we could paint designs on it with colored clay in the woods when we had nothing more important to do!

It made a largish bundle, but we did not intend to travel much. We thought we could find a good place by a lake somewhere and put up the tent, and set a few snares, and locate the nearest berry-bushes and mushroom-patches, and then, while the rabbits were catching themselves, we should have time to get acquainted with our souls again.

Tish put it in her terse manner most intelligently. "We intend to prove," she stated to Mrs. Ostermaier, the minister's wife, who came to call and found us all sitting on the floor trying to get used to it, for of course there would be no chairs, "we shall prove that the trappings of civilization are a delusion and a snare. We shall bring back 'Mens sana in corpore sano'."

The minister's wife thought this was a disease, for she said, "I hope not, I'm sure," very hastily.

"We shall make our own fire and our own shelter," said Tish from the floor. "We shall wear one garment, loose enough to allow entire freedom of movement. We shall bathe in Nature's pools and come out cleansed. On the Sabbath we shall attend divine service under the Gothic arches of the trees, read sermons in stones, and instead of that whining tenor in the choir we shall listen to the birds singing praise, overhead."

Mrs. Ostermaier looked rather bewildered. "I'm sure I hope so," she said vaguely. "I don't like camping myself. There are so many bugs."

As Tish said, some ideas are so large that the average person cannot see them at all.

We had fixed on Maine. It seemed to combine all the necessary qualities: woods and lakes, rabbits, game and fish, and-solitude. Besides, Aggie's hay fever is better the farther north she gets. On the day we were leaving, Mr. Ostermaier came to see us.

"I—I really must protest, ladies," he said. "That sort of thing may be all right for savages, but —"

"Are we not as intelligent as savages?" Tish demanded.

"Primitive people are inured to hardships, and besides, they have methods of their own. They can make fire —" "So can I," retorted Tish. "Any fool can make a fire with a rubbing-stick. It's been done in thirty-one seconds."

"If you would only take some matches," he wailed, "and a good revolver, Miss Letitia. And-you must pardon this, but I have your well-being at heart-if I could persuade you to take along some-er-flannels and warm clothing!"

"Clothing," said Tish loftily, "is a matter of habit, Mr. Ostermaier."

I think he got the idea from this that we intended to discard clothing altogether, for he went away almost immediately, looking rather upset, and he preached on the following Sunday from "Consider the lilies of the field....Even Solomon in all his glory was not arrayed like one of these."

We left on Monday evening, and by Tuesday at noon we were at our destination, as far as the railroad was concerned. Tish had a map with the lake we'd picked out, and we had figured that we'd drive out to within ten miles or so of it and then send the driver back. The lake was in an uninhabited neighborhood, with the nearest town twenty-five miles away. We had one suitcase containing our blankets, sandals, short dresses, soap, hairpins, salt-box, knives, scissors, and a compass, and the leather thongs for rabbit snares that we had had cut at a harness shop. In the other suitcase was the tepee.

We ate a substantial breakfast at Tish's suggestion, because we expected to be fairly busy the first day, and there would be no time for hunting. We had to walk ten miles, set up the tent, make a fire and gather nuts and berries. It was about that time, I think, that I happened to recall that it was early for nuts. Still there would be berries, and Tish had added mushrooms to our menu.

We found a man with a spring wagon to drive us out and Tish showed him the map.

"I guess I can get you out that way," he said, "but I ain't heard of no camp up that direction."

"Who said anything about a camp?" snapped Tish. "How much to drive us fifteen miles in that direction?"

"Fifteen miles! Well, about five dollars, but I think —"

"How much to drive us fifteen miles without thinking?"

"Ten dollars," said the man; and as he had the only wagon in the town we had to pay it.

It was a lovely day, although very warm. The morning sun turned the woods to fairylike glades. Tish sat on the front seat, erect and staring ahead.

Aggie bent over and touched my arm lightly. "Isn't she wonderful!" she whispered; "like some adventurer of old-Balboa discovering the Pacific Ocean, or Joan of Arc leading the what-you-call-'ems."

But somehow my enthusiasm was dying. The sun was hot and there were no berry-bushes to be seen. Aggie's fairy glades in the woods were filled, not with dancing sprites, but with gnats. I wanted a glass of iced tea, and some chicken salad, and talcum powder down my neck. The road was bad, and the driver seemed to have a joke to himself, for every now and then he chuckled, and kept his eyes on the woods on each side, as if he expected to see something. His manner puzzled us all.

"You can trust me not to say anything, ladies," he said at last, "but don't you think you're playing it a bit low down? This ain't quite up to contract, is it?"

"You've been drinking!" said Tish shortly.

After that he let her alone, but soon after he turned round to me and made another venture.

"In case you need grub, lady," he said," —and them two suitcases don't hold a lot, —I'll bring out anything you say: eggs and butter and garden truck at market prices. I'm no phylanthropist," he said, glaring at Tish, "but I'd be glad to help the girl, and that's the truth. I been married to this here wife o' mine quite a spell, and to my first one for twenty years, and I'm a believer in married life."

"What girl?" I asked.

He turned right round in the seat and winked at me.

"All right," he said. "I'll not butt in unless you need me. But I'd like to know one thing: He hasn't got a mother, he says, so I take it you're his aunts. Am I on, ladies?"

We didn't know what he was talking about, and we said so. But he only smiled. A mile or so from our destination the horse scared up a rabbit, and Tish could hardly be restrained from running after it with a leather thong. Aggie, however, turned a little pale.

"I'll never be able to eat one, never!" she confided to me. "Did you see its eyes? Lizzie, do you remember Mr. Wiggins's eyes? and the way he used to move his nose, just like that?"

At the end of fifteen miles the driver drew up his horses and took a fresh chew of tobacco.

"I guess this is about right," he said. "That trail there'll take you to the lake. How long do you reckon it'll be before you'll need some fresh eggs?"

"We are quite able to look after ourselves," said Tish with hauteur, and got out of the wagon. She paid him off at once and sat down on her suitcase until he had driven out of sight. He drove slowly, looking back every now and then, and his last view of us must have been impressive-three middle-aged and determined women ready to conquer the wilderness, as Tish put it, and two suitcases.

It was as solitary a place as we could have wished. We had not seen a house in ten miles, and when the last creak of the wagon had died away there was a silence that made our city-broke ears fairly ache. Tish waited until the wagon was out of sight; then she stood up and threw out her arms.

"At last!" she said. "Free to have a lodge in some vast wilderness-to think, to breathe, to expand! Lizzie, do you suppose if we go back we can get that rabbit?"

I looked at my watch. It was one o'clock and there was not a berry-bush in sight. The drive had made me hungry, and I'd have eaten a rabbit that looked like Mr. Wiggins and called me by name if I'd had it. But there was absolutely no use going back for the one we'd seen on our drive.

Aggie was opening her suitcase and getting out her costume, which was a blue calico with short sleeves and a shoe-top skirt.

"Where'll I put it on?" she asked, looking about her.

"Right here!" Tish replied. "For goodness sake, Aggie, try to discard false modesty and false shame. We're here to get close to the great beating heart of Nature. Take off your switch before you do another thing."

None of us looked particularly well, I admit; but it was wonderful how much more comfortable we were. Aggie, who is very thin, discarded a part of her figure, and each of us parted with some pet hypocrisy. But I don't know that I have ever felt better. Only, of course we were hungry.

We packed our things in the suitcases and hid them in a hollow tree, and Tish suggested looking for a spring. She said water was always the first requisite and fire the second.

"Fire!" said Aggie. "What for? We've nothing to cook."

Well, that was true enough, so we sent Aggie to look for water and Tish and I made a rabbit snare. We made a good many snares and got to be rather quick at it. They were all made like this illustration.

First Tish, with her book open in front of her, made a running noose out of one of the buckskin thongs. Next we bent down a sapling and tied the noose to it, and last of all we bound the free part of the thong round a snag and thus held the sapling down. The idea is that a rabbit, bounding along, presumably with his eyes shut, will stick his head through the noose, kick the line clear of the snag and be drawn violently into the air. Tish figured that by putting up half a dozen snares we'd have three or four rabbits at least each day.

It was about three when we finished, and we drew off to a safe distance to watch the rabbit bound to his doom. But no rabbits came along.

I was very empty and rather faint, but Tish said she had never been able to think so clearly, and that we were all overfed and stodgy and would be better for fasting.

Aggie came in at three-thirty with a hornet sting and no water. She said there were no springs, but that she had found a place where a spring had existed before the dry spell, and there was a naked footprint in the mud, quite fresh! We all went to look at it, and Tish was quite positive it was not a man's footprint at all, but only a bear's.

"A bear!" said Aggie.

"What of it?" Tish demanded. "The 'Young Woodsman' says that no bear attacks a human unless he is hungry, and at this time of the year with the woods full of food —"

"Humph!" —I could not restrain myself—"I wish you would show me a little of it. If no rabbit with acute melancholia comes along to commit suicide by hanging on that gallows of yours, I think we'll starve to death."

"There will be a rabbit," Tish said tersely; and we started back to the snare.

I was never so astonished in my life. There was a rabbit! It seems we had struck a runway without knowing it, although Tish said afterward that she had recognized it at once from the rabbit tracks. Anyhow, whether it died of design or curiosity, our supper was kicking at the top of the sapling, and Tish pretended to be calm and to have known all along that we'd get one. But it was not dead.

We got it down somehow or other and I held it by the ears while it kicked and scratched. I was hungry enough to have eaten it alive, but Aggie began to cry.

"You'll be murderers, nothing else," she wailed. "Look at his little white tail and pitiful baby eyes!"

"Good gracious, Aggie," Tish snapped, "get a knife and cut its throat while I make a fire. If it's any help to you, we're not going to eat either its little white tail or its pitiful baby eyes."

As a matter of fact Aggie wouldn't touch the rabbit and I did not care much about it myself. I do not like to kill things. My Aunt Sarah Mackintosh once killed a white hen that lived twenty minutes without its head; two weeks later she dreamed that that same hen, without a head, was sitting on the footboard of the bed, and the next day she got word that her cousin's husband in Sacramento had died of the hiccoughs.

It ended with Tish giving me the fire-making materials and stalking off into the woods with the rabbit in one hand and the knife in the other.

Tish is nothing if not thorough, but she seemed to me inconsistent. She brought blankets and a canvas tepee and sandals and an aluminum kettle, but she disdained matches. I rubbed with that silly drill and a sort of bow arrangement until my wrists ached, but I did not get even a spark of fire. When Tish came back with the rabbit there was no fire, and Aggie had taken out her watch crystal and was holding it in the sun over a pile of leaves.

Tish got out the "Young Woodsman" from the suitcase. It seems I had followed cuts I and II, but had neglected cut III, which is: Hold the left wrist against the left shin, and the left foot on the fireblock. I had got my feet mixed and was trying to hold my left wrist against my right shin, which is exceedingly difficult. Tish got a fire in fourteen minutes and thirty-one seconds by Aggie's watch, and had to wear a bandage on her hand for a week.

But we had a fire. We cooked the rabbit, which proved to be much older than Aggie had thought, and ate what we could. Personally I am not fond of rabbit, and our enjoyment was rather chastened by the fear that some mushrooms Tish had collected and added to the stew were toadstools *incognito*. To make things worse, Aggie saw some goldenrod nearby and began to sneeze.

It was after five o'clock, but it seemed wisest to move on toward the lake.

"Even if we don't make it," said Tish, "we'll be on our way, and while that bear is likely harmless we needn't thrust temptation in his way."

We carried the fire with us in the kettle and we took turns with the tepee, which was heavy. Our suitcases with our city clothes in them we hid in a hollow tree, and one after the other, with Aggie last, we started on.

The trail, which was a sort of wide wagon road at first, became a footpath; as we went on even that disappeared at times under fallen leaves. Once we lost it entirely, and Aggie, falling over a hidden root, stilled the fire. She became exceedingly disagreeable at about that time, said she was sure Tish's mushrooms were toadstools because she felt very queer, and suddenly gave a yell and said she had seen something moving in the bushes.

We all looked, and the bushes were moving.

III

It was dusk by that time and the path was only a thread between masses of undergrowth. Tish said if it was the bear he would be afraid of the fire, so we put dry leaves in the kettle and made quite a blaze. By its light Tish read that bears in the summer are full fed and really frolicsome and that they are awful cowards. We felt quite cheered and brave, and Tish said if he came near to throw the fire kettle at him and he'd probably die of fright.

It was too late to put up the tepee, so we found a clearing near the path and decided to spend the night there. Aggie still watched the bushes and wanted to spend the night in a tree; but Tish's calmness was a reproach to us both, and after we had emptied the kettle and made quite a fire to keep off animals, we unrolled our blankets and prepared for sleep. I could have slept anywhere, although I was still rather hungry. My last view was of Tish in the firelight grimly bending down a sapling and fastening a rabbit snare to it.

During the night I was wakened by somebody clutching my arm. It was Aggie who lay next to me. When I raised my head she pointed off into the woods to our left. At a height of perhaps four feet from the ground a ghastly red glow was moving rapidly away from us. It was not a torch; it was more a radiance, and it moved not evenly, but jerkily. I could feel the very hair rising on my head and it was all I could do to call Tish. When we had roused her, however, the glow had faded entirely and she said we had had a nightmare.

The snare the next morning contained a skunk, and we moved on as quickly as possible, without attempting to secure the thong, of which we had several. We gathered some puffballs to soak for breakfast and in a clearing I found some blackberry bushes. We were very cheerful that morning, for if we could capture rabbits and skunks, we were sure of other things, also, and soon we would be able to add fish to our menu. True, we had not had much time to commune with our souls, and Aggie's arms were so sunburned that she could not bend them at the elbows. But, as Tish said, we had already proved our contention that we could get along without men or houses or things. Things, she said, were the curse of modern life; we filled our lives with things instead of thoughts.

It was when we were ready to cook the puffballs that we missed the kettle! Tish was very angry; she said it was evident that the bear was mischievous and that all bears were thieves. (See the "Young Woodsman.") But I recalled the glow of the night before, and more than once I caught Aggie's eyes on me, filled with consternation. For we had seen that kettle leaving the camp with some of our fire in it, and bears are afraid of fire!

We reached the lake at noon and it seemed as if we might soon have time to sit down and rest. But there was a great deal to do. Aggie was of no assistance on account of her arms, so Tish and I put up the tent. The "Young Woodsman" said it was easy. First you tied three long poles together near the top and stood them up so they made a sort of triangle. Then you cut about a dozen and filled in between the three. That looked easy, but it took an afternoon, and our first three looked like this first cut.

As the First
Three Looked As They Should
Have Looked

We had caught a rabbit by noon, and Aggie being unfit for other work, and the kettle being gone, Tish set her to roasting it. It was not very good, but we ate some, being ravenous. The method was simplicity itself-two forked sticks in the ground, one across to hang the rabbit to and a fire beneath. It tasted rather smoky.

In the afternoon we finished putting up the tepee, and Tish made a fishhook out of a hairpin and tied it to a strong creeper I had found. But we caught no fish. We had more rabbit for supper, with some puffballs smoked and a few huckleberries. But by that time the very sight of a rabbit sickened me, and Aggie began to talk about broiled beefsteak and fried spring chicken.

We had seen no sign of the bear, or whatever it was, all day, and it seemed likely we were not to be again disturbed. But a most mysterious thing occurred that very night.

As I have said, we had caught no fish. The lake was full of them. We sat on a bank that evening and watched them playing leapfrog, and talked about frying them on red-hot stones, but nothing came near the hairpin. At last Tish made a suggestion.

"We need worms," she said. "A grasshopper loses all his spirit after he's been immersed for an hour, but a worm will keep on wriggling and attracting attention for half a day."

"I wanted to bring a spade," said I.

But Tish had read of a scheme for getting worms that she said the game warden of some place or other had guaranteed officially.

"You stick a piece of wood about two feet into the ground in a likely spot," she said, "and rub a rough piece of bark or plank across the top. This man claims, and it sounds reasonable, that the worms think it is raining and come up for water. All you have to do is to gather them up."

Tish found a pole for the purpose on the beach and set to work, while Aggie and I prepared several hooks and lines. The fish were jumping busily, and it seemed likely we should have more than we could do to haul them in.

The experiment, however, failed entirely, for not a single worm appeared. Tish laid it to the fact that it was very late and that the worms were probably settled down for the night. It may have been that, or it may have been the wrong kind of wood.

The mysterious happening was this: We rose quite early because the tepee did not seem to be well anchored and fell down on us at daybreak. Tish went down to the beach to examine the lines that had been out all night, and found nothing. She was returning rather dispirited to tell us that it would be rabbit again for breakfast, when she saw lying on a flat stone half a dozen beautiful fish, one or two still gasping, in our lost kettle!

Tish said she stood there, opening and shutting her mouth like the fish. Then she gave a whoop and we came running. At first we thought they might have been jumping and leaped out on to the beach by accident, but, as Tish said, they would hardly have landed all together and into a kettle that had been lost for two nights and a day. The queer thing was that they had not been caught with a hook at all. They hadn't a mark on them.

We were so hungry that we ate every one of them for breakfast. It was only when we had eaten, and were sitting gorged and not caring whether the tent was set up again or not, that we fell to wondering about the fish. Tish fancied it might have been the driver of the spring wagon, but decided he'd have sold us the fish at thirty cents a pound live weight.

All day long we watched for a sign of our benefactor, but we saw nothing. Tish set up more rabbit snares; not that she wanted rabbits, but it had become a mania with her, and there were so many of them that as they grew accustomed to us they sat round our camp in a ring and criticized our housekeeping. She thought if she got a good many skins she could have a fur robe made for her automobile. As a matter of fact she found another use for them.

It was that night, then, that we were sitting round the camp-fire on stones that we had brought up from the beach. We had seen nothing more of the bear, and if we had been asked we should have said that the nearest human being was twenty-five miles away.

Suddenly a voice came out of the woods just behind us, a man's voice.

"Please don't be alarmed," said the voice. "But may I have a little of your fire? Mine has gone out again."

"G-g-g-good gracious!" said Aggie. "T-Tish, get your revolver!"

This was for effect. Tish had no revolver.

All of us had turned and were staring into the woods behind, but we could see no one. After Aggie's speech about the revolver it was some time before the voice spoke again.

"Never mind, Aggie," Tish observed, very loud. "The revolver is here and loaded-as nice a little thirty-six as any one needs here in the woods."

She said afterward that she knew all the time there was no thirty-six caliber revolver, but in the excitement she got it mixed with her bust measure. Having replied to Aggie, Tish then turned in the direction of the voice.

"Don't skulk back there," she called. "Come out, where we can see you. If you look reliable, we'll give you some fire, of course."

There was another pause, as if the stranger were hesitating. Then: —

"I think I'd better not," he said with reluctance in his voice. "Can't you toss a brand this way?"

By that time we had grown accustomed to the darkness, and I thought I could see in the shadow of a tree a lightish figure. Aggie saw it at the same instant and clutched my arm.

"Lizzie!" she gasped.

It was at that moment that Tish tossed the brand. It fell far short, but her movement caught the stranger unawares. He ducked behind the tree, but the flare of light had caught him. With the exception of what looked like a pair of bathing-trunks he was as bare as my hand!

There was a sort of astonished silence. Then the voice called out: —"Why in the world didn't you warn me?" it said, aggrieved. "I didn't know you were going to throw the blamed thing."

We had all turned our backs at once and Tish's face was awful.

"Take it and go," she said, without turning. "Take it and go."

From the crackling of leaves and twigs we judged that he had come out and got the brand, and when he spoke again it was from farther back in the woods.

"You know," he said, "I don't like this any more than you do. I've got forty-two mosquito bites on my left arm."

He waited, as if for a reply; but getting none he evidently retreated. The sound of rustling leaves and crackling twigs grew fainter, fainter still, died away altogether. We turned then with one accord and gazed through the dark arches of the forest. A glowing star was retreating there —a smouldering fire, that seemed to move slowly and with an appearance of dejection.

It was the second time Aggie and I had seen fire thus carried through the wood; but whereas about the kettle there had been a glow and radiance that was almost triumphant, the brand we now watched seemed smouldering, dejected, ashamed. Even Tish felt it.

"The wretch!" she exclaimed. "Daring to come here like that! No wonder he's ashamed."

But Aggie, who is very romantic, sat staring after the distant torch.

"Mr. Wiggins suffered so from mosquitoes," she said softly.

IV

The next morning we found more fish awaiting us, and on the smooth sand of the beach was a message written with a stick: —

> If you will leave a wire hairpin or two on this stone I can get bigger fish. What do you mean to do with all those rabbit skins?

> (Signed) P.

Tish was touched by the fish, I think. She smoothed off the sand carefully and wrote a reply: —

> Here are the hairpins. Thank you. Do you want the rabbit skins?

> L.C.

All day we were in a state of expectancy. The mosquitoes were very bad, and had it not been for the excitement of the P —— person I should have given up and gone home. I wanted mashed potatoes and lima beans with butter dressing, and a cup of hot tea, and muffins, and ice-in fact, I cannot think of anything I did not want, except rabbits and fish and puffballs and such blackberries as the birds did not fancy. Although we were well enough-almost too well-the better I felt the hungrier I got.

Tish thought the time had now come to rest and invite our souls. She set the example that day by going out on a flat rock in the lake and preparing to think all the things she'd been waiting most of her life to consider.

"I am ready to form my own opinions about some things," she said. "I realize now that all my life the newspapers and stupid people and books have formed my opinions. Now I'm going to think along my own lines. Is there another life after this? Do I really desire the suffrage? Why am I a Baptist?"

Aggie said she would like to invite her soul that day also, not to form any opinions, —Tish always does that for her, —but she had to get some clothes in September and she might as well think them out.

So it happened that I was alone when I met the P —— person's young woman.

I had intended to wander only a short way along the trail, but after I had gone a mile or two it occurred to me as likely that the spring-wagon driver would come back that way before long out of curiosity, and I thought I might leave a message for him to bring out some fresh eggs and leave them there. I could tell Tish I had found a nest, or perhaps, since that would be lying, I could put them in a nest and let her find them. I'd have ordered tea, too, if I could have thought of any way to account for it.

"I'm going to do some meditating myself to-day," I remarked, "but I think better when I'm moving. If I don't come back in an hour or so don't imagine I've been kidnaped."

Tish turned on her stone and looked at me.

"You will not be kidnaped," she said shortly. "I cannot imagine any one safer than you are in that costume."

Well, I made my way along the trail as rapidly as I could. It was twenty miles there and back and I've seen the day when two city blocks would send me home to soak my feet in hot water. But the sandals were easy to walk in and my calico skirt was short and light.

I had no paper to write my message on, of course, but on the way I gathered a large white fungus and I scraped a note on it with a pin. With the fungus under my arm I walked briskly along, planning an omelet with the eggs, if we got any, and gathering mushrooms here and there. It was the mushrooms that led me to the discovery of a camping-place that was prehistoric in its primitiveness —a clearing, surrounded by low bushes, and in the center a fireplace of stones with a fire smouldering. At one side a heap of leaves and small twigs for a bed, a stump for a seat, and lying on top of it a sort of stone axe, made by inserting a sharp stone into the cleft of a sapling and tying it into place with a wild-grape tendril. Pegged out on the ground to cure was a rabbit skin, indifferently scraped. It made our aluminum kettle and canvas tepee look like a marble-vestibuled apartment on Riverside Drive.

The whole thing looked pitiful, hungry. I thought of Tish sitting on a stone inviting her soul, while rabbits came from miles round to stick their heads through our nooses and hang themselves for our dinner; and it seemed to me that we should share our plenty. I thought it probable that the gentleman of the woods lived here, and from the appearance of the place he carried all his possessions with him when he wore his bathing-trunks. If I had been in any doubt, the sight of Aggie's wire hairpin, sharpened and bent into a serviceable fishhook, decided me. I scratched a message for him on another fungus and left it: —

> If you need anything come to the Indian tepee at the lake. We have no clothing
> to spare, but are always glad to help in time of trouble.

(Signed) ONE OF THE SIMPLE LIFERS.

I went on after that and about noon reached our point of exodus from the wagon. I was tired and hot and I kept thinking of my little dining-room at home, with the electric fan going, and iced cantaloupe, and nobody worrying about her soul or thinking her own thoughts, and no rabbits.

Our suitcases were safe enough in the hollow tree, and I thought the spring wagon had been back already, for there were fresh tracks. This discouraged me and I sat down on a log to rest. It was then that I heard the girl crying.

She was crying softly, but in the woods sounds travel. I found her on her face on the pine needles about twenty yards away, wailing her heart out into a pink automobile veil, and she was so absorbed in her misery that I had to stoop and touch her before she looked up.

"Don't cry," I said. "If you are lost, I can direct you to a settlement."

She looked up at me, and from being very red and suffused she went quite pale. It seems that with my bare legs and sandals and my hair down, which was Tish's idea for making it come in thick and not gray, and what with my being sunburned and stained with berries, she thought I was a wild woman. I realized what was wrong.

"Don't be alarmed," I said somewhat grimly. "I'm rational enough; if I hop about instead of walking, it's because I'm the tomb of more rabbits than I care to remember, but aside from that I'm all right. Are you lost?"

She sat up, still staring, and wiped her eyes.

"No. I have a machine over there among the trees. Are there-are there plenty of rabbits in the woods?"

"Thousands." She was a pretty little thing, very young, and dressed in a white motor coat with white shoes and hat.

"And-and berries?"

"There aren't many berries," I admitted. "The birds eat 'em. We get the ones they don't fancy."

Now I didn't think for a moment that she was worried about my diet, but she was worried about the food supply in the woods, that was sure. So I sat down on a stump and told her about puffballs, and what Tish had read about ants being edible but acid, and that wood mice, roasted and not cooked too dry, were good food, but that Aggie had made us liberate the only ones we had caught, because a man she was once engaged to used to carry a pet mouse in his pocket.

Nothing had really appealed to her until I mentioned Mr. Wiggins. Then unexpectedly she began to cry again. And after that I got the whole story.

It seems she was in love with a young man who was everything a young man ought to be and had money as well. But the money was the barrier really, for the girl's father wouldn't believe that a youth who played polo, and did not have to work for a living, and led cotillons, and paid calls in the afternoon could have really good red blood in him. He had a man in view for her, she said, one who had made his money himself, and had to have his valet lay out his clothes for fear he'd make a mistake. Once the valet had to go to have a tooth pulled and the man had to decline a dinner.

"Father said," finished the little girl tearfully, "that if Percy-that's his name, and it counted against him too-that if Percy was a real man he'd do something. And then he hap-happened on a book of my small brother's, telling how people used to live in the woods, and kill their own food and make their own fire —"

"The 'Young Woodsman,' of course," I put in.

"And how the strong survived, but the weak succumbed, and he said if Percy was a man, and not a t-tailor's dummy, he'd go out in the woods, j-just primitive man, without anything but a pair of bathing trunks, and keep himself alive for a month. If he s-stood the test father was willing to forget the 'Percy.' He said that he knew Mr. Willoughby could do it-that's the other man-and that he'd come in at the end of the time with a deed for the forest and mortgages on all the surrounding camps."

"And Percy agreed?"

"He didn't want to. He said it took mentality and physical endurance as well as some courage to play polo. Father said it did-on the part of the pony. Then s-some of the men heard of it, and there were bets on it-ten to one he wouldn't do it and twenty to one he couldn't do it. So Percy decided to try. Father was so afraid that some of the campers and guides would help him that he had notices sent out at Mr. Willoughby's suggestion offering a reward if Percy could be shown to have asked any assistance. Oh, I know he's sick in there somewhere, or starving or-dead!"

I had had a great light break over me, and now I stooped and patted the girl on the shoulder.

"Dead! Certainly not," I said. "I saw him last night."

"Saw him!"

"Well, not exactly saw him-there wasn't much light. But he's alive and well, and-do you really want him to win?"

"Do I?" She sat up with shining eyes. "I don't care whether he owns anything in the world but the trunks. If I didn't think I'd add to his troubles I'd go into the woods this minute and find him and suffer with him."

"You'd have to be married to him first," I objected, rather startled.

But she looked at me with her cheeks as red strawberries. "Why?" she demanded. "Father's crazy about primitive man-did primitive man take his woman to church to be married, with eight brides maids and a reception after the ceremony? Of course not. He grabbed her and carried her off."

"Good Heavens! You're not in earnest?" "I think I am," she said slowly. "I'd rather live in the woods with Percy and no ceremony than live without him anywhere in the world. And I'll bet primitive man would have been wiped off the earth if he hadn't had primitive woman to add her wits to his strength. If Percy only had a woman to help him!"

"My dear," I said solemnly, "he has! He has, not one, but three!"

It took me some time to explain that Percy was not supporting a harem in the Maine woods; but when at last she got my idea and that the other two classed with me in beauty and attractiveness, she was overjoyed.

"But Percy promised not to ask for help," she said suddenly.

"He needn't. My dear, go away and stop worrying about Percy-he's all right. When is the time up?"

"In three weeks."

"I suppose father and the Willoughby person will come to meet him?"

"Yes, and all the fellows from the club who have put money up on him. We're going to motor over and father's bringing the physical director of the athletic club. He's not only got to survive, but he's got to be in good condition."

"He'll be in good condition," I said grimly. "Does he drink and smoke?"

"A little, not too much. Oh, yes, I had forgotten!" She opened up a little gold cigarette case, which she took from her pocket, and extracted a handful of cigarettes.

"If you are going to see him," she said, "you might put them where he'll find them?"

"Certainly not."

"But that's not giving them to him."

"My dear child," I said sternly, "Percy is going to come out of these woods so well and strong that he may not have to work, but he'll want to. And he'll not smoke anything stronger than corn-silk, if we're to take charge of this thing."

She understood quickly enough and I must say she was grateful. She was almost radiant with joy when I told her how capable Tish was, and that she was sure to be interested, and about Aggie's hay fever and Mr. Wiggins and the rabbit snares. She leaned over and kissed me impulsively.

"You dear old thing!" she cried. "I know you'll look after him and make him comfortable and-how old is Miss Letitia?"

"Something over fifty and Aggie Pilkington's about the same, although she won't admit it."

She kissed me again at that, and after looking at her wrist watch she jumped to her feet.

"Heavens!" she said. "It's four o'clock and my engine has been running all this time!"

She got a smart little car from somewhere up the road, and the last I saw of her she was smiling back over her shoulder and the car running on the edge of a ditch.

"You are three darlings!" she called back. "And tell Percy I love him-love him-love him!"

I thought I'd never get back to the lake. I was tired to begin with, and after I'd gone about four miles and was limping with a splinter in my heel and no needle to get it out with, I found I still had the fungus message to the spring-wagon person under my arm.

It was dark when I got back and my nerves were rather unstrung, what with wandering from the path here and there, with nothing to eat since morning, and running into a tree and taking the skin off my nose. When I limped into camp at last, I didn't care whether Percy lived or died, and the thought, of rabbit stew made my mouth water.

It was not rabbit, however. Aggie was sitting alone by the fire, waving a brand round her head to keep off mosquitoes, and in front of her, dangling from the spit, were a dozen pairs of frogs' legs in a row.

I ate six pairs without a question and then I asked for Tish.

"Catching frogs," said Aggie laconically, and flourished the brand.

"Where?"

"Pulling them off the trees. Where do you think she gets them?" she demanded.

A large mosquito broke through her guard at that moment and she flung the torch angrily at the fire.

"I'm eaten alive!" she snapped. "I wish to Heaven I had smallpox or something they could all take and go away and die."

The frogs' legs were heavenly, although in a restaurant I loathe the things. I left Aggie wondering if her hay fever wasn't contagious through the blood and hoping the mosquitoes would get it and sneeze themselves to death, and went to find Tish.

She was standing in the margin of the lake up to her knees in water, with a blazing torch in one hand and one of our tent poles in the other. Tied to the end the pole was a grapevine line, and a fishing-hook made of a hairpin was attached to it.

Her method, which it seems she'd heard from Charlie Sands and which was not in the "Young Woodsman," was simple and effectual.

"Don't move," she said tensely when she heard me on the bank. "There's one here as big as a chicken!"

She struck the flare forward, and I could see the frog looking at it and not blinking. He sat in a sort of heavenly ecstasy, like a dog about to bay at the moon, while the hook dangled just at his throat.

"I'm half-ashamed to do it, Lizzie, it's so easy," she said calmly, still tickling the thing's throat with the hook. "Grab him as I throw him at you. They slip off sometimes."

The next instant she jerked the hook up and caught the creature by the lower jaw. It was the neatest thing I have ever seen. Tish came wading over to where I stood and examined the frog.

"If we only had some Tartare sauce!" she said regretfully. "I wish you'd look at my ankle, Lizzie. There's something stuck to it."

The something was a leech. It refused to come off, and so she carried both frog and leech back to the camp. Aggie said on no account to pull a leech off, it left its teeth in and the teeth went on burrowing, or laid eggs or something. One must leave it on until it was full and round and couldn't hold any more, and then it dropped off.

So all night Tish kept getting up and going to the fire to see if it was swelling. But toward morning she fell asleep and it dropped off, and we had a terrible feeling that it was somewhere in our blankets.

But the leech caused less excitement that evening than my story of Percy and the little girl in the white coat. Aggie was entranced, and Tish had made Percy a suit of rabbit skin with a cap to match and outlined a set of exercises to increase his chest measure before I was half through with my story.

But Percy did not appear, although we had an idea that he was not far off in the woods. We could hear a crackling in the undergrowth, but when we called there was no reply. Tish was eating a frog's leg when the idea came to her.

"He'll never come out under ordinary circumstances in that-er-costume," she said. "Suppose we call for help. He'll probably come bounding. Help!" she yelled, between bites, as one may say.

"Help! Fire! Police!"

"Help!" cried Aggie. "Percy, help!" It sounded like "Mercy, help!"

It worked like a charm. The faint cracking became louder, nearer, turned from a suspicion to a certainty and from a certainty to a fact. The bushes parted and Percy stood before us. All he saw was three elderly women eating frogs' legs round a fire under a cloud of mosquitoes. He stopped, dumbfounded, and in that instant we saw that he didn't need the physical exercises, but that, of course, he did need the rabbit-skin suit.

"Great Scott!" he panted. "I thought I heard you calling for help."

"So we did," said Tish, "but we didn't need it. Won't you sit down?"

He looked dazed and backed toward the bushes.

"I —I think," he said, "if there's nothing wrong I'd better not —"

"Fiddlesticks!" Tish snapped. "Are you ashamed of the body the Lord gave you? Don't you suppose we've all got skins? And didn't I thrash my nephew, Charlie Sands, when he was almost as big as you and had less on, for bathing in the river? Sit down, man, and don't be a fool."

He edged toward the fire, looking rather silly, and Aggie passed him a frog's leg on a piece of bark.

"Try this, Percy," she said, smiling.

At the name he looked ready to run. "I guess you've seen the notices," he said, "so you'll understand I cannot accept any food or assistance. I'm very grateful to you, anyhow."

"You may take what food you find, surely," said Aggie. "If you find a roasted frog's leg on the ground-so-there's nothing to prevent you eating it, is there?"

"Nothing at all," said Percy, and picked it up. "Unless, of course —"

"It's not a trap, young man," said Tish. "Eat it and enjoy it. There are lots more where it came from."

He relaxed at that, and on Tish's bringing out a blanket from the tent to throw over his shoulders he became almost easy. He was much surprised to learn that we knew his story, and when I repeated the "love him" message, he seemed to grow a foot taller and his eyes glowed.

"I'm holding out all right," he said. "I'm fit physically. But the thing that gets my goat is that I'm to come out clothed. Dorothea's father says that primitive man, with nothing but his hands and perhaps a stone club, fed himself, made himself a shelter, and clothed himself in skins. Skins! I'm so big that two or three bears would hardly be enough. I did find a hole that I thought a bear or two might fall into, and got almost stung to death robbing a bee tree to bait the thing with honey. But there aren't any bears, and if there were how'd I kill 'em? Wait until they starve to death?"

"Rabbits!" said Tish.

He looked down at himself and he seemed very large in the firelight. "Dear lady," he said, "there aren't enough rabbits in the county to cover me, and how'd I put 'em together? I was a fool to undertake the thing, that's all."

"But aren't you in love with her?" asked Aggie.

"Well, I guess I am. It isn't that, you know. I'm a good bit worse than crazy about her. A man might be crazy about a mint julep or a power boat, but-he'd hardly go into the woods in his skin and live on fish until he's scaly for either of them. If I don't get her, I don't want to live. That's all."

He looked so gloomy and savage that we saw he meant it, and Aggie was perceptibly thrilled. Trish, however, was thinking hard, her eyes on the leech. "Was there anything in the agreement to prevent your accepting any suggestions?"

He pondered. "No, I was to be given no food, drink, shelter, or any weapon. The old man forgot fire-that's how I came to beg some."

"Fire and brains," reflected Tish. "We've given you the first and we've plenty of the second to offer. Now, young man, this is my plan. We'll give you nothing but suggestions. If now and then you find a cooked meal under that tree, that's accident, not design, and you'd better eat it. Can you sew?"

"I'm like the Irishman and the fiddle —I never tried, but I guess I can." He was much more cheerful.

"Do you have to be alone?"

"I believe he took that for granted, in this costume."

"Will it take you long to move over here?"

"I think I can move without a van," he said, grinning. "My sole worldly possessions are a stone hatchet and a hairpin fishhook."

"Get them and come over," commanded Tish. "When you leave this forest at the end of the time you are going to be fed and clothed and carry a tent; you will have with you smoked meat and fish; you will carry under your arm an Indian clock or sundial; you will have a lamp-if we can find a clamshell or a broken bottle-and you will have a fire-making outfit with your monogram on it."

"But, my dear friend," he said, "I am not supposed to have any assistance and—"

"Assistance!" Tish snapped. "Who said assistance? I'm providing the brains, but you'll do it all yourself."

He moved over an hour or so later and Tish and I went into the tent to bed. Somewhat later, when she limped to the fire to see how the leech was filling up, he and Aggie were sitting together talking, he of Dorothea and Aggie of Mr. Wiggins. Tish said they were both talking at the same time, neither one listening to the other, and that it sounded like this: —"She's so sweet and trusting and honest-well, I'd believe what she said if she —"

" —fell off a roof on a rainy day and was picked up by a man with a horse and buggy quite unconscious."

V

The next three weeks were busy times for Percy. He wore Tish's blanket for two days, and then, finding it in the way, he discarded it altogether. Seen in daylight it was easy to understand why little Dorothea was in love with him. He was a handsome young giant, although much bitten by mosquitoes and scratched with briers.

The arrangement was a good one all round. He knew of things in the wood we'd never heard of-wild onions and artichokes, and he had found a clump of wild cherry trees. He made snares of the fibers of tree bark, and he brought in turtles and made plates out of the shells. And all the time he was working on his outfit, curing rabbit skins and sewing them together with fibers under my direction.

When he'd made one sleeve of his coat we had a sort of celebration. He'd found an empty bottle somewhere in the woods, and he had made a wild-cherry decoction that he declared was cherry brandy, keeping it in the sun to ferment. Well, he insisted on opening the brandy that day and passing it round. We had cups made of leaves and we drank to his sleeve, although the stuff was villainous. He had put the sleeve on, and it looked rather inadequate. "Here's fun," he said joyously. "If my English tailor could see this sleeve he'd die of envy. A sleeve's not all of a coat, but what's a coat without a sleeve? Look at it-grace, ease of line, and beauty of material."

Aggie lifted her leaf.

"To Dorothea!" she said. "And may the sleeve soon be about her."

Tish thought this toast was not delicate, but Percy was enchanted with it.

It was on the evening of the fourth day of Percy's joining our camp that the Willoughby person appeared. It happened at a most inauspicious time. We had eaten supper and were gathered round the camp-fire and Tish had put wet leaves on the blaze to make a smudge that would drive the mosquitoes away. We were sitting there, Tish and I coughing and Aggie sneezing in the smoke, when Percy came running through the woods and stopped at the foot of a tree near by.

"Bring a club, somebody," he yelled. "I've treed the back of my coat."

Tish ran with one of the tent poles. A tepee is inconvenient for that reason. Every time any one wants a fishing-pole or a weapon, the tent loses part of its bony structure and sags like the face of a stout woman who has reduced. And it turned out that Percy had treed a coon. He climbed up after it, taking Tish's pole with him to dislodge it, and it was at that moment that a man rode into the clearing and practically fell off his horse. He was dirty and scratched with brambles, and his once immaculate riding-clothes were torn. He was about to take off his hat when he got a good look at us and changed his mind.

"Have you got anything to eat?" he asked. "I've been lost since noon yesterday and I'm about all in."

The leaves caught fire suddenly and sent a glow into Percy's tree. I shall never forget Aggie's agonized look or the way Tish flung on more wet leaves in a hurry.

"I'm sorry," she said, "but supper's over."

"But surely a starving man —"

"You won't starve inside of a week," Tish snapped. "You've got enough flesh on you for a month."

He stared at her incredulously.

"But, my good woman," he said, "I can pay for my food. Even you itinerant folk need money now and then, don't you? Come, now, cook me a fish; I'll pay for it. My name is Willoughby — J.K. Willoughby. Perhaps you've heard of me."

Tish cast a swift glance into the tree. It was in shadow again and she drew a long breath. She said afterward that the whole plan came to her in the instant of that breath.

"We can give you something," she said indifferently. "We have a stewed rabbit, if you care for it."

There was a wild scramble in the tree at that moment, and we thought all was over. We learned later that Percy had made a move to climb higher, out of the firelight, and the coon had been so startled that he almost fell out. But instead of looking up to investigate, the stranger backed toward the fire.

"Only a wildcat," said Tish. "They'll not come near the fire."

"Near!" exclaimed Mr. Willoughby. "If they came any nearer, they'd have to get into it!"

"I think," said Tish, "that if you are afraid of them-although you are safe enough if you don't get under the trees; they jump down, you know-that you would better stay by the fire to-night. In the morning we'll start you toward a road."

All night with Percy in the tree! I gave her a savage glance, but she ignored me.

The Willoughby looked up nervously, and of course there were trees all about.

"I guess I'll stay," he agreed. "What about that rabbit?"

I did not know Tish's plan at that time, and while Aggie was feeding the Willoughby person and he was grumbling over his food, I took Tish aside.

"Are you crazy?" I demanded. "Just through your idiocy Percy will have to stay in that tree all night-and he'll go to sleep, likely, and fall out."

Tish eyed me coldly.

"You are a good soul, Lizzie," she observed, "but don't overwork your mind. Go back and do something easy-let the Willoughby cross your palm with silver, and tell his fortune. If he asks any questions I'm queen of the gypsies, and give him to understand that we're in temporary hiding from the law. The worse he thinks of us the better. Remember, we haven't seen Percy."

"I'm not going to lie," I said sternly.

"Pooh!" Tish sneered. "That wretch came into the woods to gloat over his rival's misery. The truth's too good for him."

I did my best, and I still have the silver dollar he gave me. I told him I saw a small girl, who loved him but didn't realize it yet, and there was another man.

"Good gracious," I said, "there must be something wrong with your palm. I see the other man, but he seems to be in trouble. His clothing has been stolen, for he has none, and he is hungry, very hungry."

"Ha!" said Mr. Willoughby, looking startled. "You old gypsies beat the devil! Hungry, eh? Is that all?"

The light flared up again and I could see clearly the pale spot in the tree, which was Percy. But Mr. Willoughby's eyes were on his palm.

"He has about decided to give up something —I cannot see just what," I said loudly. "He seems to be in the air, in a tree, perhaps. If he wishes to be safe he should go higher."

Percy took the hint and moved up, and I said that was all there was in the palm. Soon after that Mr. Willoughby stretched out on the ground by the fire, and before long he was asleep.

During the night I heard Tish moving stealthily about in the tepee and she stepped on my ankle as she went out. I fell asleep again as soon as it stopped aching. Just at dawn Tish came back and touched me on the shoulder.

"Where's the blackberry cordial?" she whispered I sat up instantly.

"Has Percy fallen out of the tree?"

"No. Don't ask any questions, Lizzie. I want it for myself. That dratted horse fell on me."

She refused to say any more and lay down groaning. But I was too worried to sleep again. In the morning Percy was gone from the tree. Mr. Willoughby had more rabbit and prepared to leave the forest. He offered Tish a dollar for the two meals and a bed, and Tish, who was moving about stiffly, said that she and her people took no money for their hospitality. Telling fortunes was one thing, bread and salt was another. She looked quite haughty, and the Willoughby person apologized and went into the woods to get his horse.

The horse was gone!

It was rather disagreeable for a time. He plainly thought we'd taken it, although Tish showed him that the end of the strap had been chewed partly through and then jerked free.

"If the creature smelled a wildcat," she said, "nothing would hold it. None of my people ever bring a horse into this part of the country."

"Humph!" said Mr. Willoughby. "Well, I'll bet they take a few out!"

He departed on foot shortly after, very disgusted and suspicious. We showed him the trail, and the last we saw of him he was striding along, looking up now and then for wildcats.

When he was well on his way, Percy emerged from the bushes. I had thought that he had helped Tish to take the Willoughby horse, but it seems he had not, and he was much amazed when Tish came through the wood leading the creature by the broken strap.

"I'll turn it loose," she said to Percy, "and you can capture it. It will make a good effect for you to emerge from the forest on horseback, and anyhow, what with the rabbit skin, the tent, and the sundial and the other things, you have a lot to carry. You can say you found it straying in the woods and captured it."

Percy looked at her with admiration not unmixed with reverence. "Miss Letitia," he said solemnly, "if it were not for Dorothea, I should ask you to marry me. I'd like to have you in my family."

I am very nearly to the end of my narrative.

Toward the last Percy was obliged to work far into the night, for of course we could not assist him. He made a full suit of rabbit skins sewed with fibers, and a cap and shoes of coonskin to match. The shoes were cut from a bedroom-slipper pattern that Tish traced in the sand on the beach, and the cap had an eagle feather in it. He made a birch-bark knapsack to hold the fish he smoked and a bow and arrow that looked well but would not shoot. When he had the outfit completed, he put it on, with the stone hatchet stuck into a grapevine belt and the bow and arrow over his shoulder, and he looked superb.

"The question is," he reflected, trying to view himself in the edge of the lake: "Will Dorothea like it? She's very keen about clothes. And gee, how she hates a beard!"

"You could shave as the Indians do," Tish said.

"How?"

"With a clamshell."

He looked dubious, but Tish assured him it was feasible. So he hunted a clamshell, a double one, Tish requested, and brought it into camp.

"I'd better do it for you," said Tish. "It's likely to be slow, but it is sure."

He was eyeing the clamshell and looking more and more uneasy.

"You're not going to scrape it off?" he asked anxiously. "You know, pumice would be better for that, but somehow I don't like the idea."

"Nothing of the sort," said Tish. "The double clamshell merely forms a pair of Indian nippers. I'm going to pull it out."

But he made quite a fuss about it, and said he didn't care whether the Indians did it or not, he wouldn't. I think he saw how disappointed Tish was and was afraid she would attempt it while he slept, for he threw the Indian nippers into the lake and then went over and kissed her hand.

"Dear Miss Tish," he said; "no one realizes more than I your inherent nobility of soul and steadfastness of purpose. I admire them both. But if you attempt the Indian nipper business, or to singe me like a chicken while I sleep, I shall be-forgive me, but I know my impulsiveness of disposition —I shall be really vexed with you."

Toward the last we all became uneasy for fear hard work was telling on him physically. He used to sit cross-legged on the ground, sewing for dear life and singing Hood's "Song of the Shirt" in a doleful tenor.

"You know," he said, "I've thought once or twice I'd like to do something-have a business like other fellows. But somehow dressmaking never occurred to me. Don't you think the expression of this right pant is good? And shall I make this gore bias or on the selvage?"

He wanted to slash one trouser leg.

"Why not?" he demanded when Tish frowned him down. "It's awfully fetching, and beauty half-revealed, you know. Do you suppose my breastbone will ever straighten out again? It's concave from stooping."

It was after this that Tish made him exercise morning and evening and then take a swim in the lake. By the time he was to start back, he was in wonderful condition, and even the horse looked saucy and shiny, owing to our rubbing him down each day with dried grasses.

The actual leave-taking was rather sad. We'd grown to think a lot of the boy and I believe he liked us. He kissed each one of us twice, once for himself and once for Dorothea, and flushed a little over doing it, and Aggie's eyes were full of tears.

He rode away down the trail like a mixture of Robinson Crusoe and Indian brave, his rubbing-fire stick, his sundial with burned figures, and his bow and arrow jingling, his eagle feather blowing back in the wind, and his moccasined feet thrust into Mr. Willoughby's stirrups, and left us desolate. Tish watched him out of sight with set lips and Aggie was whimpering on a bank.

"Tish," she said brokenly, "does he recall anything to you?"

"Only my age," said Tish rather wearily, "and that I'm an elderly spinster teaching children to defy their parents and committing larceny to help them."

"To me," said Aggie softly, "he is young love going out to seek his mate. Oh, Tish, do you remember how Mr. Wiggins used to ride by taking his work horses to be shod!"

We went home the following day, which was the time the spring-wagon man was to meet us. We started very early and were properly clothed and hatted when we saw him down the road.

The spring-wagon person came on without hurry and surveyed us as he came.

"Well, ladies," he said, stopping before us, "I see you pulled it off all right."

"We've had a very nice time, thank you," said Tish, drawing on her gloves. "It's been rather lonely, of course."

The spring-wagon person did not speak again until he had reached the open road. Then he turned round.

"The horse business was pretty good," he said. "You ought to hev seen them folks when he rode out of the wood. Flabbergasted ain't the word. They was ding-busted."

Tish whispered to us to show moderate interest and to say as little as possible, except to protest our ignorance. And we got the story at last like this: —

It seems the newspapers had been full of the attempt Percy was to make, and so on the day before quite a crowd had gathered to see him come out of the wood.

"Ten of these here automobiles," said the spring-wagon person, "and a hay-wagon full of newspaper fellows from the city with cameras, and about half the village back home walked out or druv and brought their lunches-sort of a picnic. I kep' my eye on the girl and on a Mr. Willoughby.

"The story is that Willoughby who was the father's choice-Willoughby was pale and twitching and kep' moving about all the time. But the girl, she just kep' her eyes on the trail and waited. Noon was the time set, or as near it as possible.

"The father talked to the newspaper men mostly. 'I don't think he'll do it, boys!' he said. 'He's as soft as milk and he's surprised me by sticking it out as long as he has. But mark my words, boys,' he said, 'he's been living on berries and things he could pick up off the ground, and if his physical condition's bad he loses all bets!"

It seems that, just as he said it, somebody pulled out a watch and announced "noon." And on the instant Percy was seen riding down the trail and whistling. At first they did not know it was he, as they had expected him to arrive on foot, staggering with fatigue probably. He rode out into the sunlight, still whistling, and threw an unconcerned glance over the crowd.

He looked at the trees, and located north by the moss on the trunks, the S.-W.P. said, and unslinging his Indian clock he held it in front of him, pointing north and south. It showed exactly noon. It was then, and not until then, that Percy addressed the astonished crowd.

"Twelve o'clock, gentlemen," he said. "My watch is quite accurate."

Nobody said anything, being, as the S.-W.P. remarked, struck dumb. But a moment afterward the hay-wagon started a cheer and the machines took it up. Even the father "let loose," as we learned, and the little girl sat back in her motor car and smiled through her tears.

But Willoughby was furious. It seems he had recognized the horse. "That's my horse," he snarled. "You stole it from me."

"As a matter of fact," Percy retorted, "I found the beast wandering loose among the trees and I'm perfectly willing to return him to you. I brought him out for a purpose."

"To make a Garrison finish!"

"Not entirely. To prove that you violated the contract by going into the forest to see if you could find me and gloat over my misery. Instead you found-By the way, Willoughby, did you see any wild-cats?"

"Those three hags are in this!" said Willoughby furiously. "Are you willing to swear you made that silly outfit?"

"I am, but not to you."

"And at that minute, if you'll believe me," said the S.-W.P., "the girl got out of her machine and walked right up to the Percy fellow. I was standing right by and I heard what she said. It was, curious, seeing he'd had no help and had gone in naked, as you may say, and came out clothed head to foot, with a horse and weapons and a watch, and able to make fire in thirty-one seconds, and a tent made of about a thousand rabbit skins."

Tish eyed him coldly.

"What did she say?" she demanded severely. "She said: 'Those three dear old things!'" replied the S.-W.P. "And she said: 'I hope you kissed them for me.'"

"He did indeed," said Aggie dreamily, and only roused when Tish nudged her in a rage.

Charlie Sands came to have tea with us yesterday at Tish's. He is just back from England and full of the subject.

"But after all," he said, "the Simple Lifers take the palm. Think of it, my three revered and dearly beloved spinster friends; think of the peace, the holy calm of it! Now, if you three would only drink less tea and once in a while would get back to Nature a bit, it would be good for you. You're all too civilized."

"Probably," said Tish, pulling down her sleeves to hide her sunburned hands. "But do you think people have so much time in the-er-woods?"

"Time!" he repeated. "Why, what is there to do?"

Just then the doorbell rang and a huge box was carried in. Tish had a warning and did not wish to open it, but Charlie Sands insisted and cut the string. Inside were three sets of sable furs, handsomer than any in the church, Tish says, and I know I've never seen any like them.

Tish and I hid the cards, but Aggie dropped hers and Charlie Sands pounced on it.

" 'The sleeve is now about Dorothea,' " he read aloud, and then, turning, eyed us all sternly.

"Now, then," said Charlie Sands, "out with it! What have you been up to this time?"

Tish returned his gaze calmly. "We have been in the Maine woods in the holy calm," she said. "As for those furs, I suppose a body may buy a set of furs if she likes." This, of course, was not a lie. "As for that card, it's a mistake." Which it was indeed.

"But-Dorothea!" persisted Charlie Sands.

"Never in my life knew anybody named Dorothea. Did you, Aggie?"

"Never," said Aggie firmly.

Charlie Sands apologized and looked thoughtful. On Tish's remaining rather injured, he asked us all out to dinner that night, and almost the first thing he ordered was frogs' legs. Aggie got rather white about the lips.

"I —I think I'll not take any," she said feebly. "I —I keep thinking of Tish tickling their throats with the hairpin, and how Percy —"

We glared at her, but it was too late. Charlie Sands drew up his chair and rested his elbows on the table.

"So there was a Percy as well as a Dorothea!" he said cheerfully. "I might have known it. Now we'll have the story!"

Tish's Spy

The Adventure of the Red-headed Detective, the Lady Chauffeur, and the Man Who Could Not Tell the Truth

I

It is easy enough, of course, to look back on our Canadian experience and see where we went wrong. What I particularly resent is the attitude of Charlie Sands.

I am writing this for his benefit. It seems to me that a clean statement of the case is due to Tish, and, in less degree, to Aggie and myself.

It goes back long before the mysterious cipher. Even the incident of our abducting the girl in the pink tam-o'-shanter was, after all, the inevitable result of the series of occurrences that preceded it.

It is my intention to give this series of occurrences in their proper order and without bias. Herbert Spencer says that every act of one's life is the unavoidable result of every act that has preceded it.

Naturally, therefore, I begin with the engagement by Tish of a girl as chauffeur; but even before that there were contributing causes. There was the faulty rearing of the McDonald youth, for instance, and Tish's æsthetic dancing. And afterward there was Aggie's hay fever, which made her sneeze and let go of a rope at a critical moment. Indeed, Aggie's hay fever may be said to be one of the fundamental causes, being the reason we went to Canada.

It was like this: Along in June of the year before last, Aggie suddenly announced that she was going to spend the summer in Canada.

"It's the best thing in the world for hay fever," she said, avoiding Tish's eye. "Mrs. Ostermaier says she never sneezed once last year. The Northern Lights fill the air with ozone, or something like that."

"Fill the air with ozone!" Tish scoffed. "Fill Mrs. Ostermaier's skull with ozone, instead of brains, more likely!"

Tish is a good woman —a sweet woman, indeed; but she has a vein of gentle irony, which she inherited from her maternal grandfather, who was on the Supreme Bench of his country. However, that spring she was inclined to be irritable. She could not drive her car, and that was where the trouble really started.

Tish had taken up æsthetic dancing in Mareb, wearing no stays and a middy blouse and short skirt; and during a fairy dance, where she was to twirl on her right toes, keeping the three other limbs horizontal, she twisted her right lower limb severely. Though not incapacitated, she could not use it properly; and, failing one day to put on the brake quickly, she drove into an open-front butter-and-egg shop.

(This was the time one of the newspapers headed the article: "Even the Eggs Scrambled.")

When Tish decided to have a chauffeur for a time she advertised. There were plenty of replies, but all of the applicants smoked cigarettes —a habit Tish very properly deplores. The idea of securing a young woman was, I must confess, mine.

"Plenty of young women drive cars," I said, "and drive well. And, at least, they don't light a cigarette every time one stops to let a train go by."

"Huh!" Tish commented. "And have a raft of men about all the time!"

Nevertheless, she acted on the suggestion, advertising for a young woman who could drive a car and had no followers. Hutchins answered.

She was very pretty and not over twenty; but, asked about men, her face underwent a change, almost a hardening. "You'll not be bothered with men," she said briefly. "I detest them!"

And this seemed to be the truth. Charlie Sands, for instance, for whose benefit this is being written, absolutely failed to make any impression on her. She met his overtures with cold disdain. She was also adamant to the men at the garage, succeeding in having the gasoline filtered through a chamois skin to take out the water, where Tish had for years begged for the same thing without success.

Though a dashing driver, Hutchins was careful. She sat on the small of her back and hurled us past the traffic policemen with a smile.

(Her name was really Hutchinson; but it took so long to say it at the rate she ran the car that Tish changed it to Hutchins.)

Really the whole experiment seemed to be an undoubted success, when Aggie got the notion of Canada into her head. Now, as it happened, owing to Tish's disapproval, Aggie gave up the Canada idea in favor of Nantucket, some time in June; but she had not reckoned with Tish's subconscious self. Tish was interested that spring in the subconscious self.

You may remember that, only a year or so before, it had been the fourth dimension.

(She became convinced that if one were sufficiently earnest one could go through closed doors and see into solids. In the former ambition she was unsuccessful, obtaining only bruises and disappointment; but she did develop the latter to a certain extent, for she met the laundress going out one day and, without a conscious effort, she knew that she had the best table napkins pinned to her petticoat. She accused the woman sternly-and she had six!)

"Nantucket!" said Tish. "Why Nantucket?"

"I have a niece there, and you said you hated Canada."

"On the contrary," Tish replied, with her eyes partly shut, "I find that my subconscious self has adopted and been working on the Canadian suggestion. What a wonderful thing is this buried and greater ego! Worms, rifles, fishing-rods, 'The Complete Angler,' mosquito netting, canned goods, and sleeping-bags, all in my mind and in orderly array!"

"Worms!" I said, with, I confess, a touch of scorn in my voice. "If you will tell me, Tish Carberry —"

"Life preservers," chanted Tish's subconscious self, "rubber blankets, small tent, folding camp-beds, a camp-stove, a meat-saw, a wood-saw, and some beads and gewgaws for placating the Indians." Then she opened her eyes and took up her knitting. "There are no worms in Canada, Lizzie, just as there are no snakes in Ireland. They were all destroyed during the glacial period."

"There are plenty of worms in the United States," I said with spirit. "I dare say they could crawl over the border-unless, of course, they object to being British subjects."

She ignored me, however, and, getting up, went to one of her bureau drawers. We saw then that her subconscious self had written down lists of various things for the Canadian excursion. There was one headed Foodstuffs. Others were: Necessary Clothing: Camp Outfit; Fishing-Tackle; Weapons of Defense: and Diversions. Under this last heading it had placed binoculars, yarn and needles, life preservers, a prayer-book, and a cribbage-board.

"Boats," she said, "we can secure from the Indians, who make them, I believe, of hollow logs. And I shall rent a motor boat. Hutchins says she can manage one. When she's not doing that she can wash dishes."

(We had been rather chary of motor boats, you may remember, since the time on Lake Penzance, when something jammed on our engine, and we had gone madly round the lake a number of times, with people on various docks trying to lasso us with ropes.)

Considering that it was she who had started the whole thing, and got Tish's subconscious mind to working, Aggie was rather pettish.

"Huh!" she said. "I can't swim, and you know it, Tish. Those canoe things turn over if you so much as sneeze in them."

"You'll not sneeze," said Tish. "The Northern Lights fill the air with ozone."

Aggie looked at me helplessly; but I could do nothing. Only the year before, Tish, as you may recall, had taken us out into the Maine woods without any outfit at all, and we had lived on snared rabbits, and things that no Christian woman ought to put into her stomach. This time we were at least to go provisioned and equipped.

"Where are we going?" Aggie asked.

"Far from a white man," said Tish. "Away from milk wagons and children on velocipedes and the grocer calling up every morning for an order. We'll go to the Far North, Aggie, where the red man still treads his native forests; we'll make our camp by some lake, where the deer come at early morning to drink and fish leap to see the sunset."

Well, it sounded rather refreshing, though I confess that, until Tish mentioned it, I had always thought that fish leaped in the evening to catch mosquitoes.

We sent for Hutchins at once. She was always respectful, but never subservient. She stood in the doorway while Tish explained.

"How far north?" she said crisply. Tish told her. "We'll have no cut-and-dried destination," she said. "There's a little steamer goes up the river I have in mind. We'll get off when we see a likely place."

"Are you going for trout or bass?"

Tish was rather uncertain, but she said bass on a chance, and Hutchins nodded her approval.

"If it's bass, I'll go," she said. "I'm not fond of trout-fishing."

"We shall have a motor boat. Of course I shall not take the car."

Hutchins agreed indifferently. "Don't you worry about the motor boat," she said. "Sometimes they go, and sometimes they don't. And I'll help round the camp; but I'll not wash dishes."

"Why not?" Tish demanded.

"The reason doesn't really matter, does it? What really concerns you is the fact."

Tish stared at her; but instead of quailing before Tish's majestic eye she laughed a little.

"I've camped before," she said. "I'm very useful about a camp. I like to cook; but I won't wash dishes. I'd like, if you don't mind, to see the grocery order before it goes."

Well, Aggie likes to wash dishes if there is plenty of hot water; and Hannah, Tish's maid, refusing to go with us on account of Indians, it seemed wisest to accept Hutchins's services.

Hannah's defection was most unexpected. As soon as we reached our decision, Tish ordered beads for the Indians; and in the evenings we strung necklaces, and so on, while one of us read aloud from the works of Cooper. On the second evening thus occupied, Hannah, who is allowed to come into Tish's sitting-room in the evening and knit, suddenly burst into tears and refused to go.

"My scalp's as good to me as it is to anybody, Miss Tish," she said hysterically; and nothing would move her.

She said she would run no risk of being cooked over her own camp-fire; and from that time on she would gaze at Tish for long periods mournfully, as though she wanted to remember how she looked when she was gone forever.

Except for Hannah, everything moved smoothly. Tish told Charlie Sands about the plan, and he was quite enthusiastic.

"Great scheme!" he said. "Eat a broiled black bass for me. And take the advice of one who knows: don't skimp on your fishing-tackle. Get the best. Go light on the canned goods, if necessary; but get the best reels and lines on the market. Nothing in life hurts so much," he said impressively, "as to get a three-pound bass to the top of the water and have your line break. I've had a big fellow get away like that and chase me a mile with its thumb on its nose." This last, of course, was purely figurative.

He went away whistling. I wish he had been less optimistic. When we came back and told him the whole story, and he sat with his mouth open and his hair, as he said, crackling at the roots, I reminded him with some bitterness that he had encouraged us. His only retort was to say that the excursion itself had been harmless enough; but that if three elderly ladies, church members in good standing, chose to become freebooters and pirates the moment they got away from a corner policeman, they need not blame him.

The last thing he said that day in June was about fishing-worms.

"Take 'em with you," he said. "They charge a cent apiece for them up there, assorted colors, and there's something stolid and British about a Canadian worm. The fish aren't crazy about 'em. On the other hand, our worms here are-er-vivacious, animated. I've seen a really brisk and on-to-its-job United States worm reach out and clutch a bass by the gills."

I believe it was the next day that Tish went to the library and read about worms. Aggie and I had spent the day buying tackle, according to Charlie Sands's advice. We got some very good rods with nickel-plated reels for two dollars and a quarter, a dozen assorted hooks for each person, and a dozen sinkers. The man wanted to sell us what he called a "landing net," but I took a good look at it and pinched Aggie.

"I can make one out of a barrel hoop and mosquito netting," I whispered; so we did not buy it.

Perhaps he thought we were novices, for he insisted on showing us all sorts of absurd things-trolling-hooks, he called them; gaff hooks for landing big fish and a spoon that was certainly no spoon and did not fool us for a minute, being only a few hooks and a red feather. He asked a dollar and a quarter for it!

(I made one that night at home, using a bit of red feather from a duster. It cost me just three cents. Of that, as of Hutchins, more later.)

Aggie, whose idea of Canada had been the Hotel Frontenac, had grown rather depressed as our preparations proceeded. She insisted that night on recalling the fact that Mr. Wiggins had been almost drowned in Canada.

"He went with the Roof and Gutter Club, Lizzie," she said, "and he was a beautiful swimmer; but the water comes from the North Pole, freezing cold, and the first thing he knew —"

The telephone bell rang just then. It was Tish.

"I've just come from the library, Lizzie," she said. "We'd better raise the worms. We've got a month to do it in. Hutchins and I will be round with the car at eight o'clock to-night. Night is the time to get them."

She refused to go into details, but asked us to have an electric flash or two ready and a couple of wooden pails. Also she said to wear mackintoshes and rubbers. Just before she rang off, she asked me to see that there was a package of oatmeal on hand, but did not explain. When I told Aggie she eyed me miserably.

"I wish she'd be either more explicit or less," she said. "We'll be arrested again. I know it!"

(Now and then Tish's enthusiasms have brought us into collision with the law-not that Tish has not every respect for law and order, but that she is apt to be hasty and at times almost unconventional.)

"You remember," said Aggie, "that time she tried to shoot the sheriff, thinking he was a train robber? She started just like this-reading up about walking-tours, and all that. I —I'm nervous, Lizzie."

I was staying with Aggie for a few days while my apartment was being papered. To soothe Aggie's nerves I read aloud from Gibbon's "Rome" until dinner-time, and she grew gradually calmer.

"After all, Lizzie," she said, "she can't get us into mischief with two wooden pails and a package of oatmeal."

Tish and Hutchins came promptly at eight and we got into the car. Tish wore the intent and dreamy look that always preceded her enterprises. There was a tin sprinkling-can, quite new, in the tonneau, and we placed our wooden pails beside it and the oatmeal in it. I confess I was curious, but to my inquiries Tish made only one reply: —

"Worms!"

Now I do not like worms. I do not like to touch them. I do not even like to look at them. As the machine went along I began to have a creepy loathing of them. Aggie must have been feeling the same way, for when my hand touched hers she squealed.

Over her shoulder Tish told her plan. She said it was easy to get fishing-worms at night and that Hutchins knew of a place a few miles out of town where the family was away and where there would be plenty.

"We'll put them in boxes of earth," she said, "and feed them coffee or tea grounds one day and oatmeal water the next. They propagate rapidly. We'll have a million to take with us. If we only have a hundred thousand at a cent apiece, that's a clear saving of a thousand dollars."

"We could sell some," I suggested sarcastically; for Tish's enthusiasms have a way of going wrong.

But she took me seriously. "If there are any fishing clubs about," she said, "I dare say they'll buy them; and we can turn the money over to Mr. Ostermaier for the new organ."

Tish had bought the organ and had an evening concert with it before we turned off the main road into a private drive.

"This is the place," Hutchins said laconically.

Tish got out and took a survey. There was shrubbery all round and a very large house, quite dark, in the foreground.

"Drive onto the lawn, Hutchins," she said. "When the worms come up, the lamps will dazzle them and they'll be easy to capture."

We bumped over a gutter and came to a stop in the middle of the lawn.

"It would be better if it was raining," Tish said. "You know, yourself, Lizzie, how they come up during a gentle rain. Give me the sprinkling-can."

I do not wish to lay undue blame on Hutchins, who was young; but it was she who suggested that there would probably be a garden hose somewhere and that it would save time. I know she went with Tish round the corner of the house, and that they returned in ten minutes or so, dragging a hose.

"I broke a tool-house window," Tish observed, "but I left fifty cents on the sill to replace it. It's attached at the other end. Run back, Hutchins, and turn on the water; but not too much. We needn't drown the little creatures."

Well, I have never seen anything work better. Aggie, who had refused to put a foot out of the car, stood up in it and held the hose. As fast as she wet a bit of lawn, we followed with the pails. I spread my mackintosh out and knelt on it.

The thing took skill. The worms had a way of snapping back into their holes like lightning.

Tish got about three to my one, and talked about packing them in moss and ice, and feeding them every other day. Hutchins, however, stood on the lawn, with her hands in her pockets, and watched the house.

Suddenly, without warning, Aggie turned the hose directly on my left ear and held it there.

"There's somebody coming!" she cried. "Merciful Heavens, what'll I do with the hose?"

"You can turn it away from me!" I snapped.

So she did, and at that instant a young man emerged from the shrubbery.

He did not speak at once. Probably he could not. I happened to look at Hutchins, and, for all her usual *savoir-faire*, as Charlie Sands called it, she was clearly uncomfortable.

Tish, engaged in a struggle at that moment and sitting back like a robin, did not see him at once.

"Well!" said the young man; and again: "Well, upon my word!"

He seemed out of breath with surprise; and he took off his hat and mopped his head with a handkerchief. And, of course, as though things were not already bad enough, Aggie sneezed at that instant, as she always does when she is excited; and for just a second the hose was on him.

It was unexpected and he almost staggered. He looked at all of us, including Hutchins, and ran his handkerchief round inside his collar. Then he found his voice.

"Really," he said, "this is awfully good of you. We do need rain-don't we?"

Tish was on her feet by that time, but she could not think of anything to say.

"I'm sorry if I startled you," said the young man. "I —I'm a bit startled myself."

"There is nothing to make a fuss about!" said Hutchins crisply. "We are getting worms to go fishing."

"I see," said the young man. "Quite natural, I'm sure. And where are you going fishing?"

Hutchins surprised us all by rudely turning her back on him. Considering we were on his property and had turned his own hose on him, a little tact would have been better.

Tish had found her voice by that time. "We broke a window in the tool-house," she said; "but I put fifty cents on the sill."

"Thank you," said the young man.

Hutchins wheeled at that and stared at him in the most disagreeable fashion; but he ignored her.

"We are trespassing," said Tish; "but I hope you understand. We thought the family was away."

"I just happened to be passing through," he explained. "I'm awfully attached to the place-for various reasons. Whenever I'm in town I spend my evenings wandering through the shrubbery and remembering-er-happier days."

"I think the lamps are going out," said Hutchins sharply. "If we're to get back to town —"

"Ah!" he broke in. "So you have come out from the city?"

"Surely," said Hutchins to Tish, "it is unnecessary to give this gentleman any information about ourselves! We have done no damage —"

"Except the window," he said.

"We've paid for that," she said in a nasty tone; and to Tish: "How do we know this place is his? He's probably some newspaper man, and if you tell him who you are this whole thing will be in the morning paper, like the eggs."

"I give you my word of honor," he said, "that I am nothing of the sort; in fact, if you will give me a little time I'd —I'd like to tell all about myself. I've got a lot to say that's highly interesting, if you'll only listen."

Hutchins, however, only gave him a cold glance of suspicion and put the pails in the car. Then she got in and sat down.

"I take it," he said to her, "that you decline either to give or to receive any information."

"Absolutely!"

He sighed then, Aggie declares.

"Of course," he said, "though I haven't really the slightest curiosity, I could easily find out, you know. Your license plates —"

"Are under the cushion I'm sitting on," said Hutchins, and started the engine.

"Really, Hutchins," said Tish, "I don't see any reason for being so suspicious. I have always believed in human nature and seldom have I been disappointed. The young man has done nothing to justify rudeness. And since we are trespassing on his place —"

"Huh!" was all Hutchins said.

The young man sauntered over to the car, with his hands thrust into this coat pockets. He was nice-looking, especially then, when he was smiling.

"Hutchins!" he said. "Well, that's a clue anyhow. It-it's an uncommon name. You didn't happen to notice a large 'No-Trespassing!' sign by the gate, did you?"

Hutchins only looked ahead and ignored him. As Tish said afterward, we had a good many worms, anyhow; and, as the young man and Hutchins had clearly taken an awful dislike to each other at first sight, the best way to avoid trouble was to go home. So she got into the car. The young man helped her and took off his hat.

"Come out any time you like," he said affably. "I'm not here at all in the daytime, and the grounds are really rather nice. Come out and get some roses. We've some pretty good ones-English importations. If you care to bring some children from the tenements out for a picnic, please feel free to do it. We're not selfish."

Hutchins rudely started the car before he had finished; but he ignored her and waved a cordial farewell to the rest of us.

"Bring as many as you like," he called. "Sunday is a good day. Ask Miss-Miss Hutchins to come out and bring some friends along."

We drove back at the most furious rate. Tish was at last compelled to remonstrate with Hutchins.

"Not only are we going too fast," she said, "but you were really rude to that nice young man."

"I wish I had turned the hose on him and drowned him!" said Hutchins between her teeth.

II

Hutchins brought a newspaper to Tish the next morning at breakfast, and Tish afterwards said her expression was positively malevolent in such a young and pretty woman.

The newspaper said that an attempt had been made to rob the Newcomb place the night before, but that the thieves had apparently secured nothing but a package of oatmeal and a tin sprinkling-can, which they had abandoned on the lawn. Some color, however, was lent to the fear that they had secured an amount of money, from the fact that a silver half-dollar had been found on the window sill of a tool-house. The Newcomb family was at its summer home on the Maine coast.

"You see," Hutchins said to Tish, "that man didn't belong there at all. He was just impertinent and-laughing in his sleeve."

Tish was really awfully put out, having planned to take the Sunday school there for a picnic. She was much pleased, however, at Hutchins's astuteness.

"I shall take her along to Canada," she said to me. "The girl has instinct, which is better than reason. Her subconsciousness is unusually active."

Looking back, as I must, and knowing now all that was in her small head while she whistled about the car, or all that was behind her smile, one wonders if women really should have the vote. So many of them are creatures of sex and guile. A word from her would have cleared up so much, and she never spoke it!

Well, we spent most of July in getting ready to go. Charlie Sands said the mosquitoes and black flies would be gone by August, and we were in no hurry.

We bought a good tent, with a diagram of how to put it up, some folding camp-beds, and a stove. The day we bought the tent we had rather a shock, for as we left the shop the suburban youth passed us. We ignored him completely, but he lifted his hat. Hutchins, who was waiting in Tish's car, saw him, too, and went quite white with fury.

Shortly after that, Hannah came in one night and said that a man was watching Tish's windows. We thought it was imagination, and Tish gave her a dose of sulphur and molasses-her liver being sluggish.

"Probably an Indian, I dare say," was Tish's caustic comment.

In view of later developments, however, it is a pity we did not investigate Hannah's story; for Aggie, going home from Tish's late one night in Tish's car, had a similar experience, declaring that a small machine had followed them, driven by a heavy-set man with a mustache. She said, too, that Hutchins, swerving sharply, had struck the smaller machine a glancing blow and almost upset it.

It was about the middle of July, I believe, that Tish received the following letter: —

> *Madam*: Learning that you have decided to take a fishing-trip in Canada, I
> venture to offer my services as guide, philosopher, and friend. I know Canada

thoroughly; can locate bass, as nearly as it lies in a mortal so to do; can manage a motor launch; am thoroughly at home in a canoe; can shoot, swim, and cook-the last indifferently well; know the Indian mind and my own-and will carry water and chop wood.

I do not drink, and such smoking as I do will, if I am engaged, be done in the solitude of the woods.

I am young and of a cheerful disposition. My object is not money, but only expenses paid and a chance to forget a recent and still poignant grief. I hope you will see the necessity for such an addition to your party, and allow me to subscribe myself, madam,

Your most obedient servant,

J. UPDIKE.

Tish was much impressed; but Hutchins, in whose judgment she began to have the greatest confidence, opposed the idea.

"I wouldn't think of it," she said briefly.

"Why? It's a frank, straightforward letter."

"He likes himself too much. And you should always be suspicious of anything that's offered too cheap."

So the Updike application was refused. I have often wondered since what would have been the result had we accepted it!

The worms were doing well, though Tish found that Hannah neglected them, and was compelled to feed them herself. On the day before we started, we packed them carefully in ice and moss, and fed them. That was the day the European war was declared.

"Canada is at war," Tish telephoned. "The papers say the whole country is full of spies, blowing up bridges and railroads."

"We can still go to the seashore," I said. "The bead things will do for the missionary box to Africa."

"Seashore nothing!" Tish retorted. "We're going, of course, —just as we planned. We'll keep our eyes open; that's all. I'm not for one side or the other, but a spy's a spy."

Later that evening she called again to say there were rumors that the Canadian forests were bristling with German wireless outfits.

"I've a notion to write J. Updike, Lizzie, and find out whether he knows anything about wireless telegraphy," she said, "only there's so little time. Perhaps I can find a book that gives the code."

(This is only pertinent as showing Tish's state of mind. As a matter of fact, she did not write to Updike at all.)

Well, we started at last, and I must say they let us over the border with a glance; but they asked us whether we had any firearms. Tish's trunk contained a shotgun and a revolver; but she had packed over the top her most intimate personal belongings, and they were not disturbed.

"Have you any weapons?" asked the inspector.

"Do we look like persons carrying weapons?" Tish demanded haughtily. And of course we did not. Still, there was an untruth of the spirit and none of us felt any too comfortable. Indeed, what followed may have been a punishment on us for deceit and conspiracy.

Aggie had taken her cat along-because it was so fond of fish, she said. And, between Tish buying ice for the worms and Aggie getting milk for the cat, the journey was not monotonous;

but on returning from one of her excursions to the baggage-car, Tish put a heavy hand on my shoulder.

"That boy's on the train, Lizzie!" she said. "He had the impudence to ask me whether I still drive with the license plates under a cushion. English roses-importations!" said Tish, and sniffed. "You don't suppose he went into that tent shop and asked about us?"

"He might," I retorted; "but, on the other hand, there's no reason why our going to Canada should keep the rest of the United States at home!"

However, the thing did seem queer, somehow. Why had he told us things that were not so? Why had he been so anxious to know who we were? Why, had he asked us to take the Sunday-school picnic to a place that did not belong to him?

"He may be going away to forget some trouble. You remember what he said about happier days," said Tish.

"That was Updike's reason too," I relied. "Poignant grief!"

For just a moment our eyes met. The same suspicion had occurred to us both. Well, we agreed to say nothing to Aggie or Hutchins, for fear of upsetting them, and the next hour or so was peaceful.

Hutchins read and Aggie slept. Tish and I strung beads for the Indians, and watched the door into the next car. And, sure enough, about the middle of the afternoon he appeared and stared in at us. He watched us for quite a time, smoking a cigarette as he did so. Then he came in and bent down over Tish.

"You didn't take the children out for the picnic, did you?" he said.

"I did not!" Tish snapped.

"I'm sorry. Never saw the place look so well!"

"Look here," Tish said, putting down her beads; "what were you doing there that night anyhow? You don't belong to the family."

He looked surprised and then grieved.

"You've discovered that, have you?" he said. "I did, you know-word of honor! They've turned me off; but I love the old place still, and on summer nights I wander about it, recalling happier days."

Hutchins closed her book with a snap, and he sighed.

"I perceive that we are overheard," he said. "Some time I hope to tell you the whole story. It's extremely sad. I'll not spoil the beginning of your holiday with it."

All the time he had been talking he held a piece of paper in his hand. When he left us Tish went back thoughtfully to her beads.

"It just shows, Lizzie," she said, "how wrong we are to trust to appearances. That poor boy —"

I had stooped into the aisle and was picking up the piece of paper which he had accidentally dropped as he passed Hutchins. I opened it and read aloud to Tish and Aggie, who had wakened: —

"'Afraid you'll not get away with it! The red-haired man in the car behind is a plain-clothes man.'"

Tish has a large fund of general knowledge, gained through Charlie Sands; so what Aggie and I failed to understand she interpreted at once.

"A plain-clothes man," she explained, "is a detective dressed as a gentleman. It's as plain as pikestaff! The boy's received this warning and dropped it. He has done something he shouldn't and is escaping to Canada!"

I do not believe, however, that we should have thought of his being a political spy but for the conductor of the train. He proved to be a very nice person, with eight children and a toupee; and he said that Canada was honeycombed with spies in the pay of the German Government.

"They're sending wireless messages all the time, probably from remote places," he said. "And, of course, their play now is to blow up the transcontinental railroads. Of course the railroads have an army of detectives on the watch."

"Good Heavens!" Aggie said, and turned pale.

Well, our pleasure in the journey was ruined. Every time the whistle blew on the engine we quailed, and Tish wrote her will then and there on the back of an envelope. It was while she was writing that the truth came to her.

"That boy!" she said. "Don't you see it all? That note was a warning to him. He's a spy and the red-haired man is after him."

None of us slept that night though Tish did a very courageous thing about eleven o'clock, when she was ready for bed. I went with her. We had put our dressing-gowns over our nightrobes, and we went back to the car containing the spy.

He had not retired, but was sitting alone, staring ahead moodily. The red-haired man was getting ready for bed, just opposite. Tish spoke loudly, so the detective should hear.

"I have come back," Tish said, "to say that we know everything. A word to the wise, Mister Happier Days! Don't try any of your tricks!"

He sat, with his mouth quite open, and stared at us: but the red-haired man pretended to hear nothing and took off his other shoe.

None of us slept at all except Hutchins. Though we had told her nothing, she seemed inherently to distrust the spy. When, on arriving at the town where we were to take the boat, he offered to help her off with Aggie's cat basket, which she was carrying, she snubbed him.

"I can do it myself," she said coldly; "and if you know when you're well off you'll go back to where you came from. Something might happen to you here in the wilderness."

"I wish it would," he replied in quite a tragic manner.

(As Tish said then, a man is probably often forced by circumstances into hateful situations. No spy can really want to be a spy with every brick wall suggesting, as it must, a firing-squad.)

Well, to make a long story short, we took the little steamer that goes up the river three times a week to take groceries and mail to the logging-camps, and the spy and the red-haired detective went along. The spy seemed to have quite a lot of luggage, but the detective had only a suitcase.

Tish, watching the detective, said his expression grew more and more anxious as we proceeded up the river. Cottages gave place to logging-camps and these to rocky islands, with no sign of life; still, the spy stayed on the steamer, and so, of course, did the detective.

Tish went down and examined the luggage. She reported that the spy was traveling under the name of McDonald and that the detective's suitcase was unmarked. Mr. McDonald had some boxes and a green canoe. The detective had nothing at all. There were no other passengers.

We let Aggie's cat out on the boat and he caught a mouse almost immediately, and laid it in the most touching manner at the detective's feet; but he was in a very bad humor and flung it over the rail. Shortly after that he asked Tish whether she intended to go to the Arctic Circle.

"I don't know that that's any concern of yours," Tish said. "You're not after me, you know."

He looked startled and muttered something into his mustache.

"It's perfectly clear what's wrong with him," Tish said. "He's got to stick to Mr. McDonald, and he hasn't got a tent in that suitcase, or even a blanket. I don't suppose he knows where his next meal's coming from."

She was probably right, for I saw the crew of the boat packing a box or two of crackers and an old comfort into a box; and Aggie overheard the detective say to the captain that if he would sell him some fishhooks he would not starve anyhow.

Tish found an island that suited her about three o'clock that afternoon, and we disembarked. Mr. McDonald insisted on helping the crew with our stuff, which they piled on a large flat rock; but the detective stood on the upper deck and scowled down at us. Tish suggested that he was a woman-hater.

"They know so many lawbreaking women," she said, "it's quite natural."

Having landed us, the boat went across to another island and deposited Mr. McDonald and the green canoe. Tish, who had talked about a lodge in some vast wilderness, complained at that; but when the detective got off on a little tongue of the mainland, in sight of both islands, she said the place was getting crowded and she had a notion to go farther.

The first thing she did was to sit on a box and open a map. The Canadian Pacific was only a few miles away through the woods!

Hutchins proved herself a treasure. She could work all round the three of us; she opened boxes and a can of beans for supper with the same hatchet, and had tea made and the beans heated while Tish was selecting a site for the tent.

But-and I remembered this later-she watched the river at intervals, with her cheeks like roses from the exertion. She was really a pretty girl-only, when no one was looking, her mouth that day had a way of setting itself firmly, and she frowned at the water.

We, Hutchins and I, set up the stove against a large rock, and when the teakettle started to boil it gave the river front a homey look. Sitting on my folding-chair beside the stove, with a cup of tea in my hand and a plate of beans on a doily on a packing-box beside me, I was entirely comfortable. Through the glasses I could see the red-haired man on the other shore sitting on a rock, with his head in his hands; but Mr. McDonald had clearly located on the other side of his island and was not in sight.

Aggie and Tish were putting up the tent, and Hutchins was feeding the tea grounds to the worms, which had traveled comfortably, when I saw a canoe coming up the river. I called to Tish about it.

"An Indian!" she said calmly. "Get the beads, Aggie; and put my shotgun on that rock, where he can see it." She stood and watched him. "Primitive man, every inch of him!" she went on. "Notice his uncovered head. Notice the freedom, almost the savagery, of the way he uses that paddle. I wish he would sing. You remember, in Hiawatha, how they sing as they paddle along?"

She got the beads and went to the water's edge; but the Indian stooped just then and, picking up a Panama hat, put it on his head.

"I have called," he said, "to see whether I can interest you in a set of books I am selling. I shall detain you only a moment. Sixty-three steel engravings by well-known artists; best hand-made paper; and the work itself is of high educational value."

Tish suddenly put the beads behind her back and said we did not expect to have any time to read. We had come into the wilderness to rest our minds.

"You are wrong, I fear," said the Indian. "Personally I find that I can read better in the wilds than anywhere else. Great thoughts in great surroundings! I take Nietzsche with me when I go fishing."

Tish had the wretched beads behind her all the time; and, to make conversation, more than anything else, she asked about venison. He shrugged his shoulders. J. Fenimore Cooper had not prepared us for an Indian who shrugged his shoulders.

"We Indians are allowed to kill deer," he said; "but I fear you are prohibited. I am not even permitted to sell it."

"I should think," said Tish sharply, "that, since we are miles from a game warden, you could safely sell us a steak or two."

He gazed at her disapprovingly. "I should not care to break the law, madam," he said.

Then he picked up his paddle and took himself and his scruples and his hand-made paper and his sixty-three steel engravings down the river.

"Primitive man!" I said to Tish, from my chair. "Notice the freedom, almost the savagery, with which he swings that paddle."

We had brought a volume of Cooper along, not so much to read as to remind us how to address the Indians. Tish said nothing, but she got the book and flung it far out into the river.

There were a number of small annoyances the first day or two. Hutchins was having trouble with the motor launch, which the steamer had towed up the day we came, and which she called the "Mebbe." And another civilized Indian, with a gold watch and a cigarette case, had rented us a leaky canoe for a dollar a day.

(We patched the leak with chewing gum, which Aggie always carried for indigestion; and it did fairly well, so long as the gum lasted.)

Then, on the second night, there was a little wind, and the tent collapsed on us, the ridge-pole taking Aggie across the chest. It was that same night, I think, when Aggie's cat found a porcupine in the woods, and came in looking like a pincushion.

What with chopping firewood for the stove, and carrying water, and bailing out the canoe, and with the motor boat giving one gasp and then dying for every hundred times somebody turned over the engine, we had no time to fish for two days.

The police agent fished all day from a rock, for, of course, he had no boat; but he seemed to catch nothing. At times we saw him digging frantically, as though for worms. What he dug with I do not know; but, of course, he got no worms. Tish said if he had been more civil she would have taken something to him and a can of worms; but he had been rude, especially to Aggie's cat, and probably the boat would bring him things.

What with getting settled and everything, we had not much time to think about the spy. It was on the third day, I believe, that he brought his green canoe to the open water in front of us and anchored there, just beyond earshot.

He put out a line and opened a book; and from that time on he was a part of the landscape every day from 10 A.M. to 4 P.M. At noon he would eat some sort of a lunch, reading as he ate.

He apparently never looked toward us, but he was always there. It was the most extraordinary thing. At first we thought he had found a remarkable fishing-place; but he seemed to catch very few fish. It was Tish, I think, who found the best explanation.

"He's providing himself with an alibi," she stated. "How can he be a spy when we see him all day long? Don't you see how clever it is?"

It was the more annoying because we had arranged a small cove for soap-and-water bathing, hanging up a rod for bath-towels and suspending a soap-dish and a sponge-holder from an over-hanging branch. The cove was well shielded by brush and rocks from the island, but naturally was open to the river.

It was directly opposite this cove that Mr. McDonald took up his position.

This compelled us to bathe in the early morning, while the water was still cold, and resulted in causing Aggie a most uncomfortable half-hour on the fourth morning of our stay.

She was the last one in the pool, and Tish absent-mindedly took her bathrobe and slippers back to the camp when she went. Tish went out in the canoe shortly after. She was learning to use one, with a life preserver on-Tish, of course, not the canoe. And Mr. McDonald arriving soon after, Aggie was compelled to sit in the water for two hours and twenty minutes. When Hutchins found her she was quite blue.

This was the only disagreement we had all summer: Aggie's refusing to speak to Tish that entire day. She said Mr. McDonald had seen her head and thought it was some sort of swimming animal, and had shot at her.

Mr. McDonald said afterward he knew her all the time, and was uncertain whether she was taking a cure for something or was trying to commit suicide. He said he spent a wretched morning. At five o'clock that evening we began to hear a curious tapping noise from the spy's island. It would last for a time, stop, and go on.

Hutchins said it was woodpeckers; but Tish looked at me significantly.

"Wireless!" she said. "What did I tell you?"

That decided her next move, for that evening she put some tea and canned corn and a rubber blanket into the canoe; and in fear and trembling I went with her.

"It's going to rain, Lizzie," she said, "and after all, that detective may be surly; but he's doing his duty by his country. It's just as heroic to follow a spy up here, and starve to death watching him, as it is to storm a trench-and less showy. And I've something to tell him."

The canoe tilted just then, and only by heroic effort, were we able to calm it.

"Then why not go comfortably in the motor boat?"

Tish stopped, her paddle in the air. "Because I can't make that dratted engine go," she said, "and because I believe Hutchins would drown us all before she'd take any help to him. It's my belief that she's known him somewhere. I've seen her sit on a rock and look across at him with murder in her eyes."

A little wind had come up, and the wretched canoe was leaking, the chewing gum having come out. Tish was paddling; so I was compelled to sit over the aperture, thus preventing water from coming in. Despite my best efforts, however, about three inches seeped in and washed about me. It was quite uncomfortable.

The red-haired man was asleep when we landed. He had hung the comfort over a branch, like a tent, and built a fire at the end of it. He had his overcoat on, buttoned to the chin, and his head was on his suit-case. He sat up and looked at us, blinking.

"We've brought you some tea and some canned corn," Tish said; "and a rubber blanket. It's going to rain."

He slid out of the tent, feet first, and got up; but when he tried to speak he sneezed. He had a terrible cold.

"I might as well say at once," Tish went on, "that we know why you are here —"

"The deuce you do!" he said hoarsely.

"We do not particularly care about you, especially since the way you acted to a friendly and innocent cat-one can always judge a man by the way he treats dumb animals; but we sympathize with your errand. We'll even help if we can."

"Then the-the person in question has confided in you?"

"Not at all," said Tish loftily. "I hope we can put two and two together. Have you got a revolver?"

He looked startled at that. "I have one," he said; "but I guess I'll not need it. The first night or two a skunk hung round; two, in fact-mother and child-but I think they're gone."

"Would you like some fish?"

"My God, no!"

This is a truthful narrative. That is exactly what he said.

"I'll tell you what I do need, ladies," he went on: "If you've got a spare suit of underwear over there, I could use it. It'd stretch, probably. And I'd like a pen and some ink. I must have lost my fountain pen out of my pocket stooping over the bank to wash my face."

"Do you know the wireless code?" Tish asked suddenly.

"Wireless?"

"I have every reason to believe," she said impressively, "that one of the great trees on that island conceals a wireless outfit."

"I see!" He edged back a little from us both.

"I should think," Tish said, eyeing him, "that a knowledge of the wireless code would be essential to you in your occupation."

"We-we get a smattering of all sorts of things," he said; but he was uneasy-you could see that with half an eye.

He accompanied us down to the canoe; but once, when Tish turned suddenly, he ducked back as though he had been struck and changed color. He thanked us for the tea and corn, and said he wished we had a spare razor-but, of course, he supposed not. Then: —

"I suppose the-the person in question will stay as long as you do?" he asked, rather nervously.

"It looks like it," said Tish grimly. "I've no intention of being driven away, if that's what you mean. We'll stay as long as the fishing's good."

He groaned under his breath. "The whole d —d river is full of fish," he said. "They crawled up the bank last night and ate all the crackers I'd saved for to-day. Oh, I'll pay somebody out for this, all right! Good gracious, ladies, your boat's full of water!"

"It has a hole in it," Tish replied and upturned it to empty it.

When he saw the hole his eyes stuck out. "You can't go out in that leaky canoe! It's suicidal!"

"Not at all," Tish assured him. "My friend here will sit on the leak. Get in quick, Lizzie. It's filling."

The last we saw of the detective that night he was standing on the bank, staring after us. Afterward, when a good many things were cleared up, he said he decided that he'd been asleep and dreamed the whole thing-the wireless, and my sitting on the hole in the canoe, and the wind tossing it about, and everything-only, of course, there was the tea and the canned corn!

We did our first fishing the next day. Hutchins had got the motor boat going, and I put over the spoon I had made from the feather duster. After going a mile or so slowly I felt a tug, and on drawing my line in I found I had captured a large fish. I wrapped the line about a part of the engine and Tish put the barrel hoop with the netting underneath it. The fish was really quite large-about four feet, I think-and it broke through the netting. I wished to hit it with the oar, but Hutchins said that might break the fin and free it. Unluckily we had not brought Tish's gun, or we might have shot it.

At last we turned the boat round and went home, the fish swimming alongside, with its mouth open. And there Aggie, who is occasionally almost inspired, landed the fish by the simple expedient of getting out of the boat, taking the line up a bank and wrapping it round a tree. By all pulling together we landed the fish successfully. It was forty-nine inches by Tish's tape measure.

Tish did not sleep well that night. She dreamed that the fish had a red mustache and was a spy in disguise. When she woke she declared there was somebody prowling round the tent.

She got her shotgun and we all sat up in bed for an hour or so.

Nothing happened, however, except that Aggie cried out that there was a small animal just inside the door of the tent. We could see it, too, though faintly. Tish turned the shotgun on it and it disappeared; but the next morning she found she had shot one of her shoes to pieces.

III

It was the day Tish began her diary that we discovered the red-haired man's signal. Tish was compelled to remain at home most of the day, breaking in another pair of shoes, and she amused herself by watching the river and writing down interesting things. She had read somewhere of the value of such records of impressions: —

> 10 A.M. Gull on rock. Very pretty. Frightened away by the McDonald person, who has just taken up his customary position. Is he reading or watching this camp?

> 10.22. Detective is breakfasting-through glasses, he is eating canned corn. Aggie-pickerel, from bank.

> 10.40. Aggie's cat, beside her, has caught a small fish. Aggie declares that the cat stole one of her worms and held it in the water. I think she is mistaken.

> 11. Most extraordinary thing-Hutchins has asked permission to take pen and ink across to the detective! Have consented.

> 11.20. Hutchins is still across the river. If I did not know differently I should say she and the detective are quarreling. He is whittling something. Through glasses, she appears to stamp her foot.

11.30. Aggie has captured a small sunfish. Hutchins is still across the river. He seems to be appealing to her for something-possibly the underwear. We have none to spare.

11.40. Hutchins is an extraordinary girl. She hates men, evidently. She has had some sort of quarrel with the detective and has returned flushed with battle. Mr. McDonald called to her as she passed, but she ignored him.

12, noon. Really, there is something mysterious about all this. The detective was evidently whittling a flagpole. He has erected it now, with a red silk handkerchief at end. It hangs out over the water. Aggie-bass, but under legal size.

1.15 P.M. The flag puzzles Hutchins. She is covertly watching it. It is evidently a signal-but to whom? Are the secret-service men closing in on McDonald?

1. Aggie-pike!

2. On consulting map find unnamed lake only a few miles away. Shall investigate to-morrow.

3. Steamer has just gone. Detective now has canoe, blue in color. Also food. He sent off his letter.

4. Fed worms. Lizzie thinks they know me. How kindness is its own reward! Mr. McDonald is drawing in his anchor, which is a large stone fastened to a rope. Shall take bath.

Tish's notes ended here. She did not take the bath after all, for Mr. McDonald made us a call that afternoon.

He beached the green canoe and came up the rocks calmly and smilingly. Hutchins gave him a cold glance and went on with what she was doing, which was chopping a plank to cook the fish on. He bowed cheerfully to all of us and laid a string of fish on a rock.

"I brought a little offering," he said, looking at Hutchins's back. "The fishing isn't what I expected but if the young lady with the hatchet will desist, so I can make myself heard, I've found a place where there are fish! This biggest fellow is three and a quarter pounds."

Hutchins chopped harder than ever, and the plank flew up, striking her in the chest; but she refused all assistance, especially from Mr. McDonald, who was really concerned. He hurried to her and took the hatchet out of her hand, but in his excitement he was almost uncivil.

"You obstinate little idiot!" he said. "You'll kill yourself yet."

To my surprise, Hutchins, who had been entirely unemotional right along, suddenly burst into tears and went into the tent. Mr. McDonald took a hasty step or two after her, realizing, no doubt, that he had said more than he should to a complete stranger; but she closed the fly of the tent quite viciously and left him standing, with his arms folded, staring at it.

It was at that moment he saw the large fish, hanging from a tree. He stood for a moment staring at it and we could see that he was quite surprised.

"It is a fish, isn't it?" he said after a moment. "I—I thought for a moment it was painted on something."

He sat down suddenly on one of our folding-chairs and looked at the fish, and then at each of us in turn.

"You know," he said, "I didn't think there were such fish! I —you mustn't mind my surprise." He wiped his forehead with his handkerchief. "Just kick those things I brought into the river, will you? I apologize for them."

"Forty-nine inches," Tish said. "We expect to do better when we really get started. This evening we shall go after its mate, which is probably hanging round."

"Its mate?" he said, rather dazed. "Oh, I see. Of course!"

He still seemed to doubt his senses, for he went over and touched it with his finger. "Ladies," he said, "I'm not going after the-the mate. I couldn't land it if I did get it. I am going to retire from the game-except for food; but I wish, for the sake of my reason, you'd tell me what you caught it with."

Well, you may heartily distrust a person; but that is no reason why you should not answer a simple question. So I showed him the thing I had made-and he did not believe me!

"You're perfectly right," he said. "Every game has its secrets. I had no business to ask. But you haven't caught me with that feather-duster thing any more than you caught that fish with it. I don't mind your not telling me. That's your privilege. But isn't it rather rubbing it in to make fun of me?"

"Nothing of the sort!" Aggie said angrily. "If you had caught it —"

"My dear lady," he said, "I couldn't have caught it. The mere shock of getting such a bite would have sent me out of my boat in a swoon." He turned to Tish. "I have only one disappointment," he said, "that it wasn't one of *our* worms that did the work."

Tish said afterward she was positively sorry for him, he looked so crestfallen. So, when he started for his canoe she followed him.

"Look here," she said; "you're young, and I don't want to see you get into trouble. Go home, young man! There are plenty of others to take your place."

He looked rather startled. "That's it exactly," he said, after a moment. "As well as I can make out there are about a hundred. If you think," he said fiercely, raising his voice, "that I'm going to back out and let somebody else in, I'm not. And that's flat."

"It's a life-and-death matter," said Tish.

"You bet it's a life-and-death matter."

"And-what about the-the red-headed man over there?"

His reply amazed us all. "He's harmless," he said. "I don't like him, naturally; but I admire the way he holds on. He's making the best of a bad business."

"Do you know why he's here?"

He looked uneasy for once.

"Well, I've got a theory," he replied; but, though his voice was calm, he changed color.

"Then perhaps you'll tell me what that signal means?"

Tish gave him the glasses and he saw the red flag. I have never seen a man look so unhappy.

"Holy cats!" he said, and almost dropped the glasses. "Why, he-he must be expecting somebody!"

"So I should imagine," Tish commented dryly. "He sent a letter by the boat to-day."

"The h —l he did!" And then: "That's ridiculous! You're mistaken. As a —as a matter of fact, I went over there the other night and commandeered his fountain pen."

So it had not fallen out of his pocket!

"I'll be frank, ladies," he said. "It's my object just now to keep that chap from writing letters. It doesn't matter why, but it's vital."

He was horribly cast down when we told him about Hutchins and the pen and ink.

"So that's it!" he said gloomily. "And the flag's a signal, of course. Ladies, you have done it out of the kindness of your hearts, I know; but I think you have wrecked my life."

He took a gloomy departure and left us all rather wrought up. Who were we, as Tish said, to imperil a fellow man? And another thing-if there was a reward on him, why should we give it to a red-haired detective, who was rude to harmless animals and ate canned corn for breakfast?

With her customary acumen Tish solved the difficulty that very evening.

"The simplest thing," she said, "of course, would be to go over during the night and take the flag away; but he may have more red handkerchiefs. Then, too, he seems to be a light sleeper, and it would be awkward to have him shoot at us."

She sat in thought for quite a while. Hutchins was watching the sunset, and seemed depressed and silent. Tish lowered her voice.

"There's no reason why we shouldn't have a red flag, too," she said. "It gives us an even chance to get in on whatever is about to happen. We can warn Mr. McDonald, for one thing, if any one comes here. Personally I think he is unjustly suspected."

(But Tish was to change her mind very soon.)

We made the flag that night, by lantern light, out of Tish's red silk petticoat. Hutchins was curious, I am sure; but we explained nothing. And we fastened it obliquely over the river, like the one on the other side.

Tish's change of heart, which occurred the next morning, was due to a most unfortunate accident that happened to her at nine o'clock. Hutchins, who could swim like a duck, was teaching Tish to swim, and she was learning nicely. Tish had put a life-preserver on, with a clothes-line fastened to it, and Aggie was sitting on the bank holding the rope while she went through the various gestures.

Having completed the lesson Hutchins went into the woods for red raspberries, leaving Tish still practicing in the water with Aggie holding the rope. Happening to sneeze, the line slipped out of her hand, and she had the agonizing experience of seeing Tish carried away by the current.

I was washing some clothing in the river a few yards down the stream when Tish came floating past. I shall never forget her expression or my own sense of absolute helplessness.

"Get the canoe," said Tish, "and follow. I'm heading for Island Eleven."

She was quite calm, though pale; but, in her anxiety to keep well above the water, she did what was almost a fatal thing-she pushed the life-preserver lower down round her body. And having shifted the floating center, so to speak, without warning her head disappeared and her feet rose in the air.

For a time it looked as though she would drown in that position; but Tish rarely loses her presence of mind. She said she knew at once what was wrong. So, though somewhat handicapped by the position, she replaced the cork belt under her arms and emerged at last.

Aggie had started back into the woods for Hutchins; but, with one thing and another, it was almost ten before they returned together. Tish by that time was only a dot on the horizon through the binocular, having missed Island Eleven, as she explained later, by the rope being caught on a submerged log, which deflected her course.

We got into the motor boat and followed her, and, except for a most unjust sense of irritation that I had not drowned myself by following her in the canoe, she was unharmed. We got her into the motor boat and into a blanket, and Aggie gave her some blackberry cordial at once. It was some time before her teeth ceased chattering so she could speak. When she did it was to announce that she had made a discovery.

"He's a spy, all right!" she said. "And that Indian is another. Neither of them saw me as I floated past. They were on Island Eleven. Mr. McDonald wrote something and gave it to the Indian. It wasn't a letter or he'd have sent it by the boat. He didn't even put it in an envelope, so far as I could see. It's probably in cipher."

Well, we took her home, and she had a boiled egg at dinner.

The rest of us had fish. It is one of Tish's theories that fish should only be captured for food, and that all fish caught must be eaten. I do not know when I have seen fish come as easy. Perhaps it was the worms, which had grown both long and fat, so that one was too much for a hook; and we cut them with scissors, like tape or ribbon. Aggie and I finally got so sick of fish that while Tish's head was turned we dropped in our lines without bait. But, even at that, Aggie, reeling in her line to go home, caught a three-pound bass through the gills and could not shake it off.

We tried to persuade Tish to lie down that afternoon, but she refused.

"I'm not sick," she said, "even if you two idiots did try to drown me. And I'm on the track of something. If that was a letter, why didn't he send it by the boat?"

Just then her eye fell on the flagpole, and we followed her horrified gaze. The flag had been neatly cut away!

Tish's eyes narrowed. She looked positively dangerous; and within five minutes she had cut another flag out of the back breadth of the petticoat and flung it defiantly in the air. Who had cut away the signal-McDonald or the detective? We had planned to investigate the nameless lake that afternoon, Tish being like Colonel Roosevelt in her thirst for information, as well as in the grim pugnacity that is her dominant characteristic; but at the last minute she decided not to go.

"You and Aggie go, Lizzie," she said. "I've got something on hand."

"Tish!" Aggie wailed. "You'll drown yourself or something."

"Don't be a fool!" Tish snapped. "There's a portage, but you and Lizzie can carry the canoe across on your heads. I've seen pictures of it. It's easy. And keep your eyes open for a wireless outfit. There's one about, that's sure!"

"Lots of good it will do to keep our eyes open," I said with some bitterness, "with our heads inside the canoe!"

We finally started and Hutchins went with us. It was Hutchins, too, who voiced the way we all felt when we had crossed the river and were preparing for what she called the portage.

"She wants to get us out of the way, Miss Lizzie," she said. "Can you imagine what mischief she's up to?"

"That is not a polite way to speak of Miss Tish, Hutchins," I said coldly. Nevertheless, my heart sank.

Hutchins and I carried the canoe. It was a hot day and there was no path. Aggie, who likes a cup of hot tea at five o'clock, had brought along a bottle filled with tea, and a small basket containing sugar and cups.

Personally I never had less curiosity about a lake. As a matter of fact I wished there was no lake. Twice-being obliged, as it were, to walk blindly and the canoe being excessively heavy —I, who led the way, ran the front end of the thing against the trunk of a tree, and both Hutchins and I sat down violently, under the canoe as a result of the impact.

To add to the discomfort of the situation Aggie declared that we were being followed by a bear, and at the same instant stepped into a swamp up to her knees. She became calm at once, with the calmness of despair.

"Go and leave me, Lizzie!" she said. "He is just behind those bushes. I may sink before he gets me-that's one comfort."

Hutchins found a log and, standing on it, tried to pull her up; but she seemed firmly fastened. Aggie went quite white; and, almost beside myself, I poured her a cup of hot tea, which she drank. I remember she murmured Mr. Wiggins's name, and immediately after she yelled that the bear was coming.

It was, however, the detective who emerged from the bushes. He got Aggie out with one good heave, leaving both her shoes gone forever; and while she collapsed, whimpering, he folded his arms and stared at all of us angrily.

"What sort of damnable idiocy is this?" he demanded in a most unpleasant tone.

Aggie revived and sat upright.

"That's our affair, isn't it?" said Hutchins curtly.

"Not by a blamed sight!" was his astonishing reply.

"The next time I am sinking in a morass, let me sink," Aggie said, with simple dignity.

He did not speak another word, but gave each of us a glance of the most deadly contempt, and finished up with Hutchins.

"What I don't understand," he said furiously, "is why you have to lend yourself to this senile idiocy. Because some old women choose to sink themselves in a swamp is no reason why you should commit suicide!"

Aggie said afterward only the recollection that he had saved her life prevented her emptying the tea on him. I should hardly have known Hutchins.

"Naturally," she said in a voice thick with fury, "you are in a position to insult these ladies, and you do. But I warn you, if you intend to keep on, this swamp is nothing. We like it here. We may stay for months. I hope you have your life insured."

Perhaps we should have understood it all then. Of course Charlie Sands, for whom I am writing this, will by this time, with his keen mind, comprehend it all; but I assure you we suspected nothing.

How simple, when you line it up: The country house and the garden hose; the detective, with no camp equipment; Mr. McDonald and the green canoe; the letter on the train; the red flag; the girl in the pink tam-o'-shanter-who has not yet appeared, but will shortly; Mr. McDonald's incriminating list-also not yet, but soon.

How inevitably they led to what Charlie Sands has called our crime!

The detective, who was evidently very strong, only glared at her. Then he swung the canoe up on his head and, turning about, started back the way we had come. Though Hutchins and Aggie were raging, I was resigned. My neck was stiff and my shoulders ached. We finished our tea in silence and then made our way back to the river.

I have now reached Tish's adventure. It is not my intention in this record to defend Tish. She thought her conclusions were correct. Charlie Sands says she is like Shaw-she has got a crooked point of view, but she believes she is seeing straight. And, after a while, if you look her way long enough you get a sort of mental astigmatism.

So I shall confess at once that, at the time, I saw nothing immoral in what she did that afternoon while we were having our adventure in the swamp.

I was putting cloths wrung out of arnica and hot water on my neck when she came home, and Hutchins was baking biscuit-she was a marvelous cook, though Aggie, who washed the dishes, objected to the number of pans she used.

Tish ignored both my neck and the biscuits, and, marching up the bank, got her shotgun from the tent and loaded it.

"We may be attacked at any time," she said briefly; and, getting the binocular, she searched the river with a splendid sweeping glance. "At any time. Hutchins, take these glasses, please, and watch that we are not disturbed."

"I'm baking biscuit, Miss Letitia."

"Biscuit!" said Tish scornfully. "Biscuit in times like these?"

She walked up to the camp stove and threw the oven door open; but, though I believe she had meant to fling them into the river, she changed her mind when she saw them.

"Open a jar of honey, Hutchins," she said, and closed the oven; but her voice was abstracted. "You can watch the river from the stove, Hutchins," she went on. "Miss Aggie and Miss Lizzie and I must confer together."

So we went into the tent, and Tish closed and fastened it.

"Now," she said, "I've got the papers."

"Papers?"

"The ones Mr. McDonald gave that Indian this morning. I had an idea he'd still have them. You can't hurry an Indian. I waited in the bushes until he went in swimming. Then I went through his pockets."

"Tish Carberry!" cried Aggie.

"These are not times to be squeamish," Tish said loftily. "I'm neutral; of course; but Great Britain has had this war forced on her and I'm going to see that she has a fair show. I've ordered all my stockings from the same shop in London, for twenty years, and squarer people never lived. Look at these-how innocent they look, until one knows!"

She produced two papers from inside her waist. I must confess that, at first glance, I saw nothing remarkable.

"The first one looks," said Tish, "like a grocery order. It's meant to look like that. It's relieved my mind of one thing-McDonald's got no wireless or he wouldn't be sending cipher messages by an Indian."

It was written on a page torn out of a pocket notebook and the page was ruled with an inch margin at the left. This was the document: —

1
20
1 pkg.
1 doz.
3 lbs.
1 bot.
3

1

Dozen eggs.
Yards fishing-line.
Needles-anything to sew a button on.
A B C bass hooks.
Meat-anything so it isn't fish.
Ink for fountain pen.
Tins sardines.
Extractor.

Well, I could not make anything of it; but, of course, I have not Tish's mind. Aggie was almost as bad.

"What's an extractor?" she asked.

"Exactly!" said Tish. "What is an extractor? Is the fellow going to pull teeth? No! He needed an *e*; so he made up a word."

She ran her finger down the first letters of the second column. "D-y-n-a-m-i-t-e!" she said triumphantly. "Didn't I tell you?"

IV

Well, there it was-staring at us. I felt positively chilled. He looked so young and agreeable, and, as Aggie said, he had such nice teeth. And to know him for what he was-it was tragic! But that was not all.

"Add the numbers!" said Tish. "Thirty-one tons, perhaps, of dynamite! And that's only part," said Tish. "Here's the most damning thing of all—a note to his accomplice!"

"Damning" is here used in the sense of condemnatory. We are none of us addicted to profanity.

We read the other paper, which had been in a sealed envelope, but without superscription. It is before me as I write, and I am copying it exactly: —

I shall have to see you. I'm going crazy! Don't you realize that this is a matter of life and death to me? Come to Island Eleven to-night, won't you? And give me a chance to talk, anyhow. Something has got to be done and done soon. I'm desperate!

Aggie sneezed three times in sheer excitement; for anyone can see how absolutely incriminating the letter was. It was not signed, but it was in the same writing as the list.

Tish, who knows something about everything, said the writing denoted an unscrupulous and violent nature.

"The *y* is especially vicious," she said. "I wouldn't trust a man who made a *y* like that to carry a sick child to the doctor!"

The thing, of course, was to decide at once what measures to take. The boat would not come again for two days, and to send a letter by it to the town marshal or sheriff, or whatever the official is in Canada who takes charge of spies, would be another loss of time.

"Just one thing," said Tish. "I'll plan this out and find some way to deal with the wretch; but I wouldn't say anything to Hutchins. She's a nice little thing, though she is a fool about a motor boat. There's no case in scaring her."

For some reason or other, however, Hutchins was out of spirits that night.

"I hope you're not sick, Hutchins?" said Tish.

"No, indeed, Miss Tish."

"You're not eating your fish."

"I'm sick of fish," she said calmly. "I've eaten so much fish that when I see a hook I have a mad desire to go and hang myself on it."

"Fish," said Tish grimly, "is good for the brain. I do not care to boast, but never has my mind been so clear as it is to-night."

Now certainly, though Tish's tone was severe, there was nothing in it to hurt the girl; but she got up from the cracker box on which she was sitting, with her eyes filled with tears.

"Don't mind me. I'm a silly fool," she said; and went down to the river and stood looking out over it.

It quite spoiled our evening. Aggie made her a hot lemonade and, I believe, talked to her about Mr. Wiggins, and how, when he was living, she had had fits of weeping without apparent cause. But if the girl was in love, as we surmised, she said nothing about it. She insisted that it was too much fish and nervous strain about the Mebbe.

"I never know," she said, "when we start out whether we're going to get back or be marooned and starve to death on some island."

Tish said afterward that her subconscious self must have taken the word "marooned" and played with it; for in ten minutes or so her plan popped into her head.

"'Full-panoplied from the head of Jove,' Lizzie," she said. "Really, it is not necessary to think if one only has faith. The supermind does it all without effort. I do not dislike the young man; but I must do my duty."

Tish's plan was simplicity itself. We were to steal his canoe.

"Then we'll have him," she finished. "The current's too strong there for him to swim to the mainland."

"He might try it and drown," Aggie objected. "Spy or no spy, he's somebody's son."

"War is no time to be chicken-hearted," Tish replied.

I confess I ate little all that day. At noon Mr. McDonald came and borrowed two eggs from us.

"I've sent over to a store across country, by my Indian guide, philosopher, and friend," he said, "for some things I needed; but I dare say he's reading Byron somewhere and has forgotten it."

"Guide, philosopher, and friend!" I caught Tish's eye. McDonald had written the Updike letter! McDonald had meant to use our respectability to take him across the border!

We gave him the eggs, but Tish said afterward she was not deceived for a moment.

"The Indian has told him," she said, "and he's allaying our suspicions. Oh, he's clever enough! 'Know the Indian mind and my own!'" she quoted from the Updike letter. "'I know Canada thoroughly.' 'My object is not money.' I should think not!"

Tish stole the green canoe that night. She put on the life preserver and we tied the end of the rope that Aggie had let slip to the canoe. The life-preserver made it difficult to paddle, Tish said, but she felt more secure. If she struck a rock and upset, at least she would not drown; and we could start after her at dawn with the Mebbe.

"I'll be somewhere down the river," she said, "and safe enough, most likely, unless there are falls."

Hutchins watched in a puzzled way, for Tish did not leave until dusk.

"You'd better let me follow you with the launch, Miss Tish," she said. "Just remember that if the canoe sinks you're tied to it."

"I'm on serious business to-night, Hutchins," Tish said ominously. "You are young, and I refuse to trouble your young mind; but your ears are sharp. If you hear any shooting, get the boat and follow me."

The mention of shooting made me very nervous. We watched Tish as long as we could see her; then we returned to the tent, and Aggie and I crocheted by the hanging lantern. Two hours went by. At eleven o'clock Tish had not returned and Hutchins was in the motor boat, getting it ready to start.

"I like courage, Miss Lizzie," she said to me; "but this thing of elderly women, with some sort of bug, starting out at night in canoes is too strong for me. Either she's going to stay in at night or I'm going home."

"Elderly nothing!" I said, with some spirit. "She is in the prime of life. Please remember, Hutchins, that you are speaking of your employer. Miss Tish has no bug, as you call it."

"Oh, she's rational enough," Hutchins retorted: "but she is a woman of one idea and that sort of person is dangerous."

I was breathless at her audacity.

"Come now, Miss Lizzie," she said, "how can I help when I don't know what is being done? I've done my best up here to keep you comfortable and restrain Miss Tish's recklessness; but I ought to know something."

She was right; and, Tish or no Tish, then and there I told her. She was more than astonished. She sat in the motor boat, with a lantern at her feet, and listened.

"I see," she said slowly. "So the-so Mr. McDonald is a spy and has sent for dynamite to destroy the railroad! And-and the red-haired man is a detective! How do you know he is a detective?"

I told her then about the note we had picked up from beside her in the train, and because she was so much interested she really seemed quite thrilled. I brought the cipher grocery list and the other note down to her.

"It's quite convincing, isn't it?" she said. "And-and exciting! I don't know when I've been so excited."

She really was. Her cheeks were flushed. She looked exceedingly pretty.

"The thing to do," she said, "is to teach him a lesson. He's young. He mayn't always have had to stoop to such-such criminality. If we can scare him thoroughly, it might do him a lot of good."

I said I was afraid Tish took a more serious view of things and would notify the authorities. And at that moment there came two or three shots-then silence.

I shall never forget the ride after Tish and how we felt when we failed to find her; for there was no sign of her. The wind had come up, and, what with seeing Tish tied to that wretched canoe and sinking with it or shot through the head and lying dead in the bottom of it, we were about crazy. As we passed Island Eleven we could see the spy's camp-fire and his tent, but no living person.

At four in the morning we gave up and started back, heavy-hearted. What, therefore, was our surprise to find Tish sitting by the fire in her bathrobe, with a cup of tea in her lap and her feet in a foot-tub of hot water! Considering all we had gone through and that we had obeyed orders exactly, she was distinctly unjust. Indeed, at first she quite refused to speak to any of us.

"I do think, Tish," Aggie said as she stood shivering by the fire, "that you might at least explain where you have been. We have been going up and down the river for hours, burying you over and over."

Tish took a sip of tea, but said nothing.

"You said," I reminded her, "that if there was shooting, we were to start after you at once. When we heard the shots, we went, of course."

Tish leaned over and, taking the teakettle from the fire, poured more water into the foot-tub. Then at last she turned to speak.

"Bring some absorbent cotton and some bandages, Hutchins," she said. "I am bleeding from a hundred wounds. As for you" —she turned fiercely on Aggie and me —"the least you could have done was to be here when I returned, exhausted, injured, and weary; but, of course, you were gallivanting round the lake in an upholstered motor boat."

Here she poured more water into the foot-tub and made it much too hot. This thawed her rather, and she explained what was wrong. She was bruised, scratched to the knees, and with a bump the size of an egg on her forehead, where she had run into a tree.

The whole story was very exciting. It seems she got the green canoe without any difficulty, the spy being sound asleep in his tent; but about that time the wind came up and Tish said she could not make an inch of progress toward our camp.

The chewing gum with which we had repaired our canoe came out at that time and the boat began to fill, Tish being unable to sit over the leak and paddle at the same time. So, at last, she gave up and made for the mainland.

"The shooting," Tish said with difficulty, "was by men from the Indian camp firing at me. I landed below the camp, and was making my way as best I could through the woods when they heard me moving. I believe they thought it was a bear."

I think Tish was more afraid of the Indians, in spite of their sixty-three steel engravings and the rest of it, than she pretended, though she said she would have made herself known, but at that moment she fell over a fallen tree and for fifteen minutes was unable to speak a word. When at last she rose the excitement was over and they had gone back to their camp.

"Anyhow," she finished, "the green canoe is hidden a couple of miles down the river, and I guess Mr. McDonald is safe for a time. Lizzie, you can take a bath to-morrow safely."

Tish sat up most of the rest of the night composing a letter to the authorities of the town, telling them of Mr. McDonald and enclosing careful copies of the incriminating documents she had found.

During the following morning the river was very quiet. Through the binocular we were able to see Mr. McDonald standing on the shore of his island and looking intently in our direction, but naturally we paid no attention to him.

The red-haired man went in swimming that day and necessitated our retiring to the tent for an hour and a half; but at noon Aggie's naturally soft heart began to assert itself.

"Spy or no spy," she said to Tish, "we ought to feed him."

"Huh!" was Tish's rejoinder. "There is no sense is wasting good food on a man whose hours are numbered."

We were surprised, however, to find that Hutchins, who had detested Mr. McDonald, was rather on Aggie's side.

"The fact that he has but a few more hours," she said to Tish, "is an excellent reason for making those hours as little wretched as possible."

It was really due to Hutchins, therefore, that Mr. McDonald had a luncheon. The problem of how to get it to him was a troublesome one, but Tish solved it with her customary sagacity.

"We can make a raft," she said, "a small one, large enough to hold a tray. By stopping the launch some yards above the island we can float his luncheon to him quite safely."

That was the method we ultimately pursued and it worked most satisfactorily.

Hutchins baked hot biscuits; and, by putting a cover over the pan, we were enabled to get them to him before they cooled.

We prepared a really appetizing luncheon of hot biscuits, broiled ham, marmalade, and tea, adding, at Aggie's instructions, a jar of preserved peaches, which she herself had put up.

Tish made the raft while we prepared the food, and at exactly half-past twelve o'clock we left the house. Mr. McDonald saw us coming and was waiting smilingly at the upper end of the island.

"Great Scott!" he said. "I thought you were never going to hear me. Another hour and I'd have made a swim for it, though it's suicidal with this current. I'll show you where you can come in so you won't hit a rock."

Hutchins had stopped the engine of the motor boat and we threw out the anchor at a safe distance from the shore.

"We are not going to land," said Tish, "and I think you know perfectly well the reason why."

"Oh, now," he protested; "surely you are going to land! I've had an awfully uncomfortable accident-my canoe's gone."

"We know that," Tish said calmly. "As a matter of fact, we took it."

Mr. McDonald sat down suddenly on a log at the water's edge and looked at us.

"Oh!" he said.

"You may not believe it," Tish said, "but we know everything-your dastardly plot, who the red-haired man is, and all the destruction and wretchedness you are about to cause."

"Oh, I say!" he said feebly. "I wouldn't go as far as that. I'm —I'm not such a bad sort."

"That depends on the point of view," said Tish grimly.

Aggie touched her on the arm then and reminded her that the biscuits were getting cold; but Tish had a final word with him.

"Your correspondence has fallen into my hands, young man," she said, "and will be turned over to the proper authorities."

"It won't tell them anything they don't know," he said doggedly. "Look here, ladies: I am not ashamed of this thing. I —I am proud of it. I am perfectly willing to yell it out loud for everybody to hear. As a matter of fact, I think I will."

Mr. McDonald stood up suddenly and threw his head back; but here Hutchins, who had been silent, spoke for the first time.

"Don't be an idiot!" she said coldly. "We have something here for you to eat if you behave yourself."

He seemed to see her then for the first time, for he favored her with a long stare.

"Ah!" he said. "Then you are not entirely cold and heartless?"

She made no reply to this, being busy in assisting Aggie to lower the raft over the side of the boat.

"Broiled ham, tea, hot biscuits, and marmalade," said Aggie gently. "My poor fellow, we are doing what we consider our duty; but we want you to know that it is hard for us-very hard."

When he saw our plan, Mr. McDonald's face fell; but he stepped out into the water up to his knees and caught the raft as it floated down.

Before he said "Thank you" he lifted the cover of the pan and saw the hot biscuits underneath.

"Really," he said, "it's very decent of you. I sent off a grocery order yesterday, but nothing has come."

Tish had got Hutchins to start the engine by that time and we were moving away. He stood there, up to his knees in water, holding the tray and looking after us. He was really a pathetic figure, especially in view of the awful fate we felt was overtaking him.

He called something after us. On account of the noise of the engine, we could not be certain, but we all heard it the same way.

"Send for the whole d —d outfit!" was the way it sounded to us. "It won't make any difference to me."

V

The last thing I recall of Mr. McDonald that day is seeing him standing there in the water,
holding the tray, with the teapot steaming under his nose, and gazing after us with an air of
bewilderment that did not deceive us at all.

As I look back, there is only one thing we might have noticed at the time. This was the
fact that Hutchins, having started the engine, was sitting beside it on the floor of the boat
and laughing in the cruelest possible manner. As I said to Aggie at the time: "A spy is a spy
and entitled to punishment if discovered; but no young woman should laugh over so desperate
a situation."

I come now to the denouement of this exciting period. It had been Tish's theory that the
red-haired man should not be taken into our confidence. If there was a reward for the capture
of the spy, we ourselves intended to have it.

The steamer was due the next day but one. Tish was in favor of not waiting, but of at
once going in the motor boat to the town, some thirty miles away, and telling of our capture;
but Hutchins claimed there was not sufficient gasoline for such an excursion. That afternoon
we went in the motor launch to where Tish had hidden the green canoe and, with a hatchet,
rendered it useless.

The workings of the subconscious mind are marvelous. In the midst of chopping, Tish
suddenly looked up.

"Have you noticed," she said, "that the detective is always watching our camp?"

"That's all he has to do," Aggie suggested.

"Stuff and nonsense! Didn't he follow you into the swamp? Does Hutchins ever go out in
the canoe that he doesn't go out also? I'll tell you what has happened: She's young and pretty,
and he's fallen in love with her."

I must say it sounded reasonable. He never bothered about the motor boat, but the instant
she took the canoe and started out he was hovering somewhere near.

"She's noticed it," Tish went on. "That's what she was quarreling about with him yesterday."

"How are we to know," said Aggie, who was gathering up the scraps of the green canoe and
building a fire under them —"how are we to know they are not old friends, meeting thus in the
wilderness? Fate plays strange tricks, Tish. I lived in the same street with Mr. Wiggins for years,
and never knew him until one day when my umbrella turned wrong side out in a gust of wind."

"Fate fiddlesticks!" said Tish. "There's no such thing as fate in affairs of this sort. It's all
instinct-the instinct of the race to continue itself."

This Aggie regarded as indelicate and she was rather cool to Tish the balance of the day.

Our prisoner spent most of the day at the end of the island toward us, sitting quietly, as
we could sec through the glasses. We watched carefully, fearing at any time to see the Indian
paddling toward him.

(Tish was undecided what to do in such an emergency, except to intercept him and explain,
threatening him also with having attempted to carry the incriminating papers. As it happened,
however, the entire camp had gone for a two-days' deer hunt, and before they returned the
whole thing had come to its surprising end.)

Late in the afternoon Tish put her theory of the red-haired man to the test.

"Hutchins," she said, "Miss Lizzie and I will cook the dinner if you want to go in the canoe
to Harvey's Bay for water-lilies."

Hutchins at once said she did not care a rap for water-lilies; but, seeing a determined glint
in Tish's eye, she added that she would go for frogs if Tish wanted her out of the way.

"Don't talk like a child!" Tish retorted. "Who said I wanted you out of the way?"

It is absolutely true that the moment Hutchins put her foot into the canoe the red-haired man put down his fishing-rod and rose. And she had not taken three strokes with the paddle before he was in the blue canoe.

Hutchins saw him just then and scowled. The last we saw of her she was moving rapidly up the river and the detective was dropping slowly behind. They both disappeared finally into the bay and Tish drew a long breath.

"Typical!" she said curtly. "He's sent here to watch a dangerous man and spends his time pursuing the young woman who hates the sight of him. When women achieve the suffrage they will put none but married men in positions of trust."

Hutchins and the detective were still out of sight when supper-time came. The spy's supper weighed on us, and at last Tish attempted to start the motor launch. We had placed the supper and the small raft aboard, and Aggie was leaning over the edge untying the painter, —not a man, but a rope, —when unexpectedly the engine started at the first revolution of the wheel.

It darted out to the length of the rope, where it was checked abruptly, the shock throwing Aggie entirely out and into the stream. Tish caught the knife from the supper tray to cut us loose, and while Tish cut I pulled Aggie in, wet as she was. The boat was straining and panting, and, on being released, it sprang forward like a dog unleashed.

Aggie had swallowed a great deal of water and was most disagreeable; but the Mebbe was going remarkably well, and there seemed to be every prospect that we should get back to the camp in good order. Alas, for human hopes! Mr. McDonald was not very agreeable.

"You know," he said as he waited for his supper to float within reach, "you needn't be so blamed radical about everything you do! If you object to my hanging round, why not just say so? If I'm too obnoxious I'll clear out."

"Obnoxious is hardly the word," said Tish. "How long am I to be a prisoner?"

"I shall send letters off by the first boat."

He caught the raft just then and examined the supper with interest.

"Of course things might be worse," he said; "but it's dirty treatment, anyhow. And it's darned humiliating. Somebody I know is having a good time at my expense. It's heartless! That's what it is-heartless!"

Well, we left him, the engine starting nicely and Aggie being wrapped in a tarpaulin; but about a hundred yards above the island it began to slow down, and shortly afterward it stopped altogether. As the current caught us, we luckily threw out the anchor, for the engine refused to start again. It was then we saw the other canoes.

The girl in the pink tam-o'-shanter was in the first one.

They glanced at us curiously as they passed, and the P.T.S. —that is the way we grew to speak of the pink tam-o'-shanter-raised one hand in the air, which is a form of canoe greeting, probably less upsetting to the equilibrium than a vigorous waving of the arm.

It was just then, I believe, that they saw our camp and headed for it. The rest of what happened is most amazing. They stopped at our landing and unloaded their canoes. Though twilight was falling, we could see them distinctly. And what we saw was that they calmly took possession of the camp.

"Good gracious!" Tish cried. "The girls have gone into the tent! And somebody's working at the stove. The impertinence!"

Our situation was acutely painful. We could do nothing but watch. We called, but our voices failed to reach them. And Aggie took a chill, partly cold and partly fury. We sat there while they ate the entire supper!

They were having a very good time. Now and then somebody would go into the tent and bring something out, and there would be shrieks of laughter.

(We learned afterward that part of the amusement was caused by Aggie's false front, which one of the wretches put on as a beard.)

It was while thus distracted that Aggie suddenly screamed, and a moment later Mr. McDonald climbed over the side and into the boat, dripping.

"Don't be alarmed!" he said. "I'll go back and be a prisoner again just as soon as I've fired the engine. I couldn't bear to think of the lady who fell in sitting here indefinitely and taking cold." He was examining the engine while he spoke. "Have visitors, I see," he observed, as calmly as though he were not dripping all over the place.

"Intruders, not visitors!" Tish said angrily. "I never saw them before."

"Rather pretty, the one with the pink cap. May I examine the gasoline supply?" There was no gasoline. He shrugged his shoulders. "I'm afraid no amount of mechanical genius I intended to offer you will start her," he said; "but the young lady-Hutchins is her name, I believe? —will see you here and come after you, of course."

Well, there was no denying that, spy or no spy, his presence was a comfort. He offered to swim back to the island and be a prisoner again, but Tish said magnanimously that there was no hurry. On Aggie's offering half of her tarpaulin against the wind, which had risen, he accepted.

"Your Miss Hutchins is reckless, isn't she?" he said when he was comfortably settled. "She's a strong swimmer; but a canoe is uncertain at the best."

"She's in no danger," said Tish. "She has a devoted admirer watching out for her."

"The deuce she has!" His voice was quite interested. "Why, who on earth —"

"Your detective," said Aggie softly. "He's quite mad about her. The way he follows her and the way he looks at her-it's thrilling!"

Mr. McDonald said nothing for quite a while. The canoe party had evidently eaten every-thing they could find, and somebody had brought out a banjo and was playing.

Tish, unable to vent her anger, suddenly turned on Mr. McDonald. "If you think," she said, "that the grocery list fooled us, it didn't!"

"Grocery list?"

"That's what I said."

"How did you get my grocery list?"

So she told him, and how she had deciphered it, and how the word "dynamite" had only confirmed her early suspicions.

His only comment was to say, "Good Heavens!" in a smothered voice.

"It was the extractor that made me suspicious," she finished. "What were you going to ex-tract? Teeth?"

"And so, when my Indian was swimming, you went through his things! It's the most as-tounding thing I ever-My dear lady, an extractor is used to get the hooks out of fish. It was no cipher, I assure you. I needed an extractor and I ordered it. The cipher you speak of is only a remarkable coincidence."

"Huh!" said Tish. "And the paper you dropped in the train-was that a coincidence?"

"That's not my secret," he said, and turned sulky at once.

"Don't tell me," Tish said triumphantly, "that any young man comes here absolutely alone without a purpose!"

"I had a purpose, all right; but it was not to blow up a railroad train."

Apparently he thought he had said too much, for he relapsed into silence after that, with an occasional muttering.

It was eight o'clock when Hutchins's canoe came into sight. She was paddling easily, but the detective was far behind and moving slowly.

She saw the camp with its uninvited guests, and then she saw us. The detective, however, showed no curiosity; and we could see that he made for his landing and stumbled exhaustedly up the bank. Hutchins drew up beside us. "He'll not try that again, I think," she said in her crisp voice. "He's out of training. He panted like a motor launch. Who are our visitors?"

Here her eyes fell on Mr. McDonald and her face set in the dusk.

"You'll have to go back and get some gasoline, Hutchins."

"What made you start out without looking?"

"And send the vandals away. If they wait until I arrive, I'll be likely to do them some harm. I have never been so outraged."

"Let me go for gasoline in the canoe," said Mr. McDonald. He leaned over the thwart and addressed Hutchins. "You're worn out," he said. "I promise to come back and be a perfectly well-behaved prisoner again."

"Thanks, no."

"I'm wet. The exercise will warm me."

"Is it possible," she said in a withering tone that was lost on us at the time, "that you brought no dumb-bells with you?"

If we had had any doubts they should have been settled then; but we never suspected. It is incredible, looking back.

The dusk was falling and I am not certain of what followed. It was, however, something like this: Mr. McDonald muttered something angrily and made a motion to get into the canoe. Hutchins replied that she would not have help from him if she died for it. The next thing we knew she was in the launch and the canoe was floating off on the current. Aggie squealed; and Mr. McDonald, instead of swimming after the thing, merely folded his arms and looked at it.

"You know," he said to Hutchins, "you have so unpleasant a disposition that somebody we both know of is better off than he thinks he is!"

Tish's fury knew no bounds, for there we were marooned and two of us wet to the skin. I must say for Hutchins, however, that when she learned about Aggie she was bitterly repentant, and insisted on putting her own sweater on her. But there we were and there we should likely stay.

It was quite dark by that time, and we sat in the launch, rocking gently. The canoeing party had lighted a large fire on the beach, using the driftwood we had so painfully accumulated.

We sat in silence, except that Tish, who was watching our camp, said once bitterly that she was glad there were three beds in the tent. The girls of the canoeing party would be comfortable.

After a time Tish turned on Mr. McDonald sharply. "Since you claim to be no spy," she said, "perhaps you will tell us what brings you alone to this place? Don't tell me it's fish —I've seen you reading, with a line out. You're no fisherman."

He hesitated. "No," he admitted. "I'll be frank, Miss Carberry. I did not come to fish."

"What brought you?"

"Love," he said, in a low tone. "I don't expect you to believe me, but it's the honest truth."

"Love!" Tish scoffed.

"Perhaps I'd better tell you the story," he said. "It's long and-and rather sad."

"Love stories," Hutchins put in coldly, "are terribly stupid, except to those concerned."

"That," he retorted, "is because you have never been in love. You are young and-you will pardon the liberty? —attractive; but you are totally prosaic and unromantic."

"Indeed!" she said, and relapsed into silence.

"These other ladies," Mr. McDonald went on, "will understand the strangeness of my situation when I explain that the-the young lady I care for is very near; is, in fact, within sight."

"Good gracious!" said Aggie. "Where?"

"It is a long story, but it may help to while away the long night hours; for I dare say we are here for the night. Did any one happen to notice the young lady in the first canoe, in the pink tam-o'-shanter?"

We said we had-all except Hutchins, who, of course, had not seen her. Mr. McDonald got a wet cigarette from his pocket and, finding a box of matches on the seat, made an attempt to dry it over the flames; so his story was told in the flickering light of one match after another.

VI

"I am," Mr. McDonald said, as the cigarette steamed, "the son of poor but honest parents. All my life I have been obliged to labor. You may say that my English is surprisingly pure, under such conditions. As a matter of fact, I educated myself at night, using a lantern in the top of my father's stable."

"I thought you said he was poor," Hutchins put in nastily. "How did he have a stable?"

"He kept a livery stable. Any points that are not clear I will explain afterward. Once the thread of a narrative is broken, it is difficult to resume, Miss Hutchins. Near us, in a large house, lived the lady of my heart."

"The pink tam-o'-shanter girl!" said Aggie. "I begin to understand."

"But," he added, "near us also lived a red-headed boy. She liked him very much, and even in the long-ago days I was fiercely jealous of him. It may surprise you to know that in those days I longed-fairly longed-for red hair and a red mustache."

"I hate to interrupt," said Hutchins; "but did he have a mustache as a boy?"

He ignored her. "We three grew up together. The girl is beautiful-you've probably noticed that-and amiable. The one thing I admire in a young woman is amiability. It would not, for instance, have occurred to her to isolate an entire party on the bosom of a northern and treacherous river out of pure temper."

"To think," said Aggie softly, "that she is just over there by the camp-fire! Don't you suppose, if she loves you, she senses your nearness?"

"That's it exactly," he replied in a gloomy voice, "if she loves me! But does she? In other words, has she come up the river to meet me or to meet my rival? She knows we are here. Both of us have written her. The presence of one or the other of us is the real reason for this excursion of hers. But again the question is-which?"

Here the match he was holding under the cigarette burned his fingers and he flung it overboard with a violent gesture.

"The detective, of course," said Tish. "I knew it from the beginning of your story."

"The detective," he assented. "You see his very profession attracts. There's an element of romance in it. I myself have kept on with my father and now run the-er-livery stable. My business is a handicap from a romantic point of view.

"I am aware," Mr. McDonald went on, "that it is not customary to speak so frankly of affairs of this sort; but I have two reasons. It hurts me to rest under unjust suspicion. I am no spy, ladies. And the second reason is even stronger. Consider my desperate position: In the morning my rival will see her; he will paddle his canoe to the great rock below your camp and sing his love song from the water. In the morning I shall sit here helpless-ill, possibly-and see all that I value in life slip out of my grasp. And all through no fault of my own! Things are so evenly balanced, so little will shift the weight of her favor, that frankly the first one to reach her will get her."

I confess I was thrilled. And even Tish was touched; but she covered her emotion with hard common sense.

"What's her name?" she demanded.

"Considering my frankness I must withhold that. Why not simply refer to her as the pink tam-o'-shanter-or, better still and more briefly, the P.T.S.? That may stand for pink tam-o'-shanter, or the Person That Smiles, —she smiles a great deal, —or-or almost anything."

"It also stands," said Hutchins, with a sniff, "for Pretty Tall Story."

Tish considered her skepticism unworthy in one so young, and told her so; on which she relapsed into a sulky silence.

In view of what we knew, the bonfire at our camp and the small figure across the river took on a new significance.

As Aggie said, to think of the red-haired man sleeping calmly while his lady love was so near and his rival, so to speak, *hors de combat!* Shortly after finishing his story, Mr. McDonald went to the stern of the boat and lifted the anchor rope.

"It is possible," he said, "that the current will carry us to my island with a little judicious management. Even though we miss it, we'll hardly be worse off than we are."

It was surprising we had not thought of it before, for the plan succeeded admirably. By moving a few feet at a time and then anchoring, we made slow but safe progress, and at last touched shore. We got out, and Mr. McDonald built a large fire, near which we put Aggie to steam. His supper, which he had not had time to eat, he generously divided, and we heated the tea. Hutchins, however, refused to eat.

Warmth and food restored Tish's mind to its usual keenness. I recall now the admiration in Mr. McDonald's eyes when she suddenly put down the sandwich she was eating and exclaimed: —

"The flags, of course! He told her to watch for a red flag as she came up the river; so when the party saw ours they landed. Perhaps they still think it is his camp and that he is away overnight."

"That's it, exactly," he said. "Think of the poor wretch's excitement when he saw your flag!"

Still, on looking back, it seems curious that we overlooked the way the red-headed man had followed Hutchins about. True, men are polygamous animals, Tish says, and are quite capable of following one woman about while they are sincerely in love with somebody else. But, when you think of it, the detective had apparently followed Hutchins from the start, and had gone into the wilderness to be near her, with only a suitcase and a mackintosh coat; which looked like a mad infatuation.

(Tish says she thought of this at the time, and that; from what she had seen of the P.T.S., Hutchins was much prettier. But she says she decided that men often love one quality in one girl and another in another; that he probably loved Hutchins's beauty and the amiability of the P.T.S. Also, she says, she reflected that the polygamy of the Far East is probably due to this tendency in the male more than to a preponderance of women.)

Tish called me aside while Mr. McDonald was gathering firewood. "I'm a fool and a guilty woman, Lizzie," she said. "Because of an unjust suspicion I have possibly wrecked this poor boy's life."

I tried to soothe her. "They might have been wretchedly unhappy together, Tish," I said; "and, anyhow, I doubt whether he is able to support a wife. There's nothing much in keeping a livery stable nowadays."

"There's only one thing that still puzzles me," Tish observed: "granting that the grocery order was a grocery order, what about the note?"

We might have followed this line of thought, and saved what occurred later, but that a new idea suddenly struck Tish. She is curious in that way; her mind works very rapidly at times, and because I cannot take her mental hurdles, so to speak, she is often impatient.

"Lizzie," she said suddenly, "did you notice that when the anchor was lifted, we drifted directly to this island? Don't stare at me like that. Use your wits."

When I failed instantly to understand, however, she turned abruptly and left me, disappearing in the shadows.

For the next hour nothing happened. Tish was not in sight and Aggie slept by the fire. Hutchins sat with her chin cupped in her hands, and Mr. McDonald gathered driftwood.

Hutchins only spoke once. "I'm awfully sorry about the canoe, Miss Lizzie," she said; "it was silly and-and selfish. I don't always act like a bad child. The truth is, I'm rather upset and nervous. I hate to be thwarted —I'm sorry I can't explain any further."

I was magnanimous. "I'm sure, until to-night, you've been perfectly satisfactory," I said; "but it seems extraordinary that you should dislike men the way you do."

She only eyed me searchingly.

It is my evening custom to prepare for the night by taking my switch off and combing and braiding my hair; so, as we seemed to be settled for the night, I asked Mr. McDonald whether the camp afforded an extra comb. He brought out a traveling-case at once from the tent and opened it.

"Here's a comb," he said. "I never use one. I'm sorry this is all I can supply."

My eyes were glued to the case. It was an English traveling-case, with gold-mounted fittings. He saw me staring at it and changed color.

"Nice bag, isn't it?" he said. "It was a gift, of course. The-the livery stable doesn't run much to this sort of thing."

But the fine edge of suspicion had crept into my mind again.

––––––––––––––––––––––––––––––

Tish did not return to the fire for some time. Before she came back we were all thoroughly alarmed. The island was small, and a short search convinced us that she was not on it!

We wakened Aggie and told her, and the situation was very painful. The launch was where we had left it. Mr. McDonald looked more and more uneasy.

"My sane mind tells me she's perfectly safe," he said. "I don't know that I've ever met a person more able to take care of herself; but it's darned odd-that's all I can say."

Just as he spoke a volley of shots sounded from up the river near our camp, two close together and then one; and somebody screamed.

It was very dark. We could see lanterns flashing at our camp and somebody was yelling hoarsely. One lantern seemed to run up and down the beach in mad excitement, and then, out of the far-off din, Aggie, whose ears are sharp, suddenly heard the splash of a canoe paddle.

I shall tell Tish's story of what happened as she told it to Charlie Sands two weeks or so later.

"It is perfectly simple," she said, "and it's stupid to make such a fuss over it. Don't talk to me about breaking the law! The girl came; I didn't steal her."

Charlie Sands, I remember, interrupted at that moment to remind her that she had shot a hole in the detective's canoe; but this only irritated her.

"Certainly I did," she snapped; "but it's perfectly idiotic of him to say that it took off the heel of his shoe. In that stony country it's always easy to lose a heel."

But to return to Tish's story: —

"It occurred to me," she said, "that, if the launch had drifted to Mr. McDonald's island, the canoe might have done so too; so I took a look round. I'd been pretty much worried about having called the boy a spy when he wasn't, and it worried me to think that he couldn't get away from the place. I never liked the red-haired man. He was cruel to Aggie's cat-but we've told you that.

"I knew that in the morning the detective would see the P.T.S., as we called her, and he could get over and propose before breakfast. But when I found the canoe-yes, I found it —I didn't intend to do anything more than steal the detective's boat."

"Is that all?" said Charlie Sands sarcastically. "You disappoint me, Aunt Letitia! With all the chances you had-to burn his pitiful little tent, for instance, or steal his suitcase —"

"But on my way," Tish went on with simple dignity, "it occurred to me that I could move things a step farther by taking the girl to Mr. McDonald and letting him have his chance right away. Things went well from the start, for she was standing alone, looking out over the river. It was dark, except for the starlight, and I didn't know it was she. I beached the canoe and she squealed a little when I spoke to her."

"Just what," broke in Charlie Sands, "does one say under such circumstances? Sometime I may wish to abduct a young woman and it is well to be prepared."

"I told her the young man she had expected was on Island Eleven and had sent me to get her. She was awfully excited. She said they'd seen his signal, but nothing of him. And when they'd found a number of feminine things round they all felt a little-well, you can understand. She went back to get a coat, and while she was gone I untied the canoes and pushed them out into the river. I'm thorough, and I wasn't going to have a lot of people interfering before we got things fixed."

It was here, I think, that Charlie Sands gave a low moan and collapsed on the sofa. "Certainly!" he said in a stifled voice. "I believe in being thorough. And, of course, a few canoes more or less do not matter."

"Later," Tish said, "I knew I'd been thoughtless about the canoes; but, of course, it was too late then."

"And when was it that you assaulted the detective?"

"He fired first," said Tish. "I never felt more peaceable in my life. It's absurd for him to say that he was watching our camp, as he had every night we'd been there. Who asked him to guard us? And the idea of his saying he thought we were Indians stealing things, and that he fired into the air! The bullets sang past me. I had hardly time to get my revolver out of my stocking."

"And then?" asked Charlie Sands.

"And then," said Tish, "we went calmly down the river to Island Eleven. We went rapidly, for at first the detective did not know I had shot a hole in his canoe, and he followed us. It stands to reason that if I'd shot his heel off he'd have known there was a hole in the boat. Luckily the girl was in the bottom of the canoe when she fainted or we might have been upset."

It was at this point, I believe, that Charlie Sands got his hat and opened the door.

"I find," he said, "that I cannot stand any more at present, Aunt Tish. I shall return when I am stronger."

So I shall go back to my own narrative. Really my justification is almost complete. Any one reading to this point will realize the injustice of the things that have been said about us.

We were despairing of Tish, as I have said, when we heard the shots and then the approach of a canoe. Then Tish hailed us.

"Quick, somebody!" she said. "I have a cramp in my right leg."

(The canoeing position, kneeling as one must, had been always very trying for her. She frequently developed cramps, which only a hot footbath relieved.)

Mr. McDonald waded out into the water. Our beach fire illuminated the whole scene distinctly, and when he saw the P.T.S. huddled in the canoe he stopped as though he had been shot.

"How interesting!" said Hutchins from the bank, in her cool voice.

I remember yet Tish, stamping round on her cramped limb and smiling benevolently at all of us. The girl, however, looked startled and unhappy, and a little dizzy. Hutchins helped her to a fallen tree.

"Where-where is he?" said the P.T.S.

Tish stared at her. "Bless the girl!" she said. "Did you think I meant the other one?"

"I —What other one?"

Tish put her hand on Mr. McDonald's arm. "My dear girl," she said, "this young man adores you. He's all that a girl ought to want in the man she loves. I have done him a grave injustice and he has borne it nobly. Come now-let me put your hand in his and say you will marry him."

"Marry him!" said the P.T.S. "Why, I never saw him in my life before!"

We had been so occupied with this astounding scene that none of us had noticed the arrival of the detective. He limped rapidly up the bank-having lost his heel, as I have explained-and, dripping with water, confronted us. When a red-haired person is pale, he is very pale. And his teeth showed.

He ignored all of us but the P.T.S., who turned and saw him, and went straight into his arms in the most unmaidenly fashion.

"By Heaven," he said, "I thought that elderly lunatic had taken you off and killed you!"

He kissed her quite frantically before all of us; and then, with one arm round her, he confronted Tish.

"I'm through!" he said. "I'm done! There isn't a salary in the world that will make me stay within gunshot of you another day." He eyed her fiercely. "You are a dangerous woman, madam," he said. "I'm going to bring a charge against you for abduction and assault with intent to kill. And if there's any proof needed I'll show my canoe, full of water to the gunwale."

Here he kissed the girl again.

"You-you know her?" gasped Mr. McDonald, and dropped on a tree-trunk, as though he were too weak to stand.

"It looks like it, doesn't it?"

Here I happened to glance at Hutchins, and she was convulsed with mirth! Tish saw her, too, and glared at her; but she seemed to get worse. Then, without the slightest warning, she walked round the camp-fire and kissed Mr. McDonald solemnly on the top of his head.

"I give it up!" she said. "Somebody will have to marry you and take care of you. I'd better be the person."

"But why was the detective watching Hutchins?" said Charlie Sands. "Was it because he had heard of my Aunt Letitia's reckless nature? I am still bewildered."

"You remember the night we got the worms?"

"I see. The detective was watching all of you because you stole the worms."

"Stole nothing!" Tish snapped. "That's the girl's house. She's the Miss Newcomb you read about in the papers. Now do you understand?"

"Certainly I do. She was a fugitive from justice because the cat found dynamite in the woods. Or-perhaps I'm a trifle confused, but-Now I have it! She had stolen a gold-mounted traveling-bag and given it to McDonald. Lucky chap! I was crazy about Hutchins myself. You might tip her the word that I'm badly off for a traveling-case myself. But what about the P.T.S.? How did she happen on the scene?"

"She was engaged to the detective, and she was camping down the river. He had sent her word where he was. The red flag was to help her find him."

Tish knows Charlie Sands, so she let him talk. Then: —

"Mr. McDonald was too wealthy, Charlie," she said; "so when she wanted him to work and be useful, and he refused, she ran off and got a situation herself to teach him a lesson. She could drive a car. But her people heard about it, and that wretched detective was responsible for her safety. That's why he followed her about."

"I should like to follow her about myself," said Charlie Sands. "Do you think she's unalterably decided to take McDonald, money and all? He's still an idler. Lend me your car, Aunt Tish. There's a theory there; and-who knows?"

"He is going to work for six months before she marries him," Tish said. "He seems to like to work, now he has started."

She rang the bell and Hannah came to the door.

"Hannah," said Tish calmly, "call up the garage and tell McDonald to bring the car round. Mr. Sands is going out."

My Country Tish of Thee —

I

We had meant to go to Europe this last summer, and Tish would have gone anyhow, war or no war, if we had not switched her off onto something else. "Submarines fiddlesticks!" she said. "Give me a good life preserver, with a bottle of blackberry cordial fastened to it, and the sea has no terrors for me."

She said the proper way to do, in case the ship was torpedoed, was to go up on an upper deck, and let the vessel sink under one.

"Then without haste," she explained, "as the water rises about one, strike out calmly. The life-belt supports one, but swim gently for the exercise. It will prevent chilling. With a waterproof bag of crackers, and mild weather, one could go on comfortably for a day or two."

I still remember the despairing face Aggie turned to me. It was December then, and very cold.

However, she said nothing more until January. Early in that month Charlie Sands came to Tish's to Sunday dinner, and we were all there. The subject came up then.

It was about the time Tish took up vegetarianism, I remember that, because the only way she could induce Charlie Sands to come to dinner was to promise to have two chops for him. Personally I am not a vegetarian. I am not and never will be. I took a firm stand except when at Tish's home. But Aggie followed Tish's lead, of course, and I believe lived up to it as far as possible, although it is quite true that, stopping in one day unexpectedly to secure a new crochet pattern, I smelled broiling steak. But Aggie explained that she merely intended to use the juice from a small portion, having had one of her weak spells, the balance to go to the janitor's dog.

However, this is a digression.

"Europe!" said Charlie Sands. "Forget it! What in the name of the gastric juice is this I'm eating?"

It was a mixture of bran, raisins, and chopped nuts, as I recall it, moistened with water and pressed into a compact form. It was Tish's own invention. She called it "Bran-Nut," and was talking of making it in large quantities for sale.

Charlie Sands gave it up with a feeble gesture. "I'm sorry, Aunt Letitia," he said at last; "I'm a strong man ordinarily, but by the time I've got it masticated I'm too weak to swallow it. If-if one could have a stream of water playing on it while working, it would facilitate things."

"The Ostermaiers," said Aggie, "are going West."

"Good for the Ostermaiers," said Charlie Sands. "Great idea. See America first. 'My Country Tish of Thee,' etc. Why don't you three try it?"

Tish relinquished Europe slowly.

"One would think," Charlie Sands said, "that you were a German being asked to give up Belgium."

"What part of the West?" she demanded. "It's all civilized, isn't it?"

"The Rocky Mountains," said Charlie Sands, "will never be civilized."

Tish broke off a piece of Bran-Nut, and when she thought no one was looking poured a little tea over it. There was a gleam in her eye that Aggie and I have learned to know.

"Mountains!" she said. "That ought to be good for Aggie's hay fever."

"I'd rather live with hay fever," Aggie put in sharply, "than cure it by falling over a precipice."

"You'll have to take a chance on that, of course," Charlie Sands said. "I'm not sure it will be safe, but I am sure it will be interesting."

Oh, he knew Tish well enough. Tell her a thing was dangerous, and no power could restrain her.

I do not mind saying that I was not keen about the thing. I had my fortune told years ago, and the palmist said that if a certain line had had a bend in it I should have been hanged. But since it did not, to be careful of high places.

"It's a sporting chance," said Charlie Sands, although I was prodding him under the table. "With some good horses and a bag of this-er-concentrated food, you would have the time of your young lives."

This was figurative. We are all of us round fifty.

"The-the Bran-Nut," he said, "would serve for both food and ammunition. I can see you riding along, now and then dropping a piece of it on the head of some unlucky mountain goat, and watching it topple over into eternity. I can see —"

"Riding!" said Aggie. "Then I'm not going. I have never been on a horse and I never intend to be."

"Don't be a fool," Tish snapped. "If you've never been on a horse, it's time and to spare you got on one."

Hannah had been clearing the table with her lips shut tight. Hannah is an old and privileged servant and has a most unfortunate habit of speaking her mind. So now she stopped beside Tish.

"You take my advice and go, Miss Tish," she said. "If you ride a horse round some and get an appetite, you'll go down on your knees and apologize to your Maker for the stuff we've been eating the last four weeks." She turned to Charlie Sands, and positively her chin was quivering. "I'm a healthy woman," she said, "and I work hard and need good nourishing food. When it's come to a point where I eat the cat's meat and let it go hungry," she said, "it's time either I lost my appetite or Miss Tish went away."

Well, Tish dismissed Hannah haughtily from the room, and the conversation went on. None of us had been far West, although Tish has a sister-in-law in, Toledo, Ohio. But owing to a quarrel over a pair of andirons that had been in the family for a time, she had never visited her.

"You'll like it, all of you," Charlie Sands said as we waited for the baked apples. "Once get started with a good horse between your knees, and —"

"I hope," Tish interrupted him, "that you do not think we are going to ride astride!"

"I'm darned sure of it."

That was Charlie Sands's way of talking. He does not mean to be rude, and he is really a young man of splendid character. But, as Tish says, contact with the world, although it has not spoiled him, has roughened his speech.

"You see," he explained, "there are places out there where the horses have to climb like goats. It's only fair to them to distribute your weight equally. A side saddle is likely to turn and drop you a mile or two down a crack."

Aggie went rather white and sneezed violently.

But Tish looked thoughtful. "It sounds reasonable," she said. "I've felt for along time that I'd be glad to discard skirts. Skirts," she said, "are badge of servitude, survivals of the harem, reminders of a time when nothing was expected of women but parasitic leisure."

I tried to tell her that she was wrong about the skirts. Miss MacGillicuddy, our missionary in India, had certainly said that the women in harems wore bloomers. But Tish left the room abruptly, returning shortly after with a volume of the encyclopædia, and looked up the Rocky Mountains.

I remember it said that the highest ranges were, as compared with the size and shape of the earth, only as the corrugations on the skin of an orange. Either the man who wrote that had never seen an orange or he had never seen the Rocky Mountains. Orange, indeed! If he had said the upper end of a pineapple it would have been more like it. I wish the man who wrote it would go to Glacier Park. I am not a vindictive woman, but I know one or two places where I would like to place him and make him swallow that orange. I'd like to see him on a horse, on the brink of a cañon a mile deep, and have his horse reach over the edge for a stray plant or two, or standing in a cloud up to his waist, so that, as Aggie so plaintively observed, "The lower half of one is in a snowstorm while the upper part is getting sunburned."

For we went. Oh, yes, we went. It is not the encyclopædia's fault that we came back. But now that we are home, and nothing wrong except a touch of lumbago that Tish got from sleeping on the ground, and, of course, Aggie's unfortunate experience with her teeth, I look back on our various adventures with pleasure. I even contemplate a return next year, although Aggie says she will die first. But even that is not to be taken as final. The last time I went to see her, she had bought a revolver from the janitor and was taking lessons in loading it.

The Ostermaiers went also. Not with us, however. The congregation made up a purse for the purpose, and Tish and Aggie and I went further, and purchased a cigar-case for Mr. Ostermaier and a quantity of cigars. Smoking is the good man's only weakness.

I must say, however, that it is absurd to hear Mrs. Ostermaier boasting of the trip. To hear her talk, one would think they had done the whole thing, instead of sitting in an automobile and looking up at the mountains. I shall never forget the day they were in a car passing along a road, and we crossed unexpectedly ahead of them and went on straight up the side of a mountain.

Tish had a sombrero on the side of her head, and was resting herself in the saddle by having her right leg thrown negligently over the horse's neck. With the left foot she was kicking our pack-horse, a creature so scarred with brands that Tish had named her Jane, after a cousin of hers who had had so many operations that Tish says she is now entirely unfurnished.

Mr. Ostermaier's face was terrible, and only two days ago Mrs. Ostermaier came over to ask about putting an extra width in the skirt to her last winter's suit. But it is my belief that she came to save Tish's soul, and nothing else.

"I'm so glad wide skirts have come in," she said. "They're so modest, aren't they, Miss Tish?"

"Not in a wind," Tish said, eying her coldly.

"I do think, dear Miss Tish," she went on with her eyes down, "that to-to go about in riding-breeches before a young man is-well, it is hardly discreet, is it?"

I saw Tish glancing about the room. She was pretty angry, and I knew perfectly well what she wanted. I put my knitting-bag over Charlie Sands's tobacco-pouch.

Tish had learned to roll cigarettes out in Glacier Park. Not that she smoked them, of course, but she said she might as well know how. There was no knowing when it would come in handy. And when she wishes to calm herself she reaches instinctively for what Bill used to call, strangely, "the makings."

"If," she said, her eye still roving, —"if it was any treat to a twenty-four-year-old cowpuncher to see three elderly women in riding-breeches, Mrs. Ostermaier, —and it's kind of you to think so, —why, I'm not selfish."

Mrs. Ostermaier's face was terrible. She gathered up her skirt and rose. "I shall not tell Mr. Ostermaier what you have just said," she observed with her mouth set hard. "We owe you a great deal, especially the return of my earrings. But I must request, Miss Tish, that you do not voice such sentiments in the Sunday school."

Tish watched her out. Then she sat down and rolled eleven cigarettes for Charlie Sands, one after the other. At last she spoke.

"I'm not sure," she said tartly, "that if I had it to do over again I'd do it. That woman's not a Christian. I was thinking," she went on, "of giving them a part of the reward to go to Asbury Park with. But she'd have to wear blinders on the bathing-beach, so I'll not do it."

However, I am ahead of my recital.

For a few days Tish said nothing more, but one Sunday morning, walking home from church, she turned to me suddenly and said: —

"Lizzie, you're fat."

"I'm as the Lord made me," I replied with some spirit.

"Fiddlesticks!" said Tish. "You're as your own sloth and overindulgence has made you. Don't blame the Good Man for it."

Now, I am a peaceful woman, and Tish is as my own sister, and indeed even more so. But I was roused to anger by her speech.

"I've been fleshy all my life," I said. "I'm no lazier than most, and I'm a dratted sight more agreeable than some I know, on account of having the ends of my nerves padded."

But she switched to another subject in her characteristic manner.

"Have you ever reflected, either of you," she observed, "that we know nothing of this great land of ours? That we sing of loving 'thy rocks and rills, thy woods and templed hills' — although the word 'templed' savors of paganism and does not belong in a national hymn? And that it is all balderdash?"

Aggie took exception to this and said that she loved her native land, and had been south to Pinehurst and west to see her niece in Minneapolis, on account of the baby having been named for her.

But Tish merely listened with a grim smile. "Travel from a car window," she observed, "is no better than travel in a nickelodeon. I have done all of that I am going to. I intend to become acquainted with my native land, closely acquainted. State by State I shall wander over it, refreshing soul and body and using muscles too long unused."

"Tish!" Aggie quavered. "You are not going on another walking-tour?"

Only a year or two before Tish had read Stevenson's "Travels with a Donkey," and had been possessed to follow his example. I have elsewhere recorded the details of that terrible trip. Even I turned pale, I fear, and cast a nervous eye toward the table where Tish keeps her reading-matter.

Tish is imaginative, and is always influenced by the latest book she has read. For instance, a volume on "Nursing at the Front" almost sent her across to France, although she cannot make a bed and never could, and turns pale at the sight of blood; and another time a book on flying machines sent her up into the air, mentally if not literally. I shall never forget the time she secured some literature on the Mormon Church, and the difficulty I had in smuggling it out under my coat.

Tish did not refute the walking-tour at once, but fell into a deep reverie.

It is not her custom to confide her plans to us until they are fully shaped and too far on to be interfered with, which accounts for our nervousness.

On arriving at her apartment, however, we found a map laid out on the table and the Rocky Mountains marked with pins. We noticed that whenever she straightened from the table she grunted.

"What we want," Tish said, "is isolation. No people. No crowds. No servants. If I don't get away from Hannah soon I'll murder her."

"It wouldn't hurt to see somebody now and then, Tish," Aggie objected.

"Nobody," Tish said firmly. "A good horse is companion enough." She forgot herself and straightened completely, and she groaned.

"We might meet some desirable people, Tish," I put in firmly. "If we do, I don't intend to run like a rabbit."

"Desirable people!" Tish scoffed. "In the Rocky Mountains! My dear Lizzie, every desperado in the country takes refuge in the Rockies. Of course, if you want to take up with that class —"

Aggie sneezed and looked wretched. As for me, I made up my mind then and there that if Letitia Carberry was going to such a neighborhood, she was not going alone. I am not much with a revolver, but mighty handy with a pair of lungs.

Well, Tish had it all worked out. "I've found the very place," she said. "In the first place, it's Government property. When our country puts aside a part of itself as a public domain we should show our appreciation. In the second place, it's wild. I'd as soon spend a vacation in Central Park near the Zoo as in the Yellowstone. In the third place, with an Indian reservation on one side and a national forest on the other, it's bound to be lonely. Any tourist," she said scornfully, "can go to the Yosemite and be photographed under a redwood tree."

"Do the Indians stay on the reservation?" Aggie asked feebly.

"Probably not," Tish observed coldly. "Once for all, Aggie-if you are going to run like a scared deer every time you see an Indian or a bear, I wish you would go to Asbury Park."

She forgot herself then and sat down quickly, an action which was followed by an agonized expression.

"Tish," I said sharply, "you have been riding a horse!

"Only in a cinder ring," she replied with unwonted docility. "The teacher said I would be a trifle stiff."

"How long did you ride?"

"Not more than twenty minutes," she said. "The lesson was to be an hour, but somebody put a nickel in a mechanical piano, and the creature I was on started going sideways."

Well, she had fallen off and had to be taken home in a taxicab. When Aggie heard it she simply took the pins out of the map and stuck them in Tish's cushion. Her mouth was set tight.

"I didn't really fall," Tish said. "I sat down, and it was cinders, and not hard. It has made my neck stiff, that's all."

"That's enough," said Aggie. "If I've got to seek pleasure by ramming my spinal column up into my skull and crowding my brains, I'll stay at home."

"You can't fall out of a Western saddle," Tish protested rather bitterly. "And if I were you, Aggie, I wouldn't worry about crowding my brains."

However, she probably regretted this speech, for she added more gently: "A high altitude will help your hay fever, Aggie."

Aggie said with some bitterness that her hay fever did not need to be helped. That, as far as she could see, it was strong and flourishing. At that matters rested, except for a bit of conversation just before we left. Aggie had put on her sweater vest and her muffler and the jacket of her winter suit and was getting into her fur coat, when Tish said: "Soft as mush, both of you!"

"If you think, Tish Carberry," I began, "that I —"

"Apple dumplings!" said Tish. "Sofa pillows! Jellyfish! Not a muscle to divide between you!" I drew on my woolen tights angrily.

"Elevators!" Tish went on scornfully. "Street cars and taxicabs! No wonder your bodies are mere masses of protoplasm, or cellulose, or whatever it is."

"Since when," said Aggie, "have you been walking to develop yourself, Tish? I must say —" Here anger brought on one of her sneezing attacks, and she was unable to finish.

Tish stood before us oracularly. "After next September," she said, "you will both scorn the sloth of civilization. You will move about for the joy of moving about. You will have cast off the shackles of the flesh and be born anew. That is, if a plan of mine goes through. Lizzie, you will lose fifty pounds!"

Well, I didn't want to lose fifty pounds. After our summer in the Maine woods I had gone back to find that my new tailor-made coat, which had fitted me exactly, and being stiffened with haircloth kept its shape off and looked as if I myself were hanging to the hook, had caved in on me in several places. Just as I had gone to the expense of having it taken in I began to put on flesh again, and had to have it let out. Besides, no woman over forty should ever reduce, at least not violently. She wrinkles. My face that summer had fallen into accordion plaits, and I had the curious feeling of having enough skin for two.

Aggie had suggested at that time that I have my cheeks filled out with paraffin, which I believe cakes and gives the appearance of youth. But Mrs. Ostermaier knew a woman who had done so, and being hit on one side by a snowball, the padding broke in half, one part moving up under her eye and the second lodging at the angle of her jaw. She tried lying on a hot-water bottle to melt the pieces and bring them together again, but they did not remain fixed, having developed a wandering habit and slipping unexpectedly now and then. Mrs. Ostermaier says it is painful to watch her holding them in place when she yawns.

Strangely enough, however, a few weeks later Tish's enthusiasm for the West had apparently vanished. When several weeks went by and the atlas had disappeared from her table, and she had given up vegetarianism for Swedish movements, we felt that we were to have a quiet summer after all, and Aggie wrote to a hotel in Asbury Park about rooms for July and August.

There was a real change in Tish. She stopped knitting abdominal bands for the soldiers in Europe, for one thing, although she had sent over almost a dozen very tasty ones. In the evenings, when we dropped in to chat with her, she said very little and invariably dozed in her chair.

On one such occasion, Aggie having inadvertently stepped on the rocker of her chair while endeavoring by laying a hand on Tish's brow to discover if she was feverish, the chair tilted back and Tish wakened with a jerk.

She immediately fell to groaning and clasped her hands to the small of her back, quite ignoring poor Aggie, whom the chair had caught in the epigastric region, and who was compelled for some time to struggle for breath.

"Jumping Jehoshaphat!" said Tish in an angry tone. It is rare for Tish to use the name of a Biblical character in this way, but she was clearly suffering. "What in the world are you doing, Aggie?"

"T-t-trying to breathe," poor Aggie replied.

"Then I wish," Tish said coldly, "that you would make the effort some place else than on the rocker of my chair. You jarred me, and I am in no state to be jarred."

But she refused to explain further, beyond saying, in reply to a question of mine, that she was not feverish and that she had not been asleep, having merely closed her eyes to rest them. Also she affirmed that she was not taking riding-lessons. We both noticed however, that she did not leave her chair during the time we were there, and that she was sitting on the sofa cushion I had made her for the previous Christmas, and on which I had embroidered the poet Moore's beautiful words: "Come, rest in this bosom."

As Aggie was still feeling faint, I advised her to take a mouthful of blackberry cordial, which Tish keeps for emergencies in her bathroom closet. Immediately following her departure the calm of the evening was broken by a loud shriek.

It appeared, on my rushing to the bathroom, while Tish sat heartlessly still, that Aggie, not seeing a glass, had placed the bottle to her lips and taken quite a large mouthful of liniment, which in color resembled the cordial. I found her sitting on the edge of the bathtub in a state of collapse.

"I'm poisoned!" she groaned. "Oh, Lizzie, I am not fit to die!"

I flew with the bottle to Tish, who was very calm and stealthily rubbing one of her ankles.

"Do her good," Tish said. "Take some of the stiffness out of her liver, for one thing. But you might keep an eye on her. It's full of alcohol."

"What's the antidote?" I asked, hearing Aggie's low groans.

"The gold cure is the only thing I can think of at the moment," said Tish coldly, and started on the other ankle.

I merely record this incident to show the change in Tish. Aggie was not seriously upset, although dizzy for an hour or so and very talkative, especially about Mr. Wiggins.

Tish was changed. Her life, which mostly had been an open book to us, became filled with mystery. There were whole days when she was not to be located anywhere, and evenings, as I have stated, when she dozed in her chair.

As usual when we are worried about Tish, we consulted her nephew, Charlie Sands. But like all members of the masculine sex he refused to be worried.

"She'll be all right," he observed. "She takes these spells. But trust the old lady to come up smiling."

"It's either Christian Science or osteopathy," Aggie said dolefully. "She's not herself. The fruit cake she sent me the other day tasted very queer, and Hannah thinks she put ointment in instead of butter."

"Ointments!" observed Charlie thoughtfully. "And salves! By George, I wonder —I'll tell you," he said: "I'll keep an eye open for a few days. The symptoms sound like-But never mind. I'll let you know."

We were compelled to be satisfied with this, but for several days we lingered in anxiety. During that painful interval nothing occurred to enlighten us, except one conversation with Tish.

We had taken dinner with her, and she seemed to be all right again and more than usually active. She had given up the Bran-Nut after breaking a tooth on it, and was eating rare beef, which she had heard was digested in the spleen or some such place, thus resting the stomach for a time. She left us, however, immediately after the meal, and Hannah, her maid, tiptoed into the room.

"I'm that nervous I could scream," she said. "Do you know what she's doing now?"

"No, Hannah," I said with bitter sarcasm. "Long ago I learned never to surmise what Miss Tish is doing."

"She's in the bathroom, standing on one foot and waving the other in the air. She's been doing it," Hannah said, "for weeks. First one foot, then the other. And that ain't all."

"You've been spying on Miss Tish," Aggie said. "Shame on you, Hannah!"

"I have, Miss Aggie. Spy I have and spy I will, while there's breath in my body. Twenty years have I —Do you know what she does when she come home from these sneakin' trips of hers? She sits in a hot bath until the wonder is that her blood ain't turned to water. And after that she uses liniment. Her underclothes is that stained up with it that I'm ashamed to hang 'em out."

Here Tish returned and, after a suspicious glance at Hannah, sat down. Aggie and I glanced at each other. She did not, as she had for some time past, line the chair with pillows, and there was an air about her almost of triumph.

She did not, however, volunteer any explanation. Aggie and I were driven to speculation, in which we indulged on our way home, Aggie being my guest at the time, on account of her janitor's children having measles, and Aggie never having had them, although recalling a severe rash as a child, with other measly symptoms.

"She has something in mind for next summer," said Aggie apprehensively, "and she is preparing her strength for it. Tish is forehanded if nothing else."

"Well," I remarked with some bitterness, "if we are going along it might be well to prepare us too."

"Something," Aggie continued, "that requires landing on one foot with the other in the air."

"Don't drivel," said I. "She's not likely going into the Russian ballet. She's training her muscles, that's all."

But the mystery was solved the following morning when Charlie Sands called me up.

"I've got it, beloved aunt," he said.

"Got what?" said I.

"What the old lady is up to. She's a wonder, and no mistake. Only I think it was stingy of her not to let you and Aunt Aggie in."

He asked me to get Aggie and meet him at the office as soon as possible, but he refused to explain further. And he continued to refuse until we had arrived at our destination, a large brick building in the center of the city.

"Now," he said, "take a long breath and go in. And mind-no excitement."

We went in. There was a band playing and people circling at a mile a minute. In the center there was a cleared place, and Tish was there on ice skates. An instructor had her by the arm, and as we looked she waved him off, gave herself a shove forward with one foot, and then, with her arms waving, she made a double curve, first on one foot and then on the other.

"The outside edge, by George!" said Charlie Sands. "The old sport!"

Unluckily at that moment Tish saw us, and sat down violently on the ice. And a quite nice-looking young man fell over her and lay stunned for several seconds. We rushed round the arena, expecting to see them both carried out, but Tish was uninjured, and came skating toward us with her hands in her pockets. It was the young man who had to be assisted out.

"Well," she said, fetching up against the railing with a bang, "of course you had to come before I was ready for you! In a week I'll really be skating."

We said nothing, but looked at her, and I am afraid our glances showed disapproval, for she straightened her hat with a jerk.

"Well?" she said. "You're not tongue-tied all of a sudden, are you? Can't a woman take a little exercise without her family and friends coming snooping round and acting as if she'd broken the Ten Commandments?"

"Breaking the Ten Commandments!" I said witheringly. "Breaking a leg more likely. If you could have seen yourself, Tish Carberry, sprawled on that ice at your age, and both your arteries and your bones brittle, as the specialist told you,—and I heard him myself,—you'd take those things off your feet and go home and hide your head."

"I wish I had your breath, Lizzie," Tish said. "I'd be a submarine diver."

Saying which she skated off, and did not come near us again. A young gentleman went up to her and asked her to skate, though I doubt if she had ever seen him before. And as we left the building in disapproval they were doing fancy turns in the middle of the place, and a crowd was gathering round them.

Owing to considerable feeling being roused by the foregoing incident, we did not see much of Tish for a week. If a middle-aged woman wants to make a spectacle of herself, both Aggie and I felt that she needed to be taught a lesson. Besides, we knew Tish. With her, to conquer a thing is to lose interest.

On the anniversary of the day Aggie became engaged to Mr. Wiggins, Tish asked us both to dinner, and we buried the hatchet, or rather the skates. It was when dessert came that we realized how everything that had occurred had been preparation for the summer, and that we were not going to Asbury Park, after all.

"It's like this," said Tish. "Hannah, go out and close the door, and don't stand listening. I have figured it all out," she said, when Hannah had slammed out. "The muscles used in skating are the ones used in mountain-climbing. Besides, there may be times when a pair of skates would be handy going over the glaciers. It's not called Glacier Park for nothing, I dare say. When we went into the Maine woods we went unprepared. This time I intend to be ready for any emergency."

But we gave her little encouragement. We would go along, and told her so. But further than that I refused to prepare. I would not skate, and said so.

"Very well, Lizzie," she said. "Don't blame me if you find yourself unable to cope with mountain hardships. I merely felt this way: if each of us could do one thing well it might be helpful. There's always snow, and if Aggie would learn to use snowshoes it might be valuable."

"Where could I practice?" Aggie demanded.

But Tish went on, ignoring Aggie's sarcastic tone. "And if you, Lizzie, would learn to throw a lasso, or lariat,—I believe both terms are correct,—it would be a great advantage, especially in case of meeting ferocious animals. The park laws will not allow us to kill them, and it would be mighty convenient, Lizzie. Not to mention that it would be an accomplishment few women possess."

I refused to make the attempt, although Tish sent for the clothesline, and with the aid of the encyclopædia made a loop in the end of it. Finally she became interested herself, and when we left rather downhearted at ten o'clock she had caught the rocking-chair three times and broken the clock.

Aggie and I prepared with little enthusiasm, I must confess. We had as much love for the rocks and rills of our great country as Tish, but, as Aggie observed, there were rocks and rocks, and one could love them without climbing up them or falling off them.

The only comfort we had was that Charlie Sands said that we should ride ponies, and not horses. My niece's children have a pony which is very gentle and not much larger than a dog, which comes up on the porch for lumps of sugar. We were lured to a false sense of security, I must say.

As far as we could see, Tish was making few preparations for the trip. She said we could get everything we needed at the park entrance, and that the riding was merely sitting in a saddle and letting the pony do the rest. But on the 21st of June, the anniversary of the day Aggie was to have been married, we went out to decorate Mr. Wiggins's last resting-place, and coming out of the cemetery we met Tish.

She was on a horse, astride!

She was not alone. A gentleman was riding beside her, and he had her horse by a long leather strap.

She pretended not to see us, and Aggie unfortunately waved her red parasol at her. The result was most amazing. The beast she was on jerked itself free in an instant, and with the same movement, apparently, leaped the hedge beside the road. One moment there was Tish, in a derby hat and breeches, and the next moment there was only the gentleman, with his mouth open.

Aggie collapsed, moaning, in the road, and beyond the hedge we could hear the horse leaping tombstones in the cemetery.

"Oh, Tish!" Aggie wailed.

I broke my way through the hedge to find what was left of her, while the riding-master bolted for the gate. But to my intense surprise Tish was not on the ground. Then I saw her. She was still on the creature, and she was coming back along the road, with her riding-hat on the back of her head and a gleam in her eye that I knew well enough was a gleam of triumph.

She halted the thing beside me and looked down with a patronizing air.

"He's a trifle nervous this morning," she said calmly. "Hasn't been worked enough. Good horse, though, —very neat jump."

Then she rode on and out through the gates, ignoring Aggie's pitiful wail and scorning the leading-string the instructor offered.

We reached Glacier Park without difficulty, although Tish insisted on talking to the most ordinary people on the train, and once, losing her, we found her in the drawing-room learning to play bridge, although not a card-player, except for casino. Though nothing has ever been said, I believe she learned when too late that they were playing for money, as she borrowed ten dollars from me late in the afternoon and was looking rather pale.

"What do you think?" she said, while I was getting the money from the safety pocket under my skirt. "The young man who knocked me down on the ice that day is on the train. I've just exchanged a few words with him. He was not much hurt, although unconscious for a short time. His name is Bell-James C. Bell."

Soon after that Tish brought him to us, and we had a nice talk. He said he had not been badly hurt on the ice, although he got a cut on the forehead from Tish's skate, requiring two stitches.

After a time he and Aggie went out on the platform, only returning when Aggie got a cinder in her eye.

"Just think," she said as he went for water to use in my eye-cup, "he is going to meet the girl he is in love with out at the park. She has been there for four weeks. They are engaged. He is very much in love. He didn't talk of anything else."

She told him she had confided his tender secret to us, and instead of looking conscious he seemed glad to have three people instead of one to talk to about her.

"You see, it's like this," he said: "She is very good looking, and in her town a moving-picture company has its studio. That part's all right. I suppose we have to have movies. But the fool of a director met her at a party, and said she would photograph well and ought to be with them. He offered her a salary, and it went to her head. She's young," he added, "and he said she could be as great a hit as Mary Pickford."

"How sad!" said Aggie. "But of course she refused?"

"Well, no, she liked the idea. It got me worried. Worried her people too. Her father's able to give her a good home, and I'm expecting to take that job off his hands in about a year. But girls are queer. She wanted to try it awfully."

It developed that he had gone to her folks about it, and they'd offered her a vacation with some of her school friends in Glacier Park.

"It's pretty wild out there," he went on, "and we felt that the air, and horseback riding and everything, would make her forget the movies. I hope so. She's there now. But she's had the bug pretty hard. Got so she was always posing, without knowing it."

But he was hopeful that she would be cured, and said she was to meet him at the station.

"She's an awfully nice girl, you understand," he finished. "It's only that this thing got hold of her and needed driving out."

Well, we were watching when the train drew in at Glacier Park Station, and she was there. She was a very pretty girl, and it was quite touching to see him look at her. But Aggie observed something and remarked on it.

"She's not as glad to see him as he is to see her," she said. "He was going to kiss her, and she moved back."

In the crowd we lost sight of them, but that evening, sitting in the lobby of the hotel, we saw Mr. Bell wandering round alone. He looked depressed, and Aggie beckoned to him.

"How is everything?" she asked. "Is the cure working?"

He dropped into a chair and looked straight ahead.

"Not so you could notice it!" he said bitterly. "Would you believe that there's a moving-picture outfit here, taking scenes in the park?"

"No!"

"There is. They've taken two thousand feet of her already, dressed like an Indian," he said in a tone of suppressed fury. "It makes me sick. I dare say if we tied her in a well some fool would lower a camera on a rope."

Just at that moment she sauntered past us with a reddish-haired young man. Mr. Bell ignored her, although I saw her try to catch his eye.

"That's the moving-picture man with her," he said in a low, violent tone when they had passed. "Name's Oliver." He groaned. "He's told her she ought to go in for the business. She'd be a second Mary Pickford! I'd like to kill him!" He rose savagely and left us.

We spent the night in the hotel at the park entrance, and I could not get to sleep. Tish was busy engaging a guide and going over our supplies, and at eleven o'clock Aggie came into my room and sat down on the bed.

"I can't sleep, Lizzie," she said. "That poor Mr. Bell is on my mind. Besides, did you see those ferocious Indians hanging round?"

Well, I had seen them, but said nothing.

"They would scalp one as quick as not," Aggie went on. "And who's to know but that our guide will be in league with them? I've lost my teeth," she said with a flash of spirit, "but so far I've kept my hair, and mean to if possible. That old Indian has a scalp tied to the end of a stick. Lizzie, I'm nervous."

"If it is only hair they want, I don't mind their taking my switch," I observed, trying to be facetious, although uneasy. As to the switch, it no longer matched my hair, and I would have parted from it without a pang.

"And another thing," said Aggie: "Tish can talk about ponies until she is black in the face. The creatures are horses. I've seen them."

Well, I knew that, too, by that time. As we walked to the hotel from the train I had seen one of than carrying on. It was arching its back like a cat that's just seen a strange dog, and with every arch it swelled its stomach. At the third heave it split the strap that held the saddle on, and then it kicked up in the rear and sent saddle and rider over its head. So far as I had seen, no casualty had resulted, but it had set me thinking. Given a beast with an India-rubber spine and no sense of honor, I felt I would be helpless.

Tish came in just then and we confronted her.

"Ponies!" I said bitterly. "They are horses, if I know a horse. And, moreover, it's well enough for you, Tish Carberry, to talk about gripping a horse with your knees. I'm not built that way, and you know it. Besides, no knee grip will answer when a creature begins to act like a cat in a fit."

Aggie here had a bright idea. She said that she had seen pictures of pneumatic jackets to keep people from drowning, and that Mr. McKee, a buyer at one of the stores at home, had taken one, fully inflated, when he crossed to Paris for autumn suits.

"I would like to have one, Tish," she finished. "It would break the force of a fall anyhow, even if it did puncture."

Tish, who was still dressed, went out to the curio shop in the lobby, and returned with the sad news that there was nothing of the sort on sale.

We were late in getting started the next morning owing partly to Aggie's having put her riding-breeches on wrong, and being unable to sit down when once in the saddle. But the main reason was the guide we had engaged. Tish heard him using profane language to one of the horses and dismissed him on the spot.

The man who was providing our horses and outfit, however, understood, and in a short time returned with another man.

"I've got a good one for you now, Miss Carberry," he said. "Safe and perfectly gentle, and as mild as milk. Only has one fault, and maybe you won't mind that. He smokes considerably."

"I don't object, as long as it's in the open air," Tish said.

So that was arranged. But I must say that the new man did not look mild. He had red hair, although a nice smile with a gold tooth, and his trousers were of white fur, which looked hot for summer.

"You are sure that you don't use strong language?" Tish asked.

"No, ma'am," he said. "I was raised strict, and very particular as to swearing. Dear, dear now, would you look at that cinch! Blow up their little tummies, they do, when they're cinched, and when they breathe it out, the saddle's as loose as the tongues of some of these here tourists."

Tish swung herself up without any trouble, but owing to a large canvas bag on the back of my saddle I was unable to get my leg across, and was compelled to have it worked over, a little at a time. At last, however, we were ready. A white pack-horse, carrying our tents and cooking-utensils, was led by Bill, which proved to be the name of our cowboy guide.

Mr. Bell came to say good-bye and to wish us luck. But he looked unhappy, and there was no sign whatever of the young lady, whose name we had learned was Helen.

"I may see you on the trail," he said sadly. "I'm about sick of this place, and I'm thinking of clearing out."

Aggie reminded him that faint heart never won fair lady, but he only shook his head.

"I'm not so sure that I want to win," he said. "Marriage is a serious business, and I don't know that I'd care to have a wife that followed a camera like a street kid follows a brass band. It wouldn't make for a quiet home."

We left him staring wistfully into the distance.

Tish sat in her saddle and surveyed the mountain peaks that rose behind the hotel.

"Twenty centuries are looking down upon us!" she said. "The crest of our native land lies before us. We will conquer those beetling crags, or die trying. All right, Bill. Forward!"

Bill led off, followed by the pack-horse, then Tish, Aggie and myself. We kept on in this order for some time, which gave me a chance to observe Aggie carefully. I am not much of a horsewoman myself, having never been on a horse before. But my father was fond of riding, and I soon adapted myself to the horse's gait, especially when walking. On level stretches, however, where Bill spurred his horse to a trot, I was not so comfortable, and Aggie appeared to strike the saddle in a different spot every time she descended.

Once, on her turning her profile to me in a glance of despair, I was struck by the strange and collapsed appearance of her face. This was explained, however, when my horse caught up to hers on a wider stretch of road, and I saw that she had taken out her teeth and was holding them in her hand.

"Al-almost swallowed them," she gasped. "Oh, Lizzie, to think of a summer of this!"

At last we left the road and turned onto a footpath, which instantly commenced to rise. Tish called back something about the beauties of nature and riding over a carpet of flowers, but my horse was fording a small stream at the time and I was too occupied to reply. The path-or trail, which is what Bill called it-grew more steep, and I let go of the lines and held to the horn of my saddle. The horses were climbing like goats.

"Tish," Aggie called desperately, "I can't stand this. I'm going back! I'm —Lordamighty!"

Fortunately Tish did not hear this. We had suddenly emerged on the brink of a precipice. A two-foot path clung to the cliff, and along the very edge of this the horses walked, looking down in an interested manner now and then. My blood turned to water and I closed my eyes.

"Tish!" Aggie shrieked.

But the only effect of this was to start her horse into a trot. I had closed my eyes, but I opened them in time to see Aggie give a wild clutch and a low moan.

In a few moments the trail left the edge, and Aggie turned in her saddle and looked back at me.

"I lost my lower set back there," she said. "They went over the edge. I suppose they're falling yet."

"It's a good thing it wasn't the upper set," I said, to comfort her. "As far as appearance goes —"

"Appearance!" she said bitterly. "Do you suppose we'll meet anybody but desperadoes and Indians in a place like this? And not an egg with us, of course."

The eggs referred to her diet, as at different times, when having her teeth repaired, she can eat little else.

"Ham," she called back in a surly tone, "and hard tack, I suppose! I'll starve, Lizzie, that's all. If only we had brought some junket tablets!"

With the exception of this incident the morning was quiet. Tish and Bill talked prohibition, which he believed in, and the tin pans on the pack-horse clattered, and we got higher all the time, and rode through waterfalls and along the edge of death. By noon I did not much care if the horses fell over or not. The skin was off me in a number of places, and my horse did not like me, and showed it by nipping back at my leg here and there.

At eleven o'clock, riding through a valley on a trail six inches wide, Bill's horse stepped on a hornets' nest. The insects were probably dazed at first, but by the time Tish's horse arrived they were prepared, and the next thing we knew Tish's horse was flying up the mountain-side as if it had gone crazy, and Bill was shouting to us to stop.

The last we saw of Tish for some time was her horse leaping a mountain stream, and jumping like a kangaroo, and Bill was following.

"She'll be killed!" Aggie cried. "Oh, Tish, Tish!"

"Don't yell," I said. "You'll start the horses. And for Heaven's sake, Aggie," I added grimly, "remember that this is a pleasure trip."

It was a half-hour before Tish and Bill returned. Tish was a chastened woman. She said little or nothing, but borrowed some ointment from me for her face, where the branches of trees had scraped it, while Bill led the horses round the fatal spot. I recall, however, that she said she wished now that we had brought the other guide.

"Because I feel," she observed, "that a little strong language would be a relief."

We had luncheon at noon in a sylvan glade, and Aggie was pathetic. She dipped a cracker in a cup of tea, and sat off by herself under a tree. Tish, however, had recovered her spirits.

"Throw out your chests, and breathe deep of this pure air unsullied by civilization," she cried. "Aggie, fill yourself with ozone."

"Humph!" said Aggie. "It's about all I will fill myself with."

"Think," Tish observed, "of the fools and dolts who are living under roofs, struggling, contending, plotting, while all Nature awaits them."

"With stings," Aggie said nastily, "and teeth, and horns, and claws, and every old thing! Tish, I want to go back. I'm not happy, and I don't enjoy scenery when I'm not happy. Besides, I can't eat the landscape."

As I look back, I believe it would have been better if we had returned. I think of that day, some time later, when we made the long descent from the Piegan Pass under such extraordinary circumstances, and I realize that, although worse for our bodies, which had grown strong and agile, so that I have, later on, seen Aggie mount her horse on a run, it would have been better for our nerves had we returned.

We were all perfectly stiff after luncheon, and Aggie was sulking also. Bill was compelled to lift us into our saddles, and again we started up and up. The trail was now what he called a "switchback." Halfway up Aggie refused to go farther, but on looking back decided not to return either.

"I shall not go another step," she called. "Here I am, and here I stay till I die."

"Very well," Tish said from overhead. "I suppose you don't expect us all to stay and die with you. I'll tell your niece when I see her."

Aggie thought better of it, however, and followed on, with her eyes closed and her lips moving in prayer. She happened to open them at a bad place, although safe enough, according to Bill, and nothing to what we were coming to a few days later. Opening them as she did on a ledge of rock which sloped steeply for what appeared to be several miles down on each side, she uttered a piercing shriek, followed by a sneeze. As before, her horse started to run, and Aggie is, I believe Bill said, the only person in the world who ever took that place at a canter.

We were to take things easy the first day, Bill advised. "Till you get your muscles sort of eased up, ladies," he said. "If you haven't been riding astride, a horse's back seems as wide as the roof of a church. But we'll get a rest now. The rest of the way is walking."

"I can't walk," Aggie said. "I can't get my knees together."

"Sorry, ma'am," said Bill. "We're going down now, and the animals has to be led. That's one of the diversions of a trip like this. First you ride and than you walk. And then you ride again. This here's one of the show places, although easy of access from the entrance. Be a good place for a holdup, I've always said."

"A holdup?" Tish asked. Her enthusiasm seemed to have flagged somewhat, but at this she brightened up.

"Yes'm. You see, we're near the Canadian border, and it would be easy for a gang to slip over and back again. Don't know why we've never had one. Yellowstone can boast of a number."

I observed tartly that I considered it nothing to boast of, but Bill did not agree with me.

"It doesn't hurt a neighborhood none," he observed. "Adds romance, as you might say."

He went on and, happening to slide on a piece of shale at that moment, I sat down unexpectedly and the horse put its foot on me.

I felt embittered and helpless, but the others kept on.

"Very well," I said, "go on. Don't mind me. If this creature wants to sit in my lap, well and good. I expect it's tired."

But as they went on callously, I was obliged to shove the creature off and to hobble on. Bill was still babbling about holdups, and Aggie was saying that he was sunstruck, but of course it did not matter.

We made very slow progress, owing to taking frequent rests, and late in the afternoon we were overtaken by Mr. Bell, on foot and carrying a pack. He would have passed on without stopping, but Aggie hailed him.

"Not going to hike, are you?" she said pleasantly. Aggie is fond of picking up the vernacular of a region.

"No," he said in a surly tone quite unlike his former urbane manner, "I'm merely taking this pack out for a walk."

But he stopped and mopped his face.

"To tell you the truth, ladies," he said, "I'm working off a little steam, that's all. I was afraid, if I stayed round the hotel, I'd do something I'd be sorry for. There are times when I am not a fit companion for any one, and this is one of them."

We invited him to join us, but he refused.

"No, I'm better alone," he said. "When things get too strong for me on the trail I can sling things about. I've been throwing boulders down the mountain every now and then. I'd just as soon they hit somebody as not. Also," he added, "I'm safer away from any red-headed men."

We saw him glance at Bill, and understood. Mr. Oliver was red-headed.

"Love's an awful thing," said Bill as the young man went on, kicking stones out of his way. "I'm glad I ain't got it."

Tish turned and eyed him. "True love is a very beautiful thing," she rebuked him. "Although a single woman myself, I believe in it. 'Come live with me and be my love,'" she quoted, sitting down to shake a stone out of her riding-boot.

Bill looked startled. "I might say," he said hastily, "that I may have misled you, ladies. I'm married."

"You said you had never been in love," Tish said sharply.

"Well, not to say real love," he replied. "She was the cook of an outfit I was with and it just came about natural. She was going to leave, which meant that I'd have to do the cooking, which I ain't much at, especially pastry. So I married her."

Tish gave him a scornful glance but said nothing and we went on.

We camped late that afternoon beside Two Medicine Lake, and while Bill put up the tents the three of us sat on a log and soaked our aching feet in the water which was melted glacier, and naturally cold.

What was our surprise, on turning somewhat, to see the angry lover fishing on a point near by. While we stared he pulled out a large trout, and stalked away without a glance in our direction. As Tish, with her usual forethought, had brought a trout rod, she hastily procured it, but without result.

"Of course," Aggie said, "no fish! I could eat a piece of broiled fish. I dare say I shall be skin and bone at the end of this trip-and not much skin."

Bill had set up the sleeping-tent and built a fire, and it looked cozy and comfortable. But Tish had the young man on her mind, and after supper she put on a skirt which she had brought along and went to see him.

"I'd take him some supper, Bill," she said, "but you are correct: you are no cook."

She disappeared among the bushes, only to return in a short time, jerking off her skirt as she came.

"He says all he wants is to be let alone," she said briefly. "I must say I'm disappointed in him. He was very agreeable before."

I pass without comment over the night. Bill had put up the tent over the root of a large tree, and we disposed ourselves about it as well as we could. In the course of the night one of the horses broke loose and put its head inside the tent. Owing to Aggie's thinking it was a bear, Tish shot at it, fortunately missing it.

But the frightened animal ran away, and Bill was until noon the next day finding it. We cooked our own breakfast, and Tish made some gems, having brought the pan along. But the morning dragged, although the scenery was lovely.

At twelve Bill brought the horse back and came over to us.

"If you don't mind my saying it, Miss Carberry," he observed, "you're a bit too ready with that gun. First thing you know you'll put a hole through me, and then where will you be?"

"I've got along without men most of my life," Tish said sharply. "I reckon we'd manage."

"Well," he said, "there's another angle to it. Where would I be?"

"That's between you and your Creator," Tish retorted.

We went on again that afternoon, and climbed another precipice. We saw no human being except a mountain goat, although Bill claimed to have seen a bear. Tish was quite calm at all times, and had got so that she could look down into eternity without a shudder. But Aggie and I were still nervous, and at the steepest places we got off and walked.

The unfortunate part was that the exercise and the mountain air made Aggie hungry, and there was little that she could eat.

"If any one had told me a month ago," she said, mopping her forehead, "that I would be scaling the peaks of my country on crackers and tea, I wouldn't have believed it. I'm done out, Lizzie. I can't climb another inch."

Bill was ahead with the pack horse, and Tish, overhearing her, called back some advice.

"Take your horse's tail and let him pull you up, Aggie," she said. "I've read it somewhere."

Aggie, although frequently complaining, always does as Tish suggests. So she took the horse's tail, when a totally unexpected thing happened. Docile as the creature generally was, it objected at once, and kicked out with both rear feet. In a moment, it seemed to me, Aggie was gone, and her horse was moving on alone.

"Aggie!" I called in a panic.

Tish stopped, and we both looked about. Then we saw her, lying on a ledge about ten feet below the trail. She was flat on her back, and her riding-hat was gone. But she was uninjured, although shaken, for as we looked she sat up, and an agonized expression came over her face.

"Aggie!" I cried. "Is anything broken?"

"Damnation!" said Aggie in an awful voice. "The upper set is gone!"

I have set down exactly what Aggie said. I admit that the provocation was great. But Tish was not one to make allowances, and she turned and went on, leaving us alone. She is not without feeling, however, for from the top of the pass she sent Bill down with a rope, and we dragged poor Aggie to the trail again. Her nerves were shaken and she was repentant also, for when she found that her hat was gone she said nothing, although her eyes took on a hunted look.

At the top of the pass Tish was sitting on a stone. She had taken her mending-box from the saddle, where she always kept it handy, and was drawing up a hole in her stocking. I observed to her pleasantly that it was a sign of scandal to mend clothing while still on, but she ignored me, although, as I reflected bitterly, I had not been kicked over the cliff.

It was a subdued and speechless Aggie who followed us that afternoon along the trail. As her hat was gone, I took the spare dish towel and made a turban for her, with an end hanging down to protect the back of her neck. But she expressed little gratitude, beyond observing that as she was going over the edge piecemeal, she'd better have done it all at once and be through with it.

The afternoon wore away slowly. It seemed a long time until we reached our camping-place, partly because, although a small eater ordinarily, the air and exercise had made me feel famished. But the disagreement between Tish and Aggie, owing to the latter's unfortunate exclamation while kicked over the cliff, made the time seem longer. There was not the usual exchange of pleasant nothings between us.

But by six o'clock Tish was more amiable, having seen bear scratches on trees near the camp, and anticipating the sight of a bear. She mixed up a small cup cake while Bill was putting up our tent, and then, taking her rod, proceeded to fish, while Aggie and I searched for grasshoppers. These were few, owing to the altitude, but we caught four, which we imprisoned in a match-box.

With them Tish caught four trout and, broiling them nicely, she offered one to poor Aggie. It was a peace offering, and taken as such, so that we were soon on our former agreeable footing, and all forgotten.

The next day it rained, and we were obliged to sit in the tent. Bill sat with us, and talked mainly of desperadoes.

"As I observed before," he said, "there hasn't been any tourist holdup yet. But it's bound to come. Take the Yellowstone, now, —one holdup a year's the average, and it's full of soldiers at that."

"It's a wonder people keep on going," I observed moving out of a puddle.

"Oh, I don't know," he said. "In one way it's good business. I take it this way: When folks come West they want the West they've read about. What do they care for irrigation and apple orchards? What they like is danger and a little gunplay, the sort of thing they see in these here moving pictures."

"I'm sure I don't," Aggie remarked. It was growing dusk, and she peered out into the forest round us. "There is something crackling out there now," she said.

"Only a bear, likely," Bill assured her. "We have a sight of bears here. No, ma'am, they want danger. And every holdup's an advertisement. You see, the Government can't advertise these here parks; not the way it should, anyhow. But a holdup's news, so the papers print it, and it sets people to thinking about the park. Maybe they never thought of the place and are arranging to go elsewhere. Then along comes a gang and raises h —, raises trouble, and the park's in every one's mouth, so to speak. We'd get considerable business if there was one this summer."

At that moment the crackling outside increased, and a shadowy form emerged from the bushes. Even Bill stood up, and Aggie screamed.

It was, however, only poor Mr. Bell.

"Mind if I borrow some matches?" he said gruffly.

"We can't lend matches," Tish replied. "At least, I don't see the use of sending them back after they've been lighted. We can give you some."

"My mistake," he said.

That was all he said, except the word "Thanks" when I reached him a box.

"He's a surly creature," Tish observed as he crackled through the brush again. "More than likely that girl's better off without him."

"He looks rather downhearted," Aggie remarked. "Much that we think is temper is due to unhappiness."

"Much of your charitable view is due to a good dinner too," Tish said. "Here we are, in the center of the wilderness, with great peaks on every hand, and we meet a fellow creature who speaks nine words, and begrudges those. If he's as stingy with money as with language she's hard a narrow escape."

"He's had kind of a raw deal," Bill put in. "The girl was stuck on him all right, until this moving-picture chap came along. He offered to take some pictures with her in them, and it was all off. They're making up a play now, and she's to be in it."

"What sort of a play?" Tish demanded.

"Sorry not to oblige," Bill replied. "Can't say the nature of it."

But all of us felt that Bill knew and would not say.

Tish, to whom a mystery is a personal affront, determined to find out for herself; and when later in the evening we saw the light of Bell's camp-fire, it was Tish herself who suggested that we go over and visit with him.

"We can converse about various things," she said, "and take his mind from his troubles. But it would be better not to mention affairs of the heart. He's probably sensitive."

So we left Bill to look after things, and went to call on Mr. Bell. It was farther to his camp than it had appeared, and Tish unfortunately ran into a tree and bruised her nose badly. When it had stopped bleeding, however, we went on, and at last arrived.

He was sitting on a log by the fire, smoking a pipe and looking very sad. Behind him was a bit of a tent not much larger than an umbrella.

Aggie touched my arm. "My heart aches for him," she said. "There is despair in his very eyes."

I do not believe that at first he was very glad to see us, but he softened somewhat when Tish held out the cake she had brought.

"That's very nice of you," he said, rising. "I'm afraid I can't ask you to sit down. The ground's wet and there is only this log."

"I've sat on logs before," Tish replied. "We thought we'd call, seeing we are neighbors. As the first comers it was our place to call first, of course."

"I see," he said, and poked up the fire with a piece of stick.

"We felt that you might be lonely," said Aggie.

"I came here to be lonely," he replied gloomily. "I want to be lonely."

Tish, however, was determined to be cheerful, and asked him, as a safe subject, how he felt about the war.

"War?" he said. "That's so, there is a war. To tell the truth, I had forgotten about it. I've been thinking of other things."

We saw that it was going to be difficult to cheer him. Tish tried the weather, which brought us nowhere, as he merely grunted. But Aggie broached the subject of desperadoes, and he roused somewhat.

"There are plenty of shady characters in the park," he said shortly. "Wolves in sheep's clothing, that's what they are."

"Bill, our guide, says there may be a holdup at any time."

"Sure there is," he said calmly. "There's one going to be pulled off in the next day or two."

We sat petrified, and Aggie's eyes were starting out of her head.

"All the trimmings," he went on, staring at the fire. "Innocent and unsuspecting tourists, lunch, laughter, boiled coffee, and cold ham. Ambush. The whole business-followed by highwaymen in flannel shirts and revolvers. Dead tourist or two, desperate resistance-everything."

Aggie rose, pale as an aspen. "You-you are joking!" she cried.

"Do I look like it?" he demanded fiercely. "I tell you there is going to be the whole thing. At the end the lovely girl will escape on horseback and ride madly for aid. She will meet the sheriff and a posse, who are out for a picnic or some such damfool nonsense, and —"

"Young man," Tish said coldly, "if you know all this, why are you sitting here and not alarming the authorities?"

"Pooh!" he said disagreeably. "It's a put-up scheme, to advertise the park. Yellowstone's got ahead of them this year, and has had its excitement, with all the papers ringing with it. That was a gag, too, probably."

"Do you mean —"

"I mean considerable," he said. "That red-headed movie idiot will be on a rise, taking the tourists as they ride through. Of course he doesn't expect the holdup-not in the papers anyhow. He happens to have the camera trained on the party, and gets it all. Result —a whacking good picture, revolvers firing blank cartridges, everything which people will crowd to see. Oh, it's good business all right. I don't mind admitting that."

Tish's face expressed the greatest rage. She rose, drawing herself to her full height.

"And the tourists?" she demanded. "They lend themselves to this imposition? To this infamy? To this turpitude?"

"Certainly not. They think it's the real thing. The whole business hangs on that. And as the sheriff, or whoever it is in the fool plot, captures the bandits, the party gets its money back, and has material for conversation for the next twenty years."

"To think," said Tish, "of our great National Government lending itself to such a scheme!"

"Wrong," said the young man. "It's a combination of Western railroads and a movie concern acting together."

"I trust," Tish observed, setting her lips firmly, "that the tourists will protest."

"The more noise, the better." The young man, though not more cheerful as to appearance, was certainly more talkative. "Trust a clergyman for yelling when his pocket's picked."

With one voice the three of us exclaimed: "Mr. Ostermaier!"

He was not sure of the name, but "Helen" had pointed the clergyman out to him, and it was Mr. Ostermaier without a doubt.

We talked it over with Bill when we got back, and he was not as surprised as we'd expected.

"Knew they were cooking up something. They've got some Indians in it too. Saw them rehearsing old Thunder Mountain the other day in nothing but a breech-clout."

Tish reproved him for a lack of delicacy of speech, and shortly afterward we went to bed. Owing to the root under the tent, and puddles here and there, we could not go to sleep for a time, and we discussed the "nefarious deed," as Tish aptly termed it, that was about to take place.

"Although," Tish observed, "Mr. Ostermaier has been receiving for so many years that it might be a good thing, for his soul's sake, to have him give up something, even if to bandits." I dozed off after a time, but awakened to find Tish sitting up, wide awake.

"I've been thinking that thing over, Lizzie," she said in a low tone. "I believe it's our duty to interfere."

"Of course," I replied sarcastically; "and be shown all over the country in the movies making fools of ourselves."

"Did you notice that that young man said they would be firing blank cartridges?"

Well, even a blank cartridge can be a dangerous thing. Then and there I reminded her of my niece's boy, who was struck on the Fourth of July by a wad from one, and had to be watched for lockjaw for several weeks.

It was at that moment that we heard Bill, who had no tent, by choice, and lay under a tree, give a loud whoop, followed by what was unmistakably an oath.

"Bear!" he yelled. "Watch out, he's headed for the tent! It's a grizzly."

Tish felt round wildly for her revolver, but it was gone! And the bear was close by. We could hear it snuffing about, and to add to the confusion Aggie wakened and commenced to sneeze with terror.

"Bill!" Tish called. "I've lost my revolver!"

"I took it, Miss Carberry. But I've been lying in a puddle, and it won't go off."

All hope seemed gone. The frail walls of our tent were no protection whatever, and as we all knew, even a tree was no refuge from a bear, which, as we had seen in the Zoological Garden at home, can climb like a cat, only swifter. Besides, none of us could climb a tree.

It was at that moment that Tish had one of those inspirations that make her so dependable in emergencies. Feeling round in the tent for a possible weapon, she touched a large ham, from which we had broiled a few slices at supper. In her shadowy form there was both purpose and high courage. With a single sweeping gesture she flung the ham at the bear so accurately that we heard the thud with which it struck.

"What the hell are you doing?" Bill called from a safe distance. Even then we realized that his restraint of speech was a pose, pure and simple. "If you make him angry he'll tear up the whole place."

But Tish did not deign to answer. The rain had ceased, and suddenly the moon came out and illuminated the whole scene. We saw the bear sniffing at the ham, which lay on the ground. Then he picked it up in his jaws and stood looking about.

Tish said later that the moment his teeth were buried in the ham she felt safe. I can still see the majestic movement with which she walked out of the tent and waved her arms.

"Now, scat with you!" she said firmly. "Scat!"

He "scatted." Snarling through his nose, for fear of dropping the ham, he turned and fled up the mountainside. In the open space Tish stood the conqueror. She yawned and glanced about.

"Going to be a nice night, after all," she said. "Now, Bill, bring me that revolver, and if I catch you meddling with it again I'll put that pair of fur rugs you are so proud of in the fire."

Bill, who was ignorant of the ham, emerged sheepishly into the open. "Where the-where the dickens did you hit him, Miss Tish?" he asked.

"In the stomach," Tish replied tartly, and taking her revolver went back to the tent.

All the next day Tish was quiet. She rode ahead, hardly noticing the scenery, with her head dropped on her chest. At luncheon she took a sardine sandwich and withdrew to a tree, underneath which she sat, a lonely and brooding figure.

When luncheon was over and Aggie and I were washing the dishes and hanging out the dish towels to dry on a bush, Tish approached Bill, who was pouring water on the fire to extinguish it.

"Bill," she stated, "you came to us under false pretenses. You swear, for one thing."

"Only under excitement, Miss Tish," he said. "And as far as that goes, Miss Aggie herself said —"

"Also," Tish went on hastily, "you said you could cook. You cannot cook."

"Now, look here, Miss Tish," he said in a pleading tone, "I can cook. I didn't claim to know the whole cookbook. I can make coffee and fry bacon. How'd I know you ladies wanted pastry? As for them canned salmon croquettes with white sauce, I reckon to make them with a little showing, and —"

"Also," said Tish, cutting in sternly, "you took away my revolver, and left us helpless last night, and in peril of wild beasts."

"Tourists ain't allowed to carry guns."

He attempted to look injured, but Tish ignored him.

"Therefore," she said, "if I am not to send you back-which I have been considering all day, as I've put up a tent myself before this, and you are only an extra mouth to feed, which, as we are one ham short, is inconvenient-you will have to justify my keeping you."

"If you will just show me once about them gems, Miss Tish —" he began.

But Tish cut him off. "No," she said firmly, "you are too casual about cooking. And you are no dish-washer. Setting a plate in a river and letting the current wash it may satisfy cow-punchers. It doesn't go with me. The point is this: You know all about the holdup that is going to take place. Don't lie. I know you know. Now, you take us there and tell us all you know about it."

He scratched his head reflectively. "I'll tell you," he said. "I'm a slow thinker. Give me about twenty minutes on it, will you? It's a sort of secret, and there's different ways of looking at it."

Tish took out her watch. "Twenty minutes," she said. "Start thinking now."

He wandered off and rolled a cigarette. Later on, as I have said, he showed Tish how to do it-not, of course, that she meant to smoke, but Tish is fond of learning how to do things. She got so she could roll them with one hand, and she does it now in the winter evenings, instead of rolling paper spills as formerly. When Charlie Sands comes, she always has a supply ready for him, although occasionally somewhat dry from waiting for a few weeks.

At the end of twenty minutes Tish snapped her watch shut.

"Time!" she called, and Bill came back.

"Well, I'll do it," he said. "I don't know as they'll put you in the picture, but I'll see what I can do."

"Picture nothing!" Tish snapped. "You take us there and hide us. That's the point. There must be caves round to put us in, although I don't insist on a cave. They're damp usually."

Well, he looked puzzled, but he agreed. I caught Aggie's eye, and we exchanged glances. There was trouble coming, and we knew it. Our long experience with Tish had taught us not to ask questions. "Ours but to do and die," as Aggie later said. But I confess to a feeling of uneasiness during the remainder of that day.

We changed our course that afternoon, turning off at Saint Mary's and spending the night near the Swiss Chalet at Going-to-the-Sun. Aggie and I pleaded to spend the night in the chalet, but Tish was adamant.

"When I am out camping, I camp," she said. "I can have a bed at home, but I cannot sleep under the stars, on a bed of pine needles, and be lured to rest by the murmur of a mountain stream."

Well, we gave it up and went with her. I must say that the trip had improved us already. Except when terrified or kicked by a horse, Aggie was not sneezing at all, and I could now climb into the saddle unassisted. My waistbands were much looser, too, and during a short rest that afternoon I put a dart in my riding-breeches, during the absence of Bill after the pack-horse, which had strayed.

It was on that occasion that Tish told us as much of her plan as she thought it wise for us to know.

"The holdup," she explained, "is to be the day after to-morrow on the Piegan Pass. Bill says there is a level spot at the top with rocks all about. That is the spot. The Ostermaiers and their party leave the automobiles at Many Glaciers and take horses to the pass. It will be worth coming clear to Montana to see Mrs. Ostermaier on a horse."

"I still don't see," Aggie observed in a quavering voice, "what we have to do with it."

"Naturally not," said Tish. "You'll know as soon as is good for you."

"I don't believe it will ever be good for me," said poor Aggie. "It isn't good for anybody to be near a holdup. And I don't want to be in a moving picture with no teeth. I'm not a vain woman," she said, "but I draw the line at that."

But Tish ignored her. "The only trouble," she said, "is having one revolver. If we each had one-Lizzie, did you bring any ink?"

Well, I had, and said so, but that I needed it for postcards when we struck a settlement.

Tish waved my objection aside. "I guess it can be managed," she observed. "Bill has a knife. Yes, I think it can be done."

She and Bill engaged in an earnest conference that afternoon. At first Bill objected. I could see him shaking his head. Then Tish gave him something which Aggie said was money. I do not know. She had been short of cash on the train, but she may have had more in her trunk. Then I saw Bill start to laugh. He laughed until he had to lean against a tree, although Tish was quite stern and serious.

We reached Piegan Pass about three that afternoon, and having inspected it and the Garden Wall, which is a mile or two high at that point, we returned to a "bench" where there were some trees, and dismounted.

Here, to our surprise, we found Mr. Bell again. As Tish remarked, he was better at walking than at talking. He looked surprised at seeing us, and was much more agreeable than before.

"I'm afraid I was pretty surly the other night," he said. "The truth is, I was so blooming unhappy that I didn't give a damn for anything."

But when he saw that Bill was preparing to take the pack off the horse he looked startled.

"I say," he said, "you don't mean to camp here, do you?"

"Such is my intention," Tish observed grimly.

"But look here. Just beyond, at the pass, is where the holdup is to take place to-morrow."

"So I believe," said Tish. "What has that to do with us? What are you going to do?"

"Oh, I'm going to hang round."

"Well, we intend to hang round also."

He stood by and watched our preparations for camp. Tish chose a small grove for the tent, and then left us, clambering up the mountain-side. She finally disappeared. Aggie mixed some muffins for tea, and we invited the young man to join us. But he was looking downhearted again and refused.

However, when she took them out of the portable oven, nicely browned, and lifting the tops of each one dropped in a teaspoonful of grape jelly, he changed his mind.

"I'll stay, if you don't mind," he said. "Maybe some decent food will make me see things clearer."

When Tish descended at six o'clock, she looked depressed. "There is no cave," she said, "although I have gone where a mountain goat would get dizzy. But I have found a good place to hide the horses, where we can get them quickly when we need them."

Aggie was scooping the inside out of her muffin, being unable to eat the crust, but she went quite pale.

"Tish," she said, "you have some desperate plan in view, and I am not equal to it. I am worn with travel and soft food, and am not as young as I once was."

"Desperate nothing!" said Tish, pouring condensed milk into her tea. "I am going to teach a lot of idiots a lesson, that's all. There should be one spot in America free from the advertising man and his schemes, and this is going to be it. Commercialism," she went on, growing oratorical, "does not belong here among these mighty mountains. Once let it start, and these towering cliffs will be defaced with toothpowder and intoxicating-liquor signs."

The young man knew the plans for the holdup even letter than Bill. He was able to show us the exact spot which had been selected, and to tell us the hour at which the Ostermaier party was to cross the pass.

"They'll lunch on the pass," he said, "and, of course, they suspect nothing. The young lady of whom I spoke to you will be one of their party. She, however, knows what is coming, and is, indeed, a party to it. The holdup will take place during luncheon."

Here his voice broke, and he ate an entire muffin before he went on: "The holdup will take place on the pass, the bandits having been hidden on this 'bench' right here. Then the outlaws, having robbed the tourists, will steal the young lady and escape down the trail on the other side. The guide, who is in the plot, will ride ahead in this direction and raise the alarm. You understand," he added, "that as it's a put-up job, the tourists will get all their stuff back. I don't know how that's to be arranged."

"But the girl?" Tish asked.

"She's to make her escape later," Mr. Bell said grimly, "and will be photographed galloping down the trail, by another idiot with a camera, who, of course, just happens to be on the spot. She'll do it too," he added with a pathetic note of pride in his voice. "She's got nerve enough for anything."

He drew a long breath, and Aggie poured him a third cup of tea.

"I dare say this will finish everything," he said dejectedly. "I can't offer her any excitement like this. We live in a quiet suburb, where nobody ever fires a revolver except on the Fourth of July."

"What she needs," Tish said, bending forward, "is a lesson, Mr. Bell-something to make her hate the very thought of a moving picture and shudder at the sound of a shot."

"Exactly," said Mr. Bell. "I've thought of that. Something to make her gun-shy and camera-shy. It's curious about her. In some ways she's a timid girl. She's afraid of thunder, for one thing."

Tish bent forward. "Do you know," she said, "the greatest weapon in the world?"

"Weapon? Well, I don't know. These new German guns —"

"The greatest weapon in the world," Tish explained, "is ridicule. Man is helpless against it. To be absurd is to be lost. When the bandits take the money, where do they go?"

"Down the other side from the pass. A photographer will photograph them there, making their escape with the loot."

"And the young lady?"

"I've told you that," he said bitterly. "She is to be captured by the attacking party."

"They will all be armed?"

"Sure, with blanks. The Indians have guns and arrows, but the arrows have rubber tips."

Tish rose majestically. "Mr. Bell," she said, "you may sleep to-night the sleep of peace. When I undertake a thing, I carry it through. My friends will agree with me. I never fail, when my heart is set on it. By the day after to-morrow the young lady in the case will hate the sight of a camera."

Although not disclosing her plan, she invited the young man to join us. But his face fell and he shook his head.

Tish said that she did not expect to need him, but that, if the time came, she would blow three times on a police whistle, which she had, with her usual foresight, brought along. He agreed to that, although looking rather surprised, and we parted from him.

"I would advise," Tish said as he moved away, "that you conceal yourself in the valley below the pass on the other side."

He agreed to this, and we separated for the night. But long after Aggie and I had composed ourselves to rest Tish sat on a stone by the camp-fire and rolled cigarettes.

At last she came into the tent and wakened us by prodding us with her foot.

"Get all the sleep you can," she said. "We'll leave here at dawn to-morrow, and there'll be little rest for any of us to-morrow night."

At daylight next morning she roused us. She was dressed, except that she wore her combing-jacket, and her hair was loose round her face.

"Aggie, you make an omelet in a hurry, and, Lizzie, you will have to get the horses."

"I'll do nothing of the sort," I said, sitting up on the ground. "We've got a man here for that. Besides, I have to set the table."

"Very well," Tish replied, "we can stay here, I dare say. Bill's busy at something I've set him to doing."

"Whose fault is it," I demanded, "that we are here in 'Greenland's Icy Mountains'? Not mine. Id never heard of the dratted place. And those horses are five miles away by now, most likely."

"Go and get a cup of tea. You'll have a little sense then," said Tish, not unkindly. "And as for what Bill's doing, he's making revolvers. Where's your writing ink?"

I had none! I realized it that moment. I had got it out at the first camp to record in my diary the place, weather, temperature, and my own pulse rate, which I had been advised to watch, on account of the effect of altitude on the heart, and had left the bottle sitting on a stone.

When I confessed this to Tish, she was unjustly angry and a trifle bitter.

"It's what I deserve, most likely, for bringing along two incompetents," was her brief remark. "Without ink we are weaponless."

But she is a creature of resource, and a moment later she emerged from the tent and called to Bill in a cheerful tone.

"No ink, Bill," she said, "but we've got blackberry cordial, and by mixing it with a little soot we may be able to manage."

Aggie demurred loudly, as there are occasions when only a mouthful of the cordial enables her to keep doing. But Tish was firm. When I went to the fire, I found Bill busily carving wooden revolvers, copying Tish's, which lay before him. He had them done well enough, and could have gone for the horses as easy as not, but he insisted on trimming them up. Mine, which I still have, has a buffalo head carved on the handle, and Aggie's has a wreath of leaves running round the barrel.

In spite of Aggie's wails Tish poured a large part of the blackberry cordial into a biscuit pan, and put in a chip of wood.

"It makes it red," she said doubtfully. "I never saw a red revolver, Bill."

"Seems like an awful waste," Bill said. But having now completed the wreath he placed all three weapons-he had made one for himself-in the pan. The last thing I saw, as I started for the horses, was the three of them standing about, looking down, and Aggie's face was full of misery.

I was gone for a half-hour. The horses had not wandered far, and having mounted mine, although without a saddle, I copied as well as I could the whoop Bill used to drive them in, and rounded them up. When I returned, driving them before me, the pack was ready, and on Tish's face was a look of intense satisfaction. I soon perceived the reason.

Lying on a stone by the fire were three of the shiniest black revolvers any one could want. I eyed Tish and she explained.

"Stove polish," she said. "Like a fool I'd forgot it. Gives a true metallic luster, as it says on the box."

Tish is very particular about a stove, and even on our camping-trips we keep the portable stove shining and clean.

"Does it come off?"

"Well, more or less," she admitted. "We can keep the box out and renew when necessary. It is a great comfort," she added, "to feel that we are all armed. We shall need weapons."

"In an emergency," I observed rather tartly, "I hope you will not depend on us too much. While I don't know what you intend to do, if it is anything desperate, just remember that the only way Aggie or I can do any damage with these things is to thrust them down somebody's throat and strangle him to death."

She ignored my remark, however, and soon we were on our horses and moving along the trail toward the pass.

II

It will be unnecessary to remind those familiar with Glacier Park of the trail which hugs the mountain above timber-line, and extends toward the pass for a mile or so, in a long semicircle which curves inward.

At the end it turns to the right and mounts to an acre or so of level ground, with snow and rocks but no vegetation. This is the Piegan Pass. Behind it is the Garden Wall, that stupendous mass of granite rising to incredible heights. On the other side the trail drops abruptly, by means of stepladders which I have explained.

Tish now told us of her plan.

"The unfortunate part is," she said, "that the Ostermaiers will not see us. I tried to arrange it so they could, but it was impossible. We must content ourselves with the knowledge of a good deed done."

Her plan, in brief, was this: The sham attacking party was to turn and ride away down the far side of the pass, up which the Ostermaiers had come. They were, according to the young man, to take the girl with them, with the idea of holding her for ransom. She was to escape, however, while they were lunching in some secluded fastness, and, riding back to the pass, was to meet there a rescue party, which the Ostermaiers were to meet on the way down to Gunsight Chalet.

Tish's idea was this: We would ride up while they were lunching, pretend to think them real bandits, paying no attention to them if they fired at us, as we knew they had only blank cartridges, and, having taken them prisoners, make them walk in ignominy to the nearest camp, some miles farther.

"Then," said Tish, "either they will confess the ruse, and the country will ring with laughter, or they will have to submit to arrest and much unpleasantness. It will be a severe lesson."

We reached the pass safely, and on the way down the other side we passed Mr. Oliver, the moving-picture man, with his outfit on a horse. He touched his hat politely and moved out on a ledge to let us by.

"Mind if I take you as you go down the mountain?" he called. "It's a bully place for a picture." He stared at Aggie, who was muffled in a cape and had the dish towel round her head. "I'd particularly like to get your Arab," he said. "The Far East and the Far West, you know."

Aggie gave him a furious glance. "Arab nothing!" she snapped. "If you can't tell a Christian lady from a heathen, on account of her having lost her hat, then you belong in the dirty work you're doing."

"Aggie, be quiet!" Tish said in an awful voice.

But wrath had made Aggie reckless. "'Dirty work' was what I said," she repeated, staring at the young man.

"I beg your pardon. I'm sure I —"

"Don't think," Aggie went on, to Tish's fury, "that we don't know a few things. We do."

"I see," he said slowly. "All right. Although I'd like to know —"

"Good-morning," said Aggie, and kicked her horse to go on.

I shall never forget Tish's face. Round the next bend she got off her horse and confronted Aggie.

"The older I get, Aggie Pilkington," she said, "the more I realize that to take you anywhere means ruin. We are done now. All our labor is for nothing. There will be no holdup, no nothing. They are scared off."

But Aggie was still angry. "Just let some one take you for a lousy Bedouin, Tish," she said, "and see what you would do. I'm not sorry anyhow. I never did like the idea."

But Tish dislikes relinquishing an idea, once it has taken hold. And, although she did not speak to Aggie again for the next hour, she went ahead with her preparations.

"There's still a chance, Lizzie," she said. "It's not likely they'll give up easy, on account of hiring the Indians and everything."

About a mile and a half down the trail, she picked out a place to hide. This time there was a cave. We cleared our saddles for action, as Tish proposed to let them escape past us with the girl, and then to follow them rapidly, stealing upon them if possible while they were at luncheon, and covering them with the one real revolver and the three wooden ones.

The only thing that bothered us was Bill's attitude. He kept laughing to himself and muttering, and when he was storing things in the cave, Tish took me aside.

"I don't like his attitude, Lizzie," she said. "He's likely to giggle or do something silly, just at the crucial moment. I cannot understand why he thinks it is funny, but he does. We'd be much better without him."

"You'd better talk to him, Tish," I said. "You can't get rid of him now."

But to tell Tish she cannot do a thing is to determine her to do it.

It was still early, only half-past eight, when she came to me with an eager face.

"I've got it, Lizzie," she said. "I'll send off Mona Lisa, and he will have to search for her. The only thing is, she won't move unless she's driven. If we could only find a hornet's nest again, we could manage. It may be cruel, but I understand that a hornet's sting is not as painful to a horse as to a human being."

Mona Lisa, I must explain, was the pack-horse. Tish had changed her name from Jane to Mona Lisa because in the mornings she was constantly missing, and having to be looked for.

Tish disappeared for a time, and we settled down to our long wait. Bill put another coat of stove polish on the weapons, and broke now and then into silent laughter. On my giving him a haughty glance, however, he became sober and rubbed with redoubled vigor.

In a half-hour, however, I saw Tish beckoning to me from a distance, and I went to her. I soon saw that she was holding her handkerchief to one cheek, but when I mentioned the fact she ignored me.

"I have found a nest, Lizzie," she cried. "Slip over and unfasten Mona Lisa. She's not near the other horses, which is fortunate."

I then perceived that Tish's yellow slicker was behind her on the ground and tied into a bundle, from which emerged a dull roaring. I was wondering how Tish expected to open it, when she settled the question by asking me to cut a piece from the mosquito netting which we put in the doorway of the tent at night, and to bring her riding-gloves.

Aggie was darning a hole in the tablecloth when I went back and Bill was still engaged with the weapons. Having taken what she required to Tish, under pretense of giving Mona Lisa a lump of sugar, I untied her. What followed was exactly as Tish had planned. Mona Lisa, not realizing her freedom, stood still while Tish untied the slicker and freed its furious inmates. She then dropped the whole thing under the unfortunate animal, and retreated, not too rapidly, for fear of drawing Bill's attention. For possibly sixty seconds nothing happened, except that Mona Lisa raised her head and appeared to listen. Then, with a loud scream, she threw up her head and bolted. By the time Bill had put down the stove brush she was out of sight among the trees, but we could hear her leaping and scrambling through the wood.

"Jumping cats!" said Bill, and ran for his horse. "Acts as though she'd started for the Coast!" he yelled to me, and flung after her.

When he had disappeared, Tish came out of the woods, and, getting a kettle of boiling water, poured it over the nest. In spite of the netting, however, she was stung again, on the back of the neck, and spent the rest of the morning holding wet mud to the affected parts.

Her brain, however, was as active as ever, and by half-past eleven, mounting a boulder, she announced that she could see the Ostermaier party far down the trail, and that in an hour they would probably be at the top. She had her field-glasses, and she said that Mrs. Ostermaier was pointing up to the pass and shaking her head, and that the others were arguing with her.

"It would be just like the woman," Tish said bitterly, "to refuse to come any farther and spoil everything."

But a little later she announced that the guide was leading Mrs. Ostermaier's horse and that they were coming on.

We immediately retreated to the cave and waited, it being Tish's intention to allow them to reach the pass without suspecting our presence, and only to cut off the pseudo-bandits in their retreat, as I have explained.

It was well that we had concealed the horses also, for the party stopped near the cave, and Mrs. Ostermaier was weeping. "Not a step farther!" she said. "I have a family to consider, and Mr. Ostermaier is a man of wide usefulness and cannot be spared."

We did not dare to look out, but we heard the young lady speaking, and as Aggie remarked later, no one would have thought, from the sweetness of her voice, that she was a creature of duplicity.

"But it is perfectly safe, dear Mrs. Ostermaier," she said "And think, when you go home, of being able to say that you have climbed a mountain pass."

"Pass!" sniffed Mrs. Ostermaier. "Pass nothing! I don't call a wall a mile high a pass."

"Think," said the girl, "of being able to crow over those three old women who are always boasting of the things they do. Probably you are right, and they never do them at all, but you-there's a moving-picture man waiting, remember, and you can show the picture before the Dorcas Society. No one can ever doubt that you have done a courageous thing. You'll have the proof."

"George," said Mrs. Ostermaier in a small voice, "if anything happens, I have told you how I want my things divided."

"Little devil!" whispered Aggie, referring to the girl. "If that young man knows when he is well off, he'll let her go."

But beyond rebuking her for the epithet, Tish made no comment, and the party moved on. We lost them for a time among the trees, but when they moved out above timber-line we were able to watch them, and we saw that Mrs. Ostermaier got off her horse, about halfway up, and climbed slowly on foot. Tish, who had the glasses, said that she looked purple and angry, and that she distinctly saw the guide give her something to drink out of a bottle. It might, however, have been vichy or some similar innocent beverage, and I believe in giving her the benefit of the doubt.

When at last they vanished over the edge of the pass, we led out our horses and prepared for what was to come. Bill had not returned, and, indeed, we did not see him until the evening of the second day after that, when, worn but triumphant, we emerged from the trail at the Many Glaciers Hotel. That, however, comes later in this narrative.

With everything prepared, Tish judged it best to have luncheon. I made a few mayonnaise-and-lettuce sandwiches, beating the mayonnaise in the cool recesses of the cave, and we drank some iced tea, to which Aggie had thoughtfully added sliced lemon and a quantity of ginger ale. Feeling much refreshed, we grasped our weapons and waited.

At half-past twelve we heard a loud shriek on the pass, far overhead, followed almost immediately by a fusillade of shots. Then a silence, followed by more shots. Then a solitary horseman rode over the edge of the pass and, spurring his horse, rode recklessly down the precipitous trail. Aggie exclaimed that it was Mr. Ostermaier, basely deserting his wife in her apparent hour of need. But Tish, who had the glasses, reported finally that it was the moving-picture man.

We were greatly surprised, as it had not occurred to us that this would be a part of the program.

As he descended, Tish announced that there must be another photographer on top, as he was "registering" signs of terror—a moving-picture expression which she had acquired from Charlie Sands-and looking back frequently over his shoulder.

We waited until he reached timber-line, and then withdrew to a group of trees. It was not our intention to allow him to see us and spoil everything. But when he came near, through the woods, and his horse continued at unabated speed, Tish decided that the animal, frightened by the shots, was running away.

She therefore placed herself across the trail to check its headlong speed, but the animal merely rushed round her. Mr. Oliver yelled something at us, which we were, however, unable to hear, and kept madly on.

Almost immediately four men, firing back over their shoulders, rode into sight at the pass and came swiftly down toward us.

"Where's the girl?" Tish cried with her glasses to her eyes. "The idiots have got excited and have forgotten to steal her."

That was plainly what had happened, but she was determined to be stolen anyhow, for the next moment she rode into view, furiously following the bandits.

"She's kept her head anyhow," Tish observed with satisfaction. "Trust a lot of men to go crazy and do the wrong thing. But they'll have to change the story and make her follow them."

At timber-line the men seemed to realize that she was behind them, and they turned and looked up. They seemed to be at a loss to know what to do, in view of the picture. But they were quick thinkers, too, we decided. Right then and there they took her prisoner, surrounding her.

She made a desperate resistance, even crying out, as we could plainly see. But Tish was irritated. She said she could not see how the story would hold now. Either the girl should have captured them, they being out of ammunition, or the whole thing should have been done again, according to the original plan. However, as she said, it was not our affair. Our business was to teach them a lesson not to impose on unsuspecting tourists, for although not fond of Mrs. Ostermaier, we had been members of Mr. Ostermaier's church, and liked him, although his sermons were shorter than Tish entirely approved of.

We withdrew again to seclusion until they had passed, and Tish gave them ten minutes to get well ahead. Then we rode out.

Tish's face was stern as she led off. The shriek of Mrs. Ostermaier was still, as she said in a low tone, ringing in her ears. But before we had gone very far, Tish stopped and got off her horse. "We've got to pad the horses' feet," she said. "How can we creep up on them when on every stony place we sound like an artillery engagement?"

Here was a difficulty we had not anticipated. But Tish overcame it with her customary resource, by taking the blanket from under her saddle and cutting it into pieces with her scissors, which always accompany her. We then cut the leather straps from our saddles at her direction, and each of us went to work. Aggie, however, protested.

"I never expected," she said querulously, "to be sitting on the Rocky Mountains under a horse, tying a piece of bed quilt on his feet. I wouldn't mind," she added, "if the creature liked me. But the way he feels toward me he's likely to haul off and murder me at any moment."

However, it was done at last, and it made a great change. We moved along silently, and all went well except that, having neglected to draw the cinch tight, and the horse's back being slippery without the padding, my saddle turned unexpectedly, throwing me off into the trail. I bruised my arm badly, but Tish only gave me a glance of scorn and went on.

Being above carelessness herself, she very justly resents it in others.

We had expected, with reason, that the so-called highwaymen, having retreated to a certain distance, would there pause and very possibly lunch before returning. It was, therefore, a matter of surprise to find that they had kept on.

Moreover, they seemed to have advanced rapidly, and Tish, who had read a book on signs of the trail, examined the hoofprints of their horses in a soft place beside a stream, and reported that they had been going at a lope.

"Now, remember," she said as she prepared to mount again, "to all intents and purposes these are real bandits and to be treated accordingly. Our motto is 'No quarter.' I shall be harsh, and I expect no protest from either of you. They deserve everything they get."

But when, after another mile or two, we came to a side trail, leading, by Tish's map, not to Many Glaciers, but up a ravine to another pass, and Tish saw that they had taken that direction, we were puzzled.

But not for long.

"I understand now," she said. "It is all clear. The photographer was riding ahead to get them up this valley somewhere. They've probably got a rendezvous all ready, with another camera in place. I must say," she observed, "that they are doing it thoroughly."

We rode for two hours, and no sign of them. The stove polish had come off the handles of our revolvers by that time, and Aggie, having rubbed her face ever and anon to remove perspiration, presented under her turban a villainous and ferocious expression quite at variance with her customary mildness.

I urged her to stop and wash, but Tish, after a glance, said to keep on.

"Your looking like that's a distinct advantage, Aggie," she said. "Like as not they'll throw up their hands the minute they see you. I know I should. You'd better ride first when we get near."

"Like as not they'll put a hole in me," Aggie objected. "And as to riding first, I will not. This is your doing, Tish Carberry, and as for their having blank cartridges-how do we know someone hasn't made a mistake and got a real one?"

Tish reflected on that. "It's a possibility," she agreed. "If we find that they're going to spend the night out, it might be better to wait until they've taken off all the hardware they're hung with."

But we did not come up with them. We kept on finding traces of the party in marshy spots, and once Tish hopped off her horse and picked up a small handkerchief with a colored border and held it up to us.

"It's hers," she said. "Anybody would know she is the sort to use colored borders. They're ahead somewhere."

But it seemed strange that they would go so far, and I said so.

"We're far enough off the main trail, Tish," I said. "And it's getting wilder every minute. There's nothing I can see to prevent a mountain lion dropping on us most any time."

"Not if it gets a good look at Aggie!" was Tish's grim response.

It began to grow dark in the valley, and things seemed to move on either side of the trail. Aggie called out once that we had just passed a grizzly bear, but Tish never faltered. The region grew more and more wild. The trail was broken with mudholes and crossed by fallen logs. With a superb disdain Tish rode across all obstacles, not even glancing at them. But Aggie and I got off at the worst places and led our horses. At one mudhole I was unfortunate enough to stumble. A horse with a particle of affection for a woman who had ridden it and cared for it for several days would have paused.

Not so my animal. With a heartlessness at which I still shudder the creature used me as a bridge, and stepped across, dryfoot, on my back. Owing to his padded feet and to the depth of the mud-some eight feet, I believe —I was uninjured. But it required ten minutes of hard labor on the part of both Tish and Aggie to release me from the mud, from which I was finally raised with a low, hissing sound.

"Park!" said Aggie as she scraped my obliterated features with a small branch. "Park, indeed! It's a howling wilderness. I'm fond of my native land," she went on, digging out my nostrils, so I could breathe, "but I don't calculate to eat it. As for that unfeeling beast of yours, Lizzie, I've never known a horse to show such selfishness. Never."

Well, we went on at last, but I was not so enthusiastic about teaching people lessons as I had been. It seemed to me that we might have kept on along the trail and had a mighty good time, getting more and more nimble and stopping now and then to bake a pie and have a decent meal, and putting up our hair in crimps at night, without worrying about other folks' affairs.

Late in the afternoon of that day, when so far as I could see Tish was lost, and not even her gathering a bunch of wild flowers while the horses rested could fool me, I voiced my complaint.

"Let me look at the map, Tish," I suggested. "I'm pretty good at maps. You know how I am at charades and acrostics. At the church supper —"

"Nonsense, Lizzie," she returned. "You couldn't make head or tail of this map. It's my belief that the man who made it had never been here. Either that or there has been an earthquake since. But," she went on, more cheerfully, "if we are lost, so are the others."

"If we even had Bill along!"

"Bill!" Tish said scornfully. "It's my belief Bill is in the whole business, and that if we hadn't got rid of him we'd have been the next advertising dodge. As far as that goes," she said thoughtfully, "it wouldn't surprise me a particle to find that we've been taken, without our knowing it, most any time. Your horse just now, walking across that bridge of size, for one thing."

Tish seldom makes a pun, which she herself has said is the lowest form of humor. The dig at my figure was unkind, also, and unworthy of her. I turned and left her.

At last, well on in the evening, I saw Tish draw up her horse and point ahead.

"The miscreants!" she said.

True enough, up a narrow side cañon we could see a camp-fire. It was a small one, and only noticeable from one point. But Tish's keen eye had seen it. She sat on her horse and gazed toward it.

"What a shameful thing it is," she said, "to prostitute the beauties of this magnificent region to such a purpose. To make of these beetling crags a joke! To invade these vast gorges with the spirit of commercialism and to bring a pack of movie actors to desecrate the virgin silence with ribald jests and laughter! Lizzie, I wish you wouldn't wheeze!"

"You would wheeze, too, Tish Carberry," I retorted, justly indignant, "if a horse had just pressed your spinal column into your breast bone. Goodness knows," I said, "where my lungs are. I've missed them ever since my fall."

However, she was engrossed with larger matters, and ignored my petulance. She is a large-natured woman and above pettiness.

We made our way slowly up the cañon. The movie outfit was securely camped under an overhanging rock, as we could now see. At one point their position commanded the trail, which was hardly more than a track through the wilderness, and before we reached this point we dismounted and Tish surveyed the camp through her glasses.

"We'd better wait until dark," Tish said. "Owing to the padding they have not heard us, but it looks to me as if one of them is on a rock, watching."

It seemed rather strange to me that they were keeping a lookout, but Tish only shrugged her shoulders.

"If I know anything of that red-headed Oliver man," she said, "he hates to let a camera rest. Like as not he's got it set up among the trees somewhere, taking flashlights of wild animals. It's rather a pity," she said, turning and surveying Aggie and myself, "that he cannot get you two. If you happen to see anything edible lying on the ground, you'd better not pick it up. It's probably attached to the string that sets off the flash."

We led our horses into the woods, which were very thick at that point, and tied them. My beast, however, lay down and rolled, saddle and all, thus breaking my mirror —a most unlucky omen-and the bottle of olive oil which we had brought along for mayonnaise dressing. Tish is fond of mayonnaise, and, besides, considers olive oil most strengthening. However, it was gone, and although Aggie comforted me by suggesting that her boiled salad dressing is quite tasty, I was disconsolate.

It was by that time seven o'clock and almost dark. We held a conference. Tish was of the opinion that we should first lead off their horses, if possible.

"I intend," she said severely, "to make escape impossible. If they fire, when taken by surprise, remember that they have only blank cartridges. I must say," she added with a confession of unusual weakness, "that I am glad the Indians escaped the other way. I would hardly know what to do with Indians, even quite tame ones. While I know a few letters of the deaf-and-dumb language, which I believe all tribes use in common, I fear that in a moment of excitement I would forget what I know."

The next step, she asserted, was to secure their weapons.

"After all," she said, "the darkness is in our favor. I intend to fire once, to show them that we are armed and dangerous. And if you two will point the guns Bill made, they cannot possibly tell that they are not real."

"But we will know it," Aggie quavered. Now that the quarry was in sight she was more and more nervous, sneezing at short intervals in spite of her menthol inhaler. "I am sorry, Tish, but I cannot feel the same about that wooden revolver as I would about a real one. And even when I try to forget that it is only wood the carving reminds me."

But Tish silenced her with a glance. She had strangely altered in the last few minutes. All traces of fatigue had gone, and when she struck a match and consulted her watch I saw in her face that high resolve, that stern and matchless courage, which I so often have tried to emulate and failed.

"Seven o'clock," she announced. "We will dine first. There is nothing like food to restore failing spirits."

But we had nothing except our sandwiches, and Tish suggested snaring some of the stupid squirrels with which the region abounded.

"Aggie needs broth," she said decidedly. "We have sandwiches, but Aggie is frail and must be looked to."

Aggie was pathetically grateful, although sorry for the squirrels, which were pretty and quite tame. But Tish was firm in her kindly intent, and proceeded at once to set a rabbit snare, a trick she had learned in the Maine woods. Having done this, and built a small fire, well hidden, we sat down to wait.

In a short time we heard terrible human cries proceeding from the snare, and, hurrying thither, found in it a young mountain lion. It looked dangerous, and was biting in every direction. I admit that I was prepared to leave in haste, but not so Tish. She fetched her umbrella, without which she never travels, and while the animal set its jaws in it —a painful necessity, as it was her best umbrella-Tish hit it on the head-not the umbrella, but the lion-with a large stone.

Tish's satisfaction was unbounded. She stated that the flesh of the mountain lion was much like veal, and so indeed it proved. We made a nourishing soup of it, with potatoes and a can of macédoine vegetables, and within an hour and a half we had dined luxuriously, adding to our repast what remained of the sandwiches, and a tinned plum pudding of English make, very nutritious and delicious.

For twenty minutes after the meal we all stood. Tish insists on this, as aiding digestion. Then we prepared for the night's work.

I believe that our conduct requires no defense. But it may be well again to explain our position. These people, whose camp-fire glowed so brazenly against the opposite cliff, had for purely mercenary motives committed a cruel hoax. They had posed as bandits, and as bandits they deserved to be treated. They had held up our own clergyman, of a nervous temperament, on a mountain pass, and had taken from him a part of his stipend. It was heartless. It was barbarous. It was cruel.

My own courage came back with the hot food, which I followed by a charcoal tablet. And the difference in Aggie was marked. Possibly some of the courage of the mountain lion, that bravest of wild creatures, had communicated itself to her through the homely medicine of digestion.

"I can hardly wait to get after them," she said.

However, it was still too early for them to have settled for the night. We sat down, having extinguished our fire, and I was just dozing off when Tish remembered the young man who was to have listened for the police whistle.

"I absolutely forgot him," she said regretfully. "I suppose he is hanging round the foot of Piegan's Pass yet. I'm sorry to have him miss this. I shall tell him, when I see him, that no girl worth having would be sitting over there at supper with four moving-picture actors without a chaperon. The whole proceeding is scandalous. I have noticed," she added, "that it is the girls from quiet suburban towns who are really most prone to defy the conventions when the chance comes."

We dozed for a short time.

Then Tish sat up suddenly. "What's that?" she said.

We listened and distinctly heard the tramp of horses' feet. We started up, but Tish was quite calm.

"They've turned their horses out," she said. "Fortune is with us. They are coming this way."

But at first it did not seem so fortunate, for we heard one of the men following them, stumbling along, and, I regret to say, using profane language. They came directly toward us, and Aggie beside me trembled. But Tish was equal to the emergency.

She drew us behind a large rock, where, spreading out a raincoat to protect us from the dampness, we sat down and waited.

When one of the animals loomed up close to the rock Aggie gave a low cry, but Tish covered her mouth fiercely with an ungentle hand.

"Be still!" she hissed.

It was now perfectly dark, and the man with the horses was not far off. We could not see him, but at last he came near enough so that we could see the flare of a match when he lighted a cigarette. I put my hand on Aggie, and she was shaking with nervousness.

"I am sure I am going to sneeze, Lizzie," she gasped.

And sneeze she did. She muffled it considerably, however, and we were not discovered. But, Tish, I knew, was silently raging.

The horses came nearer.

One of them, indeed, came quite close, and took a nip at the toe of my riding-boot. I kicked at it sharply, however, and it moved away.

The man had gone on. We watched the light of his cigarette, and thus, as he now and then turned his head, knew where he was. It was now that I felt, rather than heard, that Tish was crawling out from the shelter of the rock. At the same time we heard, by the crunching of branches, that the man had sat down near at hand.

Tish's progress was slow but sure. For a half-hour we sat there. Then she returned, still crawling, and on putting out my hand I discovered that she had secured the lasso from her saddle and had brought it back. How true had been her instinct when she practiced its use! How my own words, that it was all foolishness, came back and whispered lessons of humility in my ear!

At this moment a deep, resonant sound came from the tree where the movie actor sat. At the same moment a small creature dropped into my lap from somewhere above, and ran up my sleeve. I made frantic although necessarily silent efforts to dislodge it, and it bit me severely.

The necessity for silence taxed all my strength, but managing finally to secure it by the tail, I forcibly withdrew it and flung it away. Unluckily it struck Aggie in the left eye and inflicted a painful bruise.

Tish had risen to her feet and was standing, a silent and menacing figure, while this event transpired. The movements of the horses as they grazed, the soft breeze blowing through the pines, were the only sounds. Now she took a step forward.

"He's asleep!" she whispered. "Aggie, sit still and watch the horses. Lizzie, come with me."

As I advanced to her she thrust her revolver into my hand.

"When I give the word," she said in a whisper, "hold it against his neck. But keep your finger off the trigger. It's loaded."

We advanced slowly, halting now and then to listen. Although brush crackled under our feet, the grazing horses were making a similar disturbance, and the man slept on. Soon we could see him clearly, sitting back against a tree, his head dropped forward on his breast. Tish surveyed the scene with her keen and appraising eye, and raised the lasso.

The first result was not good. The loaded end struck a branch, and, being deflected, the thing wrapped itself perhaps a dozen times round my neck. Tish, being unconscious of what had happened, drew it up with a jerk, and I stood helpless and slowly strangling. At last, however, she realized the difficulty and released me. I was unable to breathe comfortably for some time, and my tongue felt swollen for several hours.

Through all of this the movie actor had slept soundly. At the second effort Tish succeeded in lassoing him without difficulty. We had feared a loud outcry before we could get to him, but owing to Tish's swiftness in tightening the rope he was able to make, at first, only a low, gurgling sound. I had advanced to him, and was under the impression that I was holding the revolver to his neck. On discovering, however, that I was pressing it to the trunk of the tree, to which he was now secured by the lariat, I corrected the error and held it against his ear.

He was now wide awake and struggling violently. Then, I regret to say, he broke out into such language as I have never heard before. At Tish's request I suppress his oaths, and substitute for them harmless expressions in common use.

"Good gracious!" he said. "What in the world are you doing anyhow? Jimminy crickets, take that thing away from my neck! Great Scott and land alive, I haven't done anything! My word, that gun will go off if you aren't careful!"

I am aware that much of the strength of what he said is lost in this free translation. But it is impossible to repeat his real language.

"Don't move," Tish said, "and don't call out. A sound, and a bullet goes crashing through your brain."

"A woman!" he said in most unflattering amazement. "Great Jehoshaphat, a woman!"

This again is only a translation of what he said.

"Exactly," Tish observed calmly. She had cut the end off the lasso with her scissors, and was now tying his feet together with it. "My friend, we know the whole story, and I am ashamed, ashamed," she said oratorically, "of your sex! To frighten a harmless and well-meaning preacher and his wife for the purpose of publicity is not a joke. Such hoaxes are criminal. If you must have publicity, why not seek it in some other way?"

"Crazy!" he groaned to himself. "In the hands of lunatics! Oh, my goodness!" Again these were not exactly his words.

Having bound him tightly, hand and foot, and taken a revolver from his pocket, Tish straightened herself.

"Now we'll gag him, Lizzie," she said. "We have other things to do to-night than to stand here and converse." Then she turned to the man and told him a deliberate lie. I am sorry to record this. But a tendency to avoid the straight and narrow issues of truth when facing a crisis is one of Tish's weaknesses, the only flaw in an otherwise strong and perfect character.

"We are going to leave you here," she said. "But one of our number, fully armed, will be near by. A sound from you, or any endeavor to call for succor, will end sadly for you. A word to the wise. Now, Lizzie, take that bandanna off his neck and tie it over his mouth."

Tish stood, looking down at him, and her very silhouette was scornful.

"Think, my friend," she said, "of the ignominy of your position! Is any moving picture worth it? Is the pleasure of seeing yourself on the screen any reward for such a shameful position as yours now is? No. A thousand times no."

He made a choking sound in his throat and writhed helplessly. And so we left him, a hopeless and miserable figure, to ponder on his sins.

"That's one," said Tish briskly. "There are only three left. Come, Aggie," she said cheerfully—"to work! We have made a good beginning."

It is with modesty that I approach that night's events, remembering always that Tish's was the brain which conceived and carried out the affair. We were but her loyal and eager assistants. It is for this reason that I thought, and still think, that the money should have been divided so as to give Tish the lion's share. But she, dear, magnanimous soul, refused even to hear of such a course, and insisted that we share it equally.

Of that, however, more anon.

We next proceeded to capture their horses and to tie them up. We regretted the necessity for this, since the unfortunate animals had traveled far and were doubtless hungry. It went to my heart to drag them from their fragrant pasture and to tie them to trees. But, as Tish said, "Necessity knows no law," not even kindness. So we tied them up. Not, however, until we had moved them far from the trail.

Tish stopped then, and stared across the cañon to the enemy's camp-fire.

"No quarter, remember," she said. "And bring your weapons."

We grasped our wooden revolvers and, with Tish leading, started for the camp. Unluckily there was a stream between us, and it was necessary to ford it. It shows Tish's true generalship that, instead of removing her shoes and stockings, as Aggie and I were about to do, she suggested getting our horses and riding across. This we did, and alighted on the other side dryshod.

It was, on consulting my watch, nine o'clock and very dark. A few drops of rain began to fall also, and the distant camp-fire was burning low. Tish gave us each a little blackberry cordial, for fear of dampness, and took some herself. The mild glow which followed was very comforting.

It was Tish, naturally, who went forward to reconnoiter. She returned in an hour, to report that the three men were lying round the fire, two asleep and one leaning on his elbow with a revolver handy. She did not see Mr. Oliver, and it was possible that it was he we had tied to the tree. The girl, she said, was sitting on a log, with her chin propped in her hands.

"She looked rather low-spirited," Tish said. "I expect she liked the first young man better than she thought she did. I intend to give her a piece of my mind as soon as I get a chance. This playing hot and cold isn't maidenly, to say the least."

We now moved slowly forward, after tying our horses. Toward the last, following Tish's example, we went on our hands and knees, and I was thankful then for no skirts. It is wonderful the freedom a man has. I was never one to approve of Doctor Mary Walker, but I'm not so sure she isn't a wise woman and the rest of us fools. I haven't put on a skirt braid since that time without begrudging it.

Well, as I have stated, we advanced, and at last we were in full sight of the camp. I must say I'd have thought they'd have a tent. We expected something better, I suppose, because of the articles in the papers about movie people having their own limousines, and all that. But there they were, open to the wrath of the heavens, and deserving it, if I do say so.

The girl was still sitting, as Tish had described her. Only now she was crying. My heart was downright sore for her. It is no comfort, having made a wrong choice, to know that it is one's own fault.

Having now reached the zone of firelight Tish gave the signal, and we rose and pointed our revolvers at them. Then Tish stepped forward and said: —

"Hands up!"

I shall never forget the expression on the man's face.

He shouted something, but he threw up his hands also, with his eyes popping out of his head. The others scrambled to their feet, but he warned them.

"Careful, boys!" he yelled. "They're got the drop on us."

Just then his eyes fell on Aggie, and he screeched: —

"Two women and a Turk, by — —." The blank is mine.

"Lizzie," said Tish sternly, as all of them, including the girl, held their hands up, "just give me your weapon and go over them."

"Go over them?" I said, not understanding.

"Search them," said Tish. "Take everything out of their pockets. And don't move," she ordered them sternly. "One motion, and I fire. Go on, Lizzie."

Now I have never searched a man's pockets, and the idea was repugnant to me. I am a woman of delicate instincts. But Tish's face was stern. I did as commanded, therefore, the total result being: —

Four revolvers.

Two large knives.

One small knife.

One bunch of keys.

One plug of chewing-tobacco.

Four cartridge belts.

Two old pipes.

Mr. Ostermaier's cigar-case, which I recognized at once, being the one we had presented to him.

Mrs. Ostermaier's wedding-ring and gold bracelet, which her sister gave her on her last birthday.

A diamond solitaire, unknown, as Mrs. Ostermaier never owned one, preferring instead earrings as more showy.

And a considerable sum of money, which I kept but did not count.

There were other small articles, of no value.

"Is that all the loot you secured during the infamous scene on Piegan Pass?" Tish demanded, "You need not hide anything from us. We know the facts, and the whole story will soon be public."

"That's all, lady," whined one of the men. "Except a few boxes of lunch, and that's gone. Lady, lemme take my hands down. I've got a stiff shoulder, and I —"

"Keep them up," Tish snapped. "Aggie, see that they keep them up."

Until that time we had been too occupied to observe the girl, who merely stood and watched in a disdainful sort of way. But now Tish turned and eyed her sternly.

"Search her, Lizzie," she commanded.

"Search me!" the girl exclaimed indignantly. "Certainly not!"

"Lizzie," said Tish in her sternest manner, "go over that girl. Look in her riding-boots. I haven't come across Mrs. Ostermaier's earrings yet."

At that the girl changed color and backed off.

"It's an outrage," she said. "Surely I have suffered enough."

"Not as much," Tish observed, "as you are going to suffer. Go over her, Lizzie."

While I searched her, Tish was lecturing her.

"You come from a good home, I understand," she said, "and you ought to know better. Not content with breaking an honest heart, you join a moving-picture outfit and frighten a prominent divine-for Mr. Ostermaier is well known-into what may be an illness. You cannot deny," she accused her, "that it was you who coaxed them to the pass. At least you needn't. We heard you."

"How was I to know —" the girl began sullenly.

But at that moment I found Mrs. Ostermaier' chamois bag thrust into her riding-boot, and she suddenly went pale.

Tish held it up before her accusingly. "I dare say you will not deny this," she exclaimed, and took Mrs. Ostermaier's earrings out of it.

The men muttered, but Aggie was equal to the occasion. "Silence!" she said, and pointed the revolver at each in turn.

The girl started to speak. Then she shrugged her shoulders. "I could explain," she said, "but I won't. If you think I stole those hideous earrings you're welcome to."

"Of course not," said Tish sarcastically. "No doubt she gave them to you-although I never knew her to give anything away before."

The girl stood still, thinking. Suddenly she said "There's another one, you know. Another man."

"We have him. He will give no further trouble," Tish observed grimly. "I think we have you all, except your Mr. Oliver."

"He is not my Mr. Oliver," said the girl. "I never want to see him again. I —I hate him."

"You haven't got much mind or you couldn't change it so quickly."

She looked sulky again, and said she'd thank us for the ring, which was hers and she could prove it.

But Tish sternly refused. "It's my private opinion," she observed, "that it is Mrs. Ostermaier's, and she has not worn it openly because of the congregation talking quite considerably about her earrings, and not caring for jewelry on the minister's wife. That's what I think."

Shortly after that we heard a horse loping along the road. It came nearer, and then left the trail and came toward the fire. Tish picked up one of the extra revolvers and pointed it. It was Mr. Oliver!

"Throw up your hands!" Tish called. And he did it. He turned a sort of blue color, too, when he saw us, and all the men with their hands up. But he looked relieved when he saw the girl.

"Thank Heaven!" he said. "The way I've been riding this country—"

"You rode hard enough away from the pass," she replied coldly.

We took a revolver away from him and lined him up with the others. All the time he was paying little attention to us and none at all to the other men. But he was pleading with the girl.

"Honestly," he said, "I thought I could do better for everybody by doing what I did. How did I know," he pleaded, "that you were going to do such a crazy thing as this?"

But she only stared at him as if she hated the very ground he stood on.

"It's a pity," Tish observed, "that you haven't got your camera along. This would make a very nice picture. But I dare say you could hardly turn the crank with your hands in the air."

We searched him carefully, but he had only a gold watch and some money. On the chance, however, that the watch was Mr. Ostermaier's, although unlikely, we took it.

I must say he was very disagreeable, referring to us as highwaymen and using uncomplimentary language. But, as Tish observed, we might as well be thorough while we were about it.

For the nonce we had forgotten the other man. But now I noticed that the pseudo-bandits wore a watchful and not unhopeful air. And suddenly one of them whistled—a thin, shrill note that had, as Tish later remarked, great penetrative power without being noisy.

"That's enough of that," she said. "Aggie, take another of these guns and point them both at these gentlemen. If they whistle again, shoot. As to the other man, he will not reply, nor will he come to your assistance. He is gagged and tied, and into the bargain may become at any time the victim of wild beasts."

The moment she had said it, Tish realized that it was but too true, and she grew thoughtful. Aggie, too, was far from comfortable. She said later that she was uncertain what to do. Tish had said to fire if they whistled again. The question in her mind was, had it been said purely for effect or did Tish mean it? After all, the men were not real bandits, she reflected, although guilty of theft, even if only for advertising purposes. She was greatly disturbed, and as agitation always causes a return of her hay fever, she began to sneeze violently.

Until then the men had been quiet, if furious. But now they fell into abject terror, imploring Tish, whom they easily recognized as the leader, to take the revolvers from her.

But Tish only said: "No fatalities, Aggie, please. Point at an arm or a leg until the spasm subsides."

Her tone was quite gentle.

Heretofore this has been a plain narrative, dull, I fear, in many places. But I come now to a not unexciting incident-which for a time placed Tish and myself in an unpleasant position.

I refer to the escape of the man we had tied.

We held a brief discussion as to what to do with our prisoners until morning, a discussion which Tish solved with her usual celerity by cutting from the saddles which lay round the fire a number of those leather thongs with which such saddles are adorned and which are used in case of necessity to strap various articles to the aforesaid saddles.

With these thongs we tied them, not uncomfortably, but firmly, their hands behind them and their feet fastened together. Then, as the night grew cold, Tish suggested that we shove them near the fire, which we did.

The young lady, however, offered a more difficult problem. We compromised by giving her her freedom, but arranging for one of our number to keep her covered with a revolver.

"You needn't be so thoughtful," she said angrily, and with a total lack of appreciation of Tish's considerate attitude. "I'd rather be tied, especially if the Moslem with the hay fever is going to hold the gun."

It was at that moment that we heard a whistle from across the stream, and each of the prostrate men raised his head eagerly. Before Tish could interfere one of them had whistled three times sharply, probably a danger signal.

Without a word Tish turned and ran toward the stream, calling to me to follow her.

"Tish!" I heard Aggie's agonized tone. "Lizzie! Come back. Don't leave me here alone. I —"

Here she evidently clutched the revolver involuntarily, for there was a sharp report, and a bullet struck a tree near us.

Tish paused and turned. "Point that thing up into the air, Aggie," she called back. "And stay there. I hold you responsible."

I heard Aggie give a low moan, but she said nothing, and we kept on.

The moon had now come up, flooding the valley with silver radiance. We found our horses at once, and Tish leaped into the saddle. Being heavier and also out of breath from having stumbled over a log, I was somewhat slower.

Tish was therefore in advance of me when we started, and it was she who caught sight of him first.

"He's got a horse, Lizzie," she called back to me. "We can get him, I think. Remember, he is unarmed."

Fortunately he had made for the trail, which was here wider than ordinary and gleamed white in the moonlight. We had, however, lost some time in fording the stream, and we had but the one glimpse of him as the trail curved.

Tish lashed her horse to a lope, and mine followed without urging. I had, unfortunately, lost a stirrup early in the chase, and was compelled, being unable to recover it, to drop the lines and clutch the saddle.

Twice Tish fired into the air. She explained afterward that she did this for the moral effect on the fugitive, but as each time it caused my horse to jump and almost unseat me, at last I begged her to desist.

We struck at last into a straight piece of trail, ending in a wall of granite, and up this the trail climbed in a switchback. Tish turned to me.

"We have him now," she said. "When he starts up there he is as much gone as a fly on the wall. As a matter of fact," she said as calmly as though we had been taking an afternoon stroll, "his taking this trail shows that he is a novice and no real highwayman. Otherwise he would have turned off into the woods."

At that moment the fugitive's horse emerged into the moonlight and Tish smiled grimly.

"I see why now," she exclaimed. "The idiot has happened on Mona Lisa, who must have returned and followed us. And no pack-horse can be made to leave the trail unless by means of a hornet. Look, he's trying to pull her off and she won't go."

It was true, as we now perceived. He saw his danger, but too late. Mona Lisa, probably still disagreeable after her experience with the hornets, held straight for the cliff.

The moon shone full on it, and when he was only thirty feet up its face Tish fired again, and the fugitive stopped.

"Come down," said Tish quietly.

He said a great many things which, like his earlier language, I do not care to repeat. But after a second shot he began to descend slowly.

Tish, however, approached him warily, having given her revolver to me.

"He might try to get it from me, Lizzie," she observed. "Keep it pointed in our direction, but not at us. I'm going to tie him again."

This she proceeded to do, tying his hands behind him and fastening his belt also to the horn of the saddle, but leaving his feet free. All this was done to the accompaniment of bitter vituperation. She pretended to ignore this, but it made an impression evidently, for at last she replied.

"You have no one to blame but yourself," she said. "You deserve your present humiliating position, and you know it. I've made up my mind to take you all in and expose your cruel scheme, and I intend to do it. I'm nothing if I am not thorough," she finished.

He made no reply to this, and, in fact, he made only one speech on the way back, and that, I am happy to say, was without profanity.

"It isn't being taken in that I mind so much," he said pathetically. "It's all in the game, and I can stand up as well under trouble as any one. It's being led in by a crowd of women that makes it painful."

I have neglected to say that Tish was leading Mona Lisa, while I followed with the revolver.

It was not far from dawn when we reached the camp again. Aggie was as we had left her, but in the light of the dying fire she looked older and much worn. As a matter of fact, it was some weeks before she looked like her old self.

The girl was sitting where we had left her, and sulkier than ever. She had turned her back to Mr. Oliver, and Aggie said afterward that the way they had quarreled had been something terrible.

Aggie said she had tried to make conversation with the girl, and had, indeed, told her of Mr. Wiggins and her own blasted life. But she had remained singularly unresponsive.

The return of our new prisoner was greeted by the other men with brutal rage, except Mr. Oliver, who merely glanced at him and then went back to his staring at the fire. It appeared that they had been counting on him to get assistance, and his capture destroyed their last hope. Indeed, their language grew so unpleasant that at last Tish hammered sharply on a rock with the handle of her revolver.

"Please remember," she said, "that you are in the presence of ladies!"

They jeered at her, but she handled the situation with her usual generalship.

"Lizzie," she said calmly, "get the tin basin that is hanging to my saddle, and fill it with the water from that snowbank. On the occasion of any more unseemly language, pour it over the offender without mercy."

It became necessary to do it, I regret to state. They had not yet learned that Tish always carries out her threats. It was the one who we felt was the leader who offended, and I did as I had been requested to. But Aggie, ever tender-hearted, feared that it would give the man a severe cold, and got Tish's permission to pour a little blackberry cordial down his throat.

Far from this kindness having a salubrious effect, it had the contrary. They all fell to bad language again, and, realizing that they wished the cordial, and our supply being limited, we were compelled to abandon the treatment.

It had been an uncomfortable night, and I confess to a feeling of relief when "the rift of dawn" broke the early skies.

We were, Tish calculated, some forty miles from breakfast, and Aggie's diet for some days had been light at the best, even the mountain-lion broth having been more stimulating than staying. We therefore investigated the camp, and found behind a large stone some flour, baking-powder, and bacon. With this equipment and a frying-pan or two we were able to make some very fair pancakes-or flapjacks, as they are called in the West.

Tish civilly invited the girl to eat with us, but she refused curtly, although, on turning once, I saw her eyeing us with famished eyes. I think, however, that on seeing us going about the homely task of getting breakfast, she realized that we were not the desperate creatures she had fancied during the night, but three gentlewomen on a holiday-simple tourists, indeed.

"I wish," she said at last almost wistfully —"I wish that I could understand it all. I seem to be all mixed up. You don't suppose I want to be here, do you?"

But Tish was not in a mood to make concessions. "As for what you want," she said, "how are we to know that? You are here, aren't you? —here as a result of your own cold-heartedness. Had you remained true to the very estimable young man you jilted you would not now be in this position."

"Of course he would talk about it!" said the girl darkly.

"I am convinced," Tish went on, dexterously turning a pancake by a swift movement of the pan, "that sensational movies are responsible for much that is wrong with the country to-day. They set false standards. Perfectly pure-minded people see them and are filled with thoughts of crime."

Although she had ignored him steadily, the girl turned now to Mr. Oliver.

"They don't believe anything I tell them. Why don't you explain?" she demanded.

"Explain!" he said in a furious voice. "Explain to three lunatics? What's the use?"

"You got me into this, you know."

"I did! I like that! What in the name of Heaven induced you to ride off the way you did?"

Tish paused, with the frying-pan in the air. "Silence!" she commanded. "You are both only reaping what you have sowed. As far as quarreling goes, you can keep that until you are married, if you intend to be. I don't know but I'd advise it. It's a pity to spoil two houses."

But the girl said that she wouldn't marry him if he was the last man on earth, and he fell back to sulking again.

As Aggie observed later, he acted as if he had never cared for her, while Mr. Bell, on the contrary, could not help his face changing when he so much as mentioned her name.

We made some tea and ate a hearty breakfast, while the men watched us. And as we ate, Tish held the moving-picture business up to contumely and scorn.

"Lady," said one of the prostrate men, "aren't you going to give us anything to eat?"

"People," Tish said, ignoring him, "who would ordinarily cringe at the sight of a wounded beetle sit through bloody murders and go home with the obsession of crime."

"I hope you won't take it amiss," said the man again, "if I say that, seeing it's our flour and bacon, you either ought to feed us or take it away and eat it where we can't see you."

"I take it," said Tish to the girl, pouring in more batter, "that you yourself would never have thought of highway robbery had you not been led to it by an overstimulated imagination."

"I wish," said the girl rudely, "that you wouldn't talk so much. I've got a headache."

When we had finished Tish indicated the frying-pan and the batter. "Perhaps," she said, "you would like to bake some cakes for these friends of yours. We have a long trip ahead of us."

But the girl replied heartlessly that she hoped they would starve to death, ignoring their pitiful glances. In the end it was our own tender-hearted Aggie who baked pancakes for them and, loosening their hands while I stood guard, saw that they had not only food but the gentle refreshment of fresh tea. Tish it was, however, who, not to be outdone in magnanimity, permitted them to go, one by one, to the stream to wash. Escape, without horses or weapons, was impossible, and they realized it.

By nine o'clock we were ready to return. And here a difficulty presented itself. There were six prisoners and only three of us. The men, fed now, were looking less subdued, although they pretended to obey Tish's commands with alacrity.

Aggie overheard a scrap of conversation, too, which seemed to indicate that they had not given up hope. Had Tish not set her heart on leading them into the great hotel at Many Glaciers, and there exposing them to the taunts of angry tourists, it would have been simpler for one of us to ride for assistance, leaving the others there.

In this emergency Tish, putting her hand into her pocket for her scissors to trim a hangnail, happened to come across the policeman's whistle.

"My gracious!" she said. "I forgot my promise to that young man!"

She immediately put it to her lips and blew three shrill blasts. To our surprise they were answered by a halloo, and a moment later the young gentleman himself appeared on the trail. He was no longer afoot, but was mounted on a pinto pony, which we knew at once for Bill's.

He sat on his horse, staring as if he could not believe his eyes. Then he made his way across the stream toward us.

"Good Heavens!" he said. "What in the name of—" Here his eyes fell on the girl, and he stiffened.

"Jim!" cried the girl, and looked at him with what Aggie afterward characterized as a most touching expression.

But he ignored her. "Looks as though you folks have been pretty busy," he observed, glancing at our scowling captives. "I'm a trifle surprised. You don't mind my being rather breathless, do you?"

"My only regret," Tish said loftily, "is that we have not secured the Indians. They too should be taught a lesson. I am sure that the red man is noble until led away by civilized people who might know better."

It was at this point that Mr. Bell's eyes fell on Mr. Oliver, who with his hands tied behind him was crouching over the fire.

"Well!" he said. "So you're here too! But of course you would be." This he said bitterly.

"For the love of Heaven, Bell," Mr. Oliver said, "tell those mad women that I'm not a bandit."

"We know that already," Tish observed.

"And untie my hands. My shoulders are about broken."

But Mr. Bell only looked at him coldly. "I can't interfere with these ladies," he said. "They're friends of mine. If they think you are better tied, it's their business. They did it."

"At least," Mr. Oliver said savagely, "you can tell them who I am, can't you?"

"As to that," Mr. Bell returned, "I can only tell them what you say you are. You must remember that I know nothing about you. Helen knows much more than I do."

"Jim," cried the girl, "surely you are going to tell these women that we are not highway robbers. Tell them the truth. Tell them I am not a highway robber. Tell them that these men are not my accomplices, that I never saw them before."

"You must remember," he replied in an icy tone, "that I no longer know your friends. It is some days since you and I parted company. And you must admit that one of them is a friend of yours-as well as I can judge, a very close friend."

She was almost in tears, but she persisted. "At least," she said, "you can tell them that I did not rob that woman on the pass. They are going to lead us in to Many Glaciers, and-Jim, you won't let them, will you? I'll die of shame."

But he was totally unmoved. As Aggie said afterward, no one would have thought that, but a day or two before, he had been heartbroken because she was in love with someone else.

"As to that," he said, "it is questionable, according to Mrs. Ostermaier, that nothing was taken from you, and that as soon as the attack was over you basely deserted her and followed the bandits. A full description of you, which I was able to correct in one or two trifling details, is now in the hands of the park police."

She stared at him with fury in her eyes. "I hope you will never speak to me again," she cried.

"You said that the last time I saw you, Helen. If you will think, you will remember that you addressed me first just now."

She stamped her foot.

"Of course," he said politely, "you can see my position. You maintain and possibly believe that these-er-acquaintances of yours" —he indicated the men —"are not members of the moving-picture outfit. Also that your being with them is of an accidental nature. But, on the other hand —"

She put her fingers in her ears and turned her back on him.

"On the other hand," he went on calmly, "I have the word of these three respectable ladies that they are the outfit, or part of it, that they have just concluded a cruel hoax on unsuspecting tourists, and that they justly deserve to be led in as captives and exposed to the full ignominy of their position."

Here she faced him again, and this time she was quite pale. "Ask those-those women where they found my engagement ring," she said. "One of those wretches took it from me. That ought to be proof enough that they are not from the moving-picture outfit."

Tish at once produced the ring and held it out to him. But he merely glanced at it and shook his head.

"All engagement rings look alike," he observed. "I cannot possibly say, Helen, but I think it is unlikely that it is the one I gave you, as you told me, you may recall, that you had thrown it into a crack in a glacier. It may, of course, be one you have recently acquired."

He glanced at Mr. Oliver, but the latter only shrugged his shoulders.

Well, she shed a few tears, but he was adamant, and helped us saddle the horses, ignoring her utterly. It was our opinion that he no longer cared for her, and that, having lost him, she now regretted it. I know that she watched him steadily when he was not looking her way. But he went round quite happily, whistling a bit of tune, and not at all like the surly individual we had at first thought him.

The ride back was without much incident. Our prisoners rode with their hands tied behind them, except the young lady.

"We might as well leave her unfastened," the young man said casually. "While I dare say she would make her escape if possible, and particularly if there was any chance of getting filmed while doing it, I will make myself personally responsible."

As a matter of fact she was exceedingly rude to all of us, and during our stop for luncheon, which was again bacon and pancakes, she made a dash for her horse. The young man saw her, however, in time, and brought her back. From that time on she was more civil, but I saw her looking at him now and then, and her eyes were positively terrified.

It was Aggie, at last, who put in a plea for her with him, drawing him aside to do so. "I am sure," she said, "that she is really a nice girl, and has merely been led astray by the search for adventure. Naturally my friends, especially Miss Tish, have small sympathy with such a state of mind. But you are younger-and remember, you loved her once."

"Loved her once!" he replied. "Dear lady, I'm so crazy about her at this minute that I can hardly hold myself in."

"You are not acting much like it."

"The fact is," he replied, "I'm afraid to let myself go. And if she's learned a lesson, I have too. I've been her doormat long enough. I tried it and it didn't work. She's caring more for me now, at this minute, than she has in eleven months. She needs a strong hand, and, by George! I've got it-two of them, in fact."

We reached Many Glaciers late that afternoon, and Tish rode right up to the hotel. Our arrival created the most intense excitement, and Tish, although pleased, was rather surprised. It was not, however, until a large man elbowed his way through the crowd and took possession of the prisoners that we understood.

"I'll take them now," he said. "Well, George, how are you?"

This was to the leader, who merely muttered in reply.

"I'd like to leave them here for a short time," Tish stated. "They should be taught a severe lesson and nothing stings like ridicule. After that you can turn them free, but I think they ought to be discharged."

"Turn them free!" he said in a tone of amazement. "Discharged! My dear madam, they will get fifteen years' hard labor, I hope. And that's too good for them."

Then suddenly the crowd began to cheer. It was some time before Tish realized that they were cheering us. And even then, I shall have to confess, we did not understand until the young man explained to me.

"You see," he said, "I didn't like to say anything sooner, for fear of making you nervous. You'd done it all so well that I wanted you to finish it. You're been in the right church all along, but the wrong pew. Those fellows aren't movie actors, except Oliver, who will be freed now, and come after me with a gun, as like as not! They're real dyed-in-the-wool desperadoes and there's a reward of five thousand dollars for capturing them."

Tish went rather white, but said nothing. Aggie, however, went into a paroxysm of sneezing, and did not revive until given aromatic ammonia to inhale.

"I was fooled at first too," the young man said. "We'd been expecting a holdup and when it came we thought it was the faked one. But the person"—he paused and looked round—"the person who had the real jolt was Helen. She followed them, since they didn't take her for ransom, as had been agreed in the plot.

"Then, when she found her mistake, they took her along, for fear she'd ride off and raise the alarm. All in all," he said reflectively, "it has been worth about a million dollars to me."

We went into the hotel, with the crowd following us, and the first thing we saw was Mrs. Ostermaier, sitting dejectedly by the fire. When she saw us, she sprang to her feet and came to meet us.

"Oh, Miss Tish, Miss Tish!" she said. "What I have been through! Attacked on a lonely mountain-top and robbed of everything. My reason is almost gone. And my earrings, my beautiful earrings!"

Tish said nothing, but, reaching into her reticule, which she had taken from the horn of her saddle, she drew out a number of things.

"Here," she said. "Are your earrings. Here also is Mr. Ostermaier's cigar-case, but empty. Here is some money too. I'll keep that, however, until I know how much you lost."

"Tish!" screeched Mrs. Ostermaier. "You found them!"

"Yes," Tish said somewhat wearily, "we found them. We found a number of things, Mrs. Ostermaier,—four bandits, and two lovers, or rather three, but so no longer, and your things, and a reward of five thousand dollars, and an engagement ring. I think," she said, "that I'd like a hot bath and something to eat."

Mrs. Ostermaier was gloating over her earrings, but she looked up at Tish's tired and grimy face, at the mud encrusted on me from my accident the day before, at Aggie in her turban.

"Go and wash, all of you," she said kindly, "and I'll order some hot tea."

But Tish shook her head. "Tea nothing!" she said firmly. "I want a broiled sirloin steak and potatoes. And"—she looked Mrs. Ostermaier full in the eye—"I am going to have a cocktail. I need it."

Late that evening Aggie came to Tish's room, where I was sitting with her. Tish was feeling entirely well, and more talkative than I can remember her in years. But the cocktail, which she felt, she said, in no other way, had gone to her legs.

"It is not," she observed, "that I cannot walk. I can, perfectly well. But I am obliged to keep my eyes on my feet, and it might be noticed."

"I just came in," Aggie said, "to say that Helen and her lover have made it up. They are down by the lake now, and if you will look out you can see them."

I gave Tish an arm to the window, and the three of us stood and looked out. The moon was rising over the snow-capped peaks across the lake, and against its silver pathway the young people stood outlined. As we looked he stooped and kissed her. But it was a brief caress, as if he had just remembered the strong hand and being a doormat long enough.

Tish drew a long breath.

"What," she said, "is more beautiful than young love? It will be a comfort to remember that we brought them together. Let go of me now, Lizzie. If I keep my eye on the bedpost I think I can get back."

More Tish

by

Mary Roberts Rinehart

The Cave on Thunder Cloud

I

It is doubtful if Aggie and I would have known anything about Tish's plan had Aggie not seen the advertisement in the newspaper. She came to my house at once in violent excitement and with her bonnet over her ear, and gave me the newspaper clipping to read. It said:

> "Wanted: A small donkey. Must be gentle, female, and if possible answer to the name of Modestine. Address X 27, Morning News."

"Well," I said when I had read it, "did you insert the advertisement or do you propose to answer it?"

Aggie was preparing to take a drink of water, but, the water being cold and the weather warm, she was dabbing a little on her wrists first to avoid colic. She looked up at me in surprise.

"Do you mean to say, Lizzie," she demanded, "that you don't recognize that advertisement?"

"Modestine?" I reflected. "I've heard the name before somewhere. Didn't Tish have a cook once named Modestine?"

But it seemed that that was not it. Aggie sat down opposite me and took off her bonnet. Although it was only the first of May, the weather, as I have said, was very warm.

"To think," she said heavily, "that all the time while I was reading it aloud to her when she was laid up with neuralgia she was scheming and planning and never saying a word to me! Not that I would have gone; but I could have sent her mail to her, and at least have notified the authorities if she had disappeared."

"Reading what aloud to her-her mail?" I asked sharply.

"'Travels with a Donkey,'" Aggie replied. "Stevenson's 'Travels with a Donkey.' It isn't safe to read anything aloud to Tish any more. The older she gets the worse she is. She thinks that what any one else has done she can go and do. If she should read a book on poultry-farming she would think she could teach a young hen to lay an egg."

As Aggie spoke a number of things came back to me. I recalled that the Sunday before, in church, Tish had appeared absorbed and even more devout than usual, and had taken down the headings of the sermon on her missionary envelope; but that, on my leaning over to see if she had them correctly, she had whisked the paper away before I had had more than time to see the first heading. It had said "Rubber Heels."

Aggie was pacing the floor nervously, holding the empty glass.

"She's going on a walking tour with a donkey, that's what, Lizzie," she said, pausing before me. "I could see it sticking out all over her while I read that book. And if we go to her now and tax her with it she'll admit it. But if she says she is doing it to get thin don't you believe it."

That was all Aggie would say. She shut her lips and said she had come for my recipe for caramel custard. But when I put on my wraps and said I was going to Tish's she said she would come along.

Tish lives in an apartment, and she was not at home. Miss Swift, the seamstress, opened the door and stood in the doorway so we could not enter.

"I'm sorry, Miss Aggie and Miss Lizzie," she said, putting out her left elbow as Aggie tried to duck by her; "but she left positive orders to admit nobody. Of course if she had known you were coming-but she didn't."

"What are you making, Miss Letitia?" Aggie asked sweetly. "Summer clothes?"

"Yes. Some little thin things-it's getting so hot!"

"Humph! I see you are making them with an upholsterer's needle!" said Aggie, and marched down the hall with her head up.

I was quite bewildered. For even if Tish had decided on a walking tour I couldn't imagine what an upholsterer's needle had to do with it, unless she meant to upholster the donkey.

We got down to the entrance before Aggie spoke again. Then:

"What did I tell you?" she demanded. "That woman's making her a— —"

But at that very instant there was a thud under our feet and something came "ping" through the floor not six inches from my toe, and lodged in the ceiling. Aggie and I stood looking up. It had made a small round hole over our heads, and a little cloud of plaster dust hung round it.

"Somebody shot at us!" declared Aggie, clutching my arm. "That was a bullet!"

I stooped down and felt the floor. There was a hole in it, and from somewhere below I thought I heard voices. It was not very comfortable, standing there on top of Heaven knows what; but we were divided between fear and outrage, and our indignation won. With hardly a word we went back to the rear staircase and so to the cellar. Halfway down the stairs both of us remembered the same thing-that it was Tish's day to use the basement laundry, and that perhaps — —

Tish was not in the laundry, nor was Hannah, her maid. But Tish's blue-and-white dressing sacque was on the line, and the blue had run, as I had said it would when she bought it. In the furnace room beyond we heard voices, and Aggie opened the door.

Tish and Hannah were both there. They had not heard us.

"Nonsense!" Tish was saying. "If anybody had been hit we'd have heard a scream; or if they were killed we'd have heard 'em fall."

"I heard a sort of yell," said poor Hannah. "I don't like it, Miss Tish. The time before you just missed me."

"Why did you stick your arm out?" demanded Tish. "Now take that broomstick and we'll start again. Did you score that?"

"How'll I score it?" asked Hannah. "Hit or miss?" She went to the cellar wall and stood waiting, with a piece of charcoal in her hand. The whitewashed wall was marked with rows of X's and ciphers. The ciphers predominated.

"Mark it a miss."

"But I heard a yell— —"

"Fiddle-de-dee! Are you ready?" Tish had lifted a small rifle into position and was standing, with her feet apart, pointing it at a white target hanging by a string from a rafter. As she gave the signal. Hannah sighed, and, picking up a broomhandle, started the target to swaying, pendulum fashion; Tish followed it with the gun.

I thought things had gone far enough, so I stepped into the cellar and spoke in ringing tones.

"Letitia Carberry!" I said sternly.

Tish pulled the trigger at that moment and the bullet went into the furnace pipe. It was absurd, of course, for Tish to blame me for it, but she turned on me in a rage.

"Look what you made me do!" she snapped. "Can't a person have a moment's privacy?"

"What I think you need," I retorted, "is six months' complete seclusion in a sanitarium."

"You nearly shot us in the upper hall," Aggie put in warmly.

"Well, as long as I didn't shoot you in the upper hall or any other place, I guess you needn't fuss," said Tish. "Ready, Hannah."

This time she shot Hannah in the broomhandle, and practically put her *hors de combat*; but the shot immediately after was what Tish triumphantly called a clean bull's-eye-that is, it hit the center of the target.

That is the time to stop, when one has made a bull's-eye in any sort of achievement, I take it. And Tish is nobody's fool. She took off her spectacles and wiped the perspiration and gunpowder streaks from her face. She was immediately in high good humor.

"Every unprotected female should know how to handle a weapon," she said oracularly, and, sitting down on the edge of the coal-bin, proceeded to swab out the gun with a wad of cotton on the end of a stick.

"The poker has been good enough for you for fifty years," I retorted. "And if you think you look sporty, or anything but idiotic, sitting there in a flowered kimono and swabbing out the throat of that gun — —?"

Just then the janitor came down, and Tish gave him a dollar for the use of the cellar and did not mention the furnace pipe. Aggie and I glanced at each other. Tish's demoralization had begun. From that minute, to the long and entirely false story she told the red-bearded man in Thunder Cloud Glen several days later, she trod, as Aggie truthfully said, the downward path of mendacity, bringing up in the county jail and hysterics.

We went upstairs, Tish ahead and Aggie and I two flights behind, believing that Tish with an unloaded gun was a thousand times more dangerous than any outlaw with an entire arsenal loaded to the muzzle.

We had a cup of tea in Tish's parlor, but she kept us out of the bedroom, where we could hear Miss Swift running the sewing machine. Finally Aggie said out of a clear sky:

"Have you had any answers to your advertisement?"

Tish, who had been about to put a slice of lemon in her tea, put it in her mouth instead and stared at us both.

"What advertisement?"

"We know all about it, Tish," I said. "And if you think it proper for a woman of your age to go adventuring with only a donkey for company — —"

"I've had worse!" Tish snapped. "And I'm not feeble yet, as far as my age goes. If I want to take a walking tour it's my affair, isn't it?"

"You can't walk with your bad knee," I objected. Tish sniffed.

"You're envious, that's what," she sneered. "While you are sitting at home, overeating and oversleeping and getting fat in mind and body, I shall be on the broad highway, walking between hedgerows of flowering-flowering-well, between hedgerows. While you sleep in stuffy, upholstered rooms I shall lie in woodland glades in my sleeping-bag and see overhead the constellation of-of what's its name. I shall talk to the birds and the birds will talk to me."

Sleeping-bag! That was what Aggie had meant that Miss Swift was making.

"What are you going to do when it rains?"

"It doesn't rain much in May. Anyhow, a friendly farmhouse and a glass of milk-even a barn — —"

Aggie got up with the light of desperation in her eyes. Aggie hates woods and gnats, has no eye for Nature, and for almost half a century has pampered her body in a featherbed poultice, with the windows closed, until the first of June each year. Yet Aggie rose to the crisis.

"You shan't go alone, Tish," she said stoutly. "You'll forget to change your stockings when your feet are wet and you can't make a cup of coffee fit to drink. I'm going too."

Tish made a gesture of despair, but Aggie was determined. Tish glanced at me.

"Well?" she snapped. "We might as well make it a family excursion. Aren't you coming along, too, to look after Aggie?"

"Not at all," I observed calmly. "I'll have enough to do looking after myself. But I like the idea, and since you've invited me I'll come, of course."

At first I am afraid Tish was not particularly pleased. She said she had it all planned to make four miles an hour, or about forty miles a day; and that any one falling back would have to be left by the wayside. And that if we were not prepared to sleep on the ground, or were going to talk rheumatism every time she found a place to camp, she would thank us to remember that we had really asked ourselves.

But she grew more cheerful finally and seemed to be glad to talk over the details of the trip with somebody. She said it was a pity we had not had some practice with firearms, for we would each have to take a weapon, the mountains being full of outlaws, more than likely.

Neither Aggie nor I could use a gun at all, but, as Tish observed, we could pot at trees and fenceposts along the road by way of practice.

When I suggested that the sight of three women of our age-we are all well on toward fifty; Aggie insists that she is younger than I am, but we were in the same infant class in Sunday-school —three women of our age "potting" at fences was hardly dignified, Tish merely shrugged her shoulders.

She asked us not to let Charlie Sands learn of the trip. He would be sure to be fussy and want to send a man along, and that would spoil it all.

What with the secrecy, and the guns and everything, I dare say we were like a lot of small boys getting ready to run away out West and kill Indians. In fact, Tish said it reminded her of the time, years ago, when Charlie Sands and some other boys had run away, with all the carving knives and razors they could gather together, and were found a week later in a cave in the mountains twenty miles or so from town.

Tish showed us her sleeping-bag, which was felt outside and her old white fur rug within. Aggie planned hers immediately on the same lines, with her fur coat as a lining; but I had mine made of oilcloth outside, my rheumatism having warned me that we were going to have rain. I was right about the rain.

I had an old army revolver that had belonged to my father, and of course Tish had her coal-cellar rifle, but Aggie had nothing more dangerous than a bayonet from the Mexican War. This being too heavy to carry, and dull-being only possible as a weapon by bringing the handle down on one's opponent's head-Aggie was forced to buy a revolver.

The man in the shop tried to sell her a small pearl-handled one, but she would not look at it. She bought one of the sort that goes on shooting as long as one holds a finger on the trigger —a snub-nosed thing that looked as deadly as it was. She was in terror of it from the moment she got it home, and during most of the trip it was packed in excelsior, with the barrel stuffed with cotton, on Modestine's back.

Which brings me to Modestine.

Tish received three answers to her advertisement: One was a mule, one a piebald pony with a wicked eye, and the third was a donkey. It seemed that Stevenson had said that the pack animal of such a trip should be "cheap, small and hardy," and that a donkey best of all answered these requirements.

The donkey in question was, however, not a female. Tish was firm about this; but on no more donkeys being offered, she bought this one and called him Modestine anyhow. He was very dirty, and we paid a dollar extra to have him washed with soap powder, as our food was to be carried on his back. Also the day before we started I spent an hour or so on him with a fine comb, with gratifying results.

I must confess I entered on the adventure with a light heart. Tish had apparently given up all thought of the aeroplane; her automobile was being used by Charlie Sands; the weather was warm and sunny, and the orchards were in bloom. I had no premonition of danger. The adventure, reduced to its elements of canned food, alcohol lamp, sleeping-bags and toothbrushes, seemed no adventure at all, but a peaceful and pastoral excursion by three middle-aged women into green fields and pastures new.

We reckoned, however, without Aggie's missionary dime.

Aggie's church had sent each of its members a ten-cent piece, with instructions to invest it in some way and to return it multiplied as much as possible in three months. This was on Aggie's mind, but we did not know it until later. Really, Aggie's missionary dime is the story. If she had done as she had planned at first and invested it in an egg, had hatched the egg in cotton wool on the shelf over her kitchen range and raised the chicken, eventually selling the chicken to herself for dinner at seventy-five cents, this story would never have been written.

What the dime really bought was a glass of jelly wrapped in a two-day-old newspaper. But to go back:

We were to start from Tish's at dawn on Tuesday morning. Modestine's former owner had agreed to bring him at that hour to the alley behind Tish's apartment. On Monday Aggie and I sent over what we felt we could not get along without, and about five we both arrived.

Tish was sitting on the floor, with luggage scattered all round her and heaped on the chairs and bed.

She looked up witheringly when we entered.

"You forgot your opera cloak, Lizzie," she said, "and Aggie has only sent five pairs of shoes!"

"I've got to have shoes," Aggie protested.

"If you've got to have five pairs of shoes, six white petticoats, summer underwear, intermediates and flannels, a bathrobe, six bath towels and a sunshade, not to mention other things, you want an elephant, not a donkey."

"Why do we have a donkey?" I asked. "Why don't we have a horse and buggy, and go like Christians?"

"Because you and Aggie wouldn't walk if we did," snapped Tish. "I know you both. You'd have rheumatism or a corn and you'd take your walking trip sitting. Besides, we may not always keep to the roads. I'd like to go up into the mountains."

Well, Tish was disagreeable, but right. As it turned out the donkey, being small, could only carry the sleeping-bags, our portable stove and the provisions. We each were obliged to pack a suitcase and carry that.

We started at dawn the next day. Hannah came down to the alley and didn't think much of Modestine. By the time he was loaded a small crowd had gathered, and when we finally started off, Tish ahead with Modestine's bridle over her arm and Aggie and I behind with our suitcases, a sort of cheer went up. It was, however, an orderly leave-taking, perhaps owing to the fact that Tish's rifle was packed in full view on Modestine's back.

I have a great admiration for Tish. She does not fear the pointing finger of scorn. She took the most direct route out of town, and by the time we had reached the outskirts we had a string of small boys behind us like the tail of a kite. When we reached the cemetery and sat down to rest they formed a circle round us and stared at us.

Tish looked at her watch. We had been an hour and twenty minutes going two miles!

II

We were terribly thirsty, but none of us cared to drink from the cemetery well; in fact, the question of water bothered us all that day. It was very warm, and after we left the suburban trolley-line, where motormen stopped the cars to look at us and people crowded to the porches to stare at us, the water question grew serious. Tish had studied sanitation, and at every farm we came to the well was improperly located. Generally it was immediately below the pigsty.

Luckily we had brought along some blackberry cordial, and we took a sip of that now and then. But the suitcases were heavy, and at eleven o'clock Aggie said the cordial had gone to her head and she could go no farther. Tish was furious.

"I told you how it would be!" she said. "For about forty years you haven't used your legs except to put shoes and stockings on. Of course they won't carry you."

"It isn't my feet, it's my head," Aggie sniffed. "If I had some water I'd b-be all right. If you're going to examine everything you drink with a microscope you might as well have stayed at home."

"I'd have died before I drank out of that last well," snapped Tish. "One could tell by looking at that woman that there are dead rats and things in the water."

"You are not so particular at home," Aggie asserted. "You use vinegar, don't you? And I'm sure it's full of wrigglers. You can see them when you hold the cruet to the light."

We got her to go on finally, and at the next well we boiled a pailful of water and made some tea. We found a grove beside the road and built a fire in our stove there, and while Modestine was grazing we sat and soaked our feet in a brook and looked for blisters. Tish calculated that as we had been walking for six hours we'd probably gone twenty-two miles. But I believe it was about eight.

While we drank our tea and ate the luncheon Hannah had put up we discussed our plans. Tish's original scheme had been to follow the donkey; but as he would not move without some one ahead, leading him, this was not feasible.

"We want to keep away from the beaten path," Tish said with a pickle in one hand and her cup in the other. "These days automobiles go everywhere. I'm in favor of heading straight for the mountain."

"I'm not," I said firmly. "Here in civilization we can find a barn on a rainy night."

"There are plenty of caves in the mountains," said Tish. "Besides, to get the real benefit of this we ought to sleep out, rain or shine. A gentle spring rain hurts no one."

We rested for two hours; it was very pleasant. Modestine ate all that was left of the luncheon, and Aggie took a nap with her head on her suitcase. If we had not had the suitcases we should have been quite contented. Tish, with her customary ability, solved that.

"We need only one suitcase," she declared. "We can leave the other two at this farmhouse and pack a few things for each of us in the one we take along. Then we can take turns carrying it."

Aggie wakened finally and was rather more docile about the suitcases than we had expected. Possibly she would have been more indignant; but her feet had swollen so while she had her shoes off that she could hardly get them on at all, and for the remainder of the day her mind was, you may say, in her feet.

At four we stopped again and made more tea. The road had begun to rise toward the hills and the farmhouses were fewer. Ahead of us loomed Thunder Cloud Mountain, with the Camel's Back to the right of it. The road led up the valley between.

It was hardly a road at all, being a grass-grown wagontrack with not a house in a mile. Aggie was glad of the grass, for she had taken off her shoes by that time and was carrying them slung over her shoulder on the end of her parasol. We were on the lower slope of the mountain when we heard the green automobile.

It was coming rapidly from behind us. Aggie had just time to sit on a bank-and her feet-before it came in sight. It was a long, low, bright-green car and there were four men in it. They were bent forward, looking ahead, except one man who sat so he could see behind him.

They came on us rather suddenly, and the man who was looking back yelled to us as they passed, but what with noise and dust I couldn't make out what he said. The next moment the machine flew ahead and out of sight among the trees.

"What did he say?" I asked. Aggie, who has a tendency to hay-fever, was sneezing in the dust.

"I don't know," returned Tish absently, staring after them. "Probably asked us if we wanted a ride. Lizzie, those men had guns!"

"Fiddlesticks!" I said.

"Guns!" repeated Tish firmly.

"Well, what of it? Our donkey has a gun."

And as at that instant the sleeping-bags and provisions slid gently round under Modestine's stomach, the green automobile and its occupants passed out of our minds for a while.

By the time we had got the things on Modestine's back again we were convinced he had been a mistake. He objected to standing still to be reloaded, and even with Tish at his head and Aggie at his tail he kept turning in a circle, and in fact finally kicked out at Aggie and stretched her in the road. Then, too, his back was not flat like a horse's. It went up to a sort of peak, and was about as handy to pack things on as the ridge-pole of a roof.

For an hour or so more we plodded on. Tish, who is an enthusiast about anything she does, kept pointing out wild flowers to us and talking about the unfortunates back in town under roofs. But I kept thinking of a broiled lamb chop with new potatoes, and my whole being revolted at the thought of supper out of a can.

At twilight we found a sort of recess in the valley, level and not too thickly wooded, and while Tish and I set up the stove and lighted a fire Aggie spread out the sleeping-bags and got supper ready. We had canned salmon and potato salad. We ate ravenously and then, taking off our shoes and our walking suits, and getting into our flannel kimonos and putting up our crimps-for we were determined not to lapse into slovenly personal habits-we were ready for the night.

Tish said there were all sorts of animals on Thunder Cloud, so we built a large fire to keep them away. Tish said this was the customary thing, being done in all the adventure books she had read.

Aggie had to be helped into her sleeping-bag, her fur coat having been rather skimp. But, once in, she said it was heavenly, and she was asleep almost immediately. Tish and I followed, and I found I had placed my bag over a stone. I was, however, too tired to get up.

I lay and looked at the stars twinkling above the treetops, and I felt sorry for people who had nothing better to look at than a wall-papered ceiling. Tish, next to me, was yawning.

"If there are snakes," she observed drowsily, "they are not poisonous —I should think. And, anyhow, no snake could strike through these heavy bags."

She went to sleep at once, but I lay there thinking of snakes for some time. Also I remembered that we'd forgotten to leave our weapons within reach, although, as far as that goes, I should not have slept a wink had Aggie had her Fourth-of-July celebration near at hand. Then I went to sleep. The last thing I remember was wishing we had brought a dog. Even a box of cigars would have been some protection-we could have lighted one and stuck it in the crotch of a tree, as if a man was mounting guard over the camp. This idea, of course, was not original. It was done first by Mr. Sherlock Holmes, the detective.

It must have been toward dawn that I roused, with a feeling that some one was looking down at me. The fire was very low and Aggie was sleeping with her mouth open. I got up on my elbow and stared round. There was nothing in sight, but through the trees I heard a rustling of leaves and the crackling of brushwood. Whatever it was it had gone. I turned over and before long went to sleep again.

At daylight I was roused by raindrops splashing on my face. I sat up hastily. Aggie was sleeping with the flap of her bag over her head, and Tish, under an umbrella, was sitting fully dressed on a log, poring over her road map. When I sat up she glanced over at me.

"I think I know where we are now, Lizzie," she said. "Thunder Cloud Mountain is on our left, and that hill there to the right is the Camel's Back. The road goes right up Thunder Cloud Glen."

I looked at the fire, which was out; at Modestine, standing meekly by the tree to which he was tied; at the raindrops bounding off Aggie's round and prostrate figure-and I rebelled. Every muscle was sore; it hurt me even to yawn.

"Letitia Carberry!" I said indignantly. "You don't mean to tell me that, rain or no rain, you are going on?"

"Certainly I am going on," said Tish, shutting her jaw. "You and Aggie needn't come. I'm sure you asked yourselves; I didn't."

Well, that was true, of course. I crawled out and, going over, prodded at Aggie with my foot.

"Aggie," I said, "it is raining and Tish is going on anyhow. Will you go on with her or start back home with me?"

But Aggie refused to do either. She was terribly stiff and she had slept near a bed of May-apple blossoms. In the twilight she had not noticed them, and they always bring her hay-fever.

"I'b goi'g to stay right here," she said firmly between sneezes. "You cad go back or forward or whatever you please; I shad't bove."

Tish was marking out a route on the road map by making holes with a hairpin, and now she got up and faced us.

"Very well," she said. "Then get your things out of the suitcase, which happens to be mine. Lizzie, the canned beans and the sardines are yours. Aggie, your potato salad is in those six screw-top jars. Come, Modestine."

She untied the beast and, leading him over, loaded her sleeping-bag and her share of the provisions on his back. She did not glance at us. At the last, when she was ready, she picked up her rifle and turned to us.

"I may not be back for a week or ten days," she said icily. "If I'm longer than two weeks you can start Charlie Sands out with a posse."

Charlie Sands is her nephew.

"Come, Modestine," said Tish again, and started along. It was raining briskly by that time, and thundering as if a storm was coming. Aggie broke down suddenly.

"Tish! Tish!" she wailed. "Oh, Lizzie, she'll never get back alive. Never! We've killed her."

"She's about killed us!" I snarled.

"She's coming back!"

Sure enough, Tish had turned and was stalking back in our direction.

"I ought to leave you where you are," she said disagreeably, "but it's going to storm. If you decide to be sensible, somewhere up the valley is the cave Charlie Sands hid in when he ran away. I think I can find it."

It was thundering louder now, and Aggie was giving a squeal with every peal. We were too far gone for pride. I helped her out of her sleeping-bag and we started after Tish and the donkey. The rain poured down on us. At every step torrents from Thunder Cloud and the Camel's Back soaked us. The wind howled up the ravine and the lightning played round the treetops.

We traveled for three hours in that downpour.

III

Only once did Tish speak, and then we could hardly hear her above the rush of water and the roar of the wind.

"There's one comfort," she said, wading along knee-deep in a torrent. "These spring rains give nobody cold."

An hour later she spoke again, but that was at the end of that journey.

"I don't believe this is the right valley after all," she said. "I don't see any cave." We stopped to take our bearings, as you may say, and as we stood there, looking up, I could have sworn that I saw a man with a gun peering down at us from a ledge far above. But the next moment he was gone, and neither Tish nor Aggie had seen him at all.

We found the cave soon after and climbed to it on our hands and knees, pulling Modestine up by his bridle. A more outrageous quartet it would have been impossible to find, or a more outraged one. Aggie let down her dress, which she had pinned round her waist, releasing about a quart of water from its folds, and stood looking about her with a sneer. "I don't think much of your cave," she said. "It's little and it's dirty."

"It's dry!" said Tish tartly.

"Why stop at all?" Aggie asked sarcastically. "Why not just have kept on? We couldn't get any wetter."

"Yes," I added, "between flowering hedgerows! And of course these spring rains give nobody cold!"

Tish did not say a word. She took off her shoes and her skirt, got her sleeping-bag off Modestine's back, and went to bed with the worst attack of neuralgia she had ever had.

That was on Wednesday, late in the afternoon.

It rained for two days!

We built a fire out of the wood that was in the cave, and dried out our clothes, and heated stones to put against Tish's right eye, and brought in wet branches to dry against the time when we should need them. Aggie sneezed incessantly in the smoke, and Tish groaned in her corner. I was about crazy. On Thursday, when the edge of the neuralgia was gone, Tish promised to go home the moment the rain stopped and the roads dried. Aggie and I went to her together and implored her.

But, as it turned out, we did not go home for some days, and when we did — —

By Thursday evening Tish was much better. She ate a little potato salad and we sat round the fire, listening to her telling how they had found the runaways in this very cave.

"They had taken all the hatchets and kitchen knives they could find and started to hunt Indians," she was saying. "They got as far as this cave, and one evening about this time they were sitting round the fire like this when a black bear — —"

We all heard it at the same moment. Something was scrambling and climbing up the mountainside to the cave. Tish had her rifle to her shoulder in a second, and Aggie shut her eyes. But it was not a bear that appeared at the mouth of the cave and stood blinking in the light. It was a young man!

"I beg your pardon," he said, peering into the firelight, "but-you don't happen to have a spare box of matches, do you?"

Tish lowered the rifle.

"Matches!" she said. "Why-er-certainly. Aggie, give the gentleman some matches."

The young man had edged into the cave by that time and we saw that he was limping and leaning on a stick. He looked round the cave approvingly at our three sleeping-bags in an orderly row, with our toilet things set out on a clean towel on a flat stone and a mirror hung above, and at our lantern on another stone, with magazines and books grouped round it. Aggie, finding some trailing arbutus just outside the cave that day, had got two or three empty salmon cans about filled with it, and the fur rug from Tish's sleeping-bag lay in front of the fire. The effect was really civilized.

"It looks like a drawing room," said the young man, with a long breath. "It's the first dry spot I've seen for two days, and it looks like Heaven to a lost soul."

"Where are you stopping?"

"I am not stopping. I am on a walking tour, or was until I hurt my leg."

"Don't you think you'd better wait until things dry up?"

"And starve?" he asked.

"The woods are full of nuts and berries," said Tish.

"Not in May."

"And there is plenty of game."

"Yes, if one has a weapon," he replied. "I lost my gun when I fell into Thunder Creek; in fact, I lost everything except my good name. What's that thing of Shakespeare's: 'Who steals my purse steals trash, ...but he — —'"

Aggie found the matches just then and gave him a box. He was almost pathetically grateful. Tish was still staring at him. To find on Thunder Cloud Mountain a young man who quoted Shakespeare and had lost everything but his good name-even Stevenson could hardly have had a more unusual adventure.

"What are you going to do with the matches?" she demanded as he limped to the cave mouth.

"Light a fire if I can find any wood dry enough to light. If I can't — — Well, you remember the little match-seller in Hans Christian Andersen's story, who warmed her fingers with her own matches until they were all gone and she froze to death!"

Hans Christian Andersen and Shakespeare!

"Can't you find a cave?" asked Tish.

"I had a cave," he said, "but — —"

"But what?"

"Three charming women found it while I was out on the mountainside. They needed the shelter more than I, and so — —"

"What!" Tish exclaimed. "This is your cave?"

"Not at all; it is yours. The fact that I had been stopping in it gave me no right that I was not happy to waive."

"There was nothing of yours in it," Tish said suspiciously.

"As I have told you, I have lost everything but my good name and my sprained ankle. I had them both out with me when you ———"

"We will leave immediately," said Tish. "Aggie, bring Modestine."

"Ladies, ladies!" cried the young man. "Would you make me more wretched than I already am? I assure you, if you leave I shall not come back. I should be too unhappy."

Well, nothing could have been fairer than his attitude. He wished us to stay on. But as he limped a step or two into the night Aggie turned on us both in a fury.

"That's it," she said. "Let him go, of course. So long as you are dry and comfortable it doesn't matter about him."

"Well, you are dry and comfortable too," snapped Tish. "What do you expect us to do?"

"Call him back. Let him sleep here by the fire. Give him something to eat; he looks starved. If you're afraid it isn't proper we can hang our kimonos up for curtains and make him a separate room."

But we did not need to call him. He had limped back and stood in the firelight again.

"You-you haven't seen anything of the bandits, have you?" he asked.

"Bandits!"

"Train robbers. I thought you had probably run across them."

All at once we remembered the green automobile and the four men with guns. We told him about it and he nodded.

"That would be they," he said. As Tish remarked later, we knew from that instant that he was a gentleman. Even Charlie Sands would probably have said "them." "They got away very rapidly, and I dare say an automobile would be —— Did one of them have a red beard?"

"Yes," we told him. "The one who called to us."

Well, he said that on Monday night an express car on the C. & L. Railroad had been held up. The pursuit had gone in another direction, but he was convinced from what we said that they were there in Thunder Cloud Glen!

As Tish said, the situation was changed if there were outlaws about. We were three defenseless women, and here was a man brought providentially to us! She asked him at once to join our party and look after us until we got to civilization again, or at least until the roads were dry enough to travel on.

"To look after you!" he said with a smile. "I, with a bad leg and no weapon!"

At that Aggie brought out her new revolver and gave it to him. He whistled when he looked at it. "Great Scott!" he said. "What a weapon for a woman! Why, you don't need any help. You could kill all the outlaws in the county at one loading!"

But finally he consented to take the revolver and even to accept the shelter of the cave for that night anyhow, although we had to beg him to do that. "How do you know I'll not get up in the night and take all your valuables and gallop away on your trusty steed before morning?" he asked.

"We'll take a chance," Tish said dryly. "In the first place, we have nothing more valuable than the portable stove; and in the second place, if you can make Modestine gallop you may have him."

It is curious, when I look back, to think how completely he won us all. He was young-not more than twenty-six, I think-and dressed for a walking tour, in knickerbockers, with a blue flannel shirt, heavy low shoes and a soft hat. His hands were quite white. He kept running them over his chin, which was bluish, as if a day or two's beard was bothering him.

We asked him if he was hungry, and he admitted that he could hardly remember when he had eaten. So we made him some tea and buttered toast, and opened and heated a can of baked beans. He ate them all.

"Good gracious," he said, with the last spoonful, "what a world it would be without women!"

At that he fell into a sort of study, looking at the fire, and we all saw that he looked sad again and rather forlorn.

"Yes," Tish said, "you're all ready enough to shout 'Beware of woman' until you are hungry or uncomfortable or hurt, and then you are all just little boys again, crying for somebody to kiss the bump."

"But when it is a woman who has given the-er-bump?" he asked.

Aggie is romantic. Years ago she was engaged to a Mr. Wiggins, a roofer, who met with an accident due to an icy roof. She leaned forward and looked at him with sympathy.

"That's it, is it?" she asked gently.

He tried to smile, but we could all see that he was suffering.

"Yes, that's it-partly at least," he said.

"That is, if it were not for a woman — —" He stopped abruptly. "But why should I bother you with my troubles?"

We were curious, of course; but it is hardly good taste to ask a man to confide his heartaches. As Tish said, the best cure for a masculine heartache is to make the man comfortable. We did all we could. I dried his coat by the fire, and Tish made hot arnica compresses for his ankle, which was blue and swollen. I believe Aggie would gladly have sat by and held his hand, but he had crawled into his shell of reserve again and would not be coaxed out.

"I have a nephew about your age," Tish said when he objected to her bathing his ankle. "I'm doing for you what I should do for Charlie Sands under the same circumstances."

"Charlie Sands!" he said, and I was positive he started. But he said nothing, and we only remembered that later. We were glad to have a man about. Heaven only knows why women persist in regarding men as absolute protection against fire, burglars and lightning. But they do. A sharp storm came up at that time, and ordinarily Aggie would have been in her sleeping-bag, with Modestine's saddle on top by way of extra protection. But now, from sheer bravado, she went to the mouth of the cave and stood looking out at the lightning.

"Come and look at it, Tish!" she said.

"It's — — Good gracious! There's a man across the valley with a gun!"

We all ran to the mouth of the cave except the walking-tour gentleman, who had his foot in a collapsible basin of arnica and hot water. But none of us saw Aggie's man.

When we went back: "Wouldn't it be better to darken things up a bit?" he suggested. "If there are bandits round it isn't necessary to send out a welcome to them, you know."

This seemed only sensible. We put the fire out and sat in the warm darkness. And that was when our gentleman told us his story.

"Ladies," he began, "in saying that I am on a walking tour I am telling the truth, but only part of the truth. I am on a walking tour, but not for pleasure. To be frank, I —I am after the outlaws who robbed the express car on the C. & L. Railroad Monday night."

I heard Aggie gasp in the dark.

"Did you expect to capture them with a walking-stick?" Tish demanded. She might treat his ankle as she would treat Charlie Sands' ankle, but-Tish has not Aggie's confidence in people, or mine.

"Perfectly well taken," he said good-humoredly. "I left home with an entire arsenal in my knapsack, but, as I say, I lost everything when I fell into the flooded creek. Everything, that is, but my — —"

"Good name?" Aggie suggested timidly.

"Determination. That I still have. Ladies, I'm not going back empty-handed."

"Then you are in the Government service?" Tish asked with more respect.

"Have you ever heard of George Muldoon, generally known as Felt-hat Muldoon?"

Had we? Weren't the papers full of him week after week? Wasn't it Muldoon who had brought back the communion service to my church, with nothing missing and only a dent in one of the silver pitchers? Hadn't he just sent up Tish's own Italian fruit dealer for writing blackhand letters? Wasn't he the best sheriff the county had ever had?

"Muldoon!" gasped Tish. "You Muldoon!"

"Not tonight or for the next two or three days. After that — — Tonight, ladies, and for a day or two, why not adopt me to be your nephew-what was his name-Sands? —accompanying you on a walking tour?"

Adopt him! The great Muldoon! We'd have married him if he had said the word, name and all. We sat back and stared at him, open-mouthed. To think that he had come to us for help, and that in aiding him we were furthering the cause of justice!

He talked for quite a long time in the darkness, telling us of his adventures. He remembered perfectly about getting back the silver for the church, and about Tish's Italian, and then at last, finding us good listeners, he told about the girl.

"Is it-er-money?" Aggie breathlessly asked.

"Well-partly," he admitted. "I don't make much, of course."

"But with the rewards and all that?" asked Aggie, who'd been sitting forward with her mouth open.

"Rewards? Oh, well, of course I get something that way. But it isn't steady money. A chap can't very well go to a girl's father and tell him that, if somebody murders somebody else and escapes and he captures him, he can pay the rent and the grocery bill."

"Is she pretty?" asked Aggie.

"Beautiful!" His tone was ardent enough to please even Aggie.

He sat without speaking for a time, and none of us liked to interrupt him. Outside it had stopped raining, and the moon was coming up over the Camel's Back. We could hear Modestine stirring in the thicket and a watery ray of moonlight came into the cave and threw our shadows against the wall.

"If only," said Sheriff Muldoon thoughtfully —"If only I could get my hands on that chap with the red beard!"

We all went to bed soon after. Aggie, as usual, went to sleep at once, and soon, from, behind the kimono screen across the cave, loud noises told us that Mr. Muldoon also slept. It was then that Tish crept over and put her mouth to my ear.

"That may be Muldoon all right," she whispered. "But if it is he's got a wife and two children. Mrs. Muldoon is related to Hannah."

IV

Somehow, with the morning our suspicions, if we had any, vanished. Mr. Muldoon had been up at dawn, and when we wakened he had already brought water from a near-by spring and was boiling some in the teakettle.

Seen by daylight, he was very good-looking. He had blue eyes with black lashes and dark-brown hair, and a habit of getting up when any of us did that kept him on his feet most of the time. His limp was rather better-or his ankle.

"That's what a little mothering has done for me," he said gayly, over his coffee and mackerel. "It's a long time since I've had any one to do anything like that for me."

"But surely your wife — —" began Tish. He started and changed color. We all saw it.

"My wife!"

"You've got a wife and two children, haven't you?"

He looked at us all and drew a long breath.

"Ladies," he said, "I see some of my painful history is known to you. May I ask-is it too much to beg-that-that we do not discuss that part of my life?"

Tish apologized at once. We could not tell, from what he said, whether he had been divorced or had lost them all from scarlet fever. Whichever it was, I must say he was not depressed for very long, although he had reason enough for depression, as we soon learned.

"It's like this," he said. "They know I'm here in the glen-the outlaws, I mean. The red-bearded man, Naysmith, has sworn to get me."

"Get you?" from Aggie.

"Shoot me. The other three all owe me grudges, too, but Naysmith's the worst. He's just out of the pen —I got him a ten-year sentence for this very thing, robbing an express car."

"Ten years!" I exclaimed. "You look as if you hadn't shaved in ten years!"

He looked at me and smiled.

"I'm older than you think," he said, "and, anyhow, he got a lot off for good behavior. It's outrageous, the discount that's given to a criminal for behaving himself. He got —I think I am right when I say-yes, he was sent up in '07 —he got seven years off his sentence."

We all thought that this was a grave mistake, and Tish, whose father was once warden of the penitentiary, observed that there was nothing like that in old times, and she would write to the governor about it. Tish has written to the governor several times, the last occasion being the rise in price of brooms.

"It's like this," said Mr. Muldoon. "They've got the glen guarded. There's a man at each end and the rest are covering the hilltops. A squirrel couldn't get out without their knowledge. I might have before I got this leg, but now I'm done for."

"Oh, no!" we chorused.

"It amounts to that," he said dejectedly. "They've been watching you women and they're not afraid of you. As long as I stay in the cave here I'm safe enough, but let me poke my nose out and I'm gone. It's an awful thing to have to hide behind a woman's petticoats!"

We could only silently sympathize.

It was bright and clear that day. The sun came out and dried the road below. It would have been a wonderful day to go on, but none of us thought of it. As Tish said, here was a chance to assist the law and a fellow being in peril of his life. Our place was there.

Even had we doubted Mr. Muldoon's story, we had proof of it before noon. A man with a gun came out on a ledge of rock across the valley and stood, with his hands to his eyes, peering across at our cave. Tish was hanging some of our clothing out to dry, and although she saw the outlaw as well as we did she did not flinch. After a time the man seemed satisfied and disappeared.

Tish came into the cave then and took a spoonful of blackberry cordial. As we knew, her intrepid spirit had not quailed; but, as she said, one's body is never as strong as one's soul. Her knees were shaking.

We put in a quiet and restful afternoon. Mr. Muldoon had a pack of cards with him and we played whist. He played a very fair game, but he was on the alert all the time. At every sound he started, and once or twice he slipped out into the thicket and searched the glen in every direction with his eyes.

He had asked us, if the outlaws surprised us, to say that he was Tish's nephew, Charlie Sands, and to stick to it. "Unless it's Naysmith," he said. "He knows me." From that to calling us Aunt Tish, Aunt Aggie and Aunt Lizzie was very easy. At four o'clock we stopped playing, with Mr. Muldoon easily the winner, and Aggie made fudge for everybody.

Late in the afternoon Tish called me aside. She said she did not want Mr. Muldoon to feel that he was a burden, but that we were almost out of provisions. We had expected to buy eggs, milk and bread at farmhouses, and instead we had been shut up in the cave. She thought there was a farm up the glen, having heard a cow-bell, and she wanted me to go and find out.

"Go yourself!" I said somewhat rudely. "If you want to be shot down in your tracks by outlaws, well and good. I don't."

Aggie, called aside, refused as firmly as I had. Tish stood and looked at us both with her lip curling.

"Very well," she said coldly; "I shall go. But if I get my neuralgia again from wading through the creek bottom don't blame me!"

She put on her overshoes and, taking a tin bucket for milk and her trusty rifle, she started while Mr. Muldoon was showing Aggie a new game of solitaire. I went to the cave mouth with her and listened to the crackling of twigs as she slid down into the valley. She came into view at the bottom much sooner than I had expected, having, as I learned later, slipped on a loose stone and rolled fully half the way down.

The next two hours seemed endless. Mr. Muldoon, tiring of solitaire, had rolled himself up in a corner and was peacefully sleeping, with his injured foot on Aggie's hop pillow. Aggie and I sat on guard, one on each side of the cave mouth, and stared down at the valley, which was darkening rapidly.

Tish had been gone two hours and a half and no sign of her, when Aggie began to cry softly.

"She'll never come back!" she whimpered. "The outlaws have got her and killed her. Oh, Tish, Tish!"

"Why would they kill her?" I demanded. "Because she's trying to buy milk and eggs?"

"B-because she knows too much," Aggie wailed. "We've found their lair, that's why-don't tell me this isn't an outlaw's cave. It's just b-built for it. They'll do away with her and then they'll come after us."

Aggie never carries a secret weight in her bosom. She always opens up her heart to the nearest listener. This probably relieves Aggie, but it does not make her a cheerful companion. Eight o'clock and darkness came, and still no Tish. I went into the cave and brought out my gun, and Aggie roused Mr. Muldoon and explained the situation to him. He grew quite white.

"Good heavens!" he exclaimed. "What possessed her anyhow? To the farmhouse! Why, they'll — —"

His face more than his words convinced us that the matter was really serious. He examined Aggie's revolver, which he mostly carried in his hip pocket, and, going to the mouth of the cave, listened carefully. Everything was quiet. The cave and both sides of the valley were in deep shadow, but over the ridge of the Camel's Back across from us there was still a streak of red sunset light. Mr. Muldoon looked and pointed.

Against the background of crimson cloud a man's figure stood out clearly. He was peering down toward us, although in the dusk he could hardly have seen us, and he carried a gun. Mr. Muldoon smiled faintly.

"Well, they've spotted me, I guess," he said. "I'd better move on before I get you into trouble. They won't hurt women."

"Why don't you shoot him?" Aggie asked. "It would be one bandit less. If you do arrest him, and he gets nearly all his sentence off for good behavior, he'll be out again in no time, doing more mischief."

But at that moment we saw the man on the hill throw his gun to his shoulder and aim at something moving below in the valley. Aggie screamed, and I believe I did also.

"Tish!" cried Aggie. "He's shooting at Tish!" And at that instant the bandit fired. He fired three times, and the noise of his gun echoed backward and forward among the hills. We thought we heard a yell from, the valley. Then the next second there was a faint crack from below and the outlaw's gun flew out of his hands. Mr. Muldoon's jaw dropped. "Did you see that?" he said feebly. "Did-you-see-that-shot?"

The outlaw disappeared from the skyline and perhaps ten minutes later Tish crawled up to the cave and put down a tin pail full of milk, a glass of jelly wrapped in a newspaper, and a basket of eggs. Aggie fell on her and cried with joy.

"Be careful of those eggs," Tish warned her. "That outlaw charged me forty cents a dozen."

"You gave him a good fright anyhow," said Aggie fondly.

"Fright?"

"When you shot at him."

"Oh, that one! I'm talking about the woman at the farm."

"And-the one on the hill over there?"

"Oh! Well, he fired at me and I fired back. That's all."

With an air of exaggerated indifference Tish swaggered into the cave and took off her over-shoes.

"Hurry up supper, Ag," she said-never before or since has she called Aggie "Ag" —"I'm starving."

She said she had heard little or nothing. She had found the farmhouse, had bought her supplies from a surly woman and had come away again. Asked by Mr. Muldoon if she had seen any men, she said she had seen a farmhand milking. That was all, except the outlaw on the hill.

But under her calmness Tish was terribly excited. I could tell it by her glittering eyes and the red spot in each cheek. Manlike, Mr. Muldoon did not see these signs; he ate very little and sat watching her, fascinated. Only once, however, did he broach the subject.

"I had no idea you were such a shot, Miss Letitia," he said. "It-that was a marvel."

"Oh, I shoot a little," said Tish coolly. "Only for my own amusement, of course."

Mr. Muldoon made no reply. He was very thoughtful all evening, did not care to play whist, and watched Tish whenever he could, furtively.

Tish herself was in an exalted mood, but not about the shot-she was modest enough about that.

And with cause. Months after she told us how it happened. She said she was carrying the eggs and milk with her left hand and had the gun in her right, when a shot struck a tree beside her. She was so startled that her finger pulled the trigger of her own rifle, which was pointed up, with the result we know of. She would probably never have confessed even then, had she not taken rheumatic fever and thought she was dying.

When Mr. Muldoon went out to fix Modestine for the night Tish called us to the back of the cave.

"I bought the milk and eggs," she said hurriedly, "and having a dime left-your missionary dime, Aggie, I borrowed it —I went back and bought a glass of jelly. Men like preserves. The woman wrapped it in a newspaper, and there is a full account of the robbery and of Muldoon being after the outlaws. He's after the outlaws, but he's after the reward too. They're quoted at a thousand dollars!"

"He can have the thousand dollars for all of me," said Aggie.

"A thousand dollars!" said Tish. "A thousand dollars to hand in to the church as the return from your missionary dime! And if we don't get it Muldoon will! As soon as he can get about on his leg he'll cease being hunted and begin to hunt. Why should he have it? He has plenty of chances, and we'll never have another."

That was all she had a chance to say, Muldoon joining us at that moment.

We retired early, but I did not sleep well. I wakened from time to time and I could hear Tish stirring next to me. At last I reached over and touched her.

"Can't you sleep?" I whispered.

"Don't want to," she whispered back. "I've got it all fixed, Lizzie. We'll take those outlaws back to the city, roped two by two."

It was a cool spring night, but I broke into a hot perspiration.

V

Tish began with Mr. Muldoon the next morning. He could not leave the cave to carry up water, for daylight revealed another guard across the valley and it was clear we were being watched. While Aggie and I went to the spring Tish talked to him.

She told him that he had undertaken too much, single-handed, and that he should have brought a posse with him. He agreed with her. He said he had started with a posse, but that they had split up. Also he insisted that but for his accident he could have managed easily.

"I'm up against it," he said, "and I know it. They'll get me yet. For the last day or two they've been closing up round this cave, and in a night or two they'll rush it. They've got their headquarters at that farmhouse."

"The thing for you to do then," said Tish, "is to get out while there is time. You can get help and come back."

"And leave you women here alone?"

"They're not after us," Tish replied, "and we've managed alone for a good many years. I guess we'll get along."

But when she proposed her plan, which was that he should put on Aggie's spare outfit and her sun veil and ride out of the valley on Modestine's back in daylight, he objected. He said no outlaw worthy of the name would fall for a thing like that, and he said he wouldn't wear skirts, and that was all there was to it.

But in the end Tish prevailed, as usual.

"I'm going to the farmhouse this morning and I am going to say that one of the ladies is leaving this afternoon and going back home. That will be you. I wish you had a razor, but the veil will hide that. They'll not molest you. You'll not only look like Aggie-you'll be Aggie."

Well, it seemed to be his best chance, although none of us dared to think what might happen if the hat blew off or Aggie's gray alpaca ripped at the seams.

We worked feverishly all day, letting out the dress and setting forward the buttons on her raincoat. Mr. Muldoon was inclined to be sulky. He sat at the back of the cave, playing solitaire and every now and then examining the road maps. Aggie was depressed too. But, as Tish said, getting rid of Muldoon was the first step toward the thousand dollars, and even if Aggie never got her gray alpaca again it had seen its best days.

That morning, while Aggie and I sewed and ripped and Mr. Muldoon sat back in the cave with the road map on his knees, Tish went to the farmhouse. She came back at eleven o'clock with a chicken for dinner and a flush on each cheek.

"I've fixed it, Mr. Muldoon," she said. "I talked to one of the outlaws!"

"What?" screeched Aggie.

"He'd come in for something to eat-the red-bearded one. We had quite a chat. I told him we were traveling like Stevenson-with a donkey; but that one of the ladies had an abscess on a tooth and was going home. He said it was no place for women and offered himself as an escort."

Mr. Muldoon groaned. "What am I going to do if one of them comes up and makes an ass of himself?" he demanded. "Kiss him?"

Tish looked at him coldly.

"You'll have your jaw tied up," she said. "That will cover your chin, and you needn't speak. Point to your jaw. Anyhow, they'll not bother you. I said the toothache had affected your disposition, and we were just as glad you were going. The red-haired man says he's got relatives near the mouth of the valley and you can stay there overnight. One of the men folks pulls teeth in emergencies."

It is hard, writing all this of Tish, to remember that she has always been a truthful woman. As Charlie Sands said later, when we told him the story and he had sat, open-mouthed, staring from one to the other of us, no one knows what depths of mendacity lie behind the most virtuous countenance.

We started "Aggie" off at two o'clock that afternoon, sitting sideways on Modestine, jaw tied up, veiled and sun-hatted, with Aggie's flowered-silk bag hanging to one wrist and a lunch-basket on the other arm. Tish and I saw "her" down the hill and kissed "her" good-by.

This was Tish's idea. I thought it unnecessary, but as a matter of fact, no matter what Charlie Sands may say, it was not a real kiss, going as it did through a veil and a bandage.

The man with a gun watched "her" off, and Tish, having waved "her" out of sight round a curve, looked up at him and nodded. Far away as he was, he saw that and swept his hat off with quite an air.

Tish's plan was very simple. She told us as we cleared up the cave after the day's excitement.

"When I go for the evening milk," she said, "I shall mention that we have a young man with us, a stranger, who has hurt his ankle and cannot walk. And I'll ask for arnica. That's all."

"That's all!" Aggie and I exclaimed together.

"Certainly that's all. Sometime tonight they'll rush the cave."

"You're a fool!" said Aggie shortly.

"Why?" demanded Tish. "We won't be in it. We'll be outside. The moment they are in we'll start to shoot. Not one of them will dare to stick his nose out."

When we told this to Charlie Sands he slid entirely off his chair and sat on the floor. "Not really!" he kept saying over and over. "You dreamed it! You must have! A thing like that!" I hastened to explain. "Tish planned it," I said. I remember him, looking at Tish-who was crocheting as she told the story-and moistening his lips. He was quite green in color.

VI

Clipping from the *Morning News* of May the seventh:

SHERIFF AMBUSHED

Remarkable Experience of Muldoon and Party in Thunder Cloud Glen

An extraordinary state of affairs was discovered by the relief party of constables, city and county detectives and state constabulary sent to the relief of Sheriff Muldoon and his posse, who have been on the track of the C. & L. train bandits since last Monday.

The relief party was sent out in response to a telephone message from a farmhouse in Thunder Cloud Glen, and transmitted from the farmer's line to a long-distance wire. This message was to the effect that the sheriff and his posse, shut in a cave, were being held prisoners by the outlaws, being shot at steadily, and that so far every attempt at escape had been thwarted by the terrific fire of the bandits.

A relief party in automobiles was rushed at once to the scene.

Thunder Cloud Glen is a narrow valley between the Camel's Back and Thunder Cloud Mountain. A mile or so from the entrance to the glen the road, always bad and now almost washed away by the recent heavy rains, became impassable. The party abandoned the machines and in skirmish order proceeded up the glen.

Within an hour's time firing was heard, and the rescuers doubled their pace. Passing a bend in the valley, the scene of the outrage lay spread before them: On the left the low mouth of a cave, and across the valley, on a slope of the Camel's Back, a faint cloud of smoke, showing where the outlaws had their lair. As the rescuers came in sight the firing ceased and an ominous stillness hung over the valley.

The relief expedition had been seen by the imprisoned party also. Muldoon's well-known soft felt hat, tied to the end of a pole, was thrust from the cave mouth and waved vigorously up and down, showing that some of the imprisoned party still lived. One solitary shot was aimed at the hat, followed by profound quiet.

Using every precaution, Deputy Sheriff Mulcahy deployed his men with the intention of closing in on the outlaws from, all sides at the same time.

At this time an interesting interruption occurred. From the underbrush at the foot of the Camel's Back emerged three elderly women, their clothing in tatters, and in the wildest excitement. They insisted that the outlaws were in the cave, and hysterical with fright from their terrible experience, declared that they had been holding the bandits in check and demanded the reward for their capture. They were rational enough in other ways and explained that they had been on a walking tour with a donkey. There was, however, no donkey.

Deputy Sheriff Mulcahy, who is noted for his gallantry, sent the three women to a safe place at the rear of the party and detailed a guard to make them, comfortable. It being thought possible that the women were accomplices of the outlaws, precautions were also taken to prevent their escape.

No trace of the outlaws was found. Sheriff Muldoon and his three deputies, now enabled to leave the cave, joined the searchers. Every inch of Thunder Cloud Glen was searched, but without result. Across from the cave mouth, behind a heap of fallen rocks, was found the spot from which the outlaws had been shooting. The ground was trampled and the rock chipped by the return fire from the cave. Here, too, was found a new automatic revolver, a small rifle and another gun of antique pattern. In a crevice of rock was discovered a flowered-silk bag, containing various articles of feminine use, including a packet of powders marked "hay-fever," a small bottle labeled "blackberry cordial," and a dozen or so unexploded cartridges for the revolver.

Convinced now that the three women were accomplices of the outlaws-and this corroborated by Sheriff Muldoon's statement that he had positively seen one of the three women peering over the rock and aiming a rifle at him, and that the same woman, two days before, had fired at him from the valley, knocking his gun out of his hand-Deputy Sheriff Mulcahy promptly arrested the women and had them taken in an automobile to the city.

At the jail, however, it was discovered that an unfortunate error had been made, and the ladies were released. They went at once to their homes. While their names have not been divulged it is reported that they are well known and highly esteemed members of the community, and much sympathy has been expressed for their disagreeable experience.

Up to a late hour last night no trace had been found of the outlaws. It is believed that they have left Thunder Cloud Glen and have penetrated farther into the mountains.

Charlie Sands came for us at the jail. He asked us no questions, which I thought strange, but he got a carriage and took us all to Tish's. He did not speak a word on the way, except to ask us if we had no hats. On Tish's replying meekly that we had left them in the cave, he said nothing more, but sat looking like a storm until we drew up at the house.

I dare say we did look curious. Our clothes were torn and draggled, and although we had washed at the jail we were still somewhat powder-streaked and grimy.

Charlie Sands led us into Tish's parlor and shut the door. Then he turned and surveyed the three of us.

"Sit down," he said grimly.

We sat. He stood looking down at each of us in turn.

"I'll hear the story in a minute," he said, still cold and disagreeable. "But first of all, Aunt Tish, I want to ask you if you realize that this last escapade of yours is a disgrace to the family?"

"Nothing of the sort," Tish asserted with something of her old spirit. "It was all for Aggie's missionary dime. I———"

"A moment," he said, holding up his hand. "I'm going to ask a question. I'll listen after that. *Did you or did you not hold up the C. & L. express car?*"

We were too astounded to speak.

"Because if you did," he said, "missionary dime or no missionary dime, I shall turn you over to the authorities! I have gone through a lot with you, Aunt Tish, in the past year."

Aggie and I expected to see Tish rise in majesty and point him out of the room. But to our amazement she broke down and cried.

"No," she said feebly, "we didn't rob the car. But oh, Charlie, Charlie! We nursed that wretch Muldoon, and fed him and sent him off on Modestine in Aggie's gray alpaca, and he got away; and if you say to go to jail I'll go."

"Muldoon!"

"The wretch who said he was Muldoon. The-the train robber."

Well, it took hours to tell the story, and when we had all finished and Aggie had gone to bed in Tish's spare room with hysteria, and Tish had gone to bed with tea and toast, Charlie Sands was still walking up and down the parlor, stopping now and then to mutter: "Well, I'll be — —" and then going on with his pacing.

Hannah brought me a cup of junket at eight o'clock, for none of us had eaten dinner. I was sitting there with the cup in my lap when the doorbell rang. Charlie Sands answered it. It was a letter addressed to all three of us.

We called Tish and Aggie and they crept in, very subdued and pallid. Charlie Sands opened the letter and read it:

> *Dear and Charming Ladies:* I am abject. What can I say to you, who have just come through such an experience on my account? How can I apologize or explain? Especially as I am confused myself as to what really happened. Did Muldoon actually attack the cave? Were you in it when he arrived? Or is it possible that, with my foolish fabrication in your mind, you attempted — — But that is absurd, of course.
>
> Whatever occurred and however it occurred, I am on my knees to you all. Even a real bandit would have been touched by your kindness. And I am not a real bandit any more than I am a real sheriff.
>
> I am, an ordinary citizen, usually a law-abiding citizen. But as a result of a foolish wager at my club, brought about by the ease with which numerous trains have been robbed recently, I undertook to hold up a C. & L. train with an empty revolver, and to evade capture for a certain length of time. The first part was successful. The train messenger, on seeing my gun, handed me, without a word, a fat package. I had not asked for it. It was a gift. I do not even now know what is in it. The newspapers say it is money. It might have been eggs, as far as I know. The second part would have been simple also, had I not hurt my leg.
>
> Things were looking serious for me when you found me. I shall never forget the cave, or the omelets, or the tea, or the fudge. I can never return your hospitalities, but one thing I can do.
>
> The express company offers a reward of a thousand dollars for my little package. Probably they are right and it is not eggs. Whatever it is, it is buried under the tree where we tied our noble steed, Modestine. Please return the package and claim the reward. If you have scruples against taking it remember that the express company is rich and the Fiji Islanders needy. Turn it in as the increased increment on Miss Aggie's missionary dime.
>
> (Signed)
>
> The Outlaw of Thunder Cloud.

We found the package, or Charlie Sands found it for us, and the express company paid us the reward. We gave it to Aggie, and with the exception of fifty dollars she turned it all in at the church, where it created almost a riot. With the fifty dollars we purchased, through Charlie Sands, a revolver with a silver inlaid handle, and sent it to the real Sheriff Muldoon. It eased our consciences somewhat.

That was all last spring. It is summer now. Tish is talking again of flowering hedgerows and country lanes, but Aggie and I do not care for the country, and the mere sight of a donkey gives me a chill.

Yesterday evening, on our way to prayer meeting, we heard a great noise of horns coming and stopped to see a four-in-hand go by. A young gentleman was driving, with a pretty girl beside him. As we lined up at the curb he turned smiling from the girl and he caught our eyes.

He started, and then, bowing low, he saluted us from the box.

It was "Muldoon."

Tish Does Her Bit

From the very beginning of the war Tish was determined to go to France. But she is a truthful woman, and her age kept her from being accepted. She refused, however, to believe that this was the reason, and blamed her rejection on Aggie and myself.

"Age fiddlesticks!" she said, knitting violently. "The plain truth is-and you might as well acknowledge it, Lizzie-that they would take me by myself quick enough, just to get the ambulance I've offered, if for no other reason. But they don't want three middle-aged women, and I don't know that I blame them."

That was during September, I think, and Tish had just received her third rejection. They were willing enough to take the ambulance, but they would not let Tish drive it. I am quite sure it was September, for I remember that Aggie was having hay fever at the time, and she fell to sneezing violently.

Tish put down her knitting and stared at Aggie fixedly until the paroxysm was over.

"Exactly," she observed, coldly. "Imagine me creeping out onto a battlefield to gather up the wounded, and Aggie crawling behind, going off like an alarm clock every time she met a clump of golden rod, or whatever they have in France to produce hay fever."

"I could stay in the ambulance, Tish," Aggie protested.

"I understand," Tish went on, in an inflexible tone, "that those German snipers have got so that they shoot by ear. One sneeze would probably be fatal. Not only that," she went on, turning to me, "but you know perfectly well, Lizzie, that a woman of your weight would be always stepping on brush and sounding like a night attack."

"Not at all," I replied, slightly ruffled. "And for a very good reason. I should not be there. As to my weight, Tish, my mother was always considered merely a fine figure of a woman, and I am just her size. It is only since this rage for skinny women — —"

But Tish was not listening. She drew a deep sigh, and picked up her knitting again.

"We'd better not discuss it," she said. But in these days of efficiency it seems a mistake that a woman who can drive an ambulance and can't turn the heel of a stocking properly to save her life, should be knitting socks that any soldier with sense would use to clean his gun with, or to tie around a sore throat, but never to wear.

It was, I think, along in November that Charlie Sands, Tish's nephew, came to see me. He had telephoned, and asked me to have Aggie there. So I called her up, and told her to buy some cigarettes on the way. I remember that she was very irritated when she arrived, although the very soul of gentleness usually.

She came in and slammed a small package onto my table.

"There!" she said. "And don't ever ask me to do such a thing again. The man in the shop winked at me when I said they were not for myself."

However, Aggie is never angry for any length of time, and a moment later she was remarking that Mr. Wiggins had always been a smoker, and that one of his workmen had blamed his fatal accident on the roof to smoke from his pipe getting into his eyes.

Shortly after that I was surprised to find her in tears.

"I was just thinking, Lizzie," she said. "What if Mr. Wiggins had lived, and we had had a son, and he had decided to go and fight!"

She then broke down and sobbed violently, and it was some time before I could calm her. Even then it was not the fact that she had no son which calmed her.

"Of course I'm silly, Lizzie," she said. "I'll stop now. Because of course they don't *all* get killed, or even wounded. He'd probably come out all right, and every one says the training is fine for them."

Charlie Sands came in shortly after, and having kissed us both and tried on a night shirt I was making for the Red Cross, and having found the cookie jar in the pantry and brought it into my sitting room, sat down and came to business.

"Now," he said. "What's she up to?"

He always referred to Tish as "she," to Aggie and myself.

"She has given up going to France," I replied.

"Perhaps! What does Hannah report?"

I am sorry to say that, fearing Tish's impulsive nature, we had felt obliged to have Hannah watch her carefully. Tish has a way of breaking out in unexpected places, like a boil, as Charlie Sands once observed, and by knowing her plans in advance we have sometimes prevented her acting in a rash manner. Sometimes, not always.

"Hannah says everything is quiet," Aggie said. "Dear Tish has apparently given up all thought of going abroad. At least, Hannah says she no longer practises first aid on her. Not since the time Tish gave her an alcohol bath and she caught cold. Hannah says she made her lie uncovered, with the window open, so the alcohol would evaporate. But she gave notice the next day, which was ungrateful of her, for Tish sat up all night feeding her things out of her First Aid case, and if she *did* give her a bit of iodine by mistake — —"

"She is no longer interested in First Aid," I broke in. Aggie has a way of going on and on, and it was not necessary to mention the matter of the iodine. "I know that, because I blistered my hand over there the other day, and she merely told me to stick it in the baking soda jar."

"That's curious," said Charlie Sands.

"Because — — Great Scott, what's wrong with these cigarettes?"

"They are violet-scented," Aggie explained. "The smell sticks so, and Lizzie is fond of violet."

However, he did not seem to care for them, and appeared positively ashamed. He opened a window, although it was cold outside, and shook himself in front of it like a dog. But all he said was:

"I am a meek person, Aunt Lizzie, and I like to humor whims when I can. But the next time you have a male visitor and offer him a cigarette, for the love of Mike don't tell him those brazen gilt-tipped incense things are mine."

He then ate nine cookies, and explained why he had come.

"I don't like the look of things, beloved and respected spinsters," he said. "I fear my revered aunt is again up to mischief. You haven't heard her say anything more about aeroplanes, have you?"

"No," I replied, for us both.

"Or submarines?"

"She's been taking swimming lessons again," I said, thoughtfully.

"Lizzie!" Aggie cried. "Oh, my poor Tish!"

"I think, however," said Charlie Sands, "that it is not a submarine. There are no submarine flivvers, as I understand it, and a full-size one would run into money. No, I hardly think so. The fact remains, however, that my respected and revered aunt has made away with about seven thousand dollars' worth of bonds that were, until a short time ago, giving semi-annual birth to plump little coupons. The question is, what is she up to?"

But we were unable to help him, and at last he went away. His parting words were:

"Well, there is something in the air, and the only thing to do, I suppose, is to wait until it drops. But when my beloved female relative takes to selling bonds without consulting me, and goes out, as I met her yesterday, with her hat on front side behind, there is something in the wind. I know the symptoms."

Aggie and I kept a close watch on Tish after that, but without result, unless the following incident may be called a result. Although it was rather a cause, after all, for it brought Mr. Culver into our lives.

I think it important to relate it in detail, as in a way it vindicates Tish in her treatment of Mr. Culver, although I do not mean by this statement that there was anything of personal malice in the incident of June fifth of this year. Those of us who know Tish best realize that she needs no defence. Her motives are always of the highest, although perhaps the matter of the police officer was ill-advised. But now that the story is out, and Mr. Ostermaier very uneasy about the wrong name being on the marriage license, I think an explanation will do dear Tish no harm.

I should explain, then, that Tish has retained the old homestead in the country, renting it to a reliable family. And that it has been our annual custom to go there for chestnuts each autumn. On the Sunday following Charlie Sands' visit, therefore, while Aggie and I were having dinner with Tish, I suggested that we make our annual pilgrimage the following day.

"What pilgrimage?" Tish demanded. She was at that time interested in seeing if a table could be set for thirty-five cents a day per person, and the meal was largely beans.

"For chestnuts," I explained.

"I don't think I'll go this year," Tish observed, not looking at either of us. "I'm not a young woman, and climbing a chestnut tree requires youth."

"You could get the farmer's boy," Aggie suggested, hopefully. Aggie is a creature of habit, and clings hard to the past.

"The farmer is not there any more."

We stared at her in amazement, but she was helping herself to boiled dandelion at the time, and made no further explanation.

"Why, Tish!" Aggie exclaimed.

"Aggie," she observed, severely, "if you would only remember that the world is hungry, you would eat your crusts."

"I ate crusts for twenty years," said Aggie, "because I'd been raised to believe they would make my hair curl. But I've come to a time of life when my digestion means more to me than my looks. And since I've had the trouble with my teeth — —"

"Teeth or no teeth," said Tish, firmly, "eating crusts is a patriotic duty, Aggie."

She was clearly disinclined to explain about the farm, but on being pressed said she had sent the tenants away because they kept pigs, which was absurd and she knew it.

"Isn't keeping pigs a patriotic duty?" Aggie demanded, glancing at me across the table. But Tish ignored the question.

"What about the church?" I asked.

Tish has always given the farm money to missions, and is therefore Honorary President of the Missionary Society. She did not reply immediately as she was pouring milk over her cornstarch at the time, but Hannah, her maid, spoke up rather bitterly.

"If we give the heathen what we save on the table, Miss Lizzie," she said, "I guess they'll do pretty well. I'm that fed up with beans that my digestion is all upset. I have to take baking soda after my meals, regular."

Tish looked up at her sharply.

"Entire armies fight on beans," she said

"Yes'm," said Hannah. "I'd fight on 'em too. That's the way they make me feel. And if a German bayonet is any worse than the colic I get — —"

"Leave the room," said Tish, in a furious voice, and finished her cornstarch in silence.

But she is a just woman, and although firm in her manner, she is naturally kind. After dinner, seeing that Aggie was genuinely disappointed about the excursion to the farm, she relented and observed that we would go to the farm as usual.

"After all," she said, "chestnuts are nourishing, and might take the place of potatoes in a pinch."

Here we heard a hollow groan from the pantry, but on Tish demanding its reason Hannah said, meekly enough, that she had knocked her crazy bone, and Tish, with her usual magnanimity, did not pursue the subject.

There was a heavy frost that night, and two days later Tish called me up and fixed the following day for the visit to the farm. On looking back, I am inclined to think that her usual enthusiasm was absent, but we suspected nothing. She said that Hannah would put up the luncheon, and that she had looked up the food value of chestnuts and that it was enormous. She particularly requested that Aggie should not bake a cake for the picnic, as has been her custom.

"Cakes," she said, "are a reckless extravagance. In butter, eggs and flour a single chocolate layer cake could support three men at the front for two days, Lizzie," she said.

I repeated this to Aggie, and she was rather resentful. Aggie, I regret to say, has rather a weakness for good food.

"Humph!" she said, bitterly. "Very well, Lizzie. But if she expects me to go out like Balaam's ass and eat dandelions, I'd rather starve."

Neither Aggie nor I is inclined to be suspicious, and although we noticed Tish's rather abstracted expression that morning, we laid it to the fact that Charlie Sands had been talking about going to the American Ambulance in France, which Tish opposed violently, although she was more than anxious to go herself.

Aggie put in her knitting bag the bottle of blackberry cordial without which we rarely travel, as we find it excellent in case of chilling, or indigestion, and even to rub on hornet stings. I was placing the suitcase, in which it is our custom to carry the chestnuts, in the back of the car, when I spied a very small parcel. Aggie saw it too.

"If that's the lunch, Tish," she said, "I don't know that I care to go."

"You can eat chestnuts," said Tish, shortly. "But don't go on my account. It looks like rain anyhow, and the last time I went to the farm in the mud I skidded down a hill backwards and was only stopped by running into a cow that thought I was going the other way."

"Nonsense, Tish," I said. "It hasn't an idea of raining. And if the lunch isn't sufficient, there are generally some hens from the Knowles place that lay in your barn, aren't there?"

"Certainly not," she said stiffly, although it wasn't three months since she had threatened to charge the Knowleses rent for their chickens.

Well, I was puzzled. It is not like Tish to be irritable without reason, although she has undoubtedly a temper. She was most unpleasant on the way out, remarking that if the Ostermaiers's maid continued to pare away half the potatoes, as any fool could see around their garbage can, she thought the church should reduce his salary. She also stated flatly that she considered that the nation would be better off if some one would uncork a gas bomb in the Capitol at Washington, in spite of the fact that my second cousin, once removed, the Honorable J. C. Willoughby, represents his country in its legislative halls.

It is always a bad sign when Tish talks politics, especially since the income tax.

Although it had no significance for us at the time, she did not put her car in the barn as she usually does, but left it in the road. The house was closed, and there was no cool and refreshing buttermilk with which to wash down our frugal repast, which we ate on the porch, as Tish did not offer to unlock the house. Frugal repast it was indeed, consisting of lettuce sandwiches made without butter, as Tish considered that both butter and lettuce was an extravagance. There were, of course, also beans.

Now as it happens, Aggie is not strong and requires palatable as well as substantial food to enable her to get about, especially to climb trees. We missed her during the meal, and I saw that she was going toward the barn. Tish saw it also, and called to her sharply.

"I am going to get an egg," Aggie replied, with gentle obstinacy. "I am starving, Tish, and I am certain I heard a hen cackle. Probably one of the Knowles's chickens ——"

"If it is a Knowles's chicken," Tish said, virtuously, "its egg is a Knowles's egg, and we have no right to it."

I am sorry to relate that here Aggie said: "Oh, rats!" but as she apologized immediately, and let the egg drop, figuratively, of course, peace again hovered over our little party. Only momentarily, however, for, a short time after, a hen undoubtedly cackled, and Aggie got up with an air of determination.

"Tish," she said, "that may be a Knowles's hen or it may be one belonging to this farm. I don't know, and I don't give a —I don't care. I'm going to get it."

"The barn's locked," said Tish.

"I could get in through a window."

I shall never forget Tish's look of scorn as she rose with dignity, and stalked toward the barn.

"I shall go myself, Aggie," she said, as she passed her. "You would probably fall in the rain barrel under the window. You're no climber. And you might as well eat those crusts you've hidden under the porch, if you're as hungry as you make out you are."

"Lizzie," Aggie hissed, when Tish was out of hearing, *what is in that barn?*"

"It may be anything from a German spy to an aeroplane," I said. "But it's not your business or mine."

"You needn't be so dratted virtuous," Aggie observed, scooping a hole in the petunia bed and burying the crusts in it. "Whatever's on her mind is in that barn."

"Naturally," I observed. "While Tish is in it!"

Tish returned in a short time with one egg, which she placed on the porch floor without a word. But as she made no effort to give Aggie the house key, and as Aggie has never learned to swallow a raw egg, although I have heard that they taste rather like oysters, and slip down in much the same way, Aggie was obliged to continue hungry.

It is only just to record that Tish grew more companionable after luncheon, and got into a large chestnut tree near the house by climbing on top of the hen house. We had always before had the farmer's boy to do the climbing into the upper branches, and I confess to a certain nervousness, especially as Tish, when far above the ground, decided to take off her dress skirt, which was her second best tailor-made, and climb around in her petticoats.

She had to have both hands free to unhook the band, and she very nearly overbalanced while stepping out of it.

"Drat a woman's clothes, anyhow," she said. "If we had any sense we'd wear trousers."

"I understand," I said, "that even trousers are not easy to get out of, Tish."

"Don't be a fool, Lizzie," she said tartly. "If I had trousers on I wouldn't have to take them off. Catch it!"

However, the skirt did not fall clear, but caught on a branch far out, and hung there. Tish broke off a small limb and poked at it from above, and I found a paling from a fence and threw it up to dislodge it. But it stuck tight, and the paling came down and struck Aggie on the head. Had we only known it, this fortunate accident probably saved Aggie's life, for she sat down suddenly on the ground, and said faintly that her skull was fractured.

I was bending over Aggie when I heard a sharp crack from above. I looked up, and Tish was lying full length on a limb, her arm out to reach for the skirt and a most terrible expression on her face. There was another crack, and our poor Tish came hurtling through the air, landing half in Aggie's lap and half in the suitcase.

I was quite unable to speak, and owing, as I learned later, to Tish's head catching her near the waist line, Aggie had no breath even to scream.

There was a dreadful silence. Then Tish said, without moving:

"All my property is to go to Charlie Sands."

"Tish!" I cried, in an agony, and Aggie, who still could not speak, burst into tears.

However, a moment later, Tish drew up first one limb and then the other, and observed that her back was broken. She then mentioned that Aggie was to have her cameo set and the dining room sideboard, and that I was to have the automobile, but the next instant she felt a worm on her neck and sat up, looking rather dishevelled, but far from death.

"Where are you hurt, Tish?" I asked, trembling.

"Everywhere," she replied. "Everywhere, Lizzie. Every bone in my body is broken."

But after a time the aching localized itself in her right arm, which began to swell. We led her down to the creek and got her to hold it in the cold water and Aggie, being still nervous and unsteady, slipped on a mossy stone and sat down in about a foot of water. It was then that our dear Tish became like herself again, for Aggie was shocked into saying, "Oh, damn!" and Tish gave her a severe lecture on profanity.

Tish was quite sure her arm was broken, as well as all the ribs on one side. But she is a brave woman and made little fuss, although she kept poking a finger into her flesh here and there.

"Because," she said, "the First Aid book says that if a lung is punctured the air gets into the tissues, and they crackle on pressure."

It was soon after this that I saw Aggie, who had made no complaint about Tish falling on her, furtively testing her own tissues to see if they crackled.

Leaving my injured there by the creek, I went back to the tree and secured my paling again. By covering it with straw from the barn I was quite sure I could make a comfortable splint for Tish's arm. However, I had but just reached the barn and was preparing to crawl through a window by standing on a rain barrel when I saw Tish limping after me.

"Well?" she said. "What idiotic idea is in your head, Lizzie? Because if it is more eggs — —"

"I am going to get some straw and make a splint."

"Nonsense. What for?"

"What do you suppose I intend it for?" I demanded, tartly. "To trim a hat?"

"I won't have a splint."

"Very well," I retorted. "Then I shall get some straw and start a fire to dry Aggie out."

"You'll stick in that window," Tish said, in what, in a smaller woman, would have been a vicious tone.

"Look here, Tish," I said, balancing on the edge of the rain barrel, "is there something in this barn you do not wish me to see?"

She looked at me steadily.

"Yes," she said. "There is, Lizzie. And I'll ask you to promise on your honor not to mention it."

That promise I am glad to say I have kept until now, when the need of secrecy is past, Tish herself having divulged the truth. But at the time I was greatly agitated, and indeed almost fell into the rain barrel.

"Or try to find out what it is," Tish went on, sternly.

I promised, of course, and Tish relaxed somewhat, although I caught her eye on me once or twice, as though she was daring me to so much as guess at the secret.

"Of course, Lizzie," she said, as we approached Aggie, "it is nothing I am ashamed of."

"Of course not," I replied hastily. I took my courage in my hands and faced her. "Tish, have you an aeroplane hidden in that barn?"

"No," she replied promptly. She might have enlarged on her denial, but Aggie took a violent sneezing spell just then, pressing herself between paroxysms to see if she crackled, and we decided to go home at once.

Here a new difficulty presented itself. Tish could not drive the car! I shall never forget my anguish when she turned to me and said:

"You will have to drive us home, Lizzie."

"Never!" I cried.

"It's perfectly easy," she went on. "If children can run them, and the idiots they have in garages and on taxicabs — —"

"Never," I said firmly. "It may be easy, but it took you six months, Tish Carberry, and three broken springs and any number of dead chickens and animals, besides the time you went through a bridge, and the night you drove off the end of a dock. It may be easy, but if it is, I'd rather do something hard."

"I shall sit beside you, Lizzie," she said, in a patient voice. "I daresay you know which is your right foot and which is your left. If not, I can tell you. I shall say 'left' when I want you to push out the clutch, and 'right' for the brake. As for gears, I can change them for you with my left hand."

"I could do it sitting in a chair," I said, in a despairing voice. "But Tish," I said, in a last effort, "do you remember when you tried to teach me to ride a bicycle? And that the moment I saw something to avoid I made a mad dash for it?"

"This is different," Tish said. "It is a car — —"

"And that I rode about a quarter of a mile into Lake Penzance, and would likely have ridden straight across if I hadn't run into a canoe and upset it?"

"You can always *stop* a car," said Tish. "Don't be a coward, Lizzie. All you have to do is to shove hard with your right foot."

Yet, when I did exactly that, she denied she had ever said it. Fond as I am of Tish, I must admit that she has a way of forgetting things she does not wish to remember.

In the end I consented. It was against my better judgment, and I warned Tish. I have no talent for machinery, but indeed a great fear of it, since the time when as a child I was visiting my grand-aunt's farm and almost lost a finger in a feed-cutter. In addition to that, Tish's accident and her secret had both unnerved me. I knew that calamity faced us as I took my place at the wheel.

Tish was still in her petticoat, as we were obliged to leave her dress skirt in the tree, and Aggie was wrapped in the rug to prevent her taking cold.

"When we meet a buggy," Tish said, "we'd better go past it rather fast. I don't ache to be seen in a seersucker petticoat."

"Fast," I said, bitterly. "You'd better pray that we go past it at all."

However, by going very slowly, I got the thing as far as the gate going into the road. Here there was a hill, and we began to move too rapidly.

"Slower," said Tish. "You've got to make a turn here."

"How?" I cried, frantically.

"Brake!" she yelled.

"Which foot?"

"Right foot. *Right foot!*"

However, it seems that my right foot was on the gas throttle at the time, which she had forgotten. I jammed my foot down hard, and the car seemed to lift out of the air. We went across the ditch, through a stake and rider fence, through a creek and up the other side of the bank, and brought up against a haystack with a terrific jolt.

Tish sat back and straightened her hat with a jerk.

"We'd better go back and do it again, Lizzie," she said, "because you missed one or two things."

"I did what you told me," I replied, sullenly.

"Did you?" said Tish. "I don't remember telling you to leap the creek. Of course, cross-country motoring has its advantages. Only one really should have solid tires, because barbed wire fences might be awkward."

She then sat back and rested.

"Well?" I said.

"Well?" said Tish.

"What am I to do now?"

"Oh!" she said. "I thought you preferred doing it your own way. I don't object, if you don't. You are quite right. Roads do become monotonous. Only I doubt, Lizzie, if you can get over this stack. You'd better go around it."

"Very well," I said. "My own way is to walk home, Tish Carberry. And if you think I am going to steer a runaway automobile you can think again."

Aggie had said nothing, but I now turned and saw her, pale and shaken, taking a sip of the blackberry cordial we always carry with us for emergencies. I suggested that she drive the thing home, but she only shook her head and muttered something about almost falling out of the back end of the car when we leaped up out of the creek. She had, she asserted, been clear up on the folded-back top, and had stayed there until the jolt against the haystack had thrown her forward into the seat again.

I daresay we would still be there had not a young man with a gun run suddenly around the haystack. He had a frightened look, but when he saw us all alive he relaxed. Unfortunately, however, Aggie still had the bottle of blackberry cordial in the air. His expression altered when he saw her, and he said, in a disgusted voice:

"Well, I be damned!"

Tish had not seen Aggie, and merely observed that she felt like that and even more. She then remarked that I had broken her other arm, and her nose, which had struck the wind shield. But the young man merely gave her a scornful glance, and leaning his gun against the haystack, came over to the car and inspected us all with a most scornful expression.

"I thought so!" he said. "When I saw you leaping that fence and jumping the creek, I knew what was wrong. Only I thought it was a party of men. In my wildest dreams-give me that bottle," he ordered Aggie, holding out his hand.

Now it is Aggie's misfortune to have lost her own teeth some years ago, owing to a country dentist who did not know his business. And when excited she has a way of losing her hold, as one may say, on her upper set. She then speaks in a thick tone, with a lisp.

"Thertainly not!" said Aggie.

To my horror, the young man then stepped on the running board of the car and snatched the bottle out of her hand.

"I must say," he said, glaring at us each in turn, "that it is the most disgraceful thing I have ever seen." His eyes stopped at Tish, and traveled over her. "Where is your clothing?" he demanded, fiercely.

It was then that Tish rose and fixed him with a glittering eye.

"Young man," she said, "where my dress skirt is does not concern you. Nor why we are here as we are. Give Miss Pilkington that bottle of blackberry cordial."

"Blackberry cordial!" jeered the young man.

"As for what you evidently surmise, you are a young idiot. I am the President of the local branch of the W. C. T. U."

"Of course you are," said the young man. "I'm Carrie Nation myself. Now watch."

He then selected a large stone and smashed the bottle on it.

"Now," he observed, "come over with the rest of it, and be quick." But here he seemed to realize that Tish's face was rather awful, for he stopped bullying and began to coax. "Now see here," he said. "I'm going to help you out of this if I can, because I rather think it is an accident. You've all had something on an empty stomach. Go down to the creek and get some cold water, and then walk about a bit. I'll see what I can do with the car."

Aggie was weeping in the rear seat by that time, and I shall never forget Tish's face. Suddenly she got out of the car and before he realized what was happening, she had his gun in her good hand.

"Now," she said, waving it about recklessly, "I'll teach you to insult sober and God-fearing women whose only fault is that one of them hasn't all the wit she should have and let a car run away with her. Lizzie, get out of that seat."

It was the young man's turn to look strange.

"Be careful!" he cried. *"Be careful!* It's loaded, and the safety catch — —"

"Get out, Aggie."

Aggie crawled out, still holding the rug around where she had sat down in the creek.

"Now," Tish said, addressing the stranger, "you back that car out and get it to the road. And close your mouth. Something is likely to fly into it."

"I beg of you!" said the young man. "Of course I'll do what I can, but-please don't wave that gun around."

"Just a moment," said Tish. "That blackberry cordial was worth about a dollar. Just give a dollar to the lady near you. Aggie, take that dollar. Lizzie, come here and let me rest this gun on your shoulder."

She did, keeping it pointed at the young man, and I could hear her behind me, breathing in short gasps of fury. Nothing could so have enraged Tish as the thing which had happened, and for a time I feared that she would actually do the young man some serious harm.

He sat there looking at us, and he saw, of course, that he had been mistaken. He grew very red, and said:

"I've been an idiot, of course. If you will allow me to apologize — —"

"Don't talk," Tish snapped. "You have all you can do without any conversation. Did you ever drive a car before?"

"Not through a haystack," he said in a sulky voice.

But Tish fixed him with a glittering eye, and he started the engine.

Well, he got the car backed and turned around, and we followed him through the stubble as the car bumped and rocked along. But at the edge of the creek he stopped and turned around.

"Look here," he said. "This is suicide. This car will never do it."

"It has just done it," Tish replied, inexorably. "Go on."

"I might get down, but I'll never get up the other side."

"Go on."

"Tish!" Aggie cried, anguished. "He may be killed, and you'll be responsible."

Aggie is a sentimental creature, and the young man was very good-looking. Indeed, arriving at the brink, I myself had qualms. But Tish has a will of iron, and was, besides, still rankling with insult. She merely glued her eye again to the sight of the gun on my shoulder, and said:

"Go on!"

Well, he got the car down somehow or other, but nothing would make it climb the other side. It would go up a few feet and then slide back. And at last Tish herself saw that it was hopeless, and told him to turn and go down the creek bed.

It was a very rough creek bed, and one of the springs broke almost at once. We followed along the bank, and I think Tish found a sort of grim humor in seeing the young man bouncing up into the air and coming down on the wheel, for I turned once and found her smiling faintly. However, she merely called to him to be careful of the other springs or she would have to ask him to pay for them.

He stopped then, in a pool about two feet deep, and glared up at her.

"Oh, certainly," he said. "I suppose the fact that I have permanently bent in my floating ribs on this infernal wheel doesn't matter."

At last he came to a shelving bank, and got the car out. I think he contemplated making a run for it then and getting away, but Tish observed that she would shoot into the rear tires if he did so. So he went back to the road, slowly, and there stopped the car.

However, Tish was not through with him. She made him climb the chestnut tree and bring down her dress skirt, and then turn his back while she put it on. By that time, the young man was in a chastened mood, and he apologized handsomely.

"But I think I have made amends, ladies," he said. "I feel that I shall never be the same again. When I started out today I was a blithe young thing, feeling life in every limb, as the poet says. Now what I feel in every limb does not belong in verse. May I have the shotgun, please?"

But Tish had no confidence in him, and we took the gun with us, arranging to leave it at the first signpost, about a mile away. We left him there, and Aggie reported that he stood in the road staring after us as long as we were in sight.

Tish drove the car home after all, steering with one hand and taking the wheel off a buggy on the way. I sat beside her and changed the gears, and she blamed the buggy wheel on me, owing to my going into reverse when I meant to go ahead slowly. The result was that we began to back unexpectedly, and the man only saved his horse by jumping him over a watering trough.

I have gone into this incident with some care, because the present narrative concerns itself with the young man we met, and with the secret in Tish's barn. At the time, of course, it seemed merely one of the unpleasant things one wishes to forget quickly. Tish's arm was only sprained, and although Aggie wore adhesive plaster around her ribs almost all winter, because she was afraid to have it pulled off, there were no permanent ill effects.

The winter passed quietly enough. Aggie and I made Red Cross dressings for Europe, and Tish, tiring of knitting, made pajamas. She had turned against the government, and almost left the church when she learned that Mr. Ostermaier had voted the Democratic ticket. Then in January, without telling any one, she went away for four days, and Sarah Willoughby wrote me later that the Honorable J. C., her husband, said that a woman resembling Tish had demanded from the gallery of the Senate that we declare war against Germany and had been put out by the Sergeant-at-arms.

I do not know that this was Tish. She returned as unannounced as she had gone, and went back to her pajamas, but she was more quiet than usual, and sometimes, when she was sewing, her lips moved as though she was rehearsing a speech. She observed once or twice that she wanted to do her bit, but that she considered digging trenches considerably easier than driving a sewing machine twelve miles a day.

I remember, in this connection, a conversation I had with Mrs. Ostermaier some time in January. She asked me to wait after the Red Cross meeting, and I saw trouble in her eye.

"Miss Lizzie," she said, "do you think Miss Tish really enjoys sewing?"

"Not particularly," I admitted. "But it is better than knitting, she says, because it is faster. She likes to get results."

"Exactly," Mrs. Ostermaier observed. "I'll just ask you to look at this pajama coat she has turned in."

Well, there was no getting away from it. It was wrong. Dear Tish had sewed one of the sleeves in the neck opening, and had opened the sleeve hole and faced back the opening and put buttons and buttonholes on it.

"Not only that," said Mrs. Ostermaier, "but she has made the trousers of several suits wrong side before and opened them up the back, and men are such creatures of habit. They like things the way they are used to them."

Well, I had to tell Tish, and she flew into a temper and said Mrs. Ostermaier never could cut things out properly, and she would leave the society. Which she did. But she was very unhappy over it, for Tish is patriotic to her finger tips.

All the spring, until war was declared, she was restless and discontented, and she took to long trips in the car, by herself, returning moodier than ever. But with the announcement of war she found work to do. She made enlisting speeches everywhere, and was very successful, because Tish has a magnetic and compelling eye, and she would fix on one man in the crowd and talk at him and to him until all the men around were watching him. Generally, with every one looking he was ashamed not to come forward, and Tish would take him by the arm and lead him in to the recruiting station.

It was on one of these occasions that we saw the young man of the blackberry cordial again.

Tish saw him first, from the tail of the wagon she was standing in. She fixed him with her eye at once, and a man standing near him, said:

"Go on in, boy. You're as good as in the trenches already. She landed me yesterday, but I've got six toes on one foot. Blessed if she didn't try to take me to a hospital to have one cut off."

"Now," said Tish, "does any one wish to ask any questions?"

I saw the blackberry cordial person take a step forward.

"I would like to ask you one," he said. "How do you reconcile blackberry cordial with the W. C. T. U.?"

Tish went white with anger, and would no doubt have flayed him with words, as our blackberry cordial is made from her own grandmother's recipe, and a higher principled woman never lived. But unluckily the driver of the furniture wagon we were standing in had returned without our noticing it, and drove off at that moment, taking us with him.

It was about this time that Charlie Sands came to see me one day, looking worried.

"Look here," he said, "what's this about my having appendicitis?"

"Well, you ought to know," I replied rather tartly. "Don't ask me if you have a pain."

"But I haven't," he said, looking aggrieved. "I'm all right. I never felt better."

He then said that once, when a small boy, he had been taken with a severe attack of pain, following a picnic when he had taken considerable lemonade and pickles, followed by ice cream.

"I had forgotten it entirely," he went on. "But the other day Aunt Tish recalled the incident, and suggested that I get my appendix out. It wouldn't matter if she had let it go at that. But she's set on it. I may waken up any morning and find it gone."

I could only stare at him, for he is her favorite nephew, and I could not believe that she would forcibly immolate him on a bed of suffering.

"I used to think she was fond of me," he continued. "But she's —well, she's positively grewsome about the thing. She's talked so much about it that I begin to think I *have* got a pain there. I'm not sure I haven't got it now."

Well, I couldn't understand it. I knew what she thought of him. Had she not, when she fell out of the tree, immediately left him all her property? I told him about that, and indeed about the entire incident, except the secret in the barn. He grew very excited toward the end, however, where we met the blackberry-cordial person, and interrupted me.

"I know it from there on," he said. "Only I thought Culver had made it up, especially about the gun being levelled at him, and the machine in the creek bed. He's on my paper; nice boy, too. Do you mean to say-but I might have known, of course."

He then laughed for a considerable time, although I do not consider the incident funny. But when I told him about Mr. Culver's impertinent question at the recruiting station, he sobered.

"You tell her to keep her hands off him," he said. "I need him in my business. And it won't take much to send him off to war, because he's had a disappointment in love and I'm told that he walks out in front of automobiles daily, hoping to be struck down and make the girl sorry."

"I consider her a very sensible young woman," I observed. But he was already back to his appendix.

"You see," he said, "my Aunt Letitia has a positively uncanny influence over me, and if I have it out I can't enlist. No scars taken."

I put down my knitting.

"Perhaps that is the reason she wants it done," I suggested.

"By George!" he exclaimed.

Well, that *was* the reason. I may as well admit it now. Tish is a fine and spirited woman, and as brave as a lion. But it was soon evident to all of us that she was going to keep Charlie Sands safe if she could. She was continually referring to his having been a sickly baby, and I am quite sure she convinced herself that he had been. She spoke, too, of a small cough he had as indicating weak lungs, and was almost indecently irritated when the chest specialist said that it was from smoking, and that if he had any more lung space the rest of his organs would have had to move out.

One way and another, she kept him from enlisting for quite a time, maintaining that to run a newspaper and keep people properly informed was as patriotic as carrying a gun.

I remember that on one occasion, when he had at last decided to join the navy and was going to Washington, Tish took a very bad attack of indigestion, and nothing quieted her until after train time but to have Charlie Sands beside her, feeding her peppermint and hot water.

Then, at last, the draft bill was passed, and she persuaded him to wait and take his chance.

We were at a Red Cross class, being taught how to take foreign bodies out of the ear, when the news came. Tish was not paying much attention, because she considered that if a soldier got a bullet or shrapnel in his ear, a syringe would not help him much. She had gone out of the room, therefore, and Aggie had just had a bean put in her auditory canal, and was sure it would swell before they got it again, when Tish returned. She said the bill had passed, and that the age limit was thirty-one.

Mrs. Ostermaier, who was using the syringe, let it slip and shot a stream of water into Aggie's right eye.

"Thirty-one!" she said. "Well, I suppose that includes your nephew, Miss Tish."

"Not at all," said Tish. "He will have his thirty-second birthday on the fifth of June, and he probably won't have to register at all. It's likely to be July before they're ready."

"Oh, the fifth of June!" said Mrs. Ostermaier, and gave Aggie another squirt.

Now Tish and I have talked this over since, and it may only be a coincidence. But Mrs. Ostermaier's cousin is married to a Congressman from the west, and she sends the Ostermaiers all his speeches. Mr. Ostermaier sends on his sermon, too, in exchange, and every now and then Mrs. Ostermaier comes running in to Tish with something delivered in our national legislature which she claims was conceived in our pulpit.

Anyhow, when the draft day was set, *it was the fifth of June*!

Aggie and I went to Tish at once, and found her sitting very quietly with the blinds down, and Hannah snivelling in the kitchen.

"It's that woman," Tish said. "When I think of the things I've done for them, and the way I've headed lists and served church suppers and made potato salad and packed barrels, it makes me sick."

Aggie sat down beside her and put a hand on her knee.

"I know, Tish," she said. "Mr. Wiggins was set on going to the Spanish war. He said that he could not shoot, but that he would be valuable as an observer, from church towers and things, because he was used to being in the air. He would have gone, too, but — —"

"If he goes," Tish said, "he will never come back. I know it. I've known it ever since I ran over that black cat the other day."

Well, we had to leave her, as Aggie was buying wool for the Army and Navy League. We went out, very low in our minds. What was our surprise, therefore, on returning late that afternoon, to find Tish cheerfully hoeing in the garden she had planted in the vacant lot next door, while Hannah followed her and gathered up in a basket the pieces of brick, broken bottles and buried bones that Tish unearthed.

"You poor dear!" Aggie said, going toward her. "I know just how you feel. I — —"

"Get out!" Tish yelled, in a furious tone. "Look what you're doing! Great heavens, don't you see what you've done? That was a potato plant."

We tried to get out, although I could see nothing but a few weeds, but she yelled at us every moment and at last I gave it up.

"I'd rather stay here, Tish," I said, "if you don't mind. I can keep the dogs away, and along in the autumn, when it's safe to move, you can take me home, or put me in a can, along with the other garden stuff."

Here Tish fired a brick at Hannah's basket, but struck her in the knee cap instead, and down she went on what Tish said was six egg plants. In the resulting conversation I escaped, and went up to Tish's sitting room.

Tish followed us soon after, and jerked the window shades to the top.

"There's nothing like getting close to nature," she said. "I feel like a different woman, after an hour or so of the soil."

She then took Hannah's basket and placed it on the window-sill overlooking the vacant lot, explaining that she used its contents to fling at dogs, cats and birds below.

"It makes a little extra work for Hannah," she commented. "But it's making a new woman of her. It would be good for you, too, Lizzie. There's nothing like bending over to reduce the abdomen."

But Aggie, having come to mourn, proceeded to do it.

"To think," she said, "that if they had only made it a day later, dear Charlie would have been exempt. It's too tragic, Tish."

"I don't know what you are talking about," said Tish in a cold tone. "He does not have to register. He was born at seven in the morning, June fifth."

"In the evening, Tish," said Aggie gently. "I was there, you know, and I remember — —"

Tish gave her a terrible look.

"Of course you would know," she observed, icily. "But as I was in the room, and recall distinctly going out and telling old Amanda, the cook, about breakfast — —"

"Supper," said Aggie firmly. "You were excited, naturally. But I was in the hall when you came out, and I was expecting my first gentleman caller, which no girl ever forgets, Tish. I remember that Amanda was hooking my dress, which was very tight, because we had waist lines in those days and I wanted — —"

"Aggie," Tish thundered, "he was born early in the morning of June fifth. He will be thirty-two years of age early in the morning of Registration day. And if he tries to register I shall be on hand with the facts."

Well, whether she was right or not, she was convinced that she was, and it is useless to argue with her under those circumstances. Luckily she heard a dog in the lot just then, and threw down a broken bottle and some bricks at him, and the woman in the apartment below raised a window and threatened to report her to the Humane Society. But, as usual, Tish was more than her equal.

"Come right up, then," she said. "Because I am a member of the Humane Society and have been for twenty years. I consider throwing bricks at that dog as patriotic a duty as killing a German, any day."

Here, by accident, the basket slid off the window-sill, and Tish closed the window violently.

"It hit her on the head," she said, in what I fear was an exultant tone. "I wouldn't have done it on purpose, but I guess it's no sin to be thankful."

Because the incident I am about to relate concerns not only Registration Day, but also Mr. Culver and the secret in the barn, I have been some time in getting to it. And if, in so doing, I have reflected at any time either on Tish's patriotism or her strict veracity, I am sorry. No one who knows Tish can doubt either.

In spite of Aggie, in spite of Charlie Sands, who protested violently that he distinctly remembered being born in the evening, because he had yelled all the ensuing night and no one had had a wink of sleep-in spite of all this, Tish remained firm in her conviction that 7 A. M. on Registration Day, when the precincts opened, would find him too old to register.

On the surface the days that followed passed uneventfully. Tish sewed and knitted, and once each day stood Aggie and myself on the outskirts of her garden and pointed out things which she said would be green corn, and tomatoes and peppers and so on. But there was a set look about her face, to those of us who knew and loved her. She had moments of abstraction, too, and during one of them weeded out an entire row of spring onions, according to Hannah.

On the third of June I went into the jeweller's to have my watch regulated, and found Tish at the counter. She muttered something about a main spring and went out, leaving me staring after her. I am no idiot, however, although not Tish's mental equal by any means, and I saw that she had been looking at gentlemen's gold watches.

I had a terrible thought that she intended trying to purchase Charlie Sands by a gift. But I might have known her high integrity. She would not stoop to a bribe. And, as a matter of fact, happening to stop at the Ostermaiers' that evening to show Mrs. Ostermaier how to purl, I found that dear Tish, remembering the anniversary of his first sermon to us, had presented Mr. Ostermaier with a handsome watch.

It was on the fourth of June that I had another visit from Charlie Sands. He is usually a most amiable young man, but on that occasion he came in glowering savagely, and on sitting down on Aggie's knitting, which was on steel needles, he flung it across the room, and had to spend quite a little time apologizing.

"The truth is," he said, "I'm so blooming upset that I'm not myself. Let me put these needles back, won't you? Or do they belong in some particular place?"

"They do," Aggie retorted grimly. "And for a young man who will be thirty-two tomorrow morning — —"

"Evening," he corrected her, with a sort of groan. "I see she's got you too. Look here," he went on, "I'm in trouble, and I'm blessed if I see my way out. I want to register tomorrow. I may not be drawn, because I'm an unlucky devil and always was. But —I want to do my bit."

"Well," I observed, tartly. "I guess no one can prevent you. Go and do it, and say nothing."

"Not at all," he replied, getting up and striding up and down the room. "Not a bit of it. I grant you it looks simple. Wouldn't any one in his senses think that a young and able-bodied man could go and put his name down as being willing to serve his country? Why, she herself-she's crazy to go. I'd like to bet a hat she'll get there before long, too, and into the front trenches."

"Oh, no!" Aggie wailed suddenly.

"But not I," went on Charlie Sands fiercely. "Not I. How she ever got around that old fool Ostermaier I don't know. But she has. He's appointed her an assistant registrar in his precinct, which is mine. And she'll swear until she's black in the face that I'm over age."

"Can't you have the place opened before seven in the morning?" I suggested.

"I've been to him, but he says the law is seven o'clock. Besides," he added bitterly, "she knows me, and as like as not she'll sleep there, to be on hand to forestall me."

As I look back, I am convinced that a desire to do his bit, as he termed it, was only a part of his anger that evening. The rest was the feeling that Tish's superior acumen had foiled him. He had a truly masculine hatred of being thwarted by a woman, even by a beloved aunt.

"Well," he said at last, picking up his hat. "I'll be off." He went to the door, but turned back and glowered at us both, although I am sure we had done nothing whatever. "But mark my words, and remind her of them the day after tomorrow. This thing's not over yet. She's pretty devilish clever"—(I regret to record this word, but he was greatly excited)—"but she hasn't all the brains in the family."

For a day that was to contain so much, however, the fifth of June started quietly enough. We telephoned Hannah, and she reported that Tish had left the house at five-thirty, although obliged to go only one block to the engine house which was her destination.

So far as I can learn, for Tish is very uncommunicative about the entire matter, the morning passed quietly enough. She had taken the precaution of having her folding card table and two pillows sent to the engine house, and when Aggie and I arrived at midday she was seated comfortably, with her hat hung on a lamp of the fire truck. When we arrived she was asking the sexton of the Methodist Church, whom she has known for thirty years, if he had lost a leg or an arm.

Aggie had brought a basket with some luncheon for her, and she placed it on the truck. But there was an alarm of fire soon after, and the thing went out in a rush with the lunch and also with Tish's hat.

Tish was furiously angry. Indeed, I have since thought that much of what followed was due to the loss of the luncheon, which the firemen declared they had not seen, although Aggie was positive she saw one of them eating one of the doughnuts that afternoon behind a newspaper.

But, worst of all, Tish's hat was missing. It reappeared later, however, but was brought in by the engine house dog, after having been run over by the Chief's machine, two engines and a ladder truck.

As I say, that was part of her irritation, but what really upset her was the number of married men. More than once, as she grew excited, I heard her say:

"Married? How many wives?"

When of course she meant how many children.

She had registered twenty-four married men and two single ones by one o'clock, and she was looking very discouraged. But at one o'clock the clerk from the shoe store at the corner came in, and said he had dependent on him a wife, four children, a mother-in-law, a sister-in-law and his sister-in-law's husband.

"Of course," Tish said bitterly, "you claim exemption."

"Me?" he said. "Me, Miss Carberry? My God, no."

Well, about two o'clock Charlie Sands came in. Tish saw him the moment he entered the door, and stopped work to watch him. But he made no attempt to register. He said he was doing a column of slackers for the next morning's paper.

"There's aren't many," he said, "but of course there are some. The license court is the place to nail them."

"Do you mean to tell me," Tish demanded, "that there are traitors in this country who are getting married *today?*"

"There are," said Charlie Sands, sitting down on the fire truck. "Even so, beloved aunt. They are getting married so they can claim exemption because of a dependent wife. And I'll bet the orphan asylums are full of fellows trying to get ready-made families."

Tish is a composed and self-restrained woman, but she spoke so distinctly of how she felt about such conduct that Charlie Murray, our grocer's assistant, who has four children, did not so much as mention them when she made out his card.

"Of course," Charlie Sands observed, "I don't want to dictate to you, because you're doing all that can be expected of you now. But if some one would go to the license court and tell those fellows a bit of wholesome truth, it might be valuable."

"You do it, Lizzie," Tish said.

"I? I never made a speech in my life, Tish Carberry, and you know it."

"And I never before tried to get the truth from an idiot who says he is twenty-eight and has a daughter of eighteen! See here," Tish said to a man in front of her, waving her pen and throwing a circle of ink about. "I'll have you know that I represent the government today, and if you think you are being funny, you are not."

Well, it turned out that he had married a widow with a child, but had a cork leg anyhow, so it made no difference. But Tish's mind was not on her work. However, she was undecided until Charlie Sands said:

"By the way, I saw your friend Culver among the Cupid-chasers today. And this is his district. You'd better round him up."

"Culver!" Tish said. "Do you mean that—Lizzie, where's my hat?"

Well, we had to recover it again from the engine house dog, whom we found burying it in the back yard. Tish's mind, however, was far away, and she merely brushed it absently with her hand and stuck it on her head. Then she turned to Charlie Sands.

"I'm going to the license court," she said, between clenched teeth. "And I am going to show that young fool that he is not going to hide behind any petticoats today."

"It's his privilege to get married if he wants to."

"When I finish with him," said Tish, grimly, "he won't want to."

All the way to the court house Tish's lips were moving, and I knew she was rehearsing what she meant to say. I think that even then her shrewd and active mind had some foreboding of what was to come, for she called back unexpectedly to Aggie:

"Look in the right-hand pocket and see if there is a box of tacks there."

"Tacks?" said Aggie. "Why, what in the world ——"

"I had tacks to nail up flags this morning. Well?"

"They are here, Tish, but no hammer."

"I shan't need a hammer," Tish replied, cryptically.

I am afraid I had expected Tish to lead the way into the license court and break out into patriotic fury. But how little, after all, I knew her! Already in that wonderful brain of hers was seething the plot which was so to alter certain lives, and was to leave an officer of the law—but that comes later on.

Mr. Culver was at the desk. Just as we arrived, a clerk handed him a paper, and he walked across the room to an ice-water cooler and took a drink.

"The slacker!" said Tish, from clenched teeth. "The coward! The poltroon! The ——"

At that moment Mr. Culver, with a paper cup in his hand, saw us and stared at us fixedly. The next moment he had whipped off his hat, and was coming toward us.

"Well!" he said, as he came up to us, "so it really did happen!"

Tish took a deep breath, to begin on him, but he went on blithely:

"You see, when I got back home that day, I felt it hadn't really been true. I had *not* gone rabbit-shooting, and found three ladies half-buried in a haystack. And of course I had not driven an automobile along a creek bed and through the old swimming hole, with my own gun levelled at my back."

Tish took another breath and opened her mouth.

"Then, the other day," he went on, smiling cheerfully, "I thought I had had a return of the hallucination, because I fancied I saw you all on a wagon. But the next moment the wagon was driving on, and you were nowhere in sight."

"That was because," said Aggie, "when the wagon started we all sat down unexpectedly, and ——"

"Aggie!" Tish said, in a savage tone. "Now, young man, I want to say something to you, and I'd thank you ——"

"Oh, I say!" he broke in, looking suddenly depressed, "I can see you are still down on me. But don't scold me. Please don't. Because I am a sensitive person, and you will ruin what was going to be a perfect day. I know I was wrong. I apologize. I eat my words. And now I'll leave you, because if you should vanish into thin air again I should have to go and lock myself up."

Well, with all his gaiety he did not look particularly gay, and he was rather hollow in the cheeks. I came to the conclusion that he was going to marry another young woman, partly to keep out of going to war, but partly to spite the first. I must say I felt rather sorry for him, especially when I saw the way he looked at her. Oh, yes, I picked her out at once, because she never took her eyes off him.

I didn't think she was fooled much, either, because she looked as if she needed to go off into a corner and have a good cry. Well, she got her wish later, if that was what she wanted.

But Tish is a woman of one idea. While he chattered with one eye on the girl, Tish was eyeing him coldly. At last she caught him by the arm.

"I have something to say to you, young man," she commenced. "I want to ask you what you think of any one who ——"

"I beg your pardon," he interrupted, and freed his arm. "Awfully sorry. I think a young lady over there wishes to speak to me."

He left us briskly enough, but he slowed up before he got across the room. He stopped once and half turned, too, with the unhappiest face I've ever seen on a human being. Aggie was feeling in her knitting bag for the glasses.

"Is she pretty?" she asked.

"Too pretty to be a second choice," I replied, shortly. "She's a nice little thing, and deserves something better than a warmed-over heart."

Tish had been angry enough before, but when I told her that he had been disappointed in love, and was merely making the girl a tool, her eyes were savage.

"She is pretty," Aggie observed. "Perhaps, after all, he *does* love her. Or if not he may learn to. And he cannot be very unhappy about marrying her. He said, you know, it was a perfect day."

"Go down and get into the car," Tish said, in a choking voice. "I'll fix his perfect day for him. Go down and start the engine."

I took a last glance as Aggie and I left the License Court, and if we had had any doubts they vanished then, because he was speaking to the girl with angry gestures, and she was certainly crying.

"Brute," Tish said, with her eyes on him. "A bully as well as a slacker. Never mind. She won't have to put up with him long. If I have any influence in this community that youth will be drafted and sent to a mud hole in France. Mark my words," she went on, settling her hat with a jerk, "that boy will be registered as a single man before this day's over. Go and start the engine, Lizzie. I daresay you remember that much."

Seeing that she had a plan, and "ours not to reason why, ours but to do and die," as Aggie frequently quotes, we went down to the street again. I was even then vaguely apprehensive, an apprehension not without reason, as it turned out. For, reaching over to start the engine, as Tish had taught me by turning a lever on the dashboard and moving up a throttle on the wheel, what was my horror to see the car moving slowly off, with Aggie in the rear seat and as white as chalk.

Tish, in her patriotic fervor, had stopped the thing in gear.

I ran beside it, but was unable to get onto the running board. I then saw Aggie, generally so timid, crawling over the back of the seat, and called to her to put on the brake. She did so, but not until the car had mounted the sidewalk and struck a policeman in the back.

This would not be worth recording, as there were no immediate results, had it not been for the policeman. It brought us to his attention, and came near to ruining Tish's plan. But of this later on.

I do not, even now, know just what arguments Tish used with Myrtle. Yes, that was her name. We had a great deal of time later on to learn her name, and all about her. The matter is a delicate one, and we have not since discussed the events of that day. But Aggie said later on, when we were sitting in the dark and wondering what to do next, that Tish had probably waited until Mr. Culver went out to look up a minister.

Whatever Tish said or did, the result was that only a short time after Aggie had jammed on the brake, they came out together, and Tish was carrying a suitcase. Myrtle was hanging back, but Tish had her by the arm.

At first she did not see us. When she did, however, she worked her way through the crowd and opened the rear door.

"Get in," she said, in an uncompromising tone.

"But I really think," said Myrtle, "that I should — —"

"Get in," Tish said again, firmly. "We can talk it over later."

"But are you sure he sent for me?" she demanded, looking ready to cry again. "I think it must be a mistake. He said to wait, and he would come back as soon as — —"

It was the crowd that really settled the matter, for some one yelled that the girl had been eloping and that her mother had caught her in the License Court. Most of them were men, but they called to Myrtle not to let the old lady bully her. Also one young man said that if her young man didn't come back she could have him and welcome. It frightened Myrtle, and she got into the car and asked Tish to drive away quickly.

"I know it will be in the papers," she said forlornly. "And my people think I am at a house party."

But the next moment I caught her looking at Tish's hat, and her lip quivered.

"I guess I'm nervous," she said, in a choking voice. "I had no idea it was so much trouble to get married."

Tish heard her, although she had her hands full getting the car back to the street. She said nothing until we were in the street again, and moving away slowly.

"Then you might as well settle down and be quiet," she said. "Because you are not going to be married today."

Myrtle may have suspected something before that, perhaps when she first saw Tish's hat, for she looked dazed for a moment, and then stood up in the car and yelled that she was being kidnapped. Tish threw on the gas just then, and she had to sit down, but I looked back just in time to see Mr. Culver and the policeman standing in the center of the street, gesticulating madly.

"Little fool!" Tish muttered, and bent low over the wheel.

Well, they followed us. At the top of the first hill the girl was crying hard, and there were eleven automobiles, Aggie counted, not far behind us. At the end of the next rise there were still ten. It was then that Tish, with her customary presence of mind, told us to scatter the tacks over the road behind us.

The result was that only four were to be seen when we got to the top of Graham's Hill, and they had lost time and were far away. Tish was in a terrible way. Her plan had been merely to take the girl away, because Culver belonged in her precinct and it was her business, as ordered by the government, to gather in all the slackers, matrimonial or otherwise. Then, after Culver had registered as a single man, he could, as Tish tersely observed later, either marry or go and drown himself. It was immaterial to her.

But now we were likely to be arrested for abduction, and the whole thing would get in the papers.

"Tish," Aggie begged, "do stop and put her out in the road. That Culver and the policeman are in the first car. I can see them plainly-and they can pick her up and take her back."

But Tish ignored her, and kept on. She merely asked, once, if we had any scissors with us, and on Aggie finding a pair in her knitting bag, said to get them out and have them ready.

I pause here for a moment to reflect on Tish's resourcefulness. How many times, in the years of our association, has her active brain come to our rescue in trying times? And, once the danger is over, how quickly she becomes again one of us, busy with her charities, her Sunday school class, and her knitting for the poor! Indomitable spirit and Christian soul, her only fault, if any, perhaps a slight lack of humor, that is Letitia Carberry.

"Watch for a barbed wire fence, Lizzie," she said, as we flew along. "And see how near they are."

Well, they were very close, but owing to Tish leaving the macadam at this point, they lost time at a crossroads. At the top of the next hill Aggie said she could not see anything of them. It was then that Myrtle tried to jump out, and would have succeeded had not Tish speeded up the car.

I could hear Aggie trying to soothe her, and telling her that Tish was not insane, but was merely saving her from a terrible fate.

"I have never been married, my dear, owing to an unfortunate circumstance," she said, in her gentle voice. "But to marry without love ———"

The girl sat up, startled.

"But how do you know I don't love him?" she demanded.

"I am speaking of the young man," said Aggie. "My dear child, all over this great land of ours today, here and there are wretches who would use a confiding young woman in order ———"

"Barbed wire!" said Tish exultantly, and stopped the car with a jerk. In an instant she was out in the road, cutting lengths of barbed wire from a fence with the scissors and placing them across the road behind us. Her expression was set and tense. When she had placed some six pieces of wire in position, she returned to the car.

"We can thank the war for that," she observed, coolly. "As long as the barbed wire fences hold out they'll never get us."

The first car was in sight by that time, and we could see that Mr. Culver and the policeman were in it. They shouted with joy when they saw us, but Tish merely smiled, and let in the clutch. Soon after we heard a series of small explosions, and Tish observed that the enemy attack was checked against our barbed wire, and that she reckoned we could hold the position indefinitely.

Aggie looked back and reported that they were both out of the car, and that the policeman was standing on one foot and hopping up and down.

It had been Tish's intention, as I learned later, merely to take the young woman for a country ride, and there to strive to instill into her the weakness and folly of being married by Mr. Culver as an exemption plea. But as we had been making forty-five miles an hour by the speedometer, there had been little opportunity.

However, as the last car was now standing on four rims in the barbed wire entanglement behind us, and as Tish's farm was not far ahead, she improved the occasion with a short but highly patriotic speech, flung over her shoulder.

"I don't believe it," said Myrtle, sullenly. "He loves me. We only ran away today instead of some other day later because my father is leading the parade in my town, and mother is presenting a flag at the schoolhouse."

"Very well," said Tish. "If he loves you, well and good. When your young man has registered, I'll see that you get married, if I have to kidnap a preacher to do it. But I'll tell you right now, I don't think you'll be getting anything worth having."

Well, Myrtle grew quieter then, and I heard Aggie saying Miss Tish never made a promise she could not fulfill. She then told about Mr. Wiggins, and had just reached the place where he had slipped on the eve of his wedding and fallen off a roof, when the car stopped dead.

Tish pushed a few things on the dashboard, but it only hiccoughed twice and then stopped breathing.

"No gasoline!" she exclaimed, in a rage. "We'll have to run for it."

The farmhouse was in sight now, about a half mile ahead. Aggie groaned, but got out and turned to Myrtle. But Myrtle was sitting back in the car with a gleam of triumph in her eyes.

"Certainly *not*," she said calmly.

"Very well," Tish replied. "I don't know but you are just as well where you are. That last car is done for, if I know anything about barbed wire, and they're not likely to chase a machine on foot. They're probably on their way back to town now, and I hope the policeman has to hop all the way. It's only forty miles or so."

She then started up the road, but turned:

"Bring her suitcase, Lizzie," she said. "There's no use leaving it there for tramps to come along and steal it."

She then stalked majestically up the road, and we followed. I am not a complaining woman, but if that girl had left any clothes at home they couldn't have amounted to much. Aggie refused to help with the suitcase, as she had her knitting bag, and as any exertion in summer brings on her hay fever.

It was perhaps five minutes later that I heard a faint call behind me, and turned to see Myrtle coming along behind. She was not crying now, and her mouth was shut tight.

"I suppose," she said angrily, "that it does not matter if tramps get *me*."

"Miss Tish invited you to the farm," I replied.

"Invited!" she snapped. "If this is what she calls an invitation, I'd hate to have her make it a request."

However, she seemed to be really a very nice girl, although misguided, for she took one end of the suitcase. But I learned then how difficult it is for the average mind to grasp the high moral purpose and lofty conception of a woman like Tish.

"I might as well tell you now," she said, "that I don't believe they'll pay any large sum. They're not going to be very keen about me at home, since this elopement business."

"Who'll pay what sum?"

"The ransom," she said, impatiently. "You don't suppose I fell for all that patriotic stuff, do you?"

I could only stare at her in dumb rage.

"At first, of course," she said, "I thought you were white slavers. But I've got it now. The other game is different. Oh, I may come from a small town, but I'm not unsophisticated. You people didn't send my father those black hand letters he's been getting lately, I suppose?"

"Tish!" I called sharply.

But Tish had stopped and was listening intently. Suddenly she said:

"Run!"

There was a sort of pounding noise somewhere behind, and Aggie screeched that it was the Knowleses' bull loose on the road. I thought it quite likely, and as we had once had a very unpleasant time with it, spending the entire night in the Knowleses' pig pen, with the animal putting his horns through the chinks every now and then, I dropped the suitcase and ran. Myrtle ran too, and we reached the farmhouse in safety.

It was then that we realized that the sound was the pursuing car, bumping along slowly on four flat tires. Tish shut and bolted the door, and as the windows were closed with wooden frames, nailed on, we were then in darkness. We could hear the runabout, however, thudding slowly up the drive, and the voices of Mr. Culver and the policeman as they tried the door and the window shutters.

Tish stood just inside the door, and Myrtle was just beside me. Aggie had collapsed on a hall chair. I have, I think, neglected to say that the farmhouse was furnished. Tish's mother used to go out there every summer, and she was a great woman for being comfortable.

At last Mr. Culver came to the front door and spoke through it.

"Hello, inside there!" he called, in a furious voice. As no one replied, he then banged at the door, and from the sound I fancy the policeman was hammering also, with his mace.

"Open, in the name of the law!" bellowed the policeman.

"Stop that racket," Tish replied sternly. "Or I shall fire."

Of course she had no weapon, but they did not know this. We could hear Mr. Culver telling the policeman to keep back, as he knew us, and we had any other set of desperadoes he had ever heard of beaten for recklessness with a gun.

There was a moment's silence, during which I heard Aggie's knitting needles going furiously. She learned to knit by touch once when she had iritis and was obliged to finish a slumber robe in time for Tish's birthday. So the darkness did not trouble her, and I knew she was knitting to compose herself.

Tish then stood inside the door, and delivered through it one of the most inspiring patriotic speeches I have ever heard. She spoke of our long tolerance, while the world waited. Then of the decision, and the call to arms. She said that the sons of the Nation were rising that day in their might.

"But," she finished, "there are some among us who would shirk, would avoid the high and lofty duty. There are some who would profane the name of love, and hide behind it to save their own cowardly skins. To these ignoble ones there is but one course left open. Go. Put your name on the roster of your country as a free man, unmarried and without impediments of any sort. Then return and these doors will fly open before the magic of a blue card."

It was at that time, we learned later, that the policeman, who was but a rough and untutored type, decided that Tish was insane-how often, alas, is genius thus mistaken! —and started off for the Knowles farm to bring help. Mr. Culver made no reply to Tish's speech, and we learned later had gone away in the midst of it. Later on he was reported by Aggie, who looked out from an upper window, to be sitting under the chestnut tree where he had once rescued Tish's black alpaca skirt, sulking and watching.

Tish then went up and spoke to him from the window.

"See here," she said angrily, "do you think that I did not mean what I said through that door?"

He had the audacity to yawn.

"I didn't hear all of it," he said. "But judging from what I know of you, I daresay you meant it. Would you mind tossing me a tin cup or something to drink out of?"

"You are not going back to town to register, then?"

"It's early," he replied, coolly. "If you mean do I intend to walk back, I do not. I shall wait for the Sheriff and the posse."

It was then that Tish saw the policeman crossing a field toward the Knowles farm and she tried to reason with the young man. But he dropped his pretense of indifference, and would not even listen to her.

"I've only one thing to say," he said, fiercely. "You be careful of that young lady. As to whether I register or not, that's my business and has nothing to do with the case. When you open that door and send her out, with four good tires to take the place of the ones you ruined, I'll talk to you, and not before."

He then got up and walked away, and Tish came downstairs and lighted a candle with hands that shook with rage. We had heard the entire conversation, and in the candlelight I could see that Aggie was as white as wax.

Well, the situation was really desperate, but Tish's face forbade questions. Aggie ventured to observe that perhaps it would be better to unlock the door and release the girl, but Tish only gave her a ferocious glance.

"I am doing my duty," she said, firmly. "I have done nothing for which the law can punish me. If a young lady comes willingly into my car for a ride, as you did"—she turned sharply to Myrtle—"and if a young fool chooses to sit in my front yard instead of registering to serve his country, it is not my fault. As a matter of fact, I can probably have him arrested for trespass."

As I have said, the farmhouse is still furnished with Tish's mother's things. She was a Biggs, and all the things the Biggses had not wanted for sixty years were in the house. So at least we had chairs to sit on, and if we had only had water, for we were all thirsty from excitement and dust, we could have been fairly comfortable, although Myrtle complained bitterly of thirst.

"And I want to wash," she said fretfully. "If I could wash I'd change my blouse and look like something."

"For whom?" Tish demanded. "For that slacker outside?"

Suddenly Myrtle laughed. She had been in tears for so long that it surprised us. We all stared at her, but she seemed to get worse and worse.

"She's hysterical, poor child," Aggie said, feeling for her smelling salts. "I don't know that I blame her, Tish. No one knows better than I do what it is to expect to be married, and then find the divine hand of Providence intervening."

But Myrtle suddenly walked over to Aggie and, stooping, kissed her on the top of her right ear.

"You dear thing!" she said. "I still don't get all the idea, but I don't much care if I don't. I haven't had so much excitement since I ran away from boarding school."

She then straightened and looked at Tish. It was clear that her feeling for dear Tish was still vague, but was rather more of respect than of love.

"As for the-the young man outside," she said, "I seem to gather that he hasn't registered, and that I am not to marry him until he has. Very well. I hadn't thought about it before, but that speech of yours-suppose you tell him that I won't marry him until he has a—a magic blue card. I should like to see his face."

But Tish is a woman of delicacy, and she suggested that Myrtle do it herself, from an upper window. I went up with her, and we found Mr. Culver again under the tree. The conversation ran like this:

Myrtle, (looking very pretty indeed but very firm): Look here, I—I've decided not to marry you.

Mr. Culver (rousing suddenly and staring up at her): I beg your pardon!

Myrtle: I know now that I was making a terrible mistake. No matter how much I care for you, I cannot marry a slacker.

Mr. C. (furiously angry and glaring at her): You know better than that!

Myrtle: Not at all. Can you deny that you haven't registered yet?

Mr. C.: What's that got to do with it? I daresay I'm losing my mind. It wouldn't be much wonder if I have. When I think of the way I've suffered lately-look at me!

Myrtle (in a somewhat softened voice): Have you really suffered?

Mr. C.: I? Good Lord, Myrtle-why, I haven't slept for weeks. I——

But here he stopped, with his eyes fixed on the roof overhead.

"Watch out!" he yelled. "Get back. Myrtle, she'll fall on you."

"Not at all," said Tish's calm voice from overhead. There was a rasping sound, and then a long wire fell past the window. "Now," she called triumphantly, "let your policeman telephone for the Sheriff and a posse! That was a party wire, and that farmhouse over there is on it. There isn't another telephone for ten miles."

Well, I looked around for Myrtle, and she was on the guest room bed, face down.

"Oh," she groaned, "I wouldn't have missed it for a trip to Europe. And his face! Miss Lizzie, did you see his face?" She then got up suddenly and put her arms around me. "I'm simply madly happy, Miss Lizzie," she said. "I have to kiss somebody, and since he—may I kiss you?"

Well, of course I allowed her to, but I was surprised. It was not natural, somehow.

Myrtle came down soon after and said that Mr. Culver was bringing some water from the well, and would he be allowed to come in with it? But Tish was firm on this point. She gave her consent, however, to his leaving the pail on the porch and then retiring to the chestnut tree. He did so, whistling to signify that he was at a safe distance, and I then carried it in.

"I say," he called to me when he saw me, "this situation is getting on my nerves. I carried off that policeman, for one thing. He was on duty."

"You needn't stay here."

"I daresay not," he replied rather bitterly. "But what I want to ask is this: Won't it be deucedly unpleasant for you three, when I report that you deliberately put my car out of commission so I could not get back by nine o'clock to register? Of course," he went on, "a box of tacks may have spilled itself on the road, but I never heard of a barbed wire fence trying to crawl across a road and getting run over, like a snake."

I reported this to Tish, and I saw that she was uneasy, although she merely remarked that he still had two legs, and that she had not asked him to follow us. All she had set out to do was to see that he didn't get married before he registered, and she was doing that to the best of her ability. The rest was his affair.

It was six o'clock by that time, and Tish had had nothing to eat since five in the morning, and none of us had had any luncheon. Although a woman who thinks little or nothing of food, I found her, shortly afterwards, in the pantry, looking into jars. There was nothing, however, except some salt, a little baking powder and a package of dried sage. But Aggie, going to an attic window to look for the policeman, discovered about a quart of flour in a barrel up there, and scraping it out, brought it down.

"I might bake some biscuits, Tish," she suggested. "I feel that I'll have to have some nourishment. I'm so weak that my knees shake."

"Myrtle," Tish said abruptly, with that quick decision so characteristic of her, "you might tell that worthless young man of yours to look in the granary. Sometimes the Knowleses' hens come over here, and I daresay they've eaten enough off the place to pay for the eggs."

But Myrtle, after a conference from the window, reported that Mr. Culver had said he would get the eggs, if there were any, on condition that he get his pro rata share of them.

"If there are ten eggs," she said, "he wants two. And if there is an odd number he claims the odd one."

This irritated Tish, but at last she grudgingly consented. In a short time, therefore, Mr. Culver knocked at the kitchen door.

"I am leaving," he said, "eleven eggs, eight of undoubted respectability, two questionable, and one that I should advise opening into a saucer first. Also some corn meal from the granary. And if you will set out a pail and come after me if I am wounded, I shall go after a cow that I see in yon sylvan vale."

His voice was strangely cheerful, but, indeed, the prospect of food had cheered us all, although I could see that Tish was growing more and more anxious, as time went on and no policeman appeared in the Knowleses' machine. However, we worked busily. Myrtle, building a fire and setting the table with the Biggses' dishes, and Aggie making biscuits, without shortening, while Tish stirred the corn meal mush.

"Many a soldier in the trenches," she said, "would be grateful for such a frugal meal. When one reflects that the total cost of mush and milk is but a trifle ——"

Here, however, we were interrupted by Mr. Culver outside. He spoke in gasps and we heard the pail clatter to the porch floor.

"I regretfully report ——" he said, through the keyhole. "No milk. Wrong sex. Sorry."

Ten of the eggs proving good, we placed two of them on a plate with three biscuits and a bowl of mush, and Tish carried it out, placing it on the floor of the porch, much as she would have set it out for the dog.

"Here," she called. "And when you have finished you might go after that accomplice of yours. He's probably asleep somewhere."

"Dear lady," said Mr. Culver, "I would, but I dare not. A fiery creature, breathing fury from its nostrils, is abroad and — —"

But Tish came in and slammed the door.

It was after supper that we missed Tish. She was nowhere in the house, and the kitchen door, which had been bolted, was unlocked. Aggie wrung her hands, but Myrtle was quite calm.

"I shouldn't worry about her," she said. "She's about as well able to take care of herself as any woman I ever saw."

It was now quite dark, and our fears increased. But soon afterwards Tish came in. She went to the stove and pouring out a cup of hot water, drank it in silence. Then she said:

"I've been to the Knowleses'. The dratted idiots are all away, probably to the schoolhouse, registering. The car's gone, and the house is closed."

"And the policeman?" I asked.

"I didn't see him," said Tish. But she did not look at me. She fell to pacing up and down the kitchen, deep in thought.

"What time is it, Lizzie?" she asked.

"Almost eight."

Here Tish gave what in another woman would have been a groan.

"It's raining," she observed, and fell to pacing again. At last she told me to follow her outside, and I went, feeling that she had at last made a decision. Her attitude throughout her period of cogitation had been not unlike that of Napoleon before Waterloo. There were the same bent head and clasped hands, the same melancholy mixed with determination.

Mr. Culver was sitting under his tree, with his coat collar turned up around his neck. Tish stopped and surveyed him with gentle dignity.

"You may enter the house," she said. "The country will gain nothing by your having pneumonia, although personally I am indifferent. And, after thinking over your case, I have come to this decision." She paused, as for oratorical effect. "I shall deliver you to your registration precinct by nine o'clock," she said impressively, "and immediately after that, I shall see that you two are married. I am not young," she went on, "and perhaps I do not think enough of sentiment. But it shall never be said of me that I parted two loving hearts, one of which may, before the snow flies, be still and pulseless in a foreign grave."

She then, still with that new air of melancholy majesty, led me to the barn, leaving him staring.

It was there, by means of a key hanging round her neck, that Letitia Carberry, great hearted woman and patriot that she is, bared her inner heart to me. In the barn was a large and handsome ambulance, with large red crosses on side and top, which she had offered to the government if she might drive it herself. But the government which she was even then so heroically serving had refused her permission, and Tish had buried her disappointment in the bucolic solitude of her farm.

Such, in brief, was Tish's tragic secret.

"I shall take it in to the city tonight, Lizzie," she said heavily. "And tomorrow I shall present it to the Red Cross. Some other hand than mine will steer it through shot and shell, and ultimately into Berlin. It has everything. There's a soup compartment and-well," she finished, "it is doing its work even tonight. Get in."

We found Aggie on the porch, having with her usual delicacy of feeling left the lovers alone inside. When she saw the Ambulance, however, she fell to sneezing violently, crying out between paroxysms that if Tish was going to the war, she was also. But Tish hushed her sternly.

There was a good engine in the Ambulance. Tish said she had ordered a fast one, because it was often necessary to run between shells, as it were. She then shoved on the gas as far as it would go, and we were off. After a time, finding it impossible to sit on the folding seats inside, we all sat on the floor, and I believe Mr. Culver held Myrtle's hand all of the way.

He said little, beyond observing once that he felt a trifle queer about leaving the policeman, who had been on duty when he picked him up at the Court House, and who was now lost some forty-five miles from home, in a strange land.

I am glad, in this public manner, to correct the report that on the evening of June fifth a German Zeppelin made a raid over our country, and that the wounded were hurried to the city in a Red Cross Ambulance, traveling at break-neck speed.

At nine o'clock Mr. Culver was registered at Engine House number eleven, fourteenth ward, third precinct.

At nine-fifteen Mr. Culver and Myrtle were married at the same address by Mr. Ostermaier, standing in front of the fire truck.

But this should be related in detail. So bitter was Charlie Sands, so uneasy about the license, and so on, that I feel in fairness to Tish that I should relate exactly what happened.

At ten o'clock that night everything was over, and we had gathered in Tish's apartment while Hannah broiled a steak, for Tish felt that the occasion permitted a certain extravagance, when Charlie Sands came in. Behind him was a dishevelled young man, with wild eyes and a suitcase. Charlie Sands stood and glared at us.

"Well!" he said. And then: "Where's the young lady?"

"What young lady?" asked Tish, coldly.

The young man stepped forward, with his fists clenched.

"Mine!" he bellowed. "Mine! Don't deny it. I recognize you. I saw you-the lot of you. I saw you drag her into a car and kidnap her. I saw that ass Culver and a policeman chasing you in another car. Oh, I know you, all right. Didn't I pay twenty-two dollars for a taxicab that got three punctures all at once thirty miles from the city? *Now where is she?*"

"Just a moment," said Tish's nephew, holding him back by an arm across his chest. "Just remember that whatever my aunt has done was done with the best intentions."

"D — — her intentions! I want Myrtle."

The dreadful truth must have come to Tish at that moment, as it did to the rest of us. I know that she turned pale. But she rose and pointed magnificently to the door.

"Leave my apartment," she said majestically. And to Charlie Sands: "Take that madman away and lock him up. Then, if you have anything to say to me, come back alone."

"Not a step," said the young man. "Where's my marriage license? Where's — —"

But Charlie Sands pushed him out into the hallway and closed the door on him. Then, with folded arms he surveyed us.

"That's right!" he said. "Knot! I believe most pirates knit on off days. Now, Aunt Letitia, I want the whole story."

"Story?"

"About the license. He says the girl had the license."

"What license?"

"Don't evade!" he said sternly. "Where were you this afternoon?"

"If you want the truth," said Tish, "although it's none of your business, Charlie Sands, and you can unfold your arms, because the pose has no effect on me, —I was out rounding up a young man who had not registered. I got him and brought him in to my precinct at five minutes to nine."

"And that's the truth?"

"Go and ask Mr. Ostermaier," said Tish, in a bored tone.

"But this boy outside — —"

"Look here," Tish said suddenly, "go and ask that noisy young idiot for his blue card. It's my belief he hasn't registered and more than likely he's been making all this fuss so he'll have an excuse if he's found out. How do we know," she went on, gaining force with each word, "that there *is* a Myrtle?"

"By George!" said Charlie Sands, and disappeared.

It was then, for the first time in her valiant life, that I saw our Tish weaken.

"Lizzie!" she groaned, leaning back in her chair. "That Culver was married with another man's name on the license. What's more, I married him to that flibbertygibbet who had just jilted him. What have I done? Oh, what have I done?"

"They both seemed happy, Tish," I tried to soothe her. But she refused all consolation, and merely called Hannah and asked for some blackberry cordial. She drank fully half a tumbler full and she recovered her poise by the time Charlie Sands stuck his head through the door again.

"You're right, most shrewd of aunts," he said. "He's been playing me for a sucker all right. Not a blue card on him! And he belongs out of town, so it's too late."

"It's a jail matter," said Tish, knitting calmly, although we afterwards discovered that she had put a heel on the wristlet she was making. "You'd better get his name, and I'll notify the sheriff of his county in the morning."

Charlie Sands came over to her and stood looking down at her.

"Aunt Tish," he said. "I believe you. I believe you firmly. I shall not even ask about a young man named Culver, who went to get our marriage license list at the Court House this afternoon and has not been seen since. But I want to bring a small matter to your attention. That policeman had not registered."

He then turned and went toward the door.

"But I did, dear Aunt Letitia," he said and was gone.

Tish came to see me the next afternoon, bringing the paper, which contained a glowing account of her gift to the local Red Cross of a fine ambulance. An editorial comment spoke of her public spirit, which for so many years had made her a conspicuous figure in all civic work.

"The city," it finished, "can do with many like our Miss 'Tish' Carberry."

But Tish showed no exultation. She sat in a rocking chair and rocked slowly.

"Read the next editorial, Lizzie," she said, in a low voice.

I have it before me now, cut out rather raggedly, for I confess I was far from calm when I did it.

"A SHAMEFUL INCIDENT.

"Perhaps nothing has so exposed this city to criticism as the conduct of Officer Flinn, as shown in a news item in our columns exclusively. Officer Flinn has been five years on the police force of this city. He has until now borne an excellent record. But he did not register yesterday, and on limping into the Central Station this morning told a story manifestly intended to indicate temporary insanity and thus still further disqualify him for the service of his country. His statement of seeing three elderly women kidnap a young girl from in front of the Court House, his further statement of following the kidnappers far into the country, with a young man he cannot now produce, is sufficiently outrageous.

"But, not satisfied with this, the inventive ex-officer went further and added a night in a pigpen, constantly threatened by a savage bull, and a journey of forty-five miles on foot when, early this morning, the animal retired for a belated sleep!

"Representatives of this paper, investigating this curious situation, found the farmhouse which Officer Flinn described as being the den of the kidnappers and which he stated he had left in a state of siege, the bandits and their victim within and the young man who had accompanied the officer, without. Needless to say, nothing bore out his story. A young married couple, named Culver, who are spending their honeymoon there, knew nothing of the circumstances, although stating that they believed that a neighboring family possessed a belligerent bull.

"It is a regrettable fact that the only scandal which marred a fine and patriotic outburst of national feeling yesterday should have involved the city organization. Is it not time that loyal citizens demand an investigation into — —"

"Never mind the rest, Lizzie," Tish said wearily. "I suppose I'll have to get him something to do, but I don't know what, unless I employ him to follow me around and arrest me when I act like a dratted fool."

She sighed, and rocked slowly.

"Another thing, Lizzie," she said. "I don't know but what Aggie was right about Charlie Sands. I've been thinking it over, and I guess it was evening, for I remember seeing a new moon just before he came, and wishing he would be a girl. But I guess I was too late. If I'd known about this war, I'd have wished it sooner. I'm a broken woman, Lizzie," she finished.

She put on her hat wrong side before, but I had not the heart to tell her, and went away.

However, late that evening she called me up, and her voice was not the voice of a broken creature.

"I thought you might like to come over, Lizzie," she said. "That woman below has told the janitor she is going to pour ammonia water down on my tomato plants tonight, and I am making a few small preparations."

Salvage

After Charlie Sands had gone to a training camp in Ohio there was a great change in Tish. She seemed for the first time to regret that she was a woman, and there were times when that wonderful poise and dignity that had always distinguished her, even under the most trying circumstances, almost deserted her. She wrote, I remember, a number of letters to the President, offering to go into the Secret Service, and sending a photograph of the bandits she had caught in Glacier Park. But she only received a letter from Mr. Tumulty in reply, commencing "May I not thank you," but saying that the Intelligence Department had recently been increased by practically the entire population of the country, and suggesting that she could best use her energies for the national welfare by working for the return of the Democratic Party in 1920.

However, as Tish is a Republican she was not interested in this, and for a time she worked valiantly for the Red Cross and spent her evenings learning the national anthem. But she recited it, since, as the well-known writer, Mr. Irvin Cobb, has observed, it can only be properly sung by a boy whose voice is changing. It was evident, however, that she was increasingly restive, and as I look back I wonder that we did not realize that there was danger in her very repression.

As Aggie has said, Tish is volcanic in her temperament; she remains inactive for certain preparatory periods, but when she overflows she does so thoroughly.

The most ominous sign was when, in July of 1917, she stopped knitting and took up French.

Only the other day, while house cleaning, she came across the aeroplane photograph of the French village of V——, where our extraordinary experience befell us, and she turned on us both with that satiric yet kindly gaze which we both knew so well.

"If you two idiots had had your way," she observed, "I should have been knitting so many socks for Charlie Sands that he'd have had to be a centipede to wear 'em all, instead of——"

"Tish," Aggie said in a shivering voice, "I wish you wouldn't talk about it. I can't bear it, that's all. It sets me shivering."

Tish eyed her coldly. "The body is entirely controlled by the mind, Aggie," she reminded her. "And when I remember how nearly your lack of control cost us our lives, when you insisted on sneezing——"

"Insisted! If you had been in a shell hole full of water up to your neck, Tish Carberry——"

"The difference between you and me, Aggie," Tish replied calmly, "is that I should not have been in a shell hole full of water up to my neck." The war was over then, of course, but there was still a disturbed condition in certain countries, and Tish's eyes grew reflective.

"I see they are thinking of sending a real army into Russia," she said thoughtfully. "I suppose that Russian laundress of the Ostermaiers' could teach a body to talk enough to get about with."

Shortly after that Aggie disappeared, and I found her later on in Tish's bathroom crying into a Turkish towel.

"I won't go, Lizzie," she said, "and that's flat! I've done my share, and if Tish Carberry thinks I am going to go through the rest of my life falling into shell holes and being potted at by all sort of strange men she can just think again. Besides that, I have been true to the memory of one man for a good many years, and I simply refuse to be kissed by any more of those immoral foreigners."

Aggie had in her youth been betrothed to a gentleman in the roofing business, who had met with an unfortunate accident, owing to having slipped on a tin gutter, without overshoes, one rainy day; and it is quite true that we had all been kissed by two French generals and a man in civilian clothes who had not even been introduced to us. But up to that time we had kept the osculatory incident a profound secret.

"Aggie," I said with sudden suspicion, "you haven't told Mrs. Ostermaier about that affair, have you?"

Aggie put down the towel and looked at me defiantly.

"I have, Lizzie," she said. "Not all of it, but some. She said she had gone to the moving pictures with the youngest girl, but that she had been obliged to take her away before it was over, owing to a picture from France of Tish's being kissed by a French general. She said that as soon as he had kissed her on one cheek she turned the other, and that she thinks the effect on Dolores was extremely bad."

It was a great shock to us all to learn that the incident of the town of V —— had thus been made public, and that there was a moving picture of our being decorated, et cetera, going about the country. It is, I believe, quite usual to kiss the persons receiving the Croix de Guerre, even when of the masculine sex, and I know positively that Tish never saw that French general again.

However, in view of the unfortunate publicity I have decided to make this record of the actual incident of the French town of V ——. For the story has got into the papers, and only yesterday Tish discovered that the pleasant young man who had been trying to sell her a washing machine was really a newspaper reporter in disguise.

Certain things are not true. We did not see or have any conversation with the former Emperor of the Germans; nor were any of us wounded, though Aggie got a piece of plaster in her right eye when a shell hit the church roof, and I was badly scratched by barbed wire. It is not true, either, that Aggie had her teeth knocked out by a German sentry. She unfortunately fell in the darkness and lost her upper set, and it was impossible to light a match in order to search for them.

It was, as I have said, in July of the first year of the war that both Aggie and I noticed the change in Tish. She grew moody and abstracted, and on two Sundays in succession she turned over her Sunday-school class to me and went for long walks into the country. Also, going to her apartment for Sunday dinner on, I believe, the second Sunday of the month we were startled to see the Andersons, very nice people who occupy the lower floor of the building, running out wildly into the street. They said that the janitor had been quarreling with some one in the furnace cellar, and that from high words, which they could plainly hear, they had got to shooting, and a bullet had come up through the floor and hit the phonograph.

I had a strange feeling at once, and I caught Aggie's agonized eyes on me. We remained for some time in the street, and then, everything seeming to be quiet, we ventured in, with two policemen leading the way, and the Anderson baby left outside in its perambulator for fear of accident. All was quiet, however, and we made our way upstairs to Tish's apartment. She was waiting for us, and reading the *Presbyterian Banner*, but I thought she was almost too calm when we told her of the Andersons' terrible experience.

"It's a good riddance," she said, referring to the phonograph. "Besides, what right have people over here to fuss about one bullet? Think of our boys in the trenches."

After a time she looked up suddenly and said: "It didn't go anywhere near the baby, I suppose?"

We said it had not, and she then observed that the building was a mere shell, and that people with small children should raise them in the country anyhow.

It was during dinner-Tish had been reading Horace Fletcher for some time, and meals lasted almost from one to the next-that Hannah came in and said the janitor wanted to see Tish. She went out and came back somewhat later, looking as irritated as our dear Tish ever looks, and got her pocketbook from behind the china closet and went out again.

"I expected as much," Hannah said. Hannah is Tish's maid. "She's paying blackmail. Like as not that janitor will collect a hundred dollars from her, and that phonograph never cost more than thirty-five. They're paying for it on the installment plan, and the man only gets a dollar a week."

"Hannah," I said sharply, "if you mean to insinuate ——"

"Me?" Hannah replied in a hurt tone. "I don't insinuate anything. If I was called tomorrow before a judge and jury I'd say that for all I know Miss Tish was reading the *Banner* all morning. But I'd pray they wouldn't take a trip here and look in the upper right-hand sideboard drawer."

She then went out and slammed the door.

Aggie and I make it a point of honor never to pry into Tish's secrets, so we did not, of course, look into the drawer. However, a moment later I happened to upset my glass of water and naturally went to the sideboard drawer in question for a fresh napkin. And Tish's revolver was lying underneath her best monogrammed tray cover.

"It's there, Aggie," I said. "Her revolver. She's practicing again; and you know what that means-war."

Aggie gave a low moan.

"I wish we'd let her get that aeroplane. She might have been satisfied, Lizzie," she said in a shaken voice.

"She might have been dead too," I replied witheringly.

And then Tish came back. She said nothing about the Andersons; but later on when the baby started to cry she observed rather bitterly that she didn't see why people had to have a phonograph when they had that, and that personally she felt that whoever destroyed that phonograph should have a vote of thanks instead of —— She did not complete the sentence.

It was soon after that that we went to visit Charlie Sands, Tish's nephew, at the camp where he was learning to be an officer. We called to see the colonel in command first, and Aggie gave him two extra blankets for Charlie Sands' bed and a pair of knitted bedroom slippers. He was very nice to us and promised to see personally that they went to the proper bed.

"I'm always delighted to attend to these little things," he said. "Fine to feel that our boys are comfortable. You haven't by any chance brought an eiderdown pillow?"

He seemed very regretful when he found we had not thought of one.

"That's too bad," he said. "I've discovered that there is nothing so comforting as a down pillow after a day of strenuous labor."

It was rather disappointing to find that the duties of his position kept him closely confined to the office, and that therefore he had not yet had the pleasure of meeting Tish's nephew, but he said he had no doubt they would meet before long.

"They're all brought in here sooner or later, for one thing or another," he said pleasantly.

As Tish observed going out, it was pleasant to to think of Charlie Sands' being in such good hands.

It was, however, rather a shock to find him, when we did find him, lying on his stomach in a mud puddle with a rifle in front of him. We did not recognize him at once, as a lot of men were yelling, and indeed just at first he did not seem particularly glad to see us.

"Suffering cats!" he shouted. "Don't you see we're shooting? You'll be killed. Get behind the line!"

"I guess it won't defeat the Allies if you stop shooting for two minutes," Tish observed with her splendid poise. "But if you will take charge of this homemade apple butter, which I didn't trust your colonel with, we will go to your sitting room, or wherever it is you receive visitors."

There was quite a crowd of young officers round us by that time and we waited to be introduced. But Charlie Sands did not seem to think of it, so Tish put down the apple butter on the ground and said to one of them:

"Now, young man, since we seem to be in your way, perhaps you will take us to some place to wait for my nephew." Then seeing that he looked rather strange she added: "But perhaps you have never met. This is my nephew, Mr. Sands. If you will tell me who you are ——"

"Williams is my name," he said. "I —Major Williams. I —I've met your nephew-that is —— Private Sands, take these ladies to the Y. M. C. A. hut, and report back here in an hour."

Tish did not like this; nor did I. As Tish observed later, he might have been speaking to the butler.

"He might at least have said 'Mister,' and a 'please' hurts no one," she said. As for giving him only an hour when we had come a hundred miles-it was absurd. But war does queer things.

It had indeed strangely altered Tish's nephew. We were all worried about him that day. It was his manner that was odd. He seemed, as Tish said later, suppressed. When for instance we wished to take him back to headquarters and present him to the colonel he said at once: "Who? Me? The colonel! Say, you'd better get this and get it right: I'm nothing here. I'm less than nothing. Why, the colonel could walk right over me on the parade ground and never even know he'd stepped on anything. If I was a louse and he was a can of insect powder — —"

"Now see here, Charlie Sands," Tish said firmly, "I'll trouble you to remember that there are certain words not in my vocabulary; and louse is one of them."

"Still, a vocabulary is a better place than some others I can think of," he observed.

"What is more," Tish added, "you are misjudging that charming colonel. He told us himself that he tried to be a mother to you all."

She then told him how interested the colonel had been in the blankets, and so on, but I must say Charlie Sands was very queer about it. He stopped and looked at us all in turn, and then he got out the dirtiest handkerchief I have ever seen and wiped his forehead with it.

"Perhaps you'd better say it again," he said; "I don't seem to get it altogether. You are sure it was the colonel?"

So Tish repeated it, but when she came to the eiderdown pillow he held up his hand.

"All right," he said in a strange tone. "I believe you. I —you don't mind if I go and get a drink of water, do you? My mouth is dry."

Dear Tish watched him as he went away, and shook her head.

"He is changed already," she observed sadly. "That is one of the deadliest effects of war. It takes the bright young spirit of youth and feeds it on stuff cooked by men, with not even time enough to chew properly, and puts it on its stomach in the mud, while its head is in the clouds of idealism. I think that a letter to the Secretary of War might be effective."

I must admit that we had a series of disappointments that day. The first was in finding that they had put Tish's nephew, a grandson of a former Justice of the Supreme Court, into a building with a number of other men. Not only that but without so much as a screen, or a closet in which to hang up his clothing.

"What do you mean, hang up my clothes?" he said when we protested. "They're hung up all right-on me."

"It seems rather terrible," Aggie objected gently. "No privacy or anything."

"Privacy! I haven't got anything to hide."

We found some little comfort, however, in the fact that beneath the pitiful cot that he called his bed he had a small tin trunk. Even that was destroyed, however, by the entrance of a thin young man called Smithers, who reached under the cot and dragging out the trunk proceeded to take out one of the pairs of socks that Aggie had knitted.

Charlie Sands paid no attention, but Tish fixed this person with a cold eye.

"Haven't you made a mistake?" she inquired. The young man was changing his socks, with his back to us, and he looked back over his shoulder.

"Sorry!" he said. "Didn't like to ask you to go out. Haven't any place else to go, you know."

"Aren't you putting on my nephew's socks?"

"Extraordinary!" he said. "Did you notice that?"

"I'll trouble you to take them off, young man."

"Well," he said reflectively, "I'll tell you what we'll do: I'll take off these socks if he'll return what he's got on that belongs to me. I don't remember exactly, but I'm darn sure of his underwear and his breeches. You see, while you good people at home are talking democracy we're practicing it, and Sands' idea is the best yet. He swaps an entire outfit for a pair of socks. Even the Democratic Party can't improve on that."

Tish was very thoughtful during the remainder of the afternoon, but she brightened somewhat when, later on, we sat on the steps of a building watching Charlie Sands and a number of others going through what Major Williams called setting-up exercises. She was greatly interested and made notes in her memorandum book. I have a copy of the book before me now. The letter T, S, A and B stand respectively for Toes, Stomach, Arms and Back. I shall not quote all Tish's notes, but this one, for instance, is illustrative of her thorough methods:

"Lying on B. in mud, H. flat on ground, L. rigidly extended: Rise L. in air six times. Retaining prone position rise to sitting position without aid of A., but using S. muscles. Repeat six times. (Note: Director uses language unfitting a soldier and a gentleman. Report to the Secretary of War.)"

She recorded the other movements with similar care, and after one is the thoughtful observation: "Excellent to make Lizzie look less like a bolster."

I find all of Tish's notes taken that day as very indicative of the thoroughness with which she does everything. For instance she made the following recommendations to be sent to the War Department:

"That the camp cooks be instructed to use hemmed tea towels instead of sacking, and to boil the dish towels after each meal, preferably with soap powder and soda.

"That screens be provided between cots, to give that measure of privacy necessary to a man's self-respect.

"Large, commodious clothes closets in the barracks. A bag of camphor in each one would serve to keep away moths. Also, that wearing apparel should not be borrowed.

"All army blankets should be marked as to the end to go to the top of the cot. Sheets should also be provided, as blankets scratch and have a tendency to keep the soldier awake.

"Soda fountains here and there through the camp would do a great deal to prevent the men in training from going to neighboring towns after certain deleterious liquids. (Should, however, be served by male attendants.)

"Pyjamas should be included in every soldier's equipment. (Charlie Sands had told us a startling thing. On inquiring what had become of the raw-silk pyjamas we had made him as a part of his army equipment he confessed that he did not use them, and in fact had torn them into rags to clean his gun. He went even further, and stated that it was not the custom of the men to use pyjamas at all, and that in fact on cold nights some of them merely removed their hats and shoes, and then retired.)

"Table linen, even if coarse, should be provided. Are our men to come back to us savages?"

It may have been purely coincidence, but soon after Tish's recommendations had been received at the War Department the Fosdick Commission was appointed. Yet we carried away a conviction that though certain things had been sadly neglected Charlie Sands was in good hands. The colonel came up to speak to us when, seeing the men standing in rows on the parade ground about sunset while the band played, we stood watching.

He was very pleasant, and said that they were about to bring in the flag. Some such conversation then ensued:

Tish: Do you bring in the flag every night?

The Colonel: Every night, madam.

Tish: Then you are a better housekeeper than I thought you were.

The Colonel: I beg your pardon?

Tish (magnanimously): You may not know much about dishcloths, but you are right about flags. They do fade, and I dare say dew is about as bad as rain for them.

He seemed very much gratified by her approval, and said in twenty-five years in the Army he had never failed to have the flag brought in at night. "I may fail in other things," he said wistfully. "To err is human, you know. But the flag proposition is one I stand pat on."

It was after our return visit to the camp that the real change in Tish began. We had gone to our cottage in Lake Penzance for the summer, and Tish suggested that we study French there. She had an excellent French book, with photographs in it showing where to place the tongue and how to pucker the lips for certain sounds. At first she did not allow us to do anything but practice these facial expressions, and I remember finding Hannah in the kitchen one night crying into her bread sponge and asking her what the trouble was.

"I just can't bear it, Miss Lizzie," she said; "when I look in and see the three of you sitting there making faces I nearly go crazy. I've got so I do it myself, and the milkman won't leave the bottles no nearer than the gate."

After some days of silent practice Tish considered that we could advance a lesson, and we began with syllable sounds, thus:

> *Ba* —Said with tip of tongue against lower teeth.
> *Be* —Show two upper middle teeth.
> *Bi* —Broad smile.
> *Bu* —Whistle.
> *Bon* —Pout.

It was an excellent method, though we all found difficulty in showing only two upper middle teeth.

There were also syllables which called for hollow cheeks, and I remember Tish's irritation at my failure.

"If you would eat less whipped cream, Lizzie," she said scathingly, "you might learn the French language. Otherwise you might as well give it up."

"I dare say there are plump people among the French," I retorted. "And I never heard that a Frenchwoman who put on twenty pounds or so went dumb. That woman who trims your hats isn't dumb so you could notice it. I'd thank my stars if she was. She can say forty dollars fast enough, and she doesn't suck in her cheeks either!"

In the end Aggie and I gave up the French lessons, but Tish kept them up. She learned ten nouns a day, and she made an attempt at verbs, but gave it up.

"I can secure anything I want, if I ever visit our valiant Ally," she said, "by naming it in the French and then making the appropriate gesture."

She made the experiment on Hannah, and it worked well enough. She would say "butter" or "spoon" and point to her place at the table; but Hannah almost left on the strength of it, and when she tried it on Mr. Jennings, the fishman, he told all over Penzance that she had lost either her mind or her teeth.

Aggie and I were extremely uneasy all of July, for Tish does nothing without a motive, and she was learning in French such warlike phrases as "Take the trenches," "The enemy is retiring," and "We must attack from the rear." She also took to testing out the engine of her automobile in various ways, and twice, trying to cross a plowed field with it, had to be drawn out with a rope. She took to driving at night without lights also, and had the ill luck to run into the Penzance doctor's buggy and take a wheel off it.

It was after that incident, when we had taken the doctor home and put him to bed, that I demanded an explanation.

But she only said with a far-away look in her eyes: "It may be a useful accomplishment sometime. If one were going after wounded at night it would be invaluable."

"Not if you killed all the doctors on the way!" I snapped.

The limit to our patience came soon after that. One morning about the first of August the boatman from the lake came up the path with a spade over his shoulder. Tish, we perceived, tried to take him aside, but he gave her no time.

"Well, I've done it, Miss Tish," he said, "and God only knows what'll happen if somebody runs into it between now and tomorrow morning."

"Nobody will know you did it unless you continue to shout the way you are doing now."

"Oh, I'll not tell," he observed; "I'm not so proud of it. But 'twouldn't surprise me a mite if we both did some time together in the county jail, on the head of it, Miss Tish."

Well, Aggie went pale, but Tish merely gave him five dollars and spent the rest of the day shut in the garage with her car. I went back and looked in the window during the afternoon, and she was on her back under it, hammering at something.

That night at dinner she made an announcement.

"I have for some time," she said, "been considering-go out, Hannah, and close the door-been considering the values of different engines for an ambulance which I propose to take to France."

"Tish!" Aggie cried in a heart-rending tone.

"And I have come to the conclusion that my own car has the best engine on the market. Tonight I propose to make a final test and if it succeeds I shall have an ambulance body built on it. I know this engine; I may almost say I have an affection for it. And it has served me well. Why, I ask you, should I abandon it and take some new-fangled thing that would as like as not lie down and die the minute it heard the first shell?"

"Exactly," I said with some feeling; "why should you, when you can count on me doing it anyhow?"

She ignored that, however, and said she had fully determined to go abroad and to get as near the Front as possible. She said also that she had already written General Pershing, and that she expected to start the moment his reply came.

"I told him," she observed, "that I would prefer not being assigned to any particular part of the line, as it was my intention, though not sacrificing the national good to it, to remain as near my nephew as possible. Pershing is a father and I felt that he would understand."

She then prepared to take the car out, and with a feeling of desperation Aggie and I followed her.

For some time we pursued the even tenor of our way, varied only by Tish's observing over her shoulder: "No matter what happens, do not be alarmed, and don't yell!"

Aggie was for getting out then, but we have always stood by Tish in an emergency, and we could not fail her then. She had turned into a dark lane and we were moving rapidly along it.

"When I say 'Ready!' brace yourselves for a jar," Tish admonished us. Aggie was trembling, and she had just put a small flash of blackberry cordial to her lips to steady herself when the machine went over the edge of a precipice, throwing Aggie into the road and myself forward into the front of the car.

There was complete silence for a moment. Then Aggie said in a reproachful voice: "You didn't say 'Ready!' Tish."

Tish, however, said nothing, and in the starlight I perceived her bent forward over the steering wheel. The car was standing on its forward end at the time.

"Tish!" I cried. "Tish!"

She then straightened herself and put both hands over the pit of her stomach.

"I've burst something, Lizzie," she said in a strangled tone. "My gall bladder, probably."

She then leaned back and closed her eyes. We were greatly alarmed, as it is unlike our brave Tish to give in until the very last, but finally she sat erect, groaning.

"I am going back and kill that boatman," she said. "I told him to dig a shell hole, not a cellar." Here she stood up and felt her pulse. "If I've burst anything," she announced a moment later, "it's a corset steel. That boatman is a fool, but at least he has given us a chance to see if we are of the material which France requires at this tragic juncture."

"I can tell you right away that I am not," Aggie said tartly. "I'm not and I don't want to be. Though I can't see how biting my tongue half through is going to help France anyhow."

But Tish was not listening. She had lifted three shovels out of the car, and we could see her dauntless figure outlined against the darkness.

"The Germans," she said at last, "are over there behind that chicken house. The machine is stalled in a shell hole and contains a wounded soldier. We are being shelled and there are those what-you-call-'em lights overhead. We must escape or be killed. There is only one thing to do. Lizzie, what is your idea of the next step?"

"Anybody but a lunatic would know that," I said tartly. "The thing to do is to go home and make an affidavit that we never saw that car, and that the hole in this road is where it was struck by lighting."

"Aggie," Tish said without paying any attention to me, "here is a shovel for you."

But Aggie sniffed.

"Not at all, Tish Carberry," she observed. "I am the wounded soldier, and I don't stir a foot."

In the end, however, we all went to work to dig the car out of the hole, and at three o'clock in the morning Tish climbed in and started the engine. It climbed out slowly, but as Tish observed it gave an excellent account of itself.

"And I must say," she said, "I believe we have all shown that we can meet emergency in the proper spirit. As for the hole, that driveling idiot who dug it can fill it up tomorrow morning and no one be the wiser."

I have made this explanation because of the ugly reports spread by the boatman himself. It is necessary, because it appears that he became intoxicated on the money Tish had so generously given him, and the milk wagon which supplied us going into the hole an hour or so after we had left he shamelessly told his own part and ours in the catastrophe. The result was that waking the next morning with a severe attack of lumbago I heard our splendid Tish being attacked verbally by the milkman and forced to pay an outrageous sum in damages.

By September Tish had had the old body removed from her automobile and an ambulance body built on. She made the drawings for it herself, and it contained many improvements over the standard makes. It contained, for instance, a cigarette lighter-not that Tish smokes, but because wounded men always do, and we knew that matches were scarce in France. It also contained an ice-water tank, a reading lamp, with a small portable library of improving books selected by our clergyman, Mr. Ostermaier, and a false bottom. This last Tish was rather mysterious about, merely remarking that it might be a good place for Aggie to retire to if she took a sneezing spell within earshot of the enemy.

When I look back and recall how foresighted Letitia Carberry was I am filled with admiration of those sterling qualities which have so many times brought us safely out of terrible danger.

We were, however, doomed at first to real disappointment. With everything arranged, with the ambulance ready and our costumes made, we could not get to France. Tish made a special trip to Washington to see the Secretary of War, and he remembered very well her recommendations as to the camps, and so forth, and said that he had referred the matter of pyjamas, for instance, to the Chief of Staff. He himself felt that the point was well taken. He believed in pyjamas, and wore them, but that he had an impression, though he did not care to go on record about it, that the chief of staff advocated nightshirts. He also said that he had a letter from General Pershing asking that no relatives of soldiers go to France, as he was afraid that the gentle and restraining influence of their loved ones would impair their taste for war.

Aggie and I began to have a little hope at that time, and Aggie tore up a will she had made leaving her property to the Red Cross, on condition that it kept up Mr. Wiggins' lot in the cemetery. But just as we were feeling more cheerful Aggie had a warning. She had been reading everywhere of the revival in spiritualism, and once before when she was in doubt she had been most successful with a woman who told the future with the paste letters that are used in soup. She went to a clairvoyant and he told her to be very careful of high places, and that the warning came from some one who had passed over from a high place. He thought it was an aviator, but we knew better, and Aggie looked at me with agonized eyes.

Aggie has said since that when she was in her terrible position at V —— she remembered that warning, but of course it was too late then.

It was when we had gone back to the city that we realized that Tish was still determined to get to France. Only two days after our return she came in with a book called "Military Codes and Signals," and gave it to Aggie. She had it marked at a place which told how to signal at night with an electric flashlight, and from that time on for several weeks she would sit in her window at night, with Aggie on the pavement across the street, also with a pocket flash, both of them signaling anything that came into their heads. It was rather hard on Aggie on cold evenings, and I remember very well that one night she came in and threw her flashlight on the floor, and then burst into tears.

"I'm through, Tish," she said, "and that's all there is to it! I've stood being frozen until my feet are so cold I can't tell one from the other, but I draw the line at being insulted."

"Insulted?" Tish said. "If you are going to mind trifles when your country's safety is in question you'd better stay at home. Who insulted you?"

Well, it seems that by way of conversation Aggie had flashed that the wretch with the cornet who rooms above Tish's apartment was at the window watching and she wished he'd fall out and break his neck.

He had then put out his own light and had appeared in the window again, and had flashed in the same code: "Come, birdie, fly with me."

For certain reasons I have decided not to reveal how Tish finally arranged that we should get to France. As the Secretary of War says, it might make him very unpopular with the many women he had been obliged to refuse. It is enough to say that the wonderful day finally came when we found ourselves on the very ocean which had carried Tish's nephew on his glorious mission. Aggie was particularly exalted as we went down the bay, escorted by encircling aeroplanes.

"I'm not a brave woman, Tish," she said softly, "but as I look back on that glorious sky line I feel that no sacrifice is too great to make for it. I am ready to do or die."

"Humph," said Tish. "Well, as far as I'm concerned, after the prices they charged me at that hotel the Germans are welcome to New York. I'd give it to them and say 'Thank you' when they took it."

We then went below and tried on our life-preserving suits, which the clerk at the steamship office had rented to us at fifteen dollars each.

He said they were most essential, and that when properly inflated one could float about in them for a week. Indeed, as Tish said, with a compass and a small sail one could probably make the nearest land, such as the Azores, supporting life in the meantime with ship's biscuits, and so on, in waterproof packages, carried in the pockets provided for the purpose. She did indeed go so far as to place a bottle of blackberry cordial in the pocket of each suit, and also a small tin of preserved ginger, which we have always found highly sustaining. But we were somewhat uneasy to discover that it required a considerable length of time to get into the suits.

We had barely got into them when we heard a bugle blowing and men running. Just after that an alarm bell began to ring, and Aggie said "It has come!" and as usual commenced to sneeze violently. We ran out on deck, dear Tish saying to be calm, as more lives were lost through excitement than anything else; though she herself was none too calm, for when we found afterward that it was only a lifeboat drill I discovered that she was carrying her silver-handled umbrella.

Every one was on the deck, and I must say that we were followed by envious glances. As we had inflated the suits they were not immodest, effectually concealing the lines of the figure, but making it difficult to pass through doorways.

There was a very nice young man on deck, in a Red Cross uniform, and he said that as he was the only male in our lifeboat he was pleased to see that three of the eighteen ladies in it were prepared to take care of themselves. He said that he felt he would probably have his hands full saving the fifteen others.

"Not," he added, "that I should feel comfortable until you were safely in the boat anyhow. I should not like to think of you floating about, perhaps for weeks, and possibly dodging sharks and so on."

Tish liked him at once, and said that in case of trouble if the boat were crowded we would only ask for a towing line.

It was while this conversation was going on that Aggie suddenly said: "I've changed my mind, Tish, I'm not going."

Well, we looked at her. She was a green color, and she said she'd thank us to put her off in something or other and let her go back. She wasn't seasick, but she just didn't care for the sea. She never had and she never would. And then she said "Ugh!" and the Red Cross man put his arm around her as far as it would go in the rubber suit, and said that certainly she was not seasick, but that some people found the sea air too stimulating, and she'd better go below and not get too much of it at first.

He helped us get Aggie down to her cabin, but unluckily he put her down on Tish's knitting. We had the misfortune to hear a slow hissing sound, and her inflated suit began to wilt immediately, where a steel needle had penetrated it.

Even then both Tish and I noticed that he had a sad face, and later on, when we had put Aggie to bed in her life suit, for she refused to have it taken off, we sat in Tish's cabin across, listening to Aggie's moans and to his story.

Tish had immediately demanded to know why he was not in the uniform of a fighting man, and he said at once: "I'm glad you asked me that. I've been wanting to tell the whole ship about it, but it's so darned ridiculous. I've tried every branch and they've all turned me down, for a —for a physical infirmity."

"Flat feet?" Tish asked.

"No. The truth is, I've had a milk leg. Fact. I know it is-er-generally limited to the other sex at-er-certain periods. But I've had it. Can't hike any distance. Can't run. Couldn't even kick a Hun," he added bitterly. "And what's more, there's a girl on this ship who thinks I'm a slacker, and I can't tell her about it. She wouldn't believe me if I did-though why a fellow would make up a milk leg I don't know. And she'd laugh. Everybody laughs. I've made a lot of people happy."

"Why don't you tell her you have heart disease?" Tish inquired in a gentler tone. Though not young herself she has preserved a fine interest in the love affairs of youth.

"Oh, I've got that all right," he said gloomily. "But it's not the sort that keeps a fellow out of the Army. It's —well, that doesn't matter. But suppose I told her that? She wouldn't marry me with heart disease."

"Tish!" Aggie called faintly.

In the end we were obliged to cut the rubber suit off with the scissors, as she not only refused to get up but wanted to drown if we were torpedoed. We therefore did not see the young man again until evening, and then he was with a very pretty girl in a Y. M. C. A. uniform. We had gone up on deck for air, and Tish was looking for the captain. She had a theory that if we could put Aggie in a hammock she would feel better, as the hammock would remain stationary while the ship rocked. Just as we passed them, the girl said: "He's the best-looking man on the ship anyhow. And he's a captain in the infantry. He says it is the most dangerous branch of the service."

"Oh, he does, does he?" said the Red Cross young man. "Well, you'd better wait six months before you fall too hard for him. He may get his face changed, and there isn't much behind it."

He spoke quite savagely, and both Tish and I felt that he was making a mistake, and that gentleness, with just a suggestion of the caveman beneath, would have been more efficacious. Indeed when we knew Mr. Burton better-that was his name-we ventured the suggestion, but he only shook his head.

"You don't know her," he said. "She is the sort of girl who likes to take the soft-spoken fellow and make him savage. And when she gets the cave type she wants to tame him. I've tried being both, so I know. I'm damned —I beg your pardon —I'm cursed if I know why I care for her. I suppose it's because she has about as much use for me as she has for a dose of Paris green. But if you hear of that Weber who hangs round her going overboard some night, I hope you'll understand. That's all."

That conversation, however, was later on in the voyage. That first night out Tish saw the captain and he finally agreed, if we said nothing about it, to have a sailor's hammock hung in Aggie's cabin.

"It wouldn't do to have it get about, madam," he said. "You know how it is —I'd have all the passengers in hammocks in twenty-four hours, and the crew sleeping on the decks. And you know crews are touchy these days, what with submarines and chaplains and young shave-tails of officers who expect to be kissed every time they're asked to get off a coil of rope."

We promised secrecy, and that evening a hammock was hung in Aggie's cabin. It was not much like a hammock, however, and it was so high that Tish said it looked more like a chandelier than anything else. Getting Aggie into it required the steward, the stewardess, Mr. Burton and ourselves, but it was finally done, and we all felt easier at once, except that I was obliged to stand on a chair to feed her her beef tea.

However, just after midnight Tish and I in our cabin across heard a terrible thud, followed by silence and then by low, dreadful moans. Aggie had fallen out. She did not speak at all for some time, and when she did it was to horrify Tish. For she said: "Damnation!"

Tish immediately turned and left the cabin, leaving me to press a cold knife against the lump on Aggie's head and to put her back into her berth. She refused the hammock absolutely. She said she had forgotten where she was, and had merely reached out for her bedroom slippers, which were six feet below, when the whole thing had turned over and thrown her out.

She insisted that she did not remember saying anything improper, but that the time Tish's horse had thrown her in the cemetery she had certainly used strong language, to say the least.

I remember telling Tish this, and she justified herself by the subconscious mind, which she was studying at the time. She said that the subconscious mind stored up all the wicked words and impulses which the conscious mind puts virtuously from it. And she recalled the fact that Mr. Ostermaier, our clergyman, taking laughing gas to have a tooth drawn, tried to kiss the dentist on coming out, and called him a sweet little thing-though Mrs. Ostermaier is quite a large woman.

We became quite friendly with Mr. Burton during the remainder of the voyage. He formed the habit of coming down every evening before dinner to our cabin and having a dose of blackberry cordial to prevent seasickness.

"I've had it before," he said on one occasion, "but never with such-er-medicinal qualities. You don't put anything in it but blackberries, do you?"

"Only a little alcohol to preserve it," I told him with some pride. I generally make it myself.

"I will say this for it: It's extremely well preserved," he said, and filled up the tooth mug again. It was after that that he told us that Hilda had refused to marry him, and was flirting outrageously with Captain Weber.

"I only say this," he added gloomily: "He's right when he says he belongs in the infantry. He's got the photographs of five youngsters in his cabin; or he did have. He's probably hidden them now."

"Why don't you tell her?" Tish demanded.

"Why should I? Let her make a fool of herself if she wants to," he said despondently. "What chance have I against a shipload of 'em, anyhow? If it wasn't this one it would be another. She's got her eye on a tank now, and she's only waiting for that aviator to forget his stomach to sit at his feet and worship. God only knows what would happen if we had a Croix de Guerre on board."

He sat for some time, sipping the blackberry cordial and looking into space.

"I've got it figured out this way," he said at last. "I've got to pull off something over there. That's all. Got to get in the papers and get a medal and a wooden leg. She'd stand for a wooden leg better than a milk one," he added viciously.

Both Aggie and I noticed that Tish regarded him with a contemplative eye, and from, that time on she spent at least a part of every day with him. He paid no attention at all to Hilda from that time on, and one morning while Tish and Mr. Burton were walking by her chair she dropped a book. But he did not seem to see it, and that evening the captain moved over to her table, and Mr. Burton was very gay, but ate hardly any dinner.

We all went in the same train to Paris, and he had a sort of revenge then. For the captain could not speak French, and she had to ask Mr. Burton to order her dinner for her. But he ordered only one, and the captain was furious, naturally.

"Look here, Burton," he said, "I'm here, you know."

"Why, so you are," said Mr. Burton coldly. "I hadn't noticed you."

"How the devil can I make that woman understand that I'm hungry?"

Mr. Burton reflected.

"I'll tell you," he said. "You might open your mouth and point down your throat. Most of these French know the sign language."

He turned away then, and I saw a gleam of triumph in Tish's eye. She leaned over to him.

"She's furious that he can't speak French," she said. "Talk to me in French, and don't mind what I say. The only thing I can remember is a list of a hundred nouns. I'll string them together somehow."

There was a French officer near us, and I saw him watching Tish carefully as the conversation went on. She said afterward that as near as she could make out, Mr. Burton was telling the history of the country we went through, and that when he paused she would say in French: "Handkerchief, fish, trunk, pencil, book, soup," or some such list.

But it impressed Hilda; I could see that.

It was some time before we got out of Paris, and the news we had of Charlie Sands was that he was at the Front, near V — —, which was held by the enemy. Tish went out and bought a map, and decided that she would be sent in that direction or nowhere. But for several weeks nothing happened, and she found the ambulance had come and was being used to carry ice cream to convalescent hospitals round Paris. What was more, she could not get it back.

For once I thought our dauntless Tish was daunted. How true it is that we forget past success in present failure! But after a number of mysterious absences she came into my room after Aggie had gone to bed and said: "I've found where they keep it."

"Keep what?"

"My ambulance."

I was putting my hair on wavers at the time, and I saw in the mirror that she had her hat and coat on, and the expression she wears when she has decided to break the law.

"I'm not going to spend this night in a French jail, Tish Carberry," I said.

"Very well," she retorted, and turned to go out.

But the thought of Tish alone, embarked on a dangerous enterprise, was too much for me, and I called her back.

"I'll go," I said, "and I'll steal, if that's what you're up to. But I'm a fool, and I know it. You can't deceive a lot of Frenchmen with your handkerchief-fish-trunk-pencil stuff. And you can't book-soup-oysters yourself out of jail."

"I'm taking my own, and only my own," Tish said with dignity.

Well, I dressed and we went out into the street. I tried to tell Tish that even if we got it we couldn't take it home and hide it under the bed or in a bureau drawer, but she was engrossed in her own thoughts, and besides, the streets were entirely dark and not a taxicab anywhere. She had a city map, however, and a flashlight, and at last about two in the morning we reached the street where she said it was stored in a garage.

I was limping by that time, and there were cold chills running up and down my spine, but Tish was quite calm. And just then there was a terrific outburst of noise, whistles and sirens of all sorts, and a man walking near us suddenly began to run and dived into a doorway.

"Air raid," said Tish calmly, and walked on. I clutched at her arm, but she shook me off.

"Tish!" I begged.

"Don't be a craven, Lizzie," she said. "Statistics show that the percentage of mortality from these things is considerably less than from mumps, and not to be compared with riding in an elevator or with the perils of maternity."

All sorts of people were running madly by that time, and suddenly disappearing, and a man with a bird cage in his hand bumped flat into me and knocked me down. Tish, however, had moved on without noticing, and when I caught up to her she was standing beside a wide door which was open, staring in.

"This is the place," she said. And just then half a dozen men poured out through the doorway and ran along the street. Tish drew a long breath.

"You see?" she said. "Providence watches over those whose motives are pure, even if compelled to certain methods — —"

There was a terrible crash at that moment down the street, followed by glass falling all round us.

"— —which are not entirely ethical," Tish continued calmly. "We might as well go inside, Lizzie. They may drop another, and we shall never have such a chance again."

"I can't walk, Tish," I said in a quavering voice. "My knees are bending backward."

"Fiddlesticks!" she replied scornfully and stalked inside.

I have since reflected on Tish during that air raid, on the calm manner in which she filled the gasoline tank of her ambulance, on the way in which she flung out six empty ice-cream freezers, and the perfect aplomb with which she kicked the tires to see if they contained sufficient air. For such attributes I have nothing but admiration. But I am not so certain as to the mental processes which permitted her calmly to take three spare tires from other cars and to throw them into the ambulance.

Perhaps there is with all true greatness an element of ruthlessness. Or perhaps she subsequently sent conscience money to the Red Cross anonymously. There are certain matters on which I do not interrogate her.

I was still sitting on the running board of a limousine inhaling my smelling salts when she pronounced all ready and we got into the driving seat and started. Just as we moved out a man came in from the street and began to yell at us. When Tish paid no attention to him he took a flying leap and landed on the step beside us.

"Here, what the — — do you think you are doing?" he said in English. "Where's your permit?"

Tish said nothing, but turned out into the street and threw on the gas. He was on my side and the jerk almost flung him off.

"Stop this car!" he yelled. "Hey, Grogan! Grogan!"

But whoever Grogan was he was still in some cellar probably, and by that time we were going very fast. Unluckily the glass in the street cut all four tires almost immediately, and we swung madly from one side to the other. And just then, too, we struck the hole the shell had made, and went into it with a terrible bump. The man disappeared immediately, but Tish was quite composed. She simply changed gears, and the car crawled out on the other side.

"This motor will go anywhere, Lizzie," she said easily. "I feel that my judgment is entirely vindicated. Where's that man?"

"Killed, probably," I retorted with a certain acidity.

"I hope not," she replied with kindly tolerance. "But if he is it will be supposed that a bomb did it."

As a matter of fact the *Herald* next morning reported the miraculous escape of an American found on the very edge of a shell hole, recovering, but showing one of the curious results of shell shock, being convinced that two women had stolen a car from his garage, and had run it into the hole in a deliberate attempt to kill him.

Aggie read this to us at breakfast, and Tish merely observed that it was very sad, and that she proposed studying shell shock at the Front. Not until months later did we tell Aggie the story of that night.

That morning Tish disappeared, and at noon she came back to say that she had at last secured the ambulance, and that we would start for the Front at once. Privately she told me that in a pocket of the car she had found permits to get us out of Paris, but that the car would be missed before long, and that we would better start at once.

It is strange to look back and recall with what blitheness we prepared to leave. And it is interesting, too, to remember the conversation with Mr. Burton when he called that afternoon.

"Hello!" he said, glancing about. "This looks like moving on. Where to, oh, brave and radiant spirits?"

"We haven't quite decided," Tish said. She was cleaning her revolver at the time.

"You haven't decided! Great Scott, haven't you any orders? Or any permits?"

"All that are necessary," Tish said, squinting into the barrel of her revolver. "Aggie, don't forget your hay-fever spray."

"But look here," he began, "you know this is France in wartime. I hate to throw a wrench into the machinery, but no one can travel a mile in this country without having about a million papers. You'll be arrested; you'll be — —"

"Young man," Tish said quietly, pouring oil on a rag, "I was arrested before you were born. Aggie, will you order some tea? And make mine very weak."

"Weak tea!" he repeated with a sort of groan. "Weak tea! And yet you start for the Front, picking out any trench that takes your fancy, and-weak tea! And I am going to St.-Nazaire! I, a man, with a man's stomach and a mad affection for a girl who thinks I prefer serving doughnuts to fighting! I do that, while you — —"

"Why do you go to St.-Nazaire?" Tish inquired. "You can sit with Aggie inside the ambulance, and I'm sure you could be useful, changing tires, and so on. You could simply disappear, you know. That is what we intend to do."

"I'll have a cup of tea," he said in a strange voice. "Very strong, please; I seem rather dazed."

"I figure this way," Tish went on, putting down her revolver and taking up her knitting: "I don't believe an ambulance loaded with cigarettes and stick candy and chocolate, with perhaps lemons for lemonade, is going to be stopped anywhere as long as it's headed for the Front. I understand they don't stop ambulances anyhow. If they do you can stretch out and pretend to be wounded. This is one way in which you can be very useful-being wounded."

He took all his tea at a gulp, and then looked round in an almost distracted manner.

"Certainly," he said. "Of course. It's all perfectly simple. You-you don't mind, I suppose, if I take a moment to arrange my mind? It seems to be all mussed up. Apparently I think clearly, but somehow or other — —"

"We are actuated by several motives," Tish went on, beginning to turn the heel of the sock. "First of all, my nephew is at the Front. I want to be near him. I am a childless woman, and he is all I have. Second, I fancy the more cigarettes and so on our boys have the better for them, though I disapprove of cigarettes generally. And finally, I do not intend to let the biggest thing in my lifetime go by without having been a part of it, even in the most humble manner."

"Entirely reasonable too," he said.

But he still had a strange expression on his face, and soon after that he said he'd walk round a little in the air and then come back and tell us his decision.

At five o'clock he was back and he was very pale and wore what Aggie considered a haunted look. He stalked in and stood, his cap in his hand.

"I'll go," he said. "I'll go, and I don't give a —I don't care whether I come back or not. That's clear, isn't it? I'll go as far as you will, Miss Tish, and I take it that means moving right along. I'll go there, and then I'll keep on going."

"You've seen Hilda!" Aggie exclaimed with the intuition of her own experience in matters of the heart.

"I've seen her," he said grimly. "I wasn't looking for her. I've given that up. She was with that-well, you know. If I had any sense I'd have stolen those photographs and mailed them to her, one at a time. Five days, one each day, I'd have — —"

"You might save all that hate for the Germans," Tish said. "I don't care to promise anything, but I have an idea that you may have a chance to use it."

And again, as always, our dear Tish was right.

We left Paris that evening. We made up quite comfortable beds in the ambulance, which had four new tires and which Tish with her customary forethought had filled as full as possible with cigarettes and candy. I have never inquired as to where Tish secured these articles, but I have learned that very early Tish adopted an army term called salvage, which seems to consist of taking whatever is necessary wherever it may be found. For instance, she has always referred to the night when she salvaged the ambulance and the extra tires; and the night later on, when we found the window of a warehouse open and secured seven cases of oranges for some of our boys who had no decent drinking water, she also referred to our actions at that time as salvage.

In fact, so common did the term become that I have heard her speaking of the time we salvaged the town of V———.

In re the matter of passports —*in re* is also military, and means referring to, or concerning; I find a certain tendency myself to use military terms. *In re* the matter of passports and permits, since the authenticity of our adventure has recently been challenged here at home, particularly in our church, though we have been lifelong members, it is a strange fact that we never required any. The sacred emblem on the ambulance and ourselves, including Mr. Burton, was amply sufficient. And though there were times when Mr. Burton found it expedient to lie in the back of the car and emit slow and tortured groans I have always contended that it was not really necessary in the two months which followed.

Over those two months I shall pass lightly. Our brave Tish was almost incessantly at the wheel, and we distributed uncounted numbers of cigarettes and so on. We had, naturally, no home other than the ambulance, but owing to Tish's forethought we found, among other articles in the secret compartment under the floor, a full store of canned goods and a nest of cooking kettles.

With this outfit we were able to supplement when necessary such provisions as we purchased along the way, and even now and then to make such occasional delicacies as cup custard or to bake a few muffins or small sweet cakes. More than once, too, we have drawn up beside the road where troops were passing, and turned out some really excellent hot doughnuts for them.

Indeed I may say that we became quite well known among both officers and men, being called The Three Graces.

But when so many were doing similar work on a much larger scale our poor efforts are hardly worthy of record. Only one thing is significant! We moved slowly but inevitably toward the Front, and toward that portion of the Front where Charlie Sands was serving his country.

During all this time Mr. Burton never mentioned Hilda but once, and that was to state that he had learned Captain Weber was a widower.

"Not that it makes any difference to me," he said. "She can marry him tomorrow as far as I'm concerned. I've forgotten her, practically. If I marry it will be one of these French girls. They can cook anyhow, and she can't. Her idea of a meal is a plate of fudge."

"He's really breaking his heart for her," Aggie confided to me later. "Do you notice how thin he is? And every time he looks at the moon he sighs."

"So do I," I said tartly; "and I'm not in love either. Ever since that moonlight night when that fool of a German flew over and dropped a bomb onto the best layer cake I've ever baked I've sighed at the moon too."

But he was thinner; and, when the weather grew cold and wet and we suggested flannels to him as delicately as possible, he refused to consider them.

"I'd as soon have pneumonia as not," he said. "It's quick and easy, and-anyhow we need them to cover the engine on cold nights."

It was, I believe, at the end of the seventh week that we drew in one night at a small village within sound of the guns. We limped in, indeed, for we had had one of our frequent blowouts, and had no spare tire.

Scattering as was our custom, we began a search for an extra tire, but without results. There was only one machine in the town, and that belonged to General Pershing. We knew it at once by the four stars. As we did not desire to be interrogated by the commander-in-chief we drew into a small alleyway behind a ruined house, and Aggie and I cooked a Spanish omelet and arranged some lettuce-and-mayonnaise sandwiches.

Tish had not returned, but Mr. Burton came back just as I was placing the meal on the folding table we carried for the purpose, and we saw at once that something was wrong. He wore a look he had not worn since we left Paris.

"Leg, probably," I said in an undertone to Aggie. He was subject to attacks of pain in the milk leg.

But Aggie's perceptions were more tender.

"Hilda, most likely," she said.

However, we were distracted by the arrival of Tish, who came in with her customary poise and unrolled her dinner napkin with a thoughtful air. She commented kindly on the omelet, but was rather silent.

At the end of the meal, however, she said: "If you will walk up the road past the Y. M. C. A. hut, Mr. Burton, it is just possible you will find an extra tire lying there. I am not positive, but I think it likely. I should continue walking until you find it."

"Must have seen a rubber plant up that way," Mr. Burton said, rather disagreeably for him. He was most pleasant usually.

"I have simply indicated a possibility," Tish said. "Aggie, I think I'll have a small quantity of blackberry cordial."

With Tish recourse to that remedy indicated either fatigue or a certain nervous strain. That it was the latter was shown by the fact that when Mr. Burton had gone she started the engine of the car and suggested that we be ready to leave at a moment's notice. She then took a folding chair and placed herself in a dark corner of the ruined house.

"If you see the lights of a car approaching," she called, "just tell me, will you?"

However, I am happy to say that no car came near. Somewhat later Mr. Burton appeared rolling a tire ahead of him, and wearing the dazed look he still occasionally wore when confronted with new evidences of Tish's efficiency.

"Well," he said, dropping the tire and staring at Aggie and myself, "she dreamed true. Either that or —— "

"Mr. Burton," Tish called, "do you mind hiding that tire until morning? We found it and it is ours. But it's unnecessary to excite suspicion at any time."

I am not certain that Mr. Burton's theory is right, but even if it is I contend that war is war and justifies certain practices hardly to be condoned in times of peace.

Briefly, he has always maintained that Tish being desperate and arguing that the C. in C. — which is military for commander-in-chief—was able to secure tires whenever necessary-that Tish had deliberately unfastened a spare tire from the rear of General Pershing's automobile; not of course actually salvaging it, but leaving it in a position where on the car's getting into motion it would fall off and could then be salvaged.

I do not know. I do know, however, that Tish retired very early to her bed in the ambulance. As Aggie was heating water for a bath, having found a sheltered horse trough behind a broken wall, I took Mr. Burton for a walk through the town in an endeavor to bring him to a more cheerful frame of mind. He was still very low-spirited, but he offered no confidences until we approached the only undestroyed building in sight. He stopped then and suggested turning back.

"It's a Y hut," he said. "We'll be about as welcome there as a skunk at a garden party."

I reprimanded him for this, as I had found no evidence of any jealousy between the two great welfare organizations. But when I persisted in advancing he said: "Well, you might as well know it. She's there. I saw her through a window."

"What has that got to do with my getting a bottle of vanilla extract there if they have one?"

"Oh, she'll have one probably; she uses it for fudge! I'm not going there, and that's flat."

"I thought you had forgotten her."

"I have!" he said savagely. "The way you forget the toothache. But I don't go round boring a hole in a tooth to get it again. Look here, Miss Lizzie, do you know what she was doing when I saw her? She was dropping six lumps of sugar into a cup of something for that-that parent she's gone bugs about."

"That's what she's here for."

"Oh, it is, is it?" he snarled. "Well, she wasn't doing it for the fellow with a cauliflower ear who was standing beside him. There was a line of about twenty fellows there putting in their own sugar, all right."

"I'll tell you this, Mr. Burton," I said in a serious tone, "sometimes I think things are just as well as they are. You haven't a disposition for marriage. I don't believe you'll make her happy, even if you do get her."

"Oh, I'll not get her," he retorted roughly. "As a matter of fact, I don't want her. I'm cured. I'm as cured as a ham. She can feed sugar to the whole blamed Army, as far as I'm concerned. And after that she can go home and feed sugar to his five kids, and give 'em colic and sit up at night and — —"

I left him still muttering and went into the Y hut. Hilda gave a little scream of joy when she saw me and ran round the counter, which was a plank on two barrels, and kissed me. I must say she was a nice little thing.

"Isn't France small after all?" she demanded. "And do you know I've seen your nephew-or is it Miss Tish's? He's just too dear! We had a long talk here only a day or two ago, and I was telling about you three, and suddenly he said: 'Wait a minute. You've mentioned no names, but I'll bet my tin hat my Aunt Tish was one of them!' Isn't that amazing?"

Well, I thought it was, and I took a cup of her coffee. But it was poor stuff, and right then and there I made a kettleful and showed her how. But I noticed she grew rather quiet after a while.

At last she said: "You —I don't suppose you've seen that Mr. Burton anywhere, have you?"

"We saw something of him in Paris," I replied, and glanced out the window. He was standing across what had once been the street, and if ever I've seen hungry eyes in a human being he had them.

"He was so awfully touchy, Miss Lizzie," she said. "And then I was never sure — — Why do you suppose he isn't fighting? Not that it's any affair of mine, but I used to wonder."

"He's got a milk leg," I said, and set the coffee kettle off.

"A milk leg! A milk — — Oh, how ridiculous! How — — Why, Miss Lizzie, how can he?"

"Don't ask me. They get 'em sometimes too. They're very painful. My cousin, Nancy Lee McMasters, had one after her third child and — —"

I am sorry to say that here she began to laugh. She laughed all over the hut, really, and when she had stood up and held to the plank and laughed she sat down on a box of condensed milk and laughed again. I am a truthful woman, and I had thought it was time she knew the facts, but I saw at once that I had make a mistake. And when I looked out the window Mr. Burton had gone.

I remained there with her for some time, but as any mention of Mr. Burton only started her off again we discussed other matters.

She said Charlie Sands was in the Intelligence Department at the Front, and that when he left he was about to, as she termed it, pull off a raid.

"He's gone to bring me a German as a souvenir; and that Captain Weber-you remember him-he is going to bring me another," she cried. "He gave me my choice and I took an officer, with a nice upcurled mustache and — —"

"And five children?"

"Five children? Whatever do you mean, Miss Lizzie?"

"I understand that Captain Weber has five. I didn't know but that you had a special preference for them that way."

"Why, Miss Lizzie!" she said in a strained voice. "I don't believe it. He's never said — —"

I was washing out her dish towels by that time, for she wasn't much of a housekeeper, I'll say that, though as pretty as a picture, and I never looked up. She walked round the hut, humming to herself to show how calm she was, but I noticed that when her broom fell over she kicked at it.

Finally she said: "I don't know why you think I was interested in Captain Weber. He was amusing, that's all; and I like fighting men-the bravest are the tenderest, you know. I—if you ever happen on Mr. Burton you might tell him I'm here. It's interesting, but I get lonely sometimes. I don't see a soul I really care to talk to."

Well, I promised I would, and as Mr. Burton had gone I went back alone. Tish was asleep with a hot stone under her cheek, from which I judged she'd had neuralgia, and Aggie was nowhere in sight. But round the corner an ammunition train of trucks had come in and I suddenly remembered Aggie and her horse trough. Unfortunately I had not asked her where it was.

I roused Tish but her neuralgia had ruffled her usual placid temper, and she said that if Aggie was caught in a horse trough let her sit in it. If she could take a bath in a pint of water Aggie could, instead of hunting up luxuries. She then went to sleep again, leaving me in an anxious frame of mind.

Mr. Burton was not round, and at last I started out alone with a flashlight, but as we were short of batteries I was too sparing of it and stepped down accidentally into a six-foot cellar, jarring my spine badly. When I got out at last it was very late, and though there were soldiers all round I did not like to ask them to assist me in my search, as I had every reason to believe that our dear Aggie had sought cleanliness in her nightgown.

It was, I believe, fully 2 A. M. when I finally discovered her behind a wall, where a number of our boys were playing a game with a lantern and dice —a game which consisted apparently of coaxing the inanimate objects with all sorts of endearing terms. They got up when they saw me, but I observed that I was merely taking a walk, and wandered as nonchalantly as I was able into the inclosure.

At first all was dark and silent. Then I heard the trickle of running water, and a moment later a sneeze. The lost was found!

"Aggie!" I said sternly.

"Hush, for Heaven's sake! They'll hear you."

"Where are you?"

"B-b-behind the trough," she said, her teeth chattering. "Run and get my bathrobe, Lizzie. Those d-d-dratted boys have been there for an hour."

Well, I had brought it with me, and she had her slippers; and we started back. I must say that Aggie was a strange figure, however, and one of the boys said after we had passed: "Well, fellows, war's hell, all right."

"If you saw it too I feel better," said another. "I thought maybe this frog liquor was doing things to me."

Aggie, however, was sneezing and did not hear.

I come now to that part of my narrative which relates to Charlie Sands' raid and the results which followed it. I felt a certain anxiety about telling Tish of the dangerous work in which he was engaged, and waited until her morning tea had fortified her. She was, I remember, sitting on a rock directing Mr. Burton, who was changing a tire.

"A raid?" she said. "What sort of a raid?"

"To capture Germans, Tish."

"A lot of chance he'll have!" she said with a sniff. "What does he know about raids? And you'd think to hear you talk, Lizzie, that pulling Germans out of a trench was as easy as letting a dog out after a neighbor's cat. It's like Pershing and all the rest of them," she added bitterly, "to take a left-handed newspaper man, who can't shut his right eye to shoot with the left, and start him off alone to take the whole German Army."

"He wouldn't go alone," said Mr. Burton.

"Certainly not!" Tish retorted. "I know him, and you don't, Mr. Burton. He'll not go alone. Of course not! He'll pick out a lot of men who play good bridge, or went to college with him, or belong to his fraternity, or can sing, or some such reason, and ——"

Here to my great surprise she flung down one of our two last remaining teacups and retired precipitately into the ruins. Not for us to witness her majestic grief. Rachel-or was it Naomi? — mourning for her children.

However, in a short time she reappeared and stated that she was sick of fooling round on back roads, and that we would now go directly to the Front.

"We'll never pull it off," Mr. Burton said to me in an undertone.

"She has never failed, Mr. Burton," I reminded him gravely.

Before we started Mr. Burton saw Hilda, but he came back looking morose and savage. He came directly to me.

"Look me over," he said. "Do I look queer or anything?"

"Not at all," I replied.

"Look again. I don't seem to be dying on my feet, do I? Anything wan about me? I don't totter with feebleness, do I?"

"You look as strong as a horse," I said somewhat acidly.

"Then I wish to thunder you'd tell me," he stormed, "why that girl-that-well, you know who I mean-why the deuce she should first giggle all over the place when she sees me, and then baby me like an idiot child? 'Here's a chair,' she'd say, and 'Do be careful of yourself'; and when I recovered from that enough to stand up like a man and ask for a cup of coffee she said I ought to take soup; it was strengthening!"

Fortunately Tish gave the signal to start just then, and we moved out. Hilda was standing in her doorway when we passed, and I thought she looked rather forlorn. She blew kisses to us, but Mr. Burton only saluted stiffly and looked away. I have often considered that to the uninitiated the ways of love are very strange.

It was when we were out of the village that he turned to me with a strange look in his eyes.

"She doesn't care for Weber after all," he said. "Didn't I tell you the minute she found she could have him she wouldn't want him? Do you think I'd marry a girl like that?"

"She's a nice little thing," I replied. "But you're perfectly right-she's no housekeeper."

"No housekeeper!" he said in a tone of astonishment. "That's the cleanest hut in France. And let me tell you I've had the only cup of coffee ——"

He broke off and fell into a fit of abstraction. Somewhat later he looked up and said: "I'll never see her again, Miss Lizzie."

"Why?"

"Because I told her I wouldn't come back until I could bring her a German officer as a souvenir. Some idiot had told her he was going to, and, of course, I told her if she was collecting them I'd get her one. A fat chance I have too! I don't know what made me do it. I'm only surprised I didn't make it the Crown Prince while I was at it."

But how soon were our thoughts to turn from soft thoughts of love to graver matters!

Tish, as I have said before, has a strange gift of foresight that amounts almost to prophecy.

I have never known her, for instance, to put a pink bow on an afghan and then have the subsequent development turn out to be a boy, or vice versa. And the very day before Mr. Ostermaier fell and sprained his ankle she had picked up a roller chair at an auction sale, and in twenty minutes he was in it.

At noon we stopped at a crossroads and distributed to some passing troops our usual cigarettes and chocolate. We also fried a number of doughnuts, and were given three cheers by various companies as they passed. It was when our labors were over that Tish perceived a broken machine gun abandoned by the roadside, and spent some time examining it.

"One never knows," she said, "what bits of knowledge may one day be useful."

Mr. Burton explained the mechanism to her.

"I'd be firing one of these things now," he said gloomily, "if it were not for that devilish piece of American ingenuity, the shower bath."

"Good gracious!" Aggie said.

"Fact. I got into a machine-gun school, but one day in a shower one of the officers perceived my-er-affliction, badly swollen from a hike, and reported me."

Tish was strongly inclined to tow the machine gun behind us and eventually have it repaired, but Mr. Burton said it was not worth the trouble, and shortly afterward we turned off the main road into a lane, seeking a place for our luncheon. Tish drove as usual, but she continued to lament the gun.

"I feel keenly," she said, "the necessity of being fully armed against any emergency. And I feel, too, that it is my solemn duty to salvage such weapons as come my way at any and all times."

I called to her just then, but she was driving while looking over her shoulder at Mr. Burton, and it was too late to avoid the goat. We went over it and it lay behind us in the road quite still.

"You've killed it, Tish," I said.

"Not at all," she retorted. "It has probably only fainted. As I was saying, I feel that with our near approach to the lines we should be armed to the teeth with modern engines of destruction, and should also know how to use them."

We were then in a very attractive valley, and Tish descending observed that if it were not for the noise of falling shells and so on it would have been a charming place to picnic.

She then instructed Aggie and me to prepare a luncheon of beef croquettes and floating island, and asked Mr. Burton to accompany her back to the car.

As I was sitting on the running board beating eggs for a meringue at the time I could not avoid overhearing the conversation.

First Mr. Burton, acting under orders, lifted the false bottom, and then he whistled and observed: "Great Cæsar's ghost! Looks as though there is going to be hell up Sixth Street, doesn't it?"

"I'll ask you not to be vulgar, Mr. Burton."

"But-look here, Miss Tish. We'll be jailed for this, you know. You may be able to get away with the C. in C.'s tires, but you can't steal a hundred or so grenades without somebody missing them. Besides, what the-what the dickens are you going to do with them? If it had been eggs now, or oranges-but grenades!"

"They may be useful," Tish replied in her cryptic manner. "Forearmed is forewarned, Mr. Burton. What is this white pin for?"

I believe she then pulled the pin, for I heard Mr. Burton yell, and a second later there was a loud explosion.

I sat still, unable to move, and then I heard Mr. Burton say in a furious voice: "If I hadn't grabbed that thing and thrown it you'd have been explaining this salvage system of yours to your Maker before this, Miss Carberry. Upon my word, if I hadn't known you'd blow up the whole outfit the moment I was gone I'd have left before this. I've got nerves if you haven't."

"That was an over-arm pitch you gave it," was Tish's sole reply. "I had always understood that grenades were thrown in a different manner."

I distinctly heard his groan.

"You'll have about as much use for grenades as I have for pink eye," he said almost savagely. "I don't like to criticize, Miss Tish, and I must say I think to this point we've made good. But when I see you stocking up with grenades instead of cigarettes, and giving every indication of being headed for the Rhine, I feel that it is time to ask what next?"

"Have you any complaint about the last few weeks?" Tish inquired coldly.

"Well, if we continue to leave a trail of depredations behind us —— It's bad enough to have a certain person think I'm a slacker, but if she gets the idea that I'm a first-class second-story worker I'm done, that's all."

Fortunately Aggie announced luncheon just then.

Every incident of that luncheon is fixed clearly in my mind, because of what came after it. We had indeed penetrated close to the Front, as was shown by the number of shells which fell in it while we ate. The dirt from one, in fact, quite spoiled the floating island, and we were compelled to open a can of peaches to replace it. It was while we were drinking our after-dinner coffee that Tish voiced the philosophy which upheld her.

"When my hour comes it will come," she said calmly. "Viewed from that standpoint the attempts of the enemy to disturb us become amusing-nothing more."

"Exactly," said Mr. Burton, skimming some dust from the last explosion out of his coffee cup. "Amusing is the word. Funny, I call it. Funny as a crutch. Why, look who's here!"

There was a young officer riding up the valley rapidly. I remember Tish taking a look at him and then saying quickly: "Lizzie, go and close the floor of the ambulance. Don't run. I'll explain later."

Well, the officer rode up and jumped off his horse and saluted.

"Some of our fellows said you were trapped here, Miss Carberry," he said. "I didn't believe it at first. It's a bad place. We'll have to get you out somehow."

"I'm not anxious to get out."

"But," he said, and stared at all of us —"you are — — Do you know that our trenches are just beyond this hill?"

"I wish you'd tell the Germans that; they seem to think they are in this valley."

He laughed a little and said: "They ought to make you a general, Miss Carberry." He then said to Mr. Burton: "I'd like to speak to you for a moment."

Looking back I believe that Tish had a premonition of trouble then, for during their conversation aside she got out her knitting, always with her an indication of perturbation or of deep thought, and she spoke rather sharply to Aggie about rinsing the luncheon dishes more thoroughly. Aggie said afterward that she herself had felt at that time that peculiar itching in the palms of her hands which always with her presages bad news.

"If he asks about those grenades, Lizzie, you can reply. Say you don't know anything about them. That's the truth."

"I know where they are," I said with some acidity. "And what's more, I know I'm not going to ride a foot in that ambulance with that concentrated extract of hell under my feet."

"Lizzie — —"

She began sternly, but just then the two men came back, and the officer's face was uncomfortable.

"I —from your demeanor," he said, "and-er-the fact that you haven't mentioned it I rather gather that you have not heard the er-the news, Miss Carberry."

"I didn't see the morning papers," Tish said with the dry wit so characteristic of her.

"You have a nephew, I understand, at the Front?"

Tish's face suddenly grew set and stern.

"Have-or had?" she asked in a terrible voice.

"Oh, it's not so bad as all that. In fact, he's a lot safer just now than you are, for instance. But it's rather unfortunate in a way too. He has been captured by the enemy."

Aggie ran to her then with the blackberry cordial, but Tish waved her away.

"A prisoner!" she said. "A nephew of mine has allowed himself to be captured by the Germans? It is incredible!"

"Lots of us are doing it," he said. "It's no disgrace. In fact, it's a mark of courage. A fellow goes farther than he ought to, and the first thing he knows he's got a belt of bayonet points, and it is a time for discretion."

"Leave me, please," Tish said majestically. "I am ashamed. I am humbled. I must think."

Shortly after that she called us back and said: "I have come to this conclusion: The situation is unbearable and must be rectified. Do you know where he is enduring this shameful captivity?"

"I wouldn't take it too hard, Miss Tish," said the officer. "He's very comfortable, as we happen to know. One of our runners got back at dawn this morning. He said he left your nephew in the church at V — —, playing pinochle with the German C. O. The runner was hidden in the cellar under the church, and he said the C. O. had lost all his money and his Iron Cross, and was going to hold Captain Sands until he could win them back."

He then urged her, the moment night fell, to retire from our dangerous position, and to feel no anxiety whatever.

"If I know him," were his parting words, "he'll pick that German as clean as a chicken. Pinochle will win the war," he added and rode away.

During the remainder of the afternoon Tish sat by herself, knitting and thinking. It was undoubtedly then that she formed the plan which in its execution has brought us so much hateful publicity, yet without which the town of V — —might still be in German hands.

II

We knew, of course, that Tish's fine brain was working on the problem of rescuing Charlie Sands; and Mr. Burton was on the whole rather keen about it.

"I've got to get a German officer some way," he said. "She's probably planning now to see Von Hindenburg about Sands. She generally aims high, I've discovered. And in that case I rather fancy myself taking the old chap back to Hilda as a souvenir." He then reflected and scowled. "But she'd be flirting with him in ten minutes, damn her!" he added.

Tish refused both sympathy and conversation during the afternoon.

On Aggie's offering her both she merely said: "Go away and leave me alone, for Heaven's sake. He is perfectly safe. I only hope he took his toothbrush, that's all."

It is a proof of Tish's gift of concentration that she thought out her plan so thoroughly under the circumstances, for the valley was shelled all that afternoon. We found an abandoned battery position and the three of us took refuge in it, leaving Tish outside knitting calmly. It was a poor place, but by taking in our folding table and chairs we made it fairly comfortable, and Mr. Burton taught us a most interesting game of cards, in which one formed pairs and various combinations, and counted with coffee beans. If one had four of any one kind one took all the beans.

It was dusk when Tish appeared in the doorway, and we noticed that she wore a look of grim determination.

"I have been to the top of the hill," she said, "and I believe that I know now the terrain thoroughly. In case my first plan fails we may be compelled to desperate measures-but I find my present situation intolerable. Never before has a member of my family been taken by an enemy. We die, but we do not surrender."

"You can speak for your own family, then," Aggie said. "I've got a family, too, but it's got sense enough to surrender when necessary. And if you think Libby Prison was any treat to my grandfather — —"

Tish ignored her.

"It is my intention," she went on, "to appeal to the general of his division to rescue my nephew and thus wipe out the stain on the family honor. Failing that, I am prepared to go to any length." Here she eyed Aggie coldly. "It is no time for craven spirits," she said. "We may be arrested and court-martialed for being so near the Front, to say nothing of what may eventuate in case of a refusal. I intend to leave no stone unturned, but I think it only fair to ask for a vote of confidence. Those in the affirmative will please signify by saying 'aye.'"

"Aye," I said stoutly. I would not fail my dear Tish in such a crisis. Aggie followed me a moment later, but feebly, and Mr. Burton said: "I don't like the idea any more than I do my right eye. Why bother with the general? I'm for going to V — — and breaking up the pinochle game, and bringing home the bacon in the shape of a Hun or two."

However, I have reason to think that he was joking, and that subsequent events startled him considerably, for I remember that when it was all over and we were in safety once again he kept saying over and over in a dazed voice: "Well, can you beat it? Can you beat it?"

In some way Tish had heard, from a battery on the hill, I think, that headquarters was at the foot of the hill on the other side. She made her plans accordingly.

"As soon as darkness has fallen," she said to Mr. Burton, "we three women shall visit the commanding officer and there make our plea-without you, as it will be necessary to use all the softening feminine influence possible. One of two things will then occur: Either he will rescue my nephew or —I shall."

"Now see here, Miss Tish," he protested, "you're not going to leave me out of it altogether, are you? You wouldn't break my heart, would you? Besides, you'll need me. I'm a specialist at rescuing nephews. I —I've rescued thousands of nephews in my time."

Well, she'd marked out a place that would have been a crossroads if the German shells had left any road, and she said if she failed with the C. O. he was to meet us there, with two baskets of cigarettes for the men in the trenches.

"Cigarettes!" he said. "What help will they be against the enemy? Unless you mean to wait until they've smoked themselves to death."

"Underneath the cigarettes," Tish went on calmly, "you will have a number of grenades. If only we could repair that machine gun!" she reflected. "I dare say I can salvage an automatic rifle or two," she finished; "though large-sized firecrackers would do. The real thing is to make a noise."

"We might get some paper bags and burst them," suggested Mr. Burton; "and if you feel that music would add to the martial effect I can play fairly well on a comb."

It was perhaps nine o'clock when we reached the crest of the hill, and had Tish not thoughtfully brought her wire cutters along I do not believe we would have succeeded in reaching headquarters. We got there finally, however, and it was in a cellar and-though I do not care to reflect on our gallant army-not as tidy as it should have been. Mr. Burton having remained behind temporarily the three of us made our way to the entrance, and Tish was almost bayoneted by a sentry there, who was nervous because of a number of shells falling in the vicinity.

"Take that thing away!" she said with superb scorn, pointing to the bayonet. "I don't want a hole in the only uniform I've got, young man. Watch your head, Lizzie!"

"The saints protect us!" said the sentry. "Women! Three women!"

Tish and I went down the muddy incline into the cellar, and two officers who were sitting there playing cribbage looked at us and then stood up with a surprised expression.

Tish had assumed a most lofty attitude, and picking out the general with an unfailing eye she saluted and said: "Only the most urgent matters would excuse my intrusion, sir. I ——"

Unfortunately at that moment Aggie slipped and slid into the room feet first in a sitting posture. She brought up rather dazed against the table, and for a moment both officers were too surprised to offer her any assistance. Tish and I picked her up, and she fell to sneezing violently, so that it was some time before the conversation was resumed. It was the general who resumed it.

"This is very flattering," he said in a cold voice, "but if you ladies will explain how you got here I'll make it interesting for somebody."

Suddenly the colonel who was with him said: "Suffering Crimus! It can't be! And yet-it certainly is!"

We looked at him, and it was the colonel who had been so interested in Charlie Sands at the training camp. We all shook hands with him, and he offered us chairs, and said to the general: "These are the ladies I have told you about, sir, with the nephew. You may recall the helpful suggestions sent to the Secretary of War and forwarded back to me by the General Staff. I have always wanted to explain about those dish towels, ladies. You see, you happened on us at a bad time. Our dish towels had come, but though neatly hemmed they lacked the small tape in the corner by which to hang them up. I therefore ——"

"Oh, keep still!" said the general in an angry tone. "Now, what brings you women here?"

"My nephew has been taken prisoner," Tish said coldly. "I want to know merely whether you propose to do anything about it or intend to sit here in comfort and do nothing."

He became quite red in the face at this allusion to the cribbage board, et cetera, and at first seemed unable to speak.

"Quietly, man," said the colonel. "Remember your blood pressure."

"Damn my blood pressure!" said the general in a thick tone.

I must refuse to relate the conversation that followed-hardly conversation, indeed, as at the end the general did all the talking.

At last, however, he paused for breath, and Tish said very quietly: "Then I am to understand that you refuse to do anything about my nephew?"

"Who is your nephew?"

"Charlie Sands."

"And who's Charlie Sands?"

"My nephew," said Tish.

He said nothing to this, but shouted abruptly in a loud voice: "Orderly! Raise that curtain and let some air into this rat hole."

Then he turned to the colonel and said: "Thompson, you're younger than I am. I've got a family, and my blood pressure's high. I'm going out to make a tour of the observation posts."

"Coward!" said the colonel to him in a low tone.

The colonel was very pleasant to us when the other man had gone. The general was his brother-in-law, he said, and rather nervous because they hadn't had a decent meal for a week.

"The only thing that settles his nerves is cribbage," he explained. "It helps his morale. Now-let us think about getting you back to safety. I'd offer you our humble hospitality, but somebody got in here today and stole the duckboard I've been sleeping on, and I can't offer you the general's cellar door. He's devoted to it."

"What if we refuse to go back?" Tish demanded. "We've taken a risky trip for a purpose, and I don't give up easily, young man. I'm inclined to sit here until that general promises to do something."

His face changed.

"Oh, now see here," he said in an appealing voice, "you aren't going to make things difficult for me, are you? There's a regulation against this sort of thing."

"We are welfare workers," Tish said calmly. "Behind us there stand the entire American people. If kept from the front trenches while trying to serve our boys there are ways of informing the people through the press."

"It's exactly the press I fear," he said in a sad voice. "Think of the results to you three, and to me."

"What results?" Tish demanded impatiently. "I'm not doing anything I'm ashamed of."

He was abstractedly moving the cribbage pins about.

"It's like this," he said: "Not very far behind the lines there are a lot of newspaper correspondents, and lately there hasn't been much news. But perhaps I'd better explain my own position. I am engaged to a lovely girl at home. I write to her every day, but I have been conscious recently that in her replies to me there has been an element of-shall I say suspicion? No, that is not the word. Anxiety-of anxiety, lest I shall fall in love with some charming Red Cross or Y. M. C. A. girl. Nothing could be further from my thoughts, but you can see my situation. Three feminine visitors at nightfall; news-hungry correspondents; all the rest of it. Scandal, dear ladies! And absolute ruin to my hopes!"

"Bosh!" said Tish. But I could see that she was uncomfortable. "If there's trouble I'll send her our birth certificates. Besides, I thought you said the general was your brother-in-law?"

Aggie says he changed color at that but he said hastily: "By marriage, madam, only by marriage. By that I mean —I —he-the general is married to my brother."

"Really!" said Tish. "How unusual!"

She said afterward that she saw at once then that we were only wasting time, and that neither one of them would move hand or foot to get Charlie Sands back. Aggie had been scraping her skirt with a table knife, and was now fairly tidy, so Tish prepared to depart.

"On thinking it over," she said, "I realize that I am confronting a situation which requires brains rather than brute force. I shall therefore attend to it myself. Good night, colonel. I hope you find another duckboard. And-if you are writing home present my compliments to the general's husband. Come, Aggie."

At the top of the incline I looked back. The colonel was staring after us and wiping his forehead with a khaki handkerchief.

"You see," Tish said bitterly, "that is the sort of help one gets from the Army." She drew a deep breath and looked in the general direction of the trenches. "One thing is sure and certain —I'm not going back until I've found out whether Charlie Sands is still in that town over there or whether he has been taken away so we'll have to get at him from Switzerland."

Aggie gave a low moan at this, and Tish eyed her witheringly.

"Don't be an idiot, Aggie!" she observed. "I haven't asked you to go-or Lizzie either. I'd be likely," she added, "to get through our lines unseen and into the very midst of the German Army-with one of you sneezing with hay fever and the other one panting like a locomotive from, too much flesh."

"Tish — —" I began firmly. But she waved her hand in silence and demanded Aggie's flashlight. She then led the way behind the ruins of a wall and took a bundle of papers from under her jacket.

"If the Army won't help us we have a right to help ourselves," she observed. And I perceived with a certain trepidation that the papers were some that had been lying on the table at headquarters.

"'Memorandum,'" Tish read the top one. "'Write home. Order boots. Send to British Commissary for Scotch whisky. Insect powder!' Wouldn't you know," she said bitterly, "that that general would have to make a memorandum about writing home?"

Underneath, however, there was an aeroplane picture of the Front and V — —, and also a map. Both of these she studied carefully until several bullets found their way to our vicinity, and a sentry ran up and was very rude about the light. On receiving a box of cigarettes, however, he became quite friendly.

"Haven't had a pill for a week," he said. "Got to a point now where we steal the hay from the battery horses and roll it up in leaves from my Bible. But it isn't really satisfying."

Tish gave him a brief lecture on thus mutilating his best friend, but he said that he only used the unimportant pages. "You know," he explained —"somebody begat somebody else, and that sort of thing. You haven't any more fags about you, have you?" he asked wistfully. "I'll be sandbagged and robbed if I go back without any for the other fellows."

"We can bring some," Tish suggested, "and you might show us to the trenches. I particularly wish to give some to the men in the most advanced positions."

"You're on," he said cheerfully. "Bring the life savers, and we'll see that you get forward all right."

Tish reflected.

"Suppose," she said at last —"suppose that we wish to be able on returning to our native land to state that we have not only been to our advanced positions but have even made a short excursion into the debatable territory-that is, into what is commonly known as No Man's Land?"

"All of you?" he asked doubtfully.

"All of us."

He then considered and said: "How many cigarettes have you got?"

"About a hundred packages," Tish replied. "Say, five to you, and the rest used where considered most efficacious."

"Every man has his price," he observed. "That's mine. I'm taking a chance, but I've seen you round, so I know you're not spies. And if you get an extra helmet out there you might give me one. I've been here six months and I've never seen one, on a German or off. I let a woman reporter through last week," he added, "and d'you think she thanked me? No. She gave me hell because the Germans had a raid that night and nearly got her. I'm a soldier, not a prophet."

Tish left us immediately to go back to Mr. Burton, and Aggie clutched at my arm in a frenzy of anxiety.

"She's going to do it, Lizzie!" she said with her teeth chattering. "She's going to V —— to rescue Charlie Sands, and we'll all be caught, and-Lizzie, I feel that I shall never see home again."

"Well, if you ask me, I don't think you will," I said as calmly as possible. Aggie put her head on my shoulder and wept between sneezes.

"I know I'm weak, Lizzie," she moaned, "but I'm frightened, and I'm not afraid to say so. You'd think she only had to shoo those Germans like a lot of chickens. I love Tish, but if she'd only sprain her ankle or something!"

However, Tish came back soon, bringing Mr. Burton with her and two baskets with cigarettes on top and grenades below, and also our revolvers and a supply of extra cartridges. She had not explained her plan to Mr. Burton, so we sat down behind the wall and she told him. He seemed quite willing and cheerful.

"Certainly," he said. "It is all quite clear. We simply go into No Man's Land for souvenirs, and they pass us. Perfectly natural, of course. We then continue to advance to the German lines, and then commit suicide. I've been thinking of doing it for some time anyhow, and this way has an element of the dramatic that appeals to me." I have learned since that he felt that the only thing to do was to humor Tish, and that he was convinced that about a hundred yards in No Man's Land would hurt no one, and, as he expressed it, clear the air. How little he knew our dear Tish!

As it is not my intention to implicate any of those brave boys who sought to give us merely the innocent pleasure of visiting the strip of land between the two armies I shall draw a veil over our excursion through the trenches that night, where we were met everywhere with acclaim and gratitude, and finally assisted out of the trenches by means of a ladder. As it was quite dark the grenades in the basket entirely escaped notice, and we found ourselves at last headed toward the German lines, and fully armed, though looking, as Mr. Burton observed, like a picnic party.

He persisted in making humorous sallies such as: "Did any one remember the pepper and salt?" and "I hope somebody brought pickles. What's a picnic without pickles?"

I regret to say that we were fired on by some of our own soldiers who didn't understand the situation, shortly after this, and that the bottle of blackberry cordial which I was carrying was broken to fragments.

"If they hit this market basket there'll be a little excitement," Mr. Burton said. He then stopped and said that a joke was a joke, but there was such a thing as carrying it too far, and that we'd better look for a helmet or two and then go back.

"The Germans are just on the other side of that wood," he whispered; "and they don't know a joke when they see one."

"I thought, Mr. Burton, you promised to take Hilda a German officer," Tish said scornfully.

"I did," he agreed. "I did indeed. But now I think of it, I didn't promise her a live one. The more I consider the matter the more I am sure that no stipulation was made as to the conditions of delivery. I —— —"

But when he saw Tish continuing to advance he became very serious, and even suggested that if we would only go back he would himself advance as far as possible and endeavor to reach V —— —.

Just what Tish's reply would have been I do not know, as at that moment Aggie stumbled and fell into a deep shell hole full of water. We heard the splash and waited for her voice, as we were uncertain of her exact position.

But what was our surprise on hearing a deep masculine voice say: "Hands up, you dirty swine!"

"Let go of me," came in piteous accents from Aggie.

There was then complete silence, until the other voice said: "Well, I'll be damned!" It then said: "Bill, Bill!"

"Here," said still another voice, a short distance away, in a sort of loud whisper.

"There's a mermaid in my pool," said the first voice. "Did you draw anything?"

"Lucky devil," said the other voice. "I'm drawing about eight feet of water, that's all."

Tish then advanced in the direction of the voices and said: "Aggie, are you all right?"

"I'm half drowned. And there's a man here."

The first voice then said in an aggrieved manner: "This is my puddle, you know, lady. And if my revolver wasn't wet through I'm afraid there would be one mermaid less, or whatever you are."

The Germans at that moment sent up one of their white lights, which resemble certain of our Fourth of July pieces, which float a long time and give the effect of full moonlight.

"Down," said Mr. Burton, and we all fell flat on our faces. Before doing so, however, we had a short glimpse of Aggie's head and another above the water in the shell hole, and realized that her position was very uncomfortable.

When the light died away the two men emerged, and with some difficulty dragged her out. It was while this was going on that Tish caught my arm and whispered: "Lizzie, I have heard that voice before."

Well, it had a familiar sound to me also, and when he addressed the other man as Grogan I suddenly remembered. It was the man we had thrown from the ambulance in Paris the night Tish salvaged it! I told Tish in a whisper, and she remembered the incident clearly.

"You sure gave me a scare," he said to Aggie. "For if you were a German I was gone, and if you were an officer of the A. E. F. I was gone more. Bill and I just slipped out to take a look round the town behind those woods, account of our captain being a prisoner there."

"Who is your captain?" Tish asked.

"Name's Weber. We pulled off a raid last night, and he and a fellow named Sands got grabbed."

"Weber?" said Mr. Burton, forgetting to whisper.

"You-you don't mean Captain Weber?" I asked after a sickening pause.

"That's the man."

"Oh, dear!" said Aggie.

Suddenly Mr. Burton stopped and put down the basket of grenades.

"I'm damned if I'm going to rescue him!" he said firmly. "Now look here, Miss Tish, I hate to disappoint you, but I've got private reasons for leaving Weber exactly where he is.

"I don't wish him any harm, but if they'd take him and put him to road mending for three or four years I'd be a happier man. And as far as I'm concerned, I'm going to give them the chance."

The two men had stood listening, and now Bill spoke:

"Am I to understand that this is a rescue party?" he said. "Seeing the basket I thought it was a picnic. I just want to say this: If you have any idea of going to V——, and as we were going in that direction ourselves, we might combine. My friend here and I were over last night, and we know how to get into the town."

"Very well," Tish agreed after a moment's hesitation. "I have no objection. It must be distinctly understood, however, that I am in charge. Captain Sands is my nephew."

Another light went up just then, and I perceived that he was staring at her.

"My-my word!" he gasped.

We then fell on our faces, and while lying there I heard him whispering to Bill. He then said to Tish: "I believe, lady, that we have met before."

"Very possibly," Tish said calmly. "In the course of my welfare work I have met many of our brave men."

"I wouldn't call it exactly welfare work you were doing when I saw you."

"No?" said Tish.

"You may be interested to know that if you hadn't stolen that ambulance ——"

"Salvaged."

"——salvaged that ambulance I would now be in safety in Paris, instead of——Not that I'd exchange," he added. "I wouldn't have missed this excursion for a good bit. But they made it so darned unpleasant for me that I enlisted."

The starlight having now died we rose and prepared to advance. Mr. Burton, however, was very difficult and tried to get Tish to promise to leave Captain Weber if we found him.

"It's the only bit of luck I've had since I left home, Miss Tish," he said.

Tish, however, ignored him, and with the help of our new allies briefly sketched a plan of campaign.

I make no pretensions to military knowledge, but I shall try to explain the situation at V———, as our dear Tish learned it from the general's papers and the two soldiers. The real German position—a military term meaning location and not attitude-was behind the town, but they kept enough soldiers in it to hold it, and in case of an attack they filled it up with great rapidity. So far the church tower remained standing, as the Allies wished on taking the town to use it to look out from and observe any unfriendly actions on the part of the Germans.

"If only," Tish said, "we could have repaired that machine gun and brought it the affair would be extremely simple. It has from the beginning been my intention to give the impression of an attack in force."

She then considered for a short time, and finally suggested that the two soldiers return to the allied Front and attempt to secure two automatic rifles.

"And it might be as well," she added, "to take Miss Aggie with you. She is wet through, and will undoubtedly before long have a return of her hay fever, which with her has no season. A sneeze at a critical time might easily ruin us."

Aggie, however, absolutely refused to return, and said that by holding her nostrils closed and her mouth open she could, if she felt the paroxysm coming on, sneeze almost noiselessly. She said also that though not related to her by blood Charlie Sands was as dear as her own, and that if turned back she would go to V——alone and, if captured, at least suffer imprisonment with him.

Tish was quite touched, I could see, and on the two men departing to attempt the salvage of the required weapons she assisted me in wringing out Aggie's clothing and in making her as comfortable as possible.

We waited for some time, eating chocolate to restore our strength, and attempting to comfort Mr. Burton, who was very surly.

"It has been my trouble all my life," he observed bitterly, "not to leave well enough alone. I hadn't any hope of the success of this expedition before, but now I know you'll pull it off. You'll get Sands and you'll get Weber and send him back-to-well, you understand. It's just my luck. I'm not complaining, but if I'm killed and he isn't I'm going to haunt that Y hut and make it darned unpleasant for both of them."

Tish reproved him for debasing the future life to such purposes, but he was firm.

"If you think I'm going to stand round and be walked through and sat on, and all the indignities that ghosts must suffer, without getting back," he said gloomily, "you can think again, Miss Tish!"

When the two men returned Tish gave them a brief talking-to.

"First of all," she said, "there must be no mistake as to who is in command of this expedition. If we succeed it will be by finesse rather than force, and that is distinctly a feminine quality. Second, there is to be no unnecessary fighting. We are here to secure my nephew, not the German Army."

The man we had bumped off the step of the ambulance, whose name proved to be Jim, said at once that that last sentence had relieved his mind greatly. A few prisoners wouldn't put them out seriously, but the Allies were feeding more than they could afford already.

"But a few won't matter," he added. "Say, a dozen or so. They won't kick on that."

<hr>

I have never learned where Tish learned her strategy-unless from the papers she took from the general's cellar.

Military experts have always considered the plan masterly, I believe, and have lauded the mobility of a small force and the greater element of surprise possible, as demonstrated by the incidents which followed.

Briefly Tish adhered to her plan of making the attack seem a large one, by spreading the party over a large area and having it make as much noise as possible.

"By firing from one spot, and then running rapidly either to right or left, and firing again," she said, "those who have only revolvers may easily appear to be several persons instead of one."

She then arranged that the two automatic rifles attack the town from in front, but widely separated, while Aggie and myself, endeavoring to be a platoon-or perhaps she said regiment-would advance from the left. On the right Mr. Burton was to move forward in force, firing his revolver and throwing grenades in different directions. Of her own plans she said nothing.

"Forward, the Suicide Club!" said Mr. Burton with that strange sarcasm which had marked him during the last hour.

I have since reflected that certain kinds of men seem to take love very unpleasantly. Aggie, however, maintains that the deeper the love the greater the misery, and that Mr. Wiggins once sent back a muffler she had made for him on seeing her conversing with the janitor of the church about dust in her pew.

In a short time we had passed through the wood and the remainder of the excursion was very slow, owing to being obliged to crawl on our hands and knees. We could now see the church tower, and Tish gave the signal to separate. The men left us at once, but for a short time Tish was near me, as I could tell by an irritated exclamation from her when she became entangled in the enemy's barbed wire. But soon I realized that she had gone. Looking back I believe it was just before we met the Germans who were out laying wire, but I am not quite certain. There were about ten of the enemy, and they almost stepped on Aggie. She said afterward that she was so alarmed that she sneezed, but that having buried her entire face in a mudhole they did not hear her. We lay quite still for some time, and when they had gone and we could move again Tish had disappeared.

However, we obeyed orders and went on moving steadily to the left, and before long we were able to make out the ruins of V —— directly before us. They were apparently empty and silent, and concealing ourselves behind a fallen wall we waited for the automatic rifles to give the signal. Aggie had taken cold from her wetting, and could hardly speak.

"I'b sure they've taked Tish," were her first words.

"Not alive," I said grimly.

"Lizzie! Oh, by dear Tish!"

"If you've got to worry," I said rather tartly, "worry about the Germans. It wouldn't surprise me a particle to see her bring in the lot."

Well, the attack started just then and Aggie and I got our revolvers and began shooting as rapidly as possible, firing from the end of the village, and with Mr. Burton's grenades from one side and our revolvers from the other it made a tremendous noise. Aggie and I did our best, I know, to appear to be a large number, firing and then moving to a new point and firing again. I must say from the way those Germans ran toward their own lines behind the town I was not surprised at the rapidity of the final retreat which ended the war. As Aggie said later, we were not there to kill them unless necessary, but they ran so fast at times it was difficult to avoid hitting them. They fairly ran into the bullets.

In a very short time there was not one in sight, but we kept on firing for a trifle longer, and then made for the church, meeting the two privates on the way. When we arrived Mr. Burton was already there and had unfastened a large bolt on the outside of the door. We crowded in, and somebody closed the door and we had a moment to breathe.

"Well, here we are," said Mr. Burton in a quite cheerful tone. "And not a casualty among us-or the Germans either, I fancy, save those that died of heart disease. Are we all here, by the way?"

He then struck a match, and my heart sank.

"Tish!" I cried. "Tish is not here!"

It was then that a voice from the far end of the church said: "Suffering' snakes! I'm delirious, Weber! I knew that beer would get me. I thought I heard — —"

Some one was hammering at the door with a revolver, and we heard Tish's dear voice outside saying: "Keep your hands up! *Lizzie!*"

Mr. Burton opened the door and Tish backed in, followed by a figure that was muttering in German. She had both her revolvers pointed at it, and she said: "Close the door, somebody, and get a light. I think it's a general."

Well, Charlie Sands was coming with a candle stuck in the neck of a bottle, and he seemed extremely surprised. He kept stumbling over things and saying "Wake me, Weber," until he had put a hand on my arm.

"It's real," he said then. "It's a real arm. Therefore it is, it must be. And yet — —"

"Stop driveling," Tish said sharply, "and tie up this general or whatever he is. I don't trust him. He's got a mean eye."

It has been the opinion of military experts that the reason the enemy had apparently lost its morale and failed to make a counter-attack at once was the early loss of this officer. In fact, a prisoner taken later I believe told the story that V — — had been attacked and captured by an entire division, without artillery preparation, and that he himself had seen the commanding officer killed by a shell. But the truth was that Tish, having fallen into an empty trench a moment or so before I missed her, had after recovering from the shock and surprise followed the trench for some distance, finding that she could advance more rapidly than by crawling on the surface.

She had in this manner happened on a dugout where a German officer was sitting at a table with a lighted candle marking the corners of certain playing cards with the point of a pin. He seemed to be in a very bad humor, and was muttering to himself. She waited in the darkness until he had finished, and had shoved the cards into his pocket. When he had extinguished the candle he started back along the trench toward the village, and Tish merely put her two revolvers to his back and captured him.

I pass over the touching reunion between Tish and her beloved nephew. He seemed profoundly affected, and moving out of the candlelight gave way to emotion that fairly shook him. It was when he returned wiping his eyes that he recognized the German officer. He became exceedingly grave at once.

"I trust you understand," he said to him, "that this-er-surprise party is no reflection on your hospitality. And I am glad to point out also that the pinochle game is not necessarily broken up. It can continue until you are moved back behind the Allied lines. I may not," he added, "be able to offer you a church, because if I do say it you people have been wasteful as to churches. But almost any place in our trenches is entirely safe."

He then looked round the group again and said: "Don't tell me Aunt Aggie has missed this! I couldn't bear it."

"Aggie!" I cried. "Where is Aggie?"

It was then that the painful truth dawned on us. Aggie had not entered the church. She was still outside, perhaps wandering alone among a cruel and relentless foe. It was a terrible moment.

I can still see the white and anxious faces round the candle, and Tish's insistence that a search be organized at once to find her. Mr. Burton went out immediately, and returned soon after to say that she was not in sight, and that the retiring Germans were sending up signal rockets and were probably going to rush the town at once.

We held a short council of war then, but there was nothing to do but to retire, having accomplished our purpose. Even Tish felt this, and said that it was a rule of war that the many should not suffer for the few; also that she didn't propose losing a night's sleep to rescue Charlie Sands and then have him retaken again, as might happen any minute.

We put out the candle and left the church, and not a moment too soon, for a shell dropped through the roof behind us, and more followed it at once. I was very uneasy, especially as I was quite sure that between explosions I could hear Aggie's voice far away calling Tish.

We retired slowly, taking our prisoner with us, and turning round to fire toward the enemy now and then. We also called Aggie by name at intervals, but she did not appear. And when we reached the very edge of the town the Germans were at the opposite end of it, and we were obliged to accelerate our pace until lost in the Stygian darkness of the wood.

It was there that I felt Tish's hand on my arm.

"I'm going back," she said in a low tone. "Driveling idiot that she is, I cannot think of her hiding somewhere and sneezing herself into captivity. I am going back, Lizzie."

"Then I go too," I said firmly. "I guess if she's your responsibility she's mine too."

Well, she didn't want me any more than she wanted the measles, but the time was coming when she could thank her lucky stars I was there. However, she said nothing, but I heard her suggesting that we separate, every man for himself, except the prisoner, and work back, to our own side the best way we could.

With her customary thoughtfulness, however, she held a short conversation with Mr. Burton first. I have not mentioned Captain Weber, I believe, since our first entrance into the church, but he was with us, and I had observed Mr. Burton eying him with unfriendly eyes. Indeed, I am quite convinced that the accident of our leaving the church without the captain, and finding him left behind and bolted in, was no accident at all.

Tish merely told Mr. Burton that the prisoner was his, and that if he chose and could manage to present him to Hilda he might as well do it.

"She's welcome to him," she said.

"He's not my prisoner."

"He is now; I give him to you."

Finding him obdurate, however, she resorted to argument.

"It doesn't invalidate an engagement," she said rather brusquely, "for a man to borrow the money for an engagement ring. If it did there would be fewer engagements. If you want to borrow a German prisoner for the same purpose the principle is the same."

He seemed to be weakening.

"I'd like to do it-if only to see her face," he said slowly. "Not but what it's a risk. He's a good-looking devil."

In the end, however, he agreed, and the last we saw of them he was driving the German ahead, with a grenade in one hand and his revolver in the other, and looking happier than he had looked for days.

Almost immediately after that I felt Tish's hand on my arm. We turned and went back toward V — —.

Military experts have been rather puzzled by our statement that the Germans did not reënter V — — that night, but remained just outside, and that we reached the church again without so much as a how-do-you-do from any of them. I believe the general impression is that they feared a trap. I think they are rather annoyed to learn that there was a period of several hours during which they might safely have taken the town; in fact, the irritable general who was married to the colonel's brother was most unpleasant about it. When everything was over he came to Paris to see us, and he was most unpleasant.

"If you wanted to take the damned town, why didn't you say so?" he roared. "You came in with a long story about a nephew, but it's my plain conviction, madam, that you were flying for higher game than your nephew from the start."

Tish merely smiled coldly.

"Perhaps," she said in a cryptic manner. "But, of course, in these days of war one must be very careful. It is difficult to tell whom to trust."

As he became very red at that she gently reminded him of his blood pressure, but he only hammered on the table and said:

"Another thing, madam. God knows I don't begrudge you the falderals they've been pinning on you, but it seems to me more than a coincidence that your celebrated strategy followed closely the lines of a memorandum, madam, that was missing from my table after your departure."

"My dear man," Tish replied urbanely, "there is a little military word I must remind you of-salvage. As one of your own staff explained it to me one perceives an object necessary to certain operations. If on saluting that object it fails to return the salute I believe the next step is to capture it. Am I not right?"

But I regret to say that he merely picked up his cap and went out of our sitting room, banging the door behind him.

To return. We reached the church safely, and from that working out in different directions we began our unhappy search. However, as it was still very dark I evidently lost my sense of direction, and while peering into a cellar was suddenly shocked by feeling a revolver thrust against my back.

"You are my prisoner," said a voice. "Move and I'll fire."

It was, however, only Tish. We were both despondent by that time, and agreed to give up the search. As it happened it was well we did so, for we had no more than reached the church and seated ourselves on the doorstep in deep dejection when the enemy rushed the village. I confess that my immediate impulse was flight, but Tish was of more heroic stuff.

"They are coming, Lizzie," she said. "If you wish to fly go now. I shall remain. I have too many tender memories of Aggie to desert her."

She then rose and went without haste into the church, which was sadly changed by shell fire in the last two hours, and I followed her. By the aid of the flashlight, cautiously used, we made our way to a break in the floor and Tish suggested that we retire to the cellar, which we did, descending on piles of rubbish. The noise in the street was terrible by that time, but the cellar was quiet enough, save when now and then a fresh portion of the roof gave way.

I was by this time exceedingly nervous, and Tish gave me a mouthful of cordial. She herself was quite calm.

"We must give them time to quiet down," she said. "They sound quite hysterical, and it would be dangerous to be discovered just now. Perhaps we would better find a sheltered spot and get some sleep. I shall need my wits clear in the morning."

It was fortunate for us that the French use the basements of their churches for burying purposes, for by crawling behind a marble sarcophagus we found a sort of cave made by the debris. Owing to that protection the grenades the enemy threw into the cellar did no harm whatever, save to waken Tish from a sound sleep.

"Drat them anyhow!" she said. "I was just dreaming that Mr. Ostermaier had declined a raise in his salary."

"Tish," I said, "suppose they find Aggie?"

She yawned and turned over.

"Aggie's got more brains than you think she has," was her comment. "She hates dying about as much as most people. My own private opinion is and has been that she went back to our lines hours ago."

"Tish!" I exclaimed. "Then why ——"

"I just want to try a little experiment," she said drowsily, and was immediately asleep.

At last I slept myself, and when we wakened it was daylight, and the Germans were in full possession of the town. They inspected the church building overhead, but left it quickly; and Tish drew a keen deduction from that.

"Well, that's something in our favor," she said. "Evidently they're afraid the thing will fall in on them."

At eight o'clock she complained of being hungry, and I felt the need of food myself. With her customary promptness she set out to discover food, leaving me alone, a prey to sad misgivings. In a short time, however, she returned and asked me if I'd seen a piece of wire anywhere.

"I've got considerable barbed wire sticking in me in various places," I said rather tartly, "if that will do."

But she only stood, staring about her in the semidarkness.

"A lath with a nail in the end of it would answer," she observed. "Didn't you step on a nail last night?"

Well, I had, and at last we found it. It was in the end of a plank and seemed to be precisely what she wanted. She took it away with her, and was gone some twenty minutes. At the end of that time she returned carrying carefully a small panful of fried bacon.

"I had to wait," she explained. "He had just put in some fresh slices when I got there."

While we ate she explained.

"There is a small opening to the street," she said, "where there is a machine gun, now covered with debris. Just outside I perceived a soldier cooking his breakfast. Of course there was a chance that he would not look away at the proper moment, but he stood up to fill his pipe. I'd have got his coffee too, but in the fight he kicked it over."

"What fight?" I asked.

"He blamed another soldier for taking the bacon. He was really savage, Lizzie. From the way he acted I gather that they haven't any too much to eat."

Breakfast fortified us both greatly, but it also set me to thinking sadly of Aggie, whose morning meal was a crisp slice of bacon, varied occasionally by an egg. I had not Tish's confidence in her escape. And Tish was restless. She insisted on wandering about the cellar, and near noon I missed her for two hours. When she came back she was covered with plaster dust, but she made no explanation.

"I have been thinking over the situation, Lizzie," she said, "and it divides itself into two parts. We must wait until nightfall and then search again for Aggie, in case my judgment is wrong as to her escape. And then there is a higher law than that of friendship. There is our duty to Aggie, and there is also our duty to the nation."

"Well," I said rather shortly, "I guess we've done our duty. We've taken a prisoner. I owe a duty to my backbone, which is sore from these rocks; and my right leg, which has been tied in a knot with cramp for three hours."

"When," Tish broke in, "is a railroad most safe to travel on? Just after a wreck, certainly. And when, then, is a town easiest to capture? Just after it has been captured. Do you think for one moment that they'll expect another raid tonight?"

"Do you think there will be one?" I asked hopefully.

"I know there will."

She would say nothing further, but departed immediately and was gone most of the afternoon. She came back wearing a strange look of triumph, and asked me if I remembered the code Aggie used, but I had never learned it. She was very impatient.

"It's typical of her," she said, "to disappear just when we need her most. If you knew the code and could get rid of the lookout they keep in the tower, while I ———"

She broke off and reflected.

"They've got to change the lookout in the tower," she said. "If the one comes down before the other goes up, and if we had a hatchet ———"

"Exactly," I said. "And if we were back in the cottage at Penzance, with nothing worse to fight than mosquitoes ———"

We had no midday meal, but at dusk Tish was lucky enough to capture a knapsack set down by a German soldier just outside the machine-gun aperture, and we ate what I believe are termed emergency rations. By that time it was quite dark, and Tish announced that the time had come to strike, though she refused any other explanation.

We had no difficulty in getting out of the cellar, and Tish led the way immediately to the foot of the tower.

"We must get rid of the sentry up there," she whispered. "The moment he hears a racket in the street he will signal for reënforcements, which would be unfortunate."

"What racket?" I demanded.

But she did not reply. Instead she moved into the recess below the tower and stood looking up thoughtfully. I joined her, and we could make out what seemed to be a platform above, and we distinctly saw a light on it, as though the lookout had struck a match. I suggested firing up at him, but Tish sniffed.

"And bring in the entire regiment, or whatever it is!" she said scornfully but in a whisper. "Use your brains, Lizzie!"

However, at that moment the sentry solved the question himself, for he started down. We could hear his coming. We concealed ourselves hastily, and Tish watched him go out and into a cellar across the street, where she said she was convinced they were serving beer. Indeed, there could be no doubt of it, she maintained, as the men went there in crowds, and many of them carried tin cups.

Tish's first thought was that he would be immediately relieved by another lookout, and she stationed herself inside the door, ready to make him prisoner. But finally the truth dawned on us that he had temporarily deserted his post. Tish took immediate advantage of his absence to prepare to ascend the tower, and having found a large knife in the knapsack she had salvaged she took it between her teeth and climbed the narrow winding staircase.

"If he comes back before I return, Lizzie," she said, "capture him, but don't shoot. It might make the rest suspicious."

She then disappeared and I heard her climbing the stairs with her usual agility. However, she returned considerably sooner than I had anticipated, and in a state of intense anger.

"There is another one up there," she whispered. "I heard him sneezing. Why he didn't shoot at me I don't know, unless he thought I was the other one. But I've fixed him," she added with a tinge of complacency. "It's a rope ladder at the top. I reached up as high as I could and cut it."

She then grew thoughtful and observed that cutting the ladder necessitated changing a part of her plan.

"What plan?" I demanded. "I guess my life's at stake as well as yours, Tish Carberry."

"I should think it would be perfectly clear," she said. "We've either got to take this town or starve like rats in that cellar. They've got so now that they won't even walk on the side next to the church, and some of them cross themselves. The frying pan seems to have started it, and when the knapsack disappeared —— However, here's my plan, Lizzie. From what I have observed during the day pretty nearly the entire lot, except the sentries, will be in that beer cellar across in an hour or so. The rest will run for it-take my word-the moment I open fire."

"I'll take your word, Tish," I said. "But what if they don't run?"

She merely waved her hand.

"My plan is simply this," she said: "I've been tinkering with that machine gun most of the day, and my conviction is that it will work. You simply turn a handle like a hand sewing machine. As soon as you hear me starting it you leave the church by that shell hole at the back and go as rapidly as possible back to the American lines. I'll guarantee," she added grimly, "that not a German leaves that cellar across the street until my arm's worn out."

"What shall I say, Tish?" I quavered.

I shall never forget the way she drew herself up.

"Say," she directed, "that we have captured the town of V —— and that they can come over and plant the flag."

I must profess to a certain anxiety during the period of waiting that followed. I felt keenly the necessity of leaving my dear Tish to capture and hold the town alone. And various painful thoughts of Aggie added to my uneasiness. Nor was my perturbation decreased by the reëntrance of the lookout some half hour after he had gone out. Concealed behind debris we listened to his footsteps as he ascended the tower, and could distinctly hear his ferocious mutterings when he discovered that the rope had been cut.

But strangely enough he did not call to the other man, cut off on the platform above.

"I don't believe there was another," I whispered to Tish. But she was confident that she had heard one, and she observed that very probably the two had quarreled.

"It is a well-known tendency of two men, cut off from their kind," she said, "to become violently embittered toward each other. Listen. He is coming down."

I regret to say that he raised an immediate alarm, and that we were forced to retire behind our sarcophagus in the cellar for some time. During the search the enemy was close to us a number of times, and had not one of them stepped on the nail which had served us so usefully I fear to think what might have happened. He did so, however, and retired snarling and limping.

I believe Tish has given nine o'clock in her report to G. H. Q. as the time when she opened fire. It was therefore about eight forty-five when I left the church. For some time before that the cellar across had been filling up with the enemy, and the search for us had ceased. By Tish's instructions I kept to back ways, throwing a grenade here and there to indicate that the attack was a strong one, and also firing my revolver. On hearing the firing behind them the Germans in the advanced trenches apparently considered that they had been cut off from the rear, and I understand that practically all of them ran across to our lines and surrendered. Indeed I was almost run down by three of them.

I was almost entirely out of breath when I reached our trenches, and had I not had the presence of mind to shout "Kamerad," which I had heard was the customary thing, I dare say I should have been shot.

I remember that as I reached the trenches a soldier called out: "Damned if the whole German Army isn't surrendering!"

I then fell into the trench and was immediately caught in a very rude manner. When I insisted that he let me go the man who had captured me only yelled when I spoke, and dropped his gun.

"Hey!" he called. "Fellows! Come here! The boches have taken to fighting their women."

"Don't be a fool!" I snapped. "We've taken V——, and I must see the commanding officer at once."

"You don't happen to have it in your pocket, lady, have you?" he said. He then turned a light on me and said: "Holy mackerel! It's Miss Lizzie! What's this about V——?"

"Miss Carberry has taken V——," I said.

"I believe you," was all he said; and we started for headquarters.

I recall distinctly the scene in the general's headquarters when we got there. The general was sitting, and both Charlie Sands and Mr. Burton were there, looking worried and unhappy. At first they did not see me, and I was too much out of breath to speak.

"I have already told you both that I cannot be responsible for three erratic spinsters. They are undoubtedly prisoners if they returned to V——."

"Prisoners!" said Charlie Sands. "If they were prisoners would they be signaling from the church tower for help?"

"I have already heard that story. It's ridiculous. Do you mean to tell me that with that town full of Germans those women have held the church tower since last night?"

Mr. Burton drew a piece of paper from his pocket.

"From eight o'clock to nine," he said, "the signal was 'Help,' repeated at frequent intervals; shortly after nine there was an attempt at a connected message. Allowing for corrections and for the fact that the light was growing dim, as though from an overused battery, the message runs: 'Help. Bring a ladder. They have cut the——' I am sorry that the light gave out just there, and the message was uncompleted."

How terrible were my emotions at that time, to think that our dear Tish had cut off Aggie's only hope of escape.

The general got up.

"I am, afraid you young gentlemen are indulging in a sense of humor at my expense. Unfortunately I have no sense of humor, but you may find it funny. Captain Sands to continue under arrest for last night's escapade. As Mr. Burton is a member of a welfare organization I do not find him under my direct jurisdiction, but——"

"Then I shall go to V —— myself!" Mr. Burton said angrily. "I'll capture the whole damned town single-handed, and ——"

I then entered the cellar and said: "Miss Carberry has captured V——, general. She asks me to tell you that you may come over at any time and plant the flag. The signaling is being done by Miss Pilkington, who is at present holding the tower. I am acting as runner."

I regret to say that I cannot publish the general's reply.

As the remainder of the incident is a matter of historical record I shall not describe the advance of a portion of our Army into V ——.

They found the garrison either surrendered, fled or under Tish's fire in the beer cellar, and were, I believe, at first seriously menaced by that indomitable figure. It was also extremely difficult to rescue Aggie, as at first she persisted in firing through the floor of the platform the moment she heard any one ascending. In due time, however, she was brought down, but as any mention of the tower for some time gave her a nervous chill it was several weeks before we heard her story.

I doubt if we would have heard it even then had not Mr. Burton and Hilda come to Paris on their wedding trip. We had a dinner for them at the Café de Paris, and Mr. Burton told us that we were all to have the Croix de Guerre. He insisted on ordering champagne to celebrate, and Aggie had two glasses, and then said the room was going round like the weather vane on the tower at V ——.

She then went rather white and said: "The ladder was fastened to it, you know."

"What ladder?" Tish asked sharply.

"The rope ladder I was standing on. And when the wind blew ——"

Well, we gave her another glass of wine, and she told us the tragic story. She had fallen behind me, and was round a corner, when she felt a sneezing spell coming on. So seeing a doorway she slipped in, and she sneezed for about five minutes. When she came out there was nobody in sight, and after wandering round she went back to the doorway and closed the door.

There were stairs behind her, and when the counter attack came she ran up the stairs. She knew then that she was in the church tower, but she didn't dare to come down. When the firing stopped in the streets a soldier ran down the stairs and almost touched her. A moment later she heard him coming back, so she climbed up ahead and got out on a balcony above the clock. But he started to come out on the balcony, and just as she was prepared to be shot her hand touched a rope ladder and she went up it like a shot.

"It was dark, Tish," she said with a shudder, "and I couldn't look down. But when morning came I was up beside the weather vane, and a sniper from our lines must have thought I didn't belong there, for he fired at me every now and then."

Well, it seems she hung there all day, and nobody noticed her. Luckily the wind mostly kept her from the German side, and the sentry couldn't see her from the balcony. Then at last, the next evening, she heard him going down, and she would have made her escape, but he had cut the rope ladder below. She couldn't imagine why.

Tish looked at me steadily.

"It is very strange," she said. "But who can account for the instinct of destruction in the Hun mind?"